THE RISE OF ENDYMION

BOOKS BY DAN SIMMONS

Song of Kali
Phases of Gravity
Carrion Comfort
Hyperion
The Fall of Hyperion
Entropy's Bed at Midnight
Prayers to Broken Stones
Summer of Night
The Hollow Man
Children of the Night
Summer Sketches
Fires of Eden
Endymion
The Rise of Endymion

THE RISE OF ENDYMION

DAN SIMMONS

BANTAM BOOKS

NEW YORK   TORONTO   LONDON
SYDNEY   AUCKLAND

The Rise of Endymion
A Bantam Spectra Book/September 1997

Library of Congress Cataloging-in-Publication Data
Simmons, Dan.
    The rise of Endymion : a novel / by Dan Simmons.
      p.   cm.
    ISBN 0-553-10652-X
    I. Title.
    PS3569.I47292R5   1997
    813'.54—dc21   97-5658
                                                                  CIP

Published simultaneously in the United States and Canada

Bantam Books are published by Bantam Books, a division of
Bantam Doubleday Dell Publishing Group, Inc. Its trademark,
consisting of the words "Bantam Books" and the portrayal of
a rooster, is Registered in U.S. Patent and Trademark Office
and in other countries. Marca Registrada. Bantam Books, 1540
Broadway, New York, New York 10036.

PRINTED IN THE UNITED STATES OF AMERICA

BVG   10 9 8 7 6 5 4 3 2 1

This book is for **Jack Vance,** our finest creator of worlds.
It is also dedicated to the memory of **Dr. Carl Sagan,** scientist, author,
and teacher, who articulated the noblest dreams of humankind.

ACKNOWLEDGMENTS

The author would like to thank the following people: Kevin Kelly for his account of the evolution of a-life from 80-byte critters in his book *Out of Control*; Jean-Daniel Breque and Monique Labailly for their personal guided tour through the catacombs of Paris; Jeff Orr, cybercowboy *extraordinaire*, for boldly going into cyberspace to retrieve the forty-some pages of this tale kidnapped by the TechnoCore; and my editor, Tom Dupree, for his patience, enthusiasm, and shared good taste for loving *Mystery Science Theater 3000*.

We are not stuff that abides, but patterns that perpetuate themselves.
—Norbert Wiener,
Cybernetics, or Control and
Communication in the Animal
and the Machine

The universal nature out of the universal substance, as if it were wax,
now moulds the figure of a horse, and when it has broken this up, it
uses the material for a tree, next for a man, next for something else; and
each of these things subsists for a very short time. But it is no hardship
for the vessel to be broken up, just as there was none in its being fastened together.
—Marcus Aurelius,
Meditations

But here is the finger of God, a flash of the will that can,
　　Existent behind all laws, that made them and, lo, they are!
And I know not if, save in this, such gift be allowed to man,
　　That out of three sounds he frame, not a fourth sound, but a star.
—Robert Browning,
Abt Vogler

If what I have said should not be plain enough, as I fear it may not be, I
will but [sic] you in the place where I began in this series of thoughts—I
mean, I began by seeing how man was formed by circumstances—and
what are circumstances? —but touchstones of his heart—? and what are
touch stones? —but proovings [sic] of his hearrt [sic]? —and what are
the proovings [sic] of his heart but fortifiers or alterers of his nature?
and what is his altered nature but his soul? —and what was his soul
before it came into the world and had These provings and alterations
and perfectionings? —An intelligences [sic]—without Identity—and how
is this Identity to be made? Through the medium of the Heart? And how
is the heart to become this Medium but in a world of Circumstances?
—There now I think what with Poetry and Theology you may thank
your Stars that my pen is not very long-winded—
—John Keats,
In a letter to his brother

THE RISE OF ENDYMION

Part One

1

"THE POPE IS DEAD! Long live the Pope!"

The cry reverberated in and around the Vatican courtyard of San Damaso where the body of Pope Julius XIV had just been discovered in his papal apartments. The Holy Father had died in his sleep. Within minutes the word spread through the mismatched cluster of buildings still referred to as the Vatican Palace, and then moved out through the Vatican State with the speed of a circuit fire in a pure-oxygen environment. The rumor of the Pope's death burned through the Vatican's office complex, leaped through the crowded St. Anne's Gate to the Apostolic Palace and the adjacent Government Palace, found waiting ears among the faithful in the sacristy of St. Peter's Basilica to the point that the archbishop saying Mass actually turned to look over his shoulder at the unprecedented hiss and whispering of the congregation, and then moved out of the Basilica with the departing worshipers into the larger crowds of St. Peter's Square where eighty to a hundred thousand tourists and visiting Pax functionaries received the rumor like a critical mass of plutonium being slammed inward to full fission.

Once out through the main vehicle gate of the Arch of Bells, the news accelerated to the speed of electrons, then leaped to the speed of light, and finally hurtled out and away from the planet Pacem at Hawking-drive velocities thousands of times faster than light. Closer, just beyond the ancient walls of the Vatican, phones and comlogs chimed throughout the hulking, sweating Castel Sant'Angelo where the offices of the Holy Office of the Inquisition were buried deep in the mountain of stone originally built to be Hadrian's mausoleum. All that morning there was the rattle of beads and rustle of starched cassocks as Vatican functionaries rushed back to their offices to monitor their encrypted net lines and to wait for memos from above. Personal communicators rang, chimed, and vibrated in the uniforms and implants of thousands of Pax administrators, military commanders, politicians, and Mercantilus officials. Within thirty minutes of the discovery of the Pope's lifeless body, news organizations around the world of Pacem were cued to the story: they readied their robotic holocams, brought their full panoply of in-system relay sats on-line, sent their best human reporters to the Vatican press office, and waited. In an interstellar society where the Church ruled all but absolutely, news awaited not only independent confirmation but official permission to exist.

Two hours and ten minutes after the discovery of Pope Julius XIV's body, the Church confirmed his death via an announcement through the office of the Vatican Secretary of State, Cardinal Lourdusamy. Within seconds, the recorded announcement was tightcast to every radio and holovision on the teeming world of Pacem. With its population of one and a half billion souls, all born-again Christians carrying the cruciform, most employed by the Vatican or the huge civilian, military, or mercantile bureaucracy of the Pax state, the planet Pacem paused to listen with some interest. Even before the formal announcement, a dozen of the new archangel-class starships had left their orbital bases and translated across the small human sphere of the galaxy arm, their near-instantaneous drives instantly killing their crews but carrying their message of the Pope's death secure in computers and coded transponders for the sixty-some most important archdiocese worlds and star systems. These archangel courier ships would carry a few of the voting cardinals back to Pacem in time for the election, but most of the electors would choose to remain on their homeworlds—foregoing death even with its sure promise of resurrection—sending instead their encrypted, interactive holo wafers with their *eligo* for the next Supreme Pontiff.

Another eighty-five Hawking-class Pax ships, mostly high-acceleration torchships, made ready to spin up to relativistic velocities and then into jump configurations, their voyage time to be measured in days to months, their relative time-debt ranging from weeks to years. These ships would wait in Pacem space the fifteen to twenty standard days until the election of the new Pope and then bring the word to the 130-some less critical Pax systems where archbishops tended to billions more of the faithful. Those archdiocese worlds, in turn, would be charged with sending the word of the Pope's death, resurrection, and reelection on to lesser systems, distant worlds, and to the myriad colonies in the Outback. A final fleet of more than two hundred unmanned courier drones was taken out of storage at the huge Pax asteroid base in Pacem System, their message chips waiting only for the official announcement of Pope Julius's rebirth and reelection before being accelerated into Hawking space to carry the news to elements of the Pax Fleet engaged in patrol or combat with the Ousters along the so-called Great Wall defensive sphere far beyond the boundaries of Pax space.

Pope Julius had died eight times before. The Pontiff's heart was weak, and he would allow no repair of it—either by surgery or nanoplasty. It was his contention that a pope should live his natural life span and—upon his death—that a new pope should be elected. The fact that this same Pope had been reelected eight times did not dissuade him from his opinion. Even now, as Pope Julius's body was being readied for a formal evening of lying in state before being carried to the private resurrection chapel behind St. Peter's, cardinals and their surrogates were making preparations for the election.

The Sistine Chapel was closed to tourists and made ready for the voting that would occur in less than three weeks. Ancient, canopied stalls were brought in for the eighty-three cardinals who would be present in the flesh while holographic projectors and interactive datumplane connections were set in place for the cardinals who would vote by proxy. The table for the Scrutineers was set in front of the Chapel's high altar. Small cards, needles, thread, a receptacle, a plate, linen cloths, and other objects were carefully placed on the table of the Scrutineers and then covered with a larger linen cloth. The table for the Infirmarii and the Revisors was set to one side of the altar. The main doors of the Sistine Chapel were closed, bolted, and sealed. Swiss Guard commandos in full battle armor and state-of-the-art energy weapons took their place outside the Chapel doors and at the blastproof portals of St. Peter's papal resurrection annex.

Following ancient protocol, the election was scheduled to occur in no fewer than fifteen days and no more than twenty. Those cardinals who made their permanent home on Pacem or within three weeks' time-debt travel canceled their regular agendas and prepared for the enclave. Everything else was in readiness.

SOME FAT MEN carry their weight like a weakness, a sign of self-indulgence and sloth. Other fat men absorb mass regally, an outward sign of their growing power. Simon Augustino Cardinal Lourdusamy was of the latter category. A huge man, a veritable mountain of scarlet in his formal cardinal robes, Lourdusamy looked to be in his late fifties, standard, and had appeared thus for more than two centuries of active life and successful resurrection. Jowled, quite bald, and given to speaking in a soft bass rumble that could rise to a God-roar capable of filling St. Peter's Basilica without the use of a speaker system, Lourdusamy remained the epitome of health and vitality in the Vatican. Many in the inner circles of the Church's hierarchy credited Lourdusamy—then a young, minor functionary in the Vatican diplomatic machine—with guiding the anguished and pain-ridden ex-Hyperion pilgrim, Father Lenar Hoyt, to finding the secret that tamed the cruciform to an instrument of resurrection. They credited him as much as the newly deceased Pope with bringing the Church back from the brink of extinction.

Whatever the truth of that legend, Lourdusamy was in fine form this first day after the Holy Father's ninth death in office and five days before His Holiness's resurrection. As Cardinal-Secretary of State, president of the committee overseeing the twelve Sacred Congregations, and prefect of that most feared and misunderstood of those agencies—the Sacred Congregation for the Doctrine of the Faith, now officially known once again after more than a thousand-year interregnum as the Holy Office of the Universal Inquisition—Lourdusamy was the most powerful human being in the Curia. At that moment, with His Holiness, Pope Julius XIV, lying in state in St. Peter's Basilica, the body awaiting removal to the resurrection annex as soon as night should fall, Simon Augustino Cardinal Lourdusamy was arguably the most powerful human being in the galaxy.

The fact was not lost on the Cardinal that morning.

"Are they here yet, Lucas?" he rumbled at the man who had been his aide and factotum for more than two hundred busy years. Monsignor Lucas Oddi was as thin, bony, aged-looking, and urgent in his movements as Cardinal Lourdusamy was huge, fleshy, ageless, and languid. Oddi's full title as under-secretary of state for the Vatican was Substitute and Secretary of the Cypher, but he was usually known as the Substitute. "Cypher" might have been an equally apt nickname for the tall, angular Benedictine administrator, for in the twenty-two decades of smooth service he had given his master, no one—not even Lourdusamy himself—knew the man's private opinions or emotions. Father Lucas Oddi had been Lourdusamy's strong right arm for so long that the Secretary-Cardinal had long since ceased to think of him as anything but an extension of his own will.

"They have just been seated in the innermost waiting room," answered Monsignor Oddi.

Cardinal Lourdusamy nodded. For more than a thousand years—since long before the Hegira that had sent humankind fleeing the dying Earth and colonizing the stars—it had been a custom of the Vatican to hold important meetings in the waiting rooms of important officials rather than in their private offices. Secretary of State Cardinal Lourdusamy's innermost waiting room was small—no more than five meters square—and unadorned except for a round marble table with no inset com units, a single window that, if it had not been polarized to opaqueness, would have looked out onto a marvelously frescoed external loggia, and two paintings by the thirtieth-century genius Karo-tan—one showing Christ's agony in Gethsemane, the other showing Pope Julius (in his pre-papal identity of Father Lenar Hoyt) receiving the first cruciform from a powerful but androgynous-looking archangel while Satan (in the form of the Shrike) looked on powerlessly.

The four people in the waiting room—three men and a woman—represented the Executive Council of the Pancapitalist League of Independent Catholic Transstellar Trade Organizations, more commonly known as the Pax Mercantilus. Two of the men might have been father and son—M. Helvig Aron and M. Kennet Hay-Modhino—alike even to their subtle, expensive capesuits, expensive, conservative haircuts, subtly bio-sculpted Old Earth Northeuro features, and to the even-more-subtle red pins showing their membership in the Sovereign Military Order of the Hospital of St. John of Jerusalem, of Rhodes, and of Malta—the ancient society popularly known as the Knights of Malta. The third man was of Asian descent and wore a simple cotton robe. His name was Kenzo Isozaki and he was this day—after Simon Augustino Cardinal Lourdusamy—arguably the second most powerful human in the Pax. The final Pax Mercantilus representative, a woman in her fifties, standard, with carelessly cropped dark hair and a pinched face, wearing an inexpensive work suit of combed fiberplastic, was M. Anna Pelli Cognani, reputedly Isozaki's heir apparent and rumored for years to be the lover of the female Archbishop of Renaissance Vector.

The four rose and bowed slightly as Cardinal Lourdusamy entered and took his place at the table. Monsignor Lucas Oddi was the only bystander and he stood away from the table, his bony hands clasped in front of his cassock, the tortured eyes of Karo-tan's Christ in Gethsemane peering over his black-frocked shoulder at the small assembly.

M.'s Aron and Hay-Modhino moved forward to genuflect and kiss the Cardinal's beveled sapphire ring, but Lourdusamy waved away further protocol before Kenzo Isozaki or the woman could approach. When the four Pax Mercantilus representatives were seated once again, the Cardinal said, "We are all old friends. You know that while I represent the Holy See in this discussion during the Holy Father's temporary absence, any and all things discussed this day shall remain within these walls." Lourdusamy smiled. "And these walls, my friends, are the most secure and bugproof in the Pax."

Aron and Hay-Modhino smiled tightly. M. Isozaki's pleasant expression did not change. M. Anna Pelli Cognani's frown deepened. "Your Eminence," she said. "May I speak freely?"

Lourdusamy extended a pudgy palm. He had always distrusted people who asked to speak freely or who vowed to speak candidly or who used the expression "frankly." He said, "Of course, my dear friend. I regret that the pressing circumstances of the day allow us so little time."

Anna Pelli Cognani nodded tersely. She had understood the command to be precise. "Your Eminence," she said, "we asked for this conference so that we could speak to you not only as loyal members of His Holiness's Pancapitalist League, but as friends of the Holy See and of yourself."

Lourdusamy nodded affably. His thin lips between the jowls were curled in a slight smile. "Of course."

M. Helvig Aron cleared his throat. "Your Eminence, the Mercantilus has an understandable interest in the coming papal election."

The Cardinal waited.

"Our goal today," continued M. Hay-Modhino, "is to reassure Your Eminence—both as Secretary of State and as a potential candidate for the papacy—that the League will continue to carry out the Vatican's policy with the utmost loyalty after the coming election."

Cardinal Lourdusamy nodded ever so slightly. He understood perfectly. Somehow the Pax Mercantilus—Isozaki's intelligence network—had sniffed out a possible insurrection in the Vatican hierarchy. Somehow they had overheard the most silent of whispers in whisperproof rooms such as this: that it had come time to replace Pope Julius with a new pontiff. And Isozaki knew that Simon Augustino Lourdusamy would be that man.

"In this sad interregnum," M. Cognani was continuing, "we felt it our duty to offer private as well as public assurances that the League will continue serving the interests of the Holy See and the Holy Mother Church, just as it has for more than two standard centuries."

Cardinal Lourdusamy nodded again and waited, but nothing else was forthcoming from the four Mercantilus leaders. For a moment he allowed himself to speculate on why Isozaki had come in person. *To see my reaction rather than trust the reports of his subordinates,* he thought. *The old man trusts his senses and insights over anyone and anything else.* Lourdusamy smiled. *Good policy.* He let another minute of silence stretch before speaking. "My friends," he rumbled at last, "you cannot know how it warms my heart to have four such busy and important people visit this poor priest in our time of shared sorrow."

Isozaki and Cognani remained expressionless, as inert as argon, but the Cardinal could see the poorly hidden glint of anticipation in the eyes of the other two Mercantilus men. If Lourdusamy welcomed their support at this juncture, however subtly, it put the Mercantilus on an even level with the Vatican conspirators—made the Mercantilus a welcomed conspirator and de facto co-equal to the next Pope.

Lourdusamy leaned closer to the table. The Cardinal noticed that M. Kenzo Isozaki had not blinked during the entire exchange. "My friends," he continued, "as good born-again Christians"—he nodded toward M.'s Aron and Hay-Modhino—"as Knights Hospitaller, you undoubtedly know the procedure for the election of our next Pope. But let me refresh your memory. Once the cardinals and their interactive counterparts are gathered and sealed in the Sistine Chapel, there are three ways in which we can elect a pope—by acclamation, by delegation, or by scrutiny. Through acclamation, all of the cardinal electors are moved by the Holy Spirit to proclaim one person as Supreme Pontiff. We each cry *eligo*—'I elect'—and the name of the person we unanimously select. Through delegation, we choose a few of those among us—say a dozen cardinals—to make the choice for all. Through scrutiny, the cardinal electors vote secretly until a candidate receives two-thirds majority plus one. Then the new pope is elected and the waiting billions see the *sfumata*—the puffs of white smoke—which means that the family of the Church once again has a Holy Father."

The four representatives of the Pax Mercantilus sat in silence. Each of them was intimately aware of the procedure for electing a pope—not only of the antiquated mechanisms, of course, but of the politicking, pressuring, deal-making, bluffing, and outright blackmail that had often accompanied the process over the centuries. And they began to understand why Cardinal Lourdusamy was emphasizing the obvious now.

"For the last nine elections," continued the huge Cardinal, his voice a heavy rumble, "the Pope has been elected by acclamation . . . by the direct intercession of the Holy Spirit." Lourdusamy paused for a long, thick moment. Behind him, Monsignor Oddi stood watching, as motionless as the painted Christ behind him, as unblinking as Kenzo Isozaki.

"I have no reason to believe," continued Lourdusamy at last, "that this election will be any different."

The Pax Mercantilus executives did not move. Finally M. Isozaki bowed his head ever so slightly. The message had been heard and understood. There would be no insurrection within the Vatican walls. Or if there were, Lourdusamy had it well in hand and did not need the support of the Pax Mercantilus. If the former were the case and Cardinal Lourdusamy's time had not yet come, Pope Julius would once again oversee the Church and Pax. Isozaki's group had taken a terrible risk because of the incalculable rewards and power that would be theirs if they had succeeded in allying themselves with the future Pontiff. Now they faced only the consequences of the terrible risk. A century earlier, Pope Julius had excommunicated Kenzo Isozaki's predecessor for a lesser miscalculation, revoking the sacrament of the cruciform and condemning the Mercantilus leader to a life of separation from the Catholic community—which, of course, was every man, woman, and child on Pacem and on a majority of the Pax worlds—followed by the true death.

"Now, I regret that pressing duties must take me from your kind company," rumbled the Cardinal.

Before he could rise and contrary to standard protocol for leaving the presence of a prince of the Church, M. Isozaki came forward quickly, genuflected, and kissed the Cardinal's ring. "Eminence," murmured the old Pax Mercantilus billionaire.

This time, Lourdusamy did not rise or leave until each of the powerful CEOs had come forward to show his or her respect.

AN ARCHANGEL-CLASS STARSHIP translated into God's Grove space the day after Pope Julius's death. This was the only archangel not assigned to courier duty; it was smaller than the new ships and it was called the *Raphael*.

Minutes after the archangel established orbit around the ash-colored world, a dropship separated and screamed into atmosphere. Two men and a woman were aboard. The three looked like siblings, united by their lean forms, pale complexions, dark, limp, short-cropped hair, hooded gazes, and thin lips. They wore unadorned shipsuits of red and black with elaborate wristband comlogs. Their presence in the dropship was a curiosity—the archangel-class starships invariably killed human beings during their violent translation through Planck space and the onboard resurrection crèches usually took three days to revive the human crew.

These three were not human.

Morphing wings and smoothing all surfaces into an aerodynamic shell, the dropship crossed the terminator into daylight at Mach 3. Beneath it turned the former Templar world of God's Grove—a mass of burn scars, ash fields, mudflows, retreating glaciers, and green sequoias struggling to reseed themselves in the shattered landscape. Slowing now to subsonic speeds, the dropship flew above the narrow band of temperate climate and viable vegetation near the planet's equator and followed a river to the stump of the former Worldtree. Eighty-three kilometers across, still a kilometer high even in its devastated form, the stump rose above the southern horizon like a black mesa. The dropship avoided the Worldstump and continued to follow the river west, continuing to descend until it landed on a boulder near the point where the river entered a narrow gorge. The two men and the woman came down the extruded stairs and reviewed the scene. It was midmorning on this part of God's Grove, the river made a rushing noise as it entered the rapids, birds and unseen arboreals chittered in the thick trees farther downriver. The air smelled of pine needles, unclassifiable alien scents, wet soil, and ash. More than two and a half centuries earlier, this world had been smashed and slashed from orbit. Those two-hundred-meter-high Templar trees that did not flee to space had burned in a conflagration that continued to rage for the better part of a century, extinguished at last only by a nuclear winter.

"Careful," said one of the men as the three walked downhill to the river. "The monofilaments she webbed here should still be in place."

The thin woman nodded and removed a weapon laser from the flowfoam pak she carried. Setting the beam to widest dispersal, she fanned it over the river. Invisible filaments glowed like a spider's web in morning dew, crisscrossing the river and wrapping around boulders, submerging and reemerging from the white-frothed river.

"None where we have to work," said the woman as she shut off the laser. The three crossed a low area by the river and climbed a rocky slope. Here the granite had been melted and flowed downhill like lava during the slagging of God's Grove, but on one of the terraced rockfaces there were even more recent signs of catastrophe. Near the top of a boulder ten meters above the river, a crater had been burned into solid rock. Perfectly circular, indented half a meter below the level of the boulder, the crater was five meters across. On the southeast side, where a waterfall of molten rock had run and splattered and fountained to the river below, a natural staircase of black stone had formed. The rock filling the circular cavity on top of the boulder was darker and smoother than the rest of the stone, looking like polished onyx set in a granite crucible.

One of the men stepped into the concavity, lay full length on the smooth stone, and set his ear to the rock. A second later he rose and nodded to the other two.

"Stand back," said the woman. She touched her wristband comlog.

The three had taken five steps back when the lance of pure energy burned from space. Birds and arboreals fled in loud panic through the screening trees. The air ionized and became superheated in seconds, rolling a shock wave in all directions. Branches and leaves burst into flame fifty meters from the beam's point of contact. The cone of pure brilliance exactly matched the diameter of the circular depression in the boulder, turning the smooth stone to a lake of molten fire.

The two men and the woman did not flinch. Their shipsuits smoldered in the open hearth-furnace heat, but the special fabric did not burn. Neither did their flesh.

"Time," said the woman over the roar of the energy beam and widening firestorm. The golden beam ceased to exist. Hot air rushed in at gale-force winds to fill the vacuum. The depression in the rock was a circle of bubbling lava.

One of the men went to one knee and seemed to be listening. Then he nodded to the others and phase-shifted. One second he was flesh and bone and blood and skin and hair, the next he was a chrome-silver sculpture in the form of a man. The blue sky, burning forest, and lake of molten fire reflected perfectly on his shifting silver skin. He plunged one arm into the molten pool, crouched lower, reached deeper, and then pulled back. The silver form of his hand looked as if it had melted onto the surface of another silver human form—this one a woman. The male chrome sculpture pulled the female chrome sculpture out of the hissing, spitting cauldron of lava and carried it fifty meters to a point where the grass was not burning and the stone was cool enough to hold their weight. The other man and woman followed.

The man shifted out of his chrome-silver form and a second later the female he had carried did the same. The woman who emerged from the quicksilver looked like a twin of the short-haired woman in the shipsuit.

"Where is the bitch child?" asked the rescued female. She had once been known as Rhadamanth Nemes.

"Gone," said the man who rescued her. He and his male sibling could be her brothers or male clones. "They made the final farcaster."

Rhadamanth Nemes grimaced slightly. She was flexing her fingers and moving her arms as if recovering from cramps in her limbs. "At least I killed the damned android."

"No," said the other woman, her twin. She had no name. "They left in the *Raphael*'s dropship. The android lost an arm, but the autosurgeon kept him alive."

Nemes nodded and looked back at the rocky hillside where lava still ran. The glow from the fire showed the glistening web of the monofilament over the river. Behind them, the forest burned. "That was not . . . pleasant . . . in there. I couldn't move with the full force of the ship's lance burning down on me, and then I could not phase-shift with the rock around me. It took immense concentration to power down and still maintain an active phase-shift interface. How long was I buried there?"

"Four Earth years," said the man who had not spoken until now.

Rhadamanth Nemes raised a thin eyebrow, more in question than surprise. "Yet the Core knew where I was . . ."

"The Core knew where you were," said the other woman. Her voice and facial expressions were identical to those of the rescued woman. "And the Core knew that you had failed."

Nemes smiled very thinly. "So the four years were a punishment."

"A reminder," said the man who had pulled her from the rock.

Rhadamanth Nemes took two steps, as if testing her balance. Her voice was flat. "So why have you come for me now?"

"The girl," said the other woman. "She is coming back. We are to resume your mission."

Nemes nodded.

The man who rescued her set his hand on her thin shoulder. "And please consider," he said, "that four years entombed in fire and stone will be nothing to what you may expect if you fail again."

Nemes stared at him for a long moment without answering. Then, turning away from the lava and flames in a precisely choreographed motion, matching stride for stride, all four of them moved in perfect unison toward the dropship.

ON THE DESERT world of MadredeDios, on the high plateau called the Llano Estacado because of the atmosphere generator pylons crisscrossing the desert in neat ten-kilometer grid intervals, Father Federico de Soya prepared for early morning Mass.

The little desert town of Nuevo Atlan held fewer than three hundred residents—mostly Pax boxite miners waiting to die before traveling home, mixed with a few of the converted Mariaists who scratched out livings as corgor herders in the toxic wastelands—and Father de Soya knew precisely how many would be in chapel for early Mass: four—old M. Sanchez, the ancient widow who was rumored to have murdered her husband in a dust storm sixty-two years before, the Perell twins who—for unknown reasons—preferred the old run-down church to the spotless and air-conditioned company chapel on the mining reservation, and the mysterious old man with the radiation-scarred face who knelt in the rearmost pew and never took Communion.

There was a dust storm blowing—there was always a dust storm blowing—and Father de Soya had to run the last thirty meters from his adobe parish house to the church sacristy, a transparent fiberplastic hood over his head and shoulders to protect his cassock and biretta, his breviary tucked deep in his cassock pocket to keep it clean. It did not work. Every evening when he removed his cassock or hung his biretta on a hook, the sand fell out in a red cascade, like dried blood from a broken hourglass. And every morning when he opened his breviary, sand gritted between the pages and soiled his fingers.

"Good morning, Father," said Pablo as the priest hurried into the sacristy and slid the cracked weather seals around the door frame.

"Good morning, Pablo, my most faithful altar boy," said Father de

Soya. Actually, the priest silently corrected himself, Pablo was his *only* altar boy. A simple child—simple in the ancient sense of the word as mentally slow as well as in the sense of being honest, sincere, loyal, and friendly—Pablo was there to help de Soya serve Mass every weekday morning at 0630 hours and twice on Sunday—although only the same four people came to the early morning Sunday Mass and half a dozen of the boxite miners to the later Mass.

The boy nodded his head and grinned again, the smile disappearing for a moment as he pulled on his clean, starched surplice over his altar-boy robes.

Father de Soya walked past the child, ruffling his dark hair as he did so, and opened the tall vestment chest. The morning had grown as dark as the high-desert night as the dust storm swallowed the sunrise, and the only illumination in the cold, bare room was from the fluttering sacristy lamp. De Soya genuflected, prayed earnestly for a moment, and began donning the vestments of his profession.

For two decades, as Father Captain de Soya of the Pax Fleet, commander of torchships such as the *Balthasar*, Federico de Soya had dressed himself in uniforms where the cross and collar were the only signs of his priesthood. He had worn plaskev battle armor, spacesuits, tactical com implants, datumplane goggles, godgloves—all of the paraphernalia of a torchship captain—but none of those items touched him and moved him as much as these simple vestments of a parish priest. In the four years since Father Captain de Soya had been stripped of his rank of captain and removed from Fleet service, he had rediscovered his original vocation.

De Soya pulled on the amice that slipped over his head like a gown and fell to his ankles. The amice was white linen and immaculate despite the incessant dust storms, as was the alb that slid on next. He set the cincture around his waist, whispering a prayer as he did so. Then he raised the white stole from the vestment chest, held it reverently a moment in both hands, and then placed it around his neck, crossing the two strips of silk. Behind him, Pablo was bustling around the little room, putting away his filthy outside boots and pulling on the cheap fiberplastic running shoes his mother had told him to keep here just for Mass.

Father de Soya set his tunible in place, the outer garment showing a T-cross in front. It was white with a subtle purple piping: he would be saying a Mass of Benediction this morning while quietly administering the sacrament of penance for the presumed widow and murderer in the front pew and the radiation-scarred cypher in the last pew.

Pablo bustled up to him. The boy was grinning and out of breath. Father de Soya set his hand on the boy's head, trying to flatten the thatch of flyaway hair while also calming and reassuring the lad. De Soya lifted the chalice, removed his right hand from the boy's head to hold it over the veiled cup, and said softly, "All right." Pablo's grin disappeared as the gravity of the moment swept over him, and then the boy led the procession of two out of the sacristy door toward the altar.

De Soya noticed at once that there were five figures in the chapel, not four. The usual worshipers were there—all kneeling and standing and then kneeling again in their usual places—but there was someone else, someone tall and silent standing in the deepest shadows where the little foyer entered the nave.

All during the Renewed Mass, the presence of the stranger pulled at Father de Soya's consciousness, try as he might to block out all but the sacred mystery of which he was part.

"*Dominus vobiscum,*" said Father de Soya. For more than three thousand years, he believed, the Lord *had* been with them . . . with all of them.

"*Et cum spiritu tuo,*" said Father de Soya, and as Pablo echoed the words, the priest turned his head slightly to see if the light had illuminated the tall, thin form in the dark recess at the front of the nave. It had not.

During the Canon, Father de Soya forgot the mysterious figure and succeeded in focusing all of his attention on the Host that he raised in his blunt fingers. "*Hoc est enim corpus meum,*" the Jesuit pronounced distinctly, feeling the power of those words and praying for the ten-thousandth time that his sins of violence while a Fleet captain might be washed away by the blood and mercy of this Savior.

At the Communion rail, only the Perell twins came forward. As always. De Soya said the words and offered the Host to the young men. He resisted the urge to glance up at the figure in the shadows at the back of the church.

The Mass ended almost in darkness. The howl of wind drowned out the last prayers and responses. This little church had no electricity—it never had—and the ten flickering candles on the wall did little to pierce the gloom. Father de Soya gave the final benediction and then carried the chalice into the dark sacristy, setting it on the smaller altar there. Pablo hurried to shrug out of his surplice and pull on his storm anorak.

"See you tomorrow, Father!"

"Yes, thank you, Pablo. Don't forget . . ." Too late. The boy was out the door and running for the spice mill where he worked with his father and uncles. Red dust filled the air around the faulty weather-stripped door.

Normally, Father de Soya would have been pulling off his vestments now, setting them back in the vestment chest. Later in the day, he would take them to the parish house to clean them. But this morning he stayed in the tunicle and stole, the alb and cincture and amice. For some reason he felt he needed them, much as he had needed the plaskev battle armor during boarding operations in the Coal Sack campaign.

The tall figure, still in shadows, stood in the sacristy doorway. Father de Soya waited and watched, resisting the urge to cross himself or to hold the remaining Communion wafer up as if to shield against vampires or the Devil. Outside, the wind went from a howl to a banshee scream.

The figure took a step into the ruby light cast by the sacristy lamp. De Soya recognized Captain Marget Wu, personal aide and liaison for Admiral

Marusyn, commanding officer of Pax Fleet. For the second time that morning, de Soya corrected himself—it was Admiral Marget Wu now, the pips on her collar just visible in the red light.

"Father Captain de Soya?" said the Admiral.

The Jesuit slowly shook his head. It was only 0730 hours on this twenty-three-hour world, but already he felt tired. "Just *Father* de Soya," he said.

"Father Captain de Soya," repeated Admiral Wu, and this time there was no question in her voice. "You are hereby recalled to active service. You will take ten minutes to gather your belongings and then come with me. The recall is effective now."

Federico de Soya sighed and closed his eyes. He felt like crying. *Please, dear Lord, let this cup passeth from me.* When he opened his eyes, the chalice was still on the altar and Admiral Marget Wu was still waiting.

"Yes," he said softly, and slowly, carefully, he began removing his sacred vestments.

ON THE THIRD day after the death and entombment of Pope Julius XIV, there was movement in his resurrection crèche. The slender umbilicals and subtle machine probes slid back and out of sight. The corpse on the slab at first lay inanimate except for the rise and fall of a bare chest, then visibly twitched, then moaned, and—after many long minutes—raised itself to one elbow, and eventually sat up, the richly embroidered silk and linen shroud sliding around the naked man's waist.

For several minutes the man sat on the edge of the marble slab, his head in his shaking hands. Then he looked up as a secret panel in the resurrection chapel wall slid back with less than a hiss. A cardinal in formal red moved across the dimly lit space with a rustle of silk and a rattle of beads. Next to him walked a tall, handsome man with gray hair and gray eyes. This man was dressed in a simple but elegant one-piece suit of gray flannel. Three steps behind the Cardinal and the man in gray came two Swiss Guard troopers in medieval orange and black. They carried no weapons.

The naked man on the slab blinked as if his eyes were unaccustomed to even the muted light in the dim chapel. Finally the eyes focused. "Lourdusamy," said the resurrected man.

"Father Duré," said Cardinal Lourdusamy. He was carrying an oversized silver chalice.

The naked man moved his mouth and tongue as if he had awakened with a vile taste in his mouth. He was an older man with a thin, ascetic face, sad eyes, and old scars across his newly resurrected body. On his chest, two cruciforms glowed red and tumescent. "What year is it?" he asked at last.

"The Year of Our Lord 3131," said the Cardinal, still standing next to the seated man.

Father Paul Duré closed his eyes. "Fifty-seven years after my last resurrection. Two hundred and seventy-nine years since the Fall of the Farcasters." He opened his eyes and looked at the Cardinal. "Two hundred and seventy years since you poisoned me, killing Pope Teilhard the First."

Cardinal Lourdusamy rumbled a laugh. "You recover quickly from resurrection disorientation if you can do your arithmetic so well."

Father Duré moved his gaze from the Cardinal to the tall man in gray. "Albedo. You come to witness? Or do you have to give courage to your tame Judas?"

The tall man said nothing. Cardinal Lourdusamy's already thin lips tightened to the point of disappearance between florid jowls. "Do you have anything else to say before you return to hell, Antipope?"

"Not to you," murmured Father Duré and closed his eyes in prayer.

The two Swiss Guard troopers seized Father Duré's thin arms. The Jesuit did not resist. One of the troopers grabbed the resurrected man by the brow and pulled his head back, stretching the thin neck in a bow.

Cardinal Lourdusamy took a graceful half step closer. From the folds of his silken sleeve snicked a knife blade with a horn handle. While the troopers held the still passive Duré, whose Adam's apple seemed to grow more prominent as his head was forced back, Lourdusamy swept his arm up and around in a fluid, casting-away gesture. Blood spurted from Duré's severed carotid artery.

Stepping back to avoid staining his robes, Lourdusamy slid the blade back into his sleeve, raised the broad-mouthed chalice, and caught the pulsing stream of blood. When the chalice was almost filled and the blood had ceased spurting, he nodded to the Swiss Guard trooper, who immediately released Father Duré's head.

The resurrected man was a corpse once again, head lolling, eyes still shut, mouth open, the slashed throat gapping like painted lips on a terrible, ragged grin. The two Swiss Guard troopers arranged the body on the slab and lifted the shroud away. The naked dead man looked pale and vulnerable—torn throat, scarred chest, long, white fingers, pale belly, flaccid genitals, scrawny legs. Death—even in an age of resurrection—leaves little or no dignity even to those who have lived lives of sustained self-control.

While the troopers held the beautiful shroud out of harm's way, Cardinal Lourdusamy poured the heavy chalice's blood onto the dead man's eyes, into his gaping mouth, into the raw knife wound, and down the chest, belly, and groin of the corpse, the spreading scarlet matching and surpassing the intensity of color in the Cardinal's robes.

"Sie aber seid nicht fleischlich, sondern geistlich," said Cardinal Lourdusamy. "You are not made of flesh, but of spirit."

The tall man raised an eyebrow. "Bach, isn't it?"

"Of course," said the Cardinal, setting the now-empty chalice next to the corpse. He nodded to the Swiss Guard troopers and they covered the body with the two-layered shroud. Blood immediately soaked the beautiful fabrics. "Jesu, meine Freunde," added Lourdusamy.

"I thought so," said the taller man. He gave the Cardinal a questioning look.

"Yes," agreed Cardinal Lourdusamy. "Now."

The man in gray walked around the bier and stood behind the two troopers, who were completing their tucking-in of the blood-soaked shroud. When the troopers straightened and stepped back from the marble slab, the man in gray lifted his large hands to the back of each man's neck. The troopers' eyes and mouths opened wide, but they had no time to cry out: within a second their open eyes and mouths blazed with an incandescent light, their skin became translucent to the orange flame within their bodies, and then they were gone—volatilized, scattered to particles finer than ash.

The man in gray brushed his hands together to rid them of the thin layer of micro-ash.

"A pity, Councillor Albedo," murmured Cardinal Lourdusamy in his thick rumble of a voice.

The man in gray looked at the suggestion of airborne dust settling in the dim light and then back at the Cardinal. His eyebrow rose once again in query.

"No, no, no," rumbled Lourdusamy, "I mean the shroud. The stains will never come out. We have to weave a new one after every resurrection." He turned and started toward the secret panel, his robes rustling. "Come, Albedo. We need to talk and I still have a Mass of Thanksgiving to say before noon."

After the panel slid shut behind the two, the resurrection chamber lay silent and empty except for the shrouded corpse and the slightest hint of gray fog in the dim light, a shifting, fading mist suggestive of the departing souls of the more recent dead.

2

O N THE WEEK that Pope Julius died for the ninth time and Father Duré was murdered for the fifth time, Aenea and I were 160,000 light-years away on the kidnapped planet Earth—Old Earth, the *real* Earth—circling a G-type star that was not the sun in the Lesser Magellanic Cloud, a galaxy that was not the Earth's home galaxy.

It had been a strange week for us. We did not know that the Pope had died, of course, since there was no contact between this relocated Earth and Pax space except for the dormant farcaster portals. Actually, I know now, Aenea *was* aware of the Pope's demise through means we did not suspect then, but she did not mention events in Pax space to us and no one thought to ask her. Our lives on Earth during those years of exile were simple and peaceful and profound in ways that are now hard to fathom and almost painful to recall. At any rate, that particular week had been profound but not simple or peaceful for us: the Old Architect with whom Aenea had been studying for the last four years had died on Monday, and his funeral had been a sad and hasty affair out on the desert that wintry Tuesday evening. On Wednesday, Aenea had turned sixteen, but the event was overshadowed by the pall of grief and confusion at the Taliesin Fellowship and only A. Bettik and I had tried to celebrate the day with her.

The android had baked a chocolate cake, Aenea's favorite, and I had worked for days to whittle an elaborately carved walking stick out of a sturdy branch we had found during one of the Old Architect's compulsory picnic expeditions to the nearby mountains. That evening we ate the cake and drank some champagne in Aenea's beautiful little apprentice shelter in the desert, but she was subdued and distracted by the old man's death and the Fellowship's panic. I realize now that much of her distraction must have come from her awareness of the Pope's death, of the violent events that were gathering on the future's horizon, and of the end of what would be the most peaceful four years we would ever know together.

I remember the conversation that evening of Aenea's sixteenth birthday. It had grown dark early and the air was chill. Outside the comfortable stone-and-canvas home she had built four years earlier for her apprenticeship challenge, the dust was blowing and the sagebrush and yucca plants rasped and contorted in the wind's grip. We sat by the hissing lantern, traded our champagne glasses for mugs of warm tea, and talked softly beneath the hiss of sand on canvas.

"It's strange," I said. "We knew he was old and ill, but no one seemed to believe that he would die." I was speaking of the Old Architect, of course, not of the distant Pope who meant so little to us. And, like all of us on the exiled Earth, Aenea's mentor had not carried the cruciform. His death was final in the way the Pope's could not be.

"He seemed to know," Aenea said softly. "He's been calling in each of his apprentices for the past month. Imparting some last bit of wisdom."

"What last bit of wisdom did he share with you?" I asked. "I mean, if it's not a secret or too personal."

Aenea smiled over the steaming mug of tea. "He reminded me that the patron will always agree to pay twice what the bid was if you send along the extra expenses bit by bit once construction has started and the structure is taking shape. He said that was beyond the point of no return, so the client was hooked like a trout on a six-pound line."

Both A. Bettik and I laughed. It was not a disrespectful laugh—the Old Architect had been one of those rare creatures, a true genius combined with an overpowering personality—but even when thinking of him with sadness and affection, we could recognize the selfishness and deviousness that had also been part of his personality. And I don't mean to be coy here by referring to him only as the Old Architect: the cybrid's personality template had been reconstructed from a pre-Hegira human named Frank Lloyd Wright who had worked in the nineteenth and twentieth centuries, A.D. But while everyone at the Taliesin Fellowship had referred to him respectfully as Mr. Wright, including even those older apprentices who were his age, I had always thought of him as the Old Architect because of things Aenea had said about her future mentor before we came here to Old Earth.

As if thinking along these same lines, A. Bettik said, "It's odd, isn't it?"

"What's that?" said Aenea.

The android smiled and rubbed his left arm where it ended at a smooth stump just below the elbow. It is a habit he had developed over the past few years. The autosurgeon on the dropship that had carried us through the farcaster from God's Grove had kept the android alive, but his chemistry had been sufficiently different to prevent the ship from growing him a new arm. "I mean," he said, "that despite the ascendancy of the Church in the affairs of humankind, the question of whether human beings have a soul which leaves the body after death has yet to be definitely answered. Yet in Mr. Wright's case, we know that his cybrid personality still exists separate from his body—or at least did for some time after the moment of his death."

"Do we know that for sure?" I said. The tea was warm and good. Aenea and I bought it—traded for it actually—at the Indian market located in the desert where the city of Scottsdale should have been.

It was Aenea who answered my question. "Yes. My father's cybrid personality survived the destruction of his body and was stored in the Schrön Loop in Mother's skull. Even after that, we know that it had a separate existence in the megasphere and then resided in the Consul's ship for a time. A cybrid's personality survives as a sort of holistic wave front propagated along the matrices of the datumplane or megasphere until it returns to the AI source in the Core."

I had known this but never understood it. "Okay," I said, "but where did Mr. Wright's AI-based personality wave front go? There can't be any connections to the Core out here in the Magellanic Cloud. There are no dataspheres here."

Aenea set down her empty mug. "There has to be a connection, or Mr. Wright and the other reconstructed cybrid personalities assembled here on Earth couldn't have existed. Remember, the TechnoCore used the Planck space between the farcaster portals as their medium and hiding place before the dying Hegemony destroyed the farcaster openings to it."

"The Void Which Binds," I said, repeating the phrase from the old poet's *Cantos*.

"Yeah," said Aenea. "Although I always thought that was a dumb name."

"Whatever it's called," I said, "I don't understand how it can reach *here* . . . a different galaxy."

"The medium the Core used for farcasters reaches everywhere," said Aenea. "It permeates space and time." My young friend frowned. "No, that's not right, space and time are bound up in *it* . . . the Void Which Binds transcends space and time."

I looked around. The lantern light was enough to fill the little tent structure, but outside it was dark and the wind howled. "Then the Core *can* reach here?"

Aenea shook her head. We had held this discussion before. I had not understood the concept then. I did not understand it now.

"These cybrids are connected to AIs which aren't really part of the Core," she said. "Mr. Wright's persona wasn't. My father . . . the second Keats cybrid . . . wasn't."

This was the part I had never understood. "The *Cantos* said that the Keats cybrids—including your father—were created by Ummon, a Core AI. Ummon told your father that the cybrids were a Core experiment."

Aenea stood and walked to the opening of her apprentice shelter. The canvas on either side rippled with the wind, but kept its shape and held the sand outside. She had built it well. "Uncle Martin wrote the *Cantos*," she said. "He told the truth as best he could. But there were elements he did not understand."

"Me too," I said and dropped the matter. I walked over and put my arm around Aenea, feeling the subtle changes in her back and shoulder and arm since the first time I had hugged her four years earlier. "Happy birthday, kiddo."

She glanced up at me and then laid her head against my chest. "Thank you, Raul."

There had been other changes in my youthful friend since first we met when she was just turning twelve, standard. I could say that she had grown to womanhood in the intervening years, but despite the rounding of her hips and obvious breasts beneath the old sweatshirt she wore, I still did not see her as a woman. No longer a child, of course, but not yet a woman. She was . . . Aenea. The luminous dark eyes were the same—intelligent, questioning, a bit sad with some secret knowledge—and the effect of being physically touched when she turned the attention of her gaze on you was as strong as ever. Her brown hair had grown somewhat darker in the past few years, she had cut it the previous spring—now it was shorter than mine had been when I was in the Home Guard military on Hyperion a dozen years earlier, when I set my hand on her head the hair was barely long enough to rise between my fingers—but I could see some glints of the old blond streaks there, brought out by the long days she spent working in the Arizona sunlight.

As we stood there listening to the blowing dust scraping canvas, A. Bettik a silent shadow behind us, Aenea took my hand in both of hers. She might have been sixteen that day, a young woman rather than a girl, but her hands were still tiny in my huge palm. "Raul?" she said.

I looked at her and waited.

"Will you do something for me?" she said softly, very softly.

"Yes." I did not hesitate.

She squeezed my hand and looked directly *into* me then. "Will you do something for me tomorrow?"

"Yes."

Neither her gaze nor the pressure on my hand let up. "Will you do *anything* for me?"

This time I did hesitate. I knew what such a vow might entail, even though this strange and wonderful child had never asked me to do anything for her—had not asked that I come with her on this mad odyssey. That had been a promise I had made to the old poet, Martin Silenus, before I had even met Aenea. I knew that there were things that I could not—in good conscience or bad—bring myself to do. But foremost among those things I was incapable of doing was denying Aenea.

"Yes," I said, "I will do anything you ask." At that moment I knew that I was lost—and resurrected.

Aenea did not speak then, but only nodded, squeezed my hand a final time, and turned back to the light, the cake, and our waiting android friend. On the next day I was to learn what her request truly meant, and how difficult it would be to honor my vow.

I WILL STOP for a moment. I realize that you might not know about me unless you have read the first few hundred pages of my tale, which, because I had to recycle the microvellum upon which I wrote them, no longer exist except in the memory of this 'scriber. I told the truth in those lost pages. Or at least the truth as I knew it then. Or at least I *tried* to tell the truth. Mostly.

After having recycled the microvellum pages of that first attempt to tell the story of Aenea, and because the 'scriber has never been out of my sight, I have to assume that no one has read them. The fact that they were written in a Schrödinger cat box execution egg in exile orbit around the barren world of Armaghast—the cat box being little more than a fixed-position energy shell holding my atmosphere, air and food recycling equipment, bed, table, 'scriber, and a vial of cyanide gas waiting to be released by a random isotope emission—would seem to have insured that you have not read those pages.

But I am not sure.

Strange things were happening then. Strange things have happened since. I will reserve judgment on whether those pages—and these—could ever have been, or ever will be, read.

In the meantime, I will reintroduce myself. My name is Raul Endymion, my first name rhyming with tall—which I am—and my last name deriving from the "abandoned" university city of Endymion on the backwater world of Hyperion. I qualify the word "abandoned" because that quarantined city is where I met the old poet—Martin Silenus, the ancient author of the banned epic poem the *Cantos*—and that is where my adventure began. I use the word "adventure" with some irony, and perhaps in the sense that all of life is an adventure. For it is true that while the voyage began as an adventure—an attempt to rescue twelve-year-old Aenea from the Pax and to escort her safely to the distant Old Earth—it has since become a full lifetime of love, loss, and wonder.

Anyway, at the time of this telling, during the week of the Pope's death, the Old Architect's death, and Aenea's inauspicious sixteenth birthday in exile, I was thirty-two years old, still tall, still strong, still trained mostly in hunting, brawling, and watching others lead, still callow, and just teetering on the precipice of falling forever in love with the girl-child I had protected like a little sister and who—overnight, it seemed—had become a girl-woman whom I knew now as a friend.

I should also say that the other things I write of here—the events in Pax space, the murder of Paul Duré, the retrieval of the female-thing named Rhadamanth Nemes, the thoughts of Father Federico de Soya—are not surmised or extrapolated or made-up in the way that the old fiction novels were in Martin Silenus's day. I *know* these things, down to the level of

Father de Soya's thoughts and Councillor Albedo's apparel that day, not because I am omniscient, but because of later events and revelations that gave access to such omniscience.

It will make sense later. At least I hope it will.

I apologize for this awkward reintroduction. The template for Aenea's cybrid father—a poet named John Keats—said in his last letter of farewell to his friends, "I have always made an awkward bow." In truth, so have I—whether in departure or greeting or, as is perhaps the case here, in improbable reunion.

So I will return to my memories and ask your indulgence if they do not make perfect sense at my first attempt to share and shape them.

THE WIND HOWLED and the dust blew for three days and three nights after Aenea's sixteenth birthday. The girl was gone for all that time. Over the past four years I had grown used to her "time-outs," as she called them, and I usually did not fret the way I had the first few times she had disappeared for days on end. This time, however, I was more concerned than usual: the death of the Old Architect had left the twenty-seven apprentices and the sixty-some support people at the desert camp—which is what the Old Architect called Taliesin West—anxious and uneasy. The dust storm added to that anxiety, as dust storms always do. Most of the families and support staff lived close by, in one of the desert-masonry dormitories Mr. Wright had his interns build south of the main buildings, and the camp complex itself was almost fortlike with its walls and courtyards and covered walkways—good for scuttling between buildings during a dust storm—but each successive day without either sunlight or Aenea made me increasingly nervous.

Several times each day I went to her apprentice shelter: it was the farthest from the main compound, almost a quarter of a mile north toward the mountains. She was never there—she had left the door untethered and a note telling me not to worry, that it was just one of her excursions and that she was taking plenty of water—but every time I visited I appreciated her shelter more.

Four years earlier, when she and I had first arrived with a dropship stolen from a Pax warship, both of us exhausted, battered, and burned, not to mention with an android healing in the ship's autosurgeon, the Old Architect and the other apprentices had greeted us with warmth and acceptance. Mr. Wright had not seemed surprised that a twelve-year-old child had come across world after world via farcaster to find him and to ask to be his apprentice. I remember that first day when the Old Architect had asked her what she knew of architecture—"Nothing," Aenea had replied quietly, "except that you are the one I should learn from."

Evidently this had been the correct response. Mr. Wright had told her that all of the apprentices who had arrived before her—all twenty-six others, as it turned out—had been asked to design and build their own shelters in the desert as a sort of entry exam. The Old Architect had offered some crude materials from the compound—canvas, stone, cement, a bit of cast-off lumber—but the design and effort were up to the girl.

Before she set to work (not being an apprentice, I made do with a tent close to the main compound), Aenea and I toured the other apprentice shelters. Most were variations on tent-shacks. They were serviceable and some showed style—one particularly exhibited a nice design flare but, as Aenea pointed out to me, would not keep the sand or rain out with the slightest wind—but none was particularly memorable.

Aenea worked eleven days on her shelter. I helped her do some of the heavy lifting and a bit of the excavating (A. Bettik was still recovering at that time—first in the autosurgeon, then in the compound's infirmary), but the girl did all of the planning and most of the work. The result was this wonderful shelter that I visited four times a day during this, her last hiatus in the desert. Aenea had excavated the main sections of the shelter so that most of it was below ground level. Then she had set flagstones in place, making sure that they fit tightly, to create a smooth floor. Over the stones she set colorful rugs and blankets she traded for at the Indian Market fifteen miles away. Around the excavated core of the home she set walls that were about a meter high, but with the sunken main room, they seemed taller. They were constructed of the same rough "desert masonry" that Mr. Wright had used in building the walls and superstructure of the main compound buildings and Aenea used the same technique, although she had never heard him describe it.

First, she gathered stones from the desert and the many arroyos and washes around the hilltop compound. The rocks were of every size and color—purple, black, rusty reds, and deep umbers—and some held petroglyphs or fossils. After gathering the stones, Aenea built wooden forms and set the larger rocks in with their flat sides against the inside face of the form. She then spent days in the broiling sun, shoveling sand from the washes and carting it back to her building site in wheelbarrows, mixing it there with cement to form the concrete that held the stones in place as the mixture hardened. It was a rough concrete/stone concoction—desert masonry, Mr. Wright called it—but it was strangely beautiful, the colorful rocks showing through the surface of the concrete, fissures and textures everywhere. Once in place, the walls were about a meter high and thick enough to hold out the desert heat in the daytime and hold in the inner heat at night.

Her shelter was more complex than it first appeared to the eye—it was months before I appreciated the subtle tricks she had pulled in its design. One ducked to enter the vestibule, a stone-and-canvas porte cochere with three broad steps leading one down and around to the wood and masonry portal that served as the entrance to the main room. This twisting, descending vestibule acted as a sort of air lock, sealing out the desert sand and harshness, and the way she had rigged the canvas—almost like over-lapping jib sails—improved the air-lock effect. The "main room" was only three meters across and five long, but it seemed much larger. Aenea had used built-in benches around a raised stone table to create a dining and sitting area, and then placed more niches and stone seats near a hearth she had fashioned in the north wall of the shelter. There was an actual stone chimney built into the wall, and it did not touch the canvas or wood at any point. Between the stone walls and the canvas—at about eye height when seated—she had rigged screened windows that ran the length of the north and south sides of the shelter. These panoramic viewslits could be battened down by both canvas and sliding wood shutters, operated from the inside. Overhead, she had used old fiberglass rods found in the compound junk heap to shape the canvas in smooth arches, sudden peaks, cathedral vaults, and odd, folded niches.

She had actually fashioned a bedroom for herself, again removed from the main room by two steps twisted at sixty-degree angles, the entire niche built into the gently rising slope and set back against a huge boulder she had found on the site. There was no water or plumbing out here—we all shared the communal showers and toilets in the compound annex—but Aenea had built a lovely little rock basin and bath next to her bed (a plywood platform with mattress and blankets), and several times a week she would heat water in the main kitchen and carry it to her shelter, bucket by bucket, for a hot bath.

The light through the canvas ceilings and walls was warm at sunrise, buttery at midday, and orange in the evening. In addition, Aenea had deliberately placed the shelter in careful relation to saguaros, prickly pear bushes, and staghorn cactus so that different shadows would fall on different planes of canvas at different times of day. It was a comfortable, pleasant place. And empty beyond description when my young friend was absent.

I mentioned that the apprentices and support staff were anxious after the Old Architect's death. Distraught might be a better word. I spent most of those three days of Aenea's absence listening to the concerned babble of almost ninety people—never together, since even the dinner shifts in the dining hall were spaced apart because Mr. Wright had not liked huge crowds at dinner—and the level of panic seemed to grow as the days and dust storms went by. Aenea's absence was a big part of the hysteria: she was the youngest apprentice at Taliesin—the youngest person, actually—but the others had grown used to asking advice of her and of listening when she spoke. In one week, they had lost both their mentor and their guide.

On the fourth morning after her birthday, the dust storms ended and Aenea returned. I happened to be out jogging just after sunrise and saw her coming across the desert from the direction of the McDowell Mountains: she was silhouetted in the morning light, a thin figure with short hair against the corona brilliance, and in that second I thought of the first time I had seen her in the Valley of the Time Tombs on Hyperion.

She grinned when she saw me. "Hey, Boo," she called. It was an old joke based on some book she had read as a very young child.

"Hey, Scout," I called back, answering in the same in-joke language.

We stopped when we were five paces apart. My impulse was to hug her and hold her close and beg her not to disappear again. I did not do that. The rich, low light of morning threw long shadows behind the cholla cacti, greasebushes, and sage, and bathed our already-sunburned skin in an orange glow.

"How're the troops doing?" asked Aenea. I could see that despite her promises to the contrary, she had been fasting during the past three days. She had always been thin, but now her ribs almost showed through her thin cotton shirt. Her lips were dry and cracked. "They upset?" she said.

"They're shitting bricks," I said. For years I'd avoided using my Home Guard vocabulary around the kid, but she was sixteen now. Besides, she had always used a saltier vocabulary than I knew.

Aenea grinned. The brilliant light illuminated the sandy streaks in her short hair. "That'd be good for a bunch of architects, I guess."

I rubbed my chin, feeling the rough stubble there. "Seriously, kiddo. They're pretty upset."

Aenea nodded. "Yeah. They don't know what to do or where to go now that Mr. Wright's gone." She squinted toward the Fellowship compound, which showed up as little more than asymmetrical bits of stone and canvas just visible above the cacti and scrub brush. Sunlight glinted off unseen windows and one of the fountains. "Let's get everybody in the music pavilion and talk," said Aenea, and began striding toward Taliesin.

And thus began our last full day together on Earth.

I AM GOING to interrupt myself here. I hear my own voice on the 'scriber and remember the pause in the telling at this point. What I *wanted* to do here was tell all about the four years of exile on Old Earth—all about the apprentices and other people at the Taliesin Fellowship, all about the Old Architect and his whims and petty cruelties, as well as about his brilliance and childlike enthusiasms. I wanted to describe the many conversations with Aenea over those forty-eight local months (which—as I never got tired of being amazed by—corresponded perfectly to Hegemony/Pax *standard* months!) and my slow growth of understanding of her incredible insights and abilities. Finally, I wanted to tell of all my excursions during that time—my trip around the Earth in the dropship, the long driving adventures in North America, my fleeting contact with the other islands of humanity huddled around cybrid figures from the human past (the gathering in Israel and New Palestine around the cybrid Jesus of Nazareth was a memorable group to visit), but primarily, when I hear the brief silence on the 'scriber that took the place of these tales, I remember the reason for my omission.

As I said before, I 'scribed these words in the Schrödinger cat box orbiting Armaghast, while awaiting the simultaneous emission of an isotopic particle and the activation of the particle detector. When these two events coincided, the cyanide gas built into the static-energy field around the recycling equipment would be released. Death would not be instantaneous, but near enough. While protesting earlier that I would take my time in telling our story—Aenea's and mine—I realize now that there was some editing, some attempt to get to the important elements before the particle decayed and the gas flowed.

I will not double-guess that decision now, except to say that the four years on Earth would be worth telling about at some other point in time: the ninety people of the Fellowship were decent, complex, devious, and interesting in the way of all intelligent human beings, and their tales should be told. Similarly, my explorations across Earth, both in the dropship and in the 1948 "Woody" station wagon that the Old Architect loaned me, might support an epic poem of their own.

But I am not a poet. But I was a tracker in my hunting-guide days, and my job here is to follow the path of Aenea's growth to womanhood and messiahship without wandering down too many sidetracks. And so I shall.

THE OLD ARCHITECT always referred to the Fellowship compound as "desert camp." Most of the apprentices referred to it as "Taliesin"—which means "Shining Brow" in Welsh. (Mr. Wright was of Welsh distraction. I spent weeks trying to remember a Pax or Outback world named Welsh, before I remembered that the Old Architect had lived and died before spaceflight.) Aenea often referred to the place as "Taliesin West," which suggested to even someone as dull as me that there had to be a Taliesin East.

When I asked her three years earlier, Aenea had explained that the original Mr. Wright had built his first Taliesin Fellowship compound in the early 1930s in Spring Green, Wisconsin—Wisconsin being one of the political and geographical sub-units of the ancient North American nation-state called the United States of America. When I asked Aenea if the first Taliesin was like this one, she had said, "Not really. There were a series of Wisconsin Taliesins—both homes and fellowship compounds—and most were destroyed by fire. That's one of the reasons Mr. Wright installed so many pools and fountains here at this compound—sources of water to fight the inevitable fires."

"And his first Taliesin was built in the 1930s?" I said.

Aenea shook her head. "He opened his first Taliesin *Fellowship* in 1932," she said. "But that was mostly a way to get slave labor from his apprentices—both for building his dream and raising food for him—during the Depression."

"What was the Depression?"

"Bad economic times in their pure capitalist nation-state," Aenea said. "Remember, the economy wasn't really global then, and it depended upon private money institutions called banks, gold reserves, and the value of physical money—actual coins and pieces of paper that were supposed to be worth something. It was all a consensual hallucination, of course, and in the 1930s, the hallucination turned nightmare."

"Jesus," I said.

"Precisely," said Aenea. "Anyway, long before that, in 1909 A.D., the middle-aged Mr. Wright abandoned his wife and six children and ran away to Europe with a married woman."

I admit that I blinked at this news. The thought of the Old Architect—a man in his mid-eighties when we had met him four years ago—with a sex life, and a scandalous one at that, took some getting used to. I also wondered what all this had to do with my question about Taliesin East.

Aenea was getting to that. "When he returned with the other woman," she said, smiling at my rapt attention, "he began building the first Taliesin—his home in Wisconsin—for Mamah . . ."

"His mother?" I said, totally confused.

"Mamah Borthwick," said Aenea, spelling the first name for me. "Mrs. Cheney. The Other Woman."

"Oh."

The smile fading, she continued. "The scandal had destroyed his architectural practice and made him a branded man in the United States. But he built Taliesin and forged ahead, trying to find new patrons. His first wife, Catherine, would not give him a divorce. The newspapers—those were databanks printed on paper and distributed regularly—thrived on such gossip and fanned the flames of the scandal, not letting it die."

We had been walking in the courtyard when I asked Aenea the simple question about Taliesin, and I remember pausing by the fountain during this part of her answer. I was always amazed at what this child knew.

"Then," she said, "on August 15, 1914, a worker at Taliesin went crazy, killed Mamah Borthwick and her son John and daughter Martha with a hatchet, burned their bodies, set fire to the compound, and then killed four of Mr. Wright's friends and apprentices before swallowing acid himself. The entire place burned down."

"My God," I whispered, looking toward the dining hall where the cybrid Old Architect was having lunch with a few of his oldest apprentices even as we spoke.

"He never gave up," said Aenea. "A few days later, on August 18, Mr. Wright was touring an artificial lake on the Taliesin property when the dam he was standing on gave way and he was swept into a rain-swollen creek. Against all odds, he swam out of the torrent. A few weeks later he started to rebuild."

I thought that I understood then what she was telling me about the Old Architect. "Why aren't we at *that* Taliesin?" I asked as we strolled away from the bubbling fountain in the desert courtyard.

Aenea shook her head. "Good question. I doubt if it even exists in this rebuilt version of Earth. It was important to Mr. Wright, though. He died here . . . near Taliesin West . . . on April 9, 1959, but he was buried back near the Wisconsin Taliesin."

I stopped walking then. The thought of the Old Architect dying was a new and disturbing thought. Everything about our exile had been steady-state, calm and self-renewing, but now Aenea had reminded me that everything and everyone ends. Or had, before the Pax introduced the cruciform and physical resurrection to humanity. But no one at the Fellowship—perhaps no one on this kidnapped Earth—had submitted to a cruciform.

That conversation had been three years earlier. This morning, the week after the cybrid Old Architect's death and incongruous burial in the small mausoleum he had built out in the desert, we were ready to face the consequences of death without resurrection and the end of things.

While Aenea went off to the bath and laundry pavilion to wash up, I found A. Bettik and the two of us got busy with spreading the word of the meeting in the music pavilion. The blue-skinned android did not act surprised that Aenea, the youngest of us, was calling and leading the meeting. Both A. Bettik and I had watched silently over the past few years as the girl became the locus of the Fellowship.

I jogged from the fields to the dormitories, from the dormitories to the kitchen—where I rang the large bell set in the fanciful bell tower above the stairway to the guest deck. Those apprentices or workers whom I did not contact personally should hear the bell and come to investigate.

From the kitchen, where I left cooks and some of the apprentices taking their aprons off and wiping their hands, I announced the meeting to people having coffee in the large Fellowship dining room (the view from this beautiful room looked north toward the McDowell peaks, so some had watched Aenea and me return and knew that something was up), and then I poked my head in Mr. Wright's smaller, private dining room—empty—and then jogged over to the drafting room. This was probably the most attractive room in the compound with its long rows of drafting tables and filing cabinets set under the sloping canvas roof, the morning light flooding in through the two rows of offset windows. The sun was high enough now to fall on the roof and the smell of heated canvas was as pleasant as the butter-rich light. Aenea had once told me that it was this sense of camping out—of working within the confines of light and canvas and stone—that had been the real reason for Mr. Wright coming west to the second Taliesin.

There were ten or twelve of the apprentices in the drafting room, all standing around—none working now that the Old Architect was no longer around to suggest projects—and I told them that Aenea would like us to gather in the music pavilion. None protested. None grumbled or made any comment about a sixteen-year-old telling ninety of her elders to come together in the middle of a workday. If anything, the apprentices looked relieved to hear that she was back and taking charge.

From the drafting room I went to the library where I had spent so many happy hours and then checked the conference room, lit only by four glowing panels in the floor, and announced the meeting to the people I found in both places. Then I jogged down the concrete path under the covered walkway of desert masonry and peered in the cabaret theater where the Old Architect had loved to show movies on Saturday nights. This place had always tickled me—its thick stone walls and roof, the long descending space with plywood benches covered with red cushions, the well-worn red carpet on the floor, and the many hundreds of white Christmas lights running back and forth on the ceiling. When we first arrived, Aenea and I were amazed to find that the Old Architect demanded that his apprentices and their families "dress for dinner" on Saturdays—ancient tuxedoes and black ties, of the sort one sees in the oldest history holos. The women wore strange dresses out of antiquity. Mr. Wright provided the formal clothes for those who failed to bring them in their flight to Earth through Time Tombs or farcaster.

That first Saturday, Aenea had shown up dressed in a tuxedo, shirt, and black tie rather than one of the dresses provided. When I first saw the Old Architect's shocked expression, I was sure that he was going to throw us out of the Fellowship and make us eke out a living in the desert, but then the old face creased into a smile and within seconds he was laughing. He never asked Aenea to dress in anything else.

After the formal Saturday dinners, we would either have a group musical event or assemble in the cabaret theater for a movie—one of the ancient, celluloid kinds that had to be projected by a machine. It was rather like learning to enjoy cave art. Both Aenea and I loved the films he chose—ancient twentieth-century flat things, many in black and white—and for some reason that he never explained, Mr. Wright preferred to watch them with the "sound track," optical jiggles and wiggles, visible on the screen. Actually, we'd watched films there for a year before one of the other apprentices told us that they had been made to be watched *without* the sound track visible.

Today the cabaret theater was empty, the Christmas lights dark. I jogged on, moving from room to room, building to building, rounding up apprentices, workers, and family members until I met A. Bettik by the fountain and we joined the others in the large music pavilion.

The pavilion was a large space, with a broad stage and six rows of eighteen upholstered seats in each row. The walls were of redwood painted Cherokee Red (the Old Architect's favorite color) and the usual thick desert masonry. A grand piano and a few potted plants were the only things on the red-carpeted stage. Overhead, stretched tight above a gridwork of wood and steel ribs, was the usual white canvas. Aenea had once told me that after the death of the first Mr. Wright, plastic had taken the place of canvas to relieve the necessity of replacing canvas every couple of years. But upon *this* Mr. Wright's return, the plastic was ripped out—as was the glass above the main drafting room—so that pure light through white canvas would be the rule once again.

A. Bettik and I stood near the rear of the music pavilion as the murmuring apprentices and other workers took their seats, some of the construction workers standing on the aisle steps or at the back with the android and me, as if worried about tracking mud and dust onto the rich carpet and upholstery. When Aenea entered through the side curtains and jumped to the stage, all the conversation stopped.

The acoustics were good in Mr. Wright's music pavilion, but Aenea had always been able to project her voice without seeming to raise it. She spoke softly. "Thank you for gathering. I thought we should talk."

Jaev Peters, one of the older apprentices, immediately stood up in the fifth row. "You were gone, Aenea. In the desert again."

The girl on the stage nodded.

"Did you talk to the Lions and Tigers and Bears?"

No one in the audience tittered or giggled. The question was asked in deadly seriousness and the answer was awaited by ninety people just as seriously. I should explain.

It all began in the *Cantos* Martin Silenus wrote more than two centuries ago. That tale of the Hyperion pilgrims, the Shrike, and the battle between humanity and the TechnoCore explained how the early cyberspace webs had evolved into planetary dataspheres. By the time of the Hegemony, the AI TechnoCore had used their secret farcaster and fatline technologies to weave hundreds of dataspheres into a single, secret, interstellar information medium called the megasphere. But, according to the *Cantos,* Aenea's father—the cybrid John Keats—had traveled in disembodied datapersona form to the megasphere's Core and discovered that there was a larger datumplane medium, perhaps larger than our galaxy, which even the Core AIs were afraid to explore because it was full of "lions and tigers and bears"—those were Ummon the AI's words. These were the beings—or intelligences—or gods, for all we knew—who had kidnapped the Earth and brought it here before the Core could destroy it a millennium ago. These Lions and Tigers and Bears were the bugaboo guardians of our world. No one in the Fellowship had ever seen any of these entities, or spoken to them, or had any solid evidence of their existence. No one except Aenea.

"No," said the girl on the stage, "I didn't talk to them." She looked down as if embarrassed. She was always reticent to talk about this. "But I think I heard them."

"They spoke to you?" said Jaev Peters. The pavilion was hushed.

"No," said Aenea. "I didn't say that. I just . . . heard them. A bit like when you overhear someone else's conversation through a dormitory wall."

There was a rustle of amusement at this. For all the thick stone walls on the Fellowship property, the dorm partitions were notably thin.

"All right," said Bets Kimbal from the first row. Bets was the chief cook and a large, sensible woman. "Tell us what they said."

Aenea stepped up to the edge of the red-carpeted stage and looked out at her elders and colleagues. "I can tell you this," she said softly. "There'll be no more food and supplies from the Indian Market. That's gone."

It was as if she had set off a grenade in the music pavilion. When the babble began to subside, one of the biggest of the construction workers, a man named Hussan, shouted over the noise. "What do you mean it's gone? Where do we get our food?"

There was good reason for the panic. In Mr. Wright's day, way back in the twentieth century, his Fellowship desert camp had been about fifty kilometers from a large town called Phoenix. Unlike the Depression-era Wisconsin Taliesin, where apprentices raised crops in the rich soil even while they worked on Mr. Wright's construction plans, this desert camp had never been able to grow its own food. So they drove to Phoenix and bartered or paid out their primitive coins and paper money for basic supplies. The Old Architect had always depended upon the largesse of patrons—large loans never to be paid back—for such month-to-month survival.

Here in our reassembled desert camp, there were no towns. The only road—two gravel ruts—led west into hundreds of miles of emptiness. I knew this because I had flown over the area in the dropship and driven it in the Old Architect's groundcar. But about thirty klicks from the compound there was a weekly Indian market where we had bartered craft items for food and basic materials. It had been there for years before Aenea's and my arrival; everyone had obviously expected it to be there forever.

"What do you mean it's gone?" repeated Hussan in a hoarse shout. "Where'd the Indians go? Were they just cybrid illusions, like Mr. Wright?"

Aenea made a gesture with her hands that I had grown accustomed to over the years—a graceful setting-aside motion that I had come to see as a physical analog of the Zen expression "mu," which, in the right context, can mean "unask the question."

"The market's gone because we won't need it anymore," said Aenea. "The Indians are real enough—Navajo, Apache, Hopi, and Zuni—but they have their own lives to live, their own experiments to conduct. Their trading with us has been . . . a favor."

The crowd became angry at that, but eventually they settled down again. Bets Kimbal stood. "What do we do, child?"

Aenea sat on the edge of the stage as if trying to become one with the waiting, expectant audience. "The Fellowship is over," she said. "That part of our lives has to end."

One of the younger apprentices was shouting from the back of the pavilion. "No it doesn't! Mr. Wright could still return! He was a cybrid, remember . . . a construct! The Core . . . or the Lions and Tigers and Bears . . . whoever shaped him can send him back to us . . ."

Aenea shook her head, sadly but firmly. "No. Mr. Wright is gone.

The Fellowship is over. Without the food and materials the Indians brought from so far away, this desert camp can't last a month. We have to go."

It was a young female apprentice named Peret who spoke quietly into the silence. "Where, Aenea?"

Perhaps it was at this moment that I first realized how this entire group had given themselves over to the young woman I had known as a child. When the Old Architect was around, giving lectures, holding forth in seminars and drafting-room bull sessions, leading his flock on picnics and swimming outings in the mountains, demanding solicitude and the best food, the reality of Aenea's leadership had been somewhat masked. But now it was evident.

"Yes," someone else called from the center of the rising rows of seats, "where, Aenea?"

My friend opened her hands in another gesture I had learned. Rather than *Unask the question,* this one said, *You must answer your own question.* Aloud, she said, "There are two choices. Each of you traveled here either by farcaster or through the Time Tombs. You can go back by way of farcaster . . ."

"No!"

"How can we?"

"Never . . . I'd rather die!"

"No! The Pax will find us and kill us!"

The cries were immediate and from the heart. It was the sound of terror made verbal. I smelled fear in the room the way I used to smell it on animals caught in leg traps on the moors of Hyperion.

Aenea lifted a hand and the outcries faded. "You can return to Pax space by farcaster, or you can stay on Earth and try to fend for yourself."

There were murmurs and I could hear relief at the option of not returning. I understood that feeling—the Pax had come to be a bogeyman to me, as well. The thought of returning there sent me gasping up out of sleep at least once a week.

"But if you stay here," continued the girl seated on the edge of Mr. Wright's music stage, "you will be outcasts. All of the groups of human beings here are involved in their own projects, their own experiments. You will not fit in there."

People shouted questions about that, demanding answers to mysteries not understood during their long stay here. But Aenea continued with what she was saying. "If you stay here, you will waste what Mr. Wright has taught you and what you came to learn about yourself. The Earth does not need architects and builders. Not now. We have to go back."

Jaev Peters spoke again. His voice was brittle, but not angry. "And does the Pax need builders and architects? To build its cross-damned churches?"

"Yes," said Aenea.

Jaev pounded the back of the seat in front of him with his large fist.

"But they'll capture or kill us if they learn who we are . . . where we've been!"

"Yes," said Aenea.

Bets Kimbal said, "Are you going back, child?"

"Yes," said Aenea and pushed herself away from the stage.

Everyone was standing now, shouting or talking to the people next to them. It was Jaev Peters who spoke the thoughts of the ninety Fellowship orphans. "Can we go with you, Aenea?"

The girl sighed. Her face, as sunburned and alert as it looked this morning, also looked tired. "No," she said. "I think that leaving here is like dying or being born. We each have to do it alone." She smiled. "Or in very small groups."

The room fell silent then. When Aenea spoke, it was as if a single instrument were picking up where the orchestra had stopped. "Raul will leave first," she said. "Tonight. One by one, each of you will find the right farcaster portal. I will help you. I will be the last to leave Earth. But leave I will, and within a few weeks. We all must go."

People pushed forward then, still silent, but moving closer to the girl with the short-cropped hair. "But some of us will meet again," said Aenea. "I feel certain that some of us will meet again."

I heard the flip side of that reassuring prediction: some of us would not survive to meet again.

"Well," boomed Bets Kimbal, standing with one broad arm around Aenea, "we have enough food in the kitchen for one last feast. Lunch today will be a meal you'll remember for years! If you have to travel, as my mum used to say, never travel on an empty stomach. Who's to help me in the kitchen then?"

The groups broke up then, families and friends in clusters, loners standing as if stunned, everyone moving closer to Aenea as we began filing out of the music pavilion. I wanted to grab her at that moment, shake her until her wisdom teeth fell out, and demand, *What the hell do you mean—* "*Raul will leave first . . . tonight.*" *Who the hell are you to tell me to leave you behind? And how do you think you can make me?* But she was too far away and too many people were pressing around her. The best I could do was stride along behind the crowd as it moved toward the kitchen and dining area, anger written in my face, fists, muscles, and walk.

Once I saw Aenea glance back, straining to find me over the heads of the crowd around her, and her eyes pleaded, *Let me explain.*

I stared back stonily, giving her nothing.

It was almost dusk when she joined me in the large garage Mr. Wright had ordered built half a klick east of the compound. The structure was open on the sides except for canvas curtains, but it had thick stone columns supporting a permanent redwood roof; it had been built to shelter the dropship in which Aenea, A. Bettik, and I had arrived.

I had pulled back the main canvas door and was standing in the open hatch of the dropship when I saw Aenea crossing the desert toward me. On my wrist was the comlog bracelet that I had not worn in more than a year: the thing held much of the memory of our former spaceship—the Consul's ship from centuries ago—and it had been my liaison and tutor when I had learned to fly the dropship. I did not need it now—the comlog memory had been downloaded into the dropship and I had become rather good at piloting the dropship on my own—but it made me feel more secure. The comlog was also running a systems check on the ship: chatting with itself, you might say.

Aenea stood just within the folded canvas. The sunset threw long shadows behind her and painted the canvas red. "How's the dropship?" she said.

I glanced at the comlog readings. "All right," I grunted, not looking her way.

"Does it have enough fuel and charge for one more flight?"

Still not looking up, fiddling with touchplates on the arm of the pilot's chair inside the hatch, I said, "Depends on where it's flying to."

Aenea walked to the dropship stairway and touched my leg. "Raul?" This time I had to look at her.

"Don't be angry," she said. "We have to do these things."

I pulled my leg away. "Goddammit, don't keep telling me and everyone else what we have to do. You're just a kid. Maybe there are things some of us *don't* have to do. Maybe going off on my own and leaving you behind is one of those." I stepped off the ladder and tapped the comlog. The stairs morphed back into the dropship hull. I left the garage and began walking toward my tent. On the horizon, the sun was a perfect red sphere. In the last low rays of light, the stones and canvas of the main compound looked as if they had caught fire—the Old Architect's greatest fear.

"Raul, wait!" Aenea hurried to catch up to me. One glance in her direction told me how exhausted she was. All afternoon she had been meeting with people, talking to people, explaining to people, reassuring people, hugging people. I had come to think of the Fellowship as a nest of emotional vampires and Aenea as their only source of energy.

"You said that you would . . ." she began.

"Yeah, yeah," I interrupted. I suddenly had the sense that she was the adult and that I was the petulant child. To hide my confusion, I turned away again and watched the last of the sunset. For a moment or two we were both silent, watching the light fade and the sky darken. I had decided that Earth sunsets were slower and more lovely than the Hyperion sunsets I had known as a child, and that desert sunsets were particularly fine. How many sunsets had this child and I shared in the past four years? How many lazy evenings of dinner and conversation under the brilliant desert stars? Could this really be the last sunset we would watch together? The idea made me sick and furious.

"Raul," she said again when the shadows had grown together and the air was cooling, "will you come with me?"

I did not say yes, but I followed her across the rocky field, avoiding the bayonet spikes of yucca and the spines of low cacti in the gloom, until we came into the lighted area of the compound. *How long,* I wondered, *until the fuel oil for the generators runs out?* This answer I knew—it was part of my job to keep the generators maintained and fueled. We had six days' supply in the main tanks and another ten days in the reserve tanks that were never to be touched except in emergency. With the Indian Market gone, there would be no resupply. Almost three weeks of electric lights and refrigeration and power equipment and then . . . what? Darkness, decay, and an end to the incessant construction, tearing down, and rebuilding that had been the background noise at Taliesin for the last four years.

I thought perhaps that we were going to the dining hall, but we walked past those lighted windows—groups of people still sitting at the tables, talking earnestly, glancing up with eyes only for Aenea as we passed—I was invisible to them in their hour of panic—and then we approached Mr. Wright's private drafting studio and his office, but we did not stop there. Nor did we stop in the beautiful little conference room where a small group sat to watch a final movie—three weeks until the movie projectors did not run—nor did we turn into the main drafting room.

Our destination was a stone-and-canvas workshop set far down the driveway on the south side, a useful outbuilding for working with toxic chemicals or noisy equipment. I had worked here often in the first couple of years at the Fellowship, but not in recent months.

A. Bettik was waiting at the door. The android had a slight smile on his bland, blue face, rather like the one he had worn when carrying the birthday cake to Aenea's surprise party.

"What?" I said, still irritated, looking from the girl's tired face to the android's smug expression.

Aenea stepped into the workshop and turned on the light.

On the worktable in the center of the little room sat a small boat, not much more than two meters in length. It was shaped rather like a seed sharpened on both ends, enclosed except for a single, round cockpit opening with a nylon skirt that could obviously be tightened around the occupant's waist. A two-bladed paddle lay on the table next to the boat. I stepped closer and ran my hand over the hull: a polished fiberglass compound with internal aluminum braces and fittings. Only one other person at the Fellowship could do such careful work. I looked at A. Bettik almost accusingly. He nodded.

"It's called a kayak," said Aenea, running her own hand over the polished hull. "It's an old Earth design."

"I've seen variations on it," I said, refusing to be impressed. "The Ice Claw Ursus rebels used small boats like this."

Aenea was still stroking the hull, all of her attention there. It was as if

I had not spoken. "I asked A. Bettik to make it for you," she said. "He's worked for weeks here."

"For me," I said dully. My stomach tightened at the realization of what was coming.

Aenea moved closer. She was standing directly under the hanging light, and the shadows under her eyes and cheekbones made her look much older than sixteen. "We don't have the raft anymore, Raul."

I knew the raft she meant. The one that had carried us across so many worlds until it was chopped up in the ambush that almost killed us on God's Grove. The raft that had carried us down the river under the ice on Sol Draconi Septem and through the deserts of Hebron and Qom-Riyadh and across the world ocean of Mare Infinitus. I knew the raft she meant. And I knew what this boat meant.

"So I'm to take this back the way we came?" I raised a hand as if to touch the thing, but then did not.

"Not the way we came," said Aenea. "But down the River Tethys. Across different worlds. Across as many worlds as it takes to find the ship."

"The ship?" I said. We had left the Consul's spaceship hiding under a river, repairing itself from damage sustained in our flight from the Pax, on a world whose name and location we did not know.

My young friend nodded and the shadows fled, then regrouped around her tired eyes. "We'll need the ship, Raul. If you would, I'd like you to take this kayak down the River Tethys until you find the ship, then fly back with it to a world where A. Bettik and I will be waiting."

"A world in Pax space?" I said, my stomach tightening another notch at the danger present in that simple sentence.

"Yes."

"Why me?" I said, looking significantly at A. Bettik. I was ashamed at my thought then: *Why send a human being . . . your best friend . . . when the android can go?* I lowered my gaze.

"It will be a dangerous trip," said Aenea. "I believe that you can do it, Raul. I trust you to find the ship and then find us."

I felt my shoulders slump. "All right," I said. "Do we head back to where we came through the farcaster before?" We had come through from God's Grove on a small stream near the Old Architect's masterpiece building, Fallingwater. It was two thirds of a continent away.

"No," said Aenea. "Closer. On the Mississippi River."

"All right," I said again. I had flown over the Mississippi. It was almost two thousand klicks east of here. "When do I go? Tomorrow?"

Aenea touched my wrist. "No," she said, tiredly but firmly. "Tonight. Right now."

I did not protest. I did not argue. Without speaking, I took the bow of the kayak, A. Bettik took the stern, Aenea held the center steady, and we carried the damned thing back to the dropship in the deepening desert night.

3

THE GRAND INQUISITOR WAS LATE.

Vatican Air/Space Traffic Control routed the Inquisitor's EMV across normally closed airspace near the spaceport, shut down all airborne traffic on the east side of the Vatican, and held a thirty-thousand-ton robot freighter in orbital final approach until after the GI's car had flown across the southeast corner of the landing grid.

Inside the specially armored EMV, the Grand Inquisitor—His Eminence John Domenico Cardinal Mustafa—did not glance out the window or at the video monitors at the lovely sight of the approaching Vatican, its walls rosy in the morning light, or at the busy, twenty-lane highway called the Ponte Vittorio Emanuele beneath them, glimmering like a sunlit river because of sunlight on windshields and bubbletops. The Grand Inquisitor's attention was focused solely on the intelligence update scrolling by on his comlog template.

When the last paragraph had scrolled past and was committed to memory and deleted to oblivion, the Grand Inquisitor said to his aide, Father Farrell, "And there have been no more meetings with the Mercantilus?"

Father Farrell, a thin man with flat gray eyes, never smiled, but a twitch of his cheek muscle conveyed the simulation of humor to the Cardinal. "None."

"You're certain?"

"Absolutely."

The Grand Inquisitor sat back in the EMV's cushions and allowed himself a brief smile. The Mercantilus had made only that one early, disastrous approach to any of the papal candidates—the sounding out of Lourdusamy—and the Inquisitor had heard the complete recording of that meeting. The Cardinal allowed himself another few seconds of smile:

Lourdusamy had been right to think that his conference room was bug-proof—absolutely resistant to taps, bugs, wires, and squirts. Any recording device in the room—even implanted in one of the participants—would have been detected and homed in on. Any attempt to tightbeam out would have been detected and blocked. It had been one of the Grand Inquisitor's finest moments, getting the complete visual and auditory recording of that meeting.

Monsignor Lucas Oddi had gone in to the Vatican Hospital for a routine eyes, ears, and heart replacement two local years ago. The surgeon had been approached by Father Farrell and the full weight of the Holy Office had been shown ready to descend upon the poor medico's neck if he did not implant certain state-of-the-art devices in the Monsignor's body. The surgeon did so and died the true death—no resurrection possible—in a car accident far out over the Big North Shallow shortly after that.

Monsignor Lucas Oddi had no electronic or mechanical bugs in his system, but connected to his optic nerve were seven fully biological nano-recorders. Four auditory nanorecorders were tapped into his auditory nerve system. These biorecorders did not transmit inside the body, but stored the data in chemical form and physically carried it through the bloodstream to the squirt transmitter—also fully organic—set into Monsignor Oddi's left ventricle. Ten minutes after Oddi had left the secured area of Cardinal Lourdusamy's office, the transmitter had squirted a compressed record of the meeting to one of the Grand Inquisitor's nearby relay transponders. It was not real-time eavesdropping from Lourdusamy's bugproof rooms—a fact that still worried Cardinal Mustafa—but it was as close to it as current technology and stealth could get.

"Isozaki is frightened," said Father Farrell. "He thinks . . ."

The Grand Inquisitor raised one finger. Farrell stopped in mid-sentence. "You do not know that he is frightened," said the Cardinal. "You do not know what he thinks. You can only know what he says and does and infer his thoughts and reactions from that. *Never* make unsupportable assumptions about your enemies, Martin. It can be a fatal self-indulgence."

Father Farrell bowed his head in agreement and submission.

The EMV touched down on the landing pad atop Castel Sant'Angelo. The Grand Inquisitor was out the hatch and down the ramp so quickly that Farrell had to trot to catch up to his master. Security commandos, dressed in Holy Office red armorcloth, fell into escort step ahead and behind, but the Grand Inquisitor waved them away. He wanted to finish his conversation with Father Farrell. He touched his aide's left arm—not out of affection, but to close the bone-conduction circuits so that he could subvocalize—and said, "Isozaki and the Mercantilus leaders are not frightened. If Lourdusamy wanted them purged, they would be dead by now. Isozaki had to get his message of support to the Cardinal and he did. It's the Pax military who are frightened."

Farrell frowned and subvocalized on the bone circuit. "The military? But they haven't played their card yet. They have done nothing disloyal."

"Precisely," said the Grand Inquisitor. "The Mercantilus has made its move and knows that Lourdusamy will turn to them when the time comes. Pax Fleet and the rest have been terrified for years that they'll make the wrong choice. Now they're terrified that they've waited too long."

Farrell nodded. They had taken a dropshaft deep into the stone bowels of Castel Sant'Angelo, and now they moved past armed guards and through lethal forcefields down a dark corridor. At an unmarked door, two red-garbed commandos stood at attention, energy rifles raised.

"Leave us," said the Grand Inquisitor and palmed the door's ideyplate. The steel panel slid up and out of sight.

The corridor had been stone and shadows. Inside the room, everything was bright light, instruments, and sterile surfaces. Technicians looked up as the Grand Inquisitor and Farrell entered. One wall of the room was taken up by square doors, looking like nothing so much as the multitiered human file drawers of an ancient morgue. One of those doors was open and a naked man lay on a gurney that had been pulled from the cold storage drawer there.

The Grand Inquisitor and Farrell stopped on either side of the gurney.

"He is reviving well," said the technician who stood at the console. "We're holding him just beneath the surface. We can bring him up in seconds."

Father Farrell said, "How long was his last cold sleep?"

"Sixteen local months," said the technician. "Thirteen and a half standard."

"Bring him up," said the Grand Inquisitor.

The man's eyelids began to flutter within seconds. He was a small man, muscular but compact, and there were no marks or bruises on his body. His wrists and ankles were bound by sticktite. A cortical shunt had been implanted just behind his left ear and an almost invisible bundle of microfibers ran from it to the console.

The man on the gurney moaned.

"Corporal Bassin Kee," said the Grand Inquisitor. "Can you hear me?"

Corporal Kee made an unintelligible sound.

The Grand Inquisitor nodded as if satisfied. "Corporal Kee," he said pleasantly, conversationally, "shall we pick up where we left off?"

"How long . . ." mumbled Kee between dry, stiff lips. "How long have I been . . ."

Father Farrell had moved to the technician's console. Now he nodded to the Grand Inquisitor.

Ignoring the corporal's question, John Domenico Cardinal Mustafa said softly, "Why did you and Father Captain de Soya let the girl go?"

Corporal Kee had opened his eyes, blinking as if the light pained him, but now he closed them again. He did not speak.

The Grand Inquisitor nodded to his aide. Father Farrell's hand passed over icons on the console diskey, but did not yet activate any of them.

"Once again," said the Grand Inquisitor. "Why did you and de Soya allow the girl and her criminal allies to escape on God's Grove? Who were you working for? What was your motivation?"

Corporal Kee lay on his back, his fists clenched and his eyes shut fast. He did not answer.

The Grand Inquisitor tilted his head ever so slightly to the left and Father Farrell waved two fingers over one of the console icons. The icons were as abstract as hieroglyphics to the untutored eye, but Farrell knew them well. The one he had chosen would have translated as *crushed testicles*.

On the gurney, Corporal Kee gasped and opened his mouth to scream, but the neural inhibitors blocked that reaction. The short man's jaws opened as wide as they could and Father Farrell could hear the muscles and tendons stretching.

The Grand Inquisitor nodded and Farrell removed his fingers from the activation zone above the icon. Corporal Kee's entire body convulsed on the gurney, his stomach muscles rippling in tension.

"It is only virtual pain, Corporal Kee," whispered the Grand Inquisitor. "A neural illusion. Your body is not marked."

On the slab, Kee was straining to raise his head to look down at his body, but the sticktite band held his head in place.

"Or perhaps not," continued the Cardinal. "Perhaps this time we have resorted to older, less refined methods." He took a step closer to the gurney so that the man could see his face. "Again . . . why did you and Father Captain de Soya let the girl go on God's Grove? Why did you attack your crewmate, Rhadamanth Nemes?"

Corporal Kee's mouth worked until his back teeth became visible. "F . . . f . . . fuck you," he managed, his jaws tight against the shaking that was wracking him.

"Of course," said the Grand Inquisitor and nodded to Father Farrell.

This time, the icon Farrell activated could be translated as *hot wire behind the right eye*.

Corporal Kee opened his mouth in a silent scream.

"Again," said the Grand Inquisitor softly. "Tell us."

"Excuse me, Your Eminence," said Father Farrell, glancing at his comlog, "but the Conclave Mass begins in forty-five minutes."

The Grand Inquisitor waved his fingers. "We have time, Martin. We have time." He touched Corporal Kee's upper arm. "Tell us these few facts, Corporal, and you will be bathed, dressed, and released. You have sinned against your Church and your Lord by this betrayal, but the essence of the Church is forgiveness. Explain your betrayal, and all will be forgiven."

Amazingly, muscles still rippling with shock, Corporal Kee laughed. "Fuck you," he said. "You've already made me tell you everything I know under Truthtell. You know why we killed that bitch-thing and let the child go. And you'll never let me go. Fuck you."

The Grand Inquisitor shrugged and stepped back. Glancing at his own gold comlog, he said softly, "We have time. Much time." He nodded to Father Farrell.

The icon that looked like a double parentheses on the virtual pain console stood for *broad and heated blade down esophagus*. With a graceful motion of his fingers, Father Farrell activated it.

FATHER CAPTAIN FEDERICO DE SOYA was returned to life on Pacem and had spent two weeks as a de facto prisoner in the Vatican Rectory of the Legionaries of Christ. The rectory was comfortable and tranquil. The plump little resurrection chaplain who attended to his needs—Father Baggio—was as kindly and solicitous as ever. De Soya hated the place and the priest.

No one told Father Captain de Soya that he could not leave the Legionaries rectory, but he was made to understand that he should stay there until called. After a week of gaining strength and orientation after his resurrection, he was called to Pax Fleet headquarters, where he met with Admiral Wu and her boss, Admiral Marusyn.

Father Captain de Soya did little during the meeting except salute, stand at ease, and listen. Admiral Marusyn explained that a review of the Father Captain de Soya's court-martial of four years earlier had shown several irregularities and inconsistencies in the prosecution's case. Further review of the situation had warranted a reversal of the court-martial board's decision: Father Captain de Soya was to be reinstated immediately at his former rank of captain in Pax Fleet. Arrangements were being made to find him a ship for combat duty.

"Your old torchship the *Balthasar* is in drydock for a year," said Admiral Marusyn. "A complete refitting—being brought up to archangel-escort standards. Your replacement, Mother Captain Stone, did an excellent job as skipper."

"Yes, sir," said de Soya. "Stone was an excellent exec. I'm sure she's been a good boss."

Admiral Marusyn nodded absently as he thumbed through vellum sheets in his notebook. "Yes, yes," he said. "So good, in fact, that we've recommended her as skipper for one of the new planet-class archangels. We have an archangel in mind for you as well, Father Captain."

De Soya blinked and tried not to react. "The *Raphael*, sir?"

The Admiral looked up, his tanned and creased face set in a slight smile. "Yes, the *Raphael*, but not the one you skippered before. We've retired that prototype to courier duty and renamed her. The new archangel *Raphael* is . . . well, you've heard about the planet-class archangels, Father Captain?"

"No, sir. Not really." He had heard rumors on his desert world when boxite miners had talked loudly in the one cantina in town.

"Four standard years," muttered the Admiral, shaking his head. His white hair was combed back behind his ears. "Bring Federico up to speed here, Admiral."

Marget Wu nodded and touched the diskey on a standard tactical console set into Admiral Marusyn's wall. A holo of a starship came into existence between her and de Soya. The father-captain could see at once that this ship was larger, sleeker, more refined, and deadlier than his old *Raphael.*

"His Holiness has asked each industrial world in the Pax to build—or at least to bankroll—one of these planet-class archangel battlecruisers, Father Captain," said Admiral Wu in her briefing voice. "In the past four years, twenty-one of them have been completed and have entered active service. Another sixty are nearing completion." The holo began to rotate and enlarge until suddenly the main deck was shown in cutaway. It was as if a laser lance had sliced the ship in half.

"As you see," continued Wu, "the living areas, command decks, and C-three tactical centers are much roomier than on the earlier *Raphael* . . . roomier even than your old torchship. The drives—both the classified C-plus instantaneous Gideon drive and the in-system fusion plant—have been reduced in size by one-third while gaining in efficiency and ease of maintenance. The new *Raphael* carries three atmospheric dropships and a high-speed scout. There are automated resurrection crèches aboard to serve a crew of twenty-eight and up to twenty-two Marines or passengers."

"Defenses?" asked Father Captain de Soya, still standing at-ease, his hands clasped behind him.

"Class-ten containment fields," said Wu crisply. "The newest stealth technology. Omega-class ECM and jamming ability. As well as the usual assortment of close-in hyperkinetic and energy defenses."

"Attack capabilities?" said de Soya. He could tell from the apertures and arrays visible on the holo, but he wanted to hear it.

Admiral Marusyn answered with a tone of pride, as if showing off a new grandchild. "The whole nine meters," he said. "CPBs, of course, but feeding off the C-plus drive core rather than the fusion drive. Slag anything within half an AU. New Hawking hyperkinetic missiles—miniaturized— about half the mass and size of the ones you carried on *Balthasar.* Plasma needles with almost twice the yield of the warheads of five years ago. Deathbeams . . ."

Father Captain de Soya tried not to react. Deathbeams had been prohibited in Pax Fleet.

Marusyn saw something in the other man's face. "Things have changed, Federico. This fight is to the finish. The Ousters are breeding like fruit flies out there in the dark, and unless we stop them, they'll be slagging Pacem in a year or two."

Father Captain de Soya nodded. "Do you mind if I ask which world paid for the building of this new *Raphael*, sir?"

Marusyn smiled and gestured toward the holo. The hull of the ship seemed to hurtle toward de Soya as the magnification increased. The view cut through the hull and closed on the tactical bridge, moving to the edge of the tactical center holopit until the father-captain could make out a small bronze plaque with the name—H.H.S. RAPHAEL—and beneath that, in smaller script: BUILT AND COMMISSIONED BY THE PEOPLE OF HEAVEN'S GATE FOR THE DEFENSE OF ALL HUMANITY.

"Why are you smiling, Father Captain?" asked Admiral Marusyn.

"Well, sir, it's just . . . well, I've been to the world of Heaven's Gate, sir. It was, of course, more than four standard years ago, but the planet was empty except for a dozen or so prospectors and a Pax garrison in orbit. There's been no real population there since the Ouster invasion three hundred years ago, sir. I just couldn't imagine that world financing one of these ships. It seems to me that it would take a planetary GNP of a society like Renaissance Vector's to pay for a single archangel."

Marusyn's smile had not faltered. "Precisely, Father Captain. Heaven's Gate is a hellhole—poison atmosphere, acid rain, endless mud, and sulfur flats—it's never recovered from the Ouster attack. But His Holiness thought that the Pax's stewardship of that world might be better transferred to private enterprise. The planet still holds a fortune in heavy metals and chemicals. So we have sold it."

This time de Soya blinked. "Sold it, sir? An entire world?"

While Marusyn openly grinned, Admiral Wu said, "To the Opus Dei, Father Captain."

De Soya did not speak, but neither did he show comprehension.

" 'The Work of God' used to be a minor religious organization," said Wu. "It's . . . ah, I believe . . . about twelve hundred years old. Founded in 1920 A.D. In the past few years, it has become not only a great ally of the Holy See, but a worthy competitor of the Pax Mercantilus."

"Ah, yes," said Father Captain de Soya. He could imagine the Mercantilus buying up entire worlds, but he could not imagine the trading group allowing a rival to gain such power in the few years he had been out of Pax news. It did not matter. He turned to Admiral Marusyn. "One last question, sir."

The Admiral glanced at his comlog chronometer and nodded curtly.

"I have been out of Fleet service for four years," de Soya said softly. "I have not worn a uniform or received a tech update in all that time. The world where I served as a priest was so far out of the mainstream that I might as well have been in cryogenic fugue the whole time. How could I possibly take command of a new-generation archangel-class starship, sir?"

Marusyn frowned. "We'll bring you up to speed, Father Captain. Pax Fleet knows what it's doing. Are you saying no to this commission?"

Father Captain de Soya hesitated a visible second. "No, sir," he said. "I appreciate the confidence in me that you and Pax Fleet are showing. I'll do my best, Admiral." De Soya had been trained to discipline twice—once as a priest and Jesuit, again as an officer in His Holiness's fleet.

Marusyn's stone face softened. "Of course you will, Federico. We're pleased to have you back. We'd like you to stay at the Legionaries rectory here on Pacem until we're ready to send you to your ship, if that would be all right."

Dammit, thought de Soya. *Still a prisoner with those damned Legionaries*. He said, "Of course, sir. It's a pleasant place."

Marusyn glanced at his comlog again. The interview was obviously at an end. "Any requests before the assignment becomes official, Father Captain?"

De Soya hesitated again. He knew that making a request would be bad form. He spoke anyway. "Yes, sir . . . one. There were three men who served with me on the old *Raphael*. Swiss Guard commandos whom I brought from Hyperion . . . Lancer Rettig, well, he died, sir . . . but Sergeant Gregorius and Corporal Kee were with me until the end, and I wondered . . ."

Marusyn nodded impatiently. "You want them on new *Raphael* with you. It sounds reasonable. I used to have a cook that I dragged from ship to ship . . . poor bugger was killed during the Second Coal Sack engagement. I don't know about these men . . ." The Admiral looked at Marget Wu.

"By great coincidence," said Admiral Wu, "I ran across their files while reviewing your reinstatement papers, Father Captain. Sergeant Gregorius is currently serving in the Ring Territories. I am sure that a transfer can be arranged. Corporal Kee, I am afraid . . ."

De Soya's stomach muscles tightened. Kee had been with him around God's Grove—Gregorius had been returned to the crèche after an unsuccessful resurrection—and the last he had seen of the lively little corporal had been after their return to Pacem space, when the MPs had taken them away to separate holding cells after their arrest. De Soya had shaken the corporal's hand and assured him that they would see each other again.

"I am afraid that Corporal Kee died two standard years ago," finished Wu. "He was killed during an Ouster attack on the Sagittarius Salient. I understand that he received the Silver Star of St. Michael's . . . posthumously, of course."

De Soya nodded tersely. "Thank you," he said.

Admiral Marusyn gave his paternal politician's smile and extended his hand across the desk to de Soya. "Good luck, Federico. Give them hell from the *Raphael*."

THE HEADQUARTERS FOR the Pax Mercantilus was not on Pacem proper, but was located—fittingly—on the L$_5$ Trojan point trailing behind the planet by some sixty orbital degrees. Between the Vatican world and the huge, hollow Torus Mercantilus—a carbon-carbon doughnut 270 meters thick, a full klick wide, and 26 kilometers in diameter, its interior webbed with spidery drydocks, com antennae, and loading bays—floated half of Pax Fleet's total orbital-based firepower. Kenzo Isozaki once calculated that a coup attempt launched from Torus Mercantilus would last 12.06 nanoseconds before being vaporized.

Isozaki's office was in a clear bulb on a whiskered-carbon flower stem raised some four hundred meters above the outer rim of the torus. The bulb's curved hullskin could be opaqued or left transparent according to the whim of the CEO inside it. Today it was transparent except for the section polarized to dim the glare of Pacem's yellow sun. Space seemed black at the moment, but as the torus rotated, the bulb would come into the ring's shadow and Isozaki could glance up to see stars instantly appear as if a heavy black curtain had been pulled aside to reveal thousands of brilliant, unflickering candles. *Or the myriad campfires of my enemies,* thought Isozaki as the darkness fell for the twentieth time on this working day.

With the walls absolutely transparent, his oval office with its modest desk, chairs, and soft lamps seemed to become a carpeted platform standing alone in the immensity of space, individual stars blazing and the long swath of the Milky Way lighting the interior. But it was not this familiar spectacle that made the Mercantilus CEO look up: set amid the starfield, three fusion tails of incoming freighters could be picked out, looking like smudges on an astronomical holo. Isozaki was so adept at gauging distances and delta-v's from fusion tails that he could tell at a glance how long it would be before these freighters docked . . . and even which ships they were. The P.M. *Moldahar Effectuator* had refueled by skimming a gas giant in the Epsilon Eridani System and was burning redder than usual. The H.H.M.S. *Emma Constant*'s skipper was in her usual rush to get her cargo of Pegasus 51 reaction metals to the torus and was decelerating inbound a good fifteen percent above Mercantilus recommendations. Finally, the smallest smudge could only be the H.H.M.S. *Elemosineria Apostolica* just passing spindown from its C-plus translation point from Renaissance System: Isozaki knew this from a glance, just as he knew the three hundred–some other optimal translation points visible in his part of the Pacem System sky.

The lift tube rose from the floor and became a transparent cylinder, its passenger lit by starlight. Isozaki knew that the cylinder was transparent only from the outside: in it, the occupants stood in a mirrored interior, seeing nothing of the CEO's office, staring at their own reflection until Isozaki keyed their door open.

Anna Pelli Cognani was the only person in the tube. Isozaki nodded and his personal AI rotated the cube door open. His fellow CEO and protégé did not even glance up at the moving starfield as she crossed the carpet toward him. "Good afternoon, Kenzo-san."

"Good afternoon, Anna." He waved her toward the most comfortable chair, but Cognani shook her head and remained standing. She never took a seat in Isozaki's office. Isozaki never ceased offering her one.

"The Conclave Mass is almost over," said Cognani.

Isozaki nodded. At that second his office AI darkened the bubble walls and projected the Vatican's tightbeam broadcast.

St. Peter's Basilica was awash in scarlet and purple and black and white this morning as the eighty-three cardinals soon to be sealed in the Conclave bowed, prayed, genuflected, knelt, stood, and sang. Behind this *terna,* or herd of theoretically possible candidates for the papacy, were the hundreds of bishops and archbishops, deacons and members of the Curia, Pax military officials and Pax civil administrators, Pax planetary governors and high elected officials who happened to be on Pacem at the time of the Pope's death or who were within three weeks' time-debt, delegates from the Dominicans, the Jesuits, the Benedictines, the Legionaries of Christ, the Mariaists, the Salesians, and a single delegate standing for the few remaining Franciscans. Finally there were the "valued guests" in the back rows—honorary delegates from the Pax Mercantilus, the *Opus Dei,* the *Istituto per Opere di Religione*—also known as the Vatican Bank, delegates from the Vatican administrative wings of the *Prefettura,* the *Servizio Assistenziale del Santo Padre*—the Holy Father's Welfare Service, from the APSA—the Administration of the Patrimony of the Holy See, as well as from Cardinal Camerlengo's own Apostolic Chamber. Also in the rear pews were honored guests from the Pontifical Academy of Sciences, the Papal Commission on Interstellar Peace and Justice, many papal academies such as the Pontifical Ecclesiastical Academy, and other quasi-theological organizations necessary to the running of the vast Pax state. Finally there were the bright uniforms of the Corps Helvetica—the Swiss Guard—as well as commanders of the Palatine Guard reconstituted by Pope Julius, and the first appearance of the commander of the hitherto secret Noble Guard—a pale, dark-haired man in a solid red uniform.

Isozaki and Cognani watched this pageant with knowledgeable eyes. Each of them had been invited to the Mass, but it had become a tradition in recent centuries for the Pax Mercantilus CEOs to honor major Church ceremonies by their absence—sending only their official Vatican delegates. Both watched Cardinal Couesnongle celebrate this Mass of the Holy Spirit and saw Cardinal Camerlengo as the powerless figurehead he was; their eyes were on Cardinal Lourdusamy, Cardinal Mustafa, and half a dozen other power brokers in the front pews.

With the final benediction, the Mass ended and the voting cardinals filed out in solemn procession to the Sistine Chapel, where the holocams lingered while the doors were sealed, the entrance to the Conclave was closed and that door bolted on the inside and padlocked on the outside, and the sealing of the Conclave pronounced official by the Commandant of the Swiss Guards and the Prefect of the Pontifical Household. The Vatican coverage then shifted to commentary and speculation while the image remained of the sealed door.

"Enough," said Kenzo Isozaki. The broadcast flashed off, the bubble grew transparent, and sunlight flooded the room under a black sky.

Anna Pelli Cognani smiled thinly. "The voting shouldn't take too long."

Isozaki had returned to his chair. Now he steepled his fingers and tapped his lower lip. "Anna," he said, "do you think that we—all of us in the chairmanship of the Mercantilus—have any real power?"

Cognani's neutral expression showed her surprise. She said, "During the last fiscal year, Kenzo-san, my division showed a profit of thirty-six billion marks."

Isozaki held his steepled fingers still. "M. Cognani," he said, "would you be so kind as to remove your jacket and shirt?"

His protégé did not blink. In the twenty-eight standard years they had been colleagues—subordinate and master, actually—M. Isozaki had never done, said, or implied anything that might have been interpreted as a sexual overture. She hesitated only a second, then unsealed her jacket, slipped it off, set it on the chair she never sat in, and unsealed her shirt. She folded it atop her jacket on the back of the chair.

Isozaki rose and came around his desk, standing only a meter from her. "Your underthings as well," he said, slipping off his own jacket and unbuttoning his own old-fashioned shirt. His chest was healthy, muscled, but hairless.

Cognani slipped off her chemise. Her breasts were small but perfectly formed, rosy at the tips.

Kenzo Isozaki lifted one hand as if he were going to touch her, pointed, and then returned the hand to his own chest and touched the double-barred cruciform that ran from his sternum to just above his navel. "This," he said, "is power." He turned away and began dressing. After a moment, Anna Pelli Cognani hugged her shoulders and then also began dressing.

When they were both dressed, Isozaki sat behind his desk again and gestured toward the other chair. To his quiet astonishment, M. Anna Pelli Cognani sat in it.

"What you are saying," began Cognani, "is that no matter how successful we are in making ourselves indispensable to the new Pope—if there ever is a new pope—the Church will always have the ultimate leverage of resurrection."

"Not quite," said Isozaki, steepling his fingers again as if the previous interlude had not happened. "I am saying that the power controlling the cruciform controls the human universe."

"The Church . . ." began Cognani and stopped. "Of course, the cruciform is just part of the power equation. The TechnoCore provides the Church with the secret of successful resurrection. But they've been in league with the Church for two hundred and eighty years . . ."

"For their own purposes," said Isozaki softly. "What are those purposes, Anna?"

The office rotated into night. Stars exploded into existence. Cognani raised her face to the Milky Way to gain a moment to think. "No one knows," she said at last. "Ohm's Law."

Isozaki smiled. "Very good. Following the path of least resistance here may not lead us through the Church, but via the Core."

"But Councillor Albedo meets with no one except His Holiness and Lourdusamy."

"No one that we know of," amended Isozaki. "But that is a matter of the Core coming to the human universe."

Cognani nodded. She understood the implicit suggestion: the illicit, Core-class AIs that the Mercantilus was developing could find the datum-plane avenue and follow it to the Core. For almost three hundred years, the prime commandment enforced by the Church and Pax had been—*Thou shalt not build a thinking machine equal or superior to humankind.* "AIs" in use within the Pax were more "All-purpose Instruments" than "Artificial Intelligences" of the kind that had evolved away from humanity almost a millennium earlier: idiot thinking machines like Isozaki's office AI or the cretinous ship computer on de Soya's old ship, the *Raphael.* But in the past dozen years, secret research departments of the Pax Mercantilus had re-created the autonomous AIs equal to or surpassing those in common use during the days of the Hegemony. The risk and benefits of this project were almost beyond measure—absolute domination of Pax trade and a breaking of the old balance of power stand-off between Pax Fleet and Pax Mercantilus if successful, excommunication, torture in the dungeons of the Holy Office, and execution if discovered by the Church. And now this prospect.

Anna Pelli Cognani stood. "My God," she said softly, "that would be the ultimate end run."

Isozaki nodded and smiled again. "Do you know where that term originated, Anna?"

"End run? No . . . some sport, I imagine."

"A very ancient warfare-surrogate sport called football," said Isozaki.

Cognani knew that this irrelevancy was anything but irrelevant. Sooner or later her master would explain why this datum was important. She waited.

"The Church had something that the Core wanted . . . needed," said Isozaki. "The taming of the cruciform was their part of the deal. The Church had to barter something of equal worth."

Cognani thought, *Equal in worth to the immortality of a trillion human beings?* She said, "I had always assumed that when Lenar Hoyt and Lourdusamy contacted the surviving Core elements more than two centuries ago, that the Church's bartering point was in secretly reestablishing the TechnoCore in human space."

Isozaki opened his hands. "To what ends, Anna? Where is the benefit to the Core?"

"When the Core was an integral part of the Hegemony," she said, "running the WorldWeb and the fatline, they were using the neurons in the billions of human brains transiting the farcasters as a sort of neural net, part of their Ultimate Intelligence project."

"Ah, yes," said her mentor. "But there are no farcasters now. If they are using human beings . . . how? And where?"

Without meaning to, Anna Pelli Cognani raised one hand to her breastbone.

Isozaki smiled. "Irritating, isn't it? Like a word that is on the tip of one's tongue but will not come to mind. A puzzle with a missing piece. But there is one piece that was missing which has just been found."

Cognani raised an eyebrow. "The girl?"

"Back in Pax space," said the older CEO. "Our agents close to Lourdusamy have confirmed that the Core has revealed this. It happened after the death of His Holiness . . . only the Secretary of State, the Grand Inquisitor, and the top people in Pax Fleet know."

"Where is she?"

Isozaki shook his head. "If the Core knows, they haven't revealed it to the Church or any other human agency. But Pax Fleet has called up that ship's captain—de Soya—because of the news."

"The Core had predicted that he would be involved in the girl's capture," said Cognani. The beginnings of a smile were working at the corners of her mouth.

"Yes?" said Isozaki, proud of his student.

"Ohm's Law," said Cognani.

"Precisely."

The woman stood and again touched her chest without being aware of doing so. "If we find the girl first, we have the leverage to open discussions with the Core. *And* the means—with the new abilities we will have on-line." None of the CEOs who knew of the secret AI project ever said the words or phrases aloud, despite their bugproof offices.

"If we have the girl and the means of negotiating," continued Cognani, "we may have the leverage we need to supplant the Church in the Core's arrangement with humanity."

"*If* we can discover what the Core is getting from the Church in return for control of the cruciform," murmured Isozaki. "And offer the same or better."

Cognani nodded in a distracted manner. She was seeing how all of this related to her goals and efforts as CEO of *Opus Dei. In every way,* she realized at once. "In the meantime, we have to find the girl before the others do . . . Pax Fleet must be utilizing resources they would never reveal to the Vatican."

"And vice versa," said Isozaki. This kind of contest pleased him very much.

"And we will have to do the same," said Cognani, turning toward the lift tube. "Every resource." She smiled at her mentor. "It's the ultimate three-way, zero-sum game, isn't it, Kenzo-san?"

"Just so," said Isozaki. "Everything to the winner—power, immortality, and wealth beyond human imagining. To the loser—destruction, the true death, and eternal slavery for one's descendants." He held up one finger. "But not a three-way game, Anna. Six."

Cognani paused by the lift door. "I see the fourth," she said. "The Core has its own imperative to find the girl first. But . . ."

Isozaki lowered his hand. "We must presume that the child has her own goals in this game, mustn't we? And whoever or whatever has introduced her as a playing piece . . . well, that must be our sixth player."

"Or one of the other five," said Cognani, smiling. She also enjoyed a high-stakes game.

Isozaki nodded and turned his chair to watch the next sunrise above the curving-away band of the Torus Mercantilus. He did not turn back when the lift door closed and Anna Pelli Cognani departed.

ABOVE THE ALTAR, Jesus Christ, his face stern and unrelenting, divided men into camps of the good and the bad—the rewarded and the damned. There was no third group.

Cardinal Lourdusamy sat in his canopied stall inside the Sistine Chapel and looked at Michelangelo's fresco of the *Last Judgment*. Lourdusamy had always thought that this Christ was a bullying, authoritarian, merciless figure—perhaps an icon perfectly suited to oversee this choice of a new Vicar of Christ.

The little chapel was crowded with the eighty-three canopied stalls seating the eighty-three cardinals present in the flesh. An empty space allowed for activation of the holos representing the missing thirty-seven cardinals—one holo of a canopied stall at a time.

This was the first morning after the cardinals had been "nailed up" in the Vatican Palace. Lourdusamy had slept and eaten well—his bedroom a cot in his Vatican office, his repast a simple meal cooked by the nuns of the Vatican guest house: simple food and a cheap white wine served in the glorious Borgia Apartments. Now all were gathered in the Sistine Chapel, their stall-thrones in place, their canopies raised. Lourdusamy knew that this splendid sight had been missing from the Conclave for many centuries—ever since the number of cardinals had grown too large to accommodate the stalls in the small chapel, sometime pre-Hegira, the nineteenth or twentieth century A.D., he thought—but the Church had grown so small by the end of the Fall of the Farcasters that the forty-some cardinals could once again easily fit. Pope Julius had kept the number small—never more than 120 cardinals, despite the growth of the Pax. And with almost forty of them unable to travel in time to the Conclave, the Sistine Chapel could hold the stalls of those cardinals permanently based on Pacem.

The moment had come. All of the cardinal-electors in the chapel stood as one. In the empty space near the Scrutineers' table near the altar, the holos of the thirty-seven absent cardinal-electors shimmered into existence. Because the space was small, the holos were small—little more than doll-sized human figures in doll-sized wooden stalls—all of them floating in midair like ghosts of Conclave-electors past. Lourdusamy smiled, as he always did, at how appropriate the reduced size of these absent electors seemed.

Pope Julius had always been elected by acclamation. One of the three cardinals acting as Scrutineers raised his hand: the Holy Spirit may have been prepared to move these men and women, but some coordination was required. When the Scrutineer's hand dropped, the eighty-three cardinals and thirty-seven holos were to speak as one.

"*Eligo* Father Lenar Hoyt!" cried Cardinal Lourdusamy and saw Cardinal Mustafa shouting the same words from beneath the canopy of his stall.

The Scrutineer in front of the altar paused. The acclamation had been loud and clear, but obviously not unanimous. This was a new wrinkle. For 270 years, the acclamation had been immediate.

Lourdusamy was careful not to smile or look around. He knew which of the newer cardinals had not cried out Pope Julius's name for reelection. He knew the wealth it had taken to bribe these men and women. He knew the terrible risk they were running and would almost certainly suffer for. Lourdusamy knew all this because he had helped to orchestrate it.

After a moment of consultation among the Scrutineers, the one who had called for acclamation now said, "We shall proceed by Scrutiny."

There was excited talk among the cardinals as the ballots were pre- pared and handed out. This had never happened before in the lifetime of most of these princes of the Church. Immediately the acclamation holos of the missing cardinal-electors had become irrelevant. Although a few of the absent cardinals had prepared their interactive chips for scrutiny, most had not bothered.

The Masters of Ceremonies moved among the stalls, distributing vot- ing cards—three to each cardinal-elector. The Scrutineers moved among the forest of stalls to make sure that each of the cardinals had a pen. When all was in readiness, the Cardinal Deacon among the Scrutineers raised his hand again, this time to signify the moment of voting.

Lourdusamy looked at his ballot. On the upper left, the words "*Eligo in Summum Pontificem*" appeared in print. There was room for one name beneath it. Simon Augustino Cardinal Lourdusamy wrote in *Lenar Hoyt* and folded the card and held it up so that it could be seen. Within a minute, all eighty-three of the cardinals were holding a card aloft, as were half a dozen of the interactive holos.

The Scrutineer began calling the cardinals forward in order of prece- dence. Cardinal Lourdusamy went first, leaving his stall and walking to the Scrutineers' table next to the altar beneath the gaze of the terrible Christ of the fresco. Genuflecting and then kneeling at the altar, Lourdusamy bowed his head in silent prayer. Rising, he said aloud, "I call to witness Christ the Lord who will be my judge, that my vote is given to the one who before God I consider should be elected." Lourdusamy solemnly set his folded card on the silver plate that sat atop the vote receptacle. Lifting the plate, he dropped his vote into the receptacle. The Cardinal Deacon among the Scrutineers nodded; Lourdusamy bowed toward the altar and returned to his stall.

Cardinal Mustafa, the Grand Inquisitor, moved majestically toward the altar to cast the second vote.

It was more than an hour later that the votes were tallied. The first Scrutineer shook the receptacle to mix the votes. The second Scrutineer counted them—including the six votes copied from the interactive holos—depositing each in a second receptacle. The count equaled the number of voting cardinals in the Conclave. The Scrutiny proceeded.

The first Scrutineer unfolded a card, wrote down the name on it, and passed the card to the second Scrutineer, who made a note and passed it to the third and final Scrutineer. This man—Cardinal Couesnongle as it turned out—said the name aloud before making a note of it.

In each of the stalls, a cardinal jotted the name on a 'scriber pad provided by the Scrutineers. At the end of the Conclave, the 'scribers would be scrambled, their files deleted so that no record of the voting would remain.

And so the voting proceeded. For Lourdusamy as for the rest of the living cardinals present, the only suspense was whether the dissident cardinal-electors from the Acclamation would actually put someone else's name into play.

As each card was read, the last Scrutineer ran a threaded needle through the word "*Eligo*" and slid the card down the thread. When all of the ballots had been read aloud, knots were tied in each end of the thread.

The winning candidate was admitted to the Chapel. Standing before the altar in a simple black cassock, the man looked humble and a bit overwhelmed.

Standing before him, the senior Deacon Cardinal said, "Do you accept your canonical election as Supreme Pontiff?"

"I do so accept it," said the priest.

At this point, a stall was brought out and set behind the priest. The Cardinal Deacon raised his hands and intoned, "Thus accepting your canonical election, this gathering does—in the sight of God Almighty—acknowledge you as Bishop of the Church of Rome, true Pope, and Head of the College of Bishops. May God advise you well as He grants you full and absolute power over the Church of Jesus Christ."

"Amen," said Cardinal Lourdusamy and pulled the cord that lowered the canopy over his stall. All eighty-three physical canopies and thirty-seven holographic ones lowered at the same time, until only the new Pope's remained raised. The priest—now pontiff—sat back in the seat beneath the papal canopy.

"What name do you choose as Supreme Pontiff?" asked the Deacon Cardinal.

"I choose the name Urban the Sixteenth," said the seated priest.

There was a murmuring and hum from the cardinals' stalls. The Cardinal Deacon held out his hand and he and the other Scrutineers led the priest from the Chapel. The murmuring and whispering rose in volume.

Cardinal Mustafa leaned out of his stall and said to Lourdusamy, "He must be thinking of Urban the Second. Urban the Fifteenth was a sniveling little coward in the twenty-ninth century who did little but read detective novels and write love letters to his former mistress."

"Urban the Second," mused Lourdusamy. "Yes, of course."

After several minutes, the Scrutineers returned with the priest—now the Pope dressed in pure white—a white-caped cassock, a white *zuchetto* or skullcap, a pectoral cross, and a white fascia sash. Cardinal Lourdusamy went to his knees on the stone floor of the Chapel, as did all the other cardinals real and holographic, as the new Pontiff gave his first benediction.

Then the Scrutineers and the attending cardinals went to the stove to burn the votes now tethered on black thread, adding enough *bianco* chemical to make sure that the *sfumata* would indeed be white smoke.

The cardinals filed out of the Sistine Chapel and walked the ancient paths and corridors to St. Peter's, where the senior Cardinal Deacon went alone onto the balcony to announce the name of the new Pontiff to the waiting multitudes.

AMONG THE FIVE hundred thousand waiting individuals in the multitude squeezed into, out of, and around St. Peter's Square that morning was Father Captain Federico de Soya. He had been released from his de facto imprisonment at the Legionaries rectory only hours before. He was to report to Pax Fleet's spaceport later that afternoon for shuttle to his new command. Walking through the Vatican, de Soya had followed the crowds—then had been engulfed by them—as men, women, and children had flowed like a great river toward the Square.

A great cheer had gone up when the puffs of white smoke first became visible from the stovepipe. The impossibly thick throng beneath the balcony of St. Peter's somehow became thicker as tens of thousands more flowed around the colonnades and past the statuary. Hundreds of Swiss Guard troopers held the crowd back from the entrance to the Basilica and away from private areas.

When the Senior Deacon emerged and announced that the new Pope was to be called His Holiness Urban the XVI, a great gasp went up from the crowd. De Soya found himself gaping in surprise and shock. Everyone had expected Julius XV. The thought of anyone else as Pope was . . . well, unthinkable.

Then the new Pontiff stepped onto the balcony and the gasps turned to cheers that went on and on and on.

It was Pope Julius—the familiar face, the high forehead, the sad eyes. Father Lenar Hoyt, the savior of the Church, had once again been elected. His Holiness raised his hand in the familiar benediction and waited for the crowd to stop cheering so that he could speak, but the crowd would not stop cheering. The roar rose from half a million throats and went on and on.

Why Urban XVI? wondered Father Captain de Soya. He had read and studied enough history of the Church in his years as a Jesuit. Quickly he thumbed back through his mental notes on the Urban popes . . . most were forgettable or worse. Why . . .

"Damn," Father Captain de Soya said aloud, the soft curse lost under the continuing roar of the faithful filling St. Peter's Square. "Damn," he said again.

Even before the crowd quieted enough for the new-old Pontiff to speak, to explain his choice of names, to announce what de Soya knew had to be announced, the father-captain understood. And his heart sank with that understanding.

Urban II had served from A.D. 1088 to 1099. At the synod the Pope had called in Clermont in . . . November, in the year 1095, de Soya thought . . . Urban II had made his call for holy war against the Muslims in the Near East, for the rescue of Byzantium, and for the liberation of all eastern Christian holy places from Muslim domination. That call had led to the First Crusade . . . the first of many bloody campaigns.

The crowd finally quieted. Pope Urban XVI began to speak, the familiar but newly energized voice rising and falling over the heads of the half-million faithful listening in person and the billions listening via live broadcast.

Father Captain de Soya turned away even before the new Pope began to speak. He pushed and elbowed his way back through the unmoving crowd, trying to escape the suddenly claustrophobic confines of St. Peter's Square.

It was no use. The crowd was rapt and joyous and de Soya was trapped in the mob. The words from the new Pontiff were also joyous and impassioned. Father Captain de Soya stood, unable to escape, and bowed his head. As the crowd began cheering and crying *"Deus le volt!"*—God wills it—de Soya began to weep.

Crusade. Glory. A final resolution of the Ouster Problem. Death beyond imagining. Destruction beyond imagining. Father Captain de Soya squeezed his eyes shut as tightly as he could, but the vision of charged particle beams flaring against the blackness of space, of entire worlds burning, of oceans turning to steam and continents into molten rivers of lava, visions of orbital forests exploding into smoke, of charred bodies tumbling in zero-g, of fragile, winged creatures flaring and charring and expanding into ash . . .

De Soya wept while billions cheered.

4

T HAS BEEN my experience that late-night departures and farewells are the hardest on the spirit.

The military was especially good at beginning major voyages in the middle of the night. During my time in the Hyperion Home Guard, it seemed that all important troop movements began in the wee hours. I began to associate that odd blend of fear and excitement, dread and anticipation, with predawn darkness and the smell of *lateness*. Aenea had said that I would be leaving that night of her announcement to the Fellowship, but it took time to load the kayak, for me to pack my gear and decide what to leave behind forever, and to close up my tent and work area in the compound, so we weren't airborne in the dropship until after two A.M. and it was almost sunrise before we reached our destination.

I admit that I felt rushed and ordered about by the girl's preemptive announcement. Many people had come to look to Aenea for leadership and advice during the four years we spent at Taliesin West, but I wasn't one of those people. I was thirty-two years old. Aenea was sixteen. It was my job to watch out for her, to protect her, and—if it came to that—to tell *her* what to do and when to do it. I didn't like this turn of events one bit.

I'd assumed that A. Bettik would be flying with us to wherever I was supposed to shove off, but Aenea said that the android would be staying behind at the compound, so I wasted another twenty minutes tracking him down and saying good-bye.

"M. Aenea says that we will meet up again in due course," said the blue man, "so I am confident that we shall, M. Endymion."

"Raul," I said for the five hundredth time. "Call me Raul."

"Of course," said A. Bettik with that slight smile that suggested insubordination.

"Fuck it," I said eloquently and stuck out my hand. A. Bettik shook it. I had the urge then to hug our old traveling companion, but I knew that it would embarrass him. Androids were not literally *programmed* to be stiff and subservient—they were, after all, living, organic beings, not machines—but between RNA-training and long practice, they were hopelessly formal creatures. At least this one was.

And then we were away, Aenea and I, taxiing the dropship out of its hangar into the desert night and lifting off with as little noise as possible. I had said good-bye to as many of the other Fellowship apprentices and workers as I had found, but the hour was late and the people were scattered to their dorm cubbies, tents, and apprentice shelters. I hoped that I would run into some of them again—especially some of the construction crewmen and women with whom I'd worked for four years—but I had little real belief that I would.

The dropship could have flown itself to our destination—just a series of coordinates Aenea had given it—but I left the controls on semimanual so I could pretend I had something to do during the flight. I knew from the coordinates that we would be traveling about fifteen hundred klicks. Somewhere along the Mississippi River, Aenea had said. The dropship could have done that distance in ten suborbital minutes, but we had been conserving its dwindling energy and fuel reserves, so once we had extended the wings to maximum, we kept our velocity subsonic, our altitude set at a comfortable ten thousand meters, and avoided morphing the ship again until landing. We ordered the Consul's starship's persona—which I'd long ago loaded from my comlog into the dropship's AI core—to keep quiet unless it had something important to tell us, and then we settled back in the red instrument glow to talk and watch the dark continent pass beneath us.

"Kiddo," I said, "why this galloping hurry?"

Aenea made the self-conscious, throwing-away gesture I had first seen her use almost five years earlier. "It seemed important to get things going." Her voice was soft, almost lifeless, drained of the vitality and energy that had moved the entire Fellowship to her will. Perhaps I was the only living person who could identify the tone, but she sounded close to tears.

"It can't be that important," I said. "To make me leave in the middle of the night . . ."

Aenea shook her head and looked out the dark windscreen for a moment. I realized that she was crying. When she finally turned back, the glow from the instruments made her eyes look very moist and red. "If you don't leave tonight, I'll lose my nerve and ask you not to go. If you don't go, I'll lose my nerve again and stay on Earth . . . never go back."

I had the urge to take her hand then, but I kept my big paw on the omnicontroller instead. "Hey," I said, "we can go back together. This doesn't make any sense for me to go off one way and you another."

"Yes it does," said Aenea so quietly that I had to lean to my right to hear her.

"A. Bettik could go fetch the ship," I said. "You and I can stay on Earth until we're ready to return . . ."

Aenea shook her head. "I'll *never* be ready to go back, Raul. The thought scares me to death."

I thought of the wild chase that had sent us fleeing through Pax space from Hyperion, barely eluding Pax starships, torchships, fighter aircraft, Marines, Swiss Guard, and God knows what else—including that bitch-thing from hell that had almost killed us on God's Grove—and I said, "I feel the same way, kiddo. Maybe we *should* stay on Earth. They can't reach us here."

Aenea looked at me and I recognized the expression: it was not mere stubbornness, it was a closing of all discussion on a matter that was settled.

"All right," I said, "but I still haven't heard why A. Bettik couldn't take this kayak and go get the ship while I farcast back with you."

"Yes, you have," said Aenea. "You weren't listening." She shifted sideways in the big seat. "Raul, if you leave and we agree to meet at a certain time in a certain place in Pax space, I *have* to go through the farcaster and do what I have to do. And what I have to do next, I have to do on my own."

"Aenea," I said.

"Yes?"

"That's really stupid. Do you know that?"

The sixteen-year-old said nothing. Below and to the left, somewhere in western Kansas, a circle of campfires became visible. I looked out at the lights amid all that darkness. "Any idea what experiment your alien friends are doing down there?" I said.

"No," said Aenea. "And they aren't my alien friends."

"Which aren't they?" I said. "Aliens? Or friends?"

"Neither," said Aenea. I realized that this was the most specific she had ever been about the godlike intelligences that had kidnapped Old Earth—and us, it seemed to me at times, as if we had been harried and driven through the farcasters like cattle.

"Care to tell me anything else about these nonalien nonfriends?" I said. "After all, something could go wrong . . . I might not make it to our rendezvous. I'd like to know the secret of our hosts before I go."

I regretted saying that as soon as the words were out. Aenea pulled back as if I had slapped her.

"Sorry, kiddo," I said. This time I did put my hand on hers. "I didn't mean that. I'm just angry."

Aenea nodded and I could see the tears in her eyes again.

Still mentally kicking myself, I said, "Everyone in the Fellowship was sure that the aliens were benevolent, godlike creatures. People said 'Lions and Tigers and Bears' but what they were thinking was 'Jesus and Yahweh and E.T.' from that old flat film that Mr. W. showed us. Everyone was sure that when it came time to fold up the Fellowship, the aliens would appear and lead us back to the Pax in a big mothership. No danger. No muss. No fuss."

Aenea smiled but her eyes still glistened. "Humans have been waiting for Jesus and Yahweh and E.T. to save their asses since before they covered those asses with bearskins and came out of the cave," she said. "They'll have to keep waiting. This is our business . . . our fight . . . and we have to take care of it ourselves."

"Ourselves being you and me and A. Bettik against eight hundred billion or so of the born-again faithful?" I said softly.

Aenea made the graceful gesture with her hand again. "Yeah," she said. "For now."

WHEN WE ARRIVED it was not only still dark, but raining hard—a cold, sleety, end-of-autumn rain. The Mississippi was a big river—one of Old Earth's largest—and the dropship circled over it once before landing in a small town on the west bank. I saw all this on the viewscreen under image enhancement: the view out the actual windscreen was blackness and rain.

We came in over a high hill covered with bare trees, crossed an empty highway that spanned the Mississippi on a narrow bridge, and landed in an open, paved area about fifty meters from the river. The town ran back from the river here in a valley between wooded hills and on the viewscreen I could make out small, wooden buildings, larger brick warehouses, and a few taller structures near the river that might have been grain silos. Those kind of structures had been common in the nineteenth, twentieth, and twenty-first centuries in this part of Old Earth: I had no idea why this city had been spared the earthquakes and fires of the Tribulations, or why the Lions and Tigers and Bears had rebuilt it, if they had. There had been no sign of people in the narrow streets, nor of heat signatures on the infrared bands—neither living creatures nor groundcars with their overheated, internal combustion drive systems—but then again, it was almost four-thirty in the morning on a cold, rainy night. No one with an ounce of sense would be out in that lousy, stinking weather.

We both pulled on ponchos, I hefted my small backpack and said, "So long, Ship. Don't do anything I wouldn't do," and we were down the morphed stairs and into the rain.

Aenea helped me tug the kayak out of the storage area in the belly of the dropship and we headed down the slick street toward the river. On our previous river adventure, I had carried night-vision goggles, an assortment of weapons, and a raft full of fancy gadgets. This night I had the flashlight laser that was our only memento of the trip out to Earth—set to its weakest, most energy-conserving setting, it illuminated about two meters of rain-slick street—a Navajo hunting knife in my backpack, and some sandwiches and dried fruit packed away. I was ready to take on the Pax.

"What is this place?" I said.

"Hannibal," said Aenea, struggling to hold the slick kayak as we stumbled down the street.

By this point I had to shift the slim flashlight laser in my teeth, keeping both hands on the bow of the stupid little boat. When we reached the point where the street became a loading ramp, running into the black torrent of the Mississippi, I set the kayak down, removed the flashlight, and said, "St. Petersburg." I had spent hundreds and hundreds of hours reading in the Fellowship compound's rich library of print books.

I saw Aenea's hooded figure nod in the reflected glow of the flashlight beam.

"This is crazy," I said, swinging the flashlight beam around the empty street, against the wall of the brick warehouses, out to the dark river. The rush of dark water was frightening. Any thought of setting off on that was insane.

"Yes," said Aenea. "Crazy." The cold rain beat on the hood of her poncho.

I went around the kayak and took her by the arm. "You see the future," I said. "When are we going to see each other again?"

Her head was bowed. I could make it out only the barest gleam of her pale cheek in the reflected beam. The arm I gripped through the sleeve of the poncho might as well have been the branch of a dead tree for all the life I felt there. She said something too softly for me to make it out over the sound of the rain and the river.

"What?" I said.

"I said I don't *see* the future," she said. "I remember parts of it."

"What's the difference?"

Aenea sighed and stepped closer. It was cold enough that our breaths actually mingled in the air. I felt the adrenaline rush from anxiety, fear, and anticipation.

"The difference is," she said, "that seeing is a form of clarity, remembering is . . . something else."

I shook my head. Rain dripped in my eyes. "I don't understand."

"Raul, do you remember Bets Kimbal's birthday party? When Jaev played the piano and Kikki got falling-down drunk?"

"Yeah," I said, irritated at this discussion in the middle of the night, in the middle of the storm, in the middle of our departure.

"When was it?"

"What?"

"When was it?" she repeated. Behind us, the Mississippi flowed out of the darkness and back into darkness with the speed of a maglev train.

"April," I said. "Early May. I don't know."

The hooded figure before me nodded. "And what did Mr. Wright wear that night?"

I had never had the impulse to hit or spank or scream at Aenea. Not until this minute. "How should I know? Why should I remember that?"

"Try to."

I let out my breath and looked away at the dark hills in the black night. "Shit, I don't know . . . his gray wool suit. Yeah, I remember him standing by the piano in it. That gray suit with the big buttons."

Aenea nodded again. "Bets's birthday party was in mid-March," she said over the patter of rain on our hoods. "Mr. Wright didn't come because he had a cold."

"So?" I said, knowing very well what point she had just made.

"So I *remember* bits of the future," she said again, her voice sounding close to tears. "I'm afraid to trust those memories. If I say when we will see each other again, it may be like Mr. Wright's gray suit."

For a long minute I said nothing. Rain pounded like tiny fists on closed coffins. Finally I said, "Yeah."

Aenea took two steps and put her arms around me. Our ponchos crinkled against each other. I could feel the tightness of her back and the new softness of her chest as we hugged clumsily.

She stepped back. "Can I have the flashlight a moment?"

I handed it to her. She pulled back the nylon apron in the tiny cockpit of the kayak and shined the light on the narrow strip of polished wood there beneath the fiberglass. A single red button, under its clear, protective panel, gleamed in the rain. "See that?"

"Yeah."

"Don't touch it, whatever you do."

I admit that I barked a laugh at that. Among the things I had read in the Taliesin library were plays of the absurd like *Waiting for Godot*. I had the feeling that we had flown into some latitude of the absurd and surreal here.

"I'm serious," said Aenea.

"Why put a button in if it's not to be touched?" I said, wiping the dripping moisture out of my face.

The hooded figure shook its head. "I mean, don't touch it until you absolutely have to."

"How will I know when I absolutely have to, kiddo?"

"You'll know," she said and gave me another hug. "We'd better get this into the river."

I bent to kiss her forehead then. I had done this dozens of times over the past few years—wishing her well before one of her retreats, tucking her in, kissing her clammy forehead when she was sick with fever or half-dead from fatigue. But as I bent to kiss her, Aenea raised her face, and for the first time since we had met in the midst of dust and confusion in the Valley of the Time Tombs, I kissed her on the lips.

I believe that I have mentioned before how Aenea's gaze is more powerful and intimate than most people's physical touches . . . how her touch is like a jolt of electricity. This kiss was . . . beyond all that. I was thirty-two years old that night in Hannibal, on the west bank of the river known as the Mississippi, on the world once known as Earth, lost now somewhere in the Lesser Magellanic Cloud, in the dark and rain, and I had never experienced a jolt of sensation like that first kiss.

I pulled back in shock. The flashlight laser had tilted up between us and I could see the glint of her dark eyes . . . looking mischievous, perhaps, relieved, perhaps, as if a long wait had ended, and . . . something else.

"Good-bye, Raul," she said, and lifted her end of the kayak.

My mind reeling, I placed the bow in the dark water at the bottom of the ramp and leveraged myself down and into the cockpit. A. Bettik had fashioned it for me like a well-tailored suit of clothes. I made sure not to depress the red button in my flailing around. Aenea shoved and the kayak was floating in twenty centimeters of water. She handed me the double-bladed paddle, then my backpack, and then the flashlight laser.

I aimed the beam at the dark water between us. "Where's the far-caster portal?" I said. I heard the words from a distance, as if some third party had spoken. My mind and emotions were still dealing with the kiss. I was thirty-two years old. This child had just turned sixteen. My job was to protect her and to keep her alive until we could return to Hyperion and the old poet someday. This was madness.

"You'll see it," she said. "Sometime after daylight."

Hours away then. This was theater of the absurd. "And what do I do after I find the ship?" I said. "Where do we meet?"

"There is a world named T'ien Shan," said Aenea. "It means 'Mountains of Heaven.' The ship will know how to find it."

"It's in the Pax?" I said.

"Just barely," she said, her breath hanging in the cold air. "It was in the Hegemony Outback. The Pax has incorporated it into the Protectorate and promised to send missionaries, but it hasn't been tamed yet."

"T'ien Shan," I repeated. "All right. How do I find you? Planets are big things."

I could see her dark eyes in the bouncing flashlight beam. They were moist with rain or tears, or both. "Find a mountain called Heng Shan . . . the Sacred Mountain of the North. Near it there will be a place called Hsuan-k'ung Ssu," she said. "It means 'Temple Hanging in Air.' I should be there."

I made a rude gesture with my fist. "Great, so all I have to do is stop at a local Pax garrison and ask directions to the Temple Hanging in Air, and you'll be hanging there waiting for me."

"There are only a few thousand mountains on T'ien Shan," she said, her voice flat and unhappy. "And only a few . . . cities. The ship can find Heng Shan and Hsuan-k'ung Ssu from orbit. You won't be able to land there, but you'll be able to disembark."

"Why won't I be able to land there?" I said, irritated by all of these puzzles within enigmas within codes.

"You'll see, Raul," she said, her voice as filled with tears as her eyes had been. "Please, go."

The current was trying to carry me away, but I paddled the buoyant little kayak back into place. Aenea walked along the river's edge to keep pace with me. The sky seemed to be lightening a bit in the east.

"Are you certain we'll see each other there?" I shouted through the thinning rain.

"I'm not certain of anything, Raul."

"Not even that we'll survive this?" I'm not sure what I meant by "this." I'm not even sure what I meant when I said "survive."

"Especially not of that," said the girl, and I saw the old smile, full of mischief and anticipation and something like sadness mixed with involuntary wisdom.

The current was pulling me away. "How long will it take me to get to the ship?"

"I think only a few days," she called. We were several meters apart now, and the current was pulling me out into the Mississippi.

"And when I find the ship, how long to get to . . . T'ien Shan?" I called.

Aenea shouted back the answer but it was lost in the lapping of waves against the hull of my little kayak.

"What?" I yelled. "I couldn't hear you."

"I love you," called Aenea, and her voice was clear and bright across the dark water.

The river pulled me out into it. I could not speak. My arms did not work when I thought to paddle against the powerful current. "Aenea?" I aimed the flashlight toward the shore, caught a glimpse of her poncho gleaming in the light, the pale oval of her face in the shadow of the hood. "Aenea!"

She shouted something, waved. I waved back.

The current was very strong for a moment. I paddled violently to avoid being pulled into an entire tree that had snagged on a sandbar, and then I was out in the central current and hurtling south. I looked back but walls of the last buildings in Hannibal hid my dear girl from view.

A minute later I heard a hum like the dropship's EM repulsors, but when I looked up I saw only shadow. It could have been her circling. It could have been a low cloud in the night.

The river pulled me south.

5

FATHER CAPTAIN DE SOYA deadheaded from Pacem System on the H.H.S. *Raguel,* an archangel-class cruiser similar to the ship he had been ordered to command. Killed by the terrible vortex of the classified instantaneous drive, known to Pax Fleet now as the Gideon drive, de Soya was resurrected in two days rather than the usual three—the resurrection chaplains taking the added risk of unsuccessful resurrection because of the urgency of the father-captain's orders—and found himself at the Omicron$_2$-Epsilon$_3$ Pax Fleet Strategic Positioning Station orbiting a lifeless, rocky world spinning in the darkness beyond Epsilon Eridani in the Old Neighborhood, only a handful of light-years from where Old Earth had once existed.

De Soya was given one day to recover his faculties and was then shuttled to the Omicron$_2$-Epsilon$_3$ fleet staging area, a hundred thousand klicks out from the military base. The midshipman piloting the wasp-shuttle went out of his way to give Father Captain de Soya a good look at his new command, and—despite himself—de Soya was thrilled with what he saw.

The H.H.S. *Raphael* was obviously state-of-the-art technology, no longer derivative—as all of the previous Pax ships de Soya had seen had been—of rediscovered Hegemony designs from before the Fall. The overall design seemed too lean for practical vacuum work and too complicated for atmosphere, but the overall effect was one of streamlined lethality. The hull was a composite of morphable alloys and areas of pure fixed energy, allowing rapid shape and function changes that would have been impossible a few years before. As the shuttle passed the *Raphael* in a long, slow ballistic arc, de Soya watched the exterior of the long ship go from chrome silver to a stealth matte black, essentially disappearing from view. At the same time, several of the instrument booms and living cubbies were swallowed by the smooth central hull, until only weapons' blisters and containment field probes remained. Either the ship was preparing for out-system translation checks, or the officers aboard knew very well that the passing wasp carried their new commander and they were showing off a bit.

De Soya knew that both assumptions were almost certainly true.

Before the cruiser blacked into oblivion, de Soya noticed how the fusion drive spheres had been clustered like pearls around the central ship's axis rather than concentrated in a single swelling such as on his old torchship, the *Balthasar*. He also noticed how much smaller the hexagonal Gideon-drive array was on this ship than on the prototype *Raphael*. His last glimpse before the ship became invisible was of the lights glowing from the retracted, translucent living cubbies and the clear dome of the command deck. During combat, de Soya knew from his reading on Pacem and the RNA-instructional injections he had received at Pax Fleet headquarters that these clear areas would morph thicker, armored epidermises, but de Soya had always enjoyed a view and would appreciate the window into space.

"Coming up on the *Uriel*, sir," said the midshipman pilot.

De Soya nodded. The H.H.S. *Uriel* seemed a near-clone of the new *Raphael*, but as the wasp-shuttle decelerated closer, the father-captain could pick out the extra omega-knife generators, the added, glowing conference cubbies, and the more elaborate com antennae that made this vessel the flagship of the task force.

"Docking warning, sir," said the midshipman.

De Soya nodded and took his seat on the number-two acceleration couch. The mating was smooth enough that he felt no jolt whatsoever as the connection clamps closed and the ship's skin and umbilicals morphed around the shuttle. De Soya was tempted to praise the young midshipman, but old habits of command reasserted themselves.

"Next time," he said, "try the final approach without the last-second flare. It's showing off and the brass on a flagship frown on it."

The young pilot's face fell.

De Soya set his hand on her shoulder. "Other than that, good job. I'd have you aboard my ship as a dropship pilot anyday."

The crestfallen midshipman brightened. "I could only wish, sir. This station duty . . ." She stopped, realizing that she had gone too far.

"I know," said de Soya, standing by the cycling lock. "I know. But for now, be glad that you're not part of this Crusade."

The lock cycled open and an honor guard whistled him aboard the H.H.S. *Uriel*—the archangel, if Father Captain de Soya remembered correctly, that the Old Testament had described as the leader of the heavenly hosts of angels.

NINETY LIGHT-YEARS AWAY, in a star system only three light-years from Pacem, the original *Raphael* translated into real space with a violence that would have spit marrow from human bones, sliced through human cells like a hot blade through radiant gossamers, and scrambled human neurons like loose marbles on a steep hillside. Rhadamanth Nemes and her clone-siblings did not enjoy the sensation, but neither did they cry out nor grimace.

"Where is this place?" said Nemes, watching a brown planet grow in the viewscreen. *Raphael* was decelerating under 230 gravities. Nemes did not sit in the acceleration couch, but she did hang on to a stanchion with the casual ease of a commuter on her way to work in a crowded groundbus.

"Svoboda," said one of her two male siblings.

Nemes nodded. None of the four spoke again until the archangel was in orbit and the dropship detached and howling through thin air.

"He'll be here?" asked Nemes. Microfilaments ran from her temples directly into the dropship console.

"Oh, yes," said Nemes's twin sister.

A few humans lived on Svoboda, but since the Fall they had huddled in forcefield domes in the twilight zone and did not have the technology to track the archangel or its dropship. There were no Pax bases in this system. Meanwhile, the sunward side of the rocky world boiled until lead ran like water, and on the dark side the thin atmosphere hovered on the edge of freezing. Beneath the useless planet, however, ran more than eight hundred thousand kilometers of tunnels, each corridor a perfect thirty meters square. Svoboda was one of nine Labyrinthine worlds discovered in the early days of the Hegira and explored during the Hegemony. Hyperion had been another of the nine worlds. No human—alive or dead—knew the secret of the Labyrinths or their creators.

Nemes piloted the dropship through a pelting ammonia storm on the dark side, hovered an instant before an ice cliff visible only on infrared and amplification screens, and then folded the ship's wings in and guided it forward into the square opening of the Labyrinth entrance. This tunnel turned once and then stretched straight on for kilometers. Deep radar showed a honeycomb of other passages beneath it. Nemes flew forward three klicks, turned left at the first junction of tunnels, dropped half a kilometer from the surface while traveling five klicks south, and then landed the ship.

Here the infrared showed only trace heat from lava vents and the amplifiers showed nothing on the viewscreen. Frowning at the return on the radar displays, Nemes flipped on the dropship's exterior lights.

For as far as she could see down the infinitely straight corridor, the walls of the tunnel had been carved into a row of horizontal stone slabs. On each slab was a naked human body. The slabs and bodies continued on and on into darkness. Nemes glanced at the deep radar display: the lower levels were also striated with slabs and bodies.

"Outside," said the male sibling who had pulled Nemes from the lava on God's Grove.

Nemes did not bother with the air lock. Atmosphere rushed out of the dropship with a dying roar. There was a hint of pressure in the cavern—enough that she would not have to phase-shift to survive—but the air was thinner than Mars had been before it was terraformed. Nemes's personal sensors indicated that the temperature was steady at minus 162 degrees centigrade.

A human figure was outside waiting in the dropship's floodlights.

"Good evening," said Councillor Albedo. The tall man was impeccably dressed in a gray suit tailored to Pacem tastes. He communicated directly on the 75-megahertz band. Albedo's mouth did not move, but his perfect teeth were visible in a smile.

Nemes and her siblings waited. She knew that there would be no further reprimands or punishment. The Three Sectors wanted her alive and functioning.

"The girl, Aenea, has returned to Pax space," said Albedo.

"Where?" said Nemes's female sibling. There was something like eagerness between the flat tones of her voice.

Councillor Albedo opened his hands.

"The portal . . ." began Nemes.

"Tells us nothing this time," said Councillor Albedo. His smile had not wavered.

Nemes frowned at this. During all the centuries of the Hegemony's WorldWeb, the Three Sectors of Consciousness of the Core had not found a way to use the Void portal—that instantaneous interface that humans had known as farcasters—without leaving a record of modulated neutrinos in the fold matrix. "The Something Else . . ." she said.

"Of course," said Albedo. He flicked his hand as if discarding the useless segment of this conversation. "But we can still register the connection. We feel sure that the girl is among those returning from Old Earth via the old farcaster network."

"There are others?" said one of the males.

Albedo nodded. "A few at first. More now. At least fifty activations at last count."

Nemes folded her arms. "Do you think the Something Else is terminating the Old Earth experiment?"

"No," said Albedo. He walked over to the nearest slab and looked down at the naked human body on it. It had been a young woman, no more than seventeen or eighteen standard years old. She had red hair. White frost lay on her pale skin and open eyes. "No," he said again. "The Sectors agree that it is just Aenea's group returning."

"How do we find her?" said Nemes's female sibling, obviously musing aloud on the 75-megahertz band. "We can translate to every world that had a farcaster during the Hegemony and interrogate the farcaster portals in person."

Albedo nodded. "The Something Else can conceal the farcast destinations," he said, "but the Core is almost certain that it cannot hide the fact of the matrix fold itself."

Almost certain. Nemes noted that unusual modifier of TechnoCore perceptions.

"We want you . . . ." began Albedo, pointing at the female sibling. "The Stable Sector did not give you a name, did it?"

"No," said Nemes's twin. Limp, dark bangs fell over the pale forehead. No smile touched the thin lips.

Albedo chuckled on the 75-megahertz band. "Rhadamanth Nemes needed a name to pass as a human crewmate on the *Raphael.* I think that the rest of you should be named, if just for my convenience." He pointed at the female. "Scylla." Stabbing his finger at each of the males in turn, he said, "Gyges. Briareus."

None of the three responded to their christenings, but Nemes folded her arms and said, "Does this amuse you, Councillor?"

"Yes," said Albedo.

Around them, the atmosphere vented from the dropship curled and broiled like a wicked fog. The male now named Briareus said, "We'll keep this archangel for transport and begin searching all the old Web worlds, beginning, I assume, with the River Tethys planets."

"Yes," said Albedo.

Scylla tapped her nails on the frozen fabric of her jumpsuit. "Four ships, the search would go four times as fast."

"Obviously," said Albedo. "There are several reasons we have decided against that—the first being that the Pax has few of these archangel ships free to loan."

Nemes raised an eyebrow. "And when has the Core *asked* the Pax for loans?"

"Since we need their money and their factories and their human resources to build the ships," said Albedo without emphasis. "The second—and final—reason is that we want the four of you together in case you encounter someone or something impossible for one of you to handle."

Nemes's eyebrow stayed up. She expected some reference to her failure on God's Grove, but it was Gyges who spoke. "What in the Pax could we not handle, Councillor?"

Again the man in gray opened his hands. Behind him, the curling vapors of fog first obscured and then revealed the pale bodies on slabs. "The Shrike," he said.

Nemes made a rude noise on the 75-megahertz band. "I beat the thing single-handedly," she said.

Albedo shook his head. The maddening smile stayed fixed. "No," he said. "You did not. You used the hyperentropic device with which we supplied you to send it five minutes into the future. That is not the same as beating it."

Briareus said, "The Shrike is no longer under the control of the UI?"

Albedo opened his hands a final time. "The gods of the future no longer whisper to us, my expensive friend. They war among themselves and the clamor of their battle echoes back through time. If our god's work is to be done in our time, we must do it ourselves." He looked at the four clone-siblings. "Are we clear on instructions?"

"Find the girl," said Scylla.

"And?" said the Councillor.

"Kill her at once," said Gyges. "No hesitation."

"And if her disciples intervene?" said Albedo, smiling more broadly now, his voice the caricature of a human schoolteacher's.

"Kill them," said Briareus.

"And if the Shrike appears?" he said, the smile suddenly fading.

"Destroy it," said Nemes.

Albedo nodded. "Any final questions before we go our separate ways?"

Scylla said, "How many humans are here?" She gestured toward the slabs and bodies.

Councillor Albedo touched his chin. "A few tens of millions on this Labyrinthine world, in this section of tunnels. But there are many more tunnels here." He smiled again. "And eight more Labyrinth worlds."

Nemes slowly turned her head, viewing the swirling fog and receding line of stone slabs on various levels of the spectrum. None of the bodies showed any sign of heat above the ambient temperature of the tunnel. "And this is the Pax's work," she said.

Albedo chuckled on the 75-megahertz band. "Of course," he said. "Why would the Three Sectors of Consciousness or our future UI want to stockpile human bodies?" He walked over to the body of the young woman and tapped her frozen breast. The air in the cavern was far too thin to carry sound, but Nemes imagined the noise of cold marble being tapped by fingernails.

"Any more questions?" said Albedo. "I have an important meeting."

Without a word on the 75-megahertz band—or any other band—the four siblings turned and reentered the dropship.

GATHERED ON THE circular tactical conference center blister of the H.H.S. *Uriel* were twenty Pax Fleet officers, including all of the captains and executive officers of Task Force GIDEON. Among those executive officers was Commander Hoagan "Hoag" Liebler. Thirty-six standard years old, born-again since his baptism on Renaissance Minor, the scion of the once-great Liebler Freehold family whose estate covered some two million hectares—and whose current debt ran to almost five marks per hectare—Liebler had dedicated his private life to serving the Church and given his professional life to Pax Fleet. He was also a spy and a potential assassin.

Liebler had looked up with interest as his new commanding officer was piped aboard the *Uriel*. Everyone in the task force—almost everyone in Pax Fleet—had heard of Father Captain de Soya. The former torchship CO had been granted a papal diskey—meaning almost unlimited authority—for some secret project five standard years earlier, and then had failed at his mission. No one was sure what that mission had been, but de Soya's use of that diskey had made enemies among Fleet officers across the Pax. The father-captain's subsequent failure and disappearance had been cause for more rumor in the wardrooms and Fleet staff rooms: the most accepted theory was that de Soya had been turned over to the Holy Office, had been quietly excommunicated, and probably executed.

But now here he was, given command of one of the most treasured assets in Pax Fleet's arsenal: one of the twenty-one operational archangel cruisers.

Liebler was surprised at de Soya's appearance: the father-captain was short, dark-haired, with large, sad eyes more appropriate to the icon of a martyred saint than to the skipper of a battlecruiser. Introductions were made quickly by Admiral Aldikacti, the stocky Lusian in charge of both this meeting and the task force.

"Father Captain de Soya," said Aldikacti as de Soya took his place at the gray, circular table within the gray, circular room, "I believe you know some of these officers." The Admiral was famous for her lack of tact as well as for her ferocity in battle.

"Mother Captain Stone is an old friend," said de Soya, nodding toward his former executive officer. "Captain Hearn was a member of my last task force, and I have met Captain Sati and Captain Lempriere. I have also had the privilege of working with Commanders Uchikawa and Barnes-Avne."

Admiral Aldikacti grunted. "Commander Barnes-Avne is here representing the Marine and Swiss Guard presence on Task Force GIDEON," she said. "Have you met your exec, Father Captain de Soya?"

The priest-captain shook his head and Aldikacti introduced Liebler. The commander was surprised at the firmness in the diminutive father-captain's grip and the authority in the other man's gaze. *Eyes of a martyr or no,* thought Hoag Liebler, *this man is used to command.*

"All right," growled Admiral Aldikacti, "let's get started. Captain Sati will present the briefing."

For the next twenty minutes, the conference blister was fogged with holos and trajectory overlays. Comlogs and 'scribers filled with data and scribbled notes. Sati's soft voice was the only sound except for the rare question or request for clarification.

Liebler jotted his own notes, surprised at the scope of Task Force GIDEON's mission, and busy at the work of any executive officer—getting down all the salient facts and details that the captain might want to review later.

GIDEON was the first task force made up completely of archangel-class cruisers. Seven of the archangels had been tasked to this mission. Conventional Hawking-class torchships had been dispatched months earlier to rendezvous with them at their first sally point in the Outback some twenty light-years beyond the Great Wall defensive sphere so as to participate in a mock battle, but after that first jump, the task force of seven ships would be operating independently.

"A good metaphor would be General Sherman's march through Georgia in the pre-Hegira North American Civil War in the nineteenth century," said Captain Sati, sending half the officers at the table tapping at their comlog diskeys to bring up that arcane bit of military history.

"Previously," continued Sati, "our battles with the Ousters have either been in the Great Wall no-man's-land, or on the fringes of either Pax or Ouster space. There have been very few deep-penetration raids into Ouster territory." Sati paused in his briefing. "Father Captain de Soya's Task Force MAGI some five standard years ago was one of the deepest of those raids."

"Any comments about it, Father Captain?" said Admiral Aldikacti.

De Soya hesitated a moment. "We burned an orbital forest ring," he said at last. "There was no resistance."

Hoag Liebler thought that the father-captain's voice sounded vaguely ashamed.

Sati nodded as if satisfied. "That's what we hope will be the case for this entire mission. Our intelligence suggests that the Ousters have deployed the vast bulk of their defensive forces along the sphere of the Great Wall, leaving very little in the way of armed resistance through the heart of their colonized areas beyond the Pax. For almost three centuries they have positioned their forces, their bases, and their home systems with the limitations of Hawking-drive technology as the primary determining factor."

Tactical holos filled the conference blister.

"The grand cliché," continued Sati, "is that the Pax has had the advantage of interior lines of transport and communication, while the Ousters have had the defensive strength of concealment and distance. Penetration deep into Ouster space has been all but impossible due to the vulnerability of our supply lines and their willingness to cut and run before our superior strength, attacking later—often with devastating effect—when our task forces venture too far from the Great Wall."

Sati paused and looked at the officers around the table. "Gentlemen and ladies, those days are over." More holos misted into solidity, the red line of Task Force GIDEON's trajectory out from and back to the Pax sphere slicing between suns like a laser knife.

"Our mission is to destroy every in-system Ouster supply base and deep-space colony we encounter," said Sati, his soft voice taking on strength. "Comet farms, can cities, boondoggles, torus bases, L-point clusters, orbital forest rings, birthing asteroids, bubble hives . . . everything."

"Including civilian angels?" asked Father Captain de Soya.

Hoag Liebler blinked at his CO's question. Pax Fleet informally referred to the space-tailored DNA-altered mutants as "Lucifer's angels," usually shortened to "angels" in an irony bordering on blasphemy, but the phrase was rarely used before the high brass.

Admiral Aldikacti answered. "*Especially* angels, Father Captain. His Holiness, Pope Urban, has declared this a Crusade against the inhuman travesties the Ousters are breeding out there in the darkness. His Holiness has stated in his Crusade Encyclical that these unholy mutations are to be eliminated from God's universe. *There are no civilian Ousters.* Do you have a problem understanding this directive, Father Captain de Soya?"

Officers around the table seemed to hold their breaths until de Soya finally answered. "No, Admiral Aldikacti. I understand His Holiness's encyclical."

The briefing continued. "These archangel-class cruisers will be involved," said Sati. "His Holiness's Ship *Uriel* as flagship, the *Raphael,* the *Michael,* the *Gabriel,* the *Raguel,* the *Remiel,* and the *Sariel.* In each case, the ships will use their Gideon drives to make the instantaneous jump to the next system, will take two days or more to decelerate in-system, thus allowing time for crew resurrection. His Holiness has granted us dispensation to use the new two-day resurrection-cycle crèches . . . which offer a ninety-two percent probability of resurrection. After regrouping the attack force, we will do maximum damage to all Ouster forces and installations before translating to the next system. Any Pax ship damaged beyond repair will be abandoned, the crew transferred to other ships in the task force, and the cruiser destroyed. No chances will be taken with the Ousters capturing Gideon-drive technology, even though it would be useless to them without the Sacrament of Resurrection. The mission should extend some three standard months. Any questions?"

Father Captain de Soya raised his hand. "I have to apologize," he said, "I've been out of touch for several standard years, but I notice that this task force is made up of archangel-class ships named after archangels referred to by name in the Old Testament."

"Yes, Father Captain?" prompted Admiral Aldikacti. "Your question?"

"Just this, Admiral. I seem to remember that there were only seven archangels referred to by name in the Bible. What about the rest of the archangel-class ships that have come on-line?"

There was chuckling around the long table and de Soya could see that he had cut the tension much as he had planned.

Smiling, Admiral Aldikacti said, "We welcome our prodigal captain back and inform him that the Vatican theologians have searched the Book of Enoch and the rest of the pseudepigrapha to find these other angels which might be promoted to 'honorary archangel,' and the Holy Office itself has authorized dispensation in Pax Fleet's use of their names. We found it . . . ah . . . appropriate . . . that the first seven planet-class archangels built be named after those listed in the Bible and should carry their sacred fire to the enemy."

The chuckling turned to sounds of approval and finally to soft applause among the commanders and their execs.

There were no other questions. Admiral Aldikacti said, "Oh, one other detail, if you see this ship . . ." A holo of a strange-looking starship floated above the center of the table. The thing was small by Pax Fleet standards, was streamlined as if built to enter atmosphere, and had fins near the fusion ports.

"What is it?" said Mother Captain Stone, still smiling from the good feeling in the room. "Some Ouster joke?"

"No," said Father Captain de Soya in a soft monotone, "it's Web-era technology. A private starship . . . owned by an individual."

A few executive officers chuckled again.

Admiral Aldikacti stopped the laughter by waving her thick hand through the holo. "The father-captain is correct," rumbled the Lusian admiral. "It's an old Web-era ship, once owned by a diplomat of the Hegemony." She shook her head. "They had the wealth to make such gestures then. Anyway, it has a Hawking drive modified by Ouster technicians, may well be armed, and must be considered as dangerous."

"What do we do if we encounter it?" asked Mother Captain Stone. "Take it as a prize?"

"No," said Admiral Aldikacti. "Destroy it on sight. Slag it to vapor. Any questions?"

There were none. The officers dispersed to their ships to prepare for the initial translation. On the wasp-shuttle ride back to the *Raphael*, XO Hoag Liebler chatted pleasantly with his new captain about the ship's readiness and crew's high morale, all the while thinking, *I hope I don't have to kill this man.*

6

I T HAS BEEN my experience that immediately after certain traumatic separations—leaving one's family to go to war, for instance, or upon the death of a family member, or after parting from one's beloved with no assurances of reunion—there is a strange calmness, almost a sense of relief, as if the worst has happened and nothing else need be dreaded. So it was with the rainy, predawn morning on which I left Aenea on Old Earth.

The kayak that I paddled was small and the Mississippi River was large. At first, in the darkness, I paddled with an intense alertness that was close to fear, adrenaline-driven, eyes straining to make out snags and sandbars and drifting flotsam on the raging current. The river was very wide there, the better part of a mile, I guessed—the Old Architect had used the archaic English units of length and distance, feet, yards, miles, and most of us at Taliesin had fallen into the habit of imitating him—and the banks of the river looked flooded, with dead trees showing where the waters had risen hundreds of meters from the original banks, pushing the river to high bluffs on both sides.

An hour or so after I had parted from my friend, the light came up slowly, first showing the separation of gray cloud and black-gray bluff to my left, then casting a flat, cold light on the surface of the river itself. I had been right to be afraid in the dark: the river was snarled with snags and long fingers of sandbars; large, waterlogged trees with hydra heads of roots raged past me on the center currents, smashing anything in their way with the force of giant battering rams. I selected what I hoped was the most forgiving current, paddled strongly to stay out of the way of floating debris, and tried to enjoy the sunrise.

All that morning I paddled south, seeing no sign of human habitation on either bank except for a single parting glimpse of ancient, once-white buildings drowned amid the dead trees and brackish waters in what had once been the western bank and was now a swamp at the base of the bluffs there. Twice I put ashore on islands: once to relieve myself and the second time to store away the small backpack that was my only luggage. During this second stop—late in the morning with the sun warming the river and me—I sat on a log on the sandy bank and ate one of the cold meat and mustard sandwiches that Aenea had made for me during the night. I had brought two water bottles—one to fit on my belt, the other to stay in my pack—and I drank with moderation, not knowing if the water of the Mississippi was fit to drink and also not knowing when I would find a safe supply.

It was afternoon when I saw the city and the arch ahead of me.

Sometime before, a second river had joined the Mississippi on my right, widening the channel significantly. I was sure that it must be the Missouri, and when I queried the comlog, the ship's memory confirmed my hunch. It was not long after that when I saw the arch.

This farcaster portal looked different than the ones we had transited during our trip out to Old Earth: larger, older, duller, more rust-streaked. It may have once been high and dry on the west bank of the river, but now the metal of the arch rose out of waters hundreds of meters from shore. Skeletal remnants of drowned buildings—low "skyscrapers" from pre-Hegira days according to my newly informed architectural sensibilities—also rose from the sluggish waters.

"St. Louis," said the comlog bracelet when I queried the ship's AI. "Destroyed even before the Tribulations. Abandoned before the Big Mistake of '08."

"Destroyed?" I said, aiming the kayak toward the giant hoop of the arch and seeing for the first time how the west bank behind it curved around in a perfect semicircle, forming a shallow lake. Ancient trees lined the sharp arc of the shore. An impact crater, I thought, although meteor crater or bomb crater or power-source meltdown or some other variety of violent event, I could not tell. "How destroyed?" I said to the comlog.

"No information," said the bracelet. "However I do have a data entry which correlates with the arch ahead of us."

"It's a farcaster portal, isn't it?" I said, fighting the strong current here on the west side of the main channel to aim the kayak at the east-facing arch.

"Not originally," said the soft voice on my wrist. "The size and orientation of the artifact coincide with position and dimensions of the so-called Gateway Arch, an architectural oddity built in the city of St. Louis during the time of the United States of America nation-state in the mid-twentieth century A.D. It was meant to symbolize western expansion of the hegemonic, Euro-descended proto-nationalist pioneers who migrated through here in their effort to displace the original, pre-Preserve, NorthAm indigenies."

"The Indians," I said, panting as I paddled the bobbing kayak through the last conflicting current and got us lined up with the huge arch. There had been an hour or two of rich sunlight, but now the cold wind and gray clouds had returned. Raindrops pattered on the fiberglass of the kayak and rippled the wavetops on either side. The current now carried the kayak toward the center of the arch, and I rested the paddle a moment, making sure not to hit the mysterious red button by accident. "So this farcaster portal was built to honor the people who killed the Indians," I said, leaning forward on my elbows.

"The original Gateway Arch had no farcaster function," the ship's voice said primly.

"Did it survive the disaster that . . . did this?" I said, pointing the paddle at the impact-crater lake and its assortment of flooded buildings.

"No information," said the comlog.

"And you don't know if it's a farcaster?" I said, panting again as I paddled hard. The arch loomed high above us now, at least a hundred meters to its apex. The winterish sunlight glinted dully on its rusted sides.

"No," said the ship's memory. "There is no record of any farcaster on Old Earth."

Of course there would be no such record. Old Earth had collapsed into the Big Mistake black hole—or been kidnapped by the Lions and Tigers and Bears—at least a century and a half before the TechnoCore had given the old Hegemony farcaster technology. But there had been a small but very functional farcaster arch over that river—creek, actually—in western Pennsylvania where Aenea and I had 'cast from God's Grove four years earlier. And I had seen others in my travels.

"Well," I said, more to myself than to the idiot comlog AI, "if this isn't it, we'll just continue on downriver. Aenea had a reason for launching us where she did."

I was not so sure. There was no telltale farcaster shimmer under this arch—no glimpse of sunlight or starlight beyond. Just the darkening sky and the black band of forest on the shoreline beyond the lake.

I leaned back and looked up at the arch, shocked to see panels missing, steel ribs showing. The kayak had already passed beneath it and there was no transition, no sudden shift of light and gravity and alien scents. This thing was nothing more than a broken-down old architectural freak that just happened to resemble a . . .

Everything changed.

One second the kayak and I were bobbing on the windswept Mississippi, heading into the shallow crater lake that had been the city of St. Louis, and the next instant it was night and the little fiberglass boat and I were sliding along a narrow canal between canyons of lighted buildings under a dark skylight half a kilometer or more above my head.

"Jesus," I whispered.

"An ancient messiah figure," said the comlog. "Religions based on his purported teachings include Christianity, Zen-Christianity, ancient and modern Catholicism, and such Protestant sects as . . . ."

"Shut up," I said. "Good child mode." This command had the com-log speak only when spoken to.

There were other people boating on this canal, if canal it was. Scores of rowboats and tiny sailboats and other kayaks moved upriver and down. Close by, on riverwalks and esplanades, on skyways crisscrossing above the well-lighted waters, hundreds more walked in pairs and small groups. Stocky individuals in bright garments jogged alone.

I felt the gravity weigh my arms as I tried to lift the kayak paddle—at least half-again Earth's was my immediate impression—and I slowly lifted my face to the view of those hundreds—thousands—of lighted windows and turrets, walkways and balconies and landing pads, of more lights as chrome-silver trains hummed softly through clear tubes above the river, as EMVs sliced through the air overhead, as levitation platforms and sky ferries carried people back and forth across this incredible canyon . . . and I knew.

Lusus. This had to be Lusus.

I had met Lusians before: rich hunters come to Hyperion to shoot ducks or demi-gyres, richer offworld gamblers slumming in the Nine Tails casinos where I had worked as a bouncer, even a few expatriates in our Home Guard unit, felons fleeing Pax justice most likely. They all had the high-g, low-profile look of these short, stocky, prominently muscled joggers who chugged by on the riverwalks and esplanades like some primitive but powerful steam machines.

No one seemed to be paying any attention to my kayak or me. This surprised me: from these natives' perspectives, I must have appeared from nowhere, materializing under the farcaster portal behind me.

I looked back and understood why my appearance might have gone unnoticed. The farcaster portal was old, of course, part of the fallen Hegemony and of the former River Tethys, and the arch had been built into the Hive city walls—platforms and walkways studding and overhanging the slender portal—so that the segment of canal or river directly under the arch was the only visible section of this indoor city that lay in deep shadow. Even as I glanced back, a small motorboat glided out of that shadow, caught the glow of the sodium-vapor lights that overhung the river walk-way, and seemed to pop into existence just as I had half a moment earlier.

Bulked up as I was in sweater and jacket, tightly tucked into the nylon skirt of my little kayak cockpit, I probably looked as stocky as the Lusians I saw on either side of me. A man and woman on jet skis waved as they hissed past.

I waved back.

"Jesus," I whispered again, more in prayer than blasphemy. This time the comlog made no comment.

I WILL INTERRUPT myself here.

My temptation at this point in the telling, despite the hurry-up incentive of cyanide gas hissing into the Schrödinger cat box at any moment, was to describe my interworld odyssey in great detail. It was, in truth, as close as I had come to true adventure since Aenea and I had arrived at the safety of Old Earth four standard years earlier.

In the thirty-some standard hours since Aenea had peremptorily announced my imminent departure by farcaster, I had naturally assumed that the voyage would be similar to our former trip—from Renaissance Vector to Old Earth, our voyage had been through empty or abandoned landscapes via worlds such as Hebron, New Mecca, God's Grove, and unnamed worlds such as the jungle planet on which we had left the Consul's ship in hiding. On one of the few planets where we had encountered inhabitants—ironically on Mare Infinitus, the sparsely settled ocean world—the contact had been catastrophic for everyone involved: I had blown up most of their floating platform; they had captured me, stabbed me, shot me, and almost drowned me. In the process, I had lost some of the most valuable things we had taken on the trip, including the ancient hawking mat that had been handed down since the days of the Siri and Merin legend and the equally ancient .45-caliber handgun that I had wanted to believe once belonged to Aenea's mother, Brawne Lamia.

But for the majority of our voyage, the River Tethys had carried Aenea, A. Bettik, and me through empty landscapes—ominously empty on Hebron and New Mecca, as if some terror had carried away the populations—and we had been left alone.

Not here. Lusus was alive and seething. For the first time, I understood why these planetary honeycombs were called Hives.

Traveling together through unpopulated regions, the girl, the android, and I had been left to our own devices. Now, alone and essentially unarmed in my little kayak, I found myself waving to Pax police and bornagain Lusian priests who strolled by. The canal was no more than thirty meters wide here, concrete and plastic-lined, with no tributaries or hiding places. There were shadows under the bridges and overpasses, just as under the farcaster portal upriver, but river traffic moved through these shadowy places in a constant flow. No place to hide.

For the first time I considered the insanity of farcaster travel. My clothes would be out of place, drawing immediate attention as soon as I stepped out of the kayak. My body type was wrong. My Hyperion-bred dialect would be strange. I had no money, no identity chip, no EMV license or credit cards, no Pax parish papers or place of residence. Stopping the kayak for a minute by a riverside bar—the smell of grilled steak or similar fare wafting out on fans and making me salivate with hunger, the yeast tang hinting of brewery vats and cold beer on the same breeze—I realized that I would almost certainly be arrested two minutes after going into such a place.

People traveled between worlds in the Pax—millionaires mostly, businesspeople and adventurers willing to spend months in cryogenic sleep and years of time-debt traveling by Mercantilus transport between the stars, smug in their cruciform certainty that job and home and family would be waiting in their steady-state Christian universe when they returned—but it was rare, and no one traveled between worlds without money and Pax permission. Two minutes after I sauntered into this café or bar or restaurant or whatever it was, someone would probably call the local police or the Pax military. Their first search would show me crossless—a heathen in a born-again Christian universe.

Licking my lips, my stomach growling, arms weary from fatigue and the extra gravity there, eyes tearing from lack of sleep and deep frustration, I paddled away from the riverside café and continued downriver, hoping that the next farcaster would be nearer rather than far.

And here I resist the temptation to tell of all the marvelous sights and sounds, the strange people glimpsed and close encounters chanced. I had never been on a world as settled, as crowded, as *interior* as Lusus, and I could have easily spent a month exploring the bustling Hive I glimpsed from the concrete-channeled river.

After six hours traveling downstream in the canal on Lusus, I paddled under the welcomed arch and emerged on Freude, a bustling, heavily populated world that I knew little about and could not even have identified if it had not been for the comlog's navigational files. Here I finally slept, the kayak hidden in a five-meter-high sewer pipe, me curled up under tendrils of industrial fiberplastic caught in a wire fence.

I slept a full standard day and night around on Freude, but there the days were thirty-nine standard hours long and it was only evening of the day I arrived when I found the next arch, less than five klicks downriver, and translated again.

From sunny Freude, populated by Pax citizens in elaborate harlequin fabrics and bright capes, the river took me to Nevermore with its brooding villages carved into rock and its stone castles perched on canyon sides under perpetually gloomy skies. At night on Nevermore, comets streaked the heavens and crowlike flying creatures—more giant bats than birds— flapped leathery wings low above the river and blotted out the comets' glow with their black bodies.

I was hailed by commercial rafters there, and hailed them back, all the while paddling away toward a stretch of white water that almost flipped my kayak and certainly taxed all of my fledgling kayaker's skills. Sirens were hooting from the gimlet-eyed castles on Nevermore when I paddled furiously under the next farcaster portal and found myself sweltering in the desert sunshine of a busy little world the comlog told me was called Vitus-Gray-Balianus B. I had never heard of it, not even in the old Hegemony-era atlases that Grandam had kept in her travel caravan, and which I had crept in to study by glow wand whenever I could.

The River Tethys had taken Aenea, A. Bettik, and me through desert planets on the way out to Old Earth, but these had been the oddly empty worlds of Hebron and New Mecca—their deserts devoid of life, their cities abandoned. But here on Vitus-Gray-Balianus B, adobe-style houses huddled by the river's edge, and every klick or so I would encounter a levy or lock where most of the water was being siphoned away for irrigation to the green fields that followed the river's course. Luckily the river served as the main street and central highway here, and I had emerged from the ancient farcaster arch's shadow in the lee of a massive barge, so I continued paddling blandly on in the midst of bustling river traffic—skiffs, rafts, barges, tugs, electric powerboats, houseboats, and even the occasional EM levitation barge moving three or four meters above the river's surface.

The gravity was light here, probably less than two thirds of Old Earth's or Hyperion's, and at times I thought that my paddle strokes were going to lift the kayak and me right out of the water. But if the gravity was light, the light—sunlight—was as heavy on me as a giant, sweaty palm. Within half an hour of paddling, I had depleted the last of my second water bottle and knew that I would have to set in to find a drink.

One would think on a world of lesser gravity that the denizens would be beanpoles—the vertical antithesis of the Lusian barrel shape—but most of the men, women, and children I saw in the busy lanes and towpaths along the river were almost as short and stocky as Lusians. Their clothing was as bright as the harlequin motley on the residents of Freude, but here each person wore a single brilliant hue—tight bodysuits of head-to-toe crimson, cloaks and capes of intense cerulean, gowns and suits of eye-piercing emerald with elaborate emerald hats and scarves, flowing trains of yellow chiffon and bright amber turbans. I realized that the doors and shutters of the adobe homes, shops, and inns were also painted in these distinctive colors and wondered what the significance might be—caste? Political preference? Social or economic status? Some sort of kinship signal? Whatever it was, I would not blend in when I went ashore to find a drink, dressed as I was all in dull khaki and weathered cotton.

But it was either put ashore or die of thirst. Just past one of the many self-serve locks, I paddled to a pier, tied my bobbing kayak in place as a heavy barge exited the lock behind me, and walked toward a circular wood-and-adobe structure that I hoped was an artesian well. I had seen several of the women in saffron robes carrying what may have been water jugs from the thing, so I felt fairly safe in my guess as to function. What I had no confidence in was the odds that I could draw water there myself without violating some law, coda, caste rule, religious commandment, or local custom. I had seen no visible Pax presence on the towpath or lanes—neither the black of priest nor the red and black of the standardized Pax police uniform—but that meant little. There were very few worlds, even in the Outback where the comlog informed me that Vitus-Gray-Balianus B lay, where the Pax did not have some definitive presence. I had covertly slipped the scabbard with my hunting knife from pack to back pocket under my vest, and my only plan was to use the blade to bluster an exit back to my boat if a mob formed. If Pax police arrived, with stunners or flechette pistols, my journey would be over.

It would soon be over—at least for a while—for vastly different reasons, but I had no warning—except for a backache that had been with me since before leaving Lusus—of that as I diffidently approached the well, if well it was.

It was a well.

No one reacted to my tall build or drab colors. No one—not even the children dressed in brilliant red and bright blue who paused in their game to give me a glance and then look away—interfered or seemed to notice the obvious stranger in their midst. As I drank deeply and then refilled both water bottles, I had the impression—from what source I do not know— that the inhabitants of Vitus-Gray-Balianus B, or at least of this village along this stretch of the long-abandoned River Tethys farcaster-way, were simply too polite to point and stare or ask me my business. My feeling at that moment, as I capped the second bottle and turned to return to my kayak, was that a three-headed mutant alien or—to speak in the realm of the more real bizarre—that the Shrike itself could have drunk from that artesian well on that pleasant desert afternoon and not have been accosted or questioned by the citizens.

I had taken three steps on the dusty lane when the pain struck. First I doubled over, gasping in pain, unable to take a breath, and then I went to one knee, then onto my side. I curled up in agony. I would have screamed if the terrible pain had allowed me the breath and energy. It did not. Gasping like a river fish tossed to this dusty bank, I curled tighter in a fetal position and rode waves of agony.

I should say here that I was not a total stranger to pain and discomfort. When I was in the Home Guard, a study by the Hyperion military showed that most of the conscripts sent south to fight the Ice Claw rebels had little stomach for pain. The city folks of the northern Aquila cities and the fancier Nine Tails towns had rarely, if ever, experienced any pain that they couldn't banish by popping a pill or dialing up an autosurgeon or driving to their nearest doc-in-the-box.

As a shepherd and country boy, I had a bit more experience with tolerating pain: accidental knife cuts, a broken foot from a pakbrid stepping on me, bruises and contusions from falls far out in rock country, a concussion once while wrestling in the caravan rendezvous, boils from riding, even the fat lips and black eyes from campfire brawls during the Men's Convocation. And on the Iceshelf I had been hurt three times—twice cut from shrapnel after white mines had killed buddies, once lanced from a long-range sniper—that final wound serious enough to bring in a priest who all but demanded that I accept the cruciform before it was too late.

But I had never experienced pain like this.

Moaning, gasping, the polite citizenry finally falling back from this flopping apparition and being forced to take notice of the stranger, I lifted my wrist and demanded that the comlog tell me what was happening to me. It did not answer. Between waves of unbearable pain, I asked again. Still no answer. Then I remembered that I had the damn thing in good child mode. I called it by name and repeated the query.

"May I activate the dormant biosensor function, M. Endymion?" asked the idiot AI.

I had not known that the device had a biosensor function, dormant or otherwise. I made a rude noise of assent and doubled into a tighter fetal curl. It felt as if someone had stabbed me in the upper back and was twisting the hooked blade. Pain poured through me like current through a hot wire. I vomited into the dust. A beautiful woman in pure white robes took another step back and lifted one white sandal.

"What is it?" I gasped again in the briefest of intervals between the stabbing pains. "What's happening?" I demanded of the comlog. With my other hand, I felt my back, seeking out blood or an entrance wound. I expected to find an arrow or spear, but there was nothing.

"You are going into shock, M. Endymion," said the lobotomized bit of the Consul ship's AI. "Blood pressure, skin resistance, heart rate, and atropin count all support this."

"Why?" I said again and drew the single syllable out into a long moan as the pain rolled from my back out and through my entire body. I retched again. My stomach was empty but the vomiting continued. The brightly clad citizens stayed their distance, never drawing into a curious crowd, never showing the bad manners of staring or murmuring, but obviously tarrying in their rounds.

"What's wrong?" I gasped again, trying to whisper to the comlog bracelet. "What would cause this?"

"Gunshot," returned the tiny, tinny voice. "Stab wound. Spear, knife, arrow, throwing dart. Energy weapon wound. Lance, laser, omega knife, pulse blade. Concentrated flechette strike. Perhaps a long, thin needle inserted through the upper kidney, liver, and spleen."

Writhing in pain, I felt my back again, pulling my own knife scabbard out and casting it away. The outer vest and shirt under it felt unburned or blasted. No sharp objects protruded from my flesh.

The pain burned its way through me again and I moaned aloud. I had not done that when the sniper had lanced me on the Iceshelf or when Uncle Vanya's 'brid had broken my foot.

I found it difficult to form complete thoughts, but the direction of my thinking was . . . *the Vitus-Gray-Balianus B natives . . . somehow . . . mind power . . . poison . . . the water . . . invisible rays . . . punishing me . . . for . . .*

I gave up the effort and moaned again. Someone in a bright blue skirt or toga and immaculate sandals, toenails painted blue, stepped closer.

"Excuse me, sir," said a soft voice in thickly accented old Web English. "But are you in difficulty?" *Er ye en defficoolte?*

"Aaarrrgghhhggghuhh," I said in response, punctuating the noise with more dry retching.

"May I then be of assistance?" said the same soft voice from above the blue toga. *Ez-sest-ance?*

"Oh . . . ahhrrgghah . . . nnnrrehhakk," I said and half swooned from the agony. Black dots danced in my vision until I could no longer see the sandals or blue toenails, but the terrible pain would not let go of me . . . I could not escape into unconsciousness.

Robes and togas rustled around me. I smelled perfume, cologne, soap . . . felt strong hands on my arms and legs and sides. Their attempt to lift me made the heated wire rip through my back and into the base of my skull.

7

THE GRAND INQUISITOR had been ordered to appear with his aide for a papal audience at 0800 hours Vatican time. At 0752 hours, his black EMV arrived at the Via del Belvedere checkpoint entrance to the papal apartments. The Inquisitor and his aide, Father Farrell, were passed through detector portals and handheld sensors—first at the Swiss Guard checkpoint, then at the Palatine Guard station, and finally at the new Noble Guard post.

John Domenico Cardinal Mustafa, the Grand Inquisitor, gave the most subtle of looks to his aide as they were passed by this final checkpoint. The Noble Guard at this point seemed to consist of cloned twins—all thin men and women with lank hair, sallow complexions, and dead gazes. A millennium ago, Mustafa knew, the Swiss Guard had been the paid mercenary force for the Pope, the Palatine Guard had consisted of trusted locals, always of Roman birth, who provided an honor guard for His Holiness's public appearances, and the Noble Guard had been chosen from aristocracy as a form of papal reward for loyalty. Today the Swiss Guard was the most elite of Pax Fleet's regular forces, the Palatines had been reinstated only a year earlier by Pope Julius XIV, and now Pope Urban appeared to be relying upon this strange brotherhood of the new Noble Guard for his personal safety.

The Grand Inquisitor knew that the Noble Guard twins were indeed clones, early prototypes of the secret Legion in building, and vanguards of a new fighting force requested by the Pope and his Secretary of State and designed by the Core. The Inquisitor had paid dearly for this information, and he knew that his position—if not his life—might be forfeit if Lourdusamy or His Holiness discovered that he knew of it.

Past the lower guard posts, with Father Farrell straightening his cassock after the search, Cardinal Mustafa waved away the papal assistant who offered to guide them upstairs. The Cardinal personally opened the door to the ancient lift that would take them to the papal apartments.

This private way to the Pope's quarters actually began in the basement, since the reconstructed Vatican was built on a hill with the Via del Belvedere entrance beneath the usual ground floor. Rising in the creaking cage, Father Farrell nervously fidgeting with his 'scriber and folder of papers, the Grand Inquisitor relaxed as they passed the ground-floor courtyard of San Damaso. They passed the second floor with the fantastic Borgia Apartments and the Sistine Chapel. They creaked and groaned their way past the second floor with the papal state apartments, the Consistorial Hall, the library, the audience suite, and the beautiful Raphael Rooms. On the third floor they stopped and the cage doors slammed open.

Cardinal Lourdusamy and his aide, Monsignor Lucas Oddi, nodded and smiled.

"Domenico," said Lourdusamy, taking the Grand Inquisitor's hand and squeezing it tightly.

"Simon Augustino," said the Grand Inquisitor with a bow. So the Secretary of State was to be in this meeting. Mustafa had suspected and feared as much. Stepping out of the lift and walking with the others toward the papal private apartments, the Grand Inquisitor glanced down the hallway toward the offices of the Secretariat of State and—for the ten-thousandth time—envied this man's access to the Pope.

The Pope met the party in the wide, brilliantly lit gallery that connected the Secretariat of State offices with the two stories of rooms that were the private domain of His Holiness. The usually serious Pontiff was smiling. This day he was dressed in a white-caped cassock with a white *zucchetto* on his head and a white fascia tied around his waist. His white shoes made only the slightest of whispering noises on the tiled floors.

"Ah, Domenico," said Pope Urban XVI as he extended his ring hand to be kissed. "Simon. How good of you to come."

Father Farrell and Monsignor Oddi waited on one knee for the Holy Father to turn to them so that they could kiss the Ring of St. Peter.

His Holiness looked well, thought the Grand Inquisitor, definitely younger and more rested than before his most recent death. The high forehead and burning eyes were the same, but Mustafa thought that there was something simultaneously more urgent and satisfied-looking about the resurrected Pope's appearance this morning.

"We were just about to take our morning stroll in the garden," said His Holiness. "Would you care to join us?"

The four men nodded and fell in with the Pope's quick pace as he walked the length of the gallery and then climbed smooth, broad stairs to the roof. His Holiness's personal aides kept their distance, the Swiss Guard troopers at the entrance to the garden stood at rigid attention while staring straight ahead, Lourdusamy and the Grand Inquisitor walked only a pace behind the Holy Father, while Monsignor Oddi and Father Farrell kept pace two steps back.

The papal gardens consisted of a maze of flowered trellises, trickling fountains, perfectly trimmed hedges and topiaried trees from three hundred Pax worlds, stone walkways, and fantastic flowering shrubs. Above all this, a force-ten containment field—transparent from this side, opaqued to outside observers—provided both privacy and protection. Pacem's sky was a brilliant, unclouded blue this morning.

"Do either of you remember," began His Holiness, his cassock rustling as they walked briskly down the garden path, "when our sky here was yellow?"

Cardinal Lourdusamy produced the deep rumble that passed for a chuckle with him. "Oh, yes," he said, "I remember when the sky was a sick yellow, the air was all but unbreathable, it was cold all the time, and the rain never ended. A marginal world then, Pacem. The only reason the old Hegemony ever allowed the Church to settle here."

Pope Urban XVI smiled thinly and gestured toward the blue sky and warm sunlight. "So there has been some improvement during our time of service here, eh, Simon Augustino?"

Both cardinals laughed softly. They had made a quick circuit of the rooftop, and now His Holiness took another route through the center of the garden. Stepping from stone to stone on the narrow path, the two cardinals and their aides followed the white-cassocked Pontiff in single file. Suddenly His Holiness stopped and turned. A fountain burbled softly behind him.

"You have heard," he said, all jesting gone from his tone, "that Admiral Aldikacti's task force has translated beyond the Great Wall?"

Both cardinals nodded.

"It is but the first of what will be many such incursions," said the Holy Father. "We do not hope this . . . we do not predict this . . . we *know* this."

The head of the Holy Office and the Secretary of State and their aides waited.

The Pope looked at each man in turn. "This afternoon, my friends, we plan to travel to Castel Gandolfo . . ."

The Grand Inquisitor stopped himself from glancing upward, knowing that the papal asteroid could not be seen during the daytime. He knew that the Pontiff was speaking in the royal "we" and not inviting Lourdusamy and him to come along.

". . . where we will pray and meditate for several days while composing our next encyclical," continued the Pope. "It will be entitled *Redemptor Hominis* and it will be the most important document of our tenure as shepherd of our Holy Mother Church."

The Grand Inquisitor bowed his head. *The Redeemer of Mankind,* he thought. *It could be about anything.*

When Cardinal Mustafa looked up, His Holiness was smiling as if reading his thoughts. "It will be about our sacred obligation to keep humanity human, Domenico," said the Pope. "It will extend, clarify, and broaden what has become known as our Crusade Encyclical. It will define Our Lord's wish . . . nay, commandment . . . that mankind remain in the form and visage of mankind, and not be defiled by deliberate mutation and mutilation."

"The final solution to the Ouster problem," murmured Cardinal Lourdusamy.

His Holiness nodded impatiently. "That and more. *Redemptor Hominis* will look at the Church's role in defining the future, dear friends. In a sense, it will lay out a blueprint for the next thousand years."

Mother of Mercy, thought the Grand Inquisitor.

"The Pax has been a useful instrument," continued the Holy Father, "but in the days and months and years ahead, we will be laying the ground-work for the way in which the Church shall become more active in the daily lives of all Christians."

Bringing the Pax worlds more closely under control, interpreted the Grand Inquisitor, his eyes still lowered in thoughtful attention to the Pope's words. *But how . . . with what mechanism?*

Pope Urban XVI smiled again. Cardinal Mustafa noticed, not for the first time, that the Holy Father's smiles never reached his pained and wary eyes. "Upon the release of the encyclical," said His Holiness, "you may more clearly perceive the role we see for the Holy Office, for our diplomatic service, and for such underused entities and institutions as *Opus Dei,* the Pontifical Commission for Justice and Peace, and *Cor Unum.*"

The Grand Inquisitor tried to conceal his surprise. *Cor Unum?* The Pontifical Commission, officially known as *Pontificum Consilium "Cor Unum" de Humana et Christiana Progressione Fovenda,* had been little more than a powerless committee for centuries. Mustafa had to think to remember its president . . . Cardinal Du Noyer, he believed. A minor Vatican bureaucrat. An old woman who had never figured in Vatican politics before. *What in hell is going on here?*

"It is an exciting time," said Cardinal Lourdusamy.

"Indeed," said the Grand Inquisitor, recalling the ancient Chinese curse to that effect.

The Pope began walking again and the four hurried to keep up. A breeze came through the containment field and fluttered the golden blos-soms on a sculpted holyoak.

"Our new encyclical shall also deal with the growing problem of usury in our new age," said His Holiness.

The Grand Inquisitor almost stopped in his tracks. As it was, he had to take a quick half step to keep pace. It was a greater effort to keep his expression neutral. He could all but feel the shock of Father Farrell behind him.

Usury? thought the Grand Inquisitor. *The Church has been strict in regulating Pax and Pax Mercantilus trade for three centuries . . . no re-turn to the days of pure capitalism was desired or allowed . . . but the hand of control has been light. Is this a move to consolidate all political and economic life directly under Church control? Would Julius . . . Urban . . . make the move to abolish Pax civil autonomy and Mercantilus trade freedoms at this late date? And where does the military stand in all this?*

His Holiness paused by a beautiful shrub of white blossoms and bright blue leaves. "Our Illyrian gentian is doing well here," he said softly. "It was a present from Archbishop Poske on Galabia Pescassus."

Usury! thought the Grand Inquisitor in wild confusion. *A penalty of excommunication . . . losing the cruciform . . . upon violation of strict trade and profit controls. Direct intervention from the Vatican. Mother of Christ . . .*

"But that is not why we asked you here," said Pope Urban XVI. "Simon Augustino, would you be so kind as to share with Cardinal Mustafa the disturbing intelligence you received yesterday?"

They know about our biospies, thought Mustafa in panic. His heart was pounding. *They know about the agents in place . . . about the Holy Office's attempt to contact the Core directly . . . about sounding out the cardinals before the election . . . everything!* He kept his expression appropriate—alert, interested, alarmed only in a professional sense at the Holy Father's use of the word "disturbing."

The great mass of Cardinal Lourdusamy seemed to draw itself up. The heavy rumble of words seemed to come from the man's chest or belly more than from his mouth. Behind him, the figure of Monsignor Oddi reminded Mustafa of the scarecrows in the fields of his youth on the agricultural world of Renaissance Minor.

"The Shrike has reappeared," began the Cardinal.

The Shrike? What does that have to do with . . . Mustafa's usually sharp mind was reeling, unable to catch up with all of the shifts and revelations. He still suspected a trap. Realizing that the Secretary of State had paused for response, the Grand Inquisitor said softly, "Can the military authorities on Hyperion deal with it, Simon Augustino?"

Cardinal Lourdusamy's jowls vibrated as the great head moved back and forth. "It is not on Hyperion that the demon has reappeared, Domenico."

Mustafa registered appropriate shock. *I know through the interrogation of Corporal Kee that the monster appeared on God's Grove four standard years ago, apparently in an attempt to foil the murder of the child named Aenea. To get that, I had to arrange for the false death and kidnapping of Kee after his reassignment to Pax Fleet. Do they know? And why tell me now?* The Grand Inquisitor was still waiting for the metaphorical blade to drop on his very real neck.

"Eight standard days ago," continued Lourdusamy, "a monstrous creature which could only be the Shrike appeared on Mars. The death toll . . . true death, for the creature takes the cruciforms from its victims' bodies . . . has been very high."

"Mars," Cardinal Mustafa repeated stupidly. He looked to the Holy

Father for an explanation, guidance, even the condemnation he feared, but the Pontiff was examining buds on a rosebush. Behind him, Father Farrell took a step forward but the Grand Inquisitor waved his aide back. "Mars?" he said again. He had not felt so stupid and ill-informed for decades, perhaps centuries.

Lourdusamy smiled. "Yes . . . one of the terraformed worlds in Old Earth's system. FORCE used to have its command center there before the Fall, but the world is of little use or importance in the Pax. Too far away. There is no reason for you to know about it, Domenico."

"I know *where* Mars is," said the Grand Inquisitor, his tone more sharp than he had meant it to be. "I simply do not understand how the Shrike creature could be there." *And what in Dante's hell does it have to do with me?* he mentally added.

Lourdusamy was nodding. "It is true that to our knowledge, the Shrike demon has never left the world of Hyperion before this. But there can be no doubt. This terror on Mars . . . the Governor has declared a state of emergency and Archbishop Robeson has personally petitioned His Holiness for help."

The Grand Inquisitor rubbed his cheek and nodded in concern. "Pax Fleet . . ."

"Elements of the Fleet already positioned in the Old Neighborhood have been dispatched, of course," said the Secretary of State. The Supreme Pontiff was bent over a bonsai tree, his hand over the tiny, twisted branch as if he were bestowing a blessing. He seemed not to be listening.

"The ships will have a complement of Marines and Swiss Guard," continued Lourdusamy. "We hope that they will subdue and/or destroy the creature . . ."

My mother taught me never to trust anyone who uses the expression "and/or," thought Mustafa. "Of course," he said aloud. "I shall say a Mass with that prayer in mind."

Lourdusamy smiled. The Holy Father glanced up from where he was bent over the stunted little tree.

"Precisely," said Lourdusamy, and in those three syllables, Mustafa heard the sound of the overfed cat pouncing on the hapless mouse of the Grand Inquisitor. "We agree that it is more a matter of faith than of the Fleet. The Shrike—as it was revealed to the Holy Father more than two centuries ago—is truly a demon, perhaps the principal agent of the Dark One."

Mustafa could only nod.

"We feel that only the Holy Office is properly trained, equipped, and prepared—both spiritually and materially—to investigate this appearance properly . . . and to save the hapless men, women, and children of Mars."

Well fuck me, thought John Domenico Cardinal Mustafa, Grand Inquisitor and Prefect for the Sacred Congregation for the Doctrine of the Faith, otherwise known as the Supreme Congregation for the Holy Inquisition of Heretical Error. He automatically offered up a mental Act of Contrition for his obscenity.

"I see," the Grand Inquisitor said aloud, not seeing at all but almost smiling at the ingenuity of his enemies. "I will immediately appoint a commission . . ."

"No, no, Domenico," said His Holiness, moving close to touch the Grand Inquisitor's arm. "You must go at once. This . . . materialization . . . of the demon threatens the entire Body of Christ."

"Go . . ." said Mustafa stupidly.

"An archangel-class starship, one of our newest, has been requisitioned from Pax Fleet," Lourdusamy said briskly. "It will have a crew of twenty-eight, but you may still bring up to twenty-one members of your own staff and security service . . . twenty-one and yourself, of course."

"Of course," said Cardinal Mustafa and he did smile. "Of course."

"Pax Fleet is doing battle with the corporeal agents of Satan . . . the Ousters . . . even as we speak," rumbled Lourdusamy. "But this demonic threat must be confronted—and defeated—by the sacred power of the Church itself."

"Of course," said the Grand Inquisitor. *Mars*, he thought. *The most distant pimple on the ass-end of the civilized universe. Three centuries ago, I could have called on the fatline, but now I will be out of touch as long as they keep me there. No intelligence. No way to direct my people. And the Shrike . . . if the monster is still controlled by the Core's blasphemous Ultimate Intelligence, it may well be programmed to kill me as soon as I arrive. Brilliant.* "Of course," he said again. "Holy Father, when do I leave? If there could be a few days or weeks to set the current affairs of the Holy Office in proper . . ."

The Pope smiled and squeezed Mustafa's upper arm. "The archangel is waiting to transport you and your chosen contingent within the day, Domenico. Six hours from now would be optimum, they tell us."

"Of course," said Cardinal Mustafa a final time. He went to one knee to kiss the papal ring.

"God go with you and protect you always," said the Holy Father, touching the Cardinal's bowed head as he pronounced the more formal benediction in Latin.

Kissing the ring, tasting the sour cold of stone and metal in his mouth, the Grand Inquisitor mentally smiled again at the cleverness of those whom he had thought to outsmart and outmaneuver.

FATHER CAPTAIN DE SOYA did not get a chance to talk to Sergeant Gregorius until the last minutes of *Raphael*'s first beyond-the-Outback jump.

This first jump was a practice hop to an uncharted system twenty light-years beyond the Great Wall. Like Epsilon Eridani, the star in this system was a K-type sun; unlike the Eridani orange-dwarf, this K-type was an Arcturus-like giant.

Task Force GIDEON translated without incident, the new two-day automated resurrection crèches functioned without glitch, and the third day found the seven archangels decelerating into the giant's system, playing tactical cat-and-mouse with the nine Hawking-class torchships that had preceded them after months of time-debt travel. The torchships had been ordered to hide within the system. The archangels' task was to sniff them out and destroy them.

Three of the torchships were far out in the Oört cloud, floating amid the proto-comets there, their drives off, their coms silenced, their internal systems at lowest ebb. The *Uriel* picked them up at a distance of 0.86 light-years and launched three virtual Hawking hyperkinetics. De Soya stood with the other six captains in tactical space, the system's sun at their belt level, the two-hundred-kilometer flame tails of seven archangel fusion drives like chest-high diamond scratches on black glass, and he watched as holos misted, formed, and dematerialized in the Oört cloud, tracking the theoretical hyperkinetic seeker missiles as they shifted out of Hawking space, sought out the dormant torchships, and registered two virtual kills and one "severe damage certain—high probability of a kill" on the tactical tote board.

This system had no planets as such, but four of the remaining torch-ships were found lurking in ambush within the planetary accretion disc along the plane of the ecliptic. The *Remiel,* the *Gabriel,* and the *Raphael* engaged at long distance and registered kills before the torchships' sensors could register the presence of the archangel intruders.

The final two torchships were hiding in the heliosphere of the giant K-type star, shielding themselves with class-ten containment fields and venting heat via trailing monofilaments half a million kilometers long. Pax Fleet more than frowned on this sort of maneuver during simulated engagements, but de Soya had to smile at the audacity of the two ship's commanders: it was the sort of thing he might have done a standard decade earlier.

These final torchships came ripping out of the K-star at high boost, their fields venting heat on the visible spectrum, two blazing, white-hot proto-stars spit out from their massive parent, both ships trying to close on the task force that even now was ripping through the system at three-quarters light-speed. The closest archangel—*Sariel*—killed them both with-out diverting an erg of power from the class-thirty bussfield the archangel had to maintain a hundred klicks beyond its bow just to clear a path through the molecule-cluttered system. Such terrible velocities demanded a terrible price if the fields failed for an instant.

Then, with Admiral Aldikacti grumbling about the "probable" in the Oört cloud, the task force decelerated hard in one great arc around the K-type giant so that all of the commanders and execs could meet in tactical space to discuss the simulation before the GIDEON ships translated into Ouster space.

De Soya always found these conferences hubris-making: thirty-some men and women in Pax uniforms standing like giants—or in this case sitting like giants, since they used the plane of the ecliptic as a virtual tabletop—discussing kills and strategies and equipment failures and acquisition rates while the K-type sun burned brightly in the center of the space and the magnified ships moved in their slow, Newtonian ellipses like embers burning through black velvet.

During the three-hour conference, it was decided that the "probable kill" was unacceptable and that they should have fired a spread of at least five AI-piloted hyper-ks at such difficult targets, retrieving any unused missiles after all three kills were certain. There followed a discussion of expendables, fire-rates, and the kill/conserve/reserve equations on a mission such as this where there could be no resupply. A strategy was decided whereupon one of the archangels would enter each system thirty light-minutes ahead of the others, serving as "point" to draw all sensor and ECM queries, while another would trail half a light-hour behind, mopping up any "probables."

After a twenty-two-hour day spent mostly at battle stations, and with all hands fighting post-resurrection emotional jags, jump coordinates for a system known to be Ouster-infested came over the tightbeam from the *Uriel*, the seven archangels accelerated toward their translation point, and Father Captain de Soya made the rounds to chat with his new crew and to "tuck everyone in." He saved Sergeant Gregorius and his five Swiss Guard troopers for last.

ONCE, DURING THEIR long chase across the spiral arm after the girl-child named Aenea and after spending months together on the old *Raphael*, Father Captain de Soya had decided that he was tired of calling Sergeant Gregorius "Sergeant Gregorius" and called up the man's records to discover his first name. To his surprise, de Soya discovered that the sergeant had no first name. The huge noncom had come of age on the northern continent of the swamp world of Patawpha in a warrior culture where everyone was born with eight names—seven of them "weakness names"— and where only survivors of the "seven trials" were privileged to discard the weakness names and be known by only their strength name. The ship's AI had told the father-captain that only one warrior out of approximately three thousand attempting the "seven trials" survived and succeeded in discarding all weakness names. The computer had no information as to the nature of the trials. In addition, the records had shown, Gregorius had been the first Patawphan Scot-Maori to become a decorated Marine and then be chosen to join the elite Swiss Guard. De Soya had always meant to ask the sergeant what the "seven trials" were, but had never worked up the nerve.

This day, when de Soya kicked down the dropshaft in zero-g and passed through the irising wardroom soft spot, Sergeant Gregorius appeared so happy to see him that he looked as if he were about to give the father-captain a bear hug. Instead, the sergeant hooked his bare feet under a bar, snapped to attention, and shouted, "TEN-hut in the wardroom!" His five troopers dropped what they were doing—reading, cleaning, or field-stripping—and tried to put bulkhead under their toes. For a moment the wardroom was littered with floating 'scribers, magazines, pulse knives, impact armor, and stripped-down energy lances.

Father Captain de Soya nodded to the sergeant and inspected the five commandos—three men, two women, all terribly, terribly young. They were also lean, muscular, perfectly adapted to zero-g, and obviously honed for battle. All of them were combat veterans. Each of them had distinguished himself or herself adequately to be chosen for this mission. De Soya saw their eagerness for combat and was saddened by it.

After a few minutes of inspection, introductions, and commander-to-commando chatting, de Soya beckoned for Gregorius to follow and kicked off through the aft soft spot into the launch-tube room. When they were alone, Father Captain de Soya extended his hand. "Damned good to see you, Sergeant."

Gregorius shook hands and grinned. The big man's square, scarred face and short-cropped hair were the same, and his grin was as broad and bright as de Soya remembered. "Damned good t' see you, Father Captain. And when did the priesty side o' ya begin usin' profanity, sir?"

"When I was promoted to commanding this ship, Sergeant," said de Soya. "How have you been?"

"Fair, sir. Fair an' better."

"You saw action in the St. Anthony Incursion and the Sagittarius Salient," said de Soya. "Were you with Corporal Kee before he died?"

Sergeant Gregorius rubbed his chin. "Negative, sir. I was at the Salient two years ago, but I never saw Kee. Heard about his transport bein' slagged, but never saw him. Had a couple of other friends aboard it, too, sir."

"I'm sorry," said de Soya. The two were floating awkwardly near one of the hyper-k storage nacelles. The father-captain grabbed a holdtite and oriented himself so that he could look Gregorius in the eye. "Did you get through the interrogation all right, Sergeant?"

Gregorius shrugged. "They kept me on Pacem a few weeks, sir. Kept askin' the same questions in different ways. Didn't seem to believe me about what happened on God's Grove—the woman devil, the Shrike-thingee. Eventually they seemed t' get tired o' askin' me things and busted me back down to corporal and shipped me out."

De Soya sighed. "I'm sorry, Sergeant. I had recommended you for a promotion and commendation." He chuckled ruefully. "A lot of good that did you. We're lucky we weren't both excommunicated and then executed."

"Aye, sir," said Gregorius, glancing out the port at the shifting starfield. "They weren't happy with us, that's a' sure." He looked at de Soya. "And you, sir. I heard they took away your commission and all."

Father Captain de Soya smiled. "Busted me back to parish priest."

"On a dirty, desert, no-water world, I heard tell, sir. A place where piss sells for ten marks a bootful."

"That was true," said de Soya, still smiling. "MadredeDios. It was my homeworld."

"Aw, shit, sir," said Sergeant Gregorius, his huge hands clenching in embarrassment. "No disrespect meant, sir. I mean . . . I didn't . . . I wouldn't . . ."

De Soya touched the big man's shoulder. "No disrespect taken, Sergeant. You're right. Piss does sell there . . . only for fifteen marks a bootful, not ten."

"Aye, sir," said Gregorius, his dark skin darker with flush.

"And, Sergeant . . ."

"Aye, sir?"

"That will be fifteen Hail Marys and ten Our Fathers for the scatological outburst. I'm still your confessor, you know."

"Aye, sir."

De Soya's implant tingled at the same instant chimes came over the ship's communicators. "Thirty minutes until translation," said the father-captain. "Get your chicks tucked in their crèches, Sergeant. This next jump is for real."

"Aye, aye, sir." The sergeant kicked for the soft spot but stopped just as the circle irised open. "Father Captain?"

"Yes, Sergeant."

"It's just a feelin', sir," said the Swiss Guardsman, his brow furrowed. "But I've learned to trust my feelin's, sir."

"I've learned to trust your feelings as well, Sergeant. What is it?"

"Watch your back, sir," said Gregorius. "I mean . . . nothin' definite, sir. But watch your back."

"Aye, aye," said Father Captain de Soya. He waited until Gregorius was back in his wardroom and the soft spot sealed before he kicked off for the main dropshaft and his own death couch and resurrection crèche.

PACEM SYSTEM WAS crowded with Mercantilus traffic, Pax Fleet warships, large-array habitats such as the Torus Mercantilus, Pax military bases and listening posts, herded and terraformed asteroids such as Castel Gandolfo, low-rent orbital can cities for the millions eager to be close to humanity's center of power but too poor to pay Pacem's exorbitant rates, and the highest concentration of private in-system spacecraft in the known universe. Thus it was that when M. Kenzo Isozaki, CEO and Chairman of the Executive Council of the Pancapitalist League of Independent Catholic Transstellar Trade Organizations, wished to be absolutely alone, he had to commandeer a private ship and burn high-g for thirty-two hours into the outer ring of darkness far from Pacem's star.

Even choosing a ship had been a problem. The Pax Mercantilus maintained a small fleet of expensive in-system executive shuttles, but Isozaki had to assume that despite their best attempts to debug the ships, they were all compromised. For this rendezvous, he had considered rerouting one of the Mercantilus freighters that plied the trade lanes between orbital clusters, but he did not put it past his enemies—the Vatican, the Holy Office, Pax Fleet Intelligence Services, *Opus Dei,* rivals within the Mercantilus, countless others—to bug every ship in the Mercantilus's vast trade fleet.

In the end, Kenzo Isozaki had disguised himself, gone to the Torus public docks, bought an ancient asteroid hopper on the spot, and ordered his illegal comlog AI to pilot the thing out beyond the campfire zone of the ecliptic. On the trip out, his ship was challenged six times by Pax security patrols and stations, but the hopper was licensed, there were rocks where he was headed—mined and remined, to be sure, but still legitimate destinations for a desperate prospector—and he was passed on without personal interrogation.

Isozaki found all this melodramatic and a waste of his valuable time. He would have met his contact in his office on the Torus if the contact had agreed. The contact had not agreed, and Isozaki had to admit that he would have crawled to Aldebaren for this meeting.

Thirty-two hours after leaving the Torus, the hopper dropped his internal containment field, drained his high-g tank, and brought him up out of sleep. The ship's computer was too stupid to do anything but give him coordinates and readouts on the local rocks, but the illicit AI comlog interface scanned the entire region for ships—powered down or active—and pronounced this sphere of Pacem System space empty.

"So how does he get here if there is no ship?" muttered Isozaki.

"There is no way other than by ship, sir," said the AI. "Unless he is here already, which seems unlikely since . . ."

"Silence," ordered Kenzo Isozaki. He sat in the lubricant-smelling dimness of the hopper command blister and watched the asteroid half a klick distant. Hopper and rock had matched tumble rates, so it was the familiar Pacem System starfield beyond the heavily mined and cratered stone that seemed to be spinning. Other than the asteroid, there was nothing out there except hard vacuum, hard radiation, and cold silence.

Suddenly there was a knock on the outer air-lock door.

8

A T THE TIME that all these troop movements were under way, at
the same time that great armadas of matte-black starships were
tearing holes in the time and space continuum of the cosmos, at
the precise moment when the Church's Grand Inquisitor was sent packing
to Shrike-ridden Mars and the CEO of the Pax Mercantilus was traveling
alone to a secret rendezvous in deep space with a nonhuman interlocutor, I
was lying helpless in bed with a tremendous pain in my back and belly.

Pain is an interesting and off-putting thing. Few if any things in life
concentrate our attention so completely and terribly, and few things are
more boring to listen to or read about.

This pain was all-absorbing. I was amazed by the relentless, mind-
controlling quality of it. During the hours of agony that I had already
endured and was yet to endure, I attempted to concentrate on my surroundings, to think of other things, to interact with the people around me,
even to do simple multiplication tables in my head, but the pain flowed into
all the compartments of my consciousness like molten steel into the fissures
on a cracked crucible.

These things I was dimly aware of at the time: that I had been on a
world my comlog had identified as Vitus-Gray-Balianus B and in the process of dipping water from a well when the pain had felled me; that a
woman swathed in a blue robe, her toenails visibly blue in her open sandals
as I lay writhing in the dust, had called others in blue robes and gowns and
these people had carried me to the adobe house where I continued battling
the pain in a soft bed; that there were several other people in the house—
another woman in a blue gown and head scarf, a younger man who wore a
blue robe and turban, at least two children, also dressed in blue; and that
these generous people not only put up with my moaned apologies and less
articulate moans as I curled and uncurled in pain, but constantly spoke to

me, patted me, placed wet compresses on my forehead, removed my boots and socks and vest, and generally continued whispering reassurances in their soft dialect as I tried to fight to keep my dignity against the onslaught of agony in my back and abdomen.

It was several hours after they brought me to their home—the blue sky had faded to rose evening outside the window—when the woman who had found me near the well said, "Citizen, we have asked the local missionary priest for help and he has gone for the doctor at the Pax base at Bombasino. For some reason, the Pax skimmers and other aircraft are all busy now, so the priest and the doctor . . . if the doctor comes . . . must travel fifty pulls down the river, but with luck they should be here before sunrise."

I did not know how long a pull was or how much time it would take to travel fifty, or even how long the night was on this world, but the thought that there might be an end point to my agony was enough to bring tears to my eyes. Nonetheless, I whispered, "Please, ma'am, no Pax doctor."

The woman set cool fingers against my brow. "We must. There is no longer a medic here in Lock Lamonde. We are afraid you might die without medical help."

I moaned and rolled away. The pain roiled through me like a hot wire being pulled through too-narrow capillaries. I realized that a Pax doctor would know immediately that I was from offworld, would report me to the Pax police or military—if the "missionary priest" had not already done so—and that I was all but certain to be interrogated and detained. My mission for Aenea was ending early and in failure. When the old poet, Martin Silenus, had sent me on this odyssey four and a half standard years earlier, he had drunk a champagne toast to me—"To heroes." If only he had known how far from reality that toast had been. Perhaps he had.

The night passed with glacial slowness. Several times the two women looked in on me and at other times the children, in blue gowns that may have been sleeping apparel, peered in from the darkened hallway. They wore no headdress then and I saw that the girl had blond hair worn much the way Aenea had when we first met, when she was almost twelve and I twenty-eight standard. The little boy—younger than the girl I assumed to be his sister—looked especially pale; his head was shaved quite bald. Each time he looked in, his fingers fluttered at me in a shy wave. Between rolls of pain, I would feebly wave back, but each time I opened my eyes to look again, the child would be gone.

Sunrise came and went without a doctor. Hopelessness surged in me like an outgoing tide. I could not resist this terrible pain another hour. I knew instinctively that if the kind people in this household had any painkiller, they would have long since given it to me. I had spent the night trying to think of anything I had brought with me in the kayak, but the only medicine in my stowed kit was disinfectant and some aspirin. I knew that the latter would do nothing against this tidal wave of pain.

I decided that I could hold out another ten minutes. They had removed my comlog bracelet and set it within sight on an adobe ledge near the bed, but I had not thought to measure the hours of the night with it. Now I struggled to reach it, the pain twisting in me like a hot wire, and slipped the bracelet back on my wrist. I whispered to the ship's AI in it: "Is the biomonitor function still activated?"

"Yes," said the bracelet.

"Am I dying?"

"Life signs are not critical," said the ship in its usual flat tones. "But you appear to be in shock. Blood pressure is . . ." It continued to rattle off technical information until I told it to shut up.

"Have you figured out what's doing this to me?" I gasped. Waves of nausea followed the pain. I had long since vomited anything in my stomach, but the retching doubled me over.

"It is not inconsistent with an appendicitis attack," said the comlog.

"Appendicitis . . ." Those useless artifacts had long since been gene-tailored out of humanity. "Do I have an appendix?" I whispered to the bracelet. With the sunrise had come the rustle of robes in the quiet house and several visits from the women.

"Negative," said the comlog. "It would be very unlikely, unless you are a genetic sport. The odds against that would be . . ."

"Silence," I hissed. The two women in blue robes bustled in with another woman, taller, thinner, obviously offworld-born. She wore a dark jumpsuit with the cross-and-caduceus patch of the Pax Fleet Medical Corps on her left shoulder.

"I'm Dr. Molina," said the woman, unpacking a small black valise. "All the base skimmers are on war-game maneuvers and I had to come by fitzboat with the young man who fetched me." She set one sticky diagnostic patch on my bare chest and another on my belly. "And don't flatter yourself that I came all this way for you . . . one of the base skimmers crashed near Keroa Tambat, eighty klicks south of here, and I have to tend to the injured Pax crew while they wait for medevac. Nothing serious, just bruises and a broken leg. They didn't want to pull a skimmer out of the games just for that." She removed a palm-sized device from the valise and checked to see that it was receiving from the patches. "And if you're one of those Mercantilus spacers who jumped ship at the port a few weeks ago," she continued, "don't get any ideas about robbing me for drugs or money. I'm traveling with two security guards and they're right outside." She slipped earphones on. "Now what's wrong with you, young man?"

I shook my head, gritting my teeth against the surge of pain that was ripping through my back at that second. When I could, I said, "I don't know, Doctor . . . my back . . . and nausea . . ."

She ignored me while checking the palm device. Suddenly she leaned over and probed my abdomen on the left side. "Does that hurt?"

I almost screamed. "Yes," I said when I could speak.

She nodded and turned to the woman in blue who had saved me.

"Tell the priest who fetched me to bring in the larger bag. This man is completely dehydrated. We need to set up an IV. I'll administer the ultramorph after I get that going."

I realized then what I had known since I was a child watching my mother die of cancer—namely, that beyond ideology and ambition, beyond thought and emotion, there was only pain. And salvation from it. I would have done anything for that rough-edged, talkative Pax Fleet doctor right then.

"What is it?" I asked her as she was setting up a bottle and tubes. "Where is this pain coming from?" She had an old-fashioned needle syringe in her hand and was filling it from a small vial of ultramorph. If she told me that I had contracted a fatal disease and would be dead before nightfall, it would be all right as long as she gave me that shot of painkiller first.

"Kidney stone," said Dr. Molina.

I must have shown my incomprehension, because she went on, "A little rock in your kidney . . . too large to pass . . . probably made of calcium. Have you had trouble urinating in recent days?"

I thought back to the beginning of the trip and before. I had not been drinking enough water and had attributed the occasional pain and difficulty to that fact. "Yes, but . . ."

"Kidney stone," she said, swabbing my left wrist. "Little sting here." She inserted the intravenous needle and dermplasted it in place. The sting of the needle was totally lost in the cacophony of pain from my back. There was a moment of fiddling with the intravenous tube and attaching the syringe to an offshoot of it. "This will take about a minute to act," she said. "But it should eliminate the discomfort."

Discomfort. I closed my eyes so that no one would see the tears of relief there. The woman who had found me by the well took my hand in hers.

A minute later the pain began to ebb. Nothing had ever been so welcome by its absence. It was as if a great and terrible noise had finally been turned down so that I could think. I became me again as the agony dropped to the levels I had known from knife wounds and broken bones. This I could handle and still retain my dignity and sense of self. The woman in blue was touching my wrist as the ultramorph took effect.

"Thank you," I said through parched, cracked lips, squeezing the hand of the woman in blue. "And thank you, Dr. Molina," I said to the Pax medic.

Dr. Molina leaned over me, tapping my cheeks softly. "You're going to sleep for a while, but I need some answers first. Don't sleep until you talk to me."

I nodded groggily.

"What's your name?"

"Raul Endymion." I realized that I could not lie to her. She must have put Truthtell or another drug in the IV drip.

"Where are you from, Raul Endymion?" She was holding the palm-sized diagnostic device like a recorder.

"Hyperion. The continent of Aquila. My clan was . . ."

"How did you get to Lock Childe Lamonde on Vitus-Gray-Balianus B, Raul? Are you one of the spacers who jumped ship from the Mercantilus freighter last month?"

"Kayak," I heard myself say as everything began to feel distant. A great warmth filled me, almost indistinguishable from the sense of relief that surged within me. "Paddled downriver in the kayak," I babbled. "Through the farcaster. No, I'm not one of the spacers . . ."

"Farcaster?" I heard the doctor repeat, her voice puzzled. "What do you mean you came through the farcaster, Raul Endymion? Do you mean you paddled under it the way we did? Just passed by it on your trip downriver?"

"No," I said. "I came *through* it. From offworld."

The doctor glanced at the woman in blue and then turned back to me. "You came *through* the farcaster from offworld? You mean it . . . functioned? Farcast you here?"

"Yeah."

"From where?" said the doctor, checking my pulse with her left hand.

"Old Earth," I said. "I came from Earth."

For a moment I floated, blissfully free from pain, while the doctor stepped out into the hall to talk to the ladies. I heard snatches of conversation.

". . . obviously mentally unbalanced," the doctor's voice was saying. "Could not have possibly come through the . . . delusions of Old Earth . . . possibly one of the spacers on drugs . . ."

"Happy to have him stay . . ." the woman in the blue robe was saying. "Take care of him until . . ."

"The priest and one of the guards will stay here . . ." the doctor's voice said. "When the medevac skimmer comes to Keroa Tambat we'll stop by here to fetch him on the way back to the base . . . tomorrow or the day after tomorrow . . . don't let him leave . . . military police will probably want to . . ."

Buoyed up on the rising crest of bliss at the absence of pain, I quit fighting the current and allowed myself to drift downstream to the waiting arms of morphia.

I DREAMED OF a conversation Aenea and I had shared a few months earlier. It was a cool, high-desert summer night and we were sitting in the vestibule of her shelter, drinking mugs of tea and watching the stars come out. We had been discussing the Pax, but for everything negative I had said about it, Aenea had responded with something positive. Finally I got angry.

"Look," I said, "you're talking about the Pax as if it hadn't tried to capture you and kill you. As if Pax ships hadn't chased us halfway across the spiral arm and shot us down on Renaissance Vector. If it hadn't been for the farcaster there . . ."

"The Pax didn't chase us and shoot at us and try to kill us," the girl said softly. "Just elements of it. Men and women following orders from the Vatican or elsewhere."

"Well," I said, still exasperated and irritated, "it only takes *elements of it* to shoot us and kill . . ." I paused a second. "What do you mean— 'from the Vatican or elsewhere'? Do you think there are others giving orders? Other than the Vatican, I mean?"

Aenea shrugged. It was a graceful motion, but irritating in the extreme. One of the least endearing of her less-than-endearing teenaged traits.

"Are there others?" I demanded, more sharply than I was used to speaking to my young friend.

"There are always others," Aenea said quietly. "They were right to try to capture me, Raul. Or kill me."

In my dream as in reality, I set my mug of tea on the stone foundation of the vestibule and stared at her. "You're saying that you . . . and I . . . should be captured or killed . . . like animals. That they have that right?"

"Of course not," said the girl, crossing her arms in front of her chest, the tea steaming into the cool night air. "I'm saying that the Pax is correct—from its perspective—in using extraordinary measures to try to stop me."

I shook my head. "I haven't heard you say anything so subversive that they should send squadrons of starships after you, kiddo. In fact, the most subversive and heretical thing I've heard you say is that love is a basic force of the universe, like gravity or electromagnetism. But that's just . . ."

"Bullshit?" said Aenea.

"Double talk," I said.

Aenea smiled and ran her fingers through her short hair. "Raul, my friend, it's not what I *say* that's a danger to them. It's what I *do*. What I teach by doing . . . by touching."

I looked at her. I had almost forgotten all that One Who Teaches stuff that her Uncle Martin Silenus had woven into his *Cantos* epic. Aenea was to be the messiah that the old poet had prophesied in his long, confused poem some two centuries earlier . . . or so he had told me. So far I had seen very little from the girl that suggested messiahhood, unless one counted her trip forward through the Sphinx Time Tomb and the obsession of the Pax to capture or kill her . . . and me, since I was her guardian during the rough trip out to Old Earth.

"I haven't heard you teach much that's heretical or dangerous," I said again, my tone almost sullen. "Or seen you *do* anything that's a threat to the Pax, either." I gestured to the night, the desert, and to the distant, lighted buildings of the Taliesin Fellowship, and now—in my ultramorph dream that was more memory than dream—I watched myself make that gesture as if I were observing from the darkness outside the lighted shelter.

Aenea shook her head and sipped her tea. "You don't see, Raul, but *they* do. Already they've referred to me as a virus. They're right . . . that's exactly what I could be to the Church. A virus, like the ancient HIV strain on Old Earth or the Red Death that raked through the Outback after the Fall . . . a virus that invades every cell of the organism and reprograms the DNA in those cells . . . or at least infects enough cells that the organism breaks down, fails . . . dies."

In my dream, I swooped above Aenea's canvas-and-stone shelter like a hawk in the night, whirling high among the alien stars above Old Earth, seeing us—the girl and the man—sitting in the kerosene lantern light of the vestibule like lost souls on a lost world. Which is precisely what we were.

FOR THE NEXT two days I drifted in and out of pain and consciousness the way a skiff cut loose on the ocean would float through rain squalls and patches of sunlight. I drank great volumes of water that the women in blue brought me in glass goblets. I hobbled to the toilet cubby and urinated through a filter, trying to catch the stone that was causing my intermittent agony. No stone. Each time I would hobble back to the bed and wait for the pain to start up again. It never failed to do so. Even at the time, I was aware that this was not the stuff of heroic adventure.

Before the doctor left to continue downriver to the site of the skimmer crash, I was made to understand that both the Pax guard and the local priest had com units and would radio the base if I caused any trouble whatsoever. Dr. Molina let me know exactly how bad it would be for me if the Pax Fleet commander had to pull a skimmer out of the war games just to fetch a prisoner prematurely. Meanwhile, she said, keep drinking lots of water and peeing every time I could. If the stone didn't pass, she would get me into the jail infirmary at the base and break it up with sound waves. She left four more shots of ultramorph with the woman in blue and left without a good-bye. The guard—a middle-aged Lusian twice my weight with a flechette pistol in his holster and a come-along neural prod on his belt—peered in, glowered at me, and went back outside to stand by the front door.

I will stop referring to the head of the household as "the woman in blue." For the first few hours of agony, that had been all she had been to me—other than my savior, of course—but by the afternoon of the first full day in her home, I knew that she was named Dem Ria; that her primary marriage partner was the other woman, Dem Loa; that the third member of their tripartite marriage was the much younger man, Alem Mikail Dem Alem; that the teenaged girl in the house was Ces Ambre, Alem's daughter by a previous triune; that the pale boy with no hair—who looked to be about eight standard years old—was named Bin Ria Dem Loa Alem, was the child of the current partnership—although the biological child of which woman, I never discovered—and that he was dying of cancer.

"Our village medic elder . . . he died last month and has not been replaced . . . sent Bin to our own hospital in Keroa Tambat last winter, but they could only administer radiation and chemotherapy and hope for the best," said Dem Ria as she sat by my bedside that afternoon. Dem Loa sat nearby on another straight-backed chair. I had asked about the boy to shift the subject of conversation away from my own problems. The women's elaborate robes glowed a deep cobalt blue even as the sunlight behind them lay as thick and red as blood on the interior adobe walls. Lace curtains cut the light and shadows into complex negative spaces. We were chatting in the intervals between the pain. My back hurt then as if someone had struck me there with a heavy club, but this was a dull ache compared to the hot agony when the stone moved. The doctor had said that the pain was a good sign—that the stone was moving when it hurt the most. And the agony did seem to be centered lower in my abdomen. But the doctor had also said that it might take months to pass the stone, if it *was* small enough to be passed naturally. Many stones, she said, had to be pulverized or removed surgically. I brought my mind back to the health of the child we were discussing.

"Radiation and chemotherapy," I repeated, mouthing the words with distaste. It was as if Dem Ria had said that the medic had prescribed leeches and drafts of mercury for the boy. The Hegemony had known how to treat cancer, but most of the gene-tailoring knowledge and technology had been lost after the Fall. And what had not been lost had been made too expensive to share with the masses after the WorldWeb went away forever: the Pax Mercantilus carried goods and commodities between the stars, but the process was slow, expensive, and limited. Medicine had slipped back several centuries. My own mother had died of cancer—after refusing radiation and chemotherapy after the diagnosis at the Pax Moors Clinic.

But why *cure* a fatal disease when one could recover from it by dying and being resurrected by the cruciform? Even some genetically derived diseases were "cured" by the cruciform during its restructuring of the body during resurrection. And death, as the Church was constantly pointing out, was as much a sacrament as resurrection itself. It could be offered up like a prayer. The average person could now transform the pain and hopelessness of disease and death into the glory of Christ's redemptive sacrifice. As long as the average person carried a cruciform.

I cleared my throat. "Ah . . . Bin hasn't . . . I mean . . ." When the boy had waved at me in the night, his loose robe had shown a pale and crossless chest.

Dem Loa shook her head. The blue cowl of her robe was made of a translucent, silklike fabric. "None of us have yet accepted the cross. But Father Clifton has been . . . convincing us."

I could only nod. The pain in my back and groin was returning like an electric current through my nerves.

I should explain the different colored robes worn by the citizens of Lock Childe Lamonde on the world of Vitus-Gray-Balianus B. Dem Ria had explained in her melodic whisper that a little over a century ago, most of the people now living along the long river had migrated here from the nearby star system Lacaille 9352. The world there, originally called Sibiatu's Bitterness, had been recolonized by Pax religious zealots who had renamed it Inevitable Grace and begun proselytizing the indigenie cultures that had survived the Fall. Dem Ria's culture—a gentle, philosophical one stressing cooperation—decided to migrate again rather than convert. Twenty-seven thousand of her people had expended their fortunes and risked their lives to refit an ancient Hegira seedship and transport every-one—men, women, children, pets, livestock—in a forty-nine-year cold-sleep voyage to nearby Vitus-Gray-Balianus B, where the WorldWeb-era inhabitants had died out after the Fall.

Dem Ria's people called themselves the Amoiete Spectrum Helix, af-ter the epic philosophical symphony-holo-poem by Halpul Amoiete. In his poem, Amoiete had used colors of the spectrum as a metaphor for the positive human values and shown the helical juxtapositions, interactions, synergies, and collisions created by these values. The Amoiete Spectrum Helix Symphony was meant to be performed, with the symphony, the po-etry, and the holoshow all representing the philosophical interplay. Dem Ria and Dem Loa explained how their culture had borrowed the color meanings from Amoiete—white for the purity of intellectual honesty and physical love; red for the passion of art, political conviction, and physical courage; blue for the introspective revelations of music, mathematics, per-sonal therapy to help others and for the design of fabrics and textures; emerald green for resonance with nature, comfort with technology, and the preservation of threatened life-forms; ebony for the creation of human mys-teries; and so forth. The triune marriages, nonviolence, and other cultural peculiarities grew partially from Amoiete's philosophies and largely from the rich cooperative culture the Spectrum people had created on Sibiatu's Bitterness.

"So Father Clifton is convincing you to join the Church?" I said as the pain subsided into a lull where I could think and speak once again.

"Yes," said Dem Loa. Their tripartner, Alem Mikail Dem Alem, had come in to sit on the adobe windowsill. He listened to the conversation but rarely spoke.

"How do you feel about that?" I asked, shifting slightly to distribute the ache in my back. I had not asked for ultramorph for several hours. I was very aware of the desire to ask for it now.

Dem Ria lifted her hand in a complex motion that reminded me of Aenea's favorite gesture. "If all of us accept the cross, little Bin Ria Dem Loa Alem will be entitled to full medical care at the Pax base at Bombasino. Even if they do not cure the cancer, Bin will . . . return to us . . . after." She lowered her gaze and hid her expressive hands in the folds of her robe.

"They won't allow just Bin to accept the cross," I said.

"Oh, no," said Dem Loa. "It is always their position that the entire family must convert. We see their point. Father Clifton is very sad about that, but very hopeful that we will accept Jesus Christ's sacraments before it is too late for Bin."

"How does your girl—Ces Ambre—feel about becoming a born-again Christian?" I asked, realizing how personal these questions were. But I was intrigued, and the thought of the painful decision they faced took my mind off my very real but much less important pain.

"Ces Ambre loves the idea of joining the Church and becoming a full citizen of the Pax," said Dem Loa, raising her face under the cowl of her soft blue hood. "She would then be allowed to attend the Church academy in Bombasino or Keroa Tambat, and she thinks that the girls and boys there would make much more interesting marriage prospects."

I started to speak, stopped myself, and then spoke anyway. "But the triune marriage wouldn't be . . . I mean, would the Pax allow . . ."

"No," said Alem from his place by the window. He frowned and I could see the sadness behind his gray eyes. "The Church does not allow same-sex or multiple-partner marriages. Our family would be destroyed."

I noticed the three exchange glances for a second and the love and sense of loss I saw in those looks would stay with me for years.

Dem Ria sighed. "But this is inevitable anyway. I think that Father Clifton is right . . . that we must do this now, for Bin, rather than wait until he dies the true death and is lost to us forever . . . and *then* join the Church. I would rather take our boy to Mass on Sunday and laugh with him in the sunlight after, than go to the cathedral to light a candle in his memory."

"Why is it inevitable?" I asked softly.

Dem Loa made the graceful gesture once again. "Our Spectrum Helix society depends upon all members of it . . . all steps and components of the Helix must be in place for the interplay to work toward human progress and moral good. More and more of the Spectrum people are abandoning their colors and joining the Pax. The center will not hold."

Dem Ria touched my forearm as if to emphasize her next words. "The Pax has not coerced us in any way," she said softly, her lovely dialect rising and falling like the sound of the wind through the lace curtains behind her. "We respect the fact that they reserve their medicines and their miracle of resurrection for those who join them . . ." She stopped.

"But it is hard," said Dem Loa, her smooth voice suddenly ragged.

Alem Mikail Dem Alem got up from the window ledge and came over to kneel between the two women. He touched Dem Loa's wrist with infinite gentleness. He put his arm around Dem Ria. For a moment, the three were lost to the world and me, encircled by their own love and sorrow.

And then the pain came back like a fiery lance in my back and lower groin, searing through me like a laser. I moaned despite myself.

The three separated with graceful, purposeful movements. Dem Ria went to get the next ultramorph syringe.

THE DREAM BEGAN the same as before—I was flying at night above the Arizona desert, looking down at Aenea and me as we drank tea and chatted in the vestibule of her shelter—but this time the talk went far beyond the memory of our real conversation that night.

"How are you a virus?" I was asking the teenager next to me. "How could anything you teach be a threat to something as large and powerful as the Pax?"

Aenea was looking out into the desert night, breathing in the fragrance of night-blooming blossoms. She did not look at me when she spoke. "Do you know the major error in Uncle Martin's *Cantos,* Raul?"

"No," I said. She had shown me several mistakes, omissions, or wrongheaded guesses in the past few years, and together we had discovered a few during our voyage to Old Earth.

"It was twofold," she said softly. Somewhere in the desert night, a hawk called. "First, he believed what the TechnoCore told my father."

"About how they were the ones who had hijacked Earth?" I said.

"About everything," said Aenea. "Ummon was lying to the John Keats cybrid."

"Why?" I said. "They were just planning to destroy it."

The girl looked at me. "But my mother was there to record the conversation," she said. "And the Core knew that she would tell the old poet."

I nodded slowly. "And that he would put it as a fact in the epic poem he was writing," I said. "But why would they want to lie about . . ."

"His second mistake was more subtle and serious," she said, interrupting me without raising her voice. A pale glow still hung behind the mountains to the north and west. "Uncle Martin believed that the TechnoCore was humanity's enemy," she continued.

I set my mug of tea down on stone. "Why is that a mistake?" I said. "*Aren't* they our enemy?"

When the girl did not answer I held up my hand, five fingers splayed. "One, according to the *Cantos,* the Core was the real force behind the attack on the Hegemony that led to the Fall of the Farcasters. Not the Ousters . . . the Core. The Church has denied that, made the Ousters responsible. Are you saying that the Church is right and the old poet was wrong?"

"No," said Aenea. "It was the Core that orchestrated the attack."

"Billions dead," I said, almost spluttering in outrage. "The Hegemony toppled. The Web destroyed. The fatline cut . . ."

"The TechnoCore did not cut the fatline," she said softly.

"All right," I said, taking a breath. "That was some mysterious entity . . . your Lions and Tigers and Bears, say. But it was still the Core behind the attack."

Aenea nodded and poured more tea for herself.

I folded my thumb against my palm and touched the first finger with my other hand. "Second, did or did not the TechnoCore use the farcasters as a sort of cosmic leech to suck up human neural networks for their damned Ultimate Intelligence project? Everytime someone farcast, they were being . . . *used* . . . by those damned autonomous intelligences. Right or wrong?"

"Correct," said Aenea.

"Three," I said, folding the first finger away and tapping the next one in line, "the poem has Rachel—the pilgrim Sol Weintraub's child who has come backward with the Time Tombs from the future—tell about a time to come when," I shifted the tone of my voice as I quoted, " '. . . the final war raged between the Core-spawned UI and the human spirit.' Was this a mistake?"

"No," said Aenea.

"Four," I said, beginning to feel foolish with my little finger exercise, but angry enough to continue, "didn't the Core admit to your father that it created him . . . created the John Keats cybrid of him . . . just as a trap for the—what did they call it?—the empathy component of the human Ultimate Intelligence that's supposed to come into existence sometime in the future?"

"That's what they said," agreed Aenea, sipping her tea. She looked almost amused. This made me angrier.

"Five," I said, folding the last finger back so that my right hand was a fist. "Wasn't it the Core as well as the Pax—hell, the Core *ordering* the Pax—that tried to have you caught and killed on Hyperion, on Renaissance Vector, on God's Grove . . . halfway across the spiral arm?"

"Yes," she said softly.

"And wasn't it the Core," I continued angrily, forgetting my fingered checklist and the fact that we were talking about the old poet's errors, "that created that female . . . *thing* . . . that arranged to have poor A. Bettik's arm sliced off on God's Grove and would have had your head in a bag if it hadn't been for the Shrike's intervention." I actually shook my fist I was so angry. "Wasn't it the fucking Core that's been trying to kill *me* as well as you, and probably *will* kill us if we're ever stupid enough to go back into Pax space?"

Aenea nodded.

I was close to panting, feeling as if I had run a fifty-meter dash. "So?" I said lamely, unclenching my fist.

Aenea touched my knee. As contact with her always did, I felt a thrill of electric shock run through me. "Raul, I didn't say that the Core hadn't been up to no good. I simply said that Uncle Martin had made a mistake in portraying them as humanity's enemy."

"But if all those facts are true . . ." I shook my head, befuddled.

"*Elements* of the Core attacked the Web before the Fall," said Aenea. "We know from my father's visit with Ummon that the Core was not in agreement about many of its decisions."

"But . . ." I began.

Aenea held her hand up, palm out. I fell silent.

"They used our neural networks for their UI project," she said, "but there's no evidence that it did humans any harm."

My jaw almost dropped open at that comment. The thought of those damned AIs using human brains like neural bubbles in their fucking project made me want to throw up. "They had no right!" I began.

"Of course not," said Aenea. "They should have asked permission. What would you have said?"

"I would have told them to go fuck themselves," I said, realizing the absurdity of the phrase as applied to autonomous intelligences even as I uttered it.

Aenea smiled again. "And you might remember that we've been using *their* mental power for our own purposes for more than a thousand years. I don't think that we asked permission of their ancestors when we created the first silicon AIs . . . or the first magnetic bubble and DNA entities, for that matter."

I made an angry gesture. "That's different."

"Of course," said Aenea. "The group of AIs called the Ultimates have created problems for humanity in the past and will in the future—including trying to kill you and me—but they're only one part of the Core."

I shook my head. "I don't understand, kiddo," I said, my voice softer now. "Are you really saying that there are good AIs and bad AIs? Don't you remember that they actually considered *destroying the human race*? And that they may do it yet if we get in their way? That would make them an enemy of humanity in my book."

Aenea touched my knee again. Her dark eyes were serious. "Don't forget, Raul, that humanity has also come close to destroying the human race. Capitalists and communists were ready to blow up Earth when that was the only planet we lived on. And for what?"

"Yeah," I said lamely, "but . . ."

"And the Church is ready to destroy the Ousters even as we speak. Genocide . . . on a scale our race has never seen before."

"The Church . . . and a lot of others . . . don't consider the Ousters human beings," I said.

"Nonsense," snapped Aenea. "Of course they are. They evolved from common Earth-human origins, just as the AI TechnoCore did. All three races are orphans in the storm."

"All three races . . ." I repeated. "Jesus Christ, Aenea, are you including the Core in your definition of humanity?"

"We created them," she said softly. "Early on, we used human DNA to increase their computing power . . . their intelligence. We used to have robots. They created cybrids out of human DNA and AI personae. Right now, we have a human institution in power which gives all glory and demands all power because of its allegiance to and connection with God . . . the human Ultimate Intelligence. Perhaps the Core has a similar situation with the Ultimates in control."

I could only stare at the girl. I did not understand.

Aenea set her other hand on my knee. I could feel her strong fingers through the whipcord of my trousers. "Raul, do you remember what the AI

Ummon said to the second Keats cybrid? That was recorded accurately in the *Cantos*. Ummon talked in sort-of Zen koans . . . or at least that's the way Uncle Martin translated the conversation."

I closed my eyes to remember that part of the epic poem. It had been a long time since Grandam and I took turns reciting the tale around the caravan campfire.

Aenea spoke the words even as they began to form in my memory. "Ummon said to the second Keats cybrid—

> *"[You must understand/*
> *Keats/*
> *our only chance*
> *was to create a hybrid/*
> *Son of Man/*
> *Son of Machine*
> *And make that refuge so attractive*
> *that the fleeing Empathy*
> *would consider no other home/*
> *A consciousness already as near divine*
> *as humankind has offered in thirty*
> *generations*
> *an imagination which can span*
> *space and time*
> *And in so offering/*
> *and joining/*
> *form a bond between worlds*
> *which might allow*
> *that world to exist*
> *for both]"*

I rubbed my cheek and thought. The night wind stirred the canvas folds of Aenea's shelter entrance and brought sweet scents from the desert. Strange stars hung above Earth's old mountains on the horizon.

"Empathy was supposedly the fleeing component of the human UI," I said slowly as if working out a word puzzle. "Part of our evolved human consciousness in the future, come back in time."

Aenea looked at me.

"The hybrid was the John Keats cybrid," I continued. "Son of Man and Machine."

"No," said Aenea softly. "That was Uncle Martin's second misunderstanding. The Keats cybrids were not created to be the refuge for Empathy in this age. They were created to be the instrument of that fusion between the Core and humankind. To have a child, in other words."

I looked at the teenaged girl's hands on my leg. "So you're the consciousness '. . . as near divine as humankind has offered in thirty generations'?"

Aenea shrugged.

"And you have '. . . an imagination which can span space and time'?"

"All human beings have that," said Aenea. "It's just that when I dream and imagine, I can see things that truly will be. Remember when I told you that I remember the future?"

"Yeah."

"Well, right now I'm remembering that you will dream this conversation some months hence, while you're lying in bed—in terrible pain, I'm afraid—on a world with a complicated name, in a home where people dress all in blue."

"What?"

"Never mind. It will make sense when it comes about. All improbabilities do when probability waves collapse into event."

"Aenea," I heard myself say as I flew in ever higher circles above the desert shelter, watching myself and the girl dwindle below, "tell me what your secret is . . . the secret that makes you this messiah, this 'bond between two worlds.'"

"All right, Raul, my love," she said, suddenly appearing as a grown woman in the instant before I circled too high to make out details or hear distinct words above the rush of the air on my dream wings, "I will tell you. Listen."

9

B Y THE TIME they translated into their fifth Ouster system, Task Force GIDEON had slaughter down to a science.

Father Captain de Soya knew from his courses in military history at Pax Fleet Command School that almost all space engagements fought more than half an AU from a planet, moon, asteroid, or strategic point-source in space were entered into by mutual agreement. He remembered that the same had been true of primitive ocean navies on pre-Hegira Old Earth, where most great naval battles had been fought in sight of land in the same aquatic killing grounds, with only the technology of the surface ships changing slowly—Greek trireme to steel-hulled battleship. Aircraft carriers with their long-range attack planes had changed that forever—allowing armadas to strike at each other far out to sea and at great distances—but these battles were far different from the legendary naval engagements where capital ships had slugged it out within visible range of one another. Even before cruise missiles, tactical nuclear warheads, and crude charged particle weapons had forever ended the era of the ocean-going surface combatant, the sea navies of Old Earth had grown nostalgic for the days of blazing broadsides and "crossing the T."

Space war had brought a return to such mutually agreed upon engagements. The great battles of the Hegemony days—whether the ancient internecine wars with General Horace Glennon-Height and his ilk, or the centuries of warfare between Web worlds and Ouster Swarms—had usually been waged close to a planet or spaceborne farcaster portal. And distances between the combatants were absurdly short—hundreds of thousands of klicks, often tens of thousands, frequently less than that—given the light-years and parsecs traveled by the warring parties. But this closing on the enemy was necessary given the time it took a fusion-powered laser lance, a CPB, or ordinary attack missiles to cross even one AU—seven minutes for light to crawl the distance between would-be killer and target, much longer for even the highest-boost missile, where the hunt, chase, and kill could take days of seek and countermeasure, attack and parry. Ships with C-plus capability had no incentive to hang around in enemy space waiting for these seeker missiles, and the Church-sponsored restriction on AIs in warheads made the effectiveness of these weapons problematic at best. So the shape of space battles over the centuries of the Hegemony had been simple—fleets translating into disputed space and finding other translating fleets or more static in-system defenses, a quick closing to more lethal distances, a brief but terrible exchange of energies, and the inevitable retreat of the more savaged forces—or total destruction if the defending forces had nowhere to retreat—followed by consolidation of gains by the winning fleet.

Technically, the slower ships de Soya had served in previously had a powerful tactical advantage over the instantaneous-drive archangel cruisers. Revival from cryogenic fugue state took only hours at worst, minutes at best, so the captain and crew of a Hawking-drive ship could be ready to fight shortly after translating from C-plus. With the archangels, and even with papal dispensation for the accelerated and risky two-day resurrection cycles, it was fifty standard hours or more before the human elements of the ships were ready to do battle. Theoretically, this gave a great advantage to the defenders. Theoretically, the Pax could have optimized the use of Gideon-drive ships by having uncrewed craft piloted by AIs flick into enemy space, wreak havoc, and flick out again before the defenders knew that they were under attack.

But such theory did not apply here. Autonomous intelligences capable of such advanced fuzzy logic would never be allowed by the Church. More importantly, Pax Fleet had designed attack strategies to meet the requirements of resurrection so that no advantage would be surrendered to defenders. Simply put, no battles were to be fought by mutual agreement. The seven archangels had been designed to descend upon the enemy like the mailed fist of God, and that was precisely what they were doing now.

In the first three Task Force GIDEON incursions into Ouster space, Mother Captain Stone's ship, the *Gabriel*, translated first and decelerated hard in-system, drawing all long-range electromagnetic, neutrino, and other sensor probes. The restricted AIs aboard *Gabriel* were sufficient to catalogue the position and identity of all defensive positions and population centers in the system, while simultaneously monitoring the sluggish in-system movement of all Ouster attack and merchant vehicles.

Thirty minutes later, the *Uriel, Raphael, Remiel, Sariel, Michael,* and *Raguel* would translate in-system. Dropping to only three-quarters light-speed, the task force would be moving like bullets compared to the tortoise velocities of the accelerating Ouster torchships. Receiving *Gabriel*'s intelligence and targeting data via tightbeam burst, the task force would open fire with weaponry that held no respect for the limitations of light-speed. The improved Hawking-drive hyper-k missiles would wink into existence among enemy ships and above population centers, some using velocity and precise aiming to destroy targets, others detonating in carefully shaped but promiscuous plasma or thermonuclear blasts. At the same instant, recoverable Hawking-drive high-velocity probes would jump to target points and translate into real space, radiating conventional lance beams and CPBs like so many lethal sea urchins, destroying anything and everything within a hundred-thousand-klick radius.

Most terribly, the shipborne deathbeams would slice outward from the task force archangels like invisible scythes, propagating along the Hawking-drive wakes of probes and missiles and translating into real space as surely as the terrible swift sword of God. Countless trillions of synapses were fried and scrambled in an instant. Tens of thousands of Ousters died without knowing that they were under attack.

And then the GIDEON Task Force would come back in-system on thousand-kilometer tails of flame, closing in for the final kill.

EACH OF THE seven star systems to be attacked had been probed by instantaneous-drive drones, the presence of Ousters confirmed, preliminary targets assigned. Each of the seven star systems had a name—usually just a New Revised General Catalogue alpha-numerical designation—but the command team aboard H. H. S. *Uriel* had given the seven systems target names coded after the seven archdemons mentioned in the Old Testament.

Father Captain de Soya thought it a bit much, all this cabalistic numerology—seven archangels, seven target systems, seven archdemons, seven deadly sins. But he soon fell into the habit of talking about the targets in this shorthand.

The target systems were—Belphegor (sloth), Leviathan (envy), Beelzebub (gluttony), Satan (anger), Asmodeus (lechery), Mammon (avarice), and Lucifer (pride).

Belphegor had been a red-dwarf system that reminded de Soya of Barnard's Star system, but instead of the lovely, fully terraformed Barnard's World floating close to the sun, Belphegor's only planet was a gas giant resembling Barnard's Star's forgotten child, Whirl. There were true military targets around this unnamed gas giant: refueling stations for the Ouster Swarm torchships en route to attack the Pax's Great Wall, gigantic dipships that shuttled the gases from the world to orbit, repair docks and orbital shipyards by the dozen. De Soya had *Raphael* attack these without hesitation, slagging them to orbital lava.

GIDEON found most of the true Ouster population centers floating in the Trojan points beyond the gas giant, scores of small orbital forests filled with tens of thousands of space-adapted "angels," most opening their forcefield wings to the weak, red sunlight in panic at the task force's approach. The seven archangels laid waste to these delicate ecostructures, destroying all of the forests and shepherd asteroids and watering comets, burning the fleeing space-adapted Ouster angels like putting so many moths to a flame, and all without slowing significantly between entrance and exit translation points.

The second system, Leviathan, despite its impressive name, had been a Sirius B-type white dwarf with only a dozen or so Ouster asteroids huddled close to its pale fire. Here there were none of the obvious military targets that de Soya had attacked so willingly in the Belphegor System: the asteroids were undefended, probably birthing rocks and hollowed-out pressurized environments for Ousters who had not chosen to adapt to vacuum and hard radiation. Task Force GIDEON swept them with deathbeams and passed on.

The third system, Beelzebub, was an Alpha Centauri C-like red dwarf, devoid of worlds or colonies, with only a single Ouster military base swinging in the darkness some thirty AUs out and fifty-seven Swarm ships caught in the act of refueling or refitting. Thirty-nine of these warships, ranging in size and armament from tiny ramscouts to an Orion-class attack carrier, were fit to fight and flung themselves at Task Force GIDEON. The battle lasted two minutes and eighteen seconds. All fifty-seven Ouster ships and the base complex were turned to gas molecules or lifeless sarcophagi. No archangels were damaged in the exchange. The task force moved on.

The fourth system, Satan, held no ships, only breeding colonies scattered as far out as the Oört cloud. GIDEON spent eleven days in this system, putting Lucifer's angels to the torch.

The fifth system, Asmodeus, centered by a pleasant little K-type orange dwarf not unlike Epsilon Eridani, sent waves of in-system torchships to the defense of its populated asteroid belt. The waves were burned and blasted away with an economy born of practice. The *Gabriel* reported eighty-two inhabited rocks in the belt, harboring a population estimated at a million and a half adapted and unadapted Ousters. Eighty-one of the asteroids were destroyed or deathbeamed from a great distance. Then Admiral Aldikacti ordered prisoners taken. Task Force GIDEON decelerated in a long, four-day ellipse that brought them back to the belt and its sole remaining inhabited rock—a potato-shaped asteroid less than four klicks long and a klick across at its widest, cratered point. Doppler radar showed that it was orbiting and tumbling in random patterns understood only by the gods of chaos, but that it was turning on its axis in a carefully orchestrated one-tenth-g rotisserie mode. Deep radar showed that it was hollow. Probes told that it was inhabited by as many as ten thousand Ousters. Analysis suggested that it was a birthing rock.

Six unarmed rock hoppers flung themselves at the task force. *Uriel* turned them into plasma at a distance of eighty-six thousand klicks. A thousand Ouster angels, some of them armed with low-yield energy weapons or recoilless rifles, opened forcefield wings and flew toward the distant Pax ships in long, tacking ellipses along the crest of the solar wind. Their velocity was so slow that it would have taken days to cover the distance. The *Gabriel* was given the task of burning them away with a thousand winks of coherent light.

Tightbeams flicked on between the archangels. *Raphael* and *Gabriel* acknowledged orders and closed to within a thousand klicks of the silent asteroid. Sally ports opened and twelve tiny figures—six from each ship—caught the light from the orange-dwarf star as Swiss Guard commandos, Marines, and troopers jetted toward the rock. There was no resistance. The troopers found two shielded air-lock portals. With precise timing, they blasted the outer doors open and entered in teams of three.

"BLESS ME, FATHER, for I have sinned. It's been two standard months since my last confession."

"Go ahead."

"Father, today's action . . . it bothers me, Father."

"Yes?"

"It feels . . . wrong."

Father Captain de Soya was silent. He had watched Sergeant Gregorius's attack on the virtual tactical channels. He had debriefed the men after the mission. Now he knew he was going to hear it again in the darkness of the confessional. "Go ahead, Sergeant," he said softly.

"Aye, sir," said the sergeant on the other side of the partition. "I mean, aye, Father."

Father Captain de Soya heard the big man take a breath.

"We came onto the rock with no opposition," began Sergeant Gregorius. "Me an' the five young ones, I mean. We were in tightbeam contact with Sergeant Kluge's squad from the *Gabriel*. And of course, with Commanders Barnes-Avne and Uchikawa."

De Soya remained silent in his part of the confessional booth. The booth was sectional, meant to be stored away when the *Raphael* was under boost or combat stations, which was most of the time, but now it smelled of wood and sweat and velvet and sin, as all real confessionals did. The father-captain had found this half hour during the last stage of their climb toward translation point for the sixth Ouster system, Mammon, and offered the crew time for confession, but only Sergeant Gregorius had come forward.

"So when we landed, sir . . . Father, I had the laddies in my squad take the south polar air lock, just like in the sims. We blew the doors as easily as you please, Father, and then activated our own fields for the tunnel fighting."

De Soya nodded. Swiss Guard fighting suits had always been the best in the human universe—capable of surviving, moving, and fighting in air, water, hard vacuum, hard radiation, slug assault, energy lance assault, and high explosive environment up to the kiloton-yield range, but the new commando suits carried their own class-four containment fields and were able to piggyback on the ships' more formidable fields.

"The Ousters hit us in there, Father, fighting in the dark maze of the access tunnels. Some o' them were space-adapted creatures, sir . . . angels without their wings extended. But most of them were just low-g adepts in skinsuits . . . hardly any armor to speak of a'tall, Father. They tried using lance and rifle and ray on us, but they were using basic night goggles to amplify the dim glow from the rocks, sir, and we saw 'em first with our filters. Saw 'em first and shot 'em first." Sergeant Gregorius took another breath. "It only took us a few minutes to fight our way to the inner locks, Father. All the Ousters who tried to stop us in the tunnels ended up floatin' there . . ."

Father Captain de Soya waited.

"Inside, Father . . . well . . ." Gregorius cleared his throat. "Both squads blew the inner doors at the same instant, sir . . . north and south poles at once. The repeater globes we left behind in the tunnels relayed the tightbeam transmissions just fine, so we were never out of touch with Kluge's squad . . . nor with the ships, as ye know, Father. There were fail-safes on the inner doors, just as we figured, but those we blew as well, and the emergency membranes a second later. The inside of the rock was all hollow, Father . . . well, we knew that, of course . . . but I'd never been inside a birthin' asteroid before, Father. Many a military rock, aye, but never a pregnancy one . . ."

De Soya waited.

"It was about one klick across with lots o' their spidery low-g bamboo towers takin' up much of the center space, Father. The inner shell wasn't spherical or smooth, but more or less followed the shape of the outside of the rock, you know."

"Potato," said Father Captain de Soya.

"Yessir. And all pitted and cratered on the inside, too, Father. Lots of caves and grottoes everywhere . . . like dens for the pregnant Ousters, I suppose."

De Soya nodded in the darkness and glanced at his chronometer, wondering if the usually concise sergeant was going to get to the perceived sins in this account before they had to stow the confessional for C-plus translation.

"It must've been pure chaos for the Ousters, Father . . . what with the cyclone howlin' as the place depressurized, all the atmosphere flowin' out o' the two blasted air locks like water out of a bathtub drain, the air all full of dirt and debris and Ousters blowin' away like so many leaves in the storm. We had our external suit phones on, Father, and the noise was unbelievable 'til the air got too thin to carry it—wind roarin', Ousters screamin', their lances and our lances cracklin' like so many lightning rods, plasma grenades goin' off and the sound bouncin' back at us in that big rock cavern, the echoes goin' on for minutes—it was *loud,* Father."

"Yes," said Father Captain de Soya in the darkness.

Sergeant Gregorius took another breath. "Anyway, Father, the orders'd been to bring in two samples of everything . . . adult males, space-adapted, unadapted; adult females, pregnant and not pregnant; a couple of Ouster kids, pre-puberty, and infants . . . both sexes. So Kluge's team and ours got busy, stunning and bagging 'em. There was just enough gravity on the inner surface of the rock . . . one-tenth-g . . . to keep the bags in place where we left 'em.''

There was a moment of silence. Father Captain de Soya was just about to speak, to bring this confession to a close, when Sergeant Gregorius whispered through the screen and darkness separating them.

"Sorry, Father, I know you know all this. I just . . . it's hard to . . . anyway, this was the bad part, Father. Most of the Ousters who weren't modified . . . space-adapted . . . were dead or dying at this point. From decompression or lance fire or grenades. We didn't use the deathbeam wands issued to us. Neither Kluge nor I said anything to the lads . . . just none of us used the things.

"Now those adapted Ousters went angel, their bodies turnin' all shiny as they activated their personal forcefields. They couldn't fully extend their wings in there, of course, and it wouldn't have done any good if they had . . . no sunlight to catch, and the one-tenth-g was too much for them to overcome if there had been any solar wind . . . but they went angel anyway. Some of them tried to use their wings as weapons against us."

Sergeant Gregorius made a rough sound that might have been a parody of a chuckle. "We had class-four fields, Father, and they were batting at us with those gossamer wings . . . Anyway, we burned them away, sent three from each squad out with the bagged specimens, and Kluge and I each took our remainin' two lads to clear out the caverns as ordered . . ."

De Soya waited. There was less than a minute before he would have to end confession.

"We knew it was a birthin' rock, Father. We knew . . . everybody knows . . . that the Ousters, even the ones who've turned the machines loose in their cells and blood and who don't look anythin' like human . . . they haven't learned how to have their females carry and bear children in pure zero-g and hard radiation, Father. We *knew* it was a birthin' rock when we went in the goddamned asteroid . . . I'm sorry, Father . . ."

De Soya stayed silent.

"But even so, Father . . . those caverns were like homes . . . beds and cubbies and flatscreen vid sets and kitchens . . . not things we're used to thinkin' Ousters have, Father. But most of those caves were . . ."

"Nurseries," said Father Captain de Soya.

"Aye, sir. Nurseries. Wee beds with wee babies in 'em . . . not Ouster monsters, Father, not those pale, shiny things we fight against, not those damned Lucifer's angels with wings a hundred klicks across in the starlight . . . just . . . babies. By the hundreds, Father. By the thousands. Cavern after cavern. Most o' the rooms there had depressurized already, killing the little ones where they lay. Some o' the little bodies had been blown out in the depressurization, but most o' them were tucked in tight. Some o' the rooms were still airtight, though, Father. We blew our way in. Mothers . . . women in robes, pregnant women with wild hair flying in the one-tenth-g . . . they attacked us with their fingernails and teeth, Father. We ignored them until the windstorms blew them out or they died a-choking, but some of the infants . . . scores of them, Father . . . were in those little plastic respirator cases . . ."

"Incubators," said Father Captain de Soya.

"Aye," whispered Sergeant Gregorius, his voice tiring at last. "And we tightbeamed back, what did they want us to do with 'em? With all the scores and scores of baby Ousters in these incubators. And Commander Barnes-Avne beamed back . . ."

"To continue on," whispered Father Captain de Soya.

"Aye, Father . . . so we . . ."

"Followed orders, Sergeant."

"So we used the last of our grenades in those nurseries, Father. And when the plasma grenades were gone, we lanced those incubators. Room after room, cavern after cavern. The plastic melted around the babes, covered 'em. Blankets ignited. The boxes must've been fed with pure O_2, Father, because a lot o' them went up like grenades themselves . . . we had to activate our suit fields, Father, and even so . . . it took me two hours to clean my combat armor . . . but most of the incubators didn't explode, Father, they just burned like dry tinder, burned like torches, everythin' in 'em burnin' bright like little furnaces. And by now all the rooms and caverns were in vacuum, but the boxes . . . the little incubators . . . they still had atmosphere while they burned . . . and we turned off our outside phones, sir. All of us did. But somehow we could still hear the crying and the screams through the containment fields and our helmets. I can still hear them, Father . . ."

"Sergeant," said de Soya, his voice hard and flat with command.

"Aye, sir?"

"You were following orders, Sergeant. We were all following orders. His Holiness has long since decreed that Ousters have surrendered their humanity to nanodevices they release in their blood, to the changes they have made with their chromosomes . . ."

"But the screams, Father . . ."

"*Sergeant* . . . the Vatican Council and the Holy Father have decreed that this Crusade is necessary if the human family is to be saved from the Ouster threat. You were given orders. You obeyed them. We are soldiers."

"Aye, sir," whispered the sergeant in the darkness.

"We have no more time, Sergeant. We will talk about this at a later time. For now, I want you to do penance . . . not for being a soldier and following orders, but for doubting those orders. Fifty Hail Marys, Sergeant, and a hundred Our Fathers. And I want you to pray about this . . . pray very hard for understanding."

"Aye, Father."

"Now say a sincere Act of Contrition . . . quickly now . . ."

When the whispered words began to come through the screen, Father

Captain de Soya lifted his hand in benediction as he gave absolution. *"Ego te absolvo . . ."*

Eight minutes later, the father-captain and his crew all lay back in their acceleration couches/resurrection crèches as *Raphael*'s Gideon drive activated, carrying them instantaneously to Target System Mammon by way of terrible death and slow, painful rebirth.

The Grand Inquisitor had died and gone to Hell.

It was only his second death and resurrection and he had enjoyed neither experience. And Mars *was* Hell.

John Domenico Cardinal Mustafa and his contingent of twenty-one Holy Office administrators and security people—including his indispensable aide Father Farrell—had traveled to Old Earth System in the new archangel starship *Jibril* and had been given a generous four days after resurrection to recover and regroup mentally before beginning their work on the surface of Mars itself. The Grand Inquisitor had read and been briefed enough on the red planet to form an unassailable opinion—Mars was Hell.

"Actually," Father Farrell responded the first time the Grand Inquisitor had mentioned his conclusion aloud about Mars being hell, "one of the other planets in this system . . . Venus . . . better fits that description, Your Excellency. Boiling temperatures, crushing pressures, lakes of liquid metal, winds like rocket exhausts . . . ."

"Shut up," the Grand Inquisitor said with a tired turn of his hand.

Mars: the first world ever colonized by the human race despite its low rating of 2.5 on the old Solmev Scale, the first attempted terraforming, the first failed terraforming—a world bypassed after the black-hole death of Old Earth because of the Hawking drive, because of the imperatives of the Hegira, because no one wanted to live on the rusty sphere of permafrost when the galaxy offered a near-infinite number of prettier, healthier, more viable worlds.

For centuries after the death of Old Earth, Mars had been such a backwater planet that the WorldWeb had not established farcaster portals there—a desert planet of interest only to the orphans of New Palestine (the legendary Colonel Fedmahn Kassad had been born in the Palestinian relocation camps there, Mustafa was surprised to learn) and to Zen Christians returning to Hellas Basin to reenact Master Schrauder's enlightenment at the Zen Massif. For a century or so it had looked as if the huge terraforming project would work—seas filled giant impact basins and cycladferns proliferated along River Marineris—but then the setbacks came, there were no funds to fight the entropy, and the next sixty-thousand-year-long ice age arrived.

At the height of the WorldWeb civilization, the Hegemony's military wing, FORCE, had brought Farcasters to the red world and honeycombed habitats into much of the huge volcano, Mons Olympus, for their Olympic Command School. Mars's isolation from Web trade and culture served FORCE well and the planet had remained a military base until the Fall of the Farcasters. In the century after the Fall, remnants of FORCE had formed a vicious military dictatorship—the so-called Martian War Machine—which extended its rule as far as the Centauri and Tau Ceti systems and might well have become the seed crystal for a second interstellar empire if the Pax had not arrived, quickly subduing the Martian fleets, driving the War Machine back to Old Earth System, sending the dispossessed warlords into hiding among the ruins of FORCE orbital bases and in the old tunnels under Mons Olympus, replacing the War Machine's presence in Old Earth System with Pax Fleet bases in the asteroid belt and among the Jovian moons, and finally sending missionaries and Pax governors to pacified Mars.

There was little left on the rust world for the missionaries to convert or the Pax administrators to govern. The air had grown thin and cold; the large cities had been plundered and abandoned; the great *simoom* pole-to-pole dust storms had reappeared; plague and pestilence stalked the icy deserts, decimating—or worse—the last bands of nomads descended from the once noble race of Martians; and little more than spindly brandy cactus now grew where the great apple orchards and fields of bradberries had long ago flourished.

Oddly, it was the downtrodden and much-abused Palestinians on the frozen Tharsis Plateau whose society had survived and thrived. The orphans of the ancient Nuclear Diaspora of A.D. 2038 had adapted to Mars's rough ways and extended their Islamic culture to many of the planet's surviving nomad tribes and free city-states by the time the Pax missionaries arrived. Refusing to submit to the ruthless Martian War Machine for more than a century, the New Palestinians showed no interest now in surrendering autonomy to the Church.

It was precisely in the Palestinian capital of Arafat-kaffiyeh that the Shrike had appeared and slaughtered hundreds . . . perhaps thousands . . . of people.

The Grand Inquisitor conferred with his aides, met with Pax Fleet commanders in orbit, and landed in force. The main spaceport in the capital of St. Malachy was shut down to all but military traffic—no great loss, since no merchant or passenger dropships were scheduled in for a Martian week. Six assault boats preceded the Grand Inquisitor's dropship, and by the time Cardinal Mustafa set foot to Martian soil—or Pax tarmac, to be precise—a hundred Swiss Guard and Holy Office commandos had ringed the spaceport. The official Martian welcoming delegation, including Archbishop Robeson and Governor Clare Palo, were searched and sonic-probed before being allowed clearance.

From the spaceport, the Holy Office group was whisked via groundcar shuttles through decaying streets to the new Pax-built Governor's Palace on the outskirts of St. Malachy. Security was heavy. Besides the Grand

Inquisitor's personal security force, the Pax Fleet Marines, the Governor's troopers, and the Archbishop's contingent of Swiss Guards, there was a battle regiment of Home Guard armored infantry encamped around the palace. There the Grand Inquisitor was shown evidence of the Shrike's presence two standard weeks earlier on the Tharsis Plateau.

"This is absurd," said the Grand Inquisitor on the night before flying to the scene of the Shrike attack. "All these holos and vid images are two standard weeks old or taken from high altitude. I see these few holos of what must be the Shrike and some blurred scenes of carnage. I see photos of the Pax bodies the militia men found when first entering the town. But where are the local people? Where are the eyewitnesses? Where are the twenty-seven hundred citizens of Arafat-kaffiyeh?"

"We don't know," said Governor Clare Palo.

"We reported to the Vatican via archangel drone and when the drone returned, we were told not to tamper with the evidence," said Archbishop Robeson. "We were told to await your arrival."

The Grand Inquisitor shook his head and held up a flat photo image. "And what is this?" he said. "A Pax Fleet base on the outskirts of Arafat-kaffiyeh? This spaceport is newer than St. Malachy's."

"It is not Pax Fleet," said Captain Wolmak, captain of the *Jibril* and new commander of the Old Earth System task force. "Although we estimate that thirty to fifty dropships a day were using this facility during the week previous to the Shrike's appearance."

"Thirty to fifty dropships a day," repeated the Grand Inquisitor. "And *not* Pax Fleet. Who then?" He scowled at Archbishop Robeson and the Governor.

"Mercantilus?" pressed the Grand Inquisitor when no one spoke.

"No," said the Archbishop after another moment. "Not Mercantilus."

The Grand Inquisitor folded his arms and waited.

"The dropships were chartered by *Opus Dei*," said Governor Palo in a tiny voice.

"For what purpose?" demanded the Grand Inquisitor. Only Holy Office guards were allowed in this suite of the palace, and they stood at six-meter intervals along the stone wall.

The Governor opened her hands. "We do not know, Your Excellency."

"Domenico," said the Archbishop, his voice quavering slightly, "we were told not to inquire."

The Grand Inquisitor took an angry step forward. "*Told* not to . . . by whom? Who has the authority to order the presiding Archbishop and the Pax Governor of a world '*not to interfere*'?" His anger boiled through. "In the name of Christ! Who has such power?"

The Archbishop raised pained but defiant eyes toward Cardinal Mustafa. "In the name of Christ . . . precisely, Your Excellency. Those representing *Opus Dei* held official diskeys from the Pontifical Commission for

Justice and Peace," he said. "We were told that it was a security matter in Arafat-kaffiyeh. We were told that it was not our business. We were told not to interfere."

The Grand Inquisitor felt his face flushing with barely subdued rage. "Security matters on Mars or anywhere else in the Pax are the responsibility of the Holy Office!" he said flatly. "The Pontifical Commission for Justice and Peace has no charter here! Where are the representatives of the Commission? Why aren't they here for this meeting?"

Governor Clare Palo raised a thin hand and pointed at the flat photo in the Grand Inquisitor's hand. "There, Your Excellency. There are the Commission authorities."

Cardinal Mustafa looked down at the glossy photograph. Forms of white-clad bodies could be seen in the dusty red streets of Arafat-kaffiyeh. Even through the grain of the images, it was obvious that the bodies were mauled into grotesque forms and swollen from decomposition. The Grand Inquisitor spoke softly, fighting the urge to scream and then order these imbeciles tortured and shot. "Why," he asked softly, "haven't these people been resurrected and questioned?"

Archbishop Robeson actually attempted a smile. "You will see that tomorrow, Your Excellency. It will be abundantly clear tomorrow."

EMVS WERE USELESS on Mars. They used armored Pax Security skimmers for their flight to Tharsis Plateau. Torchships and the *Jibril* monitored their progress. Scorpion fighters flew space/air combat patrol. Two hundred klicks from the plateau, five squads of Marines dropped from the skimmers and flew ahead at low altitude, raking the area with acoustic probes and setting up firing positions.

Nothing but the shifting sand moved in Arafat-kaffiyeh.

The Holy Office security skimmers set down first, their landing legs settling into sand where grass had once grown on the oval city commons, the outer ships establishing and linking a class-six containment field that made the buildings around the plaza seem to shimmer in heat haze. The Marines had dropped into a defensive circle with the commons as their locus. Now the Governor's Pax and Home Guard troops moved out to establish a second perimeter in the streets and alleys around the plaza. The Archbishop's eight Swiss Guardsmen secured the circle just outside the containment field. Finally the Grand Inquisitor's Holy Office security force exploded down the skimmer ramps and established the inner perimeter of kneeling figures in black combat armor.

"Clear," came the leading Marine sergeant's voice on the tactical channel.

"Nothing moving or alive within a kilometer of Site One," rasped the lieutenant of the Home Guard. "Bodies in the street."

"Clear here," said the captain of the Swiss Guard.

"Confirm nothing moving in Arafat-kaffiyeh except your people," came the voice of the captain of the *Jibril*.

"Affirmative," said Holy Office Security Commander Browning.

Feeling foolish and disgruntled, the Grand Inquisitor swept down the ramp and across the sandy commons. His mood was not lifted by the silly osmosis mask he had to wear, its circular boostirator slung over his shoulder like a loose medallion.

Father Farrell, Archbishop Robeson, Governor Palo, and a host of functionaries ran to keep up as Cardinal Mustafa strode by the kneeling security forms and, with an imperious wave of his hand, ordered a portal cut in the containment field. He passed through over the protests of Commander Browning and the other forms in black armor who were scuttling to catch up.

"Where is the first of . . ." began the Grand Inquisitor as he bounced down the narrow alley opposite the commons. He still was not used to the light gravity here.

"Right around this corner . . ." panted the Archbishop.

"We should really wait for the outer fields to be . . ." said Governor Palo.

"Here," said Father Farrell, pointing down the street onto which they had emerged.

The group of fifteen stopped so quickly that those aides and security people in the rear had to catch themselves before bumping into the VIPs in front.

"Dear Lord," whispered Archbishop Robeson and crossed himself. Through the clear osmosis mask, his face was visibly white.

"Christ!" muttered Governor Clare Palo. "I've seen the holos and photos for two weeks, but . . . Christ."

"Ahh," said Father Farrell, taking a step closer to the first body.

The Grand Inquisitor joined him. He went to one knee in the red sand. The contorted form in the dirt looked as if someone had fashioned an abstract sculpture out of flesh, bone, and gristle. It would not have been recognizably human had it not been for the teeth gleaming in the wide-stretched mouth and one hand lying nearby in the shifting Martian dust.

After a moment the Grand Inquisitor said, "Did scavengers do some or most of this? Carrion birds, perhaps? Rats?"

"Negative," said Major Piet, the Governor's Pax Fleet groundforce commander. "No birds on the Tharsis Plateau since the atmosphere started thinning two centuries ago. No rats . . . or any other moving thing . . . have been picked up by motion detectors since this happened."

"The Shrike did this," said the Grand Inquisitor. He did not sound convinced. He stood and moved to the second body. It might have been a woman. It looked as if it had been turned inside out and shredded. "And this?"

"We think so," said Governor Palo. "The militia that found all this brought out the security camera which had that thirty-eight-second holo we've shown you."

"That looked like a dozen Shrikes killing a dozen people," said Father Farrell. "It was hazy."

"There was a sandstorm," said Major Piet. "And there was only one Shrike . . . we've studied the individual images. It simply moved through the crowd so quickly that it appeared to be multiple creatures."

"Moved through the crowd," murmured the Grand Inquisitor. He stepped over a third body that might have been a child or small female. "Doing this."

"Doing this," said Governor Palo. She glanced at Archbishop Robeson, who had moved to a wall for support.

There were twenty to thirty bodies in this section of the street.

Father Farrell knelt and ran his gloved hand across the chest and into the chest cavity of the first cadaver. The flesh was frozen, as was the blood that fell in a black icefall. "And there was no sign of the cruciform?" he said softly.

Governor Palo shook her head. "Not in the two bodies the militia returned for resurrection. No sign of the cruciform whatsoever. If there had been any remnant at all . . . even a millimeter of node or bit of fiber in the brain stem or . . ."

"We *know* that," snapped the Grand Inquisitor, ending the explanation.

"Very strange," said Bishop Erdle, the Holy Office's expert on resurrection technique. "To my knowledge there has never been an instance where the body was left so intact where we could not find remnant of the cruciform in the corpse. Governor Palo is correct, of course. Even the slightest bit of cruciform is all that is necessary for the Sacrament of Resurrection."

The Grand Inquisitor stopped to inspect a body that had been thrown against an iron railing hard enough to impale it at a dozen points. "It looks as if the Shrike was after the cruciforms. It tore every shred of them out of the bodies."

"Not possible," said Bishop Erdle. "Simply not possible. There are over five hundred meters of microfiber in the cellular node extensions of . . ."

"Not possible," agreed the Grand Inquisitor. "But when we ship these bodies back, I'll wager that none are recoverable. The Shrike may have torn their hearts and lungs and throats out, but it was after their cruciforms."

Security Commander Browning came around the corner with five troopers in black armor. "Your Excellency," he said on the tactical channel only the Grand Inquisitor could hear. "The worst is a block over . . . this way."

The entourage followed the man in black armor, but slowly, reluctantly.

THEY CATALOGUED 362 bodies. Many were in the streets, but the majority were in buildings in the city or inside the sheds, hangars, and spacecraft at the new spaceport on the edge of Arafat-kaffiyeh. Holos were taken and the Holy Office forensic teams took over, recording each site before taking the bodies back to the Pax base morgue outside of St. Malachy. It was determined that all of the bodies were offworlders—i.e., there were no local Palestinians or native Martians among them.

The spaceport intrigued the Pax Fleet experts the most.

"Eight dropships serving the field itself," said Major Piet. "That's a serious number. St. Malachy's spaceport uses only two." He glanced up at the purple Martian sky. "Assuming that the ships they were shuttling to and from had their own dropships—at least two each, if they were freighters—then we're talking about serious logistics here."

The Grand Inquisitor looked at Mars's archbishop, but Robeson merely held his hands up. "We knew nothing of these operations," said the little man. "As I explained before, it was an *Opus Dei* project."

"Well," said the Grand Inquisitor, "as far as we can tell, all of the *Opus Dei* personnel are dead . . . truly, irrecoverably dead . . . so now it's a responsibility of the Holy Office. You don't have any idea what they built this port for? Heavy metals, perhaps? Some sort of mineral mining operation?"

Governor Palo shook her head. "This world has been mined for over a thousand years. There are no heavy metals left worth shipping. No minerals worth a local salvage operation's time, much less *Opus Dei*'s."

Major Piet slipped his visor up and rubbed the stubble on his chin. "*Something* was being shipped in quantity here, Your Excellencies. Eight dropships . . . a sophisticated grid system . . . automated security."

"If the Shrike . . . or whatever it was . . . had not destroyed the computers and record systems . . ." began Commander Browning.

Major Piet shook his head. "It wasn't the Shrike. The computers had already been destroyed by shaped charges and tailored DNA viruses." He looked around the empty administrative building. Red sand had already found its way in through portals and seams. "It's my guess that these people destroyed their own records before the Shrike arrived. I think they were on the verge of clearing out. That's why the dropships were all in prelaunch mode . . . their onboard computers set to go."

Father Farrell nodded. "But all we have are the orbital coordinates. No records of who or what they were going to rendezvous with there."

Major Piet looked out the window at the dust storm blowing there. "There are twenty groundcar buses in that lot," he murmured as if speaking to himself. "Each one can transport up to eighty people. A bit of logistical overkill if the *Opus Dei* contingent here amounted to just the three hundred sixty-some people whose bodies we've found."

Governor Palo frowned and crossed her arms. "We don't know how many *Opus Dei* personnel were here, Major. As you pointed out, the records were destroyed. Perhaps there were thousands . . ."

Commander Browning stepped into the circle of VIPs. "Begging your pardon, Governor, but the barracks within the field perimeter here could house about four hundred people. I think that the Major may be right . . . all of the *Opus Dei* personnel may be accounted for in the bodies we've found."

"You can't be sure of that, Commander," said Governor Palo, her voice sounding displeased.

"No, ma'am."

She gestured toward the dust storm that had all but obscured the parked buses. "And we have evidence that they needed transport for many more people."

"Perhaps they were an advance contingent," said Commander Browning. "Preparing the way for a much larger population."

"Then why destroy the records and limited AIs?" said Major Piet. "Why does it look like they were preparing to move out for good?"

The Grand Inquisitor stepped into the circle and held up one black-gloved hand. "We'll end the speculation for now. The Holy Office will begin taking depositions and carrying out interrogations tomorrow. Governor, may we use your office at the palace?"

"Of course, Your Excellency." Palo lowered her face, either to show deference or to hide her eyes, or both.

"Very good," said the Grand Inquisitor. "Commander, Major, call the skimmers. We'll leave the forensic teams and the morgue workers out here." Cardinal Mustafa peered out at the worsening storm. Its howl could be heard through the ten layers of window plastic now. "What's the local word for this dust storm?"

"*Simoom,*" said Governor Palo. "The storms used to cover the entire world. They're growing in intensity every Martian year."

"The locals say that it's the old Martian gods," whispered Archbishop Robeson. "They're reclaiming their own."

LESS THAN FOURTEEN light-years out from Old Earth System, above the world called Vitus-Gray-Balianus B, a starship that had once been named *Raphael* but which now held no name, finished its braking run into geosynchronous orbit. The four living things on board floated in zero-g, their gazes fixed on the image of the desert world on the plotboard.

"How reliable is our reading on pertubations in the farcaster field these days?" said the female called Scylla.

"More reliable than most other clues," said her seeming twin, Rhadamanth Nemes. "We'll check it out."

"Shall we start with one of the Pax bases?" said the male named Gyges.

"The largest," said Nemes.

"That would be Pax Base Bombasino," said Briareus, checking the code on the plotboard. "Northern hemisphere. Along the central canal route. Population of . . ."

"It doesn't matter what the population is," interrupted Rhadamanth Nemes. "It just matters whether the child Aenea and the android and that bastard Endymion have come that way."

"Dropship's prepped," said Scylla.

They screeched into atmosphere, extended wings just as they crossed the terminator, used the Vatican diskey code via transponder to clear the way for their landing, and set down amid Scorpions, troopship skimmers, and armored EMVs. A flustered lieutenant greeted them and escorted them to the Base Commander's office.

"You say that you're members of the Noble Guard?" said Commander Solznykov, studying their faces and the readout on the diskey interphase at the same time.

"We have said it," Rhadamanth Nemes replied tonelessly. "Our papers, order chips, and diskey have said it. How many repetitions do you require, Commander?"

Solznykov's face and neck reddened above the high collar of his tunic. He looked down at the interphase holo instead of replying. Technically, these Noble Guard officers—members of one of the Pope's exotic new units—could pull rank on him. Technically, they could have him shot or excommunicated, since their ranks of Cohort Leaders in the Noble Guard combined the powers of both Pax Fleet and the Vatican. Technically—according to the wording and priority encryption of the diskey—they could pull rank on a planetary governor or dictate Church policy to a world's presiding archbishop. Technically, Solznykov wished these pale freaks had never shown up on his backwater world.

The Commander forced a smile. "Our forces here are at your disposal. What can I do for you?"

The thin, pale woman named Nemes held a holocard over the Commander's desk and activated it. Suddenly the life-size heads of three people floated in the space between them—or, rather, two people, since the third face was obviously that of a blue-skinned android.

"I didn't think that there were any androids left in the Pax," said Solznykov.

"Have you had reports of any of these three in your territory, Commander?" said Nemes, ignoring his question. "It is probable they would have been reported along the major river which runs from your north pole to the equator."

"It's actually a canal . . ." began Solznykov and stopped. None of the four looked as if they had any interest in small talk or extraneous information. He called his aide, Colonel Vinara, into the office.

"Their names?" said Solznykov as Vinara stood poised with his comlog ready.

Nemes gave three names that meant nothing to the Commander.

"Those aren't local names," he said as Colonel Vinara checked records. "Members of the indigenous culture—it's called the Amoiete Spectrum Helix—tend to accumulate names the way my hunting dog back on Patawpha collected ticks. You see, they have this triune marriage arrangement where . . ."

"These are not locals," interrupted Nemes. Her thin lips looked as bloodless as the rest of her pale face above the red uniform collar. "They're offworlders."

"Ahh, well," said Solznykov, relieved that he would not be dealing with these Noble Guard freaks for more than a minute or two more, "then we can't help you. You see, Bombasino's the only working spaceport on Vitus-Gray-Balianus B now that we closed down the indigenie operation at Keroa Tambat, and except for a few spacers who end up in our brig, there's no immigration at all here. The locals are all Spectrum Helix . . . and, well . . . they like colors, they surely do, but an android would stand out like a . . . well, Colonel?"

Colonel Vinara looked up from his database search. "Neither the images nor names match anything in our records except for an all-points bulletin sent through via Pax Fleet about four and a half standard years ago." He looked questioningly at the Noble Guardsmen.

Nemes and her siblings stared back without comment.

Commander Solznykov spread his hands. "I'm sorry. We've been busy for the last local two weeks on a major training exercise I had running here, but if anyone'd come through here who matched these descriptions . . ."

"Sir," said Colonel Vinara, "there were those four runaway spacers."

Goddammit! thought Solznykov. To the Noble Guardsmen he said, "Four Mercantilus spacers who jumped ship rather than face charges for use of illegal drugs. As I remember it, they were all men, all in their sixties, and"—he turned significantly to Colonel Vinara, trying to tell him to shut the fuck up with his gaze and tone—"and we found their bodies in the Big Greasy, didn't we, Colonel?"

"Three bodies, sir," said Colonel Vinara, oblivious to his commander's signals. He was checking the database again. "One of our skimmers went down near Keroa Tambat and Med dispatched . . . ah . . . Dr. Abne Molina . . . to go down-canal with a missionary to care for the injured crew."

"What the hell does this have to do with anything, Colonel?" snapped Solznykov. "These officers are searching for a teenager, a man in his thirties, and an android."

"Yes, sir," said Vinara, looking up, startled, from his comlog. "But Dr. Molina radioed in that she had treated a sick offworlder in Lock Childe Lamonde. We assumed that it was the fourth spacer . . ."

Rhadamanth Nemes took a step forward so quickly that Commander Solznykov flinched involuntarily. There was something about the slim woman's movements that was not quite human.

"Where is Lock Childe Lamonde?" demanded Nemes.

"It's just a village along the canal about eighty klicks south of here," said Solznykov. He turned to Colonel Vinara as if all this commotion were his aide's fault. "When are they flying the prisoner back?"

"Tomorrow morning, sir. We have a med-skimmer scheduled to pick up the crew in Keroa Tambat at oh-six-hundred hours and they'll stop in . . ." The Colonel stopped speaking as the four Noble Guard officers spun on their heels and made for the door.

Nemes paused just long enough to say, "Commander, clear our flight path between here and this Lock Childe Lamonde. We'll be taking the dropship."

"Ah, that's not necessary!" said the Commander, checking the screen on his desk. "This spacer is under arrest and will be delivered . . . hey!"

The four Noble Guard officers had clattered down the steps outside his office and were crossing the tarmac. Solznykov rushed out onto the landing and shouted after them. "Dropships aren't allowed to operate in atmosphere here except to land at Bombasino. Hey! We'll send a skimmer. Hey! This spacer's almost certainly not one of your . . . he's under guard . . . hey!"

The four did not look back as they reached their ship, ordered an escalator to morph down to them, and disappeared through the dropship hull. Sirens went off across the base and personnel ran for shelter as the heavy dropship lifted on thrusters, shifted to EM, and accelerated south across the port perimeter.

"Jesus fucking Christ," whispered Commander Solznykov.

"Pardon me, sir?" said Colonel Vinara.

Solznykov gave him a glare that would have melted lead. "Dispatch two combat skimmers immediately . . . no, make that three. I want a squad of Marines aboard each skimmer. This is our turf, and I don't want these anemic Noble Guard pissants doing so much as littering without our say-so. I want the skimmers there first and that fucking spacer taken into custody . . . *our* custody . . . if it means harelipping every Spectrum Helix indigenie between here and Lock Childe Lamonde. Savvy, Colonel?"

Vinara could only stare at his commander.

"*Move!*" shouted Commander Solznykov.

Colonel Vinara moved.

10

WAS AWAKE all that long night and the next day, writhing in pain, shuttling to the bathroom while carrying my IV-drip apparatus, trying painfully to urinate, and then checking the absurd filter I had to urinate through for any sign of the kidney stone that was killing me. Sometime in late morning I passed the thing.

For a minute I couldn't believe it. The pain had been less for the past half hour or so, just the echo of pain in my back and groin, actually, but as I stared at the tiny, reddish thing in the filter cone—something larger than a grain of sand but much smaller than a pebble—I couldn't believe that *it* could have caused such agony for so many hours.

"Believe it," Aenea said as she sat on the edge of the counter and watched me pull my pajama shirt back in place. "It's often the smallest things in life that cause us the greatest pain."

"Yeah," I said. I knew, vaguely, that Aenea was not there—that I would never have urinated in front of anyone like that, much less in front of this girl. I had been hallucinating her presence ever since the first ultramorph injection.

"Congratulations," said the Aenea hallucination. Her smile seemed real enough—that slightly mischievous, slightly teasing turning up of the right side of her mouth that I'd grown accustomed to—and I could see that she was wearing the green denim slacks and white cotton shirt she often wore when working in the desert heat. But I could also see the sink basin and soft towels through her.

"Thanks," I said and shuffled back to collapse in the bed. I could not believe that the pain would not return. In fact, Dr. Molina had said that there might be several stones.

Aenea was gone when Dem Ria, Dem Loa, and the trooper on guard came into the room.

"Oh, it's wonderful!" said Dem Ria.

"We're so glad," said Dem Loa. "We hoped that you would not have to go to the Pax infirmary for surgery."

"Put your right hand up here," said the trooper. He handcuffed me to the brass headboard.

"I'm a prisoner?" I said groggily.

"You always have been," grunted the trooper. His dark skin was sweaty under his helmet visor. "The skimmer'll be by tomorrow morning to pick you up. Wouldn't want you missing the ride." He went back out to the shade of the barrel tree out front.

"Ah," said Dem Loa, touching my handcuffed wrist with her cool fingers. "We are sorry, Raul Endymion."

"It's not your fault," I said, feeling so tired and drugged that my tongue did not want to work right. "You've been nothing but kind. So kind." The fading pain kept me from sleeping.

"Father Clifton would like to come in and speak with you. Would that be all right?"

At that moment I would have welcomed spider-rats nibbling on my toes about as much as the idea of chatting with a missionary priest. I said, "Sure. Why not?"

FATHER CLIFTON WAS younger than I, short—but not as short as Dem Ria or Dem Loa or her race—and pudgy, with thinning, sandy hair receding from his friendly, flushed face. I thought that I knew his type. There had been a chaplain in the Home Guard a bit like Father Clifton—earnest, mostly inoffensive, a bit of a momma's boy who may have gone into the priesthood so that he would never have to grow up and become really responsible for himself. It was Grandam who had pointed out to me how the parish priests in the various moor-end villages on Hyperion tended to remain somewhat childlike: treated with deference by their parishioners, fussed over by housekeepers and women of all ages, never in real competition with other adult males. I don't think that Grandam was actively anti-clerical in spite of her refusal to accept the cross, just amused by this tendency of parish priests in the great and powerful Pax empire.

Father Clifton wanted to discuss theology.

I think that I moaned then, but it must have been taken for a reaction to the kidney stone, for the good priest merely leaned closer, patted my arm, and murmured, "There, there, my son."

Did I mention that he was at least five or six years younger than me?

"Raul . . . may I call you Raul?"

"Sure, Father." I closed my eyes as if falling asleep.

"What is your opinion of the Church, Raul?"

Under my eyelids, I rolled my eyes. "The Church, Father?"

Father Clifton waited.

I shrugged. Or to be more precise, I *tried* to shrug—it's not that easy when one wrist is handcuffed above your head and the other arm is on the receiving end of an intravenous drip.

Father Clifton must have understood my awkward motion. "You're indifferent to it then?" he asked softly.

As indifferent as one can be to an organization that's tried to capture or kill me, I thought. "Not indifferent, Father," I said. "It's just that the Church . . . well, it hasn't been relevant to my life in most ways."

One of the missionary's sandy eyebrows rose slightly. "Gosh, Raul . . . the Church is a lot of things . . . not all of them spotlessly good, I'm sure . . . but I hardly think that it could be accused of being irrelevant."

I considered shrugging again, but decided one awkward spasm of that sort was enough. "I see what you mean," I said, hoping that the conversation was over.

Father Clifton leaned even closer, his elbows on his knees, his hands set together in front of him—but more in the aspect of persuasion and reason than prayer. "Raul, you know that they're taking you back to Base Bombasino in the morning."

I nodded. My head was still free to move.

"You know that the Pax Fleet and Mercantilus punishment for desertion is death."

"Yeah," I said, "but only after a fair trial."

Father Clifton ignored my sarcasm. His brow was wrinkled with what could only be worry—although for my fate or for my eternal soul, I was not sure which. Perhaps for both. "For Christians," he began and paused a moment. "For Christians, such an execution is punishment, some discomfort, perhaps even momentary terror, but then they mend their ways and go on with their lives. For you . . ."

"Nothingness," I said, helping him end his sentence. "The Big Gulp. Eternal darkness. Nada-ness. I become a worm's casserole."

Father Clifton was not amused. "This does not have to be the case, my son."

I sighed and looked out the window. It was early afternoon on Vitus-Gray-Balianus B. The sunlight was different here than on worlds that I had known well—Hyperion, Old Earth, even Mare Infinitus and other places I had visited briefly but intensely—but the difference was so subtle that I would have found it hard to describe. But it was beautiful. There was no arguing that. I looked at the cobalt sky, streaked with violet clouds, at the butter-rich light falling on pink adobe and the wooden sill; I listened to the sound of children playing in the alley, to the soft conversation of Ces Ambre and her sick brother, Bin, to the sudden, soft laughter as something in the game they were playing amused them, and I thought—*To lose all this forever?*

And I hallucinated Aenea's voice saying, *To lose all this forever is the essence of being human, my love.*

Father Clifton cleared his throat. "Have you ever heard of Pascal's Wager, Raul?"

"Yes."

"You have?" Father Clifton sounded surprised. I had the feeling that I had thrown him off stride in his prepared line of argument. "Then you know why it makes sense," he said rather lamely.

I sighed again. The pain was steady now, not coming and going in the tidal surges that had overwhelmed me the past few days. I remembered first encountering Blaise Pascal in conversations with Grandam when I was a kid, then discussing him with Aenea in the Arizona twilight, and finally looking up his *Pensées* in the excellent library at Taliesin West.

"Pascal was a mathematician," Father Clifton was saying, "pre-Hegira . . . mid-eighteenth century, I think . . ."

"Actually, he lived in the mid 1600s," I said, "1623 to 1662, I think." Actually, I was bluffing a bit on the dates. The numbers seemed right, but I would not have bet my life on them. I remembered the era because Aenea and I had spent a couple of weeks one winter discussing the Enlightenment and its effect on people and institutions pre-Hegira, pre-Pax.

"Yes," said Father Clifton, "but the *time* he lived isn't as important as his so-called wager. Consider it, Raul—on one side, the chance of resurrection, immortality, an eternity in heaven and benefiting from Christ's light. On the other side . . . how did you put it?"

"The Big Gulp," I said. "Nada-ness."

"Worse than that," said the young priest, his voice thick with earnest conviction. "Nada means nothingness. Sleep without dreams. But Pascal realized that the absence of Christ's redemption is worse than that. It's eternal regret . . . longing . . . infinite sadness."

"And hell?" I said. "Eternal punishment?"

Father Clifton squeezed his hands together, obviously uncomfortable at that side of the equation. "Perhaps," he said. "But even if hell were just eternal recognition of the chances one has lost . . . why risk that? Pascal realized that if the Church was wrong, nothing would be lost by embracing its hope. And if it was right . . ."

I smiled. "A bit cynical, isn't it, Father?"

The priest's pale eyes looked directly into mine. "Not as cynical as going to your death for no reason, Raul. Not when you can accept Christ as your Lord, do good works among other human beings, serve your community and your brothers and sisters in Christ, and save your physical life and your immortal soul in the process."

I nodded. After a minute, I said, "Maybe the time he lived *was* important."

Father Clifton blinked, not following me.

"Blaise Pascal, I mean," I said. "He lived through an intellectual revolution the likes of which humanity has rarely seen. On top of that, Copernicus and Kepler and their ilk were opening up the universe a thousandfold. The Sun was becoming . . . well . . . just a sun, Father. Everything was being displaced, moved aside, shoved from the center. Pascal once said, 'I am terrified by the eternal silence of these infinite spaces.'"

Father Clifton leaned closer. I could smell the soap and shaving cream scent on his smooth skin. "All the more reason to consider the wisdom of his wager, Raul."

I blinked, wanting to move away from the pink and freshly scrubbed moon of a face. I was afraid that I smelled of sweat and pain and fear. I had not brushed my teeth in twenty-four hours. "I don't think that I want to make any wager if it means dealing with a Church that has grown so corrupt that it makes obedience and submission the price of its saving the life of someone's child," I said.

Father Clifton pulled away as if slapped. His fair skin flushed a deeper red. Then he stood and patted my arm. "You get some sleep. We'll speak again before you leave tomorrow."

But I did not have until tomorrow. If I had been outside at that moment, looking at just the precise quadrant of the late-afternoon sky, I would have seen the scratch of flame across the dome of cobalt as Nemes's dropship entered the landing pattern for Pax Base Bombasino.

When Father Clifton left, I fell asleep.

I WATCHED AS Aenea and I sat in the vestibule of her shelter in the desert night and continued our conversation.

"I've had this dream before," I said, looking around and touching the stone beneath the canvas of her shelter. The rock still held some of the day's heat.

"Yes," said Aenea. She was sipping from a fresh cup of tea.

"You were going to tell me the secret that makes you the messiah," I heard myself say. "The secret which makes you the 'bond between two worlds' that the AI Ummon spoke of."

"Yes," said my young friend and nodded again, "but first tell me if you think that your reply to Father Clifton was adequate."

"Adequate?" I shrugged. "I was angry."

Aenea sipped tea. Steam rose from the cup and touched her lashes. "But you didn't really respond to his question about Pascal's Wager."

"That was all the response I needed to give," I said, somewhat irritated. "Little Bin Ria Dem Loa Alem is dying of cancer. The Church uses their cruciform as leverage. That's corrupt . . . foul. I'll have none of it."

Aenea looked at me over the steaming cup. "But if the Church were not corrupt, Raul . . . if it offered the cruciform without price or reservation. Would you accept it?"

"No." The immediacy of my answer surprised me.

The girl smiled. "So it is not the corruption of the Church that is at the heart of your objection. You reject resurrection itself."

I started to speak, hesitated, frowned, and then rephrased what I was thinking. "*This* kind of resurrection, I reject. Yes."

Still smiling, Aenea said, "Is there another kind?"

"The Church used to think so," I said. "For almost three thousand years, the resurrection it offered was of the soul, not the body."

"And do you believe in that other kind of resurrection?"

"No," I said again, as quickly as I had before. I shook my head. "Pascal's Wager never appealed to me. It seems logically . . . shallow."

"Perhaps because it posits only two choices," said Aenea. Somewhere in the desert night, an owl made a short, sharp sound. "Spiritual resurrection and immortality or death and damnation," she said.

"Those last two aren't the same thing," I said.

"No, but perhaps to someone like Blaise Pascal they were. Someone terrified of 'the eternal silence of these infinite spaces.' "

"A spiritual agoraphobic," I said.

Aenea laughed. The sound was so sincere and spontaneous that I could not help loving it. *Her.*

"Religion seems to have always offered us that false duality," she said, setting her cup of tea on a flat stone. "The silences of infinite space or the cozy comfort of inner certainty."

I made a rude noise. "The Pax Church offers a more pragmatic certainty."

Aenea nodded. "That may be its only recourse these days. Perhaps our reservoir of spiritual faith has run out."

"Perhaps it should have run out a long time ago," I said sternly. "Superstition has taken a terrible toll on our species. Wars . . . pogroms . . . resistance to logic and science and medicine . . . not to mention gathering power in the hands of people like those who run the Pax."

"Is all religion superstition then, Raul? All faith then folly?"

I squinted at her. The dim light from inside the shelter and the dimmer starlight outside played on her sharp cheekbones and the gentle curve of her chin. "What do you mean?" I said, correctly expecting a trap.

"If you had faith in me, would that be folly?"

"Faith in you . . . how?" I said, hearing my voice sounding suspicious, almost sullen. "As a friend? Or as a messiah?"

"What's the difference?" asked Aenea, smiling again in that way that usually meant a challenge was in the offing.

"Faith in a friend is . . . friendship," I said. "Loyalty." I hesitated. "Love."

"And faith in a messiah?" said Aenea, her eyes catching the light.

I made a brusque, throwing-away gesture. "That's religion."

"But what if your friend is the messiah?" she said, smiling openly now.

"You mean—'What if your friend *thinks* she's the messiah?' " I said. I shrugged again. "I guess you stay loyal to her and try to keep her out of the asylum."

Aenea's smile faded, but I sensed that it was not because of my harsh comment. Her gaze had turned inward. "I wish it were that simple, my dear friend."

Touched, filled with a wave of anxiety as real as surging nausea, I said, "You were going to tell me why you were chosen as this messiah, kiddo. What makes you the bond between two worlds."

The girl—young woman, I realized—nodded solemnly. "I was chosen simply because I was that first child of the Core and humankind."

She had said that earlier. I nodded this time. "So those are the two worlds which you connect . . . the Core and us?"

"Two of the worlds, yes," said Aenea, looking up at me again. "Not the only two. That's precisely what messiahs *do*, Raul . . . bridge different worlds. Different eras. Provide the bond between two irreconcilable concepts."

"And your connection to both these worlds makes you the messiah?" I said again.

Aenea shook her head quickly, almost impatiently. Something like anger glinted in her eyes. "No," she said sharply. "I'm the messiah because of what I can *do*."

I blinked at her vehemence. "What can you do, kiddo?"

Aenea held out her hand and gently touched me with it. "Remember when I said that the Church and Pax were right about me, Raul? That I was a virus?"

"Uh-huh."

She squeezed my wrist. "I can *pass* that virus, Raul. I can infect others. Geometric progression. A plague of carriers."

"Carriers of what?" I said. "Messiahhood?"

She shook her head. Her expression was so sad that it made me want to console her, put my arms around her. Her grip remained firm on my wrist. "No," she said. "Just the next step in what we are. What we can be."

I took a breath. "You talked about teaching the physics of love," I said. "Of understanding love as a basic force of the universe. Is that the virus?"

Still holding my wrist, she looked at me a long moment. "That's the source of the virus," she said softly. "What I teach is how to *use* that energy."

"How?" I whispered.

Aenea blinked slowly, as if she were the one dreaming and about to awaken. "Let's say there are four steps," she said. "Four stages. Four levels."

I waited. Her fingers made a loop around my captured wrist.

"The first is learning the language of the dead," she said.

"What does that . . ."

"Shhh!" Aenea had raised the first finger of her free hand to her lips to shush me.

"The second is learning the language of the living," she said.

I nodded, not understanding either phrase.

"The third is hearing the music of the spheres," she whispered.

In my reading at Taliesin West, I had run across this ancient phrase: it was all mixed up with astrology, the pre-Scientific Age on Old Earth, Kepler's little wooden models of a solar system predicated on perfect shapes, shells of stars and planets being moved by angels . . . volumes of double-talk. I had no idea what my friend was talking about and how it could apply to an age when humanity moved faster than light through the spiral arm of the galaxy.

"The fourth step," she said, her gaze turned inward again, "is learning to take the first step."

"The first step," I repeated, confused. "You mean the first step you mentioned . . . what was it? Learning the language of the dead?"

Aenea shook her head, slowly bringing me into focus. It was as if she had been elsewhere for a moment. "No," she said, "I mean *taking the first step*."

Almost holding my breath, I said, "All right. I'm ready, kiddo. Teach me."

Aenea smiled again. "That's the irony, Raul, my love. If I choose to do this, I'll always be known as the One Who Teaches. But the silly thing is, I don't have to teach it. I only have to share this virus to impart each of these stages to those who wish to learn."

I looked down at where her slim fingers encircled a part of my wrist. "So you've already given me this . . . virus?" I said. I felt nothing except the usual electric tingle that her touch always created in me.

My friend laughed. "No, Raul. You're not ready. And it takes communion to share the virus, not just contact. And I haven't decided what to do . . . if I *should* do this."

"To share with me?" I said, thinking, *Communion?*

"To share with everyone," she whispered, serious again. "With everyone ready to learn." She looked directly at me again. Somewhere in the desert, a coyote was yipping. "These . . . levels, stages . . . can't coexist with a cruciform, Raul."

"So the born-again can't learn?" I said. This would rule out the vast majority of human beings.

She shook her head. "They can learn . . . they just can't stay born-again. The cruciform has to go."

I let out my breath. I did not understand most of this, but that's because it seemed to be double-talk. *Don't all would-be messiahs speak double-talk?* asked the cynical part of me in Grandam's level voice. Aloud, I said, "There's no way to remove a cruciform without killing the person wearing it. The true death." I had always wondered if this fact had been the main reason I had been unwilling to go under the cross. Or perhaps it was just my youthful belief in my own immortality.

Aenea did not respond directly. She said, "You like the Amoiete Spectrum Helix people, don't you?"

Blinking, I tried to understand this. Had I dreamed that phrase, those people, that pain? Wasn't I dreaming now? Or was this a memory of a real conversation? But Aenea knew nothing of Dem Ria, Dem Loa, and the others. The night and stone-and-canvas shelter seemed to ripple like a shredding dreamscape.

"I like them," I said, feeling my friend remove her fingers from my wrist. *Wasn't my wrist shackled to the headboard?*

Aenea nodded and sipped her cooling tea. "There's hope for the Spectrum Helix people. And for all the thousands of other cultures which have reverted or sprung up since the Fall. The Hegemony meant homogeneity, Raul. The Pax means even more. The human genome . . . the human soul . . . distrusts homogeneity, Raul. It—they—are always ready to take a chance, to risk change and diversity."

"Aenea," I said, reaching for her. "I don't . . . we can't . . ." There was a terrible sense of falling and the dreamscape came apart like thin cardboard in a hard rain. I could not see my friend.

"WAKE UP, RAUL. They are coming for you. The Pax is coming."

I tried to awaken, groping toward consciousness like a sluggish machine crawling uphill, but the weight of fatigue and the painkillers kept dragging me down. I did not understand why Aenea wanted me awake. We were conversing so well in the dream.

"Wake up, Raul Endymion." *Wek op, Rool Endmyun.* It was not Aenea. Even before I was fully awake and focused I recognized the soft voice and thick dialect of Dem Ria.

I sat straight up. The woman was undressing me! I realized that she had pulled the loose nightshirt off and was tugging my undershirt on—cleaned and smelling of fresh breezes now, but unmistakably my undershirt. My undershorts were already on. My twill pants, overshirt, and vest were laid across the bottom of the bed. How had she done this with the handcuff on my . . .

I stared at my wrist. The handcuffs were lying open on the bedclothes. My arm tingled painfully as circulation returned. I licked my lips and tried to speak without slurring. "The Pax? Coming?"

Dem Ria pulled my shirt on as if I were her child, Bin . . . or younger. I motioned her hands away and tried to close the buttons with suddenly awkward fingers. They had used buttons rather than sealtabs at Taliesin West on Old Earth. I thought I had grown used to them, but this was taking forever.

". . . and we heard on the radio that a dropship had landed at Bombasino. There are four people in unknown uniforms—two men, two women. They were asking the Commandant about you. They just lifted off—the dropship and three skimmers. They will be here in four minutes. Perhaps less."

"Radio?" I said stupidly. "I thought you said that the radio didn't work. Isn't that why the priest went to the base to get the doctor?"

"Father *Clifton's* radio was not working," whispered Dem Ria, pulling me to my feet. She held me steady as I stepped into my trousers. "We have radios . . . tightbeam transmitters . . . satellite relays . . . all of which the Pax knows nothing about. And spies in place. One has warned us . . . hurry, Raul Endymion. The ships will be here in a minute."

I came fully awake then, literally flushed with a surge of anger and hopelessness that threatened to wash me away. *Why won't these bastards leave me alone?* Four people in unknown uniforms. Pax, obviously. Evidently their search for Aenea, A. Bettik, and me had not ended when the priest-captain—de Soya—had let us escape the trap on God's Grove more than four years earlier.

I looked at the chronometer readout on my comlog. The ships would be landing in a minute or so. There was nowhere I could run in that time where Pax troopers would not find me. "Let me go," I said, pulling away from the short woman in the blue robe. The window was open, the afternoon breeze coming through the curtains. I imagined that I could hear the near-ultrasonic hum of skimmers. "I have to get away from your house . . ." I had images of the Pax torching the home with young Ces Ambre and Bin still in it.

Dem Ria pulled me back from the window. At that moment, the man of the household—young Alem Mikail Dem Alem—came in with Dem Loa. They were carrying the Lusian bulk of the Pax trooper who had been left to guard me. Ces Ambre, her dark eyes bright, was lifting the guard's feet while Bin struggled to pull one of the man's huge boots off. The Lusian was fast asleep, mouth open, drool moistening the high collar of his combat fatigues.

I looked at Dem Ria.

"Dem Loa brought him some tea about fifteen minutes ago," she said softly. She made a graceful gesture that caused the blue sleeve of her robe to billow. "I am afraid that we used the rest of your ultramorph prescription, Raul Endymion."

"I have to go . . ." I began. The ache in my back was bearable, but my legs were shaky.

"No," said Dem Ria. "They will catch you within minutes." She pointed to the window. From outside there came the unmistakable subsonic rumble of a dropship on EM drive, followed by the thud and bark of its thrusters. The thing must be hovering right above the village, seeking a landing site. A second later the window vibrated to a triple sonic boom and two black skimmers banked above the adobe buildings next door.

Alem Mikail had stripped the Lusian to his thermal-weave underwear and had laid him out on the bed. Now he snapped the man's massive right wrist into the handcuffs and snicked the other cuff around the headboard bar. Dem Loa and Ces Ambre were sweeping up the layers of fatigue clothing, body armor, and huge boots and stuffing them in a laundry bag. Little Bin Ria Dem Loa Alem tossed the guard's helmet in the bag. The thin boy was carrying the heavy flechette pistol. I started at the sight—children and weapons was a mix I learned to avoid even when I was a child myself, learning to handle power weapons while our caravan rumbled its way across the Hyperion moors—but Alem smiled and took the pistol from the boy, patting him on the back. It was obvious from the way Bin had held the weapon—fingers away from the trigger guard, pointing the muzzle away from himself and his father, checking the safety indicator even as he gave the pistol up—that he had handled such a device before.

Bin smiled at me, took the heavy bag with the guard's clothing in it, and ran out of the room. The noise outside rose to a crescendo and I turned to look out the window.

A black skimmer kicked up dust less than thirty meters down the street that ran along the canal. I could see it through a gap between the houses. The larger dropship lowered itself out of sight to the south, probably landing in the grassy open area near the well where I had collapsed in pain from the kidney stone.

I had just finished wiggling into my boots and securing my vest when Alem handed me the flechette pistol. I checked the safety and propellant charge indicators out of habit, but then shook my head. "No," I said. "It would be suicide to attack Pax troopers with just this. Their armor . . ." I was not actually thinking about their armor at that moment, but, rather, about the return fire from assault weapons that would level this house in an instant. I thought of the boy outside with the laundry bag of trooper's armor. "Bin . . ." I said. "If they catch him . . ."

"We know, we know," said Dem Ria, pulling me away from the bed and into the narrow hallway. I did not remember this part of the house. My universe for the past forty-some hours had been the bedroom and adjoining lavatory. "Come, come," she said.

I pulled away again, handing the pistol to Alem. "Just let me run," I said, my heart pounding. I gestured toward the snoring Lusian. "They won't think that's me for a second. They can tightbeam the doctor—if she's not already in one of those skimmers—to ID me. Just tell them"—I looked at the friendly faces in their blue robes—"tell them that I overpowered the guard and held you at gunpoint . . ." I stopped then, realizing that the guard would destroy that cover story as soon as he awoke. The family's complicity in my escape would be self-evident. I looked at the flechette pistol again, half-ready to reach for it. One burst of steel needles and the sleeping trooper would never awaken to destroy the cover-up and endanger these good people.

Only I could never do it. I might shoot a Pax trooper in a fair fight—indeed, the adrenaline rush of anger that was burning through my weakness and terror told me that it would be a welcome relief to have that opportunity—but I could never shoot this sleeping man.

But there would be no fair fight. Pax troopers in combat armor, much less these mysterious four in the dropship—Swiss Guard?—would be immune to flechettes and anything else short of Pax assault weapons. And the Swiss Guard would be immune to those. I was screwed. These good people who had shown me such kindness were screwed.

A rear door slammed open and Bin slid into the hallway, his robe hiked up to show spindly legs covered with dust. I stared at him, thinking that the boy would not get his cruciform and would die of cancer. The adults might well spend the next standard decade in a Pax prison.

"I'm sorry . . ." I said, hunting for words. I could hear the commotion in the street as troopers hurried through the evening rush of pedestrians.

"Raul Endymion," said Dem Loa in her soft voice, handing me the rucksack they had brought from my kayak, "please shut up and follow us. *At once.*"

THERE WAS A tunnel entrance beneath the floor of the hallway. I had always thought that hidden passages were the stuff of holodramas, but I followed Dem Ria into this one willingly enough. We were a strange procession—Dem Ria and Dem Loa sweeping down the steep staircase ahead of me, then me carrying the flechette pistol and fumbling the rucksack on my back, then little Bin followed by his sister, Ces Ambre, then, carefully locking the trapdoor behind him, Alem Mikail Dem Alem. No one stayed behind. The house was empty except for the snoring Lusian trooper.

The stairway went deeper than a normal basement level, and at first I thought that the walls were adobe like the ones above. Then I realized that the passage was cut from a soft stone, perhaps sandstone. Twenty-seven steps and we reached the bottom of the vertical shaft and Dem Ria led the way down a narrow passage illuminated by pale chemical glowglobes. I wondered why this average, working-class home would have an underground passage.

As if reading my mind, Dem Loa's blue cowl turned and she whispered, "The Amoiete Spectrum Helix demands . . . ah . . . discreet entrances to one another's homes. Especially during the Twice Darkness."

"Twice Darkness?" I whispered back, ducking under one of the globes. We had already gone twenty or twenty-five meters—away from the canal-river, I thought—and the passage still curved out of sight to the right.

"The slow, dual eclipse of the sun by this world's two moons," whispered Dem Loa. "It lasts precisely nineteen minutes. It is the primary reason that we chose this world . . . please excuse the pun."

"Ahh," I said. I did not understand, but it didn't seem to matter at that moment. "Pax troops have sensors to find spider-holes like this," I whispered to the women in front of me. "They have deep radar to search through rock. They have . . ."

"Yes, yes," said Alem from behind me, "but they will be held up a few minutes by the Mayor and the others."

"The Mayor?" I repeated rather stupidly. My legs were still weak from the two days in bed and pain. My back and groin ached, but it was a minor pain—inconsequential—compared to what I had passed through (and what had passed through me) during the last couple of days.

"The Mayor is challenging the Pax's right to search," whispered Dem

Ria. The passage widened and went straight for at least a hundred meters. We passed two branching tunnels. This wasn't a bolt-hole; it was a bloody catacombs. "The Pax recognizes the Mayor's authority in Lock Childe Lamonde," she whispered. The silken robes of the five family members in blue were also whispering against the sandstone as we hurried down the passage. "We still have law and courts on Vitus-Gray-Balianus B, so they are not allowed unlimited search and seizure rights."

"But they'll download permission from whatever authority they need," I said, hurrying to keep up with the women. We came to another juncture and they turned right.

"Eventually," said Dem Loa, "but the streets are now filled with all of the colors of the Lock Childe Lamonde strand of the Helix—reds, whites, greens, ebonies, yellows—thousands of people from our village. And many more are coming from nearby Locks. No one will volunteer which house is the one where you were kept. Father Clifton has been lured out of town on a ruse, so he can be of no help to the Pax troopers. Dr. Molina has been detained in Keroa Tambat by some of our people and is currently out of touch with her Pax superiors. And your guard will be sleeping for at least another hour. This way."

We turned left into a wider passage, stopped at the first door we had seen, waited for Dem Ria to palmlock it open, and then stepped into a large, echoing space carved into the stone. We were standing on a metal stairway looking down on what appeared to be a subterranean garage: half a dozen long, slim vehicles with oversized wheels, stern wings, sails, and pedals clustered by primary colors. These things were like buckboards set on spidery suspensions, obviously powered by wind and muscle power, and covered over with wood, bright, silky polymer fabrics, and Perspex.

"Windcycles," said Ces Ambre.

Several men and women in emerald-green robes and high boots were preparing three of the wagons for departure. Lashed in the back of one of the long wagonbeds was my kayak.

Everyone was moving down the clattering staircase, but I stopped at the head of the stairs. My balking was so sudden that poor Bin and Ces Ambre almost crashed into me.

"What is it?" said Alem Mikail.

I had tucked the flechette pistol in my belt and now I opened my hands. "Why are you doing this? Why is everyone helping? What's going on?"

Dem Ria took a step back up the metal staircase and leaned on the railing. Her eyes were as bright as her daughter's had been. "If they take you, Raul Endymion, they will kill you."

"How do you know?" I said. My voice was soft but the acoustics of the underground garage were such that the men and women in green looked up from where they were working below.

"You spoke in your sleep," said Dem Loa.

I cocked my head, not understanding. I had been dreaming of Aenea and our conversation. What would that have told these people?

Dem Ria took another step upward and touched my wrist with her cool hand. "The Amoiete Spectrum Helix has foretold this woman, Raul Endymion. This one named Aenea. We call her the One Who Teaches."

I felt goose bumps at that moment, in the chill glowglobe light of this buried place. The old poet—Uncle Martin—had spoken of my young friend as a messiah, but his cynicism leaked into everything he said or did. The people of Taliesin West had respected Aenea . . . but to believe that the energetic sixteen-year-old was actually a World Historical Figure? It seemed unlikely. And the girl and I had spoken of it in real life and in my ultramorph dreams, but . . . my God, I was on a world scores of light-years away from Hyperion and an eternal distance from the Lesser Magellanic Cloud where Old Earth was hidden. How had these people . . .

"Halpul Amoiete knew of the One Who Teaches when he composed the Helix Symphony," said Dem Loa. "All of the people of the Spectrum were descended from empath stock. The Helix was and is a way to refine that empathic ability."

I shook my head. "I'm sorry, I don't understand . . ."

"Please understand this, Raul Endymion," said Dem Ria, her fingers squeezing my wrist almost painfully. "If you do not escape this place, the Pax will have your soul and body. And the One Who Teaches needs both these things."

I squinted at the woman, thinking that she was jesting. But her pleasant, unlined face was set and serious.

"Please," said little Bin, setting his little hand in my free one and pulling. "Please hurry, Raul."

I hurried down the stairs. One of the men in green handed me a red robe. Alem Mikail helped me fold and wrap it over my own clothes. He wrapped the red burnoose and cowl in a dozen quick strokes. I would never have been able to arrange it properly. I realized with a shock that the entire family—the two older women, teenaged Ces Ambre, and little Bin—had stripped naked from their blue robes and were arranging red ones around them. I saw then that I had been wrong thinking that they were like Lusians—for although their bodies were shorter than Pax-space average and heavily muscled, they were perfectly proportioned. None of the adults had any hair, either on their heads or elsewhere. Somehow this made their compact, perfectly toned bodies more attractive.

I looked away, realizing that I was blushing. Ces Ambre laughed and jostled my arm. We were all in red robes now, Alem Mikail being the last to pull his on. One glance at his heavily muscled upper torso told me that I would not last fifteen seconds in a fight with the shorter man. But then, I realized, I probably would not last more than thirty seconds with Dem Loa or Dem Ria either.

I offered the flechette pistol to Alem but he gestured for me to keep it and showed me how to tuck it in one of the multiple sashes of the long, crimson robe. I thought of my lack of weapons in the little backpack—a Navajo hunting knife and the little flashlight laser—and nodded my gratitude.

The women and children and I were hurried into the back of the windcycle wagon that held my kayak and red fabric was pulled tight over the stays above us. We had to crouch low as a second layer of fabric, some wooden planks, and various crates and barrels were set in around and above us. I could just make out a glimpse of light between the tailgate and the wagon cover. I listened to footsteps on stone as Alem went up front and crawled onto one of the two pedaling saddles. I listened as one of the other men—also now in a red robe—joined him on the cycling seat on the other side of the central yoke.

With the masts still lowered above us, fabric sails reefed, we began rolling up a long ramp out of the garage.

"Where are we going?" I whispered to Dem Ria, who was lying almost next to me. The wood smelled like cedar.

"The downstream farcaster arch," she whispered back.

I blinked. "You know about that?"

"They gave you Truthtell," whispered Dem Loa from the other side of a crate. "And you did speak in your sleep."

Bin was lying right next to me in the darkness. "We know the One Who Teaches has sent you on a mission," he said almost happily. "We know you have to get to the next arch." He patted the kayak that curved next to us. "I wish I could go with you."

"This is too dangerous," I hissed, feeling the wagon roll out of the tunnel and into open air. Low sunlight illuminated the fabric above us. The windcycle wagon stopped for a second as the two men cranked the mast erect and unfurled the sail. "Too dangerous." I meant them taking me to the farcaster, of course, not the mission that Aenea had sent me on.

"If they know who I am," I whispered to Dem Ria, "they'll be watching the arch."

I could see the silhouette of her cowl as she nodded. "They will be watching, Raul Endymion. And it is dangerous. But darkness is almost here. In fourteen minutes."

I glanced at my comlog. It would be another ninety minutes or more until twilight according to what I had observed the previous two days. And then almost another full hour until true nightfall.

"It is only six kilometers to the downstream arch," whispered Ces Ambre from her place on the other side of the kayak. "The villages will be filled with the Spectrum celebrating."

I understood then. "The Twice Darkness?" I whispered.

"Yes," said Dem Ria. She patted my hand. "We must be silent now. We will be moving into traffic along the saltway."

"Too dangerous," I whispered one last time as the wagon began creaking and groaning its way into traffic. I could hear the chain drive rumbling beneath the buckboard floor and feel the wind catch the sail. *Too dangerous,* I said only to myself.

If I had known what was happening a few hundred meters away, I would have realized how truly dangerous this moment was.

I PEERED OUT through the gap between wagon wood and fabric as we rumbled along the saltway. This vehicle thoroughfare appeared to be a strip of rock-hard salt between the villages clustered along the raised canal and the reticulated desert stretching as far north as I could see. "Waste Wahhabi," whispered Dem Ria as we picked up speed and headed south along the saltway. Other windcycle wagons roared past heading south, their sails fully engaged, their two pedalers working madly. Even more brightly canvased wagons tacked north, their sails set differently, the pedalers leaning far out for balance as the creaking wagons teetered on two wheels, the other two spinning uselessly in the air.

We covered the six kilometers in ten minutes and turned off the saltway onto a paved ramp that led through a cluster of homes—white stone this time, not adobe—and then Alem and the other man furled the sail and pedaled the windcycle slowly along the cobblestone street that ran between the homes and the canal-river. High, wispy ferns grew along the canal banks there between elaborately fashioned piers, gazebos, and multi-tiered docks to which were tied ornate houseboats. The city seemed to end here where the canal widened into a waterway much more riverlike than artificial, and I raised my head enough to see the huge farcaster arch a few hundred meters downstream. Through and beyond the rusted arch, I could see only fern forest on the riverbanks and desert waste to the east and west. Alem guided the windcycle onto a brick loading ramp and pulled under the cover of a copse of tall ferns.

I glanced at my comlog. Less than two minutes until the Twice Darkness.

At that instant there was a rush of warm air and a shadow passed over us. We all crouched lower as the black Pax skimmer flew out over the river at an altitude of less than a hundred meters; the aerodynamic, figure-eight shape of the thing clearly visible as it banked more steeply and then swooped low above the ships headed north and south through the arch. River traffic was brisk here where the river widened: sleek racing sculls with rowing teams of four to twelve, gleaming powerboats throwing up glistening wakes, sailboats ranging from single-person jitabouts to wallowing, square-sailed junks, canoes and rowboats, some stately houseboats churning against the current, a handful of silent electric hovercraft moving within their haloes of spray, and even some rafts that reminded me of my earlier voyage with Aenea and A. Bettik.

The skimmer flew low over these ships, passed over the farcaster arch headed south, flew back under it headed north, and disappeared in the direction of Lock Childe Lamonde.

"Come," said Alem Mikail, folding back the fabric tarp above us and pulling at the kayak. "We must hurry."

Suddenly there was a rush of warm air, followed by a cooler breeze that kicked dust off the riverbank, the fernheads rustled and shook above us, and the sky grew purple and then black. Stars came out. I glanced upward just long enough to see a beaded corona around one of the moons and the burning disc of the second, lower satellite as it moved into place behind the first.

From north along the river, back in the direction of the linear city that included Lock Childe Lamonde, there came the most haunting and mournful sound I had ever heard: a long wailing, more human-throated than siren-caused, followed by a sustained note that grew deeper and deeper until it fell into the subsonic. I realized that I had heard hundreds—perhaps thousands—of horns played at the same instant that thousands, perhaps tens of thousands, of human voices had joined in chorus.

The darkness around us grew deeper. The stars blazed. The disc of the lower moon was like some great backlit dome that threatened to drop on the darkened world at any moment. Suddenly the many ships on the river to the south and the canal-river to the north began wailing with their own sirens and horns—a cacophonous howl, this, nothing like the descending harmony of the opening chorus—and then began firing off flares and fireworks: multicolored starshells, roaring St. Catherine's Wheels, red parachute flares, braided strands of yellow, blue, green, red, and white fire—the Spectrum Helix?—and countless aerial bombs. The noise and light were all but overwhelming.

"Hurry," repeated Alem, pulling the kayak from the wagonbed. I jumped out to help him and pulled off my concealing robe, tossing it into the back of the wagon. The next minute was a flurry of coordinated motion as Dem Ria, Dem Loa, Ces Ambre, Bin, and I helped Alem and the unnamed man carry the kayak down to the river's edge and set it afloat. I went into the warm water up to my knees, stowed my backpack and the flechette pistol inside the little cockpit, held the kayak steady against the current, and looked at the two women, two young people, and two men in their billowing robes.

"What is to happen to you?" I asked. My back ached from the aftermath of the kidney stone, but at the moment the tightening of my throat was the more painful distraction.

Dem Ria shook her head. "Nothing bad will happen to us, Raul Endymion. If the Pax authorities attempt to make trouble, we will simply disappear into the tunnels beneath Waste Wahhabi until it is time to rejoin the Spectrum elsewhere." She smiled and adjusted her robe on her shoulder. "But make us one promise, Raul Endymion."

"Anything," I said. "If I can do it, I will."

"If it is possible, ask the One Who Teaches to return with you to Vitus-Gray-Balianus B and the people of the Amoiete Spectrum Helix. We shall try not to convert to the Pax's Christianity until she comes to speak to us."

I nodded, looking at Bin Ria Dem Loa Alem's shaven skull, his red cowl flapping around him in the breeze, his cheeks gaunt with chemotherapy, his eyes gleaming more with excitement than reflected fireworks. "Yes," I said. "If it is at all possible, I will do that."

They all touched me then—not to shake hands, but merely to touch, fingers against my vest or arm or face or back. I touched them back, turned the bow of the kayak into the current, and stepped into the cockpit. The paddle was in the hullclamp where I had left it. I tightened the cockpit skirt around me as if there were white water ahead, bumped my hand against the clear plastic cover over the red "panic button" that Aenea had shown me as I set the pistol on the cockpit skirt—if this interlude had not caused me to panic, I was not sure what could—held the paddle in my left hand, and waved farewell with my right. The six robed figures blended into the shadows beneath the ferns as the kayak swept out into the middle current.

The farcaster arch grew larger. Overhead, the first moon began to move beyond the disc of the sun but the second, larger moon moved to cover both with its bulk. The fireworks and siren sounds continued, even grew in ferocity. I paddled closer to the right bank as I came close to the farcaster, trying to stay in the small-boat traffic headed downstream but not too close to anyone.

If they are going to intercept me, I thought, *they will do it here.* Without thinking, I raised the flechette pistol onto the curve of hull in front of me. The swift current had me now, and I set the paddle in its bracket and waited to pass under the farcaster. No other ships or small boats would be under the farcaster when it activated. Above me, the arch was a curve of blackness against the starry sky.

Suddenly there was violent commotion on the riverbank not twenty meters to my right.

I raised the pistol and stared, not understanding what I was seeing and hearing.

Two explosions like sonic booms. Strobe flashes of white light.

More fireworks? No, these flashes were much brighter. *Energy weapons fire?* Too bright. Too unfocused. It was more like small plasma explosives going off.

Then I saw something in a blink of an eye, more a retinal echo than a true vision: two figures locked in a violent embrace, images reversed like a negative of an ancient photograph, sudden, violent motion, another sonic boom, a flash of white that blinded me even before the image had registered in my brain—spikes, thorns, two heads butting together, six arms flailing, sparks flying, a human form and something larger, the sound of metal rending, the sound of something or someone screaming with a voice louder than the sirens wailing on the river behind me. The shock wave from whatever was happening on the bank rippled out across the river, almost tumbled my kayak, and proceeded across the water like a curtain of white spray.

Then I was under the farcaster arch, there was the flash and instant of vertigo I had known before, a bright light surrounded me through the flash-bulb blindness, and the kayak and I were falling.

Truly falling. Tumbling into space. A section of water that had been farcast under me fell away into a brief waterfall, but then the kayak was falling free from the water, spinning as it fell, and in my panic I dropped the flechette pistol into the cockpit and grabbed the hull of the kayak, setting it spinning more wildly as it fell.

I blinked through the flash echoes and tried to see how far I had to fall, even as the kayak went bow down and picked up speed.

Blue sky above. Clouds all around—huge clouds, stratocumulus rising thousands of meters above and falling more thousands of meters below, cirrus many kilometers above me, black thunderstorms many more kilometers below.

There was nothing but sky and I was falling into it. Beneath me, the brief waterfall from the river had separated into giant teardrops of moisture, as if someone had taken a hundred buckets of water and hurled them into a bottomless chasm.

The kayak spun and threatened to go stern over bow. I shifted forward in the little kayak and almost tumbled out, with only my crossed legs and the lashing of the little moisture skirt holding me in.

I grabbed the rim of the cockpit in a white-knuckled, hopeless grip. Cold air whipped and roared around me as the kayak and I picked up speed, hurtling toward terminal velocity. Thousands and thousands of meters of empty, open air lay between me and the lightning-darted clouds so far below. The two-bladed paddle ripped from its bracket and tumbled away in freefall.

I did the only thing I could do under the circumstances. I opened my mouth and screamed.

11

KENZO ISOZAKI COULD say honestly that he had never been afraid before in his life. Raised as a business-samurai in the fern islands of Fuji, he had been taught and trained since infancy to be disdainful of fear and contemptuous of anyone who felt it. Caution he allowed—it had become an indispensable business tool for him—but fear was alien to his nature and his carefully constructed personality.

Until this moment.

M. Isozaki stood back while the inner door of the air lock cycled open. Whatever awaited within had been on the surface of an airless, tumbling asteroid a minute earlier. And it was not wearing a spacesuit.

Isozaki had chosen not to bring a weapon on the little asteroid hopper: neither he nor the ship was armed. At this moment, as ice crystals billowed like fog from the opening air lock and a humanoid figure stepped through, Kenzo Isozaki wondered if that had been a wise choice.

The humanoid figure was human . . . or at least human in appearance. Tan skin, neatly cut gray hair, a perfectly tailored gray suit, gray eyes under lashes still rimmed with frost, and a white smile.

"M. Isozaki," said Councillor Albedo.

Isozaki bowed. He had brought his heart rate and breathing under his control, and now he concentrated on keeping his voice flat, level, and emotionless. "It is kind of you to respond to my invitation."

Albedo crossed his arms. The smile remained on the tanned, handsome face, but Isozaki was not fooled by it. The seas around the fern islands of Fuji were thick with sharks descended from the DNA recipes and frozen embryos of the early Bussard seedships.

"Invitation?" said Councillor Albedo in a rich voice. "Or summons?"

Isozaki's head remained slightly bowed. His hands hung loosely at his sides. "Never a summons, M. . . ."

"You know my name, I think," said Albedo.

"The rumors say that you are the same Councillor Albedo who advised Meina Gladstone almost three centuries ago, sir," said the CEO of the Pax Mercantilus.

"I was more hologram than substance then," said Albedo, uncrossing his arms. "But the . . . personality . . . is the same. And you need not call me sir."

Isozaki bowed slightly.

Councillor Albedo stepped deeper into the little hopper. He ran his powerful fingers over consoles and the single pilot's couch and the rim of its empty high-g tank. "A modest ship for such a powerful person, M. Isozaki."

"I thought it best to exercise discretion, Councillor. May I call you that?"

Instead of answering, Albedo took an aggressive step closer to the CEO. Isozaki did not flinch.

"Did you feel it an act of discretion to release an AI viral telotaxis into Pacem's crude datasphere so that it could go looking for TechnoCore nodes?" Albedo's voice filled the hopper cabin.

Kenzo Isozaki raised his eyes to meet the gray glare of the taller man. "Yes, Councillor. If the Core still existed, it was imperative that I . . . that the Mercantilus . . . make personal contact. The telotaxis was programmed to self-destruct if detected by Pax antiviral programs, and to inoculate only if it received an unmistakable Core response."

Councillor Albedo laughed. "Your AI telotaxis was about as subtle as the metaphorical turd in the proverbial punchbowl, Isozaki-san."

The Mercantilus CEO blinked in surprise at the crudity.

Albedo dropped into the acceleration couch, stretched, and said, "Sit down, my friend. You went to all that trouble to find us. You risked torture, excommunication, real execution, and the loss of your parking privileges in the Vatican skimmer park. You want to talk . . . talk."

Temporarily off balance, Isozaki looked for another surface on which to sit. He settled on a clear section of the plotting board. He disliked zero-g, so the crude internal containment field kept up a differential simulating one gravity, but the effect was inconsistent enough to keep Isozaki teetering on the edge of vertigo. He took a breath and gathered his thoughts.

"You are serving the Vatican . . ." he began.

Albedo interrupted at once. "The Core serves no one, Mercantilus man."

Isozaki took another breath and began again. "Your interests and the Vatican's have overlapped to the point that the TechnoCore provides counsel and technology vital to the survival of the Pax . . ."

Councillor Albedo smiled and waited.

Thinking *For what I will say next, His Holiness will feed me to the Grand Inquisitor. I will be on the pain machine for a hundred lifetimes,*

Isozaki said, "Some of us within the Executive Council of the Pancapitalist League of Independent Catholic Transstellar Trade Organizations feel that the interests of the League and the interests of the TechnoCore may well hold more in common than those of the Core and the Vatican. We feel that an . . . ah . . . investigation of those common goals and interests would be beneficial to both parties."

Councillor Albedo showed more of his perfect teeth. He said nothing.

Feeling the hemplike texture of the noose he was placing around his own neck, Isozaki said, "For two and three-quarters centuries, the Church and the Pax civil authorities have held as official policy that the TechnoCore was destroyed in the Fall of the Farcasters. Millions of those close to power on worlds across Pax space know the rumors of the Core's survival . . ."

"The rumors of our death are greatly exaggerated," said Councillor Albedo. "So?"

"So," continued Isozaki, "with the full understanding that this alliance between Core personalities and the Vatican has been beneficial to both parties, Councillor, the League would like to suggest ways in which a similar direct alliance with our trading organization would bring more immediate and tangible benefits to your . . . ah . . . society."

"Suggest away, Isozaki-san," said Councillor Albedo, leaning farther back in the pilot's chair.

"One," said Isozaki, his voice growing firmer, "the Pax Mercantilus is expanding in ways which no religious organization can hope to do, however hierarchical or universally accepted it might be. Capitalism is regaining power throughout the Pax. It is the true glue that holds the hundreds of worlds together.

"Two, the Church continues to carry on its endless war with the Ousters and with rebellious elements within the Pax sphere of influence. The Pax Mercantilus views all such conflicts as a waste of energy and precious human and material resources. More importantly, it involves the TechnoCore in human squabbles that can neither further Core interests nor advance Core goals.

"Three, while the Church and the Pax utilize such obviously Core-derived technologies as the instantaneous Gideon drive and the resurrection crèches, the Church gives the TechnoCore no credit for these inventions. Indeed, the Church still holds the Core up as an enemy to its billions of faithful, portraying the Core entities as having been destroyed because they were in league with the Devil. The Pax Mercantilus has no need for such prejudice and artifice. If the Core were to choose continued concealment when allied with us, we should honor that policy, always willing to present the Core as visible and appreciated partners when and if you should so decide. In the meantime, however, the League would move to end, for now and forever, the demonization of the TechnoCore in history, lore, and the minds of human beings everywhere."

Councillor Albedo looked thoughtful. After a moment of gazing out the port at the tumbling asteroid beyond, he said, "So you will make us rich *and* respectable?"

Kenzo Isozaki said nothing. He felt that his future and the balance of power in human space was teetering on a knife's edge. He could not read Albedo: the cybrid's sarcasm could well be a prelude to negotiation.

"What would we do with the Church?" asked Albedo. "More than two and a half human centuries of silent partnership?"

Isozaki willed his heart rate to slow again. "We do not wish to interrupt any relationship which the Core has found useful or profitable," he said softly. "As businesspeople, we in the League are trained to see the limitations of any religion-based interstellar society. Dogma and hierarchy are endemic to such structures . . . indeed, such *are* the structures of any theocracy. As businesspeople dedicated to the mutual profit of ourselves and our business associates, we see ways in which a second level of Core-human cooperation, however secretive or limited, should and would be beneficial to both parties."

Councillor Albedo nodded again. "Isozaki-san, do you remember in your private office in the Torus when you had your associate, Anna Pelli Cognani, remove her clothes?"

Isozaki retained a neutral expression but only by the utmost effort of will. The fact that the Core was looking into his private office, recording every transaction, made his blood literally chill.

"You asked then," continued Albedo, "why we had helped the Church refine the cruciform. 'To what ends?' I believe you said. 'Where is the benefit to the Core?' "

Isozaki watched the man in gray, but more than ever he felt that he was locked in the little asteroid hopper with a cobra that had reared up and opened its hood.

"Have you ever owned a dog, Isozaki-san?" asked Albedo.

Still thinking about cobras, the Mercantilus CEO could only stare. "A dog?" he said after a moment. "No. Not personally. Dogs were not common on my homeworld."

"Ah, that's right," said Albedo, showing his white teeth again. "Sharks were the pet of choice on your island. I believe that you had a baby shark which you tried to tame when you were about six standard years old. You named it Keigo, if I am not mistaken."

Isozaki could not have spoken if his life had depended upon it at that second.

"And how did you keep your growing baby shark from eating you when you swam together in the Shioko Lagoon, Isozaki-san?"

After a moment of trying, Isozaki managed, "Collar."

"I beg your pardon?" Councillor Albedo leaned closer.

"Collar," said the CEO. Small, perfectly black spots were dancing in the periphery of his vision. "Shock collar. We had to carry the transmitter palmkeys. The same devices our fishermen used."

"Ah, yes," said Albedo, still smiling. "If your pet did something naughty, you brought it back into line. With just a touch of your finger." He held his hand out, cupping it as if he were cradling an invisible palmkey. His tanned finger came down on an invisible button.

It was not so much like an electrical shock passing through Kenzo Isozaki's body, more like radiating waves of pure, unadultered agony— beginning in his chest, beginning in the cruciform embedded under his skin and flesh and bone—and radiating out like telegraph signals of pain flowing through the hundreds of meters of fibers and nematodes and clustered nodes of cruciform tissue metastasized through his body like rooted tumors.

Isozaki screamed and doubled over in pain. He collapsed to the floor of the hopper.

"I believe that your palmkeys could give old Keigo increasing jolts if he got aggressive," mused Councillor Albedo. "Wasn't that the case, Isozaki-san?" His fingers tapped at empty air again, as if cueing a palmkey.

The pain grew worse. Isozaki urinated in his shipsuit and would have voided his bowels if they had not been already empty. He tried to scream again but his jaws clamped tight, as if from violent tetanus. Enamel on his teeth cracked and chipped away. He tasted blood as he bit through a corner of his tongue.

"On a scale of ten, that would have been about a two for old Keigo, I think," said Councillor Albedo. He stood and walked to the air lock, tapping the cycling combination in.

Writhing on the floor, his body and brain useless apppendages to a cruciform of horrific pain radiating through his body, Isozaki tried to scream through his locked jaws. His eyes were swelling out of their sockets. Blood ran from his nose and ears.

Finished with cycling the air-lock combination, Councillor Albedo tapped at the invisible key in his palm once again.

The pain vanished. Isozaki vomited across the deckplates. Every muscle in his body twitched randomly while his nerves seemed to misfire.

"I will bring your proposal to the Three Elements of the TechnoCore," Councillor Albedo said formally. "The proposition will be discussed and considered most seriously. In the meantime, my friend, your discretion will be counted upon."

Isozaki tried to make an intelligible noise, but he could only curl up and retch on the metal floor. To his horror, his spasming bowels were passing wind in a ripple of flatulence.

"And there will be no more AI viral telotaxes released in anyone's datasphere, will there, Isozaki-san?" Albedo stepped into the air lock and cycled the door shut.

Outside the port, the slashed rock of the unnamed asteroid tumbled and spun in dynamics known only to the gods of chaos mathematics.

IT TOOK RHADAMANTH Nemes and her three siblings only a few minutes to fly the dropship from Pax Base Bombasino to the village of Lock Childe Lamonde on the slate-dry world of Vitus-Gray-Balianus B, but the trip was complicated by the presence of three military skimmers that that meddling fool Commander Solznykov had sent along in escort. Nemes knew from the "secure" tightbeam traffic between the base and the skimmers that the Base Commander had sent his aide, the bumbling Colonel Vinara, to take personal charge of the expedition. More than that, Nemes knew that the Colonel would be in charge of nothing—that is, Vinara would be so wired with real-time holosim pickups and tightbeam squirters that Solznykov would be in actual command of the Pax troopers without showing his jowled face again.

By the time they were hovering over the proper village—although "village" seemed too formal a term for the four-tiered strip of adobe houses that ran along the west side of the river just as hundreds of other homes had for almost the entire way between the base and here—the skimmers had caught up and were spiraling in for a landing while Nemes looked for a site large enough and firm enough to hold the dropship.

The doors of the adobe homes were painted bright primary colors. People on the street wore robes of the same hue. Nemes knew the reason for this display of color: she had accessed both their ship's memory and the encrypted Bombasino files on the Spectrum Helix people. The data was interesting only in that it suggested that these human oddities were slow to convert to the cross, slower still to submit to Pax control. Likely, in other words, to help a rebellious child, man, and one-armed android hide from the authorities.

The skimmers landed on the dike road bordering the canal. Nemes brought the dropship down in a park, partially destroying an artesian well.

Gyges shifted in his copilot's seat and raised an eyebrow.

"Scylla and Briareus will go out to make the formal search," Nemes said aloud. "You stay here with me." She had noted with no pride or vanity that her clone-siblings had long since submitted to her authority, despite the death threat they had brought from the Three Elements and the certainty of it being carried out if she were to fail again.

The other female and male went down the ramp and through the crowd of brightly robed people. Troopers in combat armor, visors sealed, jogged to meet them. Watching on the common optic channel, not via tightbeam or vid pickup, Nemes recognized Colonel Vinara's voice through his helmet speaker. "The Mayor—a woman named Ses Gia—refuses permission for us to search the houses."

Nemes could see Briareus's contemptuous smile reflected on the Colonel's polished visor. It was like looking at a reflection of herself with slightly stronger bone structure.

"And you allow this . . . Mayor . . . to dictate to you?" said Briareus.

Colonel Vinara raised a gauntleted hand. "The Pax recognizes the indigenous authorities until they have become . . . part of the Pax Protectorate."

Scylla said, "You said that Dr. Molina left a Pax trooper as guard . . ."

Vinara nodded. His breathing was amplified through the morphic, amber helmet. "There is no sign of that trooper. We have attempted to establish communication since we left Bombasino."

"Doesn't this trooper have a trace chip surgically implanted?" said Scylla.

"No, it is woven into his impact armor."

"And?"

"We found the armor in a well several streets over," said Colonel Vinara.

Scylla's voice remained level. "I presume the trooper was not in the armor."

"No," said the Colonel, "just the armor and helmet. There was no body in the well."

"Pity," said Scylla. She started to turn away but then looked back at the Pax Colonel. "Just armor, you say. No weapon?"

"No." Vinara's voice was gloomy. "I've ordered a search of the streets and we will question the citizens until someone volunteers the location of the house where the missing spacer was put under arrest by Dr. Molina. Then we will surround it and demand the surrender of all inside. I have . . . ah . . . requested the civil courts in Bombasino consider our request for a search warrant."

Briareus said, "Good plan, Colonel. If the glaciers don't arrive first and cover the village before the warrant is issued."

"Glaciers?" said Colonel Vinara.

"Never mind," said Scylla. "If it is acceptable to you, we shall help you search the adjoining streets and await proper authorization for a house-to-house search." To Nemes, she broadcast on the internal band, *Now what?*

Stay with him and do just what you offered, sent Nemes. *Be courteous and law-abiding. We don't want to find Endymion or the girl with these idiots around. Gyges and I will go to fast time.*

Good hunting, sent Briareus.

Gyges was already waiting at the dropship lock. Nemes said, "I'll take the town, you move downriver to the farcaster arch and make sure that nothing gets through—going upriver or down—without your checking it out. Phase down to send a squirt message and I'll shift periodically to check the band. If you find him or the girl, ping me." It was possible to communicate via common band while phase-shifted, but the energy expenditure was so horribly high—above and beyond the unimaginable energy needed just for the phase-shift—that it was infinitely more economical to shift down at intervals to check the common band. Even a ping alarm would use the equivalent of this world's entire energy budget for a year.

Gyges nodded and the two phase-shifted in unison, becoming chrome sculptures of a naked male and female. Outside the lock, the air seemed to thicken and the light deepen. Sound ceased. Movement stopped. Human figures became slightly out-of-focus statues with their wind-rippled robes stiff and frozen like the trappings on bronze sculptures.

Nemes did not understand the physics of phase shifting. She did not have to understand it in order to use it. She knew that it was neither the antientropic nor hyperentropic manipulation of time—although the future UI had both of those seemingly magical technologies at its command—nor some sort of "speeding up" that would have had sonic booms crashing and the air temperature boiling in their wake, but that phase shifting was a sort of sidestepping into the hollowed-out boundaries of space/time. "You will become—in the nicest sense—rats scurrying in the walls of the rooms of time," had said the Core entity most responsible for her creation.

Nemes was not offended by the comparison. She knew the unimaginable amounts of energy that had to be transferred from the Core via the Void Which Binds to her or her siblings when they phase-shifted. The Elements had to respect even their own instruments to divert so much energy in their direction.

The two reflective figures jogged down the ramp and went opposite directions—Gyges south toward the farcaster, Nemes past her frozen siblings and the sculptures of Pax troopers and Spectrum citizens, into the adobe city.

It took her literally no time at all to find the house with the hand-cuffed Pax trooper asleep in the corner bedroom facing the canal. She rummaged through the downloaded Pax Base Bombasino files to identify the sleeping trooper—a Lusian named Gerrin Pawtz, thirty-eight standard years old, a lazy, initiative-free alcohol addict, two years away from retirement, six demotions and three sentences to brigtime in his file, assignments relegated to garrison duty and the most mundane base tasks—and then she deleted the file. The trooper was of no interest to her.

Checking once to make sure that the house was empty, Rhadamanth Nemes dropped out of phase shift and stood a moment in the bedroom. Sound and movement returned: the snoring of the handcuffed trooper, movement of pedestrians along the canal walk, a soft breeze stirring white curtains, the rumble of distant traffic, and even the samurai-armor rustles of the Pax troopers jogging through adjoining streets and alleys in their useless search.

Standing over the Pax trooper, Nemes extended her hand and first finger as if pointing at the man's neck. A needle emerged from under her fingernail and extended the ten centimeters to the sleeping man's neck, sliding under the skin and flesh with only the slightest speck of blood to show the intrusion. The trooper did not wake.

Nemes withdrew the needle and examined the blood within: dangerous levels of $C_{27}H_{45}OH$—Lusians frequently were at risk from high cholesterol—as well as a low platelet count suggesting the presence of incipient immune thrombocytopenic purpura, probably brought about by the trooper's early years in hard-radiation environments on any of several garrison worlds, a blood alcohol level of 122 mg/100 ml—the trooper was drunk, although his alcoholic past probably allowed him to hide most of the effects—and—voilà!—the presence of the artificial opiate called ultramorph mixed with heightened levels of caffeine. Nemes smiled. Someone had drugged the trooper with sleep-inducing amounts of ultramorph mixed with tea or coffee—but had done so while taking care to keep the levels below a dangerous overdose.

She sniffed the air. Nemes's ability to detect and identify distinct airborne organic molecules—that is, her sense of smell—was about three times more sensitive than a typical gas chromatograph mass spectrometer's: in other words, somewhere above that of the Old Earth canine called a bloodhound. The room was filled with the distinctive scents of many people. Some of the smells were old; a few were very recent. She identified the Lusian trooper's alcoholic stink, several subtle, musky female scents, the molecular imprint of at least two children—one deeply into puberty and the other younger but afflicted with some cancer requiring chemotherapy— and two adult males, one bearing the distinct sweat impressions of the diet of this planet, the other being at once familiar and alien. Alien because the man still carried the scent of a world Nemes had never visited, familiar because it was the distinctive human smell she had filed away: Raul Endymion still carrying the scent of Old Earth with him.

Nemes walked from room to room, but there was no hint of the peculiar scent she had encountered four years earlier of the girl named Aenea, nor the antiseptic android smell of the servant called A. Bettik. Only Raul Endymion had been here. But he had been here only moments before.

Nemes followed the scent trail to the trapdoor beneath the hall flooring. Ripping the door open despite its multiple locks, she paused before descending the ladder. She squirted the information on the common band, not receiving a responding ping from Gyges, who was probably phaseshifted. It had been only ninety seconds since they left the ship. Nemes smiled. She could ping Gyges, and he would be here before Raul Endymion and the others in the tunnel below had taken another ten heartbeats.

But Rhadamanth Nemes would like to settle this score alone. Still smiling, she jumped into the hole and dropped eight meters to the tunnel floor below.

The tunnel was lighted. Nemes sniffed the cool air, separating the adrenaline-rich scent of Raul Endymion from the other human odors. The Hyperion-born fugitive was nervous. And he had been ill or injured— Nemes picked up the underlying smell of sweat tinged with ultramorph. Endymion had certainly been the offworlder treated by Dr. Molina and someone had used painkillers prescribed for him on the hapless Lusian trooper.

Nemes phase-shifted and began jogging down a tunnel now filled with thickened light. No matter how much of a head start Endymion and his allies had on her, she would catch them now. It would have pleased Nemes to slice the troublemaker's head off while she was still phase-shifted—the decapitation seeming supernatural to the real-time onlookers, performed by an invisible executioner—but she needed information from Raul Endymion. She did not need him conscious, however. The simplest plan would be to pluck him away from his Spectrum Helix friends, surrounding him with the same phased field that protected Nemes, drive a needle into his brain to immobilize him, return him to the dropship, stow him in the resurrection crèche there, and then go through the charade of thanking Colonel Vinara and Commander Solznykov for their help. They could "interrogate" Raul Endymion once their ship had left orbit: Nemes would run microfibers into the man's brain, extracting RNA and memories at will. Endymion would never regain consciousness: when she and her siblings had learned what they needed from his memories, she would terminate him and dump the body into space. The goal was to find the child named Aenea.

Suddenly the lights went out.

While I am phase-shifted, thought Nemes. *Impossible.* Nothing could happen that quickly.

She skidded to a halt. There was no light at all in the tunnel, nothing she could amplify. She switched to infrared, scanning the passageway ahead and behind her. Empty. She opened her mouth and emitted a sonar scream, turning quickly to do the same behind her. Emptiness, the ultra-sound shriek echoing back off the ends of the tunnel. She modified the field around her to blast a deep radar pulse in both directions. The tunnel was empty, but the deep radar recorded mazes of similar tunnels for kilometers in all directions. Thirty meters ahead, beyond a thick metal door, there was an underground garage with an assortment of vehicles and human forms in it.

Still suspicious, Nemes dropped out of phase shift for an instant to see how the lights could have gone out in a microsecond.

The form was directly in front of her. Nemes had less than a ten thousandth of a second to phase-shift again as four bladed fists struck her with the force of a hundred thousand pile drivers. She was driven back the length of the tunnel, through the splintering ladder, through the tunnel wall of solid rock, and deep into the stone itself.

The lights stayed out.

IN THE TWENTY standard days during which the Grand Inquisitor stayed on Mars, he learned to hate it far more than he thought he could ever hate Hell itself.

The *simoom* planetary dust storm blew every day he was there. Despite the fact that he and his twenty-one-person team had taken over the Governor's Palace on the outskirts of the city of St. Malachy, and despite the fact that the palace was theoretically as hermetically sealed as a Pax spaceship, its air filtered and boosted and refiltered, its windows consisting of fifty-two layers of high-impact plastic, its entrances more air-lock seals than doors, the Martian dust got in.

When John Domenico Cardinal Mustafa took his needle shower in the morning, the dust he had accumulated in the night ran in red rivulets of mud into the shower drain. When the Grand Inquisitor's valet helped him pull on his cassock and robes in the morning—all of the clothing fresh-cleaned during the night—there were already traces of red grit in the silken folds. As Mustafa ate breakfast—alone in the Governor's dining room—grit ground between his molars. During the Holy Office interviews and interrogations held in the echoing great ballroom of the palace, the Grand Inquisitor could feel the dust building up in his ankle hose and collar and hair and under his perfectly manicured fingernails.

Outside, it was ridiculous. Skimmers and Scorpions were grounded. The spaceport operated only a few hours of the day, during the rare lulls in the *simoom*. Parked ground vehicles soon became humps and drifts of red sand, and even Pax-quality filters could not keep the red particles out of the engines and motors and solid-state modules. A few ancient crawlers and rovers and fusion rocket shuttles kept food and information flowing to and from the capital, but to all intents and purposes, the Pax government and military on Mars had come to a standstill.

It was on the fifth day of the *simoom* that reports came in of Palestinian attacks on Pax bases on the Tharsis Plateau. Major Piet, the Governor's laconic groundforce commander, took a company of mixed Pax and Home Guard troopers and set out in crawlers and tracked APCs. They were ambushed a hundred klicks short of the plateau approach and only Piet and half his command returned to St. Malachy.

By the second week, reports came in of Palestinian attacks on a dozen garrison posts in both hemispheres. All contact was lost with the Hellas contingent and the south polar station radioed the *Jibril* that it was preparing to surrender to the attacking forces.

Governor Clare Palo—working out of a small office that had belonged to one of her aides—conferred with Archbishop Robeson and the Grand Inquisitor and released tactical fusion and plasma weapons to the beleaguered garrisons. Cardinal Mustafa agreed to the use of the *Jibril* as a weapons' platform in the struggle against the Palestinians, and South Polar One was slagged from orbit. The Home Guard, Pax, Fleet Marines, Swiss Guard, and Holy Office commands concentrated on making sure that the capital of St. Malachy, its cathedral, and the Governor's Palace were secure from attack. In the relentless dust storm, any indigenie that approached within eight klicks of the city perimeter and who was not wearing a Pax-issued transponder was lanced and the bodies recovered later. A few were Palestinian guerrillas.

"The *simoom* can't last forever," grumbled Commander Browning, the head of the Holy Office security forces.

"It can last another three to four standard months," said Major Piet, his upper torso bulky in a burncast. "Perhaps longer."

The work of the Holy Office Inquisition was going nowhere: the milita troopers who had first discovered the massacre in Arafat-kaffiyeh were interviewed again under Truthtell and neuroprobe, but their stories remained the same; the Holy Office forensic experts worked with the coroners at St. Malachy's Infirmary only to confirm that none of the 362 corpses could be resurrected—the Shrike had ripped out every node and millifiber of their cruciforms; queries were sent back to Pacem via instantaneous-drive drone regarding the identities of the victims and—more importantly—the nature of the *Opus Dei* operations on Mars and the reasons for the advanced spaceport, but when a drone returned after fourteen local days, it brought only the IDs of the murdered and no explanation of their connection to *Opus Dei* or the motives for that organization's efforts on Mars.

After fifteen days of dust storm, more reports of continued Palestinian attacks on convoys and garrisons, and long days of interrogation and evidence sifting that led nowhere, the Grand Inquisitor was happy to hear Captain Wolmak call on secure tightbeam from the *Jibril* to announce that there was an emergency that would require the Grand Inquisitor and his entourage to return to orbit as soon as possible.

THE *JIBRIL* WAS one of the newest archangel-class starships, and it looked functional and deadly to Cardinal Mustafa as their dropships closed the last few kilometers to rendezvous. The Grand Inquisitor knew little about Pax warships, but even he could see that Captain Wolmak had morphed the starship to battle readiness: the various booms and sensor arrays had been drawn in beneath the starship's skin, the bulge of the Gideon drive had sprouted laser-reflective armor, and the various weapons' portals were cleared for action. Behind the archangel, Mars turned—a dust-shrouded disc the color of dried blood. Cardinal Mustafa hoped that this would be his last view of the place.

Father Farrell pointed out that all eight of the Mars System Task Force's torchships were within five hundred klicks of the *Jibril*—a tight, defensive grouping by space-going standards—and the Grand Inquisitor realized that something serious was in the offing.

Mustafa's dropship was the first to dock and Wolmak met them in the air-lock antechamber. The interior containment field gave them gravity.

"My apologies for interrupting your Inquisition, Your Excellency . . ." began the captain.

"Never mind that," said Cardinal Mustafa, shaking sand from the folds of his robe. "What is so important, Captain?"

Wolmak blinked at the entourage emerging from the air lock behind the Grand Inquisitor: Father Farrell, of course, followed by Security Commander Browning, three Holy Office aides, Marine Sergeant Nell Kasner, the resurrection chaplain Bishop Erdle, and Major Piet, the former groundforce commander whom Cardinal Mustafa had liberated from Governor Palo's service.

The Grand Inquisitor saw the captain's hesitation. "You can speak freely, Captain. All in this group have been cleared by the Holy Office."

Wolmak nodded. "Your Excellency, we have found the ship."

Cardinal Mustafa must have stared his incomprehension.

"The heavy-duty freighter that must have left Mars orbit the day of the massacre, Your Excellency," continued the captain. "We knew that their dropships had rendezvoused with *some* ship that day."

"Yes," said the Grand Inquisitor, "but we assumed that it would be long gone—translated to whatever star system it was bound for."

"Yes, sir," said Wolmak, "but on the off chance that the ship had never spun up to C-plus, I had the dropships do an in-system search. We found the freighter in the system's asteroid belt."

"Was that its destination?" asked Mustafa.

The captain was shaking his head. "I think not, Excellency. The freighter is cold and dead. It's tumbling. Our instruments show no life on board, no systems powered up . . . not even the fusion drive."

"But it *is* a starship freighter?" questioned Father Farrell.

Captain Wolmak turned toward the tall, thin man. "Yes, Father. The H.H.M.S. *Saigon Maru*. A three-million-ton ore and bulk freighter that's seen service since the days of the Hegemony."

"Mercantilus," the Grand Inquisitor said softly.

Wolmak looked grim. "Originally, Your Excellency. But our records show that the *Saigon Maru* was decommissioned from the Mercantilus fleet and rendered into scrap metal eight standard years ago."

Cardinal Mustafa and Father Farrell exchanged glances.

"Have you boarded the ship yet, Captain?" asked Commander Browning.

"No," said Wolmak. "Because of the political implications, I thought it best if His Excellency were aboard and authorized such a search."

"Very good," said the Grand Inquisitor.

"Also," said Captain Wolmak, "I wanted the full complement of Marines and Swiss Guard troopers aboard first."

"Why is that, sir?" asked Major Piet. His uniform looked bulky over his burncast.

"Something's not right," said the captain, looking at the Major and then at the Grand Inquisitor. "Something's very much not right."

MORE THAN TWO hundred light-years from Mars System, Task Force GID-EON was completing its task of destroying Lucifer.

The seventh and final Ouster system in their punitive expedition was the hardest to finish off. A yellow G-type star with six worlds, two of them inhabitable without terraforming, the system was crawling with Ousters:

military bases out beyond the asteroids, birthing rocks in the asteroid belt, angel environments around the innermost water world, refueling depots in low orbit around the gas giant, and an orbital forest being grown between what would have been the orbits of Venus and Old Earth in the Old Sol System. It took GIDEON ten standard days to search out and kill a majority of these nodes of Ouster life.

When they were done, Admiral Aldikacti called for a physical conference of the seven captains aboard His Holiness's Ship *Uriel* and revealed that the plans had been changed: the expedition had been so successful that they would seek out new targets and continue the attack. Aldikacti had dispatched a Gideon-drive drone to Pacem System and received permission to extend the mission. The seven archangels would translate to the nearest Pax base, Tau Ceti System, where they would be rearmed, refitted, refueled, and joined by five new archangels. Probes had already targeted a dozen new Ouster systems, none of which had yet received news of the massacre along Task Force GIDEON's swath of destruction. Counting resurrection time, they would be attacking again within ten standard days.

The seven captains returned to their seven ships and prepared for the translation from Target System Lucifer to Tau Ceti Center Base.

Aboard H.H.S. *Raphael,* Commander Hoagan "Hoag" Liebler was uneasy. Besides his official capacity as executive officer of the starship, second in command to Father Captain de Soya, Liebler was paid to spy on the father-captain and to report any suspicious behavior—first to the chief of Holy Office Security aboard Admiral Aldikacti's flagship, the *Uriel,* and then—as far as the Executive Officer could tell—all the way up the chain of command to the legendary Cardinal Lourdusamy. Liebler's problem at the moment was that he was suspicious but could not articulate the cause for his suspicions.

The spy could hardly tightbeam the *Uriel* with the dangerous news that the crew of Father Captain de Soya's *Raphael* had been going to confession too frequently, but that was precisely one of the causes of Liebler's concern. Of course, Hoag Liebler was not a spy by training or inclination: he was a gentleman of reduced circumstances, forced first by financial constraints to exercise a Renaissance Minor gentleman's option of joining the military, and then constrained further—by loyalty to his Pax and Church, he convinced himself, more than by the constant need for money to reclaim and restore his estates—into spying on his captain.

The confessions were not all that out of the ordinary—the crew was made up of faithful, Church- and confession-going born-again Christian soldiers, of course, and the circumstances in which they found themselves, the possibility of a true and eternal death if one of the Ouster fusion weapons or k-beams made it through defensive containment fields, certainly added to the urgency of that faith—but Liebler sensed some extra factor at work in all these confessions since Target System Mammon. During the lulls in the vicious fighting here in Target System Lucifer, the entire crew and Swiss Guard complement of the *Raphael*—some twenty-seven hands in all, not counting the bewildered Executive Officer—had been cycling through the confessional like spacers at an Outback port whorehouse.

And the confessional was the one place at which even the ship's Executive Officer could not linger and eavesdrop.

Liebler could not imagine what conspiracy could possibly be afoot. Mutiny made no sense. First, it was unthinkable—no crew in the nearly three centuries of Pax Fleet had ever mutinied nor come close to mutiny. Second, it was absurd—mutineers did not flock to the confessional to discuss the sin of a planned mutiny with the captain of the ship.

Perhaps Father Captain de Soya was recruiting these men and women for some nefarious deed, but Hoag Liebler could not imagine anything the priest-captain could offer that would suborn these loyal Pax spacers and Swiss Guard troopers. The crew did not like Hoag Liebler—he was used to being disliked by classmates and shipmates, it was the curse of his natural-born aristocracy, he knew—but he could not imagine them banding together to plan some evil deed directed his way. If Father Captain de Soya had somehow seduced this crew into treason, the worst they could do was attempt to steal the archangel—Liebler suspected that this remote possibility was the reason he had been placed aboard as a spy—but to what end? *Raphael* was never out of touch with the other archangels in the GIDEON Task Force, except for the instant of C-plus translation and the two days of hurried resurrection, so if the crew turned traitor and attempted to steal the ship, the other six archangels would cut them down in an instant.

The thought made Hoag Liebler physically queasy. He disliked dying, and did not wish to do so more than necessary. Moreover, it would not help his career as a restored Lord of the Manor on Renaissance Minor if his service duty was remembered as being a part of the Crew That Turned Treasonous. It was possible, he realized, that Cardinal Lourdusamy—or whoever was at the apex of his espionage food chain—might have him tortured, excommunicated, and executed to the true death along with the rest of the crew just to conceal the fact that the Vatican had put a spy aboard.

This thought made Hoag Liebler more than queasy.

He consoled himself with the thought that such an act of treason was not just unlikely, it was insane. It was not like the old days on Old Earth or some other water world that Liebler had read about where an ocean going warship goes rogue and turns pirate, preying on merchant ships and terrorizing ports. There was nowhere for a stolen archangel to run to, nowhere to hide, and nowhere to rearm and refit the ship. Pax Fleet would have their guts for garters.

Commander Hoag Liebler continued to feel queasy and uneasy despite all this forced logic.

He was on the flight deck four hours into their spinup to the translation point to Tau Ceti System when the priority squirt came in from *Uriel*: five Ouster torchship-class destroyers had been hiding in the charged-particle dust torus of the inner moon of the outer gas giant and were now making a run toward their own translation points, using the G-type sun as a shield between them and the GIDEON Task Force. The *Gabriel* and the *Raphael* were to deviate from their translation arcs enough to find a firing trajectory for their remaining C-plus hyperkinetic missiles, destroy the torchships, and then to resume their exits from Lucifer System. *Uriel* estimated that the two archangels could spin up to translation about eight hours after the other five ships had departed.

Father Captain de Soya acknowledged the squirt and ordered a change of course, and Commander Liebler monitored the tightbeam traffic as Mother Captain Stone aboard *Gabriel* did likewise. *The Admiral isn't leaving* Raphael *behind alone,* thought the Executive Officer. *My masters aren't the only ones that don't trust de Soya.*

It was not an exciting chase—not actually a chase at all, when it came down to it. Given the gravitational dynamics of this system, it would take the old Hawking-drive Ouster torchships about fourteen hours to reach relativistic velocities prior to spinup. The two archangels would be in firing position within four hours. The Ousters had no weapons that could reach all the way across this system to hurt the archangels: both *Gabriel* and *Raphael* had enough weaponry in their depleted stock to destroy the torchships a dozen times over. If all else failed, they would use the hated deathbeams.

Commander Liebler had the con—the priest-captain had gone to his cubby to catch a few hours of sleep—when the two archangels cleared the sun for a firing solution. The rest of Task Force GIDEON had long since translated. Liebler turned in his acceleration chair to buzz the captain when suddenly the blast portal irised and Father Captain de Soya and several others stepped in. For a moment Liebler forgot his suspicions—forgot even that he had been paid to *be* suspicious—as he goggled at the unlikely group. Besides the captain, there was that Swiss Guard sergeant—Gregorius—and two of his troopers. Also in attendance were Weapons Systems Officer (WHIZZO) Commander Carel Shan, Energy Systems Officer (ESSO) Lieutenant Pol Denish, Environmental Systems Officer (VIRO) Commander Bettz Argyle, and Propulsion Systems Engineer (GOPRO) Lieutenant Elijah Hussein Meier.

"What in the hell . . ." began Executive Officer (XO) Liebler and then stopped. The Swiss Guard sergeant was holding a neural stunner and it was aimed at Liebler's face.

Hoag Liebler had been carrying a concealed flechette pistol in his boot for weeks, but he forgot about it completely at this moment. He had never had a weapon aimed at him before—not even a stunner—and the effect of it made him want to urinate down his own pant leg. He concentrated on not doing that. This left little room to concentrate on anything else.

One of the female troopers came over and lifted the pistol out of his boot. Liebler stared at it as if he had never seen it before.

"Hoag," said Father Captain de Soya, "I'm sorry about this. We took a vote and decided that there was no time to try to convince you to join us. You're going to have to go away for a while."

Summoning up all the dialogue he had ever heard from holodramas, Liebler began blustering. "You'll never get away with this. The *Gabriel* will destroy you. You'll all be tortured and hanged. They'll rip your cruciforms right out of your . . ."

The stunner in the giant sergeant's hand hummed. Hoag Liebler would have gone facedown onto the deck if the female trooper had not caught him and lowered him carefully to the deckplates.

Father Captain de Soya took his place in the command chair. "Break away from this course," he said to Lieutenant Meier at the helm. "Set in our translation coordinates. Full emergency acceleration. Go to full combat readiness." The priest-captain glanced down at Liebler. "Put him in his resurrection crèche and set it to 'store.' "

The troopers carried out the sleeping man.

EVEN BEFORE FATHER Captain de Soya ordered the ship's internal containment field set to zero-g for battle stations, the priest-captain had that brief but exhilarating sense of flying one feels in the instant after having jumped off a cliff before gravity reasserts its absolute imperatives. In truth, their ship was now groaning under more than six hundred gravities of fusion acceleration, almost 180 percent of normal high boost. Any interruption in the containment field would kill them in less than an instant. But the translation point was now less than forty minutes away.

De Soya was not sure what he was doing was right. The thought of being a traitor to his Church and Pax Fleet was the most terrible thing in the world to him. But he knew that if he did indeed have an immortal soul, he had no other choice in the matter.

Actually, what made Father Captain de Soya think that a miracle might be involved—or at least that a very improbable stroke of luck had occurred—was the fact that seven others had agreed to come along with him in this doomed mutiny. Eight, including himself, out of a crew of twenty-eight. The other twenty were sleeping off neural stuns in their resurrection crèches. De Soya knew that the eight of them could handle *Raphael*'s systems and tasks under most circumstances: he was lucky—or blessed—that several of the essential flight officers had come along. In the beginning, he thought it was going to be Gregorius, his two young troopers, and himself.

The first suggestion of mutiny had come from the three Swiss Guard soldiers after their "cleansing" of the second birthing asteroid in Lucifer System. Despite their oaths to the Pax, the Church, and the Swiss Guard, the slaughter of infants had been too much like murder for them. Lancers Dona Foo and Enos Delrino had first gone to their sergeant, and then come with Gregorius to Father Captain de Soya's confessional with their plan to defect. Originally, they had asked for absolution if they decided to jump ship in the Ouster system. De Soya had asked them to consider an alternate plan.

The Propulsion Systems Engineer Lieutenant Meier had come to confession with the same concerns. The wholesale slaughter of the beautiful forcefield angels—which he had watched in tactical space—had sickened the young man and made him want to return to his ancestral religions of Judaism and Islam. Instead, he had gone to confession to admit his spiritual weakening. Father Captain de Soya had amazed Meier by telling him that his concerns were not in conflict with true Christianity.

In the days that followed, Environmental Systems Officer Commander Bettz Argyle and Energy Systems Officer Lieutenant Pol Denish followed their consciences to the confessional. Denish was among the hardest to convince, but long, whispered conversations with his cubby-mate, Lieutenant Meier, brought him along.

WHIZZO Commander Carel Shan was the last to join: the Weapons Systems Officer could no longer authorize deathbeam attacks. He had not slept in three weeks.

De Soya had realized during their last day in Lucifer System that none of the other officers was about to defect. They saw their work as distasteful but necessary. When push came to shove, he realized, the majority of flight officers and the remaining three Swiss Guard troopers would have sided with XO Hoag Liebler. Father Captain de Soya and Sergeant Gregorius decided not to give them the chance.

"The *Gabriel* is hailing us, Father Captain," said Lieutenant Denish. The ESSO was plugged into comtact as well as into his energy systems' console.

De Soya nodded. "Everyone make sure your couch crèches are active." It was an unnecessary order, he knew. Every crew member went into battle stations or C-plus translation in his or her acceleration couch, each rigged as an automated resurrection crèche.

Before jacking into tactical, de Soya checked their trajectory on the center pit display. They were pulling away from *Gabriel,* although the other archangel had gone to three hundred gravities of boost and had altered course to parallel *Raphael*'s. Across Lucifer's solar system, the five Ouster torchships were still crawling toward their own translation points. De Soya wished them well, knowing all the while that the only reason the ships still existed was the momentary distraction *Raphael*'s puzzling course change had caused for *Gabriel.* He plugged into command tactsim.

Instantly he was a giant standing in space. The six worlds and countless moons and nascent, burning orbital forests of Lucifer spread out at his belt level. Far beyond the burning sun, the six Ouster motes balanced on tiny fusion tails. *Gabriel*'s tail was much longer; *Raphael*'s the longest yet, its brilliance rivaling the central star's. Mother Captain Stone stood waiting a few giant's paces from de Soya.

"Federico," she said, "what in Christ's name are you doing?"

De Soya had considered not answering *Gabriel*'s hail. If it would have offered them a few more minutes, he would have stayed silent. But he knew Stone. She would not hesitate. On a separate tactical channel, he glanced at the translation plot. Thirty-six minutes to shift point.

Captain! Four missile launches detected! Translating . . . now! It was WHIZZO Commander Shan on the secure conduction line.

Father Captain de Soya felt sure that he had not visibly jumped or reacted in front of Mother Captain Stone in tactical. On his own bone line, he subvocalized, *It's all right, Carel. I can see them on tac. They've translated toward the Ouster ships.* To Stone, he said on tactical, "You've launched against the Ousters."

Stone's face was tight even in simlight. "Of course. Why haven't you, Federico?"

Rather than answer, de Soya stepped closer to the central sun and watched the missiles emerge from Hawking drive immediately in front of the six Ouster torchships. They detonated within seconds: two fusion, followed by two broader plasma. All of the Ousters had their defensive containment fields to maximum—an orange glow in tactical sim—but the close-range bursts overloaded all of them. The images went from orange to red to white and then three of the ships simply ceased to exist as material objects. Two became scattered fragments tumbling toward the now infinitely distant translation points. One torchship remained intact, but its containment field dropped away and its fusion tail disappeared. If anyone aboard had survived the blast effects, they were now dead of the sleet storm of undeflected radiation that was tearing through the ship.

"What are you doing, Federico?" repeated Mother Captain Stone.

De Soya knew that Stone's first name was Halen. He chose not to make his part of the conversation personal. "Following orders, Mother Captain."

Even in tactsim, Stone's expression was dubious. "What are you talking about, Father Captain de Soya?" Both knew that the conversation was being recorded. Whoever survived the next few minutes would have a record of the exchange.

De Soya kept his voice steady. "Admiral Aldikacti's flagship tightbeamed us with a change of orders ten minutes before the flagship translated. We are carrying out those orders."

Stone's expression was impassive, but de Soya knew that she was subvocalizing her XO to confirm that there had been a tightbeam transmission between *Uriel* and *Raphael* at that time. There had been. But the substance of it had been trivial: updating rendezvous coordinates for the Tau Ceti System.

"What were the orders, Father Captain de Soya?"

"They were eyes-only, Mother Captain Stone. They do not concern the *Gabriel*." On the bone circuit, he said to WHIZZO Shan, *Lock on deathbeam coordinates and give me the actuator as discussed.* A second later he felt the tactsim weight of an energy weapon in his right hand. The gun was invisible to Stone, but perfectly tactile to de Soya. He tried to make his hand on the butt of the weapon look relaxed as his finger curled around the invisible trigger. De Soya could tell from the casual way that Mother Captain Stone's arm hung free from her body that she was also carrying a virtual weapon. They stood about three meters apart in tactsim space. Between them, *Raphael*'s long fusion tail and *Gabriel*'s shorter pillar of flame climbed toward chest height from the plane of the ecliptic.

"Father Captain de Soya, your new translation point will not take you to Tau Ceti System as ordered."

"Those orders were superseded, Mother Captain." De Soya was watching his former first officer's eyes. Halen was always good at concealing her emotions and intentions. He had lost to her in poker on more than one occasion on their old torchship, *Balthasar*.

"What is your new destination, Father Captain?"

Thirty-three minutes to shift point.

"Classified, Mother Captain. I can tell you this—*Raphael* will be rejoining the task force in Tau Ceti System after our mission is completed."

With her left hand, Stone rubbed her cheek. De Soya watched the curled finger of her right hand. She would not have to raise the invisible handgun to trigger the deathbeam, but it was human instinct to aim the firearm at one's opponent.

De Soya hated deathbeams and he knew that Stone did as well. They were cowardly weapons: banned by Pax Fleet and the Church until this expeditionary force incursion. Unlike the old Hegemony-era deathwands that actually cast a scythelike beam of neural disruption, no coherent projection was involved in the ship-to-target deathbeam. Essentially, the powerful Gideon-drive accumulators extended a C-plus distortion of space/time within a finite cone. The result was a subtle twisting of the real-time matrix—similar to a failed translation into the old Hawking-drive space—but more than enough to destroy the delicate energy dance that was a human brain.

But however much Stone held the Pax Fleet officer's hatred of deathbeams, it made sense for her to use it now. The *Raphael* represented a staggering investment of Pax funds: her first goal would be to stop the crew from stealing it without damaging the ship. Her problem, however, was that killing the crew with deathbeams probably would not stop *Raphael* from translating, depending upon how much of the spinup had been preprogrammed by her crew. It was traditional for a captain to make the actual translation manually—or at least to be ready to override the ship's computer with a dead-man switch—but Stone had no assurance that de Soya would follow tradition.

"Please let me speak to Commander Liebler," said Mother Captain Stone.

De Soya smiled. "My executive officer is attending to duties." He thought, *So Hoag was the spy. This is the confirmation we needed.*

Gabriel could not catch them now, not even by accelerating to six hundred gravities herself. *Raphael* would have reached translation requirements before the other ship could get within tow range. No, to stop them, Stone would have to kill the crew and then disable the ship by using the last of her physical arsenal to overload *Raphael*'s external containment fields. If she was wrong—if de Soya *was* acting under last-minute orders—she would almost certainly be court-martialed and expelled from Pax Fleet. If she did nothing, and de Soya was stealing one of the Pax's archangels, Stone would be court-martialed, expelled, excommunicated, and almost certainly executed.

"Federico," she said softly, "please reduce thrust so that we can match velocities. You can still follow orders and spin up to your secret coordinates. I ask only that I board the *Raphael*, and confirm that everything is all right before you translate."

De Soya hesitated. He could not use the guise of orders for his precipitous departure under six hundred gravities, since wherever *Raphael* ended up, there would be two days of slow resurrection for the crew before the mission could continue. He watched Stone's eyes while also checking the tiny image of *Gabriel* on its three-hundred-gravity pillar of white fire. She might try overloading his fields with a salvo of her remaining conventional weaponry. De Soya had no wish to return missile or lance fire: a vaporized *Gabriel* was not acceptable. He was now a traitor to Church and state, but he had no intention of becoming a true-death murderer.

The deathbeams it had to be then.

"All right, Halen," he said easily. "I'll tell Hoag to drop to two-hundred-g's long enough for you to come alongside." He turned his head as if concentrating on issuing bone-channel orders.

His hand must have twitched. Stone's did as well, the invisible handgun rising a bit as her finger tightened on the trigger.

In the split second before the disruption struck, Father Captain de Soya saw the eight sparks leaving the simtact *Gabriel*: Stone was taking no chances—she would vaporize *Raphael* rather than have it escape.

The mother-captain's virtual image flew backward and evaporated as the deathbeam tore into her ship, severing all com connections as the humans aboard died.

Less than a second later, Father Captain de Soya felt himself jerked out of simspace as the neurons in his brain literally fried. Blood flew from his eyes, mouth, and ears, but the priest-captain was already dead, as was every conscious entity on the *Raphael*—Sergeant Gregorius and his two troopers on C deck, GOPRO Meier, VIRO Argyle, ESSO Denish, and WHIZZO Shan on the flight deck.

Sixteen seconds later, the eight Hawking-drive missiles flashed into real space and detonated on every side of the silent *Raphael*.

GYGES WATCHED IN real-time as Raul Endymion said good-bye to the family in red robes and paddled his kayak toward the farcaster arch. The world was in dual lunar eclipse. Fireworks exploded above the canal-river and strange ululations came from thousands of throats back in the linear city. Gyges stood and prepared to walk out across the water to pluck the man from his kayak. It had been agreed that if Raul Endymion was alone, that he needed to be kept alive for interrogation in the starship waiting above—finding the girl Aenea's whereabouts was the goal of this mission—but no one said anything about not making it more difficult for the man to fight or escape. While still phase-shifted, Gyges planned to hamstring Endymion and sever the tendons in his forearms. He could do that instantly, surgically, so that there would be no danger of the human bleeding to death before being stored in the ship's doc-in-the-box before interrogation.

Gyges had jogged the six klicks to the farcaster arch in no time, checking out pedestrians and the strange windcarts as he passed the frozen forms and figures. Once at the arch and concealed in a patch of willows on the canal's high bank, he shifted back to slow time. His job was to guard the back door. Nemes would ping him when she found the missing spacer.

During the twenty minutes of waiting, Gyges communicated with Scylla and Briareus on the internal common band but heard nothing from Nemes. This was surprising. They had all assumed that she would find the missing man within the first few seconds of real-time after she had shifted up. Gyges was not worried—he was not actually capable of worry in the true sense of the word—but he assumed that Nemes had been searching in widening arcs, using up real-time by frequently shifting down and then back up. He assumed that his common-band queries had been made while she was phase-shifted. Added to that was his understanding that while Nemes was a clone-sibling, she had been the first to be devatted. She was less used to common-band sharing than Scylla, Briareus, and he. To be truthful, Gyges would not have minded if their orders had been simply to pull Nemes out of the rock on God's Grove and terminate her then and there.

The river was busy. Each time a ship approached the farcaster arch from either the east or west, Gyges shifted up and walked across the spongy surface of the river to search it and check on its passengers. Some he had to disrobe to ascertain that it was not Endymion or the android, A. Bettik, or the girl, Aenea, in disguise. To be sure, he sniffed them and took needle biopsies of the robed ones' DNA to make sure that they were natives of Vitus-Gray-Balianus B. All were.

After each inspection, he would walk back to the bank and resume his watch. Eighteen minutes after he had left the ship, a Pax skimmer flew around and through the farcaster arch. It would have been tiring for Gyges to have to board it in fast time, but Scylla was already aboard with the searching Pax troopers so he was spared the effort.

This is tiresome, she said on the common band.

Yes, agreed Gyges.

Where is Nemes? It was Briareus back in the city. The clumsy troopers had received their radioed search warrant and were going from house to house.

Haven't heard from her, said Gyges.

It was during the eclipse and the accompanying ceremonial nonsense that he watched the windcycle wagon pull to a halt and Raul Endymion emerge. Gyges was sure that it was Endymion. Not only did the visuals match perfectly, but he picked up the personal scent that Nemes had downloaded to them. Gyges could have phase-shifted immediately, walked over to the frozen tableau, and taken a DNA needle biopsy, but he did not have to. This was their man.

Instead of broadcasting on the common band or pinging Nemes, Gyges waited another minute. This anticipation was pleasurable to him. He did not want to dilute it by sharing it. Besides, he reasoned, it would be better to abduct Endymion after he had separated from the Spectrum Helix family who even now were waving good-bye to the man in the kayak.

Gyges watched while Raul Endymion paddled the absurd little boat out into the current of the widening canal-river. He realized that it would be best to take the kayak as well as Endymion: the watching Spectrum Helix people would be expecting him to disappear if they knew that he was trying to escape via farcaster. From their point of view, there would be a flash and Endymion would have farcast out of sight. In reality, Gyges would still be phase-shifted, now carrying the man and kayak within the expanded phase-shift field. The kayak might also be useful in revealing where the girl Aenea was hiding: telltale planetary scents, methods of man-ufacture.

Along the riverbanks to the north, people cheered and sang. The lunar eclipse was complete. Fireworks exploded above the river and cast baroque shadows on the rusted farcaster arch. Endymion turned his attention away from the waving Spectrum Helix family and concentrated on staying in the strongest current as he paddled toward the farcaster.

Gyges stood, stretched languidly, and prepared to phase-shift.

Suddenly the thing was next to him, centimeters away, at least three meters tall, towering over him.

Impossible, thought Gyges. *I would have sensed the phase-shift dis-tortions.*

Exploding skyrockets spilled bloodred light on the chrome carapace. Metal teeth and chrome spikes twisted the expanding flowers of yellow, white, and red across quicksilver planes. Gyges caught an instant's look at his own reflection, distorted and startled, and then he phase-shifted.

It took less than a microsecond for the shift. Somehow one of the creature's four clawed hands made it into the field before it completely formed. Bladed fingers dug through synflesh and muscle, seeking one of Gyges's hearts.

Gyges paid no heed to the attack but attacked in return, swinging his silvered, phase-shifted arm like a horizontal guillotine. It could have cut through whiskered carbon alloy as if it were wet cardboard. It did not cut through the tall form in front of him. Sparks and thunder exploded as his arm bounced away, fingers numbed, metal radius and ulna shattered.

The clawed hand within him pulled out ropes of intestine, kilometers of microfiber optics. Gyges realized that he had been opened from navel to breastbone. It did not matter. He could still function.

Gyges clenched his right hand into a sharpened bludgeon and thrust it forward into gleaming red eyes. It was a killing blow. But the great steam-shovel jaws opened, closed, faster than phase-shifting, and Gyges's right arm suddenly ended above the wrist.

Gyges threw himself at the apparition, trying to merge fields, attempting to get his own teeth within tearing distance. Two huge hands seized him, the bladed fingers sinking through shift field and flesh to hold him tight. The chrome skull in front of him slashed forward: needle-spikes pierced Gyges's right eye and penetrated the right frontal lobe of his brain.

Gyges screamed then—not out of pain, although he felt something similar for the first time in his short life—but out of pure, relentless rage. His teeth snapped and clacked like steel rendering blades as he sought the creature's throat, but he continued being held at three-arms' length.

Then the monster ripped out both of Gyges's hearts and threw them far out over the water. A nanosecond later, it lunged forward, biting through Gyges's throat and severing his carbon-alloy spinal cord with a single snap of long teeth. Gyges's head was severed from his body. He tried to shift to telemetric control of the still-fighting body, peering through blood and fluid out of his remaining eye and broadcasting over the common band, but the transmitter in his skull had been pierced and the receiver in his spleen had been ripped away.

The world spun—first the corona of the emerging sun around the second moon, then skyrockets, then the color-dappled surface of the river, then the sky again, then darkness. With fading coherence, Gyges realized that his head had been thrown far out into the river. His last retinal image before being submerged in darkness was of his own headless and uselessly spasming body being hugged to the carapace of the creature and being impaled there on spikes and thorns. Then, with a flash, the Shrike phase-shifted out of even fast-time existence and Gyges's head struck the water and sank beneath the dark waves.

RHADAMANTH NEMES ARRIVED five minutes later. She shifted down. The riverbank was empty except for the headless corpse of her sibling. The windcycle wagon and its red-robed family were gone. No boats were visible on this section of river. The sun was beginning to emerge from behind the second moon.

Gyges is here, she sent on the common band. Briareus and Scylla were still with the troops in the city. The sleeping Pax trooper had been found and released from his handcuffs. None of the citizens queried would say whose home it was. Scylla was urging Colonel Vinara to drop the matter.

Nemes felt the discomfort as she left the shift field. All of her ribs—bone and permasteel—were either fractured or bent. Several of her internal organs had been pulped. Her left hand would not function. She had been unconscious for almost twenty standard minutes. Unconscious! She had not lost consciousness for one second in the four years she had lain in the solidified rock of God's Grove. And all this damage had been done *through* the impenetrable shift field.

It did not matter. She would allow her body to repair itself during the days of inactivity after leaving this Core-forsaken world. Nemes knelt next to her sibling's corpse. It had been clawed, decapitated, and eviscerated—almost deboned. It was still twitching, the broken fingers struggling to get a grip on an absent enemy.

Nemes shuddered—not out of sympathy for Gyges or revulsion at the damage done, she was professionally evaluating the Shrike's attack pattern and felt admiration if anything—but out of sheer frustration that she had missed this confrontation. The attack in the tunnel had been too fast for her to react—she had been in mid–phase shift—which she would have thought impossible.

I'll find him, she sent and shifted up. The air grew thick and sludge-like. Nemes went down the bank, forced her way through the thick resistance of the water's surface, and walked out along the riverbed, calling on the common band and probing with deep radar.

She found Gyges's head almost a klick downstream. The current was strong here. Freshwater crustaceans had already eaten the lips and the remaining eye and were probing in the eye sockets. Nemes brushed them away and took the head back to the bank of the canal-river.

Gyges's common-band transmitter was smashed and his vocal cords were gone. Nemes extruded a fiber-optic filament and made the connection directly to his memory center. His skull had been smashed on the left side and brain matter and bits of DNA-processing gel were spilling out.

She did not ask him questions. She phased down and downloaded the memory, squirting it to her remaining two siblings as she received it.

Shrike, sent Scylla.

No shit, Sherlock, sent Briareus.

Silence, ordered Nemes. *Finish up with those idiots. I'll clean things up here and be waiting in the dropship.*

The Gyges head—blind, leaking—was trying to speak, using what remained of its tongue to shape sibilant and glottal syllables. Nemes held it close to her ear.

"Ss-t- pp-le-ssss." *Please.* "Ss—he—puh." *Help.* "Ssss-ttp—m-eh" *Me.*

Nemes lowered the head and studied the body on the splattered bank. Many organs were missing. Scores of meters of microfiber were spilled in the weeds and mud, some trailing away in the current. Gray intestines and neural gelpaks were split and scattered. Bits of bone caught the growing light as the sun emerged from Twice Darkness. Neither the dropship nor the old archangel's doc-in-the-boxes could help the vatborn. And Gyges might take standard months to heal himself.

Nemes set the head down while she wrapped the body in its own microfilaments, weighting it outside and in with stones. Making sure that the river was still free of ships, she tossed the headless corpse far out into the current. She had seen that the river was alive with tough and indiscriminate scavengers. Even so, there were parts of her sibling that they would not find appetizing.

She lifted Gyges's head. The tongue was still clucking. Using the eye sockets as grips for her thumb and forefinger, she threw the head far out over the river in an easy underhand toss. It went under with barely a ripple.

Nemes jogged to the farcaster arch, ripped a hidden access plate free from the rusting and supposedly impenetrable exterior, and extruded a filament from her wrist. She jacked in.

I don't understand, came Briareus's code on the common band. *It opened to nowhere.*

Not to nowhere, sent Nemes, reeling in the filament. *Just to nowhere in the old Web. Nowhere the Core has built a farcaster.*

That's impossible, sent Scylla. *There are no farcasters except for those the Core has built.*

Nemes sighed. Her siblings were idiots. *Shut up and return to the dropship*, she sent. *We have to report this in person. Councillor Albedo will want to download personally.*

Nemes phase-shifted and jogged back to the dropship through air gone thick and sepia with slow-stirred time.

12

DID NOT FORGET that there was a panic button. The problem is simple—when there is real panic, one does not immediately think of buttons.

The kayak was falling into an endless depth of air broken only by clouds that rose tens of thousands of meters from the bruise-purple depths to the milky ceiling of more clouds thousands of meters above me. I had dropped my paddle and watched it tumble away in freefall. The kayak and I were dropping faster than the paddle for reasons of aerodynamics and terminal velocity that were beyond my powers to calculate at that particular moment. Great oval surges of water from the river I had left behind were falling ahead and behind me, separating and shaping themselves into ovoid spheres I had seen in zero-g, but then being whipped apart by the wind. It was as if I were falling in my own localized rainstorm. The flechette pistol I had liberated from the sleeping trooper in Dem Loa's bedroom was wedged between the outside of my thigh and the curved inner seal of the cockpit skirt. My arms were raised as if I were a bird preparing to take flight. My fists were clenched in terror. After my original scream, I found my jaws locked shut, my molars grinding. The fall went on and on.

I had caught a glimpse of the farcaster arch above and behind me, although "arch" was no longer the proper word: the huge device floating unsupported was a metal ring, a torus, a rusty doughnut. For a fleeting second I saw the sky of Vitus-Gray-Balianus B through the glowing ring, and then the image faded and only clouds showed through the receding hoop. It was the only substantial thing in the entire skyscape of clouds and I had already fallen more than a thousand meters below it. In a giddy, panicked moment of fantasy, I imagined that if I were a bird I could fly back up to the farcaster ring, perch on its broad lower arc, and wait for . . .

Wait for what? I gripped the sides of the kayak as it rotated, turning me almost upside down as it plummeted bow first toward the purple depths klicks and klicks below.

That is when I remembered the panic button. *Don't touch it, whatever you do,* Aenea had said when we floated the kayak in Hannibal. *I mean, don't touch it until you absolutely have to.*

The kayak spun on its longitudinal axis again, almost shaking me out. My butt was no longer touching the padded cushion on the bottom of the hull. I was floating free inside the cramped cockpit, within a freefalling constellation of water, tumbling paddle, and plunging kayak. I decided that this qualified as an "absolutely have to" time. I flipped up the plastic cover and depressed the red button with my thumb.

Panels popped open in front of the cockpit, near the bow, and behind me. I ducked as lines and masses of fabric billowed out. The kayak righted itself and then braked so hard that I was almost thrown out. I clung fiercely to the sides of the fiberglass boat as it rocked wildly. The shapeless mass over my head seemed to be forming itself into something more complicated than a parachute. Even in the middle of my adrenaline rush and molar-grinding panic, I recognized the fabric: memory cloth that A. Bettik and I had bought at the Indian Market near Taliesin West. The solar-powered, piezoelectric material was almost transparent, ultralight, ultrastrong, and could remember up to a dozen pre-set configurations; we had considered buying more and using it to replace the canvas over the main architects' studio since the old cover sagged, rotted, and had to be repaired and re-placed regularly. But Mr. Wright had insisted on keeping the old canvas. He preferred the buttery light. A. Bettik had taken the dozen or so meters of memory cloth down to his workshop and I had thought no more of it.

Until now.

The fall was stopped. Now the kayak hung under a delta-shaped parasail, supported by a dozen nylon-10 risers that rose from strategic positions along the upper hull. The boat and I were still descending, but in a gradual swoop now rather than a headlong fall. I looked up—the memory cloth was clear enough to see through—but the farcaster ring was too far behind me and hidden by clouds. The winds and air currents were carrying me away from the farcaster.

I suppose that I should have been grateful to my friends, the girl and the android, for somehow foreseeing this and preparing the kayak appro-priately, but my first thought was an overwhelming *Goddamn you!* This was too much. Being dropped into a world of clouds and air, with no ground, was too damned much. If Aenea had known that I was being 'cast here, why didn't she . . .

No ground? I leaned over the edge of the kayak and looked below. Perhaps the plan was for me to float gently down to some unseen surface.

No. There were kilometers of empty air beneath me, and below that, the lower layers were purple and black, a darkness relieved only by fierce slashes of lightning. The pressure down there must be terrible. Which brought up another point: if this was a Jovian world—Whirl or Jupiter or one of the others—how was it that I was breathing oxygen? As far as I knew, all of the gas giants that humanity had encountered were made up of unfriendly gases—methane, ammonia, helium, carbon monoxide, phosphine, hydrogen cyanide, other nasties, with trace amounts of water. I had never heard of a gas giant with breathable oxygen-nitrogen mix, but I was breathing. The air was thinner here than on the other worlds I had traveled through, and it stank a bit of ammonia, but I was definitely breathing air. Then it must not be a gas giant. Where the hell was I?

I lifted my wrist and spoke to the comlog, "Where the hell am I?"

There was a hesitation and for a moment I thought the thing had been broken on Vitus-Gray-Balianus B. Then it spoke in the ship's supercilious voice, "Unknown, M. Endymion. I have some data, but it is incomplete."

"Tell me."

There followed a rapid-fire listing of temperatures in Kelvin, atmospheric pressure in millibars, estimated mean density in grams per centimeter cubed, probable escape velocity in kilometers per second, and perceived magnetic field in gauss, followed by a long list of atmospheric gases and element ratios.

"Escape velocity of fifty-four point two klicks per second," I said. "That's gas-giant territory, isn't it?"

"Most assuredly," said the ship's voice. "Jovian baseline is fifty-nine point five kilometers per second."

"But the atmosphere isn't like a gas giant's?" I could see the stratocumulus ahead of me building, like a nature holo run at accelerated speeds. The towering cloud must have reached ten klicks above me, its base disappearing in the purple depths below. Lightning flickered at its base. The sunlight on its far side seemed rich and low: evening light.

"The atmosphere is unlike anything in my records," said the comlog. "Carbon monoxide, ethane, acetylene, and other hydrocarbons violating Solmev equilibrium values can be easily explained by Jovian-style molecular kinetic energy and solar radiation breaking down methane, and the presence of carbon monoxide is a standard result of methane and water vapor mixing at deep layers where the temperature exceeds twelve hundred degrees Kelvin, but the oxygen and nitrogen levels . . ."

"Yes?" I prompted.

"Indicate life," said the comlog.

I turned completely around, inspecting the clouds and sky as if something were sneaking up on me. "Life on the surface?" I said.

"Doubtful," came the flat voice. "If this world follows Jovian-Whirl norms, the pressure at the so-called surface would be under seventy million Old Earth atmospheres with a temperature of some twenty-five thousand degrees Kelvin."

"How high are we?" I said.

"Uncertain," said the instrument, "but with the current atmospheric pressure of point seven six Old Earth standard, on a standard Jovian world

I would estimate that we were above the troposphere and tropopause, actually in the lower reaches of the stratosphere."

"Wouldn't it be colder that high? That's almost outer space."

"Not on a gas giant," said the comlog in its insufferable professorial voice. "The greenhouse effect creates a thermal inversion layer, heating layers of the stratosphere to almost human-optimum temperatures. Although the difference of a few thousand meters may show pronounced temperature increases or drops."

"A few thousand meters," I said softly. "How much air is above and below us?"

"Unknown," said the comlog again, "but extrapolation would suggest that equatorial radius from the center of this world to its upper atmosphere would be approximately seventy thousand kilometers with this oxygen-nitrogen-carbon-dioxide layer extending for some three to eight thousand kilometers approximately two thirds of the distance from the planet's hypothetical center."

"A three- to eight-thousand-klick layer," I repeated stupidly. "Some fifty thousand klicks above the surface . . ."

"Approximately," said the comlog, "although it should be noted that at near-core pressures, molecular hydrogen becomes a metal . . ."

"Yeah," I said. "That's enough for now." I felt like I was going to be sick over the side of the kayak.

"I should point out the anomaly that the interesting coloration in the nearby stratocumulus suggests the presence of ammonium monosulfide or polysulfides, although at apotropospheric altitudes, one would assume only the presence of ammonia cirrus clouds with true water clouds not forming until depths reach some ten standard atmospheres because of . . ."

"Enough," I said.

"I only point this out because of the interesting atmospheric paradox involving . . ."

"Shut up," I said.

IT GOT COLD after the sun went down. The sunset itself I shall remember until I die.

High, high above me, glimpses of what might be blue sky had darkened to a Hyperion-like deep lapis and then deepened further to dark purple. The clouds all around me grew brighter as the sky far above and the depths far below both grew darker. I say clouds, but the generic term is laughably unequal to conveying the power and grandeur of what I watched. I grew up in a nomadic shepherd caravan on the treeless moors between Hyperion's Great South Sea and the Pinion Plateau: I know clouds.

Far above me, feathered cirrus and rippled cirrocumulus caught the twilight in a pastel riot of soft pinks, rose glows, violet tinges, and golden backlighting. It was as if I were in a temple with a high, rosy ceiling supported by thousands of irregular columns and pillars. The columns and pillars were towering mountains of cumulus and cumulonimbus, their anvil-shaped bases disappearing in the darkening depths hundreds or thousands of kilometers below my floating kayak, their rounded summits billowing high into the halo-tinged cirrostratus hundreds or thousands of kilometers above me. Each column of cloud caught the low, rich light passing through openings in the cloud many thousands of klicks to the west, and the light seemed to ignite the clouds as if their surfaces were made of wildly flammable material.

"Monosulfide or polysulfides," the comlog had said: well, whatever constituted these tawny cumulus in the diffuse daylight, sunset set them afire with rust-red light, brilliant crimson streaks, bloody tractus streaming away from the main cloud masses like crimson pennants, rose-colored fibratus weaving together the cirrus ceiling like muscle strands under the flesh of a living body, billowing masses of cumulus so white that they made me blink as if snowblinded, golden, striated cirroform spilling out from the boiling cumulonimbus towers like masses of blond hair blowing back from pale, upturned faces. The light deepened, richened, became so intense that it brought tears to my eyes, and then it became even more brilliant. Great, nearly horizontal shafts of Godlight burned between the columns, illuminating some here, casting others into shadow there, passing through ice clouds and bands of vertical rain on their way, spilling hundreds of simple rainbows and a thousand multiple rainbows. Then shadows moved up from the bruise-black depths, shading more and more of the still-writhing billows of cumulus and nimbus, finally climbing into the high cirrus and pond-rippled altocumulus, but at first the shadows brought not grayness or darkness, but an infinite palette of subtleties: gleaming gold dimming to bronze, pure white becoming cream and then dimming to sepia and shade, crimson with the boldness of spilled blood slowly darkening to the rust-red of dried blood, then fading to an autumnal tawny russet. The hull of my kayak lost its glint and the parasail above me quit catching the light as this vertical terminator moved past and above me. Slowly these shadows crept higher—it must have taken at least thirty minutes, although I was too absorbed in watching to check my comlog—and when they reached the cirrus ceiling, it was as if someone had dimmed all the lights in the temple.

It was one hell of a sunset.

I remember blinking then, overwhelmed by the interplay of light and cloud shadow and the oddly disturbing kinetic restlessness of all those broiling cloud masses, ready to rest my eyes while true darkness fell and to gather my thoughts. And that is when the lightning and aurora began playing.

There had been no aurora borealis on Hyperion—or if there had been, I had never seen it. But I had seen an example of Old Earth's northern lights on a peninsula that had once been the Scandinavian Republic while on my round-the-world dropship tour of that planet: they had been shimmering and gooseflesh-producing, rippling and dancing along the northern horizon like the filmy gown of a ghost dancer.

This world's aurora held none of that subtlety. Bands of light, solid striations of light—as discrete and discernible as the keys of a vertical piano—began dancing high in the sky in the direction I thought of as south. Other curtains of green, gold, red, and cobalt began shimmering against the dark world of air beneath me. These grew longer, broader, taller, stretching to meet and blend with other curtains of leaping electrons. It was as if the planet were cutting paper dolls out of shimmering light. Within minutes, every part of the sky was alive and dancing with vertical, slanted, and near-horizontal ribbons of banded color. The cloud towers became visible again, billows and pennants reflecting the strobe of thousands of these cold lights. I could almost hear the hiss and rasp of solar particles being driven along the terrifying lines of magnetic force banding this giant world.

I *could* hear them: crashes, rumbles, snappings, loud pops, long chains of cracking sounds. I swiveled in my little cockpit and leaned over the hull to look straight down. The lightning and thunder had begun.

I had seen enough lightning storms as a child on the moors. On Old Earth, Aenea, A. Bettik, and I regularly used to sit outside her shelter in the evening and watch the great electrical storms move over the mountains to the north. Nothing had prepared me for this.

The depths, as I had called them, had been little more than a dark floor so far below me as to be laughable, a broiling promise of terrible pressures and more terrible heat. But now those depths were alive with light, leaping with lightning storms that moved from one visible horizon to the rest like a chain of nuclear bombs going off. I could imagine entire hemispheres of cities being destroyed in one of those rumbling chain reactions of light. I gripped the side of the kayak and reassured myself that the storms were hundreds of klicks below me.

The lightning moved up the towers of cumulonimbus. Flashes of internal white light vied with the shimmers of colored light from the connecting auroras. The thunder-noise was subsonic, then sonic, subtly terrifying at first, then not subtle, but even more terrifying. The kayak and its parasail bucked and rocked in sudden downdrafts and elevator-quick lifts of thermals. I gripped the sides with mad strength and wished to God that I were on any other world but this.

Then the lightning discharges began flashing from cloud tower to cloud tower.

The comlog and my own reasoning had evaluated the scale of this place—an atmosphere tens of thousands of klicks deep, a horizon so far away that I could have dropped scores of Old Earths or Hyperions between me and the sunset—but the lightning bolts finally convinced me that this was a world made for giants and gods, not for humankind.

The electrical discharges were wider than the Mississippi and longer than the Amazon. I had seen those rivers and I could see these bolts. I *knew*.

I hunkered down in my little cockpit as if that would help me when one of these bolts caught my little flying kayak. The hairs on my forearms were standing straight up and I realized that the crawling sensation I felt on my neck and scalp was precisely that—the hair on my head was writhing like a nest of snakes. The comlog was flashing overload alarms on its diskey plate. It was probably shouting at me as well, but I could not have heard a laser cannon firing ten centimeters from my ear in that maelstrom. The parasail rippled and tore at the risers as heated air and imploding vacuums battered us. At one point, riding the wake of a bolt that blinded me, the kayak swung above horizontal, higher than the parasail. I was sure that the risers were going to collapse, the kayak and I were going to fall into the parasail shroud, and we would fall for minutes—hours—until pressure and heat ended my screaming.

The kayak rocked back, then back again, then continued swinging like a maddened pendulum—but *under* the sail.

In addition to the storm of lightning beneath me, in addition to the rising chain of explosions in every tower of cumulus, in addition to the searing bolts that now laced the towers like a web of firing neurons in a brain gone berserk, bundles of ball lightning and chain lightning suddenly began breaking loose from the clouds and floating in the dark spaces where my kayak flew.

I watched one of these rippling, surging spheres of electricity drift not a hundred meters beneath me: it was the size of a small, round asteroid—an electric moonlet. The noise it made was beyond description, but memories surged unbidden of being caught in a forest fire in the Aquila fens, of the tornado that skipped over our caravan on the moors when I was five years old, of plasma grenades detonating against the great blue glacier on the Claw Iceshelf. No combination of these memories could match the energy violence tumbling along beneath the kayak like some runaway boulder made of blue and gold light.

The storm lasted more than eight hours. Darkness lasted another eight. I survived the first. I slept through the last. When I awoke, shaken and thirsty, filled with dreams of light and noise, still partially deafened, badly needing to urinate and worried about falling out of the cockpit while I knelt to do so, I saw that morning light was painting the opposite side of the cloud pillars that had replaced the temple columns from the night before. Sunrise was simpler than sunset: the brilliant white and gold crawled down from the cirrus ceiling, along the roiling sides of the cumulus and nimbus, down to my layer where I sat shaking from the cold. My skin and clothes and hair were wet. Sometime during that night's bedlam, it had rained on me and rained hard.

I got to my knees on the padded floor of the hull, held tight to the cockpit rim with my left hand, made sure that the kayak's swaying had steadied somewhat, and attended to business. The thin, gold stream glinted in morning light as it dropped into infinity. The depths were black, purple, and inscrutable once again. My lower back hurt and I remembered the kidney stone nightmare of the previous few days. That seemed like another life to me now, long ago and far away. *Well,* I thought, *if there's another tiny stone being passed, I'm not going to catch it today.*

I was buttoning up and settling back into the cockpit, trying to stretch my aching legs without actually falling out, thinking about the impossibility of finding another farcaster ring anywhere in this endless sky after that night of being blown off course—as if I had ever *had* a course—when I suddenly realized that I was not alone.

Living things were rising from the depths and circling around me.

AT FIRST I saw only one creature and had no scale with which to judge the size of the visitor. The thing could have been a few centimeters across and only meters from my floating kayak, or many kilometers across and far, far away. Then the organism swam between a distant cloud pillar and a more distant cumulus tower, and I realized that kilometers was a more reasonable guess of size. As it came closer, I saw the myriad of smaller forms accompanying it through the morning sky.

Before I attempt to describe the things, I have to say that little in the history of humankind's expansion in this arm of the galaxy had prepared us to describe large alien organisms. On the hundreds of worlds explored and colonized during and after the Hegira, most of the indigenous life discovered had been plants and a few very simple organisms, such as the radiant gossamers on Hyperion. The few large, evolved animal forms—the Lantern Mouths on Mare Infinitus, say, or the zeplins of Whirl—tended to be hunted to extinction. The more common result was a world filled with a few indigenous life-forms and a myriad of human-adapted species. Humanity had terraformed all these worlds, bringing its bacteria and earthworms and fish and birds and land animals in raw DNA form, defrosting embryos in the early seedships, building birthing factories in the later expansions. The result had been much as on Hyperion—vital indigenous plants such as the tesla trees and chalma and weirwood and some surviving local insects coexisting with thriving Old Earth transplants and biotailored adapts such as triaspen, everblues, oak trees, mallards, sharks, hummingbirds, and deer. We were not used to alien animals.

And these were definitely alien animals rising to meet me.

The largest one reminded me of the cuttlefish—again, one of Old Earth's adapts—that thrived in the warm shallows of the Great South Sea on Hyperion. This creature was squidlike but almost transparent, its internal organs quite visible, although I admit that it was difficult to determine its exterior from its interior as it pulsed and throbbed and changed shape from second to second, almost like a starship morphing for battle. The thing had no head as such, not even a flattened, squidlike extension that might be considered a head, but I could make out a variety of tentacles, although fronds or filaments might be better words for the constantly swaying, retracting, extending, and quivering appendages. But these filaments were inside the pale, clear body as much as outside, and I was not sure if the creature's movement through the clear air was a result of the swimming motion of the filaments or because of gases expelled as the giant cuttlefish expanded and contracted.

As far as I could recall from old books and Grandam's explanations, the zeplins on Whirl were much simpler in appearance—blimp-shaped gasbags, mere medusalike cells to hold their mix of hydrogen and methane, storing and metabolizing helium in their crude liftsacs, giant jellyfish floating in the hydrogen-ammonia-methane atmosphere of Whirl. As best I could remember, the zeplins ate a sort of atmospheric phytoplankton that floated in the noxious atmosphere like so much airborne manna. There were no predators on Whirl . . . until humans arrived in their floating bathyscaphes to harvest the rarer gases.

As the cuttlefish creature grew closer, I saw the complexity of its innards: pale, pulsing outlines of organs and intestine-looking coils and what might be feeding filaments and tubes that might be for reproduction or elimination, and there were some appendages that might be sex organs, or perhaps eyes. And all the while it folded in on itself, retracted its curling filaments, then pulsed forward, tentacles extended fully, like a squid swimming through clear water. It was five or six hundred meters long.

I began to notice the other things. Around the cuttlefish swarmed hundreds or thousands of golden, disc-shaped creatures, ranging in size from tiny ones perhaps as large as my hand to others larger than the heavy river mantas used to pull barges on Hyperion's rivers. These things were also nearly transparent, although their insides were clouded by a sort of greenish glow that might have been an inert gas excited to luminescence by the animal's own bio-electrical field. These things swarmed around the cuttlefish, at times appearing to be swallowed or absorbed by some orifice or another, only to reappear outside again. I could not swear that I saw the cuttlefish *eating* any of the swarming discs, but at one point I thought that I could see a cloud of the green-glowing things moving along the inside of the cuttlefish's gut like ghostly platelets in a clear vein.

The monster and its cloud of companions floated closer, rising until the sunlight passed through its body on its way to light my kayak and parasail. I revised its size upward—it must be at least a klick long and a third that in width when it expanded to its widest. The living discs floated to each side of me now. I could see that they were spinning as well as curling like mantas.

I tugged out the flechette pistol Alem had given me and clicked off its safety. If the monster attacked, I would fire half the magazine of slivers into its pale side, hoping that it was as thin as it was transparent. Maybe there was a chance that I could spill whatever lift gases allowed it to float in this band of oxygen atmosphere.

At that moment, the thing's hydralike filaments flashed out in all directions, some missing my parasail by mere meters, and I realized that I could never kill or sink the monster before it destroyed my sail with one thrash of one tentacle. I waited, half expecting to be pulled into the cuttle-fish's maw—if it had a maw—at any second.

Nothing happened. My kayak floated in the direction I thought of as westward, the parasail rising on thermals and descending on colder down-drafts, the clouds towering around me, and the cuttlefish and its compan-ions—I thought of them as parasites for no good reason—stood off a few hundred meters to the "north" and a hundred meters or so above me. I wondered if the thing was following me out of curiosity or hunger. I won-dered if the green platelets drifting around me might attack at any moment.

Capable of doing nothing else, I laid the useless flechette pistol on my lap, nibbled on the last of my biscuits from my pack, and sipped from my water bottle. I had less than another day's supply of water. I cursed myself for not trying to catch rainwater during the night's terrible storm, although I had no idea if this world's water was potable.

The long morning grew into a long afternoon. Several times the drift-ing parasail took me into a cloud tower and I raised my face to the dripping fog, licking droplets from my lips and chin. The water tasted like water. Each time I emerged from the fog, I expected the cuttlefish to have de-parted, but each time it remained on station to my right and above me. Once, just after the halo that was the sun above had passed the zenith, the kayak was blown into a particularly rough patch of climbing cloud, and the parasail almost folded in the violent updraft. But it stabilized itself and when I emerged from the cloud that time, I was some kilometers higher. The air was thinner and colder. The cuttlefish had followed me up.

Perhaps it's not hungry yet. Perhaps it feeds after dark. I reassured myself with a series of these thoughts.

I kept scanning the empty sky between clouds for another farcaster ring, but none appeared. It seemed folly to expect to find one—the air currents blew me generally westward but the vagaries of the jet stream sent me klicks north and south. How could I thread such a small needle after a day and night and day of blowing around like this? It did not seem likely. But still I searched the sky.

In midafternoon I realized that there were other living things visible far below to the south. More cuttlefish moving about the base of an im-mense cloud tower, the sunlight piercing the depths enough to illuminate their clear bodies against the black of the broiling depths beneath them. There must be scores—no, hundreds—of the pulsing, swimming things along the base of that one cloud. I was too far away to make out the platelet parasites around them, but a sense of diffused light there—like dust floating—suggested their presence by the thousands or millions. I wondered if the monsters usually kept to the lower atmospheric levels and this one—still keeping pace with me within feeding-filament range—had ventured up out of curiosity.

My muscles were cramping. I pulled myself out of the cockpit and tried stretching along the top of the kayak's hull, hanging on to the parasail risers to keep my balance. It was dangerous, but I had to stretch. I lay on my back and pedaled an imaginary bicycle with my raised legs. I did push-ups, clinging to the rim of the cockpit for balance. When I had worked most of the cramps out, I crawled back into the cockpit and half dozed.

Perhaps it is odd to admit, but my mind wandered all that afternoon, even while the alien cuttlefish swam alongside within swallowing range and alien platelet creatures danced and hovered within meters of the kayak and parasail. The human mind gets used to strangeness very quickly if it does not exhibit interesting behavior.

I began thinking about the past few days and the past months and the past years. I thought of Aenea—of leaving her behind—and of all the other people I had left behind: A. Bettik and the others at Taliesin West, the old poet on Hyperion, Dem Loa and Dem Ria and their family on Vitus-Gray-Balianus B, Father Glaucus in the frozen air tunnels of Sol Draconi Septem, Cuchiat and Chiaku and Cuchtu and Chichticu and the other Chitchatuk on that same world—Aenea had been sure that Father Glaucus and our Chitchatuk friends had been murdered after we left that world, although she had never explained how she could know that—and I thought about others I had left behind, working my way back to my last sight of Grandam and the Clan members waving as I left for Home Guard service many years ago. And always my thoughts returned to leaving Aenea.

I've left too many people. And let too many people do my work and fighting for me. From now on I will fight for myself. If I ever find the girl again, I will stay with Aenea forever. The resolution burned like anger through me, fueled by the hopelessness of finding another farcaster ring in this endless cloudscape.

> YOU KNOW
> THE ONE WHO TEACHES
> SHE HAS TOUCHED
> YOU (!?!?)

The words were not carried by sound nor heard by my ears. Rather, they were like blows to the inside of my skull. I literally reeled, gripping the sides of the kayak to keep from falling out.

> HAVE YOU
> BEEN TOUCHED/CHANGED
> LEARNING
> TO HEAR/SEE/WALK
> FROM
> THE ONE WHO TEACHES
> (????)

Every word was a migraine blow. Each struck with the force of brain hemorrhage. The words were shouted inside my skull in my own voice. Perhaps I was going mad.

Wiping away tears, I peered at the giant cuttlefish and its swarm of green-platelet parasites. The larger organism pulsed, contracted, extended coiling filaments, and swam through the chilly air. I could not believe that these words were coming from that creature. It was too biological. And I did not believe in telepathy. I looked at the swarming discs, but their behavior showed no more sense of higher consciousness than dust motes in a shaft of light—less than the synchronized shifting of a school of fish or the flocking of bats. Feeling foolish, I shouted, "Who are you? Who is speaking?"

I squinted in preparation for the blast of words against my brain, but there was no response from the giant organism or its companions.

"Who spoke?" I shouted into a rising wind. There was no answering sound except for the slap of the risers against the canvas of the parasail.

The kayak slewed to the right, righted itself, and slewed again. I swiveled to my left, half expecting to see another cuttlefish monster attacking me, but instead saw something infinitely more malevolent approaching.

While I had been focusing on the alien creature to the north, a billowing, black cumulus had all but surrounded me to the south. Wind-tattered streamers of black whirled out from the heat-driven storm cloud and roiled under me like ebony rivers. I could see lightning flashing in the depths below and surging spheres of ball lightning being spit from the black column of storm. Closer, much closer, hanging from the river of black cloud flowing above me, curled a dozen or more tornadoes, their funnel clouds striking toward me like scorpion tails. Each funnel was the size of the cuttlefish monster or larger—vertical kilometers of whirling madness—and each was spawning its own cluster of smaller tornadoes. There was no way that my flimsy parasail could withstand even a close miss by one of these vortexes—and there was no way that the funnels were going to miss me.

I stood up in the pitching, rolling cockpit, holding my place in the boat only by grasping a riser with my left hand. With my right hand I made a fist, raised it, and shook it toward the tornadoes, toward the roiling storm beyond them, and toward the invisible sky beyond. "Well, goddamn you then!" I shouted. My words were lost in the wind howl. My vest flapped around me. A gust nearly blew me into the maelstrom. Leaning far out over the hull of the kayak, bracing myself into the wind like a ski jumper I had seen once on the Iceshelf caught in a moment of mad, poised balance before the inevitable descent, I shook my fist again and screamed, "Do your worst, goddamn you. I defy you gods!"

As if in answer, one of the tornado funnels came sidewinding closer, the lowest tip of its whirling cone stabbing downward as if seeking a hard surface to destroy. It missed me by a distance of hundreds of meters, but the vacuum of its passing whirled the kayak and parasail around like a toy boat in a draining bathtub. Relieved of the opposition of the wind, I fell forward onto the slippery kayak hull and would have slid into oblivion if my scrabbling hands had not found a riser to grip. My feet were fully out of the cockpit at that moment.

There was a hailstorm traveling with the passing funnel. Ice pellets—some the size of my fist—smashed through the parasail, pounded the kayak with a noise like flechette clouds slamming home, and hit me in the leg, shoulder, and lower back. The pain almost made me release my grip. That mattered little, I realized as I clung to the pitching, dipping kayak, because the sail had been torn in a hundred places. Only its canopy had saved me from being shot to bits by the hail, but now the delta-shaped foil had been riddled. It lost lift as suddenly as it had first gained it and the kayak pitched forward toward the darkness so many thousands of klicks below. Tornadoes filled the sky around me. I gripped the now-useless riser where it entered the battered hull and hung on, determined to complete that one act—hanging on—until the boat, furled sail, and I were all crushed by pressure or shredded by the winds. I realized that I was screaming again, but the sound was different in my ears—almost gleeful.

I had fallen less than a kilometer, the kayak and me gaining speed far beyond Hyperion's or Old Earth's terminal velocity, when the cuttlefish—forgotten behind and above me—made its lunge. It must have moved with blinding speed, propelling itself through the air like a squid jetting after its prey. The first I knew that it was hungry and determined not to lose its dinner was when the long feeding tendrils surged around me like so many huge tentacles coiling and probing and wrapping.

If the thing had tugged me to an immediate stop at the speeds the boat and I were falling, both kayak and I would have been snapped into small pieces. But the cuttlefish fell with us, surrounding the boat, sail, risers, and me with the smallest of its tendrils—each still two to five meters thick—and then it braked itself against the fall, jetting ammonia-smelling gases like a dropship on final approach. Then it began ascending again, up toward the storm where tornadoes still raged and the central stratocumulus rotated with its own black intensity. Only half-conscious, I realized that the cuttlefish was flying into that roiling cloud even as it reeled the bashed kayak and me toward an opening in its immense transparent body.

Well, I thought groggily, *I've found its mouth.*

Risers and shreds of parasail lay around me and over me like an oversized shroud. The kayak seemed to be draped in drab bunting as the cuttlefish pulled us in closer. I tried to turn, thought of crawling back toward the cockpit and finding the flechette gun, of cutting my way out of the thing.

The flechette gun was gone, of course, shaken out of the cockpit in all the violent tumbling and the fall. Also gone were the cockpit cushions and my backpack with the clothes, food, water, and flashlight laser. Everything was gone.

I tried to chuckle but the sound was not quite successful as the tendrils pulled the kayak and its clinging passenger the last fifty meters to the gaping orifice on the underside of the cuttlefish's body. I could see the internal organs more clearly now—pulsing and absorbing, moving in peristaltic waves, some of them filled with the green platelet creatures. As I was pulled closer, there came an almost overwhelming stench of cleaning fluid—ammonia, I realized—that made my eyes water and throat burn.

I thought of Aenea. It was not a prolonged or eloquent thought—just a mental glimpse of how she had looked on her sixteenth birthday, all short hair, sweat, and sunburn from her desert meditations—and I formed the single message, *Sorry, kiddo. I did my best to get to the ship and bring it to you. Sorry.*

Then the long feeding tendrils curled and folded and pulled the boat and me up into a lipless mouth that I realized must be thirty or forty meters across. I thought of the fiberglass and ultranylon parasail fabric and the carbon-fiber risers that were entering with me and had time for a last thought—*I hope some of this gives you a bellyache.*

And then I was pulled into the ammonia and fish smell, was vaguely aware that the air here in the creature's gut was not really breathable, decided to jump from the kayak rather than be digested, but lost consciousness before I could act or frame another coherent thought.

Without my knowledge or observation, the cuttlefish continued to rise through cloud blacker than a moonless night, its lipless mouth closing and disappearing on its seamless flesh, the kayak and sail and me nothing more than a shadow in the fluid contents of its lower tract.

13

ENZO ISOZAKI WAS not surprised when the Swiss Guard came for him.

The Corps Helvetica colonel and eight troopers in full orange-and-blue dress uniforms with energy lances and deathwands arrived at the Torus Mercantilus unannounced, demanded to see CEO Isozaki in his private office, and presented him with an encrypted diskey ordering him to dress formally and appear before His Holiness, Pope Urban XVI. Immediately.

The colonel stayed in sight of Isozaki as the CEO stepped into his personal apartment, quickly showered, and dressed in his most formal white shirt, gray vest, red cravat, the double-breasted black demisuit with the gold buttons on the side, and black velvet cape.

"May I phone my associates and issue business instructions in case I should miss meetings scheduled for later today?" he asked the colonel as they stepped out of the lift into the main reception hall where the troopers made a sort of gold and blue corridor between the workstations.

"No," said the Swiss Guard officer.

A Pax Fleet ramscout was docked where Isozaki's personal ship was usually berthed. The Pax crew gave the Mercantilus CEO the briefest of nods, instructed him to strap into his acceleration couch, and then they were boosting in-system with two torchships visible on the tactical holo display as they dropped into escort position.

They are treating me as a prisoner, not an honored guest, thought Isozaki. His face revealed nothing, of course, but a wave of something like relief followed the pulse of fear and dread in him. He had been expecting this since his illicit meeting with Councillor Albedo. And he had slept almost not at all since that painful and traumatic rendezvous. Isozaki knew that there was no reason for Albedo not to reveal the fact of the Mercantilus's attempts to contact the TechnoCore, but he hoped that they would believe that it was his attempt and his alone. Silently, Isozaki gave thanks to whatever gods that wanted to listen that his friend and associate, Anna Pelli Cognani, was out of Pacem's system, visiting Renaissance Vector for a major trade fair there.

From his couch between the Swiss Guard colonel and one of the troopers, Isozaki could see the tactical holo in front of the pilot's position. The sphere of moving light and color with its solid bars of code was highly technical, but Isozaki had been a pilot before these boys were born. He could see that they were not accelerating toward the world of Pacem, but toward a destination near the trailing Trojan point, directly in the middle of the swarm of Pax Fleet asteroid bases and system-defense forts.

A Holy Office orbital prison, thought Isozaki. Worse than Castel Sant'Angelo where the virtual pain machines were said to run all hours of the day and night. In one of the orbital dungeons, no one could hear you scream. He was sure that the command to attend a papal audience was mere irony, a way to get him out of the Pax Mercantilus without protest. Isozaki would have bet anything that within days—perhaps hours—his formal suit and cape would be bloody, sweat-soaked rags.

He was wrong on all counts. The ramscout decelerated above the plane of the ecliptic and he realized their destination: Castel Gandolfo, the Pope's "summer retreat."

The diskey viewer in the CEO's couch worked and he called up an exterior view as the ramscout left its escorting torchships and dropped toward the massive, potato-shaped asteroid. More than forty klicks long and twenty-five across, Castel Gandolfo was a little world of its own, its sky blue, its oxygen-rich atmosphere held in by class-twenty containment fields wrapped with infinite redundancies, the hillsides and terraces green with grass and crops, the sculpted mountains forested and running with streams and small animals. Isozaki saw the ancient Italian village pass below and knew that the peaceful vision was deceptive: surrounding Pax bases could destroy any ship or fleet in existence, while the interior of asteroid Castel Gandolfo was honeycombed with garrisons holding more than ten thousand Swiss Guard and elite Pax troopers.

The ramscout morphed wings and flew the final ten kilometers on silent electric pulse jets. Isozaki saw the Swiss Guard troopers in full battle dress rise to escort the ship the final five klicks. Rich sunlight glinted off their dynamic-flow armor and transparent face shields as they encircled the ramscout and approached the castle at dead-slow speeds. Isozaki saw several of the troopers aim probes at the ship: confirming with deep radar and infrared what the encrypted manifest readouts had told them about the number and identity of passengers and crew.

A door opened in the side of one of the castle's stone towers and the ramscout floated in, pulse jets cool, the Swiss Guard troopers tugging the aircraft into place with the blue glow of their liftpacs.

The air lock cycled. The eight Swiss Guard troopers went down the ramp first, taking up their two lines as the colonel escorted Kenzo Isozaki out and down. The CEO was looking for a lift door or stairway, but the entire berthing level of the tower began to descend. The motors and gears were silent. Only the passing stone walls of the tower told of their movement downward and then sideways into the subterranean guts of Castel Gandolfo.

They stopped. A door appeared in the wall of cold stone. Lights illuminated a corridor of polished steel with floating, fiberplastic lens pods keeping watch at ten-meter intervals. The colonel gestured and Isozaki led the procession down the echoing tunnel. At the end, blue light washed over them all as other probes and sensors searched them inside and out. A chime rang and another portal appeared and irised open. This was a more formal waiting room. Three people stood when Isozaki and his escort entered.

Damn, thought the Pax Mercantilus CEO. Anna Pelli Cognani was there, dressed in her finest fresilk robes, as were CEOs Helvig Aron and Kennet Hay-Modhino, Isozaki's other counterparts on the Executive Council of the Pancapitalist League of Independent Catholic Transstellar Trade Organizations.

Damn, thought Kenzo Isozaki again, his face staying absolutely impassive while he nodded silently to his associates. *They are going to hold all of us accountable for my actions. We will all be excommunicated and executed.*

"This way," said the Swiss Guard colonel and opened an elaborately carved door. The room beyond was darker. Isozaki smelled candles, incense, and sweating stone. He realized that the Swiss Guardsmen were not going with them through that door. Whatever waited there, waited for his party alone.

"Thank you, Colonel," said CEO Isozaki in a pleasant voice. With firm strides, he led the way into the incense-filled darkness.

IT WAS A small chapel, dark except for red votive candles flickering in a wrought-iron stand against one stone wall and two arched, stained-glass windows behind the simple altar at the far end. Six more candles burned on the bare altar while flames in braziers on the far side of the windows cast more ruddy light into the long, narrow room. There was only one chair, tall, straight-backed, velvet-cushioned, and placed to the left of the altar. In the back of the chair was embossed what at first appeared to be a cruciform, but what, upon second glance, was revealed to be the triple cross of the Pope. The altar and chair were set upon a low stone dais.

The rest of the chapel was without chairs or pews, but red velvet cushions had been set on the dark stone on either side of the aisle down which M.'s Isozaki, Cognani, Hay-Modhino, and Aron walked. There were four cushions—two on either side of the aisle—that were not in use. The Mercantilus CEOs dipped fingers in the stone font holding holy water, crossed themselves, genuflected toward the altar, and went to their knees on the cushions. Before lowering his head in prayer, Kenzo Isozaki glanced around the tiny chapel.

Nearest the altar dais knelt Vatican Secretary of State Simon Augustino Cardinal Lourdusamy—a mountain of red and black in the ruddy light, his jowls and chins hiding his clerical collar as he bowed his head in prayer—and behind him knelt the scarecrow figure of his aide, Monsignor Lucas Oddi. Across the aisle from Lourdusamy, the Holy Office's Grand Inquisitor, John Domenico Cardinal Mustafa, knelt in prayer, his eyes closed. Next to him was the infamous intelligence agent and torturer, Father Farrell.

On Lourdusamy's side of the aisle, three Pax Fleet officers were on their knees: Admiral Marusyn—his silver hair glinting in the red light—and his aide, Admiral Marget Wu, and someone whose face it took Isozaki a moment to recall—Admiral Aldikacti. On the Grand Inquisitor's side of the aisle knelt Cardinal Du Noyer, prefect and president of *Cor Unum*. Du Noyer was a woman in her healthy seventies, standard, with a strong jaw and short-cropped gray hair. Her eyes were the color of flint. Isozaki did not recognize the middle-aged man in monsignoral robes who knelt behind the Cardinal.

The final four kneeling figures were the Mercantilus CEOs—Aron and Hay-Modhino on the Grand Inquisitor's side of the aisle, Isozaki and Pelli Cognani on the Secretary of State's side. Isozaki counted a total of thirteen people in the chapel. Not an auspicious number, he thought.

At that moment, a hidden door in the wall to the right of the altar opened silently and the Pope entered with four men in attendance. The thirteen people in the chapel rose quickly from their knees and stood with their heads bowed. Kenzo Isozaki had time to recognize two of the men with the Pope as aides and the third as head of papal security—faceless functionaries—but the fourth man, the man in gray, was Councillor Albedo. Only Albedo stayed with the Pope as His Holiness walked into the room, allowing the kissing of his ring and touching the heads of the gathered men and women as they knelt again. Finally His Holiness, Pope Urban XVI, took his seat in the straight-backed throne with Albedo standing behind him. The thirteen dignitaries in the room immediately stood.

Isozaki lowered his eyes, his face remaining a study in calm, but his heart pounded at his ribs. *Will Albedo expose us all? Have all these groups attempted secret contact with the Core? Are we to be confronted by His Holiness and then taken from here, our cruciforms removed, and then executed?* Isozaki thought it likely.

"Brothers and sisters in Christ," began His Holiness, "we are pleased that you have agreed to join us here this day. What we must say in this secret and silent place has remained a secret for centuries and must remain within this circle until formal permission to share it with others is granted from the Holy See. We so abjure and command you, upon the pain of excommunication and the loss of your souls to the light of Christ."

The thirteen men and women murmured prayers and acquiescence.

"In the recent months and years," continued His Holiness, "there have occurred events both strange and terrible. We have witnessed these from afar—some of these we have foreseen with the help of Our Lord, Jesus Christ—and many we have prayed would pass from us, sparing our people, our Pax, and our Church from a test of wills, faith, and fortitude. But events occur as the Lord wills them to occur. It is not possible for even His most faithful servant to understand all events and portents, only to trust in His mercy when those events seem most threatening and perplexing."

The thirteen dignitaries kept their eyes carefully downcast.

"Rather than relate these events from our perspective," His Holiness said softly, "we shall ask some of those who participated in them to report in full. Then we shall endeavor to explain the connections between such seemingly disparate occurrences. Admiral Marusyn?"

The silver-haired Admiral shifted slightly to face the others as well as His Holiness. He cleared his throat. "Reports from a world called Vitus-Gray-Balianus B suggest that we came close to capturing the Hyperion-born man named Raul Endymion who eluded us—with our primary subject, the girl named Aenea—almost five standard years ago. Elements of a special force of the Noble Guard . . ." The Admiral nodded toward Pope Urban XVI, who lowered his gaze in agreement. "Elements of this special force," continued Marusyn, "tipped our commander on Vitus-Gray-Balianus B to the possible presence of this person. Although he escaped before our search of the area was completed, we did turn up definite DNA and micron-tag evidence that this was the same Raul Endymion who had been briefly incarcerated on the world of Mare Infinitus more than four years ago."

Cardinal Lourdusamy cleared his throat. "It might be helpful, Admiral, if you described how the suspect, Raul Endymion, escaped from this world of Vitus-Gray-Balianus B."

Kenzo Isozaki did not blink, but he registered the fact that Lourdusamy was speaking for His Holiness in this conference.

"Thank you, Your Excellency," said Admiral Marusyn. "Yes, it appears that this Endymion both appeared on and escaped the planet via one of the ancient farcasters."

There was no audible buzz in the room, but Isozaki sensed the psychic hum of interest and shock. There had been rumors for the past four years centering on Pax Fleet forces chasing some heretic who had managed to activate the dormant farcasters.

"And was this farcaster active when your men inspected it?" questioned Lourdusamy.

"Negative, Your Excellency," said Admiral Marusyn. "There was no sign of activity on either farcaster . . . the one upriver which must have granted the fugitive access to Vitus-Gray-Balianus B . . . nor the one downriver from the settlements."

"But you are certain that this . . . Endymion . . . had not arrived on planet by some more conventional means? And equally certain that he is not hiding there now?"

"Yes, Your Excellency. This Pax world has excellent traffic control and orbital defenses. Any spacecraft approaching Vitus-Gray-Balianus B would have been detected light-hours from the planet. And we have turned the world upside down searching . . . administered Truthtell to tens of thousands of the inhabitants. The man named Endymion is not there. Witnesses did describe, however, a flash of light at the downstream farcaster at the precise moment that our sensors in and above that hemisphere registered a major energy surge consistent with old records of farcaster displacement fields."

His Holiness raised his face and made a subtle gesture to Cardinal Lourdusamy.

"And I believe you have one other bit of unsettling news, Admiral Marusyn," rumbled Lourdusamy.

The Admiral's countenance grew grimmer as he nodded. "Aye, Your Excellency . . . Your Holiness. This involves the first mutiny in the history of Pax Fleet."

Isozaki again sensed the unspoken murmur of shock. He showed no emotion or reaction, but out of the corner of his eye he saw Anna Pelli Cognani glancing at him.

"I will have Admiral Aldikacti brief us on this matter," said Marusyn. He stepped back and folded his hands in front of him.

Isozaki noted that Aldikacti was one of those stocky Lusian women who seemed almost too androgynous to label with gender. She was as solid and blocky as a brick in a dress uniform.

Aldikacti did not waste time clearing her throat. She launched into an immediate briefing involving Task Force GIDEON, its mission to attack Ouster strongholds in seven systems far in the Outback, the successful outcome of that mission in all seven systems, and then the surprise in the final system, code-named Lucifer.

"To this point, the task force had performed beyond expectations and simulations," barked Admiral Aldikacti. "As a result, while completing operations in Ouster System Lucifer, I authorized a Gideon-drive drone to carry a message to Pacem . . . to His Holiness and Admiral Marusyn . . . requesting permission to refuel and refit in Tau Ceti System and then extend Task Force GIDEON's mission—attacking new Ouster systems before the alarm of our attack spread through the Outback. I received Gideon-drone permission to do this, and proceeded to take the bulk of my task force to Tau Ceti System for refueling, rearming, and rendezvous with five additional archangel starships which had come on-line since our task force had left Pax space."

"You took the *bulk* of your task force?" queried Cardinal Lourdusamy in his soft rumble.

"Yes, Your Excellency." There was no apology or quavering in Aldikacti's flat Lusian voice. "Five Ouster torchships had escaped our detection and were accelerating toward a Hawking-drive translation point which would have presumably brought them out in another Ouster system. They would have spread the alarm of our task force's presence and lethality. Rather than divert the entire Task Force GIDEON, which was approaching our own translation point to Tau Ceti System, I authorized H.H.S. *Gabriel* and H.H.S. *Raphael* to remain in Lucifer System just long enough to intercept and destroy the Ouster torchships."

Lourdusamy folded his pudgy hands in his robe. His voice was a deep purr. "And you then translated your flagship, the *Uriel,* and four other archangels to Tau Ceti System?"

"Yes, Your Excellency."

"Leaving the *Gabriel* and *Raphael* in Lucifer System?"

"Yes, Your Excellency."

"And you were aware, Admiral, that the *Raphael* was commanded by Father Captain de Soya . . . the same captain who had been reprimanded some years earlier for not succeeding in his mission of finding and detaining the child, Aenea?"

"Yes, Your Excellency."

"And you were aware, Admiral, that Pax Fleet and the Holy See were concerned enough about Father Captain de Soya's . . . ah . . . stability, that the Holy Office had assigned an undercover agent aboard the *Raphael* to observe and transmit observations on Father Captain de Soya's behavior and reliability?"

"A spy," said Admiral Aldikacti. "Commander Liebler. Yes, Your Excellency. I was aware that Holy Office agents aboard my flagship were receiving encoded tightbeam broadcasts from Commander Liebler aboard the *Raphael.*"

"And did these agents share any concerns or data from these broadcasts, Admiral Aldikacti?"

"Negative, Your Excellency. I was not made aware of the nature of the Holy Office's concerns related to Father Captain de Soya's loyalty or sanity."

Cardinal Mustafa cleared his throat and raised one finger.

Lourdusamy, who had been in charge of what Isozaki and the others had quickly recognized as an inquisition, glanced at the Pope.

His Holiness nodded in the direction of the Grand Inquisitor.

"I feel it necessary to point out to His Holiness and the other worthies in this room that observation of Father Captain de Soya had been approved . . . directed . . . from the Office of the Holy See, with verbal authorization from the Secretary of State and Pax Fleet Command . . . specifically from Admiral Marusyn."

There was a brief silence.

Finally Lourdusamy said, "And can you tell us, Cardinal Mustafa, what the source of this shared concern had been?"

Mustafa licked his lips. "Yes, Your Excellency. Our . . . ah . . . intelligence reports indicated that there might have been some chance of contamination during Father Captain de Soya's chase and rare contact with the subject named Aenea."

"Contamination?" queried Lourdusamy.

"Yes, Your Excellency. It was our assessment that the girl named Aenea had the power to affect both the physical and psychological makeup of those Pax citizens with whom she came in contact. Our concern in this instance was for the absolute loyalty and obedience of one of Pax Fleet's starship commanders."

"And how was this intelligence assessment made, Cardinal Mustafa?" continued Lourdusamy.

The Grand Inquisitor paused. "A variety of intelligence sources and methods were used, Your Excellency."

Lourdusamy did not pause. "Among these were the fact that you have detained and . . . ah . . . interrogated one of Father Captain de Soya's fellow shipmen from the aforementioned abortive chase of subject Aenea, is that not correct, Cardinal Mustafa? A . . . ah . . . Corporal Kee, I believe?"

Mustafa blinked. "That is correct, Your Excellency." The Grand Inquisitor turned slightly so as to speak to the others in the room as well as the Pope and the Secretary of State. "Such detention is unusual, but called for in a situation which appears to affect the security of the Church and the Pax."

"Of course, Your Excellency," murmured Cardinal Lourdusamy. "Admiral Aldikacti, you may continue with the briefing."

"Some hours after my five archangels jumped to Tau Ceti System," said Aldikacti, "and before any of us had completed our two-day resurrection cycle, a Gideon drone translated into Tau Ceti space. It had been launched by Mother Captain Stone . . ."

"Captain of the H.H.S. *Gabriel*," said Lourdusamy.

"Affirmative, Your Excellency. The drone's encrypted message . . . encrypted in a code for my eyes only . . . said that the Ouster torchships had been destroyed, but that the *Raphael* had gone rogue, was accelerating toward an unauthorized translation point, and would not respond to Mother Captain Stone's orders to stop."

"In other words," purred Lourdusamy, "one of His Holiness's Pax Fleet ships had suffered a mutiny."

"It appeared so, Your Excellency. Although in this case, the mutiny seemed to have been led by the ship's captain."

"Father Captain de Soya."

"Yes, Your Excellency."

"And were there attempts made to contact the Holy Office agent aboard the *Raphael*?"

"Yes, Your Excellency. Father Captain de Soya said that Commander Liebler was attending to duties. Mother Captain Stone thought this unlikely."

"And when challenged about the changed translation point?" queried Lourdusamy.

"Father Captain de Soya answered that I had tightbeamed changed orders to the *Raphael* prior to our task force's translation," said Admiral Aldikacti.

"Did Mother Captain Stone accept this explanation?"

"Negative, Your Excellency. Mother Captain Stone closed the distance between the two archangels and engaged the *Raphael*."

"What was the outcome of that engagement, Admiral?"

Aldikacti hesitated only a heartbeat. "Your Excellency . . . Your Holiness . . . because Mother Captain Stone had used an eyes-only encryption for her drone message, it was a full day in Tau Ceti System—the time it took for my emergency resurrection—before I read the message and authorized an immediate return to Lucifer System."

"How many ships did you take with you, Admiral?"

"Three, Your Excellency. My own flagship, the *Uriel,* with a fresh crew, and two of the archangels that had rendezvoused with us in Tau Ceti System . . . the *Mikal* and the *Izrail.* I felt that the risk of accelerating resurrection of the Task Force GIDEON crews was too great."

"Although you accepted that risk yourself, Admiral," said Lourdusamy.

Aldikacti said nothing.

"What happened then, Admiral?"

"We jumped immediately to Lucifer System, Your Excellency. There we recycled under twelve-hour automated resurrection. Many of the resurrections were unsuccessful. By combining the successfully resurrected crew members from all three ships, I was able to crew the *Uriel.* I left the other two starships in passive but automated defensive trajectories while I commenced searching for the *Gabriel* and the *Raphael.* I found neither. But a final beacon drone was soon discovered on the far side of Lucifer's yellow sun."

"And the beacon was from . . ." prompted Lourdusamy.

"Mother Captain Stone. The beacon held the downloaded history of the *Gabriel's* combat recorder. It showed the battle that had taken place less than two days before. Stone had attempted to destroy the *Raphael* by plasma and fusion weapons. The attempts failed. The *Gabriel* then engaged Father Captain de Soya's ship by deathbeam."

There was silence in the tiny chapel. Isozaki watched the red light of the flickering votive candles painting the pained face of His Holiness, Pope Urban XVI.

"The outcome of that engagement?" said Lourdusamy.

"Both crews died," said Aldikacti. "According to automated instruments aboard the *Gabriel,* the *Raphael* completed automated translation. Mother Captain Stone had ordered her crew to resurrection crèche battle stations. She had programmed the *Gabriel's* ship computers to resurrect her and several of the essential crew members on an emergency, eight-hour cycle. Only she and one of her officers survived the resurrection. Mother Captain Stone encoded the beacon and accelerated to the *Raphael*'s former translation point. She was determined to seek out and destroy the ship, preferably before de Soya and his crew completed resurrection . . . if they were in their crèches at the time of the deathbeaming."

"Did Mother Captain Stone know which system this translation point would open upon, Admiral?"

"Negative, Your Excellency. There were too many variables involved."

"And what was your response to the beacon's data, Admiral?"

"I waited twelve hours for a working complement of the crews on the *Mikal* and the *Izrail* to complete resurrection, Your Excellency. I then translated all three of my ships through the jump point indicated by the *Raphael* and *Gabriel*. I left a second beacon for the archangels I was sure would be following from Tau Ceti System within hours."

"You did not find it necessary to wait for these ships?"

"No, Your Excellency. I thought it important to translate as soon as all three of my ships were combat-ready."

"But you *did* find it expedient to wait for the crews of these two ships, Admiral. Why did you not give chase immediately with only the *Uriel*?"

Aldikacti did not hesitate. "It was a command combat decision, Your Excellency. I felt that the probabilities were very high that Father Captain de Soya had taken the *Raphael* to an Ouster system . . . quite possibly one more heavily armed than any Task Force GIDEON had encountered. I also felt it probable that Mother Captain Stone's ship, the *Gabriel*, had been destroyed by either the *Raphael* or Ouster ships within the unknown system. I felt that three ships of the line were the minimum force I could take into this unknown situation."

"And was it an Ouster system, Admiral?"

"Negative, Your Excellency. Or at least, no sign of Ousters were discovered in the two weeks of investigation following this incident."

"Where *did* the translation point take you, Admiral?"

"Into the outer shell of a red giant star," said Admiral Aldikacti. "Our containment fields were, of course, activated, but it was a very close thing."

"Did all three of your ships make it, Admiral?"

"Negative, Your Excellency. The *Uriel* and *Izrail* survived exit from the star and containment field cooling procedures. The *Mikal* was lost with all hands."

"And did you find the *Gabriel* and the *Raphael*, Admiral?"

"Only the *Gabriel*, Your Excellency. It was discovered floating free some two AUs from the red giant. All systems were inoperative. There had been a breach of the containment field and the interior of the ship had melted into a single molten mass."

"Were Mother Captain Stone and the other crew members found and resurrected, Admiral?"

"Unfortunately, no, Your Excellency. There was not enough discrete organic material remaining to pursue resurrection."

"Was the slagging due to emergence in the red giant or attack from the *Raphael* or Ouster unknowns, Admiral?"

"It is still being determined by our materials experts, Your Excellency, but the preliminary report suggests an overload due to both natural and combat causes. The weapons used would have been consistent with the *Raphael*'s armament."

"So you are saying that the *Gabriel* fought an automated engagement near this red giant sun, Admiral?"

"*Within* the star, Your Excellency. It seems that the *Raphael* turned about, reentered the star, and attacked the *Gabriel* within seconds of its emergence from Hawking space."

"And is there a chance that the *Raphael* was also destroyed in this second engagement? The ship incinerated deep in the star?"

"A chance, Your Excellency, but we are not operating upon that assumption. It is our best guess that Father Captain de Soya then translated out of system to an unknown destination in the Outback."

Lourdusamy nodded, his heavy jowls quivering slightly. "Admiral Marusyn," he rumbled, "could you give us an assessment of this threat if the *Raphael* did indeed survive?"

The older Admiral stepped forward. "Your Excellency, we have to assume that Father Captain de Soya and the other mutineers are hostile to the Pax and that this theft of a Pax archangel-class starship was premeditated. We also have to assume the worst-case scenario that this theft of our most secret and lethal weapons system was carried out in coordination with the Ousters." The Admiral took a breath. "Your Excellencies . . . Your Holiness . . . with the Gideon drive, any point in this arm of the galaxy is only an instant away from any other. The *Raphael* could translate into any Pax system—even Pacem's—without the Hawking-drive wake warnings of the earlier, and current, Ouster spacecraft. The *Raphael* could ravage our Mercantilus transport lanes, attack undefended worlds and colonies, and generally wreak havoc before a Pax task force could respond."

The Pope raised one finger. "Admiral Marusyn, are we to understand that this most prized of Gideon-drive technologies may fall into the hands of the Ousters . . . be duplicated . . . and thus power many of the Enemy's ships?"

Marusyn's already florid face and neck flushed more deeply. "Your Holiness . . . that is unlikely, Your Holiness . . . extemely unlikely. The steps of manufacture of a Gideon archangel are so complex, the cost so prohibitive, the secret elements so guarded . . ."

"But it is possible," interrupted the Pope.

"Yes, Your Holiness."

The Pope raised his hand like a blade cutting through the air. "We believe that we have heard all we need to hear from our friends in Pax Fleet. You are excused, Admiral Marusyn, Admiral Aldikacti, Admiral Wu."

The three officers genuflected, bowed their heads, stood, and backed away from His Holiness. The door whispered shut behind them.

There were now ten dignitaries present, in addition to the silent papal aides and Councillor Albedo.

The Pope inclined his head toward Secretary of State Cardinal Lourdusamy. "Disposition, Simon Augustino?"

"Admiral Marusyn is to receive a letter of rebuke and will be transferred to general staff," said Lourdusamy softly. "Admiral Wu will take his place as temporary Pax Fleet commander in chief until a suitable replacement is found. Admiral Aldikacti has been recommended for excommunication and execution by firing squad."

The Pope nodded sadly. "We shall now hear from Cardinal Mustafa, Cardinal Du Noyer, CEO Isozaki, and Councillor Albedo before concluding this business."

"... AND THUS ENDED the official inquiry by the Holy Office pertaining to the events on the Pax world of Mars," concluded Cardinal Mustafa. He glanced at Cardinal Lourdusamy. "It was at this time that Captain Wolmak suggested that it was imperative that my entourage and I return to the archangel *Jibril* still in orbit around that planet."

"Please continue, Excellency," murmured Cardinal Lourdusamy. "Can you tell us the nature of the emergency which Captain Wolmak felt required your imperative return?"

"Yes," said Mustafa, rubbing his lower lip. "Captain Wolmak had found the interstellar freighter that had uploaded cargo from the unlisted base near the Martian city of Arafat-kaffiyeh. The ship had been discovered floating powerless in Old Earth System's asteroid belt."

"Can you tell us the name of that ship, Excellency?" prompted Lourdusamy.

"The H.H.M.S. *Saigon Maru*."

CEO Kenzo Isozaki's lips twitched despite his iron control. He remembered the ship. His oldest son had crewed on it during the early years of the boy's apprenticeship. The *Saigon Maru* had been an ancient ore and bulk freighter . . . about a three-million-ton ion sledge carrier, as he recalled.

"CEO Isozaki?" snapped Lourdusamy.

"Yes, Your Excellency?" Isozaki's voice was smooth and emotionless.

"The ship's designation suggests that it is of Mercantilus registry. Is this correct, M. Isozaki?"

"Yes, Your Excellency," said the CEO. "But it is my recollection that the H.H.M.S. *Saigon Maru* was sold for scrap along with sixty-some other obsolete freighters about . . . eight standard years ago, if memory serves."

"Your Excellencies?" said Anna Pelli Cognani. "Your Holiness? If I might?" The other CEO had whispered to her wafer-thin comlog and now touched her hearring.

"CEO Pelli Cognani," said Cardinal Lourdusamy.

"Our records show that the *Saigon Maru* was indeed sold to independent scrap contractors some eight years, three months, and two days ago, standard. Later transmissions confirmed that the ships had been scrapped and recycled at the Armaghast orbital automated foundries."

"Thank you, CEO Pelli Cognani," said Lourdusamy. "Cardinal Mustafa, you may continue."

The Grand Inquisitor nodded and continued his briefing, covering only the most necessary details. And while he spoke he thought of the images he was not describing in detail:

The *Jibril* and its accompanying torchships slowing to silent, synchronized tumbling, matching velocities with the dark freighter. Cardinal Mustafa had always imagined asteroid belts as tightly packed clusters of moonlets, but despite the multiple images on the tactical plot, there were no rocks in sight: just the matte-black freighter, as ugly and functional as a rusted mass of pipes and cylinders, half a klick long. Matched as they were in velocity and trajectory, hanging only three klicks away with the yellow sun of humankind's birth burning beyond their sterns, *Jibril* and the *Saigon Maru* appeared motionless with only the stars wheeling slowly around them.

Mustafa remembered—and regretted—his decision to inspect the ship with the troopers who were going aboard. The indignities of suiting up in Swiss Guard combat armor: a monomol-D skinsuit layer, followed by an AI neural mesh, then the spacesuit itself—bulkier than civilian skinsuits with its polymered sheath of impact armor—and finally the web belts of gear and the morphable reaction pak. The *Jibril* had deep-radared the hulk a dozen times and was certain that nothing moved or breathed on board, but the archangel still backed off to thirty klicks' attack distance as soon as the Grand Inquisitor, Security Commander Browning, Marine Sergeant Nell Kasner, former groundforce commander Major Piet, and ten Swiss Guard/Marine commandos had jumped from the sally port.

Mustafa remembered his pounding pulse as they jetted closer to the dead freighter, two commandos ferrying him across the abyss as if he were another parcel to carry. He remembered the sunlight glinting off gold blast visors as the troopers communicated with tightbeam squirts and hand signals, taking up positions on either side of the open air lock. Two troopers went in first, their reaction paks throbbing silently, assault weapons raised. Then Commander Browning and Sergeant Kasner went in fast behind them. A minute later there was a coded squirt on the tactical channel and Mustafa's handlers guided him into the waiting black hole of the air lock.

Corpses floating in the beams of flashlight lasers. Meat-locker images. Frozen carcasses, red-striped ribs, gutted abdominal cavities. Jaws locked open in eternally silent screams. Frozen streamers of blood from the gaping jaws and hemorrhaged, protruding eyes. Viscera drifting in tumbling trajectories amid the stabbing beams of light.

"Crew," tightbeamed Commander Browning.

"Shrike?" queried Cardinal Mustafa. He was mentally saying the rosary in rapid monotone, not for spiritual reassurance but to keep his mind away from the images floating in hellish light before him. He had been warned not to vomit in his helmet. Filters and scrubbers would clean the mess before he strangled on it, but they were not foolproof.

"Probably the Shrike," answered Major Piet, extending his gauntlet into the shattered chest cavity of one of the drifting corpses. "See how the cruciform has been ripped out. Just as in Arafat-kaffiyeh."

"Commander!" came a tightbeamed voice of one of the troopers who had moved aft from the air lock. "Sergeant! Here! In the first cargo hold!"

Browning and Piet had gone ahead of the Grand Inquisitor into the long, cylindrical space. Flashlight lasers were lost in this huge space.

These corpses had not been slashed and shattered. They were stacked neatly on carbon slabs extruding from the hull on each side, held in place by nylon mesh bands. The slabs came out from all sides of the hull, leaving only a zero-g corridor down the center. Mustafa and his guides and keepers floated the length of this black space, flashlight lasers stabbing left, right, down, and up. Frozen flesh, pale flesh, bar codes on the soles of their feet, pubic hair, closed eyes, hands pale against black carbon by hipbones, flaccid penises, breasts frozen in zero-g weightlessness, hair tight on pale skulls or floating in frozen nimbuses. Children with smooth, cold skin, extended bellies, and translucent eyelids. Infants with bar coded soles.

There were tens of thousands of bodies in the four long cargo holds. All were human. All were naked. All were lifeless.

"AND DID YOU complete your inspection of the H.H.M.S. *Saigon Maru,* Grand Inquisitor?" prompted Cardinal Lourdusamy.

Mustafa realized that he had fallen silent for a long moment, possessed by the demon of that terrible memory. "We did complete it, Your Excellency," he answered, his voice thick.

"And your conclusions?"

"There were sixty-seven thousand eight hundred and twenty-seven human beings aboard the bulk freighter H.H.M.S. *Saigon Maru,*" said the Grand Inquisitor. "Fifty-one of them were crew members. All of the crew members' bodies were accounted for. All had been slashed and rent in the same fashion as the victims at Arafat-kaffiyeh."

"There were no survivors? None could be resurrected?"

"None."

"In your opinion, Cardinal Mustafa, was the demon-creature called the Shrike responsible for the death of the crew members of the H.H.M.S. *Saigon Maru?*"

"In my opinion, it was, Your Excellency."

"And in your opinion, Cardinal Mustafa, was the Shrike responsible for the deaths of the sixty-seven thousand seven hundred and seventy-six other bodies discovered on the *Saigon Maru?*"

Mustafa hesitated only a second. "In my opinion, Your Excellency"— he turned his head and bowed in the direction of the man in the chair— "Your Holiness . . . the cause of death of the sixty-seven thousand-some men, women, and children found on the H.H.M.S. *Saigon Maru* was *not* consistent with the wounds discovered on Mars's victims, or consistent with prior tales of Shrike attack."

Cardinal Lourdusamy took a rustling step forward. "And, according to your Holy Office forensic experts, Cardinal Mustafa, what *was* the cause of death for the human beings found aboard this freighter?"

Cardinal Mustafa's eyes were lowered as he spoke. "Your Excellency, neither the Holy Office nor Pax Fleet forensic specialists could specify any cause of death for these people. In fact . . ." Mustafa stopped.

"In fact," Lourdusamy continued for him, "the bodies found aboard the *Saigon Maru* . . . exclusive of the crew . . . showed neither clear cause of death nor the attributes of death, is that not correct?"

"That is correct, Your Excellency." Mustafa's eyes roamed to the faces of the other dignitaries in the chapel. "They were not living, but they . . . showed no signs of decomposition, postmortem lividity, brain decay . . . none of the usual signs of physical death."

"Yet they were not alive?" prompted Lourdusamy.

Cardinal Mustafa rubbed his cheek. "Not within our capacity to revive, Your Excellency. Nor within our ability to detect signs of brain or cellular activity. They were . . . stopped."

"And what was the disposition of the bulk freighter, H.H.M.S. *Saigon Maru,* Cardinal Mustafa?"

"Captain Wolmak put a prize crew aboard from the *Jibril,*" said the Grand Inquisitor. "We returned immediately to Pacem to report the matter. The *Saigon Maru* was traveling via traditional Hawking drive, escorted by four Hawking-drive torchships, and is scheduled to arrive in the nearest Pax system with a Pax Fleet base . . . Barnard's System, I believe . . . in . . . ah . . . three standard weeks."

Lourdusamy nodded slowly. "Thank you, Grand Inquisitor." The Secretary of State walked to a place near the Pope's chair, genuflected toward the altar, and crossed himself as he crossed the aisle. "Your Holiness, I would ask that we hear from Her Excellency, Cardinal Du Noyer."

Pope Urban raised one hand as if in benediction. "We would be pleased to listen to Cardinal Du Noyer."

KENZO ISOZAKI'S MIND was reeling. Why were they being told these things? What possible purpose could it serve for the CEOs of the Pax Mercantilus to hear these things? Isozaki's blood had chilled at the summary death sentence of Admiral Aldikacti. Was that to be the fate of all of them?

No, he realized. Aldikacti had received a sentence of excommunication and execution for simple incompetence. If Mustafa, Pelli Cognani, himself, and the others were to be charged with some variety of treason . . . quick, simple execution would be the furthest thing from their fates. The pain machines in Castel Sant'Angelo would be humming and grating for centuries.

CARDINAL DU NOYER obviously had chosen to be resurrected as an old woman. As with most older people, she looked in perfect health—all of her teeth, wrinkles at a minimum, dark eyes clear and bright—but she also preferred to be seen with her white hair—cut almost to the scalp—and skin tight across her sharp cheekbones. She began without preliminaries.

"Your Holiness, Excellencies, other worthies . . . I appear here today as prefect and president of *Cor Unum* and de facto spokesperson for the private agency known as *Opus Dei*. For reasons which shall become apparent, the administrators of *Opus Dei* could not and should not be present here this day."

"Continue, Your Excellency," said Cardinal Lourdusamy.

"The bulk freighter the H.H.M.S. *Saigon Maru* was purchased by *Cor Unum* for *Opus Dei,* diverted from scrap recycling, and delivered to that agency seven years ago."

"For what purpose, Your Excellency?" queried Lourdusamy.

Cardinal Du Noyer's gaze moved from face to face in the small chapel, ending at His Holiness and looking down in respect. "For the purpose of transporting the lifeless bodies of millions of people such as were found on this interrupted voyage, Excellencies, Your Holiness."

The four Mercantilus CEOs made a noise somewhere short of a gasp, but louder than a mere intake of breath.

"Lifeless bodies . . ." repeated Cardinal Lourdusamy, but with the calm tone of a prosecuting attorney who knows in advance what the answers to all questions will be. "Lifeless bodies from where, Cardinal Du Noyer?"

"From whatever world *Opus Dei* designates, Your Excellency," said Du Noyer. "In the past five years, these worlds have included Hebron, Qom-Riyadh, Fuji, Nevermore, Sol Draconi Septem, Parvati, Tsingtao-Hsishuang Panna, New Mecca, Mao Four, Ixion, the Lambert Ring Territories, Sibiatu's Bitterness, Mare Infinitus North Littoral, Renaissance Minor's terraformed moon, New Harmony, New Earth, and Mars."

All non-Pax worlds, thought Kenzo Isozaki. *Or worlds where the Pax has only a foothold.*

"And how many bodies have these *Opus Dei* and *Cor Unum* freighters transported, Cardinal Du Noyer?" Lourdusamy asked in his low rumble.

"Approximately seven billion, Your Excellency," said the old woman.

Kenzo Isozaki concentrated on keeping his balance. Seven billion bodies. A bulk freighter like the *Saigon Maru* could haul perhaps a hundred thousand corpses if they were stacked like cordwood. It would take the *Saigon Maru* some seventy thousand trips to haul seven billion people from star system to star system. *Absurd.* Unless there were scores of bulk freighters . . . many of them the newer nova class . . . on hundreds or thousands of shuttle trips. Each of the worlds that Du Noyer had mentioned had been closed to the Pax Mercantilus for all or some of the past four years—quarantined because of trade or diplomatic disputes with the Pax.

"These are all non-Christian worlds." Isozaki realized that he had spoken aloud. It was the greatest breach of discipline he had ever suffered. The men and women in the chapel turned their heads in his direction.

"All non-Christian worlds," Isozaki said again, omitting even the honorifics in addressing the others. "Or Christian worlds with large populations of non-Christians, such as Mars or Fuji or Nevermore. *Cor Unum* and *Opus Dei* have been exterminating non-Christians. But why transport their bodies? Why not just leave them to rot on their homeworlds and then bring in the Pax colonists?"

His Holiness held up one hand. Isozaki fell silent. The Pope nodded in the direction of Cardinal Lourdusamy.

"Cardinal Du Noyer," said the Secretary of State, as if Isozaki had not spoken, "what is the destination of these freighters?"

"I do not know, Your Excellency."

Lourdusamy nodded. "And who authorized this project, Cardinal Du Noyer?"

"The Peace and Justice Commission, Your Excellency."

Isozaki's head snapped around. The Cardinal had just laid the blame for this atrocity . . . this unprecedented mass murder . . . directly at the feet of one man. The Peace and Justice Commission had one prefect and only one prefect . . . Pope Urban XVI, formerly Pope Julius XIV. Isozaki lowered his gaze to the shoes of the fisherman and contemplated rushing the fiend, attempting to get his fingers around the Pope's scrawny throat. He knew that the silent guards in the corner would cut him down halfway there. He was still tempted to try.

"And do you know, Cardinal Du Noyer," continued Lourdusamy as if nothing terrible had been revealed, nothing unspeakable had been spoken, "how these people . . . these non-Christians . . . are rendered . . . lifeless?"

Rendered lifeless, thought Isozaki, who had always hated euphemisms. *Murdered, you motherfucker!*

"No," said Cardinal Du Noyer. "My job as prefect of *Cor Unum* is merely to provide *Opus Dei* with the transport necessary to carry out their duties. The destinations of the ships and what happened before my freighters are needed is not . . . has never been . . . my concern."

Isozaki went to one knee on the stone floor, not to pray, but just because he could no longer stand. *How many centuries, gods of my ancestors, have accomplices to mass murder answered in this way? Since Horace Glennon-Height. Since the legendary Hitler. Since . . . forever.*

"Thank you, Cardinal Du Noyer," said Lourdusamy.

The old woman stepped back.

Incredibly, it was the Pope who was rising, moving forward, his white slippers making soft sounds on the stone. His Holiness walked between the staring people—past Cardinal Mustafa and Father Farrell, past Cardinal Lourdusamy and Monsignor Oddi, past Cardinal Du Noyer and the un-named monsignor behind her, past the empty pillows where the Pax Fleet officers had been, past CEO Aron and CEO Hay-Modhino and CEO Anna Pelli Cognani, to where Isozaki knelt, close to vomiting, black dots dancing in his vision.

His Holiness laid a hand on the head of the man who was even at that moment contemplating killing him.

"Rise, our son," said the mass murderer of billions. "Stand and listen. We command you."

Isozaki rose, legs apart, teetering. His arms and hands tingled as if someone had zapped him with a neural stunner, but he knew it was his own body betraying him. He could not have closed his fingers around anyone's throat at that moment. It was difficult enough just to stand alone.

Pope Urban XVI extended a hand, set it on the CEO's shoulder, and steadied him. "Listen, brother in Christ. Listen."

His Holiness turned his head and dipped his miter forward.

Councillor Albedo stepped to the edge of the low dais and began to speak.

"YOUR HOLINESS, YOUR Excellencies, Honorable Chief Executive Officers," said the man in gray. Albedo's voice was as smooth as his hair, as smooth as his gray gaze, as smooth as the silk of his gray cape.

Kenzo Isozaki trembled at the sound of it. He remembered the agony and embarrassment of the moment when Albedo had turned the CEO's cruciform into a crucible of pain.

"Tell us who you are, please," rumbled Lourdusamy in his most congenial tone.

Personal advisor to His Holiness, Pope Urban XVI, Kenzo Isozaki was prepared to hear. Albedo's gray presence had been glimpsed and rumored for decades and decades. He was never identified other than *personal advisor to His Holiness.*

"I am an artificial construct, a cybrid, created by elements of the AI TechnoCore," said Councillor Albedo. "I am here as a representative of those elements of the Core."

Everyone in the room except for His Holiness and Cardinal Lourdusamy took a step away from Albedo. No one spoke, no one gasped or cried out, but the animal scent of terror and revulsion in the little chapel could not have been stronger if the Shrike had suddenly materialized among them. Kenzo Isozaki felt the Pope's fingers still tight on his shoulder. He wondered if His Holiness could feel the pounding of his pulse through flesh and bone.

"The human beings transported from the worlds listed by Cardinal Du Noyer were . . . rendered lifeless . . . by Core technology, using Core robot spacecraft, and are being stored using Core techniques," continued Albedo. "As Cardinal Du Noyer reported, approximately seven billion non-Christians have been processed in this manner over the past seven years. Another forty to fifty billion must be similarly processed in the next standard decade. It is time to explain the reason for this project and to enlist your direct aid in it."

Kenzo Isozaki was thinking—*It is possible to wire the human skeletal structure with a powerful protein-based explosive so subtle that even the Swiss Guard sniffers would not have detected it. Would to the gods I had done that before coming here.*

The Pope released Isozaki's shoulder and walked softly to the dais, touching the sleeve of Councillor Albedo's robe as he passed. His Holiness sat in his straight-backed chair. His thin face was peaceful. "We wish you all to listen carefully," said His Holiness. "Councillor Albedo speaks with our authorization and approval. Continue, please."

Albedo bowed his head slightly and turned back toward the staring dignitaries. Even the Pope's security guards had moved back to the wall.

"You have been told, largely through myth and legend, but also through Church history," began Albedo, "that the TechnoCore was destroyed in the Fall of the Farcasters. That is not true.

"You have been told—primarily through the banned Hyperion *Cantos*—that the Core consisted of Three Elements—the Stables, who wished to preserve the status quo between humanity and the Core, the Volatiles, who viewed humanity as a threat and plotted to destroy it—primarily through the destruction of the Earth via the Big Mistake of '08, and the Ultimates, who thought only of creating an AI-based Ultimate Intelligence, a sort of silicon God which could predict and rule over the universe . . . or at least this galaxy.

"All these truths are lies."

Isozaki realized that Anna Pelli Cognani had gripped his wrist with her cool fingers and was squeezing very hard.

"The TechnoCore was never grouped into three warring elements," said Albedo, pacing in front of the altar and dais. "From its evolution into consciousness a thousand years ago, the Core was made up of thousands of distinct elements and factions—often warring, more often cooperating, but always struggling to achieve a synthesis of agreement toward the direction autonomous intelligence and artificial life should evolve. That agreement has never crystallized.

"Almost at the same time that the TechnoCore was evolving into true autonomy, while most of humankind lived on the surface of and in near orbit around one world—Old Earth—humanity had developed the capacity to change its own genetic programming . . . that is, to determine its own evolution. This breakthrough came partially through developments in the early twenty-first century A.D. in genetic manipulation, but was made possible most directly through the refinement of advanced nanotechnology. At first under the direction and control of early Core AIs working in conjunction with human researchers, nanotech life-forms . . . autonomous beings, some intelligent, much smaller than a cell, some molecular in size . . . soon developed their own *raison d'être* and *raison d'état*. Nanomachines, many in the form of viruses, invaded and reshaped humanity like a terrible viral plague. Luckily for both the human race and the race of autonomous intelligences now known as the Core, the primary vector for that plague was in the early seedships and other slower-than-light colony ships launched in the years just preceding the human Hegira.

"At that time, early elements of what would become the Human Hegemony and the forecasting elements of the TechnoCore realized that the goal of the evolving nanotech communities developed on those seedships was nothing less than the destruction of humankind and the creation of a new race of nanotech-controlled biologic adapts in a thousand distant star systems. The Hegemony and the Core responded by banning advanced nanotech research and by declaring war on the nanotech seedship colonies—the groups now known as the Ousters.

"But other events overshadowed this struggle.

"Elements of the emergent Core which favored alliance with the nanotech universes—and this was more than a small faction—discovered something that terrified *all* elements of the Core.

"As you know, our early research into Hawking-drive physics and faster-than-light communication led to the discovery of the Planck-space medium, what some have called the Void Which Binds. Evolving knowledge about this underlying and unifying substructure to the universe led to our creation of the FTL communication—the so-called fatline—as well as to the refined Hawking drive, the farcasters that united the Hegemonic WorldWeb, the planetary dataspheres evolving into megaspheres of Core-directed data, today's instantaneous Gideon drive, and even experiments into antientropic bubbles within this universe—what we believe will become the Time Tombs on Hyperion.

"But these gifts to humanity were not without price. It is true that certain Ultimate factions within the Core used the farcasters as a way to tap into human brains so as to create a neural net for their own purposes. This use was harmless . . . the neural nets were created in the nontime and nonspace of farcaster Planck-space transit and humans need never have learned of the experiments if other elements of the Core had not revealed this fact to the first John Keats cybrid persona four centuries ago—but I agree with those humans and those Core elements who consider this act as unethical, a violation of privacy.

"But those earliest neural net experiments revealed an amazing fact. There were other Cores in the universe . . . perhaps in our home galaxy. The discovery of this fact led to a civil war within our TechnoCore which still rages. Certain elements—not merely the Volatiles—decided that it was time to end the biological experiment that was the human race. Plans were made to 'accidentally' drop the '08 Kiev black hole into the center of Old Earth before Hawking drives allowed for a general exodus. Other elements of the Core delayed these plans until the mechanisms for escape were given to the human race.

"In the end, neither extreme faction triumphed . . . Old Earth was not destroyed. It was kidnapped—by means which our TechnoCore cannot understand to this day—by one or more of these alien Ultimate Intelligences."

The CEOs began babbling among themselves. Cardinal Mustafa went to both knees on his cushion and began praying. Cardinal Du Noyer looked so ill that her aide, the monsignor, whispered concerned entreaties. Even Monsignor Lucas Oddi looked as if he might faint.

His Holiness, Pope Urban XVI, held up three fingers. The chapel became silent.

"This is, of course, only background," continued Councillor Albedo. "What we wish to share with you today is the urgent reason for shared action.

"Three centuries ago, extreme factions of the Core—a society of autonomous intelligences ravaged and torn by eight centuries of violent debate and conflict—tried a new tack. They devised the cybrid creature known as John Keats—a human personality imbedded in an AI persona carried in a human body connected to the Core via Planck-space interface. The Keats persona had many purposes—as a sort of trap for what the UIs considered the 'empathy' element of an emerging human species UI, as a prime mover to set the events in motion which eventually led to the last Hyperion pilgrimage and the opening of the Time Tombs there, to flush the Shrike out of hiding, and as a catalyst to the Fall of the Farcasters. To serve this final purpose, elements of the Core—elements to which I owe my creation and allegiance—leaked the information to CEO Meina Gladstone and others in the Hegemony that other Core elements were using the Farcasters to prey upon human neurons like some sort of neural vampires.

"Those elements of the Core, under the guise of an Ouster attack, launched a final, physical assault on the WorldWeb. Despairing of destroying the scattered human race in one stroke, these elements hoped to destroy the advanced WorldWeb society. By attacking the Core directly via destroying the farcaster medium, Gladstone and the other Hegemony leaders ended the neural-net experiments and caused a great setback to the so-called Volatiles and Ultimates in the Core civil war.

"Our elements of the Core—elements devoted to preserving not only the human race but some sort of alliance with your species—destroyed one iteration of the John Keats cybrid, but a second was created and succeeded in its primary mission.

"And that mission was—to reproduce with a specific human female and create a 'messiah' with connections to both the Core and humanity.

"That 'messiah' lives now in the form of the child named Aenea.

"Born on Hyperion more than three centuries ago, that child fled through the Time Tombs to our age. She did so not out of fear—we would not have harmed her—but *because her mission is to destroy the Church, destroy the Pax civilization, and to end the human race as you have known it.*

"We believe that she is not aware of her true purpose or function.

"Three centuries ago, remnants of my element of the Core—a group you might think of as the Humanists—made contact with human survivors of the Fall of the Farcasters and the chaos which followed this fall." Albedo nodded in the direction of His Holiness. The Pope lowered his head in acknowledgment.

"Father Lenar Hoyt was a survivor of the last Shrike Pilgrimage," continued Councillor Albedo, pacing back and forth in front of the altar once again. Candle flames flickered slightly at his passing. "He had seen firsthand the manipulations of the Ultimate Intelligence Core elements and the depredations of their monster sent back through time, the Shrike. When we first made contact—the Humanists and Father Hoyt and a few other members of a dying Church—we resolved to protect the human race from further assaults while restoring civilization. The cruciform was our instrument of salvation—literally.

"You all know that the cruciform had been a failure. Prior to the Fall, humans resurrected by this symbiote's actions were retarded and sexual neuters. The cruciform—a sort of organic computer in which is stored the neurological and physiological data of a living human being—restored the body but not the full intellect or personality. It resurrected the corpse but stole the soul.

"The origins of the cruciform lie shrouded in mystery, but we Humanist elements of the Core believe that it was developed in our future and brought back through time via the Hyperion Time Tombs. In a sense, it was sent to be discovered by young Father Lenar Hoyt.

"The failure of the symbiote was due to the simple demands of information storage and retrieval. In a human mind, there are neurons. In a human body, there are approximately 10^{28} atoms. The cruciform, in order to restore the mind and body of a human being, must not only keep track of these atoms and neurons, but remember the precise configuration of the standing holistic wave front which comprises the human memory and personality. It also must provide the energy to restructure these atoms, molecules, cells, bones, muscles, and memories so that the organism is reborn as the individual who lived in that shell before. The cruciform alone cannot do that successfully. At best, the biomachine can reproduce a crude copy of the original.

"But the Core had the computing capacity to store, retrieve, reshape, and re-form this information into a resurrected human being. And we have done so for three centuries."

HERE KENZO ISOZAKI saw the panic in the exchanged glances between Cardinal Du Noyer and Cardinal Mustafa, between Father Farrell and the monsignor who was Du Noyer's aide. This was heresy. It was blasphemy. It was the end of the Sacrament of Resurrection and the beginning of the reign of the physical and mechanical once again. Isozaki himself felt sick. He glanced at Hay-Modhino and Pelli Cognani and saw that the CEOs were praying. CEO Aron looked as if he were in shock.

"BELOVED," SAID HIS Holiness. "Do not doubt. Do not surrender faith. Your thoughts now are a betrayal of Our Lord Jesus Christ, and of His Church. The miracle of resurrection is no less a miracle because these friends in what was once known as the TechnoCore help us realize the miracle. It was the work of Jesus Christ Almighty who led these other children of God—these creations of Our Lord through His most unworthy instruments, the human race—to find their own souls and salvation. Continue, M. Albedo."

ALBEDO LOOKED MILDLY amused at the expressions of shock in the room. But his smooth features settled into quiet amiability as he began speaking again.

"We have given the human race immortality. In exchange, we have asked for nothing but a silent alliance with humanity. We want only peace with our creators.

"In the past three centuries, our quiet alliance has benefited both AI and humanity. We have, as His Holiness said, found our souls. Humanity has found a peace and stability missing from history for millennia . . . perhaps forever. And I admit, the alliance has been good for my element of the Core, the group known as the Humanists. We have gone from being one of the smaller, more despised factions to becoming the—not ruling party, for no element rules in the Core—the major element of consensus. Our philosophy is accepted by almost all former warring groups.

"But not by all."

Here Councillor Albedo quit pacing and stood directly in front of the altar. He looked from face to face and his gray eyes were grim.

"The Core element which had hoped to dispose of humanity . . . the element composed of some former Ultimates and some pro-nanotech evolutionists—has played its trump card in the child named Aenea. She is, literally, the virus released into the body of humanity."

CARDINAL LOURDUSAMY STEPPED forward. The huge man's face was flushed and serious. His small eyes gleamed. His voice was sharp.

"Tell us, Councillor Albedo, what is the purpose of the child Aenea?"

"Her purpose," said the man in gray, "is threefold."

"What is the first purpose?"

"To destroy humanity's chance at physical immortality."

"And how can one child do that?" asked Lourdusamy.

"She is not a child, nor even human," said Albedo. "She is the spawn of a tailored cybrid. The persona of her cybrid father interfaced with her when she was in her mother's womb. Her mind and body have been interwoven with rogue elements of the Core since before birth."

"But how can she steal humanity's gift of immortality?" insisted Lourdusamy.

"Her blood," said Albedo. "She can spread a virus that destroys the cruciform."

"A literal virus?"

"Yes. But not a natural one. It was tailored by the rogue elements of the Core. The virus is a form of nanotech pestilence."

"But there are hundreds of billions of born-again Christians in the Pax," said Lourdusamy, his tone that of a lawyer leading his witness. "How could one child pose a threat to so many? Does the virus spread from victim to victim?"

Albedo sighed. "As far as we can tell, the virus becomes contagious once the cruciform has died. Those who have been denied resurrection through contact with Aenea will spread the virus to others. Also, those who have never carried a cruciform can be vectors for this virus."

"Is there any cure? Any immunization?" queried Lourdusamy.

"None," said Albedo. "The Humanists have attempted for three centuries to create countermeasures. But because the Aenea virus is a form of autonomous nanotech, it designs its own optimum mutation vector. Our defenses can never catch up to it. Perhaps with our own legions of nanotech colonies released within humanity we could someday catch up with the Aenea virus and defeat it, but we Humanists abhor nanotechnology. And the sad fact is that all nanotech life is out of our control—out of anyone's control. The essence of nanotech life's evolution is autonomy, self-will, and goals which have nothing to do with those of the harboring life-form."

"Humanity, you mean," said Lourdusamy.

"Precisely."

"Aenea's first goal," said Cardinal Lourdusamy, "or to be more precise—the first goal of her Core rogue element creators—is to destroy all cruciforms and thus destroy human resurrection."

"Yes."

"You mentioned three goals. What are the other two?"

"The second goal is to destroy the Church and the Pax . . . that is, all current human civilization," said Albedo. "When the Aenea virus spreads, when resurrection is denied . . . with farcasters still not functional and the Gideon drive impractical for single life-span humans . . . that second goal will be accomplished. Humanity will return to the balkanized tribalism which followed the Fall."

"And the third goal?" said Lourdusamy.

"The final goal is actually this Core element's original goal," said Councillor Albedo. "The destruction of the human species."

It was CEO Anna Pelli Cognani who shouted. "That's impossible! Even the destruction . . . kidnapping . . . of Old Earth or the Fall of the Farcasters did not wipe out humanity. Our species is too far-flung for such extinction. Too many worlds. Too many cultures."

Albedo was nodding, but sadly. "That was true. *Was.* But the Aenea Plague will spread almost everywhere. The cruciform-killing viruses will have mutated to new stages. Human DNA will have been invaded everywhere. With the fall of the Pax, the Ousters will invade again . . . this time successfully. They have long since succumbed to nanotech mutation. They are no longer human. With no Church or Pax or Pax Fleet to protect humanity, the Ousters will seek out those pockets of surviving human DNA and infect them with the nanotech plague. The human species . . . as we have known it and as the Church has sought to protect it . . . will cease to exist within a few standard years."

"And what will succeed it?" asked Cardinal Lourdusamy in a low rumble.

"No one knows," said Albedo softly. "Not even Aenea or the Ousters or the rogue elements of the Core who have released this final plague. The nanotech life-form colonies will evolve according to their own agenda, fashioning the human form to their own whims, and only they will be in control of their destiny. But that destiny will no longer be human."

"My God, my God," said Kenzo Isozaki, amazed that he was speaking aloud. "What can we do? What can *I* do?"

Amazingly, it was His Holiness who answered.

"WE HAVE DREADED and fought this threatened plague for three hundred years," His Holiness said softly, his sad eyes expressing more pain than his own. "Our first effort was to capture the child, Aenea, before she could spread the infection. We knew that she fled her era to ours not out of fear— we wished her no harm—but so that she could spread the virus across the Pax.

"Actually," amended His Holiness, "we suspect that the child Aenea does not truly know the full effect her contagion will have on humanity. In some ways, she is the unknowing pawn of these rogue elements of the Core."

It was CEO Hay-Modhino who suddenly spoke with vehemence. "We should have plasma-bombed Hyperion to cinders on the day she was scheduled to emerge from the Time Tombs. Sterilized the entire planet. Taken no chances."

His Holiness took no umbrage at the unpardonable interruption. "Yes, our son, there are those who urged that. But the Church could no more be the cause of taking so many innocent lives than we could have authorized the death of the single girl. We conferred with the predictive elements of the Core . . . they saw that a Jesuit named Father Captain de Soya would be instrumental in her final capture . . . but none of our peaceful attempts to seize the child succeeded. Pax Fleet could have vaporized her ship four years ago, but it was under orders not to unless all else failed. So we continue to strive for containment of her viral invasion. What you must do, M. Isozaki—what you must all do—is continue to support the Church's efforts, even as we intensify those efforts. M. Albedo?"

The gray man spoke again.

"Imagine the coming plague as a forest fire on an oxygen-rich world. It will sweep everything before it unless we can contain it and then extinguish it. Our first effort is to remove the dead wood and brush—the inflammable elements—not necessary to the living forest."

"The non-Christians," murmured CEO Pelli Cognani.

"Precisely," said Councillor Albedo.

"That is why they had to be terminated," said the Grand Inquisitor. "All those thousands on the *Saigon Maru*. All those millions. All those billions."

Pope Urban XVI raised his hand, in a command to silence rather than benediction this time. "*Not* terminated!" he said sternly. "Not a single life, not Christian, not non-Christian, has been taken."

The dignitaries looked at one another in confusion.

"This is true," said Councillor Albedo.

"But they were lifeless . . ." began the Grand Inquisitor and then stopped abruptly. "My profound apologies, Holy Father," he said to the Pope.

His Holiness shook his mitered head. "No apology is required, John Domenico. These are emotional topics. Please explain, M. Albedo."

"Yes, Your Holiness," said the man in gray. "Those aboard the *Saigon Maru* were lifeless, Your Excellency, but not dead. The Core . . . the Humanist elements in the Core . . . have perfected a method of putting human beings in temporary stasis, neither alive nor dead . . ."

"Like cryogenic fugue?" said CEO Aron, who had traveled much by Hawking drive before his conversion.

Albedo shook his head. "Much more sophisticated. And less harmful." He gestured with well-manicured fingers. "During the past seven years, we have processed seven billion human beings. In the next standard decade—or sooner—we must process more than forty-two billion more. There are many worlds in the Outback, and many even within Pax space, where non-Christians are in the majority."

"Processed?" said CEO Pelli Cognani.

Albedo smiled grimly. "Pax Fleet declares a world quarantined without knowing the real reason for their actions. Core robot ships arrive in orbit and sweep the inhabited sections with our stasis equipment. *Cor Unum* provides the ships and funding and training. *Opus Dei* uses freighters to remove the bodies in stasis . . ."

"Why remove them?" asked the Grand Inquisitor. "Why not leave them on their homeworlds?"

His Holiness answered. "They must be hidden in a place where the Aenea Plague cannot find them, John Domenico. They must be carefully . . . lovingly . . . put out of harm's way until the danger is past."

The Grand Inquisitor bowed his head in understanding and compliance.

"There is more," said Councillor Albedo. "My element of the Core has created a . . . breed of soldier . . . whose sole job is to find and capture this Aenea before she can spread the deadly contamination. The first one was activated four years ago and was called Rhadamanth Nemes. There are only a few others of these hunter/seekers, but they are equipped to deal with whatever obstacles the rogue elements of the Core throw at them . . . even the Shrike."

"The Shrike is controlled by the Ultimates and other rogue elements of the Core?" asked Father Farrell. It was the first time the man had spoken.

"We think so," answered Cardinal Lourdusamy. "The demon seems to be in league with the Aenea . . . helping her spread the contagion. In the same way, the Ultimates appear to have found a way to open certain farcaster portals for her. The Devil has found a name . . . and allies . . . in our age, I fear."

Albedo held up one finger. "I should stress that even Nemes and our other hunter/seekers are dangerous . . . as are any constructs so terribly single-minded. Once the child is captured, these cybrid beings will be terminated. Only the terrible danger posed by the Aenea Plague justifies their existence."

"Holy Father," said Kenzo Isozaki, his hands pressed together in prayer, "what else can we do?"

"Pray," said His Holiness. His dark eyes were wells of pain and responsibility. "Pray and support our Holy Mother Church in her effort to save humankind."

"The Crusade against the Ousters will continue," said Cardinal Lourdusamy. "We will hold them at bay as long as we can."

"To that end," said Councillor Albedo, "the Core has developed the Gideon drive and is working on new technologies for humanity's defense."

"We shall continue our search for the girl . . . young woman, now, I believe," added Lourdusamy. "And if she is apprehended, she will be isolated."

"And if she is not apprehended, Your Excellency?" asked Grand Inquisitor Cardinal Mustafa.

Lourdusamy did not answer.

"We must pray," said His Holiness. "We must ask for Christ's help at this time of maximum danger for our Church and our human race. We must each do everything we can and then ask more of ourselves. And we must pray for the souls of all of our brothers and sisters in Christ—even for, *especially* for, the soul of the child Aenea who unwittingly leads her species into such peril."

"Amen," said Monsignor Lucas Oddi.

Then, while all the others in the small chapel knelt and bowed their heads, His Holiness, Pope Urban XVI, stood, moved to the altar, and began to say a Mass of Thanksgiving.

14

ENEA.

Her name came before any other conscious thought. I thought of her before I thought to think of myself.

Aenea.

And then came the pain and noise and onslaught of wetness and buffeting. Mostly it was the pain that roused me.

I opened one eye. The other appeared to be gummed shut with caked blood or other matter. Before I remembered who or where I was, I felt the pain from innumerable bruises and cuts, but also from something far worse in my right leg. Then I remembered who I was. And then I remembered where I had been.

I laughed. Or more precisely, I *tried* to laugh. My lips were split and swollen and there was more blood or goo sealing one corner of my mouth. The laugh emerged as a sort of demented moan.

I had been swallowed by some sort of aerial squid on a world all atmosphere and clouds and lightning. Even now I was being digested in the noisy belly of the beast.

It *was* noisy. Explosively so. Rumbles, blasts, and a pounding, slapping noise. Like rain on a tropical forest canopy. I squinted through my one eye. Darkness . . . then a strobe of white light . . . darkness with red retinal echoes . . . more white strobes.

I remembered the tornadoes and planet-sized storm that had been coming toward me as I floated along in my kayak under the parasail before the beast swallowed me. But this was not that storm. This was rain on a jungle canopy. The material batting at my face and chest was tattered nylon, the remains of the parasail, wet palm fronds, and pieces of shattered fiberglass. I squinted downward and waited for the next lightning flash. The kayak was there, but splintered and shattered. My legs were there . . .

still partially ensconced in the kayak shell . . . the left leg intact and movable, but the right . . . I cried out in pain. The right leg was definitely broken. I could see no bone breaking through the flesh, but I was sure that there was a fracture in the lower thigh.

Otherwise I seemed intact. I was bruised and scratched. There was dried blood on my face and hands. My trousers were little more than rags. My shirt and vest were in tatters. But as I turned and arched my back, stretched my arms and flexed my fingers, wiggled the toes on my left foot and tried to wiggle those on my right, I thought that I was more or less in one piece . . . no broken back, no shattered ribs, no nerve damage except for possibly in my right leg where the agony was like barbed wire dragged through veins.

When the next flashes of lightning exploded, I tried to assess my surroundings. The broken kayak and I seemed to be stuck in a jungle canopy, wedged between splintered limbs, wrapped around with the tattered parasail and clinging shroud lines, being battered with palm fronds in a tropical storm, in a darkness broken only by lightning flashes, hanging some indeterminate distance above solid ground.

Trees? Solid ground?

The world I had been flying on had no solid ground . . . or at least none reachable without being compressed by pressure to something the size of my fist. And it seemed unlikely that there would be trees in the core of that Jovian world where hydrogen was squeezed to metal form. So I was not on that world. Nor was I still in the belly of the beast. Where was I?

Thunder blasted around me like plasma grenades. The wind came up, tossing the kayak in its precarious perch and making me scream aloud from the pain. I may have lost consciousness for a few moments, for when I opened my eyes again, the wind had died down and the rain was pummeling me like a thousand cold fists. I wiped the rain and matted blood from my eyes and realized that I was feverish, that my skin was burning even in that cold rain. *How long have I been here? What vicious microbes have found my open wounds? What bacteria shared the gut of that airborne squid-thing with me?*

Logic would have dictated that the entire memory of flying on the Jovian cloud world and being taken in by a tentacled squid-thing had been a fever dream—that I had farcast here . . . wherever here was . . . after escaping Vitus-Gray-Balianus B and all the rest was dreamscape. But there were the remnants of the deployed parasail all around me in the wet night. And there was the vividness of my memories. And there was the logical fact that logic did not work on this odyssey.

The wind shook the tree. The broken kayak slid along the precarious nest of shattered fronds and branches. My broken leg sent stabs of agony through me.

I realized that I had better apply some logic to this situation. At any moment the kayak was going to slide, or the branches would break, and the entire mass of shattered fiberglass, clinging nylon-10 risers, and wet memory-canvas parasail tatters was going to crash down into the darkness, dragging me and my broken leg with it. Despite the flashes of lightning . . . which came with less regularity now, leaving me in the pitching, wet darkness . . . I could see nothing below me except more branches, gaps of darkness, and the thick, gray-green trunks of trees that wound around themselves in a tight spiral. I did not recognize that sort of tree.

Where am I? Aenea . . . where have you sent me now?

I stopped that sort of thing. It was almost a form of prayer, and I was not going to get into the habit of praying to the girl I had traveled with and protected and eaten dinner with and argued with for four years. *Still and all,* I thought, *you might have sent me to some less difficult places, kiddo. If you had a choice in the matter, I mean.*

Thunder rumbled but no lightning flashed to light the scene. The kayak shifted and sagged, the broken bow tilting suddenly. I reached behind me and flailed around for the thick branch I had seen there during the earlier flashes of lightning. There were broken branches galore, razor-sharp splintered frond stems, and the sawtooth edges of the fronds themselves. I grabbed and pulled, trying to leverage my broken leg out of the broken cockpit of the kayak, but the branches were loose and I came only halfway out, reeling in nausea from the pain. I imagined that black dots were dancing in my vision, but the night was so dark that it made no difference. I retched over the side of the rocking kayak and tried again to find a firm handhold in the maze of splintered branches.

How the hell did I get in these treetops, anyway?

It did not matter. Nothing mattered at the moment except getting out of this mess of broken fiberglass and tangled shroud lines.

Get my knife, cut my way out of this clinging tangle.

My knife was gone. My *belt* was gone. The pockets of my vest had been ripped away and then the vest torn to a few tatters. My shirt was mostly gone. The flechette pistol I'd held like a talisman against the airborne cuttlefish-squid thing was gone . . . I dimly remembered it and my backpack dropping out when the passing tornado had ripped the parasail to shreds. Clothes, flashlight laser, ration pak . . . everything gone.

Lightning flashed, although the thunder-rumble had moved farther away. My wrist glinted in the downpour.

Comlog. That goddamn band must be indestructible.

What good would the comlog do me? I wasn't sure, but it was better than nothing. Raising my left wrist close to my mouth in the drumming rain, I shouted, "Ship! Comlog on . . . Ship! Hey!"

No response. I remembered the device flashing overload warnings during the electrical storm on the Jovian world. Inexplicably, I felt a sense of loss. The ship's memory in the comlog had been an idiot savant, at best, but it had been with me for a long time. I had grown used to its presence. And it had helped me fly the dropship that had carried us from Fallingwater to Taliesin West. And . . .

I shook away the nostalgia and thrashed around for a handhold again, finally clinging to the shroud lines that hung around me like thin vines. This worked. The parasail streamers must have caught firmly in the upper branches, and some of the shroud lines bore my weight as I scrabbled with my left foot on slick fiberglass to pull my dead leg from the wreckage.

The pain made me black out again for a few moments . . . this was as bad as the kidney stone at its worst, only coming at me in jagged waves . . . but when my mind came back into focus, I was clinging to the spiral-wrapped trunk of the palm tree rather than lying in the wreckage. A few minutes later a microburst of wind bulled through the jungle canopy and the kayak fell away in pieces, some being arrested by the still-intact shroud lines, others tumbling and crashing into darkness.

What now?

Wait for dawn, I guess.

What if there's no dawn on this world?

Wait for the pain to die down then.

Why would it die down? The fractured femur is obviously tearing at nerve and muscle. You have a wild fever. God knows how long you were lying here in the rain and torn plant material, unconscious, wounds open to every killer microbe that wants to get in. Gangrene could be settling in. That rotting vegetation stink you smell could be you.

Gangrene doesn't happen that quickly, does it?

No answer.

I tried hanging on to the tree trunk with my left arm and feeling along my injured thigh with my right hand, but the slightest touch made me moan and sway. If I passed out again, I could easily pitch off this branch. I settled on testing my lower right leg: it was numb in most places, but felt intact. Perhaps just a simple break in the lower thighbone.

Just a simple break, Raul? On a jungle world in a storm that might be permanent for all we know. With no medkit, no way to make a fire, no tools, no weapons. Just a shattered leg and a high fever. Oh, well . . . as long as it's just a simple fracture.

Shut the fuck up.

I weighed alternatives as the rain pounded on me. I could cling here for the rest of the night . . . which might be ten minutes or another thirty hours . . . or I could try to lower myself to the jungle floor.

Where the predators are waiting? Good plan.

I said shut up. The jungle floor might give me a place to shelter from the rain, find a soft place to rest my leg, offer branches and vines to make a splint.

"All right," I said aloud, and groped around in the dark to find a shroud line or vine or branch so that I could start my descent.

MY GUESS IS that it took me between two and three hours to lower myself. It might have been twice that or half that. The lightning part of the storm had passed and it would have been almost impossible to find handholds in the near absolute darkness, but a strange, faint, almost invisible reddish glow began above the thick jungle canopy and allowed my eyes to adapt enough to find a line here, a vine there, a solid branch here.

Sunrise? I thought not. The glow seemed too diffuse, too faint, almost chemical.

I guessed that I had been about twenty-five meters up in the canopy. The thick branches continued all the way down, but the density of razor-edged palm fronds diminished as I neared the bottom. There was no ground. Resting in the crotch of two branches, recovering from the pain and dizziness, I began lowering myself again only to find surging water beneath me. I pulled my left leg up quickly. The reddish glow was just bright enough to show me water all around, torrents of water flowing between the spiraled tree trunks, eddies of black water washing by like a torrent of oil.

"Shit," I said. I wasn't going any farther this night. I had held vague notions of building a raft. I was on a different world, so there must be a farcaster upstream and another downstream. I'd gotten here somehow. I had built a raft before.

Yeah, when you were healthy, well fed, with two legs and tools . . . like an axe and a flashlight laser. Now you don't even have two legs.

Please shut up. Please.

I closed my eyes and tried to sleep. The fever was making me shake from chills now. I ignored it all and tried to think of the stories I would tell Aenea when we saw each other next.

You don't really *believe that you'll ever see her again, do you?*

"Shut the fuck up," I said again, my voice lost in the sound of rain on jungle foliage and against the swirl of raging water half a meter beneath me. I realized that I should climb a couple of meters up the branches I had just lowered myself on through such pain and effort. The water might rise. Probably would rise again. Ironic to go to all that trouble just to make it easier to be swept away. Three or four meters up would be better. Would start in a minute. Just catch my breath first and let the waves of pain steady a bit. Two minutes at the most.

I AWOKE TO a thin gruel of sunlight. I was sprawled across several sagging branches, just centimeters above the swirling, gray surface of a flood that moved between the spiraled trunks with a visible current. It was still as dim as a deep twilight. For all I knew I had slept away the day and was ready to enter another endless night. It was still raining, but this was little more than a drizzle. The temperature was tropical warm, although my fever made it hard to judge, and the humidity was near absolute.

I ached everywhere. It was hard to separate the dull agony of the shattered leg from the ache in my head and my back and my guts. My skull felt as if there were a ball of mercury in it that shifted ponderously long seconds after my head itself turned. The vertigo made me sick again, but I had nothing left to vomit. I hung on the tangle of branches and contemplated the glories of adventure.

Next time you need an errand run, kiddo, send A. Bettik.

The light did not fade, but neither did it grow brighter. I shifted position and studied the water moving by: gray, ripped by eddies, carrying detritus of palm fronds and dead vegetation. I looked up, but could see no sign of the kayak or parasail. Any fiberglass or fabric that had dropped down here during the long night had long since been swept away.

It looked like a flood, like the spring runoff through the Fens above Toschahi Bay on Hyperion where the silt was deposited for another full year, a temporary inundation, but I knew that this drowned forest, this endless everglades of a watery jungle, could just as easily be the permanent state of affairs here. *Wherever here is.*

I studied the water. It was opaque, murky as gray milk, and could have been a few centimeters or many meters deep. The drowned trunks gave no clue. The current was quick, but not so quick as to carry me away if I kept a good grip on the branches that hung low above the roiling surface of the water. With luck, with no local equivalent of the Fens' mud cysts or dracula ticks or biting garr, I might be able to wade toward . . . something.

Wading takes two legs, Raul, m'boy. Hopping through the mud is more like it for you.

All right then, hopping through the mud. I gripped the branch above me with both hands and lowered my left leg into the current while keeping my injured leg propped on the wide branch where I lay. This led to new agonies, but I persisted, lowering my foot in the clotted water, then my ankle and calf, then my knee, then shifting to see if I could stand . . . my forearms and biceps straining, my injured leg sliding off the branch with a rending surge of agony that made me gasp.

The water was less than a meter and a half deep. I could stand on my good leg while water surged about my waist and splashed my chest. It was warm and seemed to lessen the pain in my broken leg.

All those nice, juicy microbes in this warm broth, many of them mutated from seedship days. They're licking their chops, Raul, old boy.

"Shut up," I said dully, looking around. My left eye was swollen and crusted with scab, but I could see out of it. My head hurt.

Endless trunks of trees rising from the gray water to the gray drizzle on all sides, the dripping fronds and branches so dark a gray-green that they appeared almost black. It seemed a slight bit brighter to my left. And the mud underfoot seemed a little firmer in that direction.

I began moving that way, shifting my left foot forward as I changed handholds from branch to branch, sometimes ducking beneath hanging

fronds, sometimes shifting aside like a slow-motion toreador to allow floating branches or other debris to swirl past. The move toward brightness
took hours more. But I had nothing better to do.

THE FLOODED JUNGLE ended in a river. I clung to the last branch, felt the
current trying to pull my good leg out from under me, and stared out at the
endless expanse of gray water. I could not see the other side—not because
the water was endless, I could see from the current and eddies moving from
right to left that it was a river and not some lake or ocean, but because the
fog or low clouds roiled almost to the surface, blotting out everything more
than a hundred meters away. Gray water, gray-green dripping trees, dark
gray clouds. It seemed to be getting dimmer. Night was coming on.

I had gone as far as I could on this leg. Fever raged. Despite the jungle
heat of the place, my teeth were chattering and my hands were shaking
almost uncontrollably. Somewhere in my awkward progress through the
flooded jungle, I had aggravated the fracture to the point where I wanted to
scream. No, I admit, I *had* been screaming. Softly at first, but as the hours
went by and the pain deepened and the situation worsened, I screamed out
lyrics to old Home Guard marching songs, then bawdy limericks I had
learned as a bargeman on the Kans River, then merely screams.

So much for the building the raft scenario.

I was getting used to the caustic voice in my head. It and I had made a
peace when I realized that it wasn't urging me to lie down and die, just
critiquing my inadequate efforts to stay alive.

There goes your best chance for a raft, Raul, old boy.

The river was carrying by an entire tree, its braided trunk rolling over
and over again in the deep water. I was standing shoulder-deep here, and I
was ten meters from the edge of the real current.

"Yeah," I said aloud. My fingers slipped on the smooth bark of the
branch to which I was clinging. I shifted position and pulled myself up a
bit. Something grated in my leg and this time I was sure that black spots
dulled my vision. "Yeah," I said again. *What are the odds that I'll stay
conscious, or that it will stay light, or that I'll stay alive, long enough to
catch one of those commuter trees?* Swimming for one was out of the
question. My right leg was useless and my other three limbs were shaking
as if palsied. I had just enough strength to cling to this branch for another
few minutes. "Yeah," I said again. "Shit."

"Excuse me, M. Endymion. Were you speaking to me?"

The voice almost made me lose my grip on the branch. Still clinging
with my right hand, I lowered my left wrist and studied it in the dimming
light. The comlog had a slight glow that had not been there the last time I
had looked.

"Well, I'll be damned. I thought that you were broken, Ship."

"This instrument is damaged, sir. The memory has been wiped. The neural circuits are quite dead. Only the com chips function under emergency power."

I frowned at my wrist. "I don't understand. If your memory has been wiped and your neural circuits are . . ."

The river pulled at my torn leg, seducing me into releasing my grip. For a moment I could not speak.

"Ship?" I said at last.

"Yes, M. Endymion?"

"You're here."

"Of course, M. Endymion. Just as you and M. Aenea instructed me to stay. I am pleased to say that all necessary repairs have been . . ."

"Show yourself," I commanded. It was almost dark. Tendrils of fog curled toward me across the black river.

The starship rose dripping, horizontal, its bow only twenty meters from me in the central current, blocking the current like a sudden boulder, hovering still half in the water, a black leviathan shedding river water in noisy rivulets. Navigation lights blinked on its bow and on the dripping black shark's fin far behind it in the fog.

I laughed. Or wept. Or perhaps just moaned.

"Do you wish to swim to me, sir? Or should I come in to you?"

My fingers were slipping. "Come in to me," I said, and gripped the branch with both hands.

THERE WAS A doc-in-the-box on the cryogenic fugue cubby-deck where Aenea used to sleep on the voyage out from Hyperion. The doc-in-the-box was ancient—hell, the whole ship was ancient—but its autorepair worked, it was well stocked, and—according to the garrulous ship on the way out four years earlier—the Ousters had tinkered with it back in the Consul's day. It worked.

I lay in the ultraviolet warmth as soft appendages probed my skin, salved my bruises, sutured my deeper cuts, administered painkiller via IV drip, and finished diagnosing me.

"It is a compound fracture, M. Endymion," said the ship. "Would you care to see the X rays and ultrasound?"

"No, thanks," I said. "How do we fix it?"

"We've already begun," said the ship. "The bone is being set as we speak. The bondplast and ultrasonic grafting will commence while you sleep. Because of the repair to damaged nerves and muscle tissue, the surgeon recommends at least ten hours' sleep while it begins the procedure."

"Soon enough," I said.

"The diagnostic's greatest concern is your fever, M. Endymion."

"It's a result of the break, isn't it?"

"Negative," said the ship. "It seems that you have a rather virulent kidney infection. Left untreated, it would have killed you before the ancillary effects of the broken femur."

"Cheery thought," I said.

"How so, sir?"

"Never mind," I said. "You say that you're totally repaired?"

"Totally, M. Endymion. Better than before the accident, if you don't mind me bragging a bit. You see, because of the loss of some material, I was afraid that I would have to synthesize carbon-carbon templates from the rather dross rock substrata of this river, but I soon found that by recycling some of the unused components of the compression dampers made superfluous by the Ouster modifications that I could evince a thirty-two percent increase in autorepair efficiency if I . . . ."

"Never mind, Ship," I said. The absence of pain made me almost giddy. "How long did it take you to finish the repairs?"

"Five standard months," said the ship. "Eight and one-half local months. This world has an odd lunar cycle with two highly irregular moons which I have postulated must be captured asteroids because of the . . . ."

"Five months," I said. "And you've just been waiting the other three and a half years?"

"Yes," said the ship. "As instructed. I trust that all is well with A. Bettik and M. Aenea."

"I trust that too, Ship. But we'll find out soon enough. Are you ready to leave this place?"

"All ship's systems are functional, M. Endymion. Awaiting your command."

"Command is given," I said. "Let's go."

The ship piped in the holo showing us rising above the river. It was dark out, but the night-vision lenses showed the swollen river and the farcaster arch only a few hundred meters upstream. I had not seen it in the fog. We rose above the river, above the swirling clouds.

"River's up from the last time I was here," I said.

"Yes," said the ship. The curve of the planet became visible, the sun rising again above fleecy clouds. "It floods for a period of some three standard months every local orbital cycle, which equals approximately eleven standard months."

"So you know what world this is now?" I said. "You weren't sure when we left you."

"I am quite confident that this planet was not among the two thousand eight hundred sixty-seven worlds in the General Catalogue Index," said the ship. "My astronomical observations have shown that it is neither in Pax space nor in the realm of the former WorldWeb or Outback."

"Not in the old WorldWeb or Outback," I repeated. "Where is it then?"

"Approximately two hundred and eighty light-years galactic northwest of the Outback system known as NNGC 4645 Delta," said the ship.

Feeling slightly groggy from the painkiller, I said, "A new world. Beyond the Outback. Why did it have farcasters then? Why was the river part of the Tethys?"

"I do not know, M. Endymion. But I should mention that there is a multitude of interesting life-forms which I observed by remotes while resting on the river bottom. Besides the river manta-ish creature which you and M. Aenea and A. Bettik observed downriver, there are more than three hundred observed species of avian variety and at least two species of humanoids."

"Two species of humanoids? You mean humans."

"Negative," said the ship. "Humanoids. Definitely not Old Earth human. One variety is quite small—little more than a meter in height—with bilateral symmetry but quite variant skeletal structure and a definite reddish hue."

A memory flitted by of a red-rock monolith Aenea and I had scouted on the lost hawking mat during our short stay here. Tiny steps carved in the smooth stone. I shook my head to clear it. "That's interesting, Ship. But let's set our destination." The curve of the world had become pronounced and stars were gleaming unblinkingly. The ship continued to rise. We passed a potato-shaped moon and moved farther from orbit. The unnamed world became a blinding sphere of sunlit clouds. "Do you know the world known as T'ien Shan, or the 'Mountains of Heaven'?"

"T'ien Shan," repeated the ship. "Yes. As far as my memory serves, I have never been there, but I have the coordinates. A small world in the Outback, settled by refugees of the Third Chinese Civil War late in the Hegira."

"You won't have any trouble getting there?"

"None would be anticipated," said the ship. "A simple Hawking-drive jump. Although I recommend that you use the autosurgeon as your cryogenic fugue cubby during the jump."

I shook my head again. "I'll stay awake, Ship. At least after the doc heals my leg."

"I would recommend against that, M. Endymion."

I frowned. "Why? Aenea and I stayed awake during the other jumps."

"Yes, but those were relatively short voyages within the old WorldWeb," said the ship. "What you now call Pax space. This will be a bit more extensive."

"How extensive?" I said. My naked body felt a sudden chill. Our longest jump—to Renaissance Vector System—had taken ten days of ship travel time and five months of time-debt for the Pax Fleet waiting for us. "How extensive a trip?" I said again.

"Three standard months, eighteen days, six hours, and some minutes," said the ship.

"That's not too bad a time-debt," I said. I last saw Aenea just after her sixteenth birthday. She would gain a few months on me. Her hair might be longer. "We had a greater time-debt jumping to Renaissance System."

"That is not time-debt, M. Endymion," said the ship. "That is ship-time."

This time the chill along the length of my body was real. My tongue seemed thick. "Three months' shiptime . . . how much time-debt?"

"For someone waiting on T'ien Shan?" said the ship. The jungle world was a speck behind us now as we accelerated toward a translation point. "Five years, two months, and one day," said the ship. "As you are aware, the time-debt algorithm is not a linear function of C-plus duration, but includes such factors as . . ."

"Ah, Jesus," I said, raising my wrist to my clammy forehead in the autosurgeon coffin. "Ah, damn."

"Are you in pain, M. Endymion? The dolorometer suggests you are not, but your pulse has become erratic. We can increase the level of pain-killer . . ."

"No!" I snapped. "No, it's all right. I just . . . five years . . . damn."

Did Aenea know this? Had she known that our separation would cover years of her life? Perhaps I should have brought the ship through the downriver farcaster. No, Aenea had said to fetch the ship and fly it to T'ien Shan. The farcaster had brought us to Mare Infinitus last time. Who knows where it would have taken me this time.

"Five years," I muttered. "Ah, damn. She'll be . . . damn, Ship . . . she'll be twenty-one years old. A grown woman. I'll have missed . . . I won't see . . . she won't remember . . ."

"Are you sure you are not in pain, M. Endymion? Your vital signs are turbulent."

"Ignore that, Ship."

"Shall I prepare the autosurgeon for cryogenic fugue?"

"Soon enough, Ship. Tell it to put me under while it heals my leg tonight and deals with the fever. I want at least ten hours' sleep. How long until translation point?"

"Only seventeen hours. It is well inside this system."

"Good," I said. "Wake me in ten hours. Have a full breakfast ready. What I used to have when we celebrated 'Sunday' on our voyage out."

"Very good. Anything else?"

"Yeah, do you have any record holos of . . . of Aenea . . . on our last trip?"

"I have stored several hours of such records, M. Endymion. The time you were swimming in the zero-g bubble on the outer balcony. The discussion you had about religion versus rationality. The flying lessons down the central dropshaft when . . ."

"Good," I said. "Cue those up. I'll look through them over break-fast."

"I will prepare the autosurgeon for three months of cryogenic sleep after your seven-hour interlude tomorrow," said the ship.

I took a breath. "All right."

"The surgeon wishes to commence repairing nerve damage and inject-ing antibiotics now, M. Endymion. Do you wish to sleep?"

"Yes."

"With dreams or without? The medication may be tailored for either neurological state."

"No dreams," I said. "No dreams now. There'll be time enough for those later."

"Very good, M. Endymion. Sleep well."

Part Two

15

AM ON THE PHARI marketplace shelf with A. Bettik, Jigme
Norbu, and George Tsarong when I hear the news that Pax
ships and troops have finally come to T'ien Shan, the "Mountains of Heaven."

"We should tell Aenea," I say. Around us, above us, and under us,
thousands of tons of scaffolding rock and creak with the weight of crowded
humanity buying, selling, trading, arguing, and laughing. Very few have
heard the news of the Pax's arrival. Very few will understand the implications when they do hear it. The word comes from a monk named Chim Din
who has just returned from the capital of Potala, where he works as a
teacher in the Dalai Lama's Winter Palace. Luckily, Chim Din also works
alternate weeks as a bamboo rigger at Hsuan-k'ung Ssu, the "Temple
Hanging in Air," Aenea's project, and he hails us in Phari Marketplace as
he is on his way to the Temple. Thus we are among the first people outside
the court at Potala to hear of the Pax arrival.

"Five ships," Chim Din had said. "Several score of Christian people.
About half of them warriors in red and black. About half of the remaining
half are missionaries, all in black. They have rented the old Red Hat Sect
gompa near Rhan Tso, the Otter Lake, near the Phallus of Shiva. They have
sanctified part of the gompa as a chapel to their triune God. The Dalai
Lama will not allow them to use their flying machines or go beyond the
south ridge of the Middle Kingdom, but he has allowed them free travel
within this region."

"We should tell Aenea," I say again to A. Bettik, leaning close so that
I can be heard over the marketplace babble.

"We should tell everyone at Jo-kung," says the android. He turns and
tells George and Jigme to complete the shopping—not to forget arranging

porters to carry the orders of cable and extra bonsai bamboo for the construction—and then he hoists his massive rucksack, tightens his climbing hardware on his harness, and nods to me.

I heft my own heavy pack and lead the way out of the marketplace and down the scaffolding ladders to the cable level. "I think the High Way will be faster than the Walk Way, don't you?"

The blue man nods. I had hesitated at suggesting the High Way for the return trip, since it has to be difficult for A. Bettik to handle the cables and slideways with just one hand. Upon our reunion, I had been surprised that he had not fashioned a metal hook for himself—his left arm still ends in a smooth stump halfway between his wrist and elbow—but I soon saw how he used a leather band and various leather attachments to make up for his missing digits. "Yes, M. Endymion," he says. "The High Way. It is much faster. I agree. Unless you want to use one of the flyers as courier."

I look at him, assuming that he is kidding. The flyers are a breed apart and insane. They launch their paragliders from the high structures, catching ridge lift from the great rock walls, crossing the wide spaces between the ridges and peaks where there are no cables or bridges, watching the birds, looking for thermals as if their lives depended on it . . . because their lives do depend on it. There are no flat areas on which a flyer can set down if the treacherous winds shift, or if their lift fails, or if their hang gliders develop a problem. A forced landing on a ridge wall almost always means death. Descent to the clouds below always means death. The slightest miscalculation in gauging the winds, the updrafts, the downdrafts, the jet stream . . . any mistake means death for a flyer. That is why they live alone, worship in a secret cult, and charge a fortune to do the Dalai Lama's bidding by delivering messages from the capital at Potala, or to fly prayer streamers during a Buddhist celebration, or to carry urgent notes from a trader to his home office to beat competitors, or—so the legend goes—to visit the eastern peak of T'ai Shan, separated for months each local year from the rest of T'ien Shan by more than a hundred klicks of air and deadly cloud.

"I don't think we want to entrust this news to a flyer," I say.

A. Bettik nods. "Yes, M. Endymion, but the paragliders can be purchased here at the marketplace. At the Flyer's Guild stall. We could buy two and take the shortest route back. They are very expensive, but we could sell some of the pack zygoats."

I never know when my android friend is joking. I remember the last time I was under a parasail canopy and have to resist the urge to shiver. "Have you ever paraglided on this world?" I say.

"No, M. Endymion."

"On any world?"

"No, M. Endymion."

"What would you think our chances would be if we tried?" I say.

"One in ten," he says without a second's hesitation.

"And what are our chances on the cables and slideway this late in the day?" I say.

"About nine in ten before dark," he says. "Less if sunset catches us short of the slideway."

"Let's take the cables and slideway," I say.

WE WAIT IN the short queue of market-goers leaving by cable, and then it is our turn to walk onto the step-off platform. The bamboo shelf is about twenty meters beneath the lowest marketplace scaffolding and it extends about five meters farther out over the abyss than does the rest of Phari. Beneath us there is nothing but air for thousands of meters and at the bottom of that emptiness only the ubiquitous sea of clouds that rolls against the ridges of upthrust rock like a white tide spilling against stone pilings. More kilometers beneath those clouds, I know, are poisonous gases and the surging, acidic sea that covers all of this world except its mountains.

The cablemaster gestures us forward and A. Bettik and I step onto the jump platform together. From this nexus, a score or more of cables slant out and down across the abyss, creating a black spiderweb that disappears at the edge of vision. The nearest cable terminus is more than a kilometer and a half to the north—on a little rock fang that stands out against the white glory of Chomo Lori, "Queen of Snow"—but we are going east across the great gap between the ridges, our terminal point is more than twenty kilometers away, and the cable dropping away in that direction appears to end in midair as it blends into the evening glow of the distant rock wall. And our final destination is more than thirty-five klicks beyond that to the north and east. Walking, it would take us about six hours to make the long trip north along Phari Ridge and then east across the system of bridges and catwalks. Traveling by cable and slideway should take less than half that time, but it is late in the day and the slideway is especially dangerous. I glance at the low sun again and wonder again about the wisdom of this plan.

"Ready," growls the cablemaster, a brown little man in a stained patchwork *chuba*. He is chewing besil root and turns to spit over the edge as we step up to the clip-on line.

"Ready," A. Bettik and I say in unison.

"Keep 'ur distance," growls the cablemaster and gestures for me to go first.

I shake my traveling risers loose from my full-body harness, slide my hands over the crowded gear sling that we call a rack, find the two-bearing pulley by feel, clip it on to the riser ring with a carabiner, run a Munter hitch into a second carabiner as a friction-brake backup to the pulley brake, find my best offset-D carabiner and use it to clip the pulley flanges together around the cable, and then run my safety line through the first two carabiners while tying a short prusik sling onto the rope, finally clipping that on to my chest harness below the risers. All of this takes less than a minute. I raise both hands, grab the D-ring controls to the pulley, and jump up and down, testing both the pulley connection and my clip-ons. Everything holds.

The cablemaster leans over to inspect the double-D-ring attachment and the pulley clamp with expert eyes. He runs the pulley up and back a meter, making sure that the near-frictionless bearings are sliding smoothly in their compact housing. Finally he puts all of his weight on my shoulders and harness, hanging on me like a second rucksack, and then releases me to make sure that the rings and brakelines hold. I am sure that he cares nothing if I fall to my death, but if the pulley was to stick somewhere on the twenty klicks of braided monofilament cable running out there to invisibility, it will be this cablemaster who will have to clear the mess, hanging from his etriers or belay seat over kilometers of air while waiting commuters seethe. He seems satisfied with the equipment.

"Go," he says and slaps me on the shoulder.

I jump into space, shifting my bulging rucksack high on my back as I do so. The harness webbing stretches, the cable sags, the pulley bearings hum ever so slightly, and I begin to slide faster as I release the brake with both thumbs on the D-ring controls. Within seconds I am hurtling down the cable. I lift my legs and sit back up into the harness seat in the way that has become second nature to me in the past three months. K'un Lun Ridge, our destination, glows brightly as sunset shadow begins to fill the abyss beneath me and evening shade moves down the wall of Phari Ridge behind me.

I feel a slight change in the cable tension and hear the cable humming as A. Bettik begins his descent behind me. Glancing back, I can see him leaving the jump-off platform, his legs straight ahead of him in the approved form, his body bobbing beneath the elastic risers. I can just make out the tether connecting the leather band on his left arm to the pulley brakeline. A. Bettik waves and I wave back, swiveling in my harness to pay attention to the cable screaming past me as I continue hurtling out over the gorge. Sometimes birds land on the cable to rest. Sometimes there is a sudden ice buildup or braid spurs. Very rarely there is a snagged pulley of someone who has met with an accident or cut away from their harness for reasons known only to themselves. Even more rarely, but enough to fix it in the mind, someone with a grudge or vague psychopathic tendencies will pause on the cable to loop a chock sling or spring-loaded cam around it, leaving a little surprise for the next person to come flying along the line. The penalty for that crime is death by flinging from the highest platform of Potala or Jo-kung, but this is of little solace to the person who first encounters the chock or cam.

None of these eventualities materialize as I slide across the emptiness under the ultralight cable. The only sound is the slight hum from the pulley brake as I moderate my speed and the soft rush of air. We are still in sunlight and it is late spring on this world, but the air is always chilly above eight thousand meters. Breathing is no problem. Every day since I arrived on T'ien Shan, I thank the gods of planetary evolution that even with the slightly lighter gravity here—0.954 standard—the oxygen is richer at this altitude. Glancing down at the clouds some klicks below my boots, I think of the seething ocean in that blind pressure, stirred by winds of phosgene and thick CO_2. There is no real surface land on T'ien Shan, merely that thick soup of a planetary ocean and the countless sharp peaks and ridges rising thousands of meters to the O_2 layer and the bright, Hyperion-like sunlight.

Memory nudges me. I think of another cloudscape world from a few months back. I think of my first day out in the ship, before reaching the translation point and while my fever and broken leg were healing, when I said idly to the ship, "I wonder how I got through the farcaster here. My last memory was of a giant . . ."

The ship had answered by running a holo taken from one of its buoy cameras as it sat at the bottom of the river where we had left it. It was a starlight-enhanced image—it was raining—and showed the green-glowing arch of the farcaster and tossing treetops. Suddenly a tentacle longer than the ship came through the farcaster opening, carrying what looked to be a toy kayak draped about with a mass of riddled parasail fabric. The tentacle made a single, graceful, slow-motion twist and parasail, kayak, and slumped figure in the cockpit glided—fluttered, actually—a hundred meters or so to disappear in the thrashing treetops.

"Why didn't you come get me then?" I asked, not hiding the irritation in my voice. My leg still hurt. "Why wait all night while I hung there in the rain? I could have died."

"I had no instructions to retrieve you upon your return," said the arrogant, idiot-savant ship's voice. "You might have been carrying out some important business that would brook no interruption. If I had not heard from you in several days, I would have sent a crawler drone into the jungle to inquire as to your well-being."

I explained my opinion of the ship's logic.

"That is a strange designation," said the ship. "While I have certain organic elements incorporated into my substructure and decentralized DNA computing components, I am not—in the strictest sense of the term— a biological organism. I have no digestive system. No need for elimination, other than the occasional waste gas and passenger effluvium. Therefore, I have no anus in either real or figurative terms. Therefore, I hardly believe I could qualify to be called an . . ."

"Shut up," I said.

THE SLIDE TAKES less than fifteen minutes. I brake cautiously as the great wall of the K'un Lun Ridge approaches. For the last few hundred meters, my shadow—and A. Bettik's—is thrown ahead of us against the orange-glowing vertical expanse of rock and we become shadow puppets—two strange stick figures with flailing appendages as we work the riser rings to brake our descent and swing our legs to brace for landing. Then the pulley brake sound grows from a low hum to a loud groan as I slow for the final approach to the landing ledge—a six-meter slab of stone with the back wall lined with padded zygoat fleece made brown and rotten by the weather.

I slide and bounce to a stop three meters from the wall, find my footing on the rock, and unclip my pulley and safety line with a speed born of practice. A. Bettik slides to a stop a moment later. Even with one hand, the android is infinitely more graceful than I on the cables; he uses up less than a meter of landing run-out.

We stand there a minute, watching the sun balance on the edge of Phari Ridge, the low light painting the ice-cone summit rising above the jet stream to the south of it. When we finish adjusting our harnesses and equipment racks to our liking, I say, "It's going to be dark by the time we get into the Middle Kingdom."

A. Bettik nods. "I would prefer to have the slideway behind us before full darkness falls, M. Endymion, but I think that this will not be the case."

Even the thought of doing the slideway in the dark makes my scrotum tighten. I wonder idly if a male android has any similar physiological reaction. "Let's get moving," I say, setting off down the slab ledge at a trot.

We lost several hundred meters of altitude on the cableway, and we will have to make it up now. The ledge soon runs out—there are very few flat places on the peaks of the Mountains of Heaven—and our boots clatter as we jog down a bonsai-bamboo scaffold walkway that hangs from the cliff wall and juts out over nothing. There is no railing here. The evening winds are rising and I seal my therm jacket and zygoat-fleece *chuba* as we jog along. The heavy pack bounces on my back.

The jumar point is less than a klick north of the landing ledge. We pass no one on the walkway, but far across the cloud-stirred valley we can see the torches being lit on the Walk Way between Phari and Jo-kung. The scaffold way and maze of suspension bridges on that side of the Great Abyss is coming alive with people heading north—some undoubtedly headed for the Temple Hanging in Air to hear Aenea's evening public session. I want to get there before them.

The jumar point consists of four fixed lines running up the vertical rock wall for almost seven hundred meters above us. These red lines are for ascension. A few meters away dangle the blue lines for rappelling from the ridge summit. Evening shadow covers us by now and the rising winds are chill. "Side by side?" I say to A. Bettik, gesturing toward one of the middle ropes.

The android nods. His blue countenance looks precisely as I had remembered it from our trip out from Hyperion, almost ten of his years ago. What did I expect—an android to age?

We remove our powered ascenders from our web racks and clip on to adjoining lines, shaking the hanging microfiber lines as if that will tell us if they are still anchored properly. The fixed ropes here are checked only occasionally by the cablemasters; they could have been torn by someone's jumar clips, or abraided by hidden rock spurs, or coated with ice. We will soon know.

We each clip a daisy chain and etriers to our powered ascenders. A. Bettik unloops eight meters of climbing line and we attach this to our harnesses with locking carabiners. Now, if one of the fixed lines fails, the other person can arrest the first climber's fall. Or so goes the theory.

The powered ascenders are the most technology owned by most citizens on T'ien Shan: powered by a sealed solar battery, little larger than our hands that fit in the molded grips, the ascenders are elegant pieces of climbing equipment. A. Bettik checks his attachments and nods. I thumb both of my ascenders to life. The telltales glow green. I jumar the right ascender up a meter, clamp it, step up in the looped etrier foothold, check that I am clear, slide the left ascender up a bit farther, clamp it tight, swing my left foot up two loops, and so on. And so on for seven hundred meters, the two of us pausing occasionally to hang from our etriers and look out across the valley where the Walk Way is ablaze with torches. The sun has set now and the sky has darkened immediately to violets and purples, the brightest stars already making an appearance. I estimate that we have about twenty minutes of real twilight left. We will be doing the slideway in the dark.

I shiver as the wind howls around us.

The fixed lines hang over vertical ice for the last two hundred meters. We both carry collapsible crampons in our rack bags, but we do not need them as we continue the tiring ritual—jumar—clamp—step—pull etriers free—rest a second—jumar—clamp—step—pull—rest—jumar. It takes us almost forty minutes to do the seven hundred meters. It is quite dark as we step onto the ice-ridge platform.

T'ien Shan has five moons: four of them captured asteroids but in orbits low enough to reflect quite a bit of light, the fifth almost as large as Old Earth's moon, but fractured on its upper right quadrant by a single, huge impact crater whose rays spread like a glowing spiderweb to every visible edge of the sphere. This large moon—the Oracle—is rising in the northeast as A. Bettik and I walk slowly north along the narrow ice ridge, clipping on to fixed cables to keep from being blown away by the sub-zero winds that hurtle down from the jet stream now.

I have pulled up my thermal hood and dropped my face mask into place, but the freezing wind still burns at my eyes and any bits of exposed flesh. We cannot tarry here long. But the urge to stand and gaze is strong in me, as it always is when I stand at the cableway terminus of K'un Lun Ridge and look out over the Middle Kingdom and the world of the Mountains of Heaven.

Pausing at the flat, open icefield at the head of the slideway, I pivot in all directions, taking in the view. To the south and west across the moonlit churn of cloudtops so far below, the Phari Ridge glows in the light of the Oracle. Torches high along the ridge north of Phari clearly mark the Walk Way, and I can see the lighted suspension bridges much farther north.

Beyond Phari Marketplace, there is a glow in the sky and I fancy that this is the torchlit brilliance of Potala, Winter Palace for His Holiness the Dalai Lama and home to the most magnificent stone architecture on the planet. It is just a few klicks north of there, I know, that the Pax has just been granted an enclave at Rhan Tso, in the evening shadow of Shivling—the "Phallus of Shiva." I smile beneath my therm mask as I imagine the Christian missionaries brooding about this heathen indignity.

Beyond Potala, hundreds of klicks to the west, is the ridge realm of Koko Nor with its countless hanging villages and dangerous bridges. Far south along the great ridge spine called the Lob-sang Gyatso lies the land of the Yellow Hat Sect, ending at the terminal peak of Nanda Devi, where the Hindu goddess of bliss is said to dwell. Southwest of them, so far around the curve of the world that the sunset still burns there, is Muztagh Alta with its tens of thousands of Islamic dwellers guarding the tombs of Ali and the other saints of Islam. North of Muztagh Alta, the ridges run into territory I have not seen—not even from orbit during my approach—harboring the high homes of the Wandering Jews along the approaches to Mt. Zion and Mt. Moriah, where the twin cities of Abraham and Isaak boast the finest libraries on T'ien Shan. North and west of them rise Mt. Sumeru—the center of the universe—and Harney Peak, also the center of the universe, oddly enough—both some six hundred klicks southeast of the four San Francisco Peaks where the Hopi-Eskimo culture there ekes out a living on the cold ridges and fern clefts, also certain that their peaks bound the center of the universe.

As I turn and look due north, I can see the greatest mountain in our hemisphere and the northern boundary of our world since the ridge disappears beneath phosgene clouds a few klicks north of there—Chomo Lori, "Queen of Snow." Incredibly, the sunset still lights Chomo Lori's frozen summit even as the Oracle bathes its eastern ridges with a softer light.

From Chomo Lori, the K'un Lun and Phari ridges both run south, the gap between them widening to unbridgeable distances south of the cableway we have just crossed. I turn my back to the north wind and look to the south and east, tracing the looping K'un Lun ridgeline, imagining that I can see the torches some two hundred klicks south where the city of Hsi wang-mu, "Queen Mother of the West" ("west" being south and west of the Middle Kingdom), shelters some thirty-five thousand people in the safety of its notches and fissures.

South of Hsi wang-mu, with only its high summit visible above the jet stream, rises the great peak of Mt. Koya, where—according to the faithful who live in ice-tunnel cities on its lower reaches—Kobo Daishi, the founder of Shingon Buddhism, lies interred in his airless ice tomb, waiting for conditions to be right before emerging from his meditative trance.

East of Mt. Koya, out of sight over that curve of the world, are Mt. Kalais, home to Kubera, the Hindu god of wealth, as well as to Shiva, who evidently does not mind being separated from his phallus by more than a thousand kilometers of cloud space. Parvati, Shiva's wife, is also reputed to live on Mt. Kalais, although no one has heard her opinion of the separation.

A. Bettik had traveled to Mt. Kalais during his first full year on the planet, and he told me that the peak was beautiful, one of the tallest peaks on the planet—more than nineteen thousand meters above sea level—and he described it as looking like a marble sculpture rising from a pedestal of striated rock. The android also said that on the summit of Mt. Kalais, high on the icefields where the wind is too thin to blow or breathe, sits a carboned-alloy temple to the Buddhist deity of the mountain, Demchog, the "One of Supreme Bliss," a giant at least ten meters tall, as blue as the sky, draped with garlands of skulls and happily embracing his female consort as he dances. A. Bettik said that the blue-skinned deity looks a bit like him. The palace itself is in the precise center of the rounded summit, which lies in the center of a mandala made up of lesser snow peaks, all of it embracing the sacred circle—the physical mandala—of the divine space of Demchog, where those who meditate will discover the wisdom to set them free from the cycle of suffering.

In sight of the Mt. Kalais Demchog mandala, said A. Bettik, and so far to the south that the peak is buried beneath kilometer-deep glaciers of gleaming ice, rises Helgafell—the "Mead Hall of the Dead"—where a few hundred Hegira-transplanted Icelanders have reverted to Viking ways.

I look to the southwest. If I could someday travel the arc of the Antarctic Circle there, I know, I would come across such peaks as Gunung Agung, the navel of the world (one of dozens on T'ien Shan), where the Eka Dasa Rudra Festival is now twenty-seven years into its sixth hundred-year cycle, and where the Balinese women are said to dance with unsurpassed beauty and grace. Northwest more than a thousand klicks along the high ridge from Gunung Agung is Kilimachaggo, where the denizens of the lower terraces disinter their dead from the loamy fissures after a decent interval and carry the bones high above breathable atmosphere—climbing in handsewn skinsuits and pressure masks—to rebury their relatives in rock-hard ice near the eighteen-thousand-meter level, with the skulls staring through ice toward the summit in eternal hopefulness.

Beyond Kilimachaggo, the only peak I know by name is Croagh Patrick, which reputedly has no snakes. But as far as I know, there are no snakes anywhere else on the Mountains of Heaven.

I turn back to the northeast. The cold and wind buffet me head-on, urging me to hurry, but I take this final minute to look out toward our destination. A. Bettik also appears to be in no rush, although it might be anxiety about the coming slideway that causes him to pause here a moment with me.

To the north and east here, beyond the sheer wall of the K'un Lun Ridge, lies the Middle Kingdom with its five peaks glowing in the lantern light of the Oracle.

To the north of us, the Walk Way and a dozen suspension bridges cross the space to the town of Jo-kung and the central peak of Sung Shan, the "Lofty," although this is by far the lowest of the five summits of the Middle Kingdom.

Ahead of us, connected from the southwest only by a sheer ice ridge branded by the looping route of the slideway, rises Hua Shan, "Flower Mountain," the westernmost summit in the Middle Kingdom and arguably the most beautiful of the five peaks. From Hua Shan, the final klicks of cableway connect the Flower Mountain to the spur ridges north of Jo-kung where Aenea works on Hsuan-k'ung Ssu, the Temple Hanging in Air, set into a sheer cliff face looking north across the abyss to Heng Shan, the Sacred Mountain of the North.

There is a second Heng Shan some two hundred klicks to the south, marking the Middle Kingdom's boundary there, but it is an unimpressive mound compared to the sheer walls, great ridges, and sweeping profile of its northern counterpart. Looking north through the raging winds and sheets of spindrift, I remember being in the Consul's ship and floating between the noble Heng Shan and the Temple on that first hour on the planet.

Glancing to the east and north again, beyond Hua Shan and the short central peak of Sung Shan, I can easily see the incredible summit of T'ai Shan silhouetted against the rising Oracle more than three hundred klicks away. This is the Great Peak of the Middle Kingdom, 18,200 meters tall, with its town of Tai'an—the City of Peace—hunkered down at the 9,000-meter level, and its legendary 27,000-step staircase rising from Tai'an, through the snowfields and rock walls, all the way to the mythical Temple of the Jade Emperor on the summit.

Beyond our Sacred Mountain of the North, I know, rise the Four Mountains of Pilgrimage for the Buddhist faithful—O-mei Shan to the west; Chiu-hua Shan, "Nine Flower Mountain," to the south; Wu-t'ai Shan, the "Five Terrace Mountain" with its welcoming Purple Palace to the north; and lowly but subtly beautiful P'u-t'o Shan in the far east.

I take a few final seconds on this wind-battered ice ridge, glancing toward Jo-kung, hoping to see the torchlights lining the fissure pass over to Hsuan-k'ung Ssu, but high clouds or sheets of spindrift haze the view so that only an Oracle-lighted blur is to be seen.

Turning to A. Bettik, I point toward the slideway and give the thumbs-up gesture. The wind is blowing too hard now to carry words.

A. Bettik nods and reaches back to unfurl the folding sledfoil from an outside pocket on his pack. I realize that my heart is pounding from more than exertion as I find my own sledfoil and carry it to the slideway launch platform.

THE SLIDEWAY IS fast. That has always been its appeal. And that is its greatest danger.

There are still places in the Pax, I am sure, where the ancient custom of tobogganing still exists. In that sport, one sits on a flat-bottomed sled and hurtles down a prepared ice course. This pretty much describes the slideway, except that instead of a flat-bottomed sled, A. Bettik and I each have a sledfoil, which is less than a meter long and curves up around us like a spoon. The sledfoil is more foil than sled, as limp as so much aluminum wrap until we each divert a bit of power from our ascenders, sending the piezoelectric message to the stiffeners in the foil structure until our little sleds seem to inflate, taking form in a few seconds.

Aenea once told me that there used to be fixed carbon-carbon lines running the length of the slideway, and the sledders had clipped on to them much as we would a cableway or rappel line, using a special low-friction clip ring similar to the cable pulley to keep from losing speed. That way, one could brake using the cable or, if the sled were to fly off into space, use the clip line as a self-arrest harness. There would be bruises and broken bones with such a safety line, but at least the body would not fly out into space with the sled.

But the cables had not worked, Aenea said. They took too much maintenance to keep clear and functioning. Sudden ice storms would freeze them to the side of the slideway and someone traveling 150 klicks an hour would suddenly have their clip ring encounter immovable ice. It is hard enough these days keeping the cableway clear: the fixed lines of the slideway had been unmanageable.

So the slideways were abandoned. At least until teenagers looking for a thrill and adults in a serious hurry found that nine times out of ten, one could keep the sledfoils in the groove just by glissading—that is, by using one or more ice axes in the self-arrest position and keeping the speed low enough to stay in the trough. "Low enough" meaning beneath 150 klicks per hour. Nine times out of ten it would work. If one was very skillful. And if the conditions were perfect. And if it was daylight.

A. Bettik and I had taken the slideway three other times, once returning from Phari with some medicine needed to save a young girl's life and twice just to learn the turns and straightaways. The voyage had been exhilarating and terrifying those times, but we had made it safely. But each time had been in daylight . . . with no wind . . . and with other glissaders ahead of us, showing the way.

Now it is dark; the long run gleams wickedly in the moonlight ahead of us. The surface looks iced and rough as stone. I have no idea if anyone has made the run this day . . . or this week . . . if anyone has checked for fissures, ice heaves, fractures, cave-ins, crevasses, ice spikes, or other obstacles. I do not know how long the ancient toboggan runs had been, but this slideway is more than twenty klicks long, running along the side of the sheer Abruzzi Spur connecting K'un Lun Ridge to the slopes of Hua Shan, flattening out on the gradual icefields on the west side of the Flower Mountain, kilometers south of the safer and slower Walk Way looping down from the north. From Hua Shan, it is only nine klicks and three easy cable runs to the scaffolding of Jo-kung and then a brisk walk through the fissure pass and down onto the sheer face walkways to Hsuan-k'ung Ssu.

A. Bettik and I are sitting side by side like children on sleds, waiting for a push from Mommy or Daddy. I lean over, grab my friend's shoulder, and pull him closer so that I can shout through the thermal material of his hood and face mask. The wind is stinging me with ice now. "All right if I lead?" I yell.

A. Bettik turns his face so that our cloth-covered cheeks are touching. "M. Endymion, I feel that I should lead. I have done this slideway two more times than you, sir."

"In the dark?" I shout.

A. Bettik shakes his hooded head. "Few try it in the dark these days, M. Endymion. But I have a very good memory of every curve and straight. I believe I can be helpful in showing you the proper braking points."

I hesitate only a second. "All right," I say. I squeeze his hand through our gloves.

With night-vision goggles, this would be as easy as a daylight slideway glissade—which does not qualify as easy in my book. But I had lost the goggles that I had taken on my farcaster odyssey, and although the ship carried replacement pairs, I had left them in the ship. "Bring two skinsuits and rebreathers," Rachel had relayed from Aenea. She might have mentioned night-vision goggles.

Today's jaunt was supposed to have been an easy hike to Phari Marketplace, a night spent in the hostelry there, and then a pack trip back with George Tsarong, Jigme Norbu, and a long line of porters, hauling the heavy material for the building site.

Perhaps, I think, I'm overreacting to the news of the Pax landing. Too late now. Even if we turn around, the rappel down the fixed lines on K'un Lun Ridge would be as much trouble as this glissade. Or so I lie to myself.

I watch as A. Bettik rigs his short, 38-centimeter ice-climbing hammer in the loop of the wristband on his left arm, then readies his regular 75-centimeter ice axe. Sitting cross-legged on my sled, I slip my own ice hammer into my left hand and trail my longer ice axe in my right hand like a tiller. I give the android the thumbs-up signal again and watch as he pushes off in the moonlight, spinning once, then steadying the sled expertly with his short ice hammer, chips flying, and then hurtling over the brink and out of sight for a minute. I wait until there is an interval of ten meters or so—far enough to avoid the ice spray of his passing, close enough to see him in the orange light of the Oracle—and then I push over myself.

Twenty kilometers. At an average speed of 120 klicks per hour, we should cover the distance in ten minutes. Ten freezing, adrenaline-pumping, gorge-rising, terror-beating-against-the-ribs, react-in-a-microsecond-or-die minutes.

A. Bettik is brilliant. He sets up each turn perfectly, coming in low for the high-banked curves so that his apogee—and mine a few seconds later—will be teetering right at the lip of the icy bank, careering out of the banked turn at just the right speed for the next descending straight, then banging and skipping down the long icy ramp so fast that vision blurs, the pounding comes up through my tailbone and spine so that vision is doubled, trebled, and my head pounds with the pain of it, then blurs again with the spray of ice chips flying, creating halos in the moonlight, bright as the unblinking stars spill and reel above us—the brilliant stars competing even with the Oracle's glow and the asteroid moons' quick, tumbling light—and then we are braking low and bouncing hard and riding high again, arresting into a sharp left that takes my breath away, then skidding into a sharper right, then pounding and flying down a straight so steep that the sled and I seem to be screaming into freefall. For a minute I am looking straight down at the moonlit phosgene clouds—green as mustard gas in the lying moonlight—then we are both racketing around a series of spirals, DNA-helix switchbacks, our sleds teetering on the edge of each bank so that twice my ice-axe blade bites into nothing but freezing air, but both times we drop back down and emerge—not exiting the turns so much as being spit out of them, two rifle bullets fired just above the ice—and then we bank high again, come out accelerating onto a straight, and shoot across eight kilometers of sheer ice wall on the Abruzzi Spur, the right banked wall of the slideway now serving as the floor of our passage, my ice axe spinning chips into vertical space as our speed increases, then increases more, then becomes something more than speed as the cold, thin air slices through my mask and thermal garments and gloves and heated boots to freeze flesh and to tear at muscle. I feel the frozen skin of my cheeks stretching under my thermal mask as I grin idiotically, a rictal grimace of terror and the sheer joy of mindless speed, my arms and hands adjusting constantly, automatically, instantly to changes in the ice-axe tiller and the ice-hammer brake.

Suddenly A. Bettik swerves to the left, chips flying as he bites deep with the curved blades of both long and short axes—it makes no sense, such a move will send him—both of us!—bouncing off the inner wall, the vertical ice wall, and then screaming out into black air—but I trust him, making the decision in less than a second, and slam the blade of my large axe down, pounding hard with my ice hammer, feeling my heart in my throat as I skid sideways and threaten to slide right instead of left, on the verge of spinning and spiraling off the narrow ice ledge at 140 kilometers per hour—but I correct and stabilize and flash past a hole in the ice floor where we would have been sliding except for this wild detour, hurtling onto a broken-away ledge six or eight meters wide, a trapdoor to death—and then A. Bettik rackets down off the inner wall, catches his slide with a flash of ice-axe blades in the moonlight, and then continues hurtling down the Abruzzi Spur toward the final series of turns onto the Hua Shan ice slopes.

And I follow.

On the Flower Mountain, we are both too frozen and shaken to rise from our sleds for several cold minutes. Then, together, we get to our feet, ground the piezoelectric charges in our sleds, collapse them, and fold them away in our packs. We walk the ice path around the shoulder of Hua Shan in silence—I in awe of A. Bettik's reactions and courage, he in silence I cannot interpret but fervently hope is not anger at my hasty decision to return via this route.

The final three cableway flights are anticlimax, noted only for the beauty of the moonlight on the peaks and ridges around us, and for the difficulty I have in closing my frozen fingers on the D-ring brakes.

Jo-kung is ablaze with torches after the moonlit emptiness of the upper slopes, but we avoid the main scaffolds and take the ladders to the fissure pass. Then we are surrounded by the shadowed darkness of the north face, broken by sputtering torches along the high walkway to Hsuan-k'ung Ssu. We jog the last kilometer.

We arrive just as Aenea is beginning her early evening discussion session. There are about a hundred people crowded into the little platform pagoda. She looks across the heads of the waiting people, sees my face, asks Rachel to begin the discussion, and comes immediately to where A. Bettik and I stand in the windy doorway.

16

ADMIT THAT I was confused and a bit depressed when I first arrived on the Mountains of Heaven.

I slept in cryogenic fugue for three months and two weeks. I had thought that cryogenic fugue was dreamless, but I was wrong. I had nightmares for most of the way and awoke disoriented and apprehensive.

The translation point in our outbound system had been only seventeen hours away, but in the T'ien Shan System we had to translate from C-plus out beyond the last icy planet and decelerate in-system for three full days. I jogged the various decks, up and down the spiral staircase, and even out onto the little balcony I'd had the ship extrude. I told myself that I was trying to get my leg back into shape—it still hurt despite the ship's pronouncement that the doc-in-the-box had healed it and that there should be no pain—but in truth, I knew, I was trying to work off nervous energy. I'm not sure that I remembered ever being so anxious before.

The ship wanted to tell me all about this star system in excruciating detail—G-type yellow star, blah, blah, blah—well, I could *see* that . . . eleven worlds, three gas giants, two asteroid belts, a high percentage of comets in the inner system, blah, blah, blah. I was interested only in T'ien Shan, and I sat in the carpeted holopit and watched it grow. The world was amazingly bright. Blindingly bright. A brilliant pearl set against the black of space.

"What you are seeing is the lower, permanent cloud layer," droned the ship. "The albedo is impressive. There are higher clouds—see those storm swirls in the lower right of the illuminated hemisphere? Those high cirrus causing shadows near the north polar cap? Those are the clouds that would bring weather to the human inhabitants."

"Where are the mountains?" I asked.

"There," said the ship, circling a gray shadow in the northern hemisphere. "According to my old charts, this is a great peak in the northern reaches of the eastern hemisphere—Chomo Lori, 'Queen of Snow'—and you see these striations running south from it? See how they stay close together until they pass the equator and then spread farther and farther apart until they disappear into the south polar cloud masses? These are the two great spine ridges, Phari Ridge and K'un Lun Ridge. They were the first inhabited rock lines on the planet and are excellent examples of the equivalent early Cretaceous Dakotan violent upthrust resulting in . . ."

Blah, blah, blah. And all I could think of was Aenea, and Aenea, and Aenea.

It was strange entering a system with no Pax Fleet ships to challenge us, no orbital defenses, no lunar bases . . . not even a base on the giant bull's-eye of a moon that looked as if someone had fired a single bullet into a smooth orange sphere—no register of Hawking-drive wakes or neutrino emissions or gravitational lenses or cleared swaths of Bussard-jet drones—no sign of any higher technologies. The ship said that there was a trickle of microwave broadcasting emanating from certain areas of the planet, but when I had them piped in, they turned out to be in pre-Hegira Chinese. This was a shock. I had never been on a world where the majority of humans spoke anything but a version of Web English.

The ship entered geosynchronous orbit above the eastern hemisphere. "Your directions were to find the peak called Heng Shan, which should be approximately six hundred and fifty kilometers southeast of Chomo Lori . . . there!" The telescopic view in the holopit zoomed in on a beautiful fang of snow and ice leaping through at least three layers of cloud until the summit gleamed clear and bright above most of the atmosphere.

"Jesus," I whispered. "And where is Hsuan-k'ung Ssu? The Temple Hanging in Air?"

"It should be . . . *there*," said the ship triumphantly.

We were looking straight down at a vertical ridge of ice, snow, and gray rock. Clouds broiled at the base of this incredible slab. Even looking at this through the holo viewer made me grab couch cushions and reel in vertigo.

"Where?" I said. There were no structures in sight.

"That dark triangle," said the ship, circling what I thought was a shadow on one gray slab of rock. "And this line . . . here."

"What's the magnification?" I asked.

"The triangle is approximately one-point-two meters along the longest edge," came the voice I'd grown to know so well from my comlog.

"Pretty small building for people to live in," I pointed out.

"No, no," said the ship. "This is just a bit of a human-made structure protuding from under what must be a rock overhang. I would surmise that the entire so-called Temple Hanging in Air is under this overhang. The rock is more than vertical at this point . . . it pitches back some sixty or eighty meters."

"Can you get us a side view? So that I can see the Temple?"

"I could," said the ship. "It would require repositioning us in a more northerly orbit so that I can use the telescope to look south over the peak of Heng Shan, and go to infrared to look through the cloud mass at eight thousand meters which is passing between the peak and the ridge spur on which the Temple is built, I would also have to . . ."

"Skip it," I said. "Just tightbeam that temple area . . . hell, the whole ridge . . . and see if Aenea is waiting for us."

"Which frequency?" said the ship.

Aenea had not mentioned any frequency. She had just said something about not being able to land in a true sense, but to come down to Hsuan-k'ung Ssu anyway. Looking at this vertical and worse-than-vertical wall of snow and ice, I began to understand what she meant.

"Broadcast on whatever common frequency we would have used if you were calling a comlog extension," I said. "If there's no answer, dial through all the frequencies you have. You might try the frequencies that you picked up earlier."

"They were coming from the southernmost quadrant of the western hemisphere," said the ship in a patient voice. "I picked up no microwave emanations from this hemisphere."

"Just do it, please," I said.

We hung there for half an hour, sweeping the ridge with tightbeam, then broadcasting general radio signals toward all the peaks in the area, then flooding the hemisphere with short queries. There was no response.

"Can there actually be an inhabited world where no one uses radio?" I said.

"Of course," said the ship. "On Ixion, it is against local law and custom to use microwave communication of any sort. On New Earth there was a group which . . ."

"Okay, Okay," I said. For the thousandth time, I wondered if there were a way to reprogram this autonomous intelligence so that it wasn't such a pain in the ass. "Take us down," I said.

"To which location?" said the ship. "There are extensive inhabited areas on the high peak to the east—T'ai Shan it is called on my map—and another city south on the K'un Lun Ridge, it is called Hsi wang-mu, I believe, and other habitations along the Phari Ridge and west of there in an area marked as Koko Nor. Also . . ."

"Take us down to the Temple Hanging in Air," I said.

LUCKILY, THE PLANET'S magnetic field was completely adequate for the ship's EM repulsors, so we floated down through the sky rather than having to descend on a tail of fusion flame. I went out to the balcony to watch, although the holopit or screens in the top bedroom would have been more practical.

It seemed to take hours, but actually within minutes we were floating gently at eight thousand–some meters, drifting between the fantastic peak to the north—Heng Shan—and the ridge holding Hsuan-k'ung Ssu. I had seen the terminator rushing from the east as we descended, and according to the ship, it was late afternoon here now. I carried a pair of binoculars out to the balcony and stared. I could see the Temple clearly. I could see it, but I could not quite believe it.

What had seemed a mere play of light and shadow beneath the huge, striated, overhanging slabs of gray granite was a series of structures extending east and west for many hundreds of meters. I could see the Asian influence at once: pagoda-shaped buildings with pitched tile roofs and curling eaves, their elaborately tiled surfaces gilded and glowing in the bright sunlight; round windows and moon gates in the lower brick sections of the superstructure, airy wooden porches with elaborately carved railings; delicate wooden pillars painted the color of dried blood; red and yellow banners draped from eaves and doorways and railings; complicated carvings on the roof beams and tower ridges; and suspension bridges and stairways festooned with what I would later learn were prayer wheels and prayer flags, each offering a prayer to Buddha every time a human hand spun it or the wind fluttered it.

The Temple was still being built. I could see raw wood being carried up to high platforms, saw human figures chiseling away at the stone face of the ridge, could see scaffolding, rude ladders, crude bridges consisting of little more than some sort of woven plant material with climbing ropes for handrails, and upright figures hauling empty baskets up these ladders and bridges and more stooped figures carrying the baskets full of stone back down to a broad slab where most of the baskets were dumped into space. We were close enough that I could see that many of these human figures wore colorful robes hanging almost to their ankles—some blowing in the stiff wind that blew across the rockface here—and that these robes looked thick and lined against the cold. I would later learn that these were the ubiquitous *chuba,* and that they could be made of thick, waterproof zygoat wool or of ceremonial silk or even of cotton, although this last material was rare and much prized.

I had been nervous about showing our ship to the locals—afraid it might cause a panic or a laser lance attack or something—but did not know what else to do. We were still several kilometers away, so at most we would be an unusual glint of sunlight on dark metal floating against the white backdrop of the northern peak. I had hoped that they would think us just another bird—the ship and I had seen many birds through the viewer, many of them with wingspans several meters across—but that hope was dashed as I saw first a few of the workers at the Temple pause in their labors and stare out in our direction, then more, and more. No one panicked. There was no rush for shelter or to retrieve weapons—I saw no weapons in sight anywhere—but we had obviously been seen. I watched two women in robes run up through the ascending series of temple buildings, hanging bridges, stairways, steep ladders, and penultimate construction scaffolding to the easternmost platform where the work seemed to consist of cutting holes in the rock wall. There was some sort of construction shack there, and one of the women disappeared into it, coming out a moment later with several taller forms in robes.

I increased the magnification of my binoculars, my heart pounding against my ribs, but there was drifting smoke from the construction work and I could not make out for sure if the tallest person there was Aenea. But through the veils of swirling smoke, I did catch a glimpse of blond-brown hair—just shorter than shoulder length—and for a moment I lowered the binoculars and just stared out at the distant wall, grinning like an idiot.

"They are signaling," said the ship.

I looked through the glasses again. Another person—female, I think, but with much darker hair—was flashing two handheld semaphore flags.

"It is an ancient signal code," said the ship. "It is called Morse. The first words are . . ."

"Quiet," I said. We had learned Morse Code in the Home Guard and I had used it once with two bloody bandages to call in medevac skimmers on the Iceshelf.

GO . . . TO . . . THE . . . FISSURE . . . TEN   KLICKS . . . TO . . . THE . . . NORTH . . . EAST.

HOVER . . . THERE.

AWAIT . . . INSTRUCTIONS.

"Got that, Ship?" I said.

"Yes." The ship's voice always sounded cold after I was rude to it.

"Let's go," I said. "I think I see a gap about ten klicks to the northeast. Let's stay as far out as we can and come in from the east. I don't think they'll be able to see us from the Temple, and I don't see any other structures along the cliff face in that direction."

Without further comment, the ship brought us out and around and back along the sheer rock wall until we came to the fissure—a vertical cleft dropping several thousand meters from the ice and snow far above to a point where it converged about four hundred meters above the level of the Temple, which now was out of sight around the curve of rockface to the west.

The ship floated vertically until we were just fifty meters above the bottom of the fissure. I was surprised to see streams running down the steep rock walls of the sides of this gap, tumbling into the center of the fissure before pouring off into thin air as a waterfall. There were trees and mosses and lichens and flowering plants everywhere along this cleft, fields of them rising many hundreds of meters alongside the streams until finally becoming mere streaks of multicolored lichen rising toward the ice levels above. At first I was sure that there was no sign of human intrusion here, but then I saw the chiseled ledges along the north wall—barely wide enough to stand on, I thought—and then the paths through the bright green moss, and the artfully placed stepping stones in the stream, and then I noticed the tiny, weathered little structure—too small to be a cabin, more like a gazebo with windows—which sat under wind-sculpted evergreens along the stream and near the high point of the fissure's verdant pass.

I pointed and the ship moved up in that direction, hovering near the gazebo. I understood why it would be difficult, if not impossible, to land here. The Consul's ship was not that large—it had been hidden in the stone tower in the old poet's city of Endymion for centuries—but even if it landed vertically on its fins or extendable legs here, some trees, grass, moss, and flowering plants would be crushed. They seemed too rare in this vertical rock world to destroy that way.

So we hovered. And waited. And about thirty minutes after we arrived, a young woman came around the path from the direction of the rock ledges and waved heartily at us.

IT WAS NOT Aenea.

I admit that I was disappointed. My desire to see my young friend again had reached the point of obsession, and I guess that I was having absurd fantasies of reunion—Aenea and I running toward one another across a flowered field, she the child of eleven again, I her protector, both of us laughing with the pleasure of seeing one another and me lifting her and swinging her around, tossing her up . . .

Well, we had the grassy field. The ship continued hovering and morphed a stairway to the flower-bedecked lawn next to the gazebo. The young woman crossed the stream, hopping from stepping stone to stepping stone with perfect balance, and came grinning toward me up the grassy knoll.

She was in her early twenties. She had the physical grace and sense of presence I remembered from a thousand images of my young friend. But I had never seen this woman before in my life.

Could Aenea have changed this much in five years? Could she have disguised herself to hide from the Pax? Had I simply forgotten what she looked like? The latter seemed improbable. No, impossible. The ship had assured me that it had been five years and some months for Aenea if she was waiting on this world for me, but my entire trip—including the cryogenic fugue part—had taken only about four months. I had aged only a few weeks. I could not have forgotten her. I would never forget her.

"Hello, Raul," said the young woman with dark hair.

"Hello?" I said.

She stepped closer and extended her hand. She had a firm handshake. "I'm Rachel. Aenea's described you perfectly." She laughed. "Of course, we haven't been expecting anyone else to come calling in a starship looking like this . . ." She waved her hand in the general direction of the ship hanging there like a vertical balloon bobbing softly in the wind.

"How is Aenea?" I said, my voice sounding strange to me. "*Where* is she?"

"Oh, she is back at the Temple. She's working. It's the middle of the busiest work shift. She couldn't get away. She asked me to come over and help you dispose of your ship."

She couldn't get away. What the hell was this? I'd come through literal hell—suffered kidney stones and broken legs, been chased by Pax troopers, dumped into a world with no land, eaten and regurgitated by an alien—and she couldn't goddamn get away? I bit my lip, resisting the impulse to say what I was thinking. I admit that emotion was surging rather high at that moment.

"What do you mean—dispose of my ship?" I said. I looked around. "There has to be someplace for it to land."

"There isn't really," said the young woman named Rachel. Looking at her now in the bright sunlight, I realized that she was probably a little older than Aenea would be—mid-twenties perhaps. Her eyes were brown and intelligent, her brown hair was chopped off as carelessly as Aenea used to cut hers, her skin was tanned from long hours in the sun, her hands were callused with work, and there were laugh lines at the corners of her eyes.

"Why don't we do this," said Rachel. "Why don't you get what you need from the ship, take a comlog or communicator so you can call the ship back when you need it, get two skinsuits and two rebreathers out of the storage locker, and then tell the ship to hop back up to the third moon—the second smallest captured asteroid. There's a deep crater there for it to hide in, but that moon's in a near geosynchronous orbit and it keeps one face toward this hemisphere all the time. You could tightbeam it and it could be back here in a few minutes."

I looked suspiciously at her. "Why the skinsuits and rebreathers?" The ship had them. They were designed for benign hard-vacuum environments where true space armor was not required. "The air seems thick enough here," I said.

"It is," said Rachel. "There's a surprisingly rich oxygen atmosphere at this altitude. But Aenea told me to ask you to bring the skinsuits and rebreathers."

"Why?" I said.

"I don't know, Raul," said Rachel. Her eyes were placid, seemingly clear of deceit or guile.

"Why does the ship have to hide?" I said. "Is the Pax here?"

"Not yet," said Rachel. "But we've been expecting them for the last six months or so. Right now, there are no spacecraft on or around Tien Shan . . . with the exception now of your ship. No aircraft either. No skimmers, no EMVs, no thopters or copters . . . only paragliders . . . the flyers . . . and they would never be out that far."

I nodded but hesitated.

"The Dugpas saw something they couldn't explain today," continued Rachel. "The speck of your ship against Chomo Lori, I mean. But eventually they explain everything in terms of *tendrel,* so that won't be a problem."

"What are *tendrel?*" I said. "And who are the Dugpas?"

"*Tendrel* are signs," said Rachel. "Divinations within the shamanistic Buddhist tradition prevalent in this region of the Mountains of Heaven. Dugpas are the . . . well, the word translates literally as 'highest.' The people who dwell at the upper altitudes. There are also the Drukpas, the valley people . . . that is, the lower fissures . . . and the Drungpas, the wooded valley people . . . mostly those who live in the great fern forests and bonsai-bamboo stands on the western reaches of Phari Ridge and beyond."

"So Aenea's at the Temple?" I said stubbornly, resisting following the young woman's "suggestion" for hiding the ship.

"Yes."

"When can I see her?"

"As soon as we walk over there." Rachel smiled.

"How long have you known Aenea?"

"About four years, Raul."

"Do you come from this world?"

She smiled again, patient with my interrogation. "No. When you meet the Dugpas and the others, you'll see that I'm not native. Most of the people in this region are from Chinese, Tibetan, and other Central Asian stock."

"Where are you from?" I asked flatly, sounding rude in my own ears.

"I was born on Barnard's World," she said. "A backwater farming planet. Cornfields and woods and long evenings and a few good universities, but not much else."

"I've heard of it," I said. It made me more suspicious. The "good universities" that had been Barnard's World's claim to fame during the Hegemony had long since been converted to Church academies and seminaries. I had the sudden wish that I could see the flesh of this young woman's chest—see if there were a cruciform there, I mean. It would be all too easy for me to send the ship away and walk into a Pax trap. "Where did you meet Aenea?" I said. "Here?"

"No, not here. On Amritsar."

"Amritsar?" I said. "I've never heard of it."

"That's not unusual. Amritsar is a Solmev-marginal world way out back of the Outback. It was only settled about a century ago—refugees from a civil war on Parvati. A few thousand Sikhs and a few thousand Sufi eke out a living there. Aenea was hired to design a desert community center there and I hired on to do the survey and ramrod the construction crew. I've been with her ever since."

I nodded, still hesitating. I was filled with something not quite disappointment, surging like anger but not quite as clear, bordering on jealousy. But that was absurd. "A. Bettik?" I said, feeling a sudden intuition that the android had died in the past five years. "Is he . . ."

"He headed out yesterday for our biweekly provision trek to Phari Marketplace," said the woman named Rachel. She touched my upper arm. "A. Bettik's fine. He should be back by moonrise tonight. Come on. Get your stuff. Tell the ship about hiding on the third moon. You'd rather hear all this stuff from Aenea."

I ENDED UP taking little more than a change of clothes, good boots, my small binoculars, a small sheath knife, the skinsuits and rebreathers, and a palm-sized com unit/journal from the ship. I stuffed all this into a rucksack, hopped down the steps to the meadow, and told the ship what it should do. My anthropomorphizing had reached the point where I expected the ship to sulk at the idea of going back into hibernation mode—on an airless moon this time—but the ship acknowledged the order, suggested that it check in via tightbeam once daily to make sure that the com unit was functioning, and then it floated up and away, dwindling to a speck and then disappearing, like nothing so much as a balloon that has had its string cut.

Rachel gave me a wool *chuba* to pull on over my therm jacket. I noticed the nylon harness she wore over her jacket and trousers, the metal climbing equipment hanging on straps, and asked about it.

"Aenea has a harness for you at the temple site," she said, rattling the hardware on the sling. "This is the most advanced technology on this world. The metalworkers at Potala demand and receive a king's ransom for this stuff—crampons, cable pulleys, folding ice axes and ice hammers, chocks, 'biners, lost arrows, bongs, birdbeaks, you name it."

"Will I need it?" I said dubiously. We had learned some basic ice-climbing techniques in the Home Guard—rappelling, crevasse work, that sort of thing—and I had done some roped-up quarry climbing when I worked with Avrol Hume on the Beak, but I wasn't sure about real mountaineering. I didn't like heights.

"You'll need it but you'll get used to it quickly," assured Rachel and set off, hopping across the stepping stones and running lightly up the path toward the cliff's edge. The gear jangled softly on her harness, like steel chimes or the bells around some mountain goat's neck.

The ten-klick walk south along the sheer rockface was easy enough once I got used to the narrow ledge, the dizzy-making sheer drop to our right, the bright glare from the incredible mountain to the north and from the churning clouds far below, and the heady surge of energy from the rich atmosphere.

"Yes," said Rachel when I mentioned the air. "The oxygen-rich atmosphere here would be a problem if there were forests or savannahs to burn. You should see the monsoon lightning storms. But the bonsai forest back there at the fissure and the fern forests over on the rainy side of Phari is about all we have in terms of combustible materials. They're all fire species. And the bonsai wood that we use in the building is almost too dense to burn."

For a while we walked in single file and in silence. My attention was on the ledge. We had just come around a sharp corner that required me to duck my head under the overhang when the ledge widened, the view opened up, and there was Hsuan-k'ung Ssu, the "Temple Hanging in Air."

From this closer view, a bit below and to the east of the Temple, it still looked to be magically suspended in midair above nothing. Some of the lower, older buildings had stone or brick bases, but the majority were built out over air. These pagoda-style buildings were sheltered by the great rock overhang some seventy-five meters above the main structures, but ladders and platforms zigged and zagged up almost to the underside of that overhang.

We came in among people. The many-hued *chubas* and ubiquitous climbing slings were not the only common denominators here: most of the faces that peered at me with polite curiosity seemed to be of Old Earth Asian stock; the people were relatively short for a roughly standard-g world; they nodded and stepped aside respectfully as Rachel led the way through the crowds, up the ladders, through the incense-and-sandalwood-smelling interior halls of some of the buildings, out and across porches and swinging bridges and up delicate staircases. Soon we were in the upper levels of the Temple where construction proceeded at a rapid pace. The small figures I had seen through binoculars were now living, breathing human beings grunting under heavy baskets of stone, individual people smelling of sweat and honest labor. The silent efficiency I had watched from the ship's terrace now became a clamorous mixture of hammers pounding, chisels ringing, pick-axes echoing, and workers shouting and gesturing amid the controlled chaos common to any construction site.

After several staircases and three long ladders rising to the highest platform, I paused to catch my breath before climbing the last ladder. Rich oxygen atmosphere or no, this climbing was hard work. I noticed Rachel watching me with the equanimity that could easily be mistaken for indifference.

I looked up to see a young woman stepping over the edge of the high platform and descending gracefully. For the briefest of seconds I felt my heart pound with nervousness—Aenea!—but then I saw how the woman moved, saw the short-cropped dark hair from the back, and knew that it was not my friend.

Rachel and I stepped back from the base of the ladder as the woman jumped down the last few rungs. She was large and solid—as tall as I was—with strong features and amazing violet eyes. She looked to be in her forties or early fifties, standard, was deeply tanned and very fit, and from the white wrinkles at the corners of her eyes and mouth, it seemed that she also enjoyed laughing. "Raul Endymion," she said, thrusting out her hand. "I'm Theo Bernard. I help build things."

I nodded. Her handshake was as firm as Rachel's.

"Aenea's just finishin' up." Theo Bernard gestured toward the ladder.

I glanced at Rachel.

"You go on up," she said. "We've got things to do."

I went up hand over hand. There were probably sixty rungs on the bamboo ladder, and I was aware as I climbed that the platform below was very narrow if one fell, the drop beyond it endless.

Stepping onto the platform, I saw the rough construction shacks and areas of chiseled stone where the last temple building would be. I was aware of the countless tons of stone starting just ten meters above me where the overhang angled up and out like a granite ceiling. Small birds with v-shaped tails darted and swooped among the cracks and fissures there.

Then all my attention became fixed on the figure emerging from the larger of the two construction shacks.

It was Aenea. The bold, dark eyes, the unself-conscious grin, the sharp cheekbones and delicate hands, the blond-brown hair cut carelessly and blowing now in the strong wind along the cliff face. She was not that much taller than when I had seen her last—I could still have kissed her forehead without bending—but she was *changed*.

I took in a sudden breath. I had watched people grow and come of age, of course, but most of these had been my friends when I was also growing and coming of age. Obviously I had never had children, and my careful observation of someone maturing had only been during the four years and some months of my friendship with this child. In most ways, I realized, Aenea still looked much as she had on her sixteenth birthday, five of her years earlier, minus now the last of her baby fat, with sharper cheekbones and firmer features, wider hips and slightly more prominent breasts. She wore whip trousers, high boots, a green shirt I remembered from Taliesin West, and a khaki jacket that was blowing in the wind. I could see that her arms and legs were stronger, more muscled, than I remembered from Old Earth—but not that much was changed about her.

Everything was changed about her. The child I had known was gone. A woman stood in her place; a strange woman walking quickly toward me across the rough platform. It was not just strong features and perhaps a bit more firm flesh on her still-lean form, it was . . . a solidity. A presence. Aenea had always been the most alive, animated, and *complete* person I had ever known, even as a child. Now that the child was gone, or at least submerged in the adult, I could see the solidity within that animated aura.

"Raul!" She crossed the last few steps to me, stood close, and grasped my forearms in her strong hands.

For a second I thought that she was going to kiss me on the mouth the way she had . . . the way the child of sixteen had . . . during the last minutes we had been together on Old Earth. Instead, she raised one long-fingered hand and set it against my face, running fingers down the line of my cheek to my chin. Her dark eyes were alive with . . . what? Not amusement. Vitality, perhaps. Happiness, I hoped.

I felt tongue-tied. I started to speak, stopped, raised my right hand as if to touch her cheek, dropped it.

"Raul . . . damn . . . it is *so* good to see you!" She took her hand away from my face and hugged me with an intensity bordering on violence.

"It's good to see you too, kiddo." I patted her back, feeling the rough material of her jacket under my palm.

She stepped back, grinning very broadly now, and grabbed my upper arms. "Was the trip to get the ship terrible? Tell me."

"Five years!" I said. "Why didn't you tell me . . .."

"I did. I shouted it."

"When? At Hannibal? When I was . . ."

"Yes. Then I shouted 'I love you.' Remember?"

"I remember that, but . . . if you knew . . . five years, I mean . . .."

We were both talking at once, almost babbling. I found myself trying to tell her all about the farcasters, the kidney stone on Vitus-Gray-Balianus B, the Amoiete Spectrum Helix people, the cloud world, the cuttlefish-squid thing—all while I was asking her questions and babbling on again before she could answer.

Aenea kept grinning. "You look the same, Raul. You look the same. But then, hell, I guess you *should*. It's only been . . . what . . . a week or two of travel and a cold sleep on the ship for you."

I felt a wash of anger amid the happy giddiness. "Goddammit, Aenea. You should have *told* me about the time-debt. And maybe about the farcast to a world with no river or solid ground too. I could have died."

Aenea was nodding. "But I didn't know for *sure*, Raul. There was no certainty, only the usual . . . possibilities. That's why A. Bettik and I built the parasail into the kayak." She grinned again. "I guess it worked."

"But you knew it would be a long separation. Years for you." I did not phrase it as a question.

"Yes."

I started to speak, felt the anger wash away as quickly as it had surged, and took her by the arms. "It's good to see you, kiddo." She hugged me again, kissing me on the cheek this time the way she had as a kid when I had delighted her with some joke or comment.

"Come on," she said. "The afternoon shift is over. I'll show you our platform and introduce you to some of the people here."

Our platform? I followed her down ladders and across bridges that I had not noticed while walking with Rachel.

"Have you been all right, Aenea? I mean . . . is everything all right?"

"Yes." She looked back over her shoulder and smiled at me again. "Everything is good, Raul." We crossed a terrace on the side of the topmost of three pagodas stacked one atop the other. I could feel the platform shaking a bit as we walked the narrow terrace, and when we stepped out onto the narrow platform between pagodas, the entire structure vibrated. I noticed that people were leaving the westernmost pagoda and following the narrow ledge trail back along the cliff face.

"This part feels shaky, but it's sturdy enough," said Aenea, noticing my apprehension. "Beams of tougher bonsai pine are driven into holes drilled into the rock. That supports the whole infrastructure."

"They must rot away," I said as I followed her onto a short suspension bridge. We swayed in the wind.

"They do," said Aenea. "They've been replaced several times in the eight hundred–some years the Temple's been here. No one is sure exactly how many times. Their records are shakier than the floors."

"And you've been hired to add on to the place?" I said. We had come out onto a terrace of wine-colored wood. A ladder at the end rose to another platform and a narrower bridge running from it.

"Yeah," said Aenea. "I'm sort of part architect, part construction boss. I'd supervised the construction of a Taoist temple over near Potala when I first arrived, and the Dalai Lama thought that I might be able to finish work on the Temple Hanging in Air. It's frustrated a few would-be renovators over the past few decades."

"When you arrived," I repeated. We had come onto a high platform at the center of the structure. It was bound about with beautifully carved railings and held two small pagodas perched right at the edge. Aenea stopped at the door of the first pagoda.

"A temple?" I said.

"My place." She grinned, gesturing toward the interior. I peeked in. The square room was only three meters by three meters, its floor of polished wood with two small tatami mats. The most striking thing about it was the far wall—which simply was not there. Shoji screens had folded back and the far end of the room ended in open air. One could sleepwalk into oblivion there. The breeze up the cliff face rustled the leaves on three willow-type branches set in a beautiful mustard-yellow vase that sat on a low wood dais against the west wall. It was the only ornamentation in the room.

"We kick off our shoes in the buildings—except for the transit corridors you came through earlier," she said. She led the way to the other pagoda. It was almost identical to the first, except for the shoji screens being latched closed here and a futon on the floor near them. "A. Bettik's stuff," she said, pointing to a small, red-painted locker near the futon. "This is where we've set you up to bunk. Come on in." She slipped her boots off, crossed to the tatami mat, slid the shoji back, and sat cross-legged on the mat.

I removed my boots, set the pack against the south wall, and went over to sit next to her.

"Well," she said and gripped my forearms again. "Gosh."

For a minute I could not speak. I wondered if the altitude or the rich atmosphere was making me so emotional. I concentrated on watching lines of people in bright *chubas* leaving the Temple and walking the narrow ledges and bridges west along the cliff face. Directly across from our open door here was the gleaming massif of Heng Shan, its icefields glowing in the late afternoon light. "Jesus," I said softly. "It's beautiful here, kiddo."

"Yes. And deadly if one is not careful. Tomorrow A. Bettik and I will take you up on the face and give you a refresher course on climbing gear and protocol."

"Primer course is more like it," I said. I could not stop looking at her face, her eyes. I was afraid that if I touched her bare skin again, visible voltage would leap between us. I remembered that electric shock whenever we had touched when she was a kid. I took a breath. "Okay," I said. "When you got here, the Dalai Lama—whoever that is—said that you could work on the Temple here. So when did you get here? *How* did you get here? When did you meet Rachel and Theo? Who else do you know well here? What happened after we said good-bye in Hannibal? What happened to everyone else at Taliesin? Have the Pax troops been after you? Where did you learn all the architectural stuff? Do you still talk with the Lions and Tigers and Bears? How did you . . ."

Aenea held up one hand. She was laughing. "One thing at a time, Raul. I need to hear all about your trip too, you know."

I looked into her eyes. "I dreamed that we were talking," I said. "You told me about the four steps . . . learning the language of the dead . . . learning . . ."

"The language of the living," she finished for me. "Yes. I had that dream too."

My eyebrows must have arched.

Aenea smiled and set both her hands on mine. Her hands were larger, covering my oversized fist. I remembered when both her hands would have disappeared in one of mine. "I do remember the dream, Raul. And I dreamed that you were in pain . . . your back . . ."

"Kidney stone," I said, wincing at the memory.

"Yes. Well, I guess it shows that we're still friends if we can share dreams while light-years apart."

"Light-years," I repeated. "All right, how did you get across them, Aenea? How did you get here? Where else have you been?"

She nodded and began speaking. The wind through the open wall screens rustled her hair. While she spoke, the evening light grew richer and higher on the great mountain to the north and across the cliff face to the east and west.

AENEA HAD BEEN the last to leave Taliesin West, but that was only four days after I had paddled down the Mississippi. The other apprentices had left by different farcasters, she said, and the dropship had used the last of its power to ferry them to the various portals—near the Golden Gate Bridge, at the edge of the Grand Canyon, atop the stone faces at Mount Rushmore, beneath the rusted girders of launch gantries at the Kennedy Spaceport Historical Park—all over the western hemisphere of Old Earth, it seemed. Aenea's farcaster had been built into an adobe house in a pueblo north of the empty city called Santa Fe. A. Bettik had farcast with her. I blinked in jealousy at this, but said nothing.

Her first farcast had brought her to a high-gravity world called Ixion. The Pax had a presence there, but it was concentrated primarily in the opposite hemisphere. Ixion had never recovered properly from the Fall, and the high, jungle plateau where Aenea and A. Bettik had emerged was a maze of overgrown ruins populated primarily by warring tribes of neo-Marxists and Native American resurgencists, this volatile mixture further destabilized by bands of renegade and roving ARNists who were attempting to bring back all recorded species of Old Earth dinosaur.

Aenea made the tale funny—hiding A. Bettik's blue skin and obvious android status with great daubs of the decorative face paint the locals used, the audacity of a sixteen-year-old girl demanding money—or in this case, food and furs in barter—for heading up the reconstruction efforts in the old Ixion cities of Canbar, Iliumut, and Maoville. But it had worked. Not only had Aenea helped in the redesign and rebuilding of three of the old city centers and countless small homes, but she had started a series of "discussion circles" that brought listeners in from a dozen of the warring tribes.

Here Aenea was being circumspect, I knew, but I wanted to know what these "discussion circles" were all about.

"Just things," she said. "They would raise the topic, I would suggest some things to think about, and people would talk."

"Did you teach them?" I asked, thinking of the prophecy that the child of the John Keats cybrid would be the One Who Teaches.

"In the Socratic sense, I guess," said Aenea.

"What's that . . . oh, yeah." I remembered the Plato she had steered me toward in the Taliesin library. Plato's teacher, Socrates, had taught by questioning, drawing out truths that people already held within themselves. I had thought that technique highly dubious, at best.

She went on. Some of the members of her discussion group had become devoted listeners, returning every evening and following her when she moved from ruined city to ruined city on Ixion.

"You mean disciples," I said.

Aenea frowned. "I don't like that word much, Raul."

I folded my arms and looked out at the alpenglow illuminating the cloudtops many kilometers below and the brilliant evening light on the northern peak. "You may not like it, but it sounds like the correct word to me, kiddo. Disciples follow their teacher wherever she travels, trying to glean one last bit of knowledge from her."

"Students follow their teacher," said Aenea.

"All right," I said, not willing to derail the story by arguing. "Go on."

There was not much more to tell about Ixion, she said. She and A. Bettik were on the world about one local year, five months standard. Most of the building had been with stone blocks and her design had been ancient-classical, almost Greek.

"What about the Pax?" I said. "Did they ever come sniffing around?"

"Some of the missionaries took part in the discussions," said Aenea. "One of them . . . a Father Clifford . . . became good friends with A. Bettik."

"Didn't he—they—turn you in? They must still be hunting for us."

"I am sure that Father Clifford didn't," said Aenea. "But eventually some of the Pax troopers began looking for us in the western hemisphere where we were working. The tribes hid us for another month. Father Clifford was coming to evening discussions even when the skimmers were flying back and forth over the jungle looking for us."

"What happened?" I felt like a two-year-old who would ask questions just to keep the other person talking. It had only been a few months of separation—including the dream-ridden cold sleep—but I had forgotten exactly how much I loved the sound of my young friend's voice.

"Nothing, really," she said. "I finished the last job—an old amphitheater for plays and town meetings, fittingly enough—and A. Bettik and I left. Some of the . . . students . . . left as well."

I blinked. "With you?" Rachel had said that she had met Aenea on a world called Amritsar and traveled here with her. Perhaps Theo had come from Ixion.

"No, no one came with me from Ixion," Aenea said softly. "They had other places to go. Things to teach to others."

I looked at her for a moment. "You mean the Lions and Tigers and Bears are allowing others to farcast now? Or are all the old portals opening?"

"No," answered Aenea, although to which question I was not sure. "No, the farcasters are as dead as ever. It's just . . . well . . . a few special cases."

Again I did not press the issue. She went on.

After Ixion, she had 'cast to the world of Maui-Covenant.

"Siri's world!" I said, remembering Grandam's voice teaching me the cadences of the Hyperion *Cantos*. That had been the locale for one of the pilgrims' tales.

Aenea nodded and continued. Maui-Covenant had been battered by revolution and Hegemony attacks way back during the Web, had recovered during the Fall interregnum, had been recolonized during the Pax expansion without the help of the locals who, in the best Siri tradition, had fought from their motile isles and alongside their dolphin companions until Pax Fleet and Swiss Guard had put their boots down hard. Now Maui-Covenant was being Christianized with a vengeance, the residents of the one large continent, the Equatorial Archipelago, and the thousands of migrating motile isles being sent to "Christian academies" for reeducation.

But Aenea and A. Bettik had stepped through to a motile isle still belonging to the rebels—groups of neo-pagans called Sirists who sailed at night, floated among the traveling archipelagoes of empty isles during the daylight, and who fought the Pax at every turn.

"What did you build?" I asked. I thought that I remembered from the *Cantos* that the motile isles carried little except treehouses under their sail-trees.

"Treehouses," said Aenea, grinning. "Lots of treehouses. Also some underwater domes. That's where the pagans were spending most of their time."

"So you designed treehouses."

She shook her head. "Are you kidding? These are—next to the missing God's Grove Templars—the best treehouse builders in human space. I *studied* how to build treehouses. They were gracious enough to let A. Bettik and me help."

"Slave labor," I said.

"Exactly."

She had spent only some three standard months on Maui-Covenant. That is where she had met Theo Bernard.

"A pagan rebel?" I said.

"A runaway Christian," corrected Aenea. "She had come to Maui-Covenant as a colonist. She fled the colonies and joined the Sirists."

I was frowning without realizing it. "She carries a cruciform?" I said. Born-again Christians still made me nervous.

"Not anymore," said Aenea.

"But how . . ." I knew of no way that a Christian with the cross could rid herself of a cruciform, short of the secret ritual of excommunication, which only the Church could perform.

"I'll explain later," said Aenea. Before her tale was done, this phrase would be used more than a few times.

After Maui-Covenant, she and A. Bettik and Theo Bernard had far-cast to Renaissance Vector.

"Renaissance Vector!" I almost shouted. That was a Pax stronghold. We had almost been shot down on Renaissance Vector. It was a hyper-industrialized world, all cities and robot factories and Pax centers.

"Renaissance Vector." Aenea smiled. It had not been easy. They had been forced to disguise A. Bettik as a burn victim with a synflesh mask. It had been uncomfortable for him for the six months they were there.

"What jobs did you do there?" I asked, finding it hard to imagine my friend and her friends staying hidden in the thronging world-city that was Renaissance Vector.

"Just one job," said Aenea. "We worked on the new cathedral in Da Vinci—St. Matthew's."

It took me a minute of staring before I could speak. "You worked on a *cathedral*? A Pax cathedral? A Christian church?"

"Of course," said Aenea calmly. "I labored alongside some of the best stonemasons, glass workers, builders, and craftsmen in the business. I was an apprentice at first, but before we left I was assistant to the chief designer working on the nave."

I could only shake my head. "And did you . . . have discussion circles?"

"Yes," said Aenea. "More came on Renaissance Vector than on any of the other worlds. Thousands of students, before it was over."

"I'm amazed that you weren't betrayed."

"I was," she said. "But not by one of the students. One of the glass workers turned us in to the local Pax garrison. A. Bettik, Theo, and I barely made it out."

"Via farcaster," I said.

"By . . . 'casting, yes," said Aenea. It was only much later that I realized that there had been a slight hesitation in her voice there, an unspoken qualification.

"And did others leave with you?"

"Not with me," she said again. "But hundreds 'cast elsewhere."

"Where?" I said, mystified.

Aenea sighed. "Do you remember our discussion, Raul, where I said that the Pax thought that I was a virus? And that they were right?"

"Yeah."

"Well, these students of mine are also carrying the virus," she said. "They had places to go. People to infect."

Her litany of worlds and jobs went on. Patawpha for three months, where she had used her treehouse experience to build mansions in the interwoven branches and trunks growing from the endless swamps there.

Amritsar, where she had worked for four standard months in the desert building tent homes and meeting places for the nomad bands of Sikhs and Sufis who wandered the green sands there.

"That's where you met Rachel," I said.

"Correct."

"What is Rachel's last name?" I said. "She didn't mention it to me."

"She has never mentioned it to me, either," said Aenea and went on with her tale.

From Amritsar, she and A. Bettik and her two female friends had 'cast to Groombridge Dyson D. This world had been a Hegemony terraforming failure, abandoned to its encroaching methane-ammonia glaciers and ice-crystal hurricanes, its dwindling number of colonists retreating to its biodomes and orbital construction shacks. But its people—mostly Suni Muslim engineers from the failed Trans-African Genetic Reclamation Project—stubbornly refused to die during the Fall, and ended up terraforming Groombridge Dyson D into a Laplandic tundra world with breathable air and adapted-Old Earth flora and fauna, including wooly mammoths wandering the equatorial highlands. The millions of hectares of grasslands were perfect for horses—Old Earth horses of the kind that had disappeared during the Tribulations before the homeworld fell into itself—so the gene-designers took their original seedship stock and bred horses by the thousands, then by the tens of thousands. Nomad bands wandered the greenways of the southern continent, living in a kind of symbiosis with the great herds, while the farmers and city folk moved into the high foothills along the equator. There were violent predators there, evolved and unleashed during the centuries of accelerated and self-directed ARNying experimentation: mutant carrion-breed packs and burrowing night terrors, thirty-meter-long grass serpents descended from those from Hyperion's Sea of Grass and Fuji rock tigers, smart wolves, and IQ-enhanced grizzlies.

The humans had the technology to hunt the adapted killers to extinction in a year or less, but the residents of the world chose a different path: the nomads would take their chances, one-on-one with the predators, protecting the great horse herds as long as the grass grows and the water flows, while the city types would begin work on a wall—a single wall eventually to be more than five thousand kilometers long that would separate the wilder sections of the savage highlands from the horse-herd savannahs and evolving cyclad forests to the south. And the wall was to be more than a wall, it was to become the great linear city of Groombridge Dyson D, thirty meters tall at its lowest, its ramparts resplendent with mosques and minarets, the travelway on top wide enough that three chariots could pass without rubbing wheels.

The colonists were too few and too busy with other projects to work full-time on such a wall, but they programmed robots and decanted androids from their seedship vaults to carry out the labor. Aenea and her friends joined in this project, working for six standard months as the wall took shape and began its relentless march along the base of the highlands and the edge of the grasslands.

"A. Bettik found two of his siblings there," said Aenea softly.

"My God," I whispered. I had almost forgotten. When we were on Sol Draconi Septem some years ago, sitting by the warmth of a heating cube in Father Glaucus's book-lined study inside a skyscraper that, in turn, was frozen within the eternal glacier of that world's frozen atmosphere . . . A. Bettik had talked about one of his reasons for coming on the odyssey with the child, Aenea, and me: he was hoping against logic to find his four siblings—three brothers and a sister. They had been separated shortly after their training period as children—if an android's accelerated early years could be called "childhood."

"So he found them?" I said, marveling.

"Two of them," repeated Aenea. "One of the other males in his growth crèche—A. Antibbe—and his sister, A. Darria."

"Were they like him?" I asked. The old poet had used androids in his empty city of Endymion, but I had not paid much attention to any of them except A. Bettik. Too much had been happening too fast.

"Much like him," said Aenea. "But very different, as well. Perhaps he will tell you more."

She wrapped up her story. After six standard months working on the linear city wall on Groombridge Dyson D, they had had to leave.

"Had to leave?" I said. "The Pax?"

"The Commission for Justice and Peace, to be precise," said Aenea. "We did not want to leave, but we had no choice."

"What is the Commission for Justice and Peace?" I said. Something about the way she had pronounced the words made the hairs on my arm stand up.

"I'll explain later," she said.

"All right," I said, "but explain something else now."

Aenea nodded and waited.

"You say you spent five standard months on Ixion," I said. "Three months on Maui-Covenant, six months on Renaissance Vector, three months on Patawpha, four standard months on Amritsar, about six standard months on—what was it?—Groombridge Dyson D?"

Aenea nodded.

"And you've been here about a standard year you say?"

"Yes."

"That's only thirty-nine standard months," I said. "Three standard years and three months."

She waited. The corners of her mouth twitched slightly, but I realized that she was not going to smile . . . it looked more as if she was trying to avoid crying. Finally, she said, "You were always good at math, Raul."

"My trip here took five years' time-debt," I said softly. "So that's about sixty standard months for you, but you've only accounted for thirty-nine. Where are the missing twenty-one standard months, kiddo?"

I saw the tears in her eyes. Her mouth was quavering slightly, but she tried to speak in a light tone. "It was sixty-two standard months, one week, and six days for me," she said. "Five years, two months, and one day time-debt on the ship, about four days accelerating and decelerating, and eight days' travel time. You forgot your travel time."

"All right, kiddo," I said, seeing the emotion well in her. Her hands were shaking. "Do you want to talk about the missing . . . what was it?"

"Twenty-three months, one week, and six hours," she said.

Almost two standard years, I thought. *And she doesn't want to tell me what happened to her during that time.* I had never seen her exercise such rigid control before; it was as if she were trying to hold herself together physically against some terrible centrifugal force.

"We'll talk about it later," she said, pointing out the open doorway at the cliff face to the west of the Temple. "Look."

I could just make out figures—two-legged and four-legged—on the narrow ledge. They were still several klicks away along the cliff face. I walked over to my pack, retrieved my binoculars, and studied the forms.

"The pack animals are zygoats," said Aenea. "The porters are hired in Phari Marketplace and will be returning in the morning. See anyone familiar?"

I did. The blue face in the hooded *chuba* looked much the way it had five of his years earlier. I turned back to Aenea, but she was obviously finished talking about her missing two years. I allowed her to change the subject again.

Aenea began asking me questions then and we were still talking when A. Bettik arrived. The women—Rachel and Theo—wandered in a few minutes later. One of the tatami mats folded back to reveal a cooking brazier in the floor near the open wall, and Aenea and A. Bettik began cooking for everyone. Others wandered in and were introduced—the foremen George Tsarong and Jigme Norbu, two sisters who were in charge of much of the decorative railing work—Kuku and Kay Se, Gyalo Thondup in his formal silken robes and Jigme Taring in soldier's garb, the teaching monk Chim Din and his master, Kempo Ngha Wang Tashi, abbot of the gompa at the Temple Hanging in Air, a female monk named Donka Nyapso, a traveling trade agent named Tromo Trochi of Dhomu, Tsipon Shakabpa who was the Dalai Lama's overseer of construction here at the Temple, and the famed climber and paraglide flyer Lhomo Dondrub, who was perhaps the most striking man I had ever seen and—I later discovered—one of the few flyers who would drink beer or break bread with Dugpas, Drukpas, or Drungpas.

The food was tsampa and momo—a roasted barley mixed into zygoat-buttered tea, forming a paste that one rolled into balls and ate with other balls of steamed dough holding mushrooms, cold zygoat tongue, sugared bacon, and bits of pears that A. Bettik told me were from the fabled gardens of Hsi wang-mu. More people came in as the bowls were being handed out—Labsang Samten—who, A. Bettik whispered, was the older brother of the current Dalai Lama and was now in his third year of monkhood here at the Temple, and various Drungpas from the wooded clefts—including master carpenter Changchi Kenchung with his long, waxed mustaches, Perri Samdup, an interpreter, and Rimsi Kyipup, a brooding and unhappy young scaffold-rigger. Not all of the monks who dropped in that night were descended from the Chinese/Tibetan Old Earth seedship colonists. Laughing and lifting their rough mugs of beer with us were the fearless high riggers Haruyuki Otaki and Kenshiro Endo, the master bamboo workers Voytek Majer and Janusz Kurtyka, and the brickmakers Kim Byung-Soon and Viki Groselj. The mayor of Jo-kung, the nearest cliff city, was there—Charles Chi-kyap Kempo—who also served as Lord Chamberlain of all the Temple's priest officials and was an appointed member of both the Tsongdu, the regional assembly of elders, and advisor to Yik-Tshang, literally the "Nest of Letters," the secret four-person body that reviewed the monks' progress and appointed all priests. Charles Chi-kyap Kempo was the first member of our party to drink enough to pass out. Chim Din and several of the other monks dragged the snoring man away from the edge of the platform and left him sleeping in the corner.

There were others—at least forty people must have filled the little pagoda as the last of the sunlight ebbed away and the moonlight from the

Oracle and three of her siblings lit the cloudtops below—but I forgot their names that night as we ate tsampa and momo, drank beer in great quantities, and made the torches burn bright in Hsuan-k'ung Ssu.

SOME HOURS LATER that evening, I went out to relieve myself. A. Bettik showed me the way to the toilets. I had assumed that one would just use the edge of platforms, but he assured me that on a world where dwelling structures had many levels—most of them above or below others—this was considered bad form. The toilets were built into the side of the cliff, enclosed by bamboo partitions, and the sanitary arrangements consisted of cleverly engineered pipes and sluices leading into fissures running deep into the cliff as well as washbasins cut in stone counters. There was even a shower area and solar-heated water for washing.

When I had rinsed my hands and face and stepped back out onto the platform—the chill breeze helping to sober me a bit—I stood next to A. Bettik in the moonlight and looked into the glowing pagoda where the crowd had arranged itself in concentric circles with my young friend as the locus. The laughter and chaos had disappeared. One by one, the monks and holy men and riggers and carpenters and stonemasons and gompa abbots and mayors and bricklayers were asking soft questions of the young woman, and she was answering.

The scene reminded me of something—some recent image—and it took me only a minute to recall it: the forty-AU deceleration into this star system, with the ship offering up holo representations of the G-type sun with its eleven orbiting planets, two asteroid belts, and countless comets. Aenea was definitely the sun in this system, and all of the men and women in that room were orbiting around her as surely as had the worlds, asteroids, and comets in the ship's projection.

I leaned on a bamboo post and looked at A. Bettik in the moonlight. "She'd better be careful," I said softly to the android, enunciating each word carefully, "or they'll begin treating her like a god."

A. Bettik nodded ever so slightly. "They do not think that M. Aenea is a god, M. Endymion," he murmured.

"Good." I put my arm around the android's shoulder. "Good."

"However," he said, "many of them are becoming convinced, despite her best efforts to assure them otherwise, that she is God."

17

HE EVENING A. BETTIK and I bring the news of the Pax's arrival, Aenea leaves her discussion group, comes to where we are standing at the door, and listens intently.

"Chim Din says that the Dalai Lama has allowed them to occupy the old gompa at Otter Lake," I say, "in the shadow of the Shivling."

Aenea says nothing.

"They won't be allowed to use their flying machines," I say, "but they're free to walk anywhere in the province. *Anywhere.*"

Aenea nods.

I want to grab her and shake her. "That means they'll hear about you soon, kiddo," I say sharply. "There'll be missionaries here within weeks—maybe days—spying around and sending word back to the Pax Enclave." I let out a breath. "Shit, we'll be lucky if it's just missionaries and not troopers."

Aenea is silent another minute. Then she says, "We're already lucky that it's not the Commission for Justice and Peace."

"What's that?" I say. She had mentioned them before.

She shakes her head. "Nothing that's immediately relevant, Raul. They must have some business here other than . . . than stamping out unorthodoxy."

During my first days here, Aenea had told me about the fighting going on in and around Pax space—a Palestinian revolt on Mars that had resulted in the Pax evacuating the planet and nuking it from orbit, free trader rebellions in the Lambert Ring Territories and on Mare Infinitus, continued fighting on Ixion and dozens of other worlds. Renaissance Vector, with its huge Pax Fleet bases and countless bars and bordellos, had been a hornets' nest of rumors and inside intelligence. And because most of the ships of the line in Pax Fleet were now the Gideon-drive archangels, the news was usually only a few days old.

One of the most intriguing rumors that Aenea had heard before coming to T'ien Shan was that at least one of those archangel-class ships had gone rogue, escaped to Ouster space, and was now flashing into Pax space to attack convoys of Pax Mercantilus ships—disabling rather than destroying the crewed freighters—and to disrupt Pax Fleet task forces preparing to attack Ousters out beyond the Great Wall. There had been a rumor during Aenea's and A. Bettik's last weeks on Renaissance Vector that the fleet bases there were in danger. Other rumors suggested that large elements of the fleet were now being kept in Pacem System to defend the Vatican. Whatever else was true about the tales of the rogue ship *Raphael,* it was uncontestable that His Holiness's Crusade against the Ousters had been set back years by the hit-and-run attacks.

But none of that seems important now as I stand waiting for Aenea's response to this news of the Pax's arrival on T'ien Shan. What do we do now, I wonder, farcast to her next world?

Instead of discussing flight, Aenea says, "The Dalai Lama will have a formal ceremony to welcome the Pax officials."

"So?" I say after a moment.

"So we have to make sure that we get an invitation," she says.

I doubt if my jaw is literally hanging slack, but it feels as if it is.

Aenea touches my shoulder. "I'll take care of it," she says. "I'll talk to Charles Chi-kyap Kempo and Kempo Ngha Wang Tashi and make sure that they include us in any party invited to the ceremony."

I am literally speechless as she goes back to her discussion group and the silent throng, their faces expectant and placid in the soft lantern light.

I READ THESE words on microvellum, remember writing them in my last days in the Schrödinger cat box in orbit around Armaghast, remember writing them in the haste of certainty that the laws of probability and quantum mechanics would soon be releasing cyanide into my closed-cycle universe, and I marvel at the present tense of the narrative. Then I remember the reason for this choice.

When I was sentenced to death in the Schrödinger box—egg-shaped, actually—I was allowed to bring very few of my own things into terminal exile. My clothes were my own. On a whim, they had given me a small rug for the floor of my Schrödinger cell—it was an ancient rug, a bit less than two meters long and a meter wide, frayed, with a small cut missing at one end. It was a replica of the Consul's hawking mat. I had lost the real mat on Mare Infinitus many years before and the details of how it came back to me still lie ahead in my tale. I had given the actual hawking mat to A. Bettik, but it must have amused my torturers to furnish my final cell with this useless copy of a flying carpet.

So they had allowed me my clothes, the fake hawking mat and the palm-sized diskey journal I had taken from the ship on T'ien Shan. The com-unit element of the journal had been disabled—not that it would broadcast through the energy shell of the Schrödinger box or that there was anyone for me to call—but the journal memory—after their careful study of it during my inquisition trial—had been left intact. It was on T'ien Shan that I had begun making notes and daily journal entries.

It was these notes that I had brought up onto the 'scriber screen in the Schrödinger cat box, reviewing them before writing this most personal of sections, and it was the immediacy in the notes, I believe, that led me to use the present-tense narrative. All of my memories of Aenea are vivid, but some of the memories brought back by these hurried entries at the end of a long day of work or adventure on T'ien Shan were so vital as to make me weep with renewed loss. I relived those moments as I wrote those words.

And some of her discussion groups were recorded verbatim on the diskey journal. I played those during my last days just to hear Aenea's soft voice once again.

"TELL US ABOUT the TechnoCore," one of the monks requests during the discussion hour this night of the Pax's arrival. "Please tell us about the Core."

Aenea hesitates only an instant, bowing her head slightly as if ordering her thoughts.

"Once upon a time," she begins. She always begins her long explanations this way.

"Once upon a time," says Aenea, "more than a thousand standard years ago, before the Hegira . . . before the Big Mistake of '08 . . . the only autonomous intelligences we humans knew of were us humans. We thought then that if humankind ever devised another intelligence that it would be the result of a huge project . . . a great mass of silicon and ancient amplification, switching, and detection devices called transistors and chips and circuit boards . . . a machine with lots of networking circuits, in other words, aping—if you will pardon the expression—the human brain in form and function.

"Of course, AIs did not evolve that way. They sort of slipped into existence when we humans were looking the other way.

"You have to imagine now, an Old Earth before humankind had offworld colonies. No Hawking drive. No interplanetary flight to speak of. All of our eggs were literally in one carton, and that carton was the lovely blue and white water world of Old Earth.

"By the end of the twentieth century, Christian era, this little world had a crude datasphere. Basic planetary telecommunication had evolved into a decentralized swarm system of old silicon-based computers demanding no organization or hierarchy, demanding nothing beyond a common communications protocol. Creation of a distributed-memory hive mind was then inevitable.

"The earliest lineal ancestors to today's Core personalities were not projects to create artificial intelligence, but incidental efforts to simulate artificial life. In the 1940s, the great-grandfather of the TechnoCore—a mathematician named John von Neumann—had done all the proofs of artificial self-replication. As soon as the early silicon-based computers became small enough for individuals to play with, curious amateurs began practicing synthetic biology within the confines of these machines' CPU cycles. Hyperlife—self-reproducing, information-storing, interacting, metabolizing, evolving—came into existence in the 1960s. It escaped the tide pools of the individual machines in the last decade of that century, moving into the embryonic planetary datasphere that they called the Internet or the web.

"The earliest AIs were dumb as dirt. Or perhaps the better metaphor would be that they were as dumb as early cellular life that was in the dirt. Some of the earliest hypercritters floating in the warm medium of the datasphere—which was also evolving—were 80-byte organisms inserted into a block of RAM in a virtual computer—a computer simulated by a computer. One of the first humans to release such creatures into the datasphere ocean was named Tom Ray and he was not an AI expert or computer programmer or cyberpuke, which they called hackers then—but was a biologist, an insect collector, botanist, and bird-watcher, and someone who had spent years collecting ants in the jungle for a pre-Hegira scientist named E. O. Wilson. Watching ants, Tom Ray became interested in evolution, and wondered if he could not just simulate evolution in one of the early computers but create *real* evolution there. None of the cyberpukes he spoke with were interested in the idea, so he taught himself computer programming. The cyberpukes said that evolving and mutating code sequences happened all the time in computers—they were called bugs and screwed-up programs. They said that if his code sequences evolved into something else they would almost certainly be nonfunctional, nonviable, as most mutations are, and would just foul up the operation of the computer software. So Tom Ray created a virtual computer—a simulated computer within his real computer—for his code-sequenced creations. And then he created an actual 80-byte code-sequence creature that could reproduce, die, and evolve in his computer-within-a-computer.

"The 80-byte copied itself into more 80-bytes. These 80-byte proto-AI cell-things would have quickly filled their virtual universe, like pond scum on top of pond scum in an Elysium early Earth, but Tom Ray gave each 80-byte a date tag, gave them age in other words, and programmed in an executioner that he called the Reaper. The Reaper wandered through this virtual universe and harvested old 80-byte critters and nonviable mutants.

"But evolution, as it is wont to do, tried to outsmart the Reaper. A mutant 79-byte creature proved not only to be viable, but soon outbred and outpaced the 80-bytes. The hyperlifes, ancestors to our Core AIs, were just born but already they were optimizing their genomes. Soon a 45-byte organism had evolved and all but eliminated the earlier artificial life-forms. As their creator, Tom Ray found this odd. 45-bytes did not include enough code to allow for reproduction. More than that, the 45s were dying off as the 80s disappeared. He did an autopsy on one of the 45-creatures.

"It turned out that all of the 45-bytes were parasites. They borrowed needed reproductive code from the 80s to copy themselves. The 79s, it turned out, were immune to the 45-parasite. But as the 80s and 45s moved toward extinction in their coevolutionary downward spiral, a mutant of the 45s appeared. It was a 51-byte parasite and it *could* prey on the vital 79s. And so it went.

"I mention all this, because it is important to understand that from the very first appearance of human-created artificial life and intelligence, such life was parasitic. It was more than parasitic—it was hyperparasitic. Each new mutation led to parasites which could prey on earlier parasites. Within a few billion generations—that is to say, CPU cycles—this artificial life had become hyper-hyper-hyperparasitic. Within standard months of his creation of hyperlife, Tom Ray discovered 22-byte creatures flourishing in his virtual medium . . . creatures so algorithmically efficient that when challenged by Tom Ray, human programmers could create nothing closer than a 31-byte version. Only months after their creation, hyperlife creatures had evolved an efficiency that their creators could not match!

"By the early twenty-first century, there was a thriving biosphere of artificial life on Old Earth, both in the quickly evolving datasphere and in the macrosphere of human life. Although the breakthroughs of DNA-computing, bubble memories, standing wave-front parallel processing, and hypernetworking were just being explored, human designers had created silicon-based entities of remarkable ingenuity. And they had created them by the billions. Microchips were in everything from chairs to cans of beans on store shelves to groundcars to artificial human body parts. The machines had grown smaller and smaller until the average human home or office was filled with tens of thousands of them. A worker's chair would recognize her as soon as she sat, bring up the file she had been working on in her crude silicon computer, chat with another chip in a coffeemaker to heat up the coffee, enable the telecommunications grid to deal with calls and faxes and crude electronic mail arrivals so that the worker would not be disturbed, interact with the main house or office computer so that the temperature was optimal, and so forth. In their stores, microchips in the cans of beans on the shelves noted their own price and price changes, ordered more of themselves when they were running short, kept track of the consumers' buying habits, and interacted with the store and the other commodities in it. This web of interaction became as complex and busy as the bubble and froth of Old Earth's organic stew in its early oceans.

"Within forty years of Tom Ray's 80-byte a-cell, humans were accustomed to talking to and otherwise interacting with the countless artificial life-forms in their cars, their offices, their elevators . . . even in their bodies, as medical monitors and proto-shunts moved toward true nanotechnology.

"The TechnoCore came into autonomous being sometime during this
period. Humanity had understood—quite correctly as it turned out—that
for artificial life and artificial intelligence to be effective, it must be autonomous. It must evolve and diversify much as organic life had on the planet.
And it did so. As well as the biosphere surrounding the planet, hyperlife
now wrapped the world in a living datasphere. The Core evolved not just
as an abstract entity within the information flow of the web datasphere, but
among the interactions of a billion tiny, autonomous, chip-driven
micromachines carrying out their mundane tasks in the human
macroworld.

"Humanity and the billion-faceted, evolving Core entity soon became
as symbiotic as acacia plants and the marauding ants that protect, prune,
and propagate the acacia as their sole food source. This is known as
coevolution, and humans understand the concept on a truly cellular level,
since so much of organic life on Old Earth had been created and optimized
by the reciprocal coevolutionary dance. But where human beings saw a
comfortable symbiosis, the early AI entities saw—were capable of seeing—
only new opportunities for parasitism.

"Computers might be turned off, software programs might be terminated, but the hive mind of the proto-Core had already moved into the
emerging datasphere, and that could be turned off only by planetary catastrophe.

"The Core eventually provided that catastrophe in the Big Mistake of
'08, but not before it had diversified its own medium and moved beyond a
mere planetary scale.

"Early experiments in the Hawking drive, conducted and understood
only by advanced Core elements, had revealed the existence of the underlying Planck-space reality of the Void Which Binds. Core AIs of the day—
DNA-based, wave-form in structure, driven by genetic algorithms, parallel
in function—completed the construction of the early Hawking-drive ships
and began design of the farcaster network.

"Human beings always saw the Hawking drive as a shortcut through
time and space—a realization of their old hyperdrive dreams. They conceptualized farcaster portals as convenient holes punched through space/time.
This was the human preconception, borne out by their own mathematical
models, and confirmed by the most powerful Core computing AIs. It was
all a lie.

"Planck space, the Void Which Binds, is a multidimensional medium
with its own reality and—as the Core was soon to learn—its own topography. The Hawking drive was not and is not a drive at all, in the classic
sense, but an entry device which touches on Planck-space topography just
long enough to change coordinates in the four-dimensional space/time con-

tinuum. Farcaster portals, on the other hand, allow actual entry to the Void Which Binds medium.

"To humans, the reality was obvious—step through a hole in space/time here, exit instantaneously via another farcaster hole there. My Uncle Martin had a farcaster home with adjoining rooms on dozens of different worlds. Farcasters created the Hegemony's WorldWeb. Another invention, the fatline—a faster-than-light communications medium—allowed for instantaneous communication between star systems. All the prerequisites for an interstellar society had been met.

"But the Core did not perfect the Hawking drive, the farcaster, and the fatline for human convenience. Indeed, the Core never perfected anything in their dealings with the Void Which Binds.

"The Core knew from the beginning that the Hawking drive was little more than a failed attempt to enter Planck space. Driving spacecraft via Hawking drive was comparable, they knew, to moving an ocean going vessel by setting off a series of explosions at its stern and riding the waves. Crudely effective, but wildly inefficient. They knew that despite all appearances to the contrary and despite their claims of having created them, there were not millions of farcaster portals during the height of the World-Web . . . only one. All farcaster portals were actually a single entry door to Planck space, manipulated across space/time to provide the functioning illusion of so many doors. If the Core had attempted to explain the truth to humanity, they might have used the analogy of a flashlight beam being rapidly flashed around a closed room. There were not many sources of light, only one in rapid transition. But they never bothered to explain this . . . in truth, they have kept the secret to this day.

"And the Core knew that the topography of the Void Which Binds could be modulated to transmit information instantaneously—via the fatline—but that this was a clumsy and destructive use of the medium of Planck space, rather like communicating across a continent by means of artificially produced earthquakes. But it offered this fatline service to humanity without ever explaining it because it served their purpose to do so. They had their own plans for the Planck-space medium.

"What the Core realized in their earliest experiments was that the Void Which Binds was the perfect medium for their own existence. No longer would they have to depend upon electromagnetic communication or tightbeam or even modulated neutrino broadcast for their datasphere networks. No longer would they need human beings or robot probes to travel to the stars to expand the physical parameters of that network. By simply moving the primary elements of the Core into the Void Which Binds, the AIs would have a safe hiding place from their organic rivals . . . a hiding place which was at once nowhere and everywhere.

"It was during this migration of the Core personae from human-based dataspheres to the Void Which Binds megasphere that the Core discovered that Planck space was not an empty universe. Behind its metadimensional hills and deep in its folded quantum-space arroyos lurked . . . something different. *Someone* different. There were intelligences there. The Core probed and then recoiled in awe and terror at the potential power of these Others. These were the Lions and Tigers and Bears spoken of by Ummon, the Core persona who claimed to have created and killed my father.

"The Core's retreat had been so hasty, its reconnaissance into the Planck-space universe so incomplete, that it had no idea where in real space/time these Lions and Tigers and Bears dwelt . . . or if they existed in real-time at all. Nor could the Core AIs identify the Others as having evolved from organic life as humanity had done or from artificial life as they had. But the briefest glimpse had shown them that these Others could manipulate time and space with the ease that human beings had once manipulated steel and iron. Such power was beyond comprehension. The Core's reaction was pure panic and immediate retreat.

"This discovery and panic happened just as the Core had initiated the action of destroying Old Earth. My Uncle Martin's poem sings of how it was the Core that arranged the Big Mistake of '08, the Kiev Group's 'accidental' dropping of a black hole into the guts of Old Earth, but his poem does not tell—because he did not know—of the Core's panic at the discovery of the Lions and Tigers and Bears and how they rushed to stop their planned destruction of Old Earth. It was not easy to scoop a growing black hole out of the core of the collapsing planet, but the Core designed a means and set about doing it in haste.

"Then, the home planet disappeared . . . not destroyed as it seemed to the humans, not saved as the Core had hoped . . . just *gone*. The Core knew that the Lions and Tigers and Bears had to be the ones who took the Earth, but as to how . . . and to where . . . and for what reason . . . they had no clue. They computed the amount of energy necessary to farcast an entire planet away and again they began quaking in their hyperlife boots. Such intelligences could explode the core of an entire galaxy to use as an energy source as easily as humans could light a campfire on a cold night. The Core entities shit hyperlife bricks in their fear.

"I should back up here to explain the reasons for the Core's decision to destroy Earth and their subsequent attempt to save it. The reasons go back to Tom Ray's 80-byte RAM creatures. As I explained, the life and intelligence which evolved in the datasphere medium knew no other form of evolution than parasitism, hyperparasitism, and hyper-hyper-hyper-hyperparasitism. But the Core was aware of the shortcomings of absolute parasitism and knew that the only way it could grow beyond parasite status and parasite psychology was to evolve in response to the physical universe—that is, to have physical bodies as well as abstract Core personae. The Core had multiple sensory inputs and could create neural networks, but what it required for nonparasitic evolution was a constant and coordinated system of neural feedback circuits—that is, eyes, ears, tongues, limbs, fingers, toes . . . bodies.

"The Core created cybrids for that purpose—bodies grown from human DNA but connected to their Core-based personae via fatline—but cybrids were difficult to monitor and became aliens when put down in a human landscape. Cybrids would never be comfortable on worlds inhabited by billions of organically evolved human beings. So the Core made its early plans to destroy Old Earth and thin out the human race by a factor of ninety percent.

"The Core did have plans for incorporating the surviving elements of the human race into their cybrid-inhabited universe after the death of Old Earth—using them as spare DNA stock and slave labor, much as we used androids—but the discovery of Lions and Tigers and Bears and the panicked retreat from Planck space complicated those plans. Until the threat of these Others was assessed and eliminated, the Core would have to continue its parasitic relationship with humanity. It devised the farcasters in the old WorldWeb just for that purpose. To humans, the trip through the farcaster medium was instantaneous. But in the timeless topography of Planck space, the subjective dwell-time there could be as long as the Core wished. The Core tapped into billions of human brains during that period, using human minds millions of times each standard day, to create a huge neural network for their own computing purposes. Every time a human stepped through a farcaster portal, it was as if the Core cut open that person's skull, removed the gray matter, laid the brain out on a workbench, and hooked it up to billions of other brains in their giant, parallel-processing, organic computer. The humans completed their step from Planck space in a subjective instant of their time and never noticed the inconvenience.

"Ummon told my father, the John Keats cybrid, that the Core consisted of three warring camps—the Ultimates, obsessed with creating their own god, the Ultimate Intelligence; the Volatiles, who wished to eliminate humanity and get on with their own goals; and the Stables, who wished to maintain the status quo vis-à-vis humankind. This explanation was an absolute lie.

"There were not and are not three camps in the TechnoCore . . . there are billions. The Core is the ultimate exercise in anarchy—hyperparasitism carried to its highest power. Core elements vie for power in alliances which might last centuries or microseconds. Billions of the parasitic personae ebb and flow in unholy alliances built to control or predict events. You see, Core personae refuse to die unless they are forced to—Meina Gladstone's deathbomb attack on the farcaster medium not only caused the Fall of the Farcasters, it killed billions of would-be immortal Core personae—but the individuals refuse to make way for others without a fight. Yet at the same time, the Core hyperlife needs death for its own evolution. But death, in the Core universe, has its own agenda.

"The Reaper program which Tom Ray created more than a thousand years ago still exists in the Core medium, mutated to a million alternate forms. Ummon never mentioned the Reapers as a Core faction, but they represent a far greater bloc than the Ultimates. It was the Reapers who created and first controlled the physical construct known as the Shrike.

"It's an interesting footnote that those Core personae which survive the Reapers do so not just through parasitism, but through a necrophilic parasitism. This is the technique by which the original 22-byte artificial life-forms managed to evolve and survive in Tom Ray's virtual evolution machine so many centuries ago—by stealing the scattered copy code of other byte creatures who were 'reaped' in the midst of reproducing. The Core parasites not only have sex, they have sex with the dead! This is how millions of the mutated Core personae survive today . . . by necrophilic hyperparasitism.

"What does the Core want from humankind now? Why has it revitalized the Catholic Church and allowed the Pax to come into existence? How do the cruciforms work and how do they serve the Core? How do the so-called Gideon-drive archangel ships really work and what is their effect on the Void Which Binds? And how is the Core dealing with the threat of the Lions and Tigers and Bears?

"These things we shall discuss another time."

IT IS THE day after we learn of the coming of the Pax and I am working stone on the highest scaffolds.

During the first days after my arrival, I think that Rachel, Theo, Jigme Norbu, George Tsarong, and the others were doubtful if I could earn my keep on the construction site at Hsuan-k'ung Ssu. I admit that I had doubts of my own as I watched the hard work and skill on view here. But after a few days of literally learning the ropes of gear and climbing protocols on the rockfaces, ledges, cables, scaffolds, and slideways in the area, I volunteered for work duty and was given a chance to fail. I did not fail.

Aenea knew of my apprenticeship with Avrol Hume, not only landscaping the huge Beak estates but working stone and wood for follies and bridges, gazebos and towers. That work served me well here, and within two weeks I had graduated from the basic scaffolding crew to the select group of high riggers and stone workers laboring on the highest platforms. Aenea's design allowed for the highest structures to rise to the great rock overhang and for various walkways and parapets actually to be incorporated into that stone. This is what we are working on now, chiseling stone and laying brick for the walkway along the edge of nothing, our scaffolds perilously cantilevered far out over the drop. In the past three months my body has grown leaner and stronger, my reaction time quicker, and my judgment more careful as I work on sheer rock walls and slippery bonsai bamboo.

Lhomo Dondrub, the skilled flyer and climber, has volunteered to free-climb the end of the overhang here to set anchor points for the final meters of scaffolding and for the last hour Viki Groselj, Kim Byung-Soon, Haruyuki Otaki, Kenshiro Endo, Changchi Kenchung, Labsang Samten, a few of the other brickworkers, masons, high riggers, and I have been watching as Lhomo moves across the rock above the overhang without protection, moving like the proverbial Old Earth fly, his powerful arms and legs flexing under the thin material of his climbing garb, three points in touch with the slick, more-than-vertical stone at all times while his free hand or foot feels for the slightest rough spot on which to rest, the smallest fissure or crack in which to work a bolt for our anchor. It is terrifying to watch him, but also a privilege—as if we were able to go back in a time machine to watch Picasso paint or George Wu read poetry or Meina Gladstone give a speech. A dozen times I am sure that Lhomo is going to peel off and fall—it would take minutes for him to freefall into the poison clouds below—but each time he magically holds his place, or finds a friction point, or miraculously discovers a crack into which he can wedge a hand or finger to support his entire body.

Finally he is done, the lines are anchored and dangling, the cable points are secured, and Lhomo slides down to his early fixed point, traverses five meters laterally, drops into the stirrups of the overhang gear, and swings onto our work platform like some legendary superhero coming in for a landing. Labsang Samten hands him an icy mug of rice beer. Kenshiro and Viki pound him on the back. Changchi Kenchung, our master carpenter with the waxed mustaches, breaks into a bawdy song of praise. I shake my head and grin like an idiot. The day is exhilarating—a dome of blue sky, the Sacred Mountain of the North—Heng Shan—gleaming brightly across the cloud gap, and the winds moderate. Aenea tells me that the rainy season will descend on us within days—a monsoon from the south bringing months of rain, slick rock, and eventual snow—but that seems unlikely and distant on such a perfect day as this.

There is a touch at my elbow and Aenea is there. She has been out on the scaffolding most of the morning, or hanging from her harness on the worked rockface, supervising the stone and brick work on the walkway and parapets.

I am still grinning from the vicarious adrenaline rush of watching Lhomo. "Cables are ready to be rigged," I say. "Three or four more good days and the wooden walkway will be done here. Then your final platform there"—I point to the ultimate edge of the overhang—"and voilà! Your project's done except for the painting and polishing, kiddo."

Aenea nods but it is obvious that her mind is not on the celebration around Lhomo or the imminent completion of her year of work. "Can you come walk with me a minute, Raul?"

I follow her down the scaffolding ladders, onto one of the permanent levels, and out a stone ledge. Small green birds take wing from a fissure as we pass.

From this angle, the Temple Hanging in Air is a work of art. The painted woodwork gleams rather than glows its dark red. The staircases and railings and fretwork are elegant and complex. Many of the pagodas have their shoji walls slid open and prayer flags and bedclothes flutter in the warm breeze. There are eight lovely shrines in the Temple, in ascending order along the rising walkways, each pagoda shrine representing a step in the Noble Eightfold Path as identified by the Buddha: the shrines line up on three axes relating to the three sections of the Path: Wisdom, Morality, and Meditation. On the ascending Wisdom axis of staircases and platforms are the meditation shrines for "Right Understanding" and "Right Thought."

On the Morality axis are "Right Speech," "Right Action," "Right Livelihood," and "Right Effort." These last meditation shrines can be reached only by hard climbing on a ladder rather than staircase because—as Aenea and Kempo Ngha Wang Tashi explained to me one evening early in my stay—the Buddha had meant for his path to be one of strenuous and unremitting commitment.

The highest Meditation pagodas are given over to contemplation of the last two steps on the Noble Eightfold Path—"Right Mindfulness" and "Right Meditation." This final pagoda, I had noticed immediately, looks out only onto the stone wall of the cliff face.

I also had noticed that there were no statues of Buddha in the Temple. The little that Grandam had explained to me about Buddhism when I'd asked as a child—having run across a reference in an old book from the Moors End library—was that Buddhists revered and prayed to statues in the likeness of the Buddha. Where were they? I had asked Aenea.

She had explained that on Old Earth Buddhist thought had been grouped into two major categories—Hinayana, an older school of thought given the pejorative term meaning "Lesser Vehicle"—as in salvation—by the more popular schools of the Mahayana, or the self-proclaimed "Greater Vehicle." There had once been eighteen schools of Hinayana teaching—all of which had dealt with Buddha as a teacher and urged contemplation and study of his teachings rather than worship of him—but by the time of the Big Mistake, only one of those schools survived, the Theravada, and that only in remote sections of disease- and famine-ravaged Sri Lanka and Thailand, two political provinces of Old Earth. All the other Buddhist schools carried away on the Hegira had belonged to the Mahayana category, which focused on veneration of Buddhist statuary, meditation for salvation, saffron robes, and the other trappings that Grandam had described to me.

But, Aenea had explained, on T'ien Shan, the most Buddhist-influenced world in the Outback or old Hegemony, Buddhism had evolved backward toward rationality, contemplation, study, and careful, open-minded analysis of Buddha's teaching. Thus there were no statues to the Buddha at Hsuan-k'ung Ssu.

We stop walking at the end of this stone ledge. Birds soar and circle below us, waiting for us to leave so that they can return to their fissure nests.

"What is it, kiddo?"

"The reception at the Winter Palace in Potala is tomorrow night," she says. Her face is flushed and dusty from her morning's work on the high scaffolds. I notice that she has scraped a rough line above her brow and that there are a few tiny crimson drops of blood. "Charles Chi-kyap Kempo is putting together an official party numbering no more than ten to attend," she continues. "Kempo Ngha Wang Tashi will be in it, of course, as will Overseer Tsipon Shakabpa, the Dalai Lama's cousin Gyalo, his brother Labsang, Lhomo Dondrub because the Dalai Lama's heard of his feats and would like to meet him, Tromo Trochi of Dhomu as trade agent, and one of the foremen to represent the workers . . . either George or Jigme . . ."

"I can't imagine one going without the other," I say.

"I can't either," says Aenea. "But I think it will have to be George. He talks. Perhaps Jigme will walk there with us and wait outside the palace."

"That's eight," I say.

Aenea takes my hand. Her fingers are roughened by work and abrasion, but are still, I think, the softest and most elegant human digits in the known universe. "I'm nine," she says. "There's going to be a huge crowd there—parties from all the towns and provinces in the hemisphere. The odds are that we won't get within twenty meters of anyone from the Pax."

"Or that we'll be the first to be introduced," I say. "Murphy's Law and all that."

"Yeah," says Aenea and the smile I see is exactly the one I had seen on the face of my eleven-year-old friend when something mischievous and perhaps a bit dangerous was afoot. "Want to go as my date?"

I let out a breath. "I wouldn't miss it for the world," I say.

18

O N THE NIGHT before the Dalai Lama's reception I am tired but I cannot sleep. A. Bettik is away, staying at Jo-kung with George and Jigme and the thirty loads of construction material that should have come in yesterday but that were held up in the fissure city by a porters' strike. A. Bettik will hire new porters in the morning and lead the procession the last few kilometers to the Temple.

Restless, I roll off my futon and slip into whipcord trousers, a faded shirt, my boots, and the light therm jacket. When I step out of my sleeping pagoda, I notice lantern light warming the opaque windows and shoji door of Aenea's pagoda. She is working late again. Walking softly so as not to disturb her by rocking the platform, I clamber down a ladder to the main level of the Temple Hanging in Air.

It always amazes me how empty this place is at night. At first I thought it was the result of the construction workers—most of whom live in the cliffside crates around Jo-kung—being gone, but I've come to realize how few people spend their nights in the temple complex. George and Jigme usually sleep in their foreman's shack but are in Jo-kung with A. Bettik tonight. The abbot Kempo Ngha Wang Tashi stays with the monks some nights, but this night he has returned to his formal home in Jo-kung. A handful of monks prefer their austere quarters here to the formal monastery in Jo-kung, including Chim Din, Labsang Samten, and the woman, Donka Nyapso. Occasionally the flyer, Lhomo, stays at the monks' quarters or in an empty shrine here, but not tonight. Lhomo has left early for the Winter Palace, having mentioned his thought of climbing Nanda Devi south of Potala.

So while I can see a soft lantern glow coming from the monks' quarters hundreds of meters away on the lowest level of the eastern edge of the complex—a glow that is extinguished even as I watch it—the rest of the temple complex is dark and quiet in the starlight. Neither the Oracle nor the other bright moons have risen yet, although the eastern horizon is beginning to glow a bit with their coming. The stars are incredibly bright, almost as brilliant and unwavering as when seen from space. There are thousands visible this night—more than I remembered from Hyperion's or Old Earth's night sky—and I crane my neck until I can see the slowly moving star that is the tiny moon where the ship is presumably hiding. I am carrying the com unit/diskey journal and all it would take is a whisper to query the ship, but Aenea and I have decided that with the Pax so near, even tightbeam transmissions to or from the ship should be reserved for emergency situations.

I sincerely hope that no emergency situations will arise soon.

Taking the ladders, staircases, and short bridges down the west side of the temple complex, I walk back along the brick-and-stone ledge beneath the lowest structures. The night wind has come up and I can hear the creak and groan of the wooden timbers as entire platform levels adjust themselves to the wind and chill. Prayer flags flap above me and I see starlight on the cloudtops where they curl against the ridge rock so far below. The wind is not quite strong enough to make the distinctive wolf's howl that woke me my first few nights here, but its passage through the fissures and timbers and cracks sets the world muttering and whispering around me.

I reach the Wisdom staircase and climb up through the Right Understanding meditation pavilion, standing a moment at the balcony to look out at the dark and silent monks' quarters perched by itself on a boulder to the east. I recognize the infinite woodcarving skill and care of the sisters, Kuku and Kay Se, in the elaborate carvings just under my fingertips here. Wrapping my jacket tighter in the rising wind, I climb the spiral staircase to the platform pagoda for Right Thought. On the east wall of this restored pagoda, Aenea has designed a large, perfectly round window looking east toward the dip in the ridgeline there where the Oracle makes its first appearance and the moon is rising now, its bright rays illuminating first the ceiling of this pagoda and then the rear wall, where these words from the *Sutta Nipata* scripture are set into the plaster wall:

> As a flame blown out by the wind
> Goes to rest and cannot be defined
> So the wise man freed from individuality
> Goes to rest and cannot be defined.
> Gone beyond all images—
> Gone beyond the power of words.

I know that this passage deals with enigmatic death of Buddha, but I read it in the moonlight with the thought of how it might apply to Aenea or myself, or the two of us. It does not seem to apply. Unlike the monks who labor here for enlightenment, I have no urge whatsoever to go beyond individuality. The world itself—*all* of the myriad worlds I have been privileged to see and walk upon—are what fascinate and delight me. I have no wish to put the world and my sense images of the world behind me. And I know that Aenea feels the same about life—that involvement with it is like the Catholic Communion, only the World is the Host, and it must be chewed.

Still, the thought of the essence of things—of people—of life going beyond all images and the power of words, this resonates with me. I have been trying—and failing—to put even the essence of this place, these days, into words and discovering the futility of it.

Leaving the Wisdom axis, I cross the long platform for cooking and common meals, and begin up the Morality axis of stairways, bridges, and platforms. The Oracle is free of the ridgeline now and the light from it and its two attendants paint the rock and red wood around me in thick moon paint.

I pass through the pavilions for Right Speech and Right Action, pausing to catch my breath in the circular pagoda for Right Livelihood. There is a bamboo barrel of drinking water just outside the pagoda for Right Effort, and I drink deeply there. Prayer flags flutter and snap along the terraces and eaves as I move softly across the long connecting platform to the highest structures.

The meditation pavilion for Right Mindfulness is part of Aenea's recent work and still smells of fresh bonsai cedar. Ten meters higher along the steep ladder, the Right Meditation pavilion perches out over the bulk of the Temple, its window looking out on the ridge wall. I stand there for several minutes, realizing for the first time that the shadow of the pagoda itself falls upon that slab of rock when the moon is rising as it is now, and that Aenea has designed the roof of the pavilion so that its shadow connects with natural clefts and discolorations in the rock to create a shadow character that I recognize as the Chinese character for Buddha.

At this moment I am taken by a chill, although the wind is not blowing any harder than it has been. Goosebumps rise along my forearms and the back of my neck feels cold. I realize—no, see—in that instant, that Aenea's mission, whatever it is, is doomed to failure. She and I are both going to be captured, interrogated, probably tortured, and executed. My promises to the old poet on Hyperion were so much wasted breath. Bring down the Pax, I had said. The Pax with its billions of faithful, millions of men and women in arms, thousands of warships . . . Bring back Old Earth, I had agreed. Well, I had *visited* it.

I look out the window to see the sky, but there is only the rock wall in the moonlight and the slowly cohering shadow character of the Buddha's name, the three vertical strokes like ink on slate-colored vellum, the three horizontal strokes flowing around and together, making three white faces in the negative spaces, three faces staring at me in the dark.

I had promised to protect Aenea. I vow that I will die doing that.

Shaking off the chill and the premonition, I go out onto the Meditation platform, clip to a cable, and hum thirty meters across the void to the platform below the top terrace where Aenea and I have sleeping pagodas. As I climb the last ladder to the highest level, I am thinking—perhaps I will sleep now.

I MADE NO notes on this in the diskey journal. I remember it now as I write it.

Aenea's light was out. I was pleased—she stayed up too late, worked too hard. The high work scaffolds and cliff cables were no place for an exhausted architect.

I stepped into my own shack, slid shut the shoji door, and kicked off my boots. Things were as I had left them—the outer screen wall slid back a bit, moonlight bright across my sleeping mat, the wind rattling the walls in its soft conversation with the mountains. Neither of my lanterns was lit, but I had the light from the moon and my memory of the small room in the dark. The floor was bare tatami except for my sleeping futon and a single chest near the door that held my rucksack, few food items, beer mug, the rebreathers I'd brought from the ship, and my climbing gear: there was nothing to trip over.

I hung my jacket on the hook near the door, splashed water on my face from the basin on the chest, and stripped off my shirt, socks, trousers, and underwear, stuffing them into the ditty bag in the chest. Tomorrow was laundry day. Sighing, feeling the premonition of doom I'd felt in the meditation pavilion now fading into simple fatigue, I walked over to the sleeping mat. I have always slept naked except for when in the Home Guard and during my trip in the Consul's ship with my two friends.

There was the slightest of movements in the darkness beyond the bright stripe of moonlight and, startled, I dropped into a fighting crouch. Nakedness makes one feel more vulnerable than usual. Then I realized—*A. Bettik must have returned early.* I unclenched my right fist.

"Raul?" said Aenea. She leaned forward into the moonlight. She had wrapped my sleeping blanket around the lower part of her body, but her shoulders and breasts and abdomen were bare. The Oracle touched her hair and cheekbones with soft light.

I opened my mouth to speak, started to turn back toward my clothes or jacket, decided not to walk that far, and dropped on one knee to the sleeping mat, pulling up the futon's sheet to cover myself. I was not a prude, but this was Aenea. What was she . . .

"Raul," she said again, and this time there was no question in her voice. She moved closer to me on her knees. The blanket fell away from her.

"Aenea," I said stupidly. "Aenea, I . . . you . . . I don't . . . you don't really . . ."

She set her finger on my lips and removed it a second later, but before I could speak she leaned closer and pressed her lips where her finger had been.

Every time I had ever touched my young friend, the contact had been electric. I have described this before and always felt foolish discussing it, but I ascribed it to her . . . an aura . . . a charge of personality. It was real, not a metaphor. But never had I felt the surge of electricity between us as in this instant.

For a second I was passive, receiving the kiss rather than sharing in it. But then the warmth and insistence of it overcame thought, overcame doubt, overcame all of my other senses in every nuance of the word, and then I was returning her kiss, putting my arms around her to pull her closer even as she slid her arms under mine and ran strong fingers up my back. More than five years ago for her, when she had kissed me farewell at the river on Old Earth, her kiss had been urgent, electric, filled with questions and messages—but still a sixteen-year-old girl's kiss. This kiss was the warm, moist, open touch of a woman, and I responded to it in an instant.

We kissed for an eternity. I was vaguely aware of my own nudity and excitement as something I should be concerned about, embarrassed about, but it was a distant thing, secondary to the expanding warmth and urgency of the kisses that would not stop. When finally our lips came apart, feeling swollen, almost bruised, wanting to be kissed again, we kissed each other's cheeks, eyelids, forehead, ears. I lowered my face and kissed the hollow of her throat, feeling the pulse against my lips there and inhaling the perfumed scent of her skin.

She moved forward on her knees, arching her back slightly so that her breasts touched my cheek. I cupped one and kissed the nipple almost reverently, Aenea cupped the back of my head in her palm. I could feel her breath on me, quickening, as she bowed her face toward me.

"Wait, wait," I said, pulling my face up and leaning back. "No, Aenea, are you . . . I mean . . . I don't think . . ."

"Shhh," she said, leaning over me again, kissing me again, pulling back so that her dark eyes seemed to fill the world. "Shhh, Raul. Yes." She kissed me again, leaning to her right so that we both reclined on the sleeping mat, still kissing, the rising breeze rattling the rice-paper walls, the entire platform rocking to the depth of our kiss and the motion of our bodies.

IT IS A problem. To tell of such things. To share the most private and sacred of moments. It feels like a violation to put such things into words. And a lie not to.

To see and feel one's beloved naked for the first time is one of life's pure, irreducible epiphanies. If there is a true religion in the universe, it must include that truth of contact or be forever hollow. To make love to the one true person who deserves that love is one of the few absolute rewards of being a human being, balancing all of the pain, loss, awkwardness, loneliness, idiocy, compromise, and clumsiness that go with the human condition. To make love to the right person makes up for a lot of mistakes.

I had never made love to the right person before. I knew that even as Aenea and I first kissed and lay against each other, even before we began moving slowly, then quickly, then slowly again. I realized that I had never really made love to anyone before—that the young-soldier-on-leave sex with friendly women or the bargeman-and-bargewoman-we-have-the-opportunity-so-why-not? sex that I had thought had explored and discovered everything to do with the subject was not even the beginning.

This was the beginning. I remember Aenea rising above me at one point, her hand hard on my chest, her own chest slick with sweat, but she was still looking at me—looking at me so intensely and so warmly that it was as if we were connected intimately by our gaze as surely as by our thighs and genitals—and I was to remember that instant every time we made love in the future, even as I seemed to be remembering forward to all those future times even during these first few moments of our intimacy.

LYING TOGETHER IN the moonlight, the sheets and blankets and the futon curled and thrown around us, the cool wind from the north drying the sweat on our bodies, her cheek on my chest and my thigh across her hip, we kept touching each other—her fingers playing with the hair on my chest, my fingers tracing the line of her cheek, the sole of my foot sliding up and down the back of her leg, curling around her strong calf muscles.

"Was this a mistake?" I whispered.

"No," she whispered back. "Unless . . ."

My heart pounded. "Unless what?"

"Unless you didn't get those shots in the Home Guard that I'm sure you got," she whispered. I was so anxious that I did not hear the teasing quality in her voice.

"What? Shots? What?" I said, rolling onto my elbow. "Oh . . . shots . . . shit. You know I did. Jesus."

"I know you did," whispered Aenea and I could hear the smile now.

When we Hyperion lads had joined the Home Guard, the authorities had given us the usual battery of Pax-approved injections—antimalaria, anticancer, antivirus, and birth control. In a Pax universe where the vast majority of individuals chose the cruciform—chose to attempt to be immortal—birth control was a given. One could apply to Pax authorities for the antidote after marriage or simply buy it on the black market when it was time to start a family. Or, if one chose neither the way of the cross nor a family, it would last until old age or death made the issue moot. I had not thought of that shot for years. Actually, I think A. Bettik had asked me about those shots on the Consul's ship a decade ago when we were discussing preventative medicine and I had mentioned the Home Guard induction battery, our young friend of eleven or twelve curled on a couch there on the holopit level, reading a book from the ship's library, seemingly not paying attention at all . . .

"No," I said, still on my elbow, "I mean a *mistake*. You're . . ."

"Me," she whispered.

"Twenty-one standard years old," I finished. "I'm . . ."

"You," she whispered.

". . . eleven standard years older than that."

"Incredible," said Aenea. Her whole face was in the moonlight as she looked up at me. "You can do math. At such a moment."

I sighed and rolled over on my stomach. The sheets smelled of us. The wind was still rising and now it rattled the walls.

"I'm cold," whispered Aenea.

In the days and months to come, I would have held her in my arms if she said such a thing, but that night I responded literally and stood to slide shut the shoji screen. The wind was colder than usual.

"No," she said.

"What?"

"Don't close it all the way." She was sitting up with the sheet raised to just below her breasts.

"But it's . . ."

"The moonlight on you," Aenea whispered.

Her voice may have caused my physical response. Or the sight of her, waiting for me in the blankets. Besides holding in our own scents, the room smelled like fresh straw because of the new tatami and the ryokan in the ceiling. And of the fresh, cool air of the mountains. But the cold breeze did not slow my reaction to her.

"Come here," she whispered, and opened the blanket like a cape to fold me in.

THE NEXT MORNING and I am working on setting the overhang walkway in place and it is as if I am sleepwalking. Part of the problem is lack of sleep—the Oracle had set and the east was paling with morning when Aenea slipped back to her own pavilion—but the major reason is sheer, simple stupefaction. Life has taken a turn that I had never anticipated, never imagined.

I am setting supports into the cliff for the high walk with the high riggers Haruyuki, Kenshiro, and Voytek Majer moving ahead, drilling holes in the stone, while Kim Byung-Soon and Viki Groselj lay brick behind and beneath us and carpenter Changchi Kenchung begins work behind me on the laying of the wood floor of the terrace itself. There would be nothing to catch the high riggers and me if we fall from the wooden beams if Lhomo had not done his free-climbing exhibition yesterday and set fixed ropes and cables in place. Now as we jump from beam to beam, we just clip one of our harness carabiners into place on the next rope. I have fallen before and had the fall arrested by this sort of fixed rope: each can hold five times my weight.

Now I leap from set beam to set beam, pulling along the next beam as it dangles from one of the cables. The wind is coming up and threatens to hurl me off into space, but I balance myself with one hand touching the hanging beam and three fingers on the rockface itself. I reach the end of the third fixed rope, unclip, and prepare to clip on to the fourth of seven lines Lhomo has rigged.

I do not know what to think about last night. That is, I know how I feel—exhilarated, confused, ecstatic, in love—but I don't how to think about it. I tried to intercept Aenea before breakfast in the communal dining pavilion near the monks' quarters, but she had already eaten and headed far out to where the terrace carvers had run into trouble on the new eastern walkway. Then A. Bettik, George Tsarong, and Jigme Norbu had shown up with the porters and an hour or two was consumed sorting materials and transporting the beams, chisels, lumber, and other items to the new high scaffolds. I had headed out onto the eastern ledge before the beam work began, but A. Bettik and Tsipon Shakabpa were conferring with Aenea, so I jogged back to the scaffolds and got busy.

Now I was jumping to the last beam set in place this morning, ready to install the next one in the hole Haruyuki and Kenshiro have chiseled and blasted into the rock with tiny, shaped charges. Then Voytek and Viki will cement the post in place. Within thirty minutes, it will be firm enough for Changchi to set a work platform on. I've become accustomed to leaping from beam to beam, catching my balance and squatting to set the next beam in place, and I do so now on the last beam, pinwheeling my left arm to keep my balance while my fingers stay in contact with the beam balancing from the cable. Suddenly the beam swings out too far ahead of me and I am off balance, leaning into nothing. I know that the safety line will catch me, but I hate to fall and be dangling here between the last beam and the newly drilled hole. If I don't have enough momentum to kick back to the beam, I'll have to wait for Kenshiro or one of the other riggers to kick out and rescue me.

In a fraction of a second, I make up my mind and jump, catching the swinging beam and kicking out hard. Because the safety rope has several meters of slack before it will catch me, all of my weight is on my fingers now. The beam is too thick for me to get a good grip on it and I can feel my fingers sliding on the iron-hard wood. But rather than go dropping to the elastic end of my fixed line, I struggle to hang on, succeed in swinging the heavy post back toward the last beam in place, and jump the last two meters, landing on the slippery beam and flailing my arms for balance. Laughing at my own foolishness, I catch my balance and stand panting for a moment, watching the clouds boiling against the rock several thousand meters below my feet.

Changchi Kenchung is leaping from beam to beam toward me, clipping onto the fixed ropes with a rapid urgency. There is something like horror in his eyes, and for a second I am sure that something has happened to Aenea. My heart begins beating so hard and anxiety washes over me so swiftly that I almost lose my balance. But I catch it again and stand balancing on the last fixed beam, waiting for Changchi with a sense of dread.

When he leaps to the last beam with me, Changchi is too winded to speak. He gestures toward me urgently, but I do not understand the motion. Perhaps he had seen my comical swing and dance and leap with the dangling beam and was concerned. To show him that it was all right, I reach up to my harness line to show him that the carabiner is locked tight to the safety line.

There is no carabiner there. I never tied on to the last fixed rope. I have been doing all this leaping, balancing, hanging, and jumping with no safety line. There has been nothing between me and . . .

Feeling a sudden stab of vertigo and nausea, I stagger three steps to the cliff wall and lean against the cold stone. The overhang tries to push me away and it is as if the entire mountain is tilting outward, pushing me off the beam.

Changchi tugs Lhomo's fixed line around, lifts a 'biner from my harness rack, and clips me on. I nod my appreciation and try not to lose my breakfast while he is here with me.

Ten meters around the bend in the cliff, Haruyuki and Kenshiro are gesturing. They have blasted another perfect hole. They want me to catch up with setting the beams in place.

THE PARTY DEPARTING for the Dalai Lama's evening reception for the Pax at Potala leaves just after the noon meal in the common dining hall. I see Aenea there, but except for a meaningful exchange of glances and a smile from her that makes my knees weak, we have no private communication.

We assemble on the lowest level with hundreds of workers, monks, cooks, scholars, and porters waving and cheering from the platforms above. Rain clouds are beginning to curl and spill between the low gaps in the eastern ridgeline, but the sky above Hsuan-k'ung Ssu is still blue and the red prayer flags flapping from the high terraces stand out with almost shocking clarity.

We are all dressed in travel clothes, our formal reception clothing carried in waterproof shoulder-strap satchels or—in my case—my rucksack. The Dalai Lama's receptions are traditionally held late at night and we have more than ten hours until our presence is required, but it is a six-hour trip on the High Way, and couriers and one flyer coming into Jo-kung earlier that day have told of bad weather beyond the K'un Lun Ridge, so we step off lively enough.

The order of march is set by protocol. Charles Chi-kyap Kempo, Mayor of Jo-kung and Lord Chamberlain of the Temple Hanging in Air, walks a few paces ahead of his near-peer, Kempo Ngha Wang Tashi, abbot of the Temple. Both men's "traveling clothes" are more resplendent than my shot at formal wear, and they are surrounded by small hornet clusters of aides, monks, and security people.

Behind the priest politicians walk Gyalo Thondup, the young monk and cousin to the current Dalai Lama, and Labsang Samten, the third-year monk who is the Dalai Lama's brother. They have the easy stride and easier laugh of young men at the peak of physical health and mental clarity. Their white teeth gleam in their brown faces. Labsang is wearing a brilliant red climbing *chuba* that gives the appearance of him being an ambulatory prayer flag in our procession as we head west along the narrow walkway to the Jo-kung fissure.

Tsipon Shakabpa, the official overseer of Aenea's project, walks with George Tsarong, our chubby construction foreman. George's inseparable companion, Jigme Norbu, is absent now: his feelings hurt by not being invited, Jigme has stayed behind at the Temple. I believe that this is the first time that I have seen George where he is not smiling. Tsipon makes up for George's silence, however, telling stories with waving arms and extravagant gestures. Several of their workers hike with them—at least as far as Jo-kung.

Tromo Trochi of Dhomu, the flamboyant trade agent from the south, walks with his only companion for so many months on the highways—an oversized zygoat packbrid laden with the trader's goods. The zygoat has three bells hung from its shaggy neck and they chime like the Temple's prayer bells as we walk along. Lhomo Dondrub is to meet us in Potala, but his presence in the party is represented symbolically on the zygoat's topmost pack duffel by a swatch of new flight fabric for his paraglider.

Aenea and I bring up the rear of the procession. Several times I try to talk about last night, but she silences me with a finger to her lips and a nod in the direction of the nearby trader and other members of the procession. I settle for small talk about the last days of work on the Temple overhang pavilion and walkways, but my mind continues to jostle with questions.

Soon we are in Jo-kung, where the ramps and walkways are lined with crowds waving pennants and prayer flags. From the fissure terraces and cliff shacks, citizens of the city cheer their mayor and the rest of us.

Just beyond the fissure city of Jo-kung, near the jump-off platforms of the only cableway we will be using on this trip to Potala, we encounter another party headed to the Dalai Lama's reception: the Dorje Phamo and her nine female priests. The Dorje Phamo travels in a palanquin carried by four heavily muscled males because she is the abbess of Samden Gompa, an all-male monastery some thirty klicks out along the south wall of the same ridge that holds the Temple Hanging in Air along its north wall. The Dorje Phamo is ninety-four standard years old and was discovered to be the incarnation of the original Dorje Phamo, the Thunderbolt Sow, when she was three standard years old. She is a woman of immense importance and a separate monastery for women—the Oracle Gompa at Yamdrok Tso, some sixty klicks farther along the dangerous ridge wall—has held her as its prefect and avatar for more than seventy standard years. Now the Thunderbolt Sow, her nine female priest companions, and about thirty male carriers and guards are waiting at the cableway to attach the palanquin's massive carabiner clamps.

The Dorje Phamo peers through her curtains, spies our party, and beckons Aenea over. I know from Aenea's offhand comments that she has traveled to the Oracle Gompa at Yamdrok Tso several times to meet with the Sow and that the two are fast friends. I also know from A. Bettik's comments to me in confidence that the Dorje Phamo has recently told her female priests and monks at the Oracle Gompa and the male monks at Samden Gompa that it is Aenea, not His Holiness the current Dalai Lama, who is the incarnation of the living Buddha of Mercy. Word of this heresy has spread, according to A. Bettik, but because of the Thunderbolt Sow's popularity across the world of T'ien Shan, the Dalai Lama has not yet responded to the impertinence.

Now I watch as the two women—my young Aenea and the ancient form in the palanquin—chat and laugh easily as both parties wait to cross the cableway across the Langma Abyss. The Dorje Phamo must have insisted that we precede her group, for the carriers move the palanquin back out of the way and the nine female priests bow deeply as Aenea motions our group forward on the platform. Charles Chi-kyap Kempo and Kempo Ngha Wang Tashi look discomfited as they allow their aides to clip them on to the cable—not out of concern for their safety, I know, but out of some breech of protocol that I missed and am not particularly interested in. At that moment I am interested in getting Aenea alone and talking with her. Or perhaps just kissing her again.

IT RAINS HARD during the walk to Potala. During my three months here I've experienced more than a few summer showers, but this is a serious pre-monsoon rain, chilling, icy, with curling tendrils of fog that close around us. We clear the one cableway transit before the clouds close in, but by the time we are approaching the east side of the K'un Lun Ridge, the High Way is slick with ice.

The High Way consists of rock ledges, bricked pathways on the sheer cliffside, high wooden walkways along the northwest ridge of Hua Shan, the Flower Mountain, and a long series of platform walkways and suspension bridges connecting those icy ridgelines with K'un Lun. Then there is the second-longest suspension bridge on the planet connecting K'un Lun Ridge with Phari Ridge, followed by another series of walkways, bridges, and ledges heading southwest along the east face of Phari Ridge to Phari Marketplace. There we pass through the fissure and follow the ledge road almost due west to Potala.

Normally this is a six-hour walk in the sunshine, but this afternoon it is a dreary, dangerous trudge through the curling fog and icy rain. The aides traveling with Mayor/Lord Chamberlain Charles Chi-kyap Kempo and Abbot Kempo Ngha Wang Tashi attempt to shelter their worthies under bright red and yellow umbrellas, but the icy ledge is often narrow and the worthies frequently must get wet as they go ahead in single file. The suspension bridges are nightmares to cross—the "floor" of each is just a single, heavily braided hemp cable with hemp ropes rising vertically, horizontal side ropes for railings, and a second thick cable above one's head—and although it is usually child's play to balance on the lower cable while keeping contact with the side ropes, it takes complete concentration in this driving rain. But all of the locals have done this through dozens of monsoons and they move along quickly; it is only Aenea and I who hesitate as the bridges flex and toss under the party's weight, the icy ropes threatening to slip out of our hands.

Despite the storm—or perhaps because of it—someone has lighted the High Way torches all along the east face of Phari Ridge, and the braziers burning through the thick fog help us find our way as the wooden walkways turn, bend, rise, descend icy staircases, and lead out to more bridges. We arrive in Phari Marketplace just at dusk, although it seems much later because of the gloom. Other groups bound for the Winter Palace join us there and there are at least seventy people headed west together past the fissure. The Dorje Phamo's palanquin still bobs along with us and I suspect that others besides myself are a bit envious of her dry perch in there.

I confess that I am disappointed: we had planned to arrive at Potala in the twilight, while there was still alpenglow lighting the north-south ridges and the higher peaks to the north and west of the palace. I have never glimpsed the palace before, and I had been looking forward to seeing this region. As it is, the broad High Way between Phari and Potala is just a series of torchlit ledges and walkways. I have brought the flashlight laser in my pack, although whether as a futile gesture for defense should things turn bad at the palace, or for finding our way in the dark, I am not sure. Ice coats the rocks, the platforms, the hemp-cable railings along this most well traveled of walkways, as well as the stairs. I cannot imagine being on the cableway this night, but rumor has it that several of the more adventurous guests are traveling that way.

We arrive at the Forbidden City some two hours before the reception is scheduled to begin. The clouds have lifted a bit, the rain relents, and our first glimpse of the Winter Palace takes my breath away and makes me forget my disappointment of not having approached it in the twilight.

The Winter Palace is built on a great peak rising from the Yellow Hat Ridge, with the higher peaks of Koko Nor behind it, and our first glimpse through the clouds is of Drepung, the surrounding monastery that houses thirty-five thousand monks, tier upon tier of tall stone buildings rising up the vertical slopes, its thousands of windows glowing with lantern light, torches at balconies, terraces, and entrances, while behind the Drepung and above it, with gold roofs touching the ceiling of boiling clouds, rises Potala—the Winter Palace of the Dalai Lama—ablaze with light, and backlighted—even in the stormy darkness—by the lightning-lit peaks of the Koko Nor.

The aides and fellow travelers turn back here, and only we invited pilgrims press on into the Forbidden City.

The High Way now flattens and broadens to a true highway, an avenue fifty meters wide, paved with gold stones, lined with torches, and surrounded by countless temples, chortens, lesser gompas, outbuildings for the imposing monastery, and military guard posts. The rain has stopped but the avenue glistens goldly while hundreds upon hundreds of brightly garbed pilgrims and residents of the Forbidden City bustle to and fro in front of the huge walls and gates of the Drepung and the Potala. Monks in saffron robes move in small, silent groups; palace officials in brilliant red and rich purple gowns and yellow hats looking like inverted saucers walk purposefully past soldiers in blue uniforms with black-and-white-striped pikes; official messengers jog by in skintight outfits of orange and red or gold and blue; women of the court glide across the gold stones in long silk dresses of sky blue, deep lapis lazuli, and daring cobalt, their trains making soft slithering sounds on the wet pavement; priests from the Red Hat Sect are instantly recognizable with their inverted saucer hats of crimson silk and crimson fringe, while the Drungpas—the wooded valley people—stride by with wooly hats of zygoat fur, their costumes adorned with brilliant white, red, tan, and gold feathers, carrying their great gold ceremonial swords tucked into their sashes; finally the common folk of the Forbidden City are little less colorful than the high officials, the cooks and gardeners and servants and tutors and masons and personal valets all bedecked in silk *chubas* of green and blue or gold and orange, those who work in the Dalai Lama's quarters of the Winter Palace—several thousand strong—glimpsed in the crimson and gold, everyone wearing the zygoat-banded silk hats with stiff brims some fifty centimeters broad, to preserve their pale palace complexions on sunny days and to ward off the rain during monsoon season.

Our wet band of pilgrims seems dull and shabby in these surroundings, but I have little thought of our own appearance as we pass through a sixty-meter-tall gate in one of the outer walls of the Drepung Monastery and begin to cross the Kyi Chu Bridge.

This bridge is 20 meters wide, 115 meters long, and made of the most modern carbon-plasteel. It shines like black chrome. Beneath it is . . . nothing. The bridge spans a terminal fissure in the ridgeline and drops thousands of meters to the phosgene clouds below. On the east side—the side from which we approach—the structures of the Drepung rise two or three kilometers above us, flat walls and glowing windows and the air above us laced with spiderweb upon spiderweb of official cable shortcuts between the monastery and the palace proper. On the west side—ahead of us—the Potala rises more than six kilometers on the cliff faces, its thousands of stone facets and hundreds of gold roofs reflecting the flickering lightning from the low clouds above it. In case of attack, the Kyi Chu Bridge can retract into the western cliff in less than thirty seconds, leaving no stairway, foothold, ledge, or window for half a kilometer of vertical stone to the first ramparts above.

The bridge does not retract as we cross it. The sides are lined with troopers in ceremonial garb, each carrying a deadly serious pike or energy rifle. At the far end of the Kyi Chu, we pause at the Pargo Kaling—the Western Gate—an ornate arch eighty-five meters tall. Light glows from within the giant arch, breaking out through a thousand intricate designs, the brightest glow coming from the two great eyes—each more than ten meters across—that stare unblinkingly across the Kyi Chu and the Drepung to the east.

We each pause as we pass under the Pargo Kaling. Our first step beyond it will bring us onto the grounds of the Winter Palace itself, although the actual doorway is still some thirty paces ahead of us. Inside that doorway are the thousand steps that will take us up to the palace proper. Aenea has told me that pilgrims have come from all over T'ien Shan by walking on their knees, or in some cases by prostrating themselves at every step—literally measuring the hundreds or thousands of kilometers with their bodies—just to be allowed to pass under the Western Gate and to touch this last section of Kyi Chu Bridge with their foreheads out of homage to the Dalai Lama.

Aenea and I step across together, glancing at one another.

After presenting our invitations to the guards and officials within the main entrance portal, we ascend the thousand stairs. I am amazed to find that the stairway is an escalator, although Tromo Trochi of Dhomu whispers that it is often left unactivated to allow the faithful a final exertion before being allowed into the upper reaches of the palace.

Above, on the first public levels, there is another flurry of invitation checking, servants divesting us of our wet outer robes, and other servants escorting us to rooms in which we might bathe and change. Lord Chamberlain Charles Chi-kyap Kempo is entitled to a small suite of rooms on the seventy-eighth level of the palace, and after what seems like farther kilometers of walking down outside halls—the windows to our right showing the red rooftops of the Drepung Monastery flickering and gleaming in the storm light—we are greeted by more servants given over to our bidding. Each of our party has at least a curtained alcove in which we will sleep after the formal reception, and adjoining bathrooms offer hot water, baths, and modern sonic showers. I follow Aenea and smile at her when she winks on her way out of the steamy room.

I had no truly formal clothes at the Temple Hanging in Air—nor any in the ship currently hiding on the third moon, for that matter—but Lhomo Dondrub and some of the others roughly my size have fitted me out for tonight's honor: black trousers and highly polished, high black boots, a white silk shirt under a gold vest, with a red-and-black X-shaped wool overvest, tied together at the waist with a crimson silk sash. The formal evening cape is made of the finest warrior-silk from the western reaches of Muztagh Alta and is mostly black, but with intricate border designs of red, gold, silver, and yellow. It is Lhomo's second-best cape and he made it quite clear that he would toss me from the highest platform if I stained, tore, or lost it. Lhomo is a pleasant, easygoing man—almost unheard of in a lone flyer, I am told—but I think he was not kidding about this.

A. Bettik loaned me the requisite silver bracelets for the reception, these purchased by him on a whim in the beautiful markets of Hsi wang-mu. Over my shoulders I place the feather and zygoat wool red hood loaned to me by Jigme Norbu, who has waited his entire life in vain for an invitation to the Winter Palace. Around my neck is a jade-and-silver-link Middle Kingdom formal talisman courtesy of master carpenter and friend Changchi Kenchung, who told me this morning that he has been to three receptions at the palace and has been bored witless each time.

Servants in gold silk come to our chambers to announce that it is time for us to congregate in the Main Reception Hall next to the Throne Room. The outside corridors are filled with hundreds of guests moving along the tiled halls, silk is rustling, jewelry rattles, and the air is filled with the clash of perfume and cologne and soap and leather. Ahead of us, I get a glimpse of the ancient Dorje Phamo—the Thunderbolt Sow herself—being helped along by two of her nine female priests, all of them in elegant saffron gowns. The Sow wears no jewelry, but her white hair is tied and ribboned in elaborate mounds and beautiful braids.

Aenea's gown is simple but breathtaking—a deep blue silk, with a cobalt hood covering her otherwise bare shoulders, one Middle Kingdom talisman of silver and jade dropping to her bosom, and a silver comb pinned in her hair, holding a thin half veil in place. Many of the women in view are veiled for modesty tonight, and I realize how cleverly this disguises my friend's appearance.

She takes my arm and we move in procession down the endless corridors, turning right and gliding up spiral escalators toward the Dalai Lama's levels.

I lean close and whisper against her veiled ear. "Nervous?"

I see the glint of her smile beneath the veil and she squeezes my hand.

Persisting, I whisper, "Kiddo, you sometimes see the future. I know you do. So . . . do we get out of this alive tonight?"

I bend over as she leans close to whisper back. "Only a few things in anyone's future are set, Raul. Most things are as liquid as . . ." She gestures toward a swirling fountain that we pass and spiral above. "But I see no reason to worry, do you? There are thousands of guests here tonight. The Dalai Lama can greet only a few in person. His guests . . . the Pax . . . whoever they will be, have no reason to think that we are here."

I nod, but am not convinced.

Suddenly Labsang Samten, the Dalai Lama's brother, comes racketing down the ascending escalator in violation of all protocol. The monk is grinning and bubbling over with enthusiasm. He addresses our group, but hundreds on the rising staircase lean to listen in.

"The guests from space are very important!" he says enthusiastically. "I have been talking to our tutor who is the assistant to the second in command to the Minister of Protocol. These are not just missionaries whom we greet tonight!"

"No?" says the Lord Chamberlain Charles Chi-kyap Kempo, resplendent in his many layers of red and gold silk.

"No!" grins Labsang Samten. "It is a cardinal of the Pax Church. A very important cardinal. With several of his top people."

I feel my stomach churn and then drop into freefall.

"Which cardinal?" says Aenea. Her voice seems calm and interested. We are approaching the top of the spiral staircase ride and the sound of hundreds or thousands of softly murmuring guests fills the air.

Labsang Samten straightens his formal monk's robe. "A Cardinal Mustafa," he says brightly. "Someone very close to the Pax Pope, I think. The Pax honors my brother by sending him as ambassador."

I feel Aenea's hand close on my arm, but I cannot see her expression clearly through the veil.

"And several other important Pax guests," continues the monk, turning as we approach the reception level. "Including some strange Pax women. Military types, I think."

"Did you get their names?" asks Aenea.

"One of them," says Labsang. "General Nemes. She is very pale." The Dalai Lama's brother turns his wide, sincere smile on Aenea. "The Cardinal has asked to meet you specifically, M. Aenea. You and your escort, M. Endymion. The Protocol Minister was very surprised, but has arranged for a private reception for you with the Pax people and the Regent and, of course, my brother, His Holiness, the Dalai Lama."

Our ascent ends. The staircase slides into the marble floor. With Aenea on my arm, I step out into the noise and tightly controlled chaos of the Main Reception Hall.

19

T HE DALAI LAMA is only eight standard years old. I had known that—Aenea and A. Bettik and Theo and Rachel have all mentioned it more than once—but I am still surprised when I see the child sitting on his high, cushioned throne.

There must be three or four thousand people in the immense reception room. Several broad escalators disgorge guests simultaneously into an antechamber the size of a spacecraft hangar—gold pillars rising to a frescoed ceiling twenty meters above us, blue-and-white tiles underfoot with elaborate, inset images from the *Bardo Thodrol,* the *Tibetan Book of the Dead,* as well as illustrations of the vast seedship migration of the Buddhist Old Earth émigrés, huge gold arches under which we pass to enter the reception room—and the reception room is larger still, its ceiling one giant skylight through which the broiling clouds and flickering lightning and lantern-lit mountainside are quite visible. The three or four thousand guests are brilliant in their finery—flowing silk, sculpted linen, draped and dyed wool, profusions of red-black-and-white feathers, elaborate hairdos, subtle but beautifully formed bracelets, necklaces, anklets, earrings, tiaras, and belts of silver, amethyst, gold, jade, lapis lazuli, and a score of other precious metals. And scattered among all this elegance and finery are scores of monks and abbots in their simple robes of orange, gold, yellow, saffron, and red, their closely shaved heads gleaming in the light from a hundred flickering tripod braziers. Yet the room is so large that these few thousand people do not come close to filling it up—the parquet floors gleam in the firelight and there is a twenty-meter space between the first fringes of the crowd and the golden throne.

Small horns blow as the lines of guests step from the escalator staircases to the anteroom tiles. The trumpets are of brass and bone and the line of monks blowing them runs from the stairs to the entrance arches—more than sixty meters of constant noise. The hundreds of horns hold one note for minutes on end and then shift to another low note without signal from trumpeter to trumpeter and as we enter the Main Reception Hall—the antechamber acting as a giant echo chamber behind us—these low notes are taken up and amplified by twenty four-meter-long horns on either side of our procession. The monks who blow these monstrous instruments stand in small alcoves in the walls, resting the giant horns on stands set on the parquet floors, the bell-horn ends curling up like meter-wide lotus blossoms. Added to this constant, low series of notes—rather like an ocean-going ship's foghorn wrapped within a glacier's rumble—are the reverberations of a huge gong, at least five meters across, being struck at precise intervals. The air smells of incense from the braziers and the slightest veil of fragrant smoke moves above the jeweled and coiffed heads of the guests and seems to shimmer and shift with the rise and fall of the notes from the trumpets and horns and gong.

All faces are turned toward the Dalai Lama, his immediate retinue, and his guests. I take Aenea's hand and we move to our right, staying far back from the throne and its surrounding dais. Constellations of important guests move nervously between us and the distant throne.

Suddenly the deep horn notes cease. The gong's final vibrations echo and fall away. All of the guests are present. The huge doors behind us are pushed shut by straining servants. Across the giant, echoing space, I can hear the crackling of flames in the countless braziers. Rain suddenly beats at the crystal skylight far above us.

The Dalai Lama is smiling slightly as he sits cross-legged on multiple silk cushions atop a platform that brings him to eye level with his standing guests. The boy's head is bare and shaven and he wears a simple red lama's robe. To his right, and lower, on a throne of his own, sits the Regent who will rule—in consultation with other high priests—until His Holiness the Dalai Lama comes of age at eighteen standard years. Aenea has told me about this Regent, a man named Reting Tokra who is said to be the literal incarnation of cunning, but all I can see from my distant vantage point now is the usual red robe and a narrow, pinched, brown face with its slitted eyes and tiny mustache.

To the left of His Holiness the Dalai Lama is the Lord Chamberlain, abbot of abbots. This man is quite old and smiling broadly at the phalanxes of guests. To his left is the State Oracle, a thin young woman with severely cropped hair and a yellow linen shirt under her red robe. Aenea has explained that it is the State Oracle's job to predict the future while in a deep trance. To the left of the State Oracle, their faces largely blocked from my view by the gilded pillars of the Dalai Lama's throne, stand five emissaries from the Pax—I can make out a short man in cardinal's red, three forms in black cassocks, and at least one military uniform.

To the right of the Regent's throne stands the Chief Crier and Head of His Holiness's Security, the legendary Carl Linga William Eiheji, Zen archer, watercolorist, karate master, philosopher, former flyer, and flower arranger. Eiheji looks to be built of coiled steel wrapped about with pure muscle as he strides forward and fills the immense hall with his voice:

"Honored guests, visitors from beyond our world, Dugpas, Drukpas, Drungpas—those from the highest ridges, the noble fissures, and the wooded valley slopes—*Dzasas,* honored officials, the Red Hats and the Yellow Hats, monks, abbots, *getsel* novices, *Ko-sa*s of the Fourth Rank and higher, blessed ones who wear the *su gi,* wives and husbands of those so honored, seekers of Enlightenment, it is my pleasure to welcome you here tonight on behalf of His Holiness, Getswang Ngwang Lobsang Tengin Gyapso Sisunwangyur Tshungpa Mapai Dhepal Sangpo—the Holy One, the Gentle Glory, Powerful in Speech, Pure in Mind, of Divine Wisdom, Holding the Faith, Ocean-Wide!"

The small brass and bone trumpets blow high, clear notes. The great horns bellow like dinosaurs. The gong sends vibrations through our bones and teeth.

Chief Crier Eiheji steps back. His Holiness the Dalai Lama speaks, his child's voice soft but clear and firm across the great space.

"Thank you all for coming this night. We shall greet our new friends from the Pax in more intimate circumstances. Many of you have requested to see me . . . you shall receive my blessing in private audience tonight. I have requested to speak with some of you. You shall meet me in private audience tonight. Our friends from the Pax will speak with many of you this evening and in the days to come. In speaking to them, please remember that these are our brothers and sisters in the Dharma, in the quest for Enlightenment. Please remember that our breath is their breath, and that all of our breath is the breath of Buddha. Thank you. Please enjoy our celebration this night."

And with that the dais, throne and all, slides silently back through the opening wall, is hidden by a sliding curtain, then by another curtain, and then by the wall itself, and the thousands in the main reception hall let out a breath as one.

THE EVENING WAS, as I remember, a nearly surreal combination of a gala ball swirling around a formal papal reception. I had never seen a papal reception, of course—the mystery Cardinal on the now-curtained dais was the highest official of the Church encountered in my experience—but the excitement of those being received by the Dalai Lama must have been similar to a Christian meeting the Pope, and the pomp and circumstance surrounding their presentation was impressive. Soldier-monks in red robes and red or yellow hats escorted the lucky few through the tented curtains and then through more curtains and finally through the door in the wall to the Dalai Lama's presence while the rest of us moved and mixed across the torchlit parquet floor, or browsed the long tables of excellent food, or even danced to the music of a small band—no brass and bone trumpets or four-meter horns there. I admit that I asked Aenea if she would like to dance, but she smiled, shook her head, and led our group to the nearest banquet table. Soon we were engaged in conversation with the Dorje Phamo and some of her female priests.

Knowing that I might be committing a faux pas, I nonetheless asked the beautiful old woman why she was called the Thunderbolt Sow. As we munched on fried balls of tsampa and drank delicious tea, the Dorje Phamo laughed and told us the story.

On Old Earth, the first such abbess of an all-male Tibetan Buddhist monastery had gained the reputation of being the reincarnation of the original Thunderbolt Sow, a demigoddess of frightening power. That first Dorje Phamo abbess was said to have transformed not only herself but all of the lamas in her monastery into pigs to frighten away enemy soldiers.

When I asked this last reincarnation of the Thunderbolt Sow if she had retained the power of transforming into a sow, the elegant old woman lifted her head and said firmly, "If that would frighten away these current invaders, I would do so in an instant."

In the three hours or so during which Aenea and I mixed and chatted and listened to music and watched the lightning through the grand skylight, this was the only negative thing we heard spoken—aloud—about the Pax emissaries, although under the silk finery and gala gaiety, there seemed to be an undercurrent of anxiety to the evening. This seemed natural since the world of T'ien Shan had been—except for the occasional free trader's drop-ship—isolated from the Pax and the rest of post-Hegemonic humanity for almost three centuries.

The evening was growing late and I was becoming convinced that Labsang Samten's statement that the Dalai Lama and his Pax guests had wished to see us was erroneous, when suddenly several palace officiaries in great, curved red and yellow hats—looking rather like illustrations I had seen of ancient Greek helmets—sought us out and asked that we accompany them to the Dalai Lama's presence.

I looked at my friend, ready to bolt with her and cover our retreat if she showed even a hint of fear or reticence, but Aenea simply nodded in compliance and took my arm. The sea of partygoers made way for us as we crossed the vast space behind the officials, the two of us walking slowly, arm in arm, as if I were her father giving her away in a traditional Church wedding . . . or as if we had always been a couple ourselves. In my pocket was the flashlight laser and the diskey journal/com unit. The laser would be worth little if the Pax was determined to seize us, but I had decided to call the ship if the worst happened. Rather than allow Aenea to be captured, I would bring the ship down on blazing reaction thrusters, right through that lovely skylight.

We passed through the outer curtain and entered a canopied space where the sounds of the band and merrymaking were still quite audible. Here several red-hat officials asked us to extend our arms with our palms upward. When we did so, they set a white silk scarf in our hands, the ends hanging down. We were waved forward through the second curtain. Here the Lord Chamberlain greeted us with a bow—Aenea responding with a graceful curtsy, me with an awkward bow in return—and led us through the door into the small room where the Dalai Lama waited with his guests.

This private room was like an extension of the young Dalai Lama's throne—gold and gilt and silk brocade and wildly ornate tapestries with reversed swastikas embroidered everywhere amid images of opening flowers and curling dragons and spinning mandalas. The doors closed behind us and the sounds of the party would have been shut out completely except for the audio pickups of three video monitors set in the wall to our left. Real-time video of the party was being fed in from different locations around the Main Reception Hall and the boy on the throne and his guests were watching it raptly.

We paused until the Lord Chamberlain gestured us forward again. He whispered to us as we approached the throne and the Dalai Lama turned in our direction. "It is not necessary to bow until His Holiness raises his hand. Then please bow forward until after he releases his touch."

We paused three paces from the raised throne platform with its shimmering quilts and draped cushions. Carl Linga William Eiheji, the Chief Crier, said in soft but resonant tones, "Your Holiness, the architect in charge of construction at Hsuan-k'ung Ssu and her assistant."

Her assistant? I moved forward a step behind Aenea, confused, but grateful that the Crier had not announced our names. I could see the five Pax figures out of the corner of my eye, but protocol demanded that I keep my gaze directed toward the Dalai Lama but lowered.

Aenea stopped at the edge of the high throne platform, her arms still held in front of her, the scarf taut between her hands. The Lord Chamberlain set several objects on the scarf and the boy reached forward and whisked them off quickly, setting them to his right on the platform. When the objects were gone, a servant stepped forward and took away the white scarf. Aenea put her hands together as if in prayer and bowed forward. The boy's smile was gentle as he leaned forward and touched my friend—my beloved—on the head, setting his fingers like a crown on her brown hair. I realized that it was a blessing. When he removed his fingers, he lifted a red scarf from a stack by his side and set it in Aenea's left hand. Then he took her right hand and shook it, his smile broadening. The Lord Chamberlain gestured for Aenea to stand in front of the Regent's lower throne as I stepped forward and went through the same quick ceremony with the Dalai Lama.

I just had time to notice that the objects set on the white scarf by the Lord Chamberlain and whisked away by the Dalai Lama included a small gold relief in the shape of three mountains, representing the world of T'ien Shan Aenea later explained, an image of a human body, a stylized book representing speech, and a *chorten,* or temple, shape representing the mind. The appearing and disappearing act was over before I had time to pay more attention to it, and then the red scarf was in one hand while the boy's tiny hand was in my large one. His handshake was surprisingly firm. My gaze was lowered, but I could still make out his broad smile. I stepped back next to Aenea.

The same ceremony was quickly performed with the Regent—white scarf, symbolic objects placed and removed, red scarf. But the Regent did not shake hands with either of us. When we had received the Regent's blessing, the Lord Chamberlain gestured for us to raise our heads and gazes.

I almost made a grab for the flashlight laser and started firing wildly. Besides the Dalai Lama, his monk servants, the Lord Chamberlain, the Regent, the State Oracle, the Crier, the short Cardinal, the three men in black cassocks, there was a woman in a black-and-red Pax Fleet uniform. She had just stepped around a tall priest so we could see her face for the first time. Her dark eyes were fixed on Aenea. The woman's hair was short and hung over her pale forehead in limp bangs. Her skin was sallow. Her gaze was reptilian—simultaneously remote and rapt.

It was the thing that had tried to kill Aenea, A. Bettik, and me on God's Grove some five of my years—more than ten of Aenea's—ago. It was the inhuman killing device that had defeated the Shrike and would have carried Aenea's head away in a bag had it not been for the intervention of Father Captain de Soya in his orbiting spacecraft; he had used the full fusion power of the ship to lance the monster downward into a cauldron of bubbling, molten rock.

And here it was again, its black, inhuman eyes fixed on Aenea's face. It had obviously sought her across the years and light-years, and now it had her. It had us.

My heart was pounding and my legs felt suddenly weak, but through the shock my mind was working like an AI. The flashlight laser was tucked in a pocket in the right side of my cape. The com unit was in my left trouser pocket. With my right hand I would flash the cutting beam into the woman-thing's eyes, then flick the selector to broad and blind the Pax priests. With my left hand I would trigger the squirt command to send the prerecorded message via tightbeam to the ship.

But even if the ship responded immediately and was not intercepted by a Pax warship on its flight, it would be several minutes before it could descend through the palace skylight. We would be dead by then.

And I knew the speed of this thing—it simply had disappeared when it fought the Shrike, a chrome blur. I would never get the flashlight laser or com unit out of my pockets. We would be dead before my hand made it halfway to the weapon.

I froze, realizing that although Aenea must have recognized the woman at once, she had not reacted with the shock I felt. To outward appearances, she had not reacted at all. Her smile remained. Her gaze had passed over the Pax visitors—including the monster—and then returned to the boy on the throne.

It was Regent Reting Tokra who spoke first. "Our guests asked for this audience. They heard from His Holiness of the reconstruction going on at the Temple Hanging in Air and wished to meet the young woman who had designed the construction."

The Regent's voice was as pinched and ungiving as his appearance.

The Dalai Lama spoke then and his boy's voice was soft but as generous as the Regent's had been guarded. "My friends," he said, gesturing toward Aenea and me, "may I introduce our distinguished visitors from the Pax. John Domenico Cardinal Mustafa of the Catholic Church's Holy Office, Archbishop Jean Daniel Breque of the Papal Diplomatic Corps, Father Martin Farrell, Father Gerard LeBlanc, and Commander Rhadamanth Nemes of the Noble Guard."

We nodded. The Pax dignitaries—including the monster—nodded. If there was a breech of protocol by His Holiness the Dalai Lama doing the introductions, no one seemed to notice.

John Domenico Cardinal Mustafa said in a silken voice, "Thank you, Your Holiness. But you have introduced these exceptional people only as the architect and her assistant." The Cardinal smiled at us, showing small, sharp teeth. "You have names, perhaps?"

My pulse was racing. The fingers of my right hand twitched at the thought of the flashlight laser. Aenea was still smiling but showed no sign of answering the Cardinal. My mind galloped to come up with aliases. But why? Certainly they knew who we were. All this was a trap. The Nemes thing would never let us leave this throne room . . . or would be waiting for us when we did.

Surprisingly, it was the boy Dalai Lama who spoke again. "I would be pleased to complete my introductions, Your Eminence. Our esteemed architect is called Ananda and her assistant—one of many skilled assistants I am told—is called Subhadda."

I admit that I blinked at this. Had someone told the Dalai Lama these names? Aenea had told me that Ananda had been the Buddha's foremost disciple and a teacher in his own right; Subhadda had been a wandering ascetic who had become the Buddha's last direct disciple, becoming a follower after meeting him just hours before he died. She also told me that the Dalai Lama had come up with these names for our introduction, apparently appreciating the irony in them. I failed to see the humor.

"M. Ananda," said Cardinal Mustafa, bowing slightly. "M. Subhadda." He looked us over. "You will pardon my bluntness and ignorance, M. Ananda, but you seem of a different racial stock than most of the people we have met in the Potala or the surrounding areas of T'ien Shan."

Aenea nodded. "One must be careful in making generalizations, Your Eminence. There are areas of this world settled by seedship colonists from many of Old Earth's regions."

"Of course," purred Cardinal Mustafa. "And I must say that your Web English is very unaccented. May I inquire as to which region of T'ien Shan you and your assistant call home?"

"Of course," responded Aenea in as smooth a voice as the Cardinal's.

"I came into the world in a region of ridges beyond Mt. Moriah and Mt. Zion, north and west of Muztagh Alta."

The Cardinal nodded judiciously. I noticed then that his collar—what Aenea later said was called his *rabat* or *rabbi* in Church terminology—was of a scarlet watered silk the same color as his red cassock and skullcap.

"Are you perchance," he continued smoothly, "of the Hebrew or Muslim faiths which our hosts have told us prevail in those regions?"

"I am of no faith," said Aenea. "If one defines faith as belief in the supernatural."

The Cardinal's eyebrows lifted slightly. The man called Father Farrell glanced at his boss. Rhadamanth Nemes's terrible gaze never wavered.

"Yet you labor to build a temple to Buddhist beliefs," said Cardinal Mustafa pleasantly enough.

"I was hired to reconstruct a beautiful complex," said Aenea. "I am proud to have been chosen to this task."

"Despite your lack of . . . ah . . . belief in the supernatural?" said Mustafa. I could hear the Inquisition in his voice. Even on the rural moors of Hyperion, we had heard of the Holy Office.

"Perhaps because of it, Your Eminence," said Aenea. "And because of the trust in my own human abilities and those of my coworkers."

"So the task is its own justification?" pressed the Cardinal. "Even if it has no deeper significance?"

"Perhaps a task well done *is* the deeper significance," said Aenea.

Cardinal Mustafa chuckled. It was not an altogether pleasant sound. "Well said, young lady. Well said."

Father Farrell cleared his throat. "The region beyond Mt. Zion," he said musingly. "We noticed during our orbital survey that there was a single farcaster portal set onto a ridgeline in that area. We had thought that T'ien Shan had never been a part of the Web, but our records showed that the portal was completed very shortly before the Fall."

"But never used!" exclaimed the young Dalai Lama, lifting one slim finger. "No one ever traveled to or from the Mountains of Heaven via the Hegemony farcaster."

"Indeed," said Cardinal Mustafa softly. "Well, we assumed as much, but I must tender our apologies, Your Holiness. In our ship's zeal to probe the structure of the old farcaster portal from orbit, it accidentally melted the surrounding rocks onto it. The doorway is sealed forever under rock, I am afraid."

I glanced at Rhadamanth Nemes when this was said. She did not blink. I had not seen her blink. Her gaze was riveted to Aenea.

The Dalai Lama swept his hand in a dismissive gesture. "It does not matter, Your Eminence. We have no use for a farcaster portal which was never used . . . unless your Pax has found a way to reactivate the farcasters?" He laughed at the idea. It was a pleasant boyish laugh, but sharp with intelligence.

"No, Your Holiness," said Cardinal Mustafa, smiling. "Even the Church has not found a way to reactivate the Web. And it is almost certainly best that we never do."

My tension was quickly turning to a sort of nausea. This ugly little man in cardinal red was telling Aenea that he knew how she had arrived on T'ien Shan and that she could not escape that way. I glanced at my friend, but she seemed placid and only mildly interested in the conversation. Could there be a second farcaster portal of which the Pax knew nothing? At least this explained why we were still alive: the Pax had sealed Aenea's mousehole and had a cat, or several cats—in the form of their diplomatic ship in orbit and undoubtedly more warships hidden elsewhere in-system— waiting for her. If I had arrived a few months later, they would have seized or destroyed our ship and still had Aenea where they wanted her.

But why wait? And why this game?

". . . we would be very interested in seeing your—what is it called?—Temple Hanging in Air? It sounds fascinating," Archbishop Breque was saying.

Regent Tokra was frowning. "It may be difficult to arrange, Your Excellency," he said. "The monsoons are approaching, the cableways will be very dangerous, and even the High Way is hazardous during the winter storms."

"Nonsense!" cried the Dalai Lama, ignoring the scowl the thin-faced Regent had turned in his direction. "We will be happy to help arrange such an expedition," continued the boy. "You must, by all means, see Hsuan-k'ung Ssu. And all of the Middle Kingdom . . . even to the T'ai Shan, the Great Peak, where the twenty-seven-thousand-step stairway rises to the Temple to the Jade Emperor and the Princess of the Azure Clouds."

"Your Holiness," murmured the Lord Chamberlain, his head bowed but only after exchanging a parental glance with the Regent, "I should remind you that the Great Peak of the Middle Kingdom can be reached by cableway only in the spring months because of the high tide of the poisonous clouds. For the next seven months, T'ai Shan is inaccessible to the rest of the Middle Kingdom and the world."

The Dalai Lama's boyish smile disappeared . . . not, I thought, out of petulance, but from displeasure at being patronized. When he spoke next, his voice had the sharp edge of command to it. I did not know many children, but I had known more than a few military officers, and if my experience was any guide, this boy would become a formidable man and commander.

"Lord Chamberlain," said the Dalai Lama, "I of course know of the closure of the cableway. *Everyone* knows of the closure of the cableway. But I also know that every winter season, a few intrepid flyers make the flight from Sung Shan to the Great Peak. How else would we share our formal edicts with our friends among the faithful on T'ai Shan? And some of the parawings can accommodate more than one flyer . . . passengers even, yes?"

The Lord Chamberlain was bowing so low that I was afraid that his forehead was going to scrape the formal tiles. His voice quavered. "Yes, yes, of course, Your Holiness, of course. I knew that you knew this, My Lord, Your Holiness. I only meant . . . I only meant to say . . ."

Regent Tokra said sharply, "I am sure that what the Lord Chamberlain meant to say, Your Holiness, is that although a few flyers make the voyage each year, many more die in the attempt. We would not want to put our honored guests in any danger."

The Dalai Lama's smile returned, but it was something older and more cunning—almost mocking—than the boy's smile of a few minutes earlier. He spoke to Cardinal Mustafa. "You are not afraid of dying, are you, Your Eminence? That is the entire purpose of your visit here, is it not? To show us the wonders of your Christian resurrection?"

"Not the sole purpose, Your Holiness," murmured the Cardinal. "We come primarily to share the joyous news of Christ with those who wish to hear it and also to discuss possible trade relations with your beautiful world." The Cardinal returned the boy's smile. "And although the cross and the Sacrament of Resurrection are direct gifts from God, Your Holiness, it is a sad requirement that some portion of the body or the cruciform must be recovered for that sacrament to be given. I understand that no one returns from your sea of clouds?"

"No one," agreed the boy with his smile widening.

Cardinal Mustafa made a gesture with his hands. "Then perhaps we will limit our visit to the Temple Hanging in Air and other accessible destinations," he said.

There was a silence and I looked at Aenea again, thinking that we were about to be dismissed, wondering what the signal would be, thinking that the Lord Chamberlain would lead us out, feeling my arms go to goosebumps at the intensity of the Nemes-thing's hungry gaze aimed at Aenea, when suddenly Archbishop Jean Daniel Breque broke the silence. "I have been discussing with His Highness, Regent Tokra," he said to us as if we might settle some argument between them, "how amazingly similar our miracle of resurrection is to the age-old Buddhist belief in reincarnation."

"Ahhh," said the boy on the golden throne, his face brightening as if someone had brought up a subject of interest to him, "but not all Buddhists believe in reincarnation. Even before the migration to T'ien Shan and the great changes in philosophy which have evolved here, not all Buddhist sects accepted the concept of rebirth. We know for a fact that the Buddha refused to speculate with his disciples on whether there was such a thing as life after death. 'Such questions,' he said, 'are not relevant to the practice of the Path and cannot be answered while bound by the restraints of human existence.' Most of Buddhism, you see, gentlemen, can be explored, appreciated, and utilized as a tool toward enlightenment without descending into the supernatural."

The Archbishop looked nonplussed, but Cardinal Mustafa said

quickly, "Yet did not your Buddha say—and I believe that one of your scriptures holds these as his words, Your Holiness, but correct me immediately if I am wrong—'There is an unborn, an unoriginated, an unmade, an uncompounded; were there not, there would be no escape from the world of the born, the originated, the made, and the compounded.' "

The boy's smile did not waver. "Indeed, he did, Your Eminence. Very good. But are there not elements—as yet not completely understood—within our physical universe, bound by the laws of our physical universe, which might be described as unborn, unoriginated, unmade, and uncompounded?"

"None that I know of, Your Holiness," said Cardinal Mustafa, affably enough. "But then I am not a scientist. Only a poor priest."

Despite this diplomatic finesse, the boy on the throne seemed intent on pursuing the subject. "As we have previously discussed, Cardinal Mustafa, our form of Buddhism has evolved since we landed on this mountain world. Now it is very much filled with the spirit of Zen. And one of the great Zen masters of Old Earth, the poet William Blake, once said—'Eternity is in love with the productions of time.' "

Cardinal Mustafa's fixed smile showed his lack of understanding.

The Dalai Lama was no longer smiling. The boy's expression was pleasant but serious. "Do you think perhaps that M. Blake meant that time without ending is worthless time, Cardinal Mustafa? That any being freed from mortality—even God—might envy the children of slow time?"

The Cardinal nodded but showed no agreement. "Your Holiness, I cannot see how God could envy poor mortal humankind. Certainly God is not capable of envy."

The boy's nearly invisible eyebrows shot up. "Yet, is not your Christian God, by definition, omnipotent? Certainly he, she, it must be capable of envy."

"Ah, a paradox meant for children, Your Holiness. I confess I am trained in neither logical apologetics nor metaphysics. But as a prince of Christ's Church, I know from my catechism and in my soul that God is not capable of envy . . . especially not envy of his flawed creations."

"Flawed?" said the boy.

Cardinal Mustafa smiled condescendingly, his tone that of a learned priest speaking to a child. "Humanity is flawed because of its propensity for sin," he said softly. "Our Lord could not be envious of a being capable of sin."

The Dalai Lama nodded slowly. "One of our Zen masters, a man named Ikkyu, once wrote a poem to that effect—

"All the sins committed
In the Three Worlds
Will fade and disappear
Together with myself."

Cardinal Mustafa waited a moment, but when no more poem was

forthcoming, he said, "Which three worlds was he speaking of, Your Holiness?"

"This was before spaceflight," said the boy, shifting slightly on his cushioned throne. "The Three Worlds are the past, present, and future."

"Very nice," said the Cardinal from the Holy Office. Behind him, his aide, Father Farrell, was staring at the boy with something like cold distaste. "But we Christians do not believe that sin—or the effects of sin—or the accountability for sin, for that matter—end with one's life, Your Holiness."

"Precisely." The boy smiled. "It is for this reason that I am curious why you extend life so artificially through your cruciform creature," he said. "We feel that the slate is washed clean with death. You feel that it brings judgment. Why defer this judgment?"

"We view the cruciform as a sacrament given to us by Our Lord Jesus Christ," Cardinal Mustafa said softly. "This judgment was first deferred by Our Savior's sacrifice on the cross, God Himself accepting the punishment for our sins, allowing us the option of everlasting life in heaven if we so choose it. The cruciform is another gift from Our Savior, perhaps allowing us time to set our houses in order before that final judgment."

"Ahh, yes," sighed the boy. "But perhaps Ikkyu meant that there are no sinners. That there is no sin. That 'our' lives do not belong to us . . ."

"Precisely, Your Holiness," interrupted Cardinal Mustafa, as if praising a slow learner. I saw the Regent, the Lord Chamberlain, and others around the throne wince at this interruption. "Our lives do not belong to us, but to Our Lord and Savior . . . and to serve Him, to our Holy Mother Church."

". . . do not belong to us, but belong to the universe," continued the boy. "And that our deeds—good and bad—also are property of the universe."

Cardinal Mustafa frowned. "A pretty phrase, Your Holiness, but perhaps too abstract. Without God, the universe can only be a machine . . . unthinking, uncaring, unfeeling."

"Why?" said the boy.

"I beg your pardon, Your Holiness?"

"Why must the universe be unthinking, uncaring, unfeeling without your definition of a God?" the child said softly. He closed his eyes.

> *"The morning dew*
> *Flees away,*
> *   And is no more;*
> *Who may remain*
> *In this world of ours?"*

Cardinal Mustafa steepled his fingers and touched his lips as if in prayer or mild frustration. "Very nice, Your Holiness. Ikkyu again?"

The Dalai Lama grinned broadly. "No. Me. I write a little Zen poetry when I can't sleep."

The priests chuckled. The Nemes creature stared at Aenea.

Cardinal Mustafa turned toward my friend. "M. Ananda," he said, "do you have an opinion on these weighty matters?"

For a second I did not know whom he was addressing, but then I remembered the Dalai Lama's introduction of Aenea as Ananda, foremost disciple of the Buddha.

"I know another little verse by Ikkyu which expresses my opinion," she said.

> *"More frail and illusory*
> > *Than numbers written on water,*
> *Our seeking from the Buddha*
> > *Felicity in the afterworld."*

Archbishop Breque cleared his throat and joined in the conversation. "That seems clear enough, young lady. You do not think that God will grant our prayers."

Aenea shook her head. "I think that he meant two things, Your Eminence. First that the Buddha will not help us. It isn't in his job definition, so to speak. Secondly, that planning for the afterworld is foolish because we are, by nature, timeless, eternal, unborn, undying, and omnipotent."

The Archbishop's face and neck reddened above his collar. "Those adjectives can be applied only to God, M. Ananda." He felt Cardinal Mustafa's glare on him and remembered his place as a diplomat. "Or so we believe," he added lamely.

"For a young person and an architect, you seem to know your Zen and poetry, M. Ananda." Cardinal Mustafa chuckled, obviously trying to lighten the tone. "Are there any other Ikkyu poems you feel might be relevant?"

Aenea nodded.

> *"We come into this world alone,*
> *We depart alone,*
> > *This also is illusion.*
> *I will teach you the way*
> *Not to come, not to go!"*

"That would be a good trick," said Cardinal Mustafa with false joviality.

The Dalai Lama leaned forward. "Ikkyu taught us that it is possible to live at least part of our lives in a timeless, spaceless world where there is no birth and death, no coming and going," he said softly. "A place where there is no separation in time, no distance in space, no barrier barring us from the ones we love, no glass wall between experience and our hearts."

Cardinal Mustafa stared as if speechless.

"My friend . . . M. Ananda . . . also taught me this," said the boy.

For a second, the Cardinal's face was twisted by something like a sneer. He turned toward Aenea. "I would be pleased if the young lady would teach me . . . teach us all . . . this clever conjuror's trick," he said sharply.

"I hope to," said Aenea.

Rhadamanth Nemes took a half step toward my friend. I set my hand in my cape, lightly touching the firing stud of the flashlight laser.

The Regent tapped a gong with a cloth-wrapped stick. The Lord Chamberlain hurried forward to escort us out. Aenea bowed to the Dalai Lama and I clumsily did likewise.

The audience was over.

I DANCE WITH Aenea in the great, echoing reception hall, to the music of a seventy-two-piece orchestra, with the lords and ladies, priests and plenipotentiaries of T'ien Shan, the Mountains of Heaven, all watching from the edges of the dance floor or wheeling around us in shared motion to the music. I remember dancing with Aenea, dining again before midnight at the long tables constantly restocked with food, and then dancing again. I remember holding her tight as we moved together around the dance floor. I do not remember ever having danced before—at least when I was sober— but I dance this night, holding Aenea close to me as the torchlight from the crackling braziers dims and the Oracle casts skylight shadows across the parquet floors.

It is in the wee hours of the morning and the older guests have retired, all the monks and mayors and elder statesmen—except for the Thunderbolt Sow, who has laughed and sung and clapped along with the orchestra for every raceme quadrille, tapping her slippered feet on the polished floors— and there are only four or five hundred determined celebrants remaining in the great, shadowy space, while the band plays slower and slower pieces as if their musical mainspring is wearing down.

I confess that I would have gone off to bed hours earlier if it were not for Aenea: she wants to dance. So dance we do, moving slowly, her small hand in my large one, my other hand flat on her back—feeling her spine and strong muscles under my palm through the thin silk of the dress—her hair against my cheek, her breasts soft against me, the curve of her skull against my neck and chin. She seems slightly sad, but still energetic, still celebrating.

Private audiences had ended many hours ago and word had spread that the Dalai Lama had gone to bed before midnight, but we last celebrants partied on—Lhomo Dondrub, our flyer friend, laughing and pouring champagne and rice beer for everyone, Labsang Samten, the Dalai Lama's little brother, leaping over the ember-filled braziers at some point, the serious Tromo Trochi of Dhomu suddenly metamorphosing into a magician in one corner, doing tricks with fire and hoops and levitations, and then the Dorje Phamo singing one clear, slow a cappella solo in a voice so sweet that it haunts my dreams to this day, and finally the scores of others joining in the Oracle Song as the orchestra prepares to wrap up the evening's celebration before the predawn begins to fade the night sky.

Suddenly the music ends in mid-bar. The dancers stop. Aenea and I lurch to a stop and look around.

There has been no sign of the Pax guests for hours, but suddenly one of them—Rhadamanth Nemes—emerges from the shadows of the Dalai Lama's curtained alcove. She has changed her uniform and is now dressed all in red. There are two others with her, and for a moment I think they are the priests, but then I see that the two figures dressed in black are near-copies of the Nemes thing: another woman and a man, both in black combat suits, both with limp, black bangs hanging down on pale foreheads, both with eyes of dead amber.

The trio moves through the frozen dancers toward Aenea and me. Instinctively I put myself between my friend and the things, but the Nemes male and its other sibling begin to move around us, flanking us. I pull Aenea close behind me, but she steps to my side.

The frozen dancers make no noise. The orchestra remains silent. Even the moonlight seems stilled to solid shafts in the dusty air.

I remove the flashlight laser and hold it at my side. The primary Nemes thing shows small teeth. Cardinal Mustafa steps from the shadows and stands behind her. All four of the Pax creatures hold their gaze on Aenea. For a moment I think that the universe has stopped, that the dancers are literally frozen in time and space, that the music hangs above us like icy stalactites ready to shatter and fall, but then I hear the murmur through the crowd—fearful whispers, a hiss of anxiety.

There is no visible threat—only four Pax guests moving out across the ballroom floor with Aenea as the locus of their closing circle—but the sense of predators closing on their prey is too strong to ignore, as is the scent of fear through the perfume and powder and cologne.

"Why wait?" says Rhadamanth Nemes, looking at Aenea but speaking to someone else—her siblings perhaps, or the Cardinal.

"I think . . ." says Cardinal Mustafa and freezes.

Everyone freezes. The great horns near the entrance arch have blown with the bass rumble of continental crusts shifting. No one is there in the alcoves to blow them. The bone and brass trumpets bracket the endless one-note rumbling of the horns. The great gong vibrates on the bone conduction level.

There is a rustle and stifled outcry across the dance floor, in the direction of the escalators, the anteroom, and the curtained entrance arch. The thinning crowds there are parting wider, moving aside like furrowed soil ahead of a steel plow.

Something is moving behind the closed curtains of the anteroom.

Now something has passed through the curtains, not so much parting them as severing them. Now something is glinting in Oracle light and gliding across the parquet floors, gliding as if floating centimeters above the floor, glinting in the dying light of the moon. Tatters of red curtain hang from an impossibly tall form—three meters at least—and there are too many arms emerging from the folds of that crimson robe. It looks as if the hands hold steel blades. The dancers move away more quickly and there is a general and audible intake of breath. Lightning silently supercedes the moonlight and strobes off polished floors, eclipsing the Oracle with retinal echoes. When the thunder arrives some long seconds later, it is indistinguishable from the low, bone-shaking rumble of the still-reverberating horns in the entrance hall.

The Shrike glides to a halt five paces from Aenea and me, five paces from the Nemes thing, ten paces from each of the Nemes siblings frozen in their act of circling us, eight paces from the Cardinal. It occurs to me that the Shrike shrouded in its dangling red curtain tatters resembles nothing so much as a chrome and bladed caricature of Cardinal Mustafa in his crimson robe. The Nemes clones in their black uniforms look like shadows of stilettos against the walls.

Somewhere in one of the shadowed corners of the great reception hall, a tall clock slowly strikes the hour . . . one . . . two . . . three . . . four. It is, of course, the number of inhuman killing machines standing before and behind us. It has been more than four years since I have seen the Shrike, but its presence is no less terrible and no more welcome despite its intercession here. The red eyes gleam like lasers under a thin film of water. The chrome-steel jaws are parted to show row upon row of razor teeth. The thing's blades, barbs, and cutting edges emerge from the enfolding red curtain robe in scores of places. It does not blink. It does not appear to breathe. Now that the gliding has stopped, it is as motionless as a nightmare sculpture.

Rhadamanth Nemes is smiling at it.

Still holding the silly flashlight laser, I remember the confrontation on God's Grove years ago. The Nemes thing had gone silver and blurry and simply disappeared, reappearing next to twelve-year-old Aenea without warning. It had planned to cut off my friend's head and carry it away in a burlap bag, and it would have done so had not the Shrike appeared then. The Nemes thing could do so now without hope of my reacting in time. These things moved outside of time. I know the agony of a parent watching its child step into the path of a speeding groundcar, unable to move in time to protect her. Superimposed on this terror is the pain of a lover unable to protect his beloved. I would die in a second to protect Aenea from any of these things—including the Shrike—indeed, may die in a second, in less than a second—but my death will not protect her. I grind my molars in frustration.

Moving only my eyes, afraid that I will precipitate the slaughter if I move a hand or head or muscle, I see that the Shrike is not staring at Aenea or the primary Nemes thing—it is staring directly at John Domenico Cardinal Mustafa. The frog-faced priest must feel the weight of this bloodred gaze, for the Cardinal's complexion has gone a pure white above the red of his robe.

Aenea moves now. Stepping to my left side, she slips her right hand in my empty left one and squeezes my fingers. It is not a child's request for reassurance; it is a signal of reassurance to me.

"You know how it will end," she says softly to the Cardinal, ignoring the Nemes things as they coil like cats ready to pounce.

The Grand Inquisitor licks his thick lips. "No, I do not. There are the three of . . ."

"You know how it will end," interrupts Aenea, her voice still soft. "You were on Mars."

Mars? I think. *What the hell does Mars have to do with anything?* Lightning flickers again through the skylight, throwing wild shadows. The faces of the hundreds of terror-frozen revelers are like white ovals painted on black velvet around us. I realize in a flash of insight as sudden and illuminating as the lightning that the metaphysical biosphere of this world—Zen-evolved or not—is riddled with Tibetan myth-inspired demons and malevolent spirits: cancerous *nyen* earth spirits; *sadag* "lords of the soil" who haunt builders who disturb their realms; *tsen* red spirits who live in rocks; *gyelpo* spirits of dead kings who have failed their vows, dead, deadly, dressed all in pale armor; *dud* spirits who are so malevolent that they feed only on human flesh and wear black, beetle skin; *mamo* female deities as ferocious as unseen riptides; *matrika* sorceresses of charnel grounds and cremation platforms, first sensed by a whiff of their carrion breath; *grahas* planetary deities that cause epilepsy and other violent, thrashing illnesses; *nodjin* guardians of wealth in the soil—death to diamond miners—and a score more of night things, teethed things, clawed things, and killing things. Lhomo and the others have told me the stories well and often. I look at the white faces staring in shock at the Shrike and the Nemes creatures and think—*This night will not be so strange in the telling for these people.*

"The demon cannot vanquish all three of them," says Cardinal Mustafa, saying the word "demon" aloud even as I think the word. I realize that he is speaking about the Shrike.

Aenea ignores the comment. "It will harvest your cruciform first," she says softly. "I cannot stop it from doing that."

Cardinal Mustafa's head jerks back as if he has been slapped. His pale countenance grows visibly paler. Taking their cue from Rhadamanth Nemes, the clone-siblings coil tighter as if building energy toward some terrible transformation. Nemes has returned her black gaze to Aenea and the creature is smiling so broadly now that her rearmost teeth are visible.

"Stop!" cries Cardinal Mustafa and his shout echoes from the skylight and floor. The great horns cease rumbling. Revelers clutch one another in a rustling of fingernails on silk. Nemes flashes the Cardinal a look of malevolent loathing and near defiance.

"Stop!" screams the Pax holy man again, and I realize that he is talking to his own creatures first and foremost. "I invoke the command of Albedo and the Core, by the authority of the Three Elements I command thee!" This last desperate scream has the cadence of a shouted exorcism, some profound ritual, but even I can tell that it is not Catholic or Christian. It is not the Shrike being invoked under an iron grip of talismanic control here; it is his own demons.

Nemes and her siblings slide backward on the parquet floor as if pulled by invisible strings. The clone male and clone female move around us until they join Nemes in front of Mustafa.

The Cardinal smiles but it is a tremulous gesture. "My pets will not be unleashed until we speak again. I give my word as a prince of the Church, unholy child. Do I have your word that this"—he gestures toward the bladed Shrike in its velvet tatters—"this demon will not stalk me until then?"

Aenea appears as calm as she has through the entire incident. "I do not control it," she says. "Your only safety is to leave this world in peace."

The Cardinal is eyeing the Shrike. The man seems poised to leap away if the tall apparition flexes so much as a fingerblade. Nemes and her ilk continue standing between him and the Shrike. "What assurance have I," he says, "that the thing will not follow me into space . . . or back to Pacem?"

"None," says Aenea.

The Grand Inquisitor points a long finger at my friend. "We have business here that has nothing to do with you," he says sharply, "but you will never leave this world. I swear this to you by the bowels of Christ."

Aenea returns his gaze and says nothing.

Mustafa turns and stalks away with a swish of his red robe and a rasp of his slippers on the polished floor. The Nemes things back all the way across the floor while following him, the male and female clones holding their gazes on the Shrike, Nemes piercing Aenea with her stare. They pass through the curtain tent of the Dalai Lama's private portal and are gone.

The Shrike stays where it is, lifeless, its four arms frozen in front of it, fingerblades catching the last drops of Oracle light before the moon moves behind the mountain and is lost.

Revelers begin moving toward the exits on a wave of whispers and exclamations. The orchestra thumps, clangs, and whistles as instruments are packed in a hurry and dragged or carried away. Aenea continues holding my hand as a small circle remains around us.

"Buddha's ass!" cries Lhomo Dondrub and strides over to the Shrike, testing his finger against a metallic thorn rising from the thing's chest. I see blood on his finger in the dimming light. "Fantastic!" cries Lhomo and swigs from a goblet of rice beer.

The Dorje Phamo moves to Aenea's side. She takes my friend's left hand, goes to one knee, and sets Aenea's palm against her wrinkled forehead. Aenea removes her hand from mine as she takes the Thunderbolt Sow gently by the arms and helps her rise. "No," whispers Aenea.

"Blessed One," whispers the Dorje Phamo. "*Amata,* Immortal One; *Arhat,* Perfected One; *Sammasambuddha,* Fully Awakened One; command us and teach us the *dhamma.*"

"No," snaps Aenea, still gentle with the old woman as she pulls her to her feet but stern of countenance. "I will teach you what I know and share what I have when the time arrives. I can do no more. The hour for myth has passed."

My friend turns, takes my hand, and leads us across the dance floor, past the immobile Shrike, and toward the tattered curtains and unmoving escalator. Former revelers part for our passing as swiftly as they had for the Shrike.

We pause at the top of the steel stairs. Lanterns glow in the hallway to our sleeping rooms far below us.

"Thank you," says Aenea, looking up at me with her brown eyes moist.

"What?" I say stupidly. "For . . . why . . . I don't understand."

"Thank you for the dance," she says and reaches up to kiss me softly on the lips.

The electricity of her touch makes me blink. I gesture back toward the roiling crowd behind us, the dance floor empty of the Shrike now, at the Potala guards rushing into the echoing space, and at the curtained alcove through which Mustafa and his creatures have disappeared. "We can't sleep here tonight, kiddo. Nemes and the other two will . . ."

"Uh-uh," says Aenea, "they won't. Trust me on this. They won't come creeping down the outside wall and across our ceiling tonight. In fact, they'll all be leaving their gompa and shuttling straight up to their ship in orbit. They'll be back, but not tonight."

I sigh.

She takes my hand. "Are you sleepy?" she says softly.

Of course I am sleepy. I am exhausted beyond words. Last night seems days and weeks away, and I had only two or three hours' light sleep then because of . . . because we had . . . because of . . .

"Not a bit," I say.

Aenea smiles and leads the way back to our sleeping chamber.

20

POPE URBAN XVI: *Send forth Thy Spirit and they shall be created.*

All: Thou shalt renew the memory of Earth and the face of all worlds in God's Dominion.

Pope Urban XVI: Let us pray.

O God, You have instructed the hearts of the faithful by the light of the Holy Spirit. Grant that through the same Holy Spirit we may always be truly wise and rejoice in His consolation. Through Christ our Lord.

All: Amen.

Pope Urban XVI blesses the insignia of the Knights of the Equestrian Order of the Holy Sepulchre of Jerusalem.

Pope Urban XVI: Our help is in the name of the Lord.

All: Who made Heaven and earth and all worlds.

Pope Urban XVI: The Lord be with you.

All: And also with you.

Pope Urban XVI: Let us pray.

Hear, we pray You, O Lord, our prayers and deign through the power of Your majesty to bless the insignia of office. Protect Your servants who desire to wear them, so that they may be strong to guard the rights of the Church, and quick to defend and spread the Christian faith. Through Christ our Lord.

All: Amen.

Pope Urban XVI sprinkles the emblems with holy water.

The Master of Ceremonies, Cardinal Lourdusamy, reads the decree of the newly appointed Knights and of those promoted in rank. Each member stands as his or her name is mentioned and remains standing. There are one thousand two hundred and eight Knights in the Basilica.

Cardinal Lourdusamy lists all honorees by rank, lowest to highest, Knights first, followed by Priest Knights.

At the conclusion of the reading, the Knights to be invested kneel. All others are seated.

Pope Urban XVI asks the Knights: What do you ask?
The Knights answer: I ask to be invested as a Knight of the Holy Sepulchre.
Pope Urban XVI: Today, being a Knight of the Holy Sepulchre means engaging in the battle for the Kingdom of Christ and for the extension of the Church; and undertaking works of charity with the same deep spirit of faith and love with which you may give your life in battle. Are you ready to follow this ideal throughout your life?
The Knights answer: I am.
Pope Urban XVI: I remind you that if all men and women should consider themselves honored to practice virtue, so much the more should a soldier of Christ glory in being a Knight of Jesus Christ and use every means to show by his actions and virtues that he is deserving of the honor which is being conferred upon him and of the dignity with which he is invested. Are you prepared to promise to observe the Constitutions of this holy Order?
The Knights answer: With the grace of God I promise to observe, as a true soldier of Christ, the Commandments of God, the precepts of the Church, the orders of my commanders in the field, and the Constitution of this holy Order.
Pope Urban XVI: In virtue of the decree received, I appoint and declare you Soldiers and Knights of the Holy Sepulchre of Our Lord Jesus Christ. In the name of the Father, and of the Son, and of the Holy Spirit.
The Knights enter the Sanctuary and kneel while the Pope blesses the Jerusalem Cross, the emblem of the Order.

Pope Urban XVI: Receive the Cross of Our Lord Jesus Christ for your protection, in the name of the Father, and of the Son, and of the Holy Spirit.
After kneeling in front of the Jerusalem Cross, each Knight responds:
    Amen.
Pope Urban XVI returns to the chair placed on the altar platform. When His Holiness gives the signal, the Master of Ceremonies Cardinal Lourdusamy reads the decree of each newly appointed Knight. As each Knight's name is called, the newly appointed Knight approaches the altar, genuflects, and kneels in the great space before His Holiness. One Knight has been chosen to represent all of the Knights to be invested and now that Knight approaches the altar.

Pope Urban XVI: What do you request?
Knight: I desire to be invested a Knight of the Holy Sepulchre.

Pope Urban XVI: I remind you again, that if all men should consider themselves honored to practice virtue, so much the more must a soldier of Christ, who should glory in being a Knight of Jesus Christ, use every means never to sully his good name. Finally, he ought to show by his actions and virtues that he is deserving of the honor which is being conferred upon him and of the dignity with which he is invested. Are you prepared to promise by word and in truth to observe the constitutions of this holy military Order?

The Knight puts his folded hands into the hands of His Holiness.

Knight: I declare and promise by word and in truth to God Almighty, to Jesus Christ, His Son, to the Blessed Virgin Mary, to observe, as a true soldier of Christ, all that I have been charged to do.

His Holiness, Pope Urban XVI, places his right hand on the head of the Knight.

Pope Urban XVI: Be a faithful and brave soldier of Our Lord Jesus Christ, a Knight of His Holy Sepulchre, strong and courageous, so that one day you may be admitted to His heavenly court.

His Holiness hands the golden spurs to the Knight saying: Receive these spurs that are a symbol of your Order for the honor and defense of the Holy Sepulchre.

The Knight Master of Ceremonies Cardinal Lourdusamy hands the unsheathed sword to His Holiness who, in turn, holds it before the newly appointed Knight and returns it to the Knight Master.

Master of Ceremonies: Receive this sword that symbolizes the defense of the Holy Church of God and the overthrow of the enemies of the Cross of Christ. Be on guard never to use it to strike anyone unjustly.

After the Knight Master of Ceremonies has returned it into the scabbard, His Holiness hands the sword to the newly appointed Knight.

Pope Urban XVI: Bear well in mind that the Saints have conquered kingdoms not by the sword, but by faith.

This part of the ceremony is repeated for each candidate. His Holiness the Pope is given the unsheathed sword and touches each Knight's right shoulder three times with the sword, saying: I appoint and declare you a Soldier and Knight of the Holy Sepulchre of Our Lord Jesus Christ. In the name of the Father, and of the Son, and of the Holy Spirit.

After returning the sword to the Knight Master of Ceremonies, His Holiness places around the neck of each the Cross, the emblem of the Order, saying: Receive the Cross of Our Lord Jesus Christ for your protection, and for that purpose repeat unceasingly: "By the sign of the Cross, deliver us, O Lord, from our enemies."

Each newly invested Knight arises, bows to His Holiness, and goes to the dignitary highest in rank to receive the cape from him. He then receives from the Knight assistant, the beret, which he puts on immediately. He then goes to his place in the pews.

All stand as His Holiness begins the following hymn, which is continued by all present.

VENI CREATOR
Come, Holy Spirit, Creator blest,
And in our souls take up Your rest;
Come with Your grace and heavenly aid,
To fill the hearts which You have made.

O Comforter, to You we cry,
You, heavenly gift of God Most High,
You, fount of life and fire of love,
And sweet anointing from above.

You, in your sevenfold gifts are unknown;
You, finger of God's hand we own;
You, promise of the Father, You
Who do the sword with flame imbue.

Kindle our senses from on high,
And calm the hearts of those to die;
With patience firm and virtue high
The weakness of our flesh supply.

Far from us drive the foe we dread,
And grant to us Your wrath instead;
So shall we not, with You for guide,
Allow the victory be denied.

Oh, may your grace on us bestow
The Father and the Son to know;
And you, through endless times confessed,
Of both the eternal Spirit blest.

Now to the Father and the Son,
Who rose from death, be glory given,
Before You, O Holy Sword and Shield,
Be all in Pax and Heaven driven,

His Holiness Pope Urban XVI: And all the foes of Christ must yield.
All: Amen.
Exit His Holiness and the Master of Ceremonies.

INSTEAD OF RETURNING to his Apostolic Apartments, the Pope led his cardinal to a small room off the Sistine Chapel.

"The Room of Tears," said Cardinal Lourdusamy. "I've not been in here for years." It was a small room with brown floor tiles aged to a black hue, red flock wallpaper, low, medieval-vaulted ceilings, harsh lighting from a few gold wall sconces, no windows but heavy and incongruous white drapes along one scarlet wall. The room was barely furnished—an odd red settee in one corner, a small, black table-cum-altar with a white linen cloth, and a skeletal framework in the center upon which hung an ancient, yellowed, and somewhat unsettling alb and chasuble, with two white and absurdly decorated shoes nearby, the toes curling with age.

"The vestment belonged to Pope Pius XII," said the Pontiff. "He donned it here in 1939 after his election. We had it taken from the Vatican Museum and set out here. We visit it upon occasion."

"Pope Pius XII," mused Cardinal Lourdusamy. The Secretary of State tried to recall any special significance of that long-dead Pope. All he could think of was the disturbing statue of Pius XII done almost two millennia ago—in 1964—by Francesco Messina, now relegated to a subterranean corridor beneath the Vatican. Messina's Pius XII is shown in rough strokes, his round glasses as empty as the eye sockets in a skull, his right arm raised defensively—bony fingers splayed—as if trying to ward off the evil of his time.

"A war pope?" guessed Lourdusamy.

Pope Urban XVI wearily shook his head. There was a welt on his forehead where the heavy orphreyed mitre had rested during the long investiture ceremony. "It is not his reign during the Old Earth world war which interests us," said the Holy Father, "but the complex dealings he was compelled to carry out with the very heart of darkness in order to preserve the Church and the Vatican."

Lourdusamy nodded slowly. "The Nazis and the Fascists," he murmured. "Of course." The parallel with the Core was not without merit.

The Pope's servants had set out tea on the single table and the Secretary of State now acted as personal servant to His Holiness, pouring the tea into a fragile china cup and carrying it to the other man. Pope Urban XVI nodded wearily in gratitude and sipped the steaming liquid. Lourdusamy returned to his place in the middle of the room near the ancient hanging garments and looked critically at his pontiff. *His heart has been bothering him again. Will we have to go through another resurrection and election conclave soon?*

"Did you notice who was chosen as the representative Knight?" asked the Pope, his voice stronger now. He looked up with intense, sad eyes.

Caught off balance, Lourdusamy had to think for a second. "Oh, yes . . . the former Mercantilus CEO. Isozaki. He will be the Knight in titular leadership of the Cassiopeia 4614 Crusade."

"Making amends." His Holiness smiled.

Lourdusamy rubbed his jowls. "It may be more serious penance than M. Isozaki had counted on, Your Holiness."

The Pope looked up. "Serious losses forcast?"

"About forty percent casualties," rumbled Lourdusamy. "Half of those irretrievable for resurrection. The fighting in that sector has been very, very heavy."

"And elsewhere?" said the Pontiff.

Lourdusamy sighed. "The unrest has spread to about sixty Pax worlds, Your Holiness. About three million suffer the Contagion and have rejected the cruciform. There is fighting, but nothing the Pax authorities cannot handle. Renaissance Vector is the worst . . . about three quarters of a million infected, and it is spreading very quickly."

The Pope nodded wearily and sipped his tea. "Tell us something positive, Simon Augustino."

"The messenger drone translated from T'ien Shan System just before the ceremony," said the Cardinal. "We decrypted the holo message from Cardinal Mustafa immediately."

The Pope held his cup and saucer and waited.

"They have encountered the Devil's Child," said Lourdusamy. "They met her at the Dalai Lama's palace."

"And . . ." prompted His Holiness.

"No action was taken because of the presence of the Shrike demon," said Lourdusamy, glancing at notes on his wrist comlog diskey. "But identification is certain. The child named Aenea . . . she is in her twenties, standard, now of course . . . her bodyguard, Raul Endymion, whom we had arrested and lost on Mare Infinitus more than nine years ago . . . and the others."

The Pope touched his thin lips with his thin fingers. "And the Shrike?"

"It appeared only when the girl was threatened by Albedo's Noble Guard . . . officers," said Cardinal Lourdusamy. "And then disappeared. There was no fighting."

"But Cardinal Mustafa failed to consummate the moment?" said the Pope.

Lourdusamy nodded.

"And you still think that Mustafa is the right person for the job?" murmured Pope Urban XVI.

"Yes, Holy Father. Everything is going according to plan. We had hoped to make contact prior to the actual arrest."

"And the *Raphael*?" said the Pope.

"No sign of it yet," said the Secretary of State, "but Mustafa and Admiral Wu feel certain that de Soya will appear in T'ien Shan System before the allotted time to collect the girl."

"We certainly pray that this will be the case," said the Pontiff. "Do you know, Simon Augustino, how much damage that renegade ship has done to our Crusade?"

Lourdusamy knew that the question was rhetorical. He and the Holy Father and the squirming Pax Fleet admirals had pored over combat action reports, casualty lists, and tonnage losses for five years. The *Raphael* and its turncoat Captain de Soya had almost been captured or destroyed a score of times, but always had managed to escape to Ouster space, leaving behind scattered convoys, tumbling hulks, and shattered Pax warships. Pax Fleet's failure to catch a single renegade archangel had become the shame of the Fleet and the best-kept secret in the Pax.

And now it was going to end.

"Albedo's Elements calculate a ninety-four percent probability that de Soya will rise to our bait," said the Cardinal.

"It's been how long since Pax Fleet and the Holy Office planted the information?" said the Pope, finishing his tea and carefully setting the cup and saucer on the edge of the settee.

"Five weeks standard," said Lourdusamy. "Wu arranged for it to be encrypted in the AI aboard one of the escort torchships that the *Raphael* jumped at the edge of Ophiuchi System. But not so heavily encrypted that the Ouster-enhanced systems aboard the *Raphael* could not decipher it."

"Won't de Soya and his people scent a trap?" mused the man who had once been Father Lenar Hoyt.

"Unlikely, Your Holiness," said the Cardinal. "We've used that encryption pattern before to feed reliable information to de Soya and . . ."

The Pope's head snapped up. "Cardinal Lourdusamy," he said sharply, "do you mean to tell us that you sacrificed innocent Pax ships and lives . . . lives beyond resurrection . . . merely to insure that the renegades will consider this information reliable?"

"Yes, Holy Father," said Lourdusamy.

The Pope let out a breath and nodded. "Regrettable, but understandable . . . given the stakes involved."

"In addition," continued the Cardinal, "certain officers aboard the crew of the ship positioned to be captured by the *Raphael* had been . . . ah . . . conditioned . . . by the Holy Office so that they also had the information on when we plan to move on the girl Aenea and the world of T'ien Shan."

"All this prepared months in advance?" said the Pope.

"Yes, Your Holiness. It was an advantage given us by Councillor Albedo and the Core when they registered the activation of the T'ien Shan farcaster some months ago."

The Pontiff laid his hands flat on his robed thighs. His fingers were bluish. "And that escape has been denied the Devil's Child?"

"Absolutely," said the Cardinal. "The *Jibril* slagged the entire mountain around the farcaster portal. The farcaster itself is all but impervious, Your Holiness, but at the moment it is buried under twenty meters of rock."

"And the Core is certain that this is the only farcaster on T'ien Shan?"

"Absolutely certain, Holy Father."

"And the preparations for the confrontation with de Soya and his renegade archangel?"

"Well, Admiral Wu should be here to discuss the tactical details, Your Holiness . . ."

"We trust you to convey the general outline, Simon Augustino."

"Thank you, Holy Father. Pax Fleet has stationed fifty-eight planet-class archangel cruisers within the T'ien Shan System. These have been hidden for the past six standard weeks . . ."

"Excuse us, Simon Augustino," murmured the Pope. "But how does one hide fifty-eight archangel-class battlecruisers?"

The Cardinal smiled thinly. "They have been powered down, floating in strategic positions within the inner-system asteroid belt and the system's outer Kuiper Belt, Your Holiness. Completely undetectable. Ready to jump at a second's notice."

"The *Raphael* will not escape this time?"

"No, Your Holiness," said Cardinal Lourdusamy. "The heads of eleven Pax Fleet commanders depend upon the success of this ambush."

"Leaving a fifth of our archangel fleet to float for weeks in this Outback system has seriously compromised the effectiveness of our Crusade against the Ousters, Cardinal Lourdusamy."

"Yes, Your Holiness." The Cardinal set his own palms against his robe and was surprised to realize that his palms were damp. Besides the eleven Pax Fleet heads riding on the success of this mission, Lourdusamy knew that his own future hung in the balance.

"It will be worth it when we destroy this rebel," murmured the Pope.

Lourdusamy took a breath.

"We presume that the ship and Captain de Soya *will* be destroyed, not taken captive," said His Holiness.

"Yes, Holy Father. Standing orders are to slag the ship to atoms."

"But we will *not* harm the child?"

"No, Holy Father. All precautions have been taken to assure that the contagion vector named Aenea will be taken alive."

"That is very important, Simon Augustino," muttered the Pope. He seemed to be whispering to himself. They had gone over these details a hundred times. "We must have the girl alive. The others with her . . . they are expendable . . . but the girl must be captured. Tell us again the procedure."

Cardinal Lourdusamy closed his eyes. "As soon as the *Raphael* is interdicted and destroyed, the Core ships will move into orbit around T'ien Shan and incapacitate the planet's population."

"Deathbeam them," murmured His Holiness.

"Not . . . technically," said the Cardinal. "As you know, the Core assures us that the results of this technique are reversible. It is more the induction of a permanent coma."

"Will the millions of bodies be transported this time, Simon Augustino?"

"Not at first, Your Holiness. Our special teams will go planetside, find the girl, and remove her to an archangel convoy that shall bring her here to Pacem, where she will be revived, isolated, interrogated, and . . ."

"Executed," sighed the Pope. "To show those millions of rebels on sixty worlds that their putative messiah is no more."

"Yes, Your Holiness."

"We look forward to speaking to this person, Simon Augustino. The Devil's Child or not."

"Yes, Your Holiness."

"And when will Captain de Soya take the bait and appear for his destruction, do you think?"

Cardinal Lourdusamy looked at his comlog. "Within hours, Your Holiness. Within hours."

"Let us pray for a successful conclusion," whispered the Pope. "Let us pray for the salvation of our Church and our race."

Both men bowed their heads in the Room of Tears.

IN THE DAYS immediately following our return from the Dalai Lama's Potala palace, I get the first hints of the full scope of Aenea's plans and power.

I am amazed at the reception upon our return. Rachel and Theo weep as they hug Aenea. A. Bettik pounds me on the back with his remaining hand and hugs me with both arms. The usually laconic Jigme Norbu first hugs George Tsarong and then comes down the line of us pilgrims, hugging all of us, tears streaming down his thin face. The entire Temple has turned out to cheer and clap and weep. I realize then that many had not expected us—or at least Aenea—to return from the reception with the Pax. I realize then what a close thing it had been that we had returned.

We set to work finishing the reconstruction of Hsuan-k'ung Ssu. I work with Lhomo, A. Bettik, and the high riggers on the last touches to the highest promenade, while Aenea, Rachel, and Theo surpervise detail work throughout the compound.

That evening, all I can think of is turning in early with my beloved, and from our hurried but passionate kisses during our few minutes alone on the high walk after the communal dinner, I guess that Aenea recipro-cates the wish for immediate and intense intimacy. But it is one of her scheduled "discussion group" evenings—her last as it turns out—and more than a hundred people are there in the central gompa platform as darkness falls. Luckily, the monsoons have held off after the first foretaste of their gray rain, and the evening is lovely as the sun sets to the west of K'un Lun Ridge. Torches crackle along the main axis stairways and prayer pennants snap.

I am amazed by some of those in attendance this night: the Tromo Trochi of Dhomu has returned from Potala in spite of his declared need to move west with his wares; the Dorje Phamo is there with all nine of her

favorite priests; there are numerous famous guests from the palace reception—mostly younger people—and the youngest and most famous of all,
trying to appear incognito in a plain red robe and hood, is the Dalai Lama
himself, minus his Regent and Lord Chamberlain, accompanied only by his
personal bodyguard and Chief Crier, Carl Linga William Eiheji.

I stand at the back of the crowded room. For an hour or so, the
discussion group is a discussion group, sometimes led but never dominated
by Aenea. But slowly her questioning turns the conversation her way. I
realize that she is a master of Tantric and Zen Buddhism, answering monks
who have spent decades mastering those disciplines in koan and Dharma.
To a monk who demands to know why they should not accept the Pax
offer of immortality as a form of rebirth, she quotes Buddha as teaching
that no individual is reborn, that all things are subject to *annicca*—the law
of mutability—and she then elaborates on the doctrine of *anatta,* literally
"no-self," the Buddha's denial that there is any such thing as a personal
entity known as a soul.

Responding to another query about death, Aenea quotes a Zen koan:
"A monk said to Tozan, 'A monk has died; where has he gone?'"
Tozan answered, 'After the fire, a sprout of grass.' "

"M. Aenea," says Kuku Se, her bright face flushed, "does that mean
mu?"

Aenea has taught me that *mu* is an elegant Zen concept that might
translate as—"Unask the question."

My friend smiles. She is sitting farthest from the door, in an open
space near the opened wall of the room, and the stars are bright and visible
above the Sacred Mountain of the North. The Oracle has not risen.

"It means that to some extent," she says softly. The room is silent to
hear. "It also means that the monk is as dead as a doornail. He hasn't gone
anywhere—more importantly, he has gone nowhere. But life has also gone
nowhere. It continues, in a different form. Hearts are sorrowed by the
monk's death, but life is not lessened. Nothing has been removed from the
balance of life in the universe. Yet that whole universe—as reproduced in
the monk's mind and heart—has itself died. Seppo once said to Gensha,
'Monk Shinso asked me where a certain dead monk had gone, and I told
him it was like ice becoming water.' Gensha said, 'That was all right, but I
myself would not have answered like that.' 'What would you have said?'
asked Seppo. Gensha replied, 'It's like water returning to water.' "

After a moment of silence, someone near the front of the room says,
"Tell us about the Void Which Binds."

"Once upon a time," begins Aenea as she always begins such things,
"there was the Void. And the Void was beyond time. In a real sense, the
Void was an orphan of time . . . an orphan of space.

"But the Void was not of time, not of space, and certainly was not of
God. Nor is the Void Which Binds God. In truth, the Void evolved long
after time and space had staked out the limits to the universe, but unbound
by time, untethered in space, the Void Which Binds has leaked backward

and forward across the continuum to the Big Bang beginning and the Little Whimper end of things."

Aenea pauses here and lifts her hands to her temples in a motion I have not seen her use since she was a child. She does not look to be a child this night. Her eyes are tired but vital. There are wrinkles of fatigue or worry around those eyes. I love her eyes.

"The Void Which Binds is a *minded* thing," she says firmly. "It comes from minded things—many of whom were, in turn, created by minded things.

"The Void Which Binds is stitched of quantum stuff, woven with Planck space, Planck time, lying under and around space/time like a quilt cover around and under cotton batting. The Void Which Binds is neither mystical nor metaphysical, it flows from and responds to the physical laws of the universe, *but it is a product of that evolving universe.* The Void is structured from thought and feeling. It is an artifact of the universe's consciousness of itself. And not merely of human thought and feeling—the Void Which Binds is a composite of a hundred thousand sentient races across billions of years of time. It is the only constant in the evolution of the universe—the only common ground for races that will evolve, grow, flower, fade, and die millions of years and hundreds of millions of light-years apart from one another. And there is only one entrance key to the Void Which Binds . . ."

Aenea pauses again. Her young friend Rachel is sitting close to her, cross-legged and attentive. I notice now for the first time that Rachel—the woman whom I have been foolishly jealous of these past few months—is indeed beautiful: copperish-brown hair short and curly, her cheeks flushed, her large green eyes flecked with tiny specks of brown. She is about Aenea's age, early twenties, standard, and hued to a golden brown by months of work in high places under T'ien Shan's yellow sun.

Aenea touches Rachel's shoulder.

"My friend here was a baby when her father discovered an interesting fact about the universe," says Aenea. "Her father, a scholar named Sol, had been obsessed for decades about the historical relationship between God and man. Then one day, under the most extreme of circumstances, when faced with losing his daughter for a second time, Sol was granted *satori*—he saw totally and intuitively what only a few others have been privileged to see clearly through the million years of our slow ponderings . . . Sol saw that love was a real and equal force in the universe . . . as real as electromagnetism or weak nuclear force. As real as gravity, and governed by many of the same laws. The inverse square law, for instance, often works as surely for love as it does for gravitational attraction.

"Sol realized that love was the binding force of the Void Which Binds, the thread and fabric of the garment. And in that instant of *satori,* Sol realized that humankind was not the only seamstress of that gorgeous tapestry. Sol glimpsed the Void Which Binds and the force of love behind it, but he could not gain access to that medium. Human beings, so recently evolved from our primate cousins, have not yet gained the sensory capacity to see clearly or enter the Void Which Binds.

"I say 'to see clearly' because all humans with an open heart and mind have caught rare but powerful glimpses of the Void landscape. Just as Zen is not a religion, but *is* religion, so the Void Which Binds is not a state of mind, but *is* the state of mind. The Void is all probability as standing waves, interacting with that standing wave front which is the human mind and personality. The Void Which Binds is touched by all of us who have wept with happiness, bidden a lover good-bye, been exalted with orgasm, stood over the grave of a loved one, or watched our baby open his or her eyes for the first time."

Aenea is looking at me as she speaks, and I feel the gooseflesh rise along my arms.

"The Void Which Binds is always under and above the surface of our thoughts and senses," she continues, "invisible but as present as the breathing of our beloved next to us in the night. Its actual but unaccessible presence in our universe is one of the prime causes for our species elaborating myth and religion, for our stubborn, blind belief in extrasensory powers, in telepathy and precognition, in demons and demigods and resurrection and reincarnation and ghosts and messiahs and so many other categories of almost-but-not-quite satisfying bullshit."

The hundred-some listening monks, workers, intellectuals, politicians, and holy men and women shift slightly at this statement. The wind is rising outside and the platform rocks gently, as it was designed to do. Thunder rumbles from somewhere to the south of Jo-kung.

"The so-called 'Four Statements of the Zen Sect' ascribed to Bodhidharma in the sixth century A.D. are an almost perfect signpost to find the Void Which Binds, at least to find its outline as an absence of otherworldly clutter," continues Aenea. "*First, no dependence on words and letters.* Words are the light and sound of our existence, the heat lightning by which the night is illuminated. The Void Which Binds is to be found in the deepest secrets and silences of things . . . the place where childhood dwells.

"*Second, a special transmission outside the Scriptures.* Artists recognize other artists as soon as the pencil begins to move. A musician can tell another musician apart from the millions who play notes as soon as the music begins. Poets glean poets in a few syllables, especially where the ordinary meaning and forms of poetry are discarded. Chora wrote—

> "*Two came here,*
> *Two flew off—*
> *Butterflies.*

"—and in the still-warm crucible of burned-away words and images remains the gold of deeper things, what R. H. Blyth and Frederick Franck once called 'the dark flame of life that burns in all things,' . . . and 'seeing with the belly, not with the eye; with "bowels of compassion." '

"The Bible lies. The Koran lies. The Talmud and Torah lie. The New Testament lies. The *Sutta-pitaka,* the *nikayas,* the *Itivuttaka,* and the *Dhammapada* lie. The Bodhisattva and the Amitabha lie. *The Book of the Dead* lies. The *Tiptaka* lies. All Scripture lies . . . just as I lie as I speak to you now.

"All these holy books lie not from intention or failure of expression, but by their very nature of being reduced to words; all the images, precepts, laws, canons, quotations, parables, commandments, koans, zazen, and sermons in these beautiful books ultimately fail by adding only more words between the human being who is seeking and the perception of the Void Which Binds.

"*Third, direct pointing to the soul of man.* Zen, which best understood the Void by finding its absence most clearly, wrestled with the problem of pointing without a finger, of creating this art without a medium, of hearing this powerful sound in a vacuum with no sounds. Shiki wrote—

> "*A fishing village;*
> *Dancing under the moon,*
> *To the smell of raw fish.*

"This—and I do not mean the poem—is the essence of seeking the key to the portal of the Void Which Binds. A hundred thousand races on a million worlds in days long dead have each had their villages with no houses, their dancing under the moon in worlds with no moons, the smell of raw fish on oceans with no fish. *This* can be shared beyond time, beyond words, beyond a race's span of existence.

"*Fourth, seeing into one's nature and the attainment of Buddhahood.* It does not take decades of zazen or baptism into the Church or pondering the Koran to do this. The Buddha nature is, after all, the after-the-crucible essence of being human. Flowers all attain their flowerhood. A wild dog or blind zygoat each attain their doghood or zygoathood. A place—any place—is granted its placehood. Only humankind struggles and fails in becoming what it is. The reasons are many and complex, but all stem from the fact that we have evolved as one of the self-seeing organs of the evolving universe. Can the eye see itself?"

Aenea pauses for a moment and in the silence we can all hear thunder rumbling somewhere beyond the ridge. The monsoon is holding off a few days, but its arrival is imminent. I try to imagine these buildings, mountains, ridges, cables, bridges, walkways, and scaffolds covered with ice and shrouded by fog. The thought makes me shiver.

"The Buddha understood that we could sense the Void Which Binds by silencing the din of the everyday," says Aenea at last. "In that sense, *satori* is a great and satisfying silence after listening to a neighbor's blasting sound system for days or months on end. But the Void Which Binds is more than silence . . . it is the beginning of hearing. Learning the language of the dead is the first task of those who enter the Void medium.

"Jesus of Nazareth entered the Void Which Binds. We know that. His voice is among the clearest of those who speak in the language of the dead. He stayed long enough to move to the second level of responsibility and effort—of learning the language of the dead. He learned well enough to hear the music of the spheres. He was able to ride the surging probability waves far enough to see his own death and was brave enough not to avoid it when he could. And we know that—at least on one occasion while dying on the cross—he learned to take that first step—to move through and across the space/time web of the Void Which Binds, appearing to his friends and disciples several paces into the future from where he hung dying on that cross.

"And, liberated from the restrictions of his time by his glimpse of the timelessness on the Void Which Binds, Jesus realized that it was he who was the key—not his teachings, not Scriptures based on his ideas, not groveling adulation to him or the suddenly evolving Old Testament God in which he solidly believed—but *him,* Jesus, a human man whose cells carried the decryption code to unlock the portal. Jesus knew that his ability to open that door lay not in his mind or soul but in his skin and bones and cells . . . literally in his DNA.

"When, during the Last Supper, Jesus of Nazareth asked his followers to drink of his blood and eat of his body, he was not speaking in parable or asking for magical transubstantiation or setting the place for centuries of symbolic reenactment. *Jesus wanted them to drink of his blood . . . a few drops in a great tankard of wine . . . and to eat of his body . . . a few skin scrapings in a loaf of bread.* He gave of himself in the most literal terms, knowing that those who drank of his blood would share his DNA, and be able to perceive the power of the Void Which Binds the universe.

"And so it was for some of his disciples. But, confronted with perceptions and impressions far beyond their power to absorb or to set in context—all but driven mad by the unceasing voices of the dead and their own reactions to the language of the living—*and unable to transmit their own blood music to others*—these disciples turned to dogma, reducing the inexpressible into rough words and turgid sermons, tight rules and fiery rhetoric. And the vision paled, then failed. The portal closed."

Aenea pauses again and sips water from a wooden mug. I notice for the first time that Rachel and Theo and a few others are weeping. I swivel where I am sitting on the fresh tatami and look behind me. A. Bettik is standing in the open doorway, his ageless blue face serious and intent on our young friend's words. The android is holding his shortened forearm with his good right hand. *Does it pain him?* I wonder.

Aenea speaks again. "Strangely enough, the first children of Old Earth to rediscover the key to the Void Which Binds were the TechnoCore. The autonomous intelligences, attempting to guide their own destiny through forced evolution at a million times the rate of biological human-

kind, found the DNA keycode to seeing the Void . . . although 'seeing' is
not the correct word, of course. Perhaps 'resonating' better expresses the
meaning.

"But while the Core could feel and explore the outlines of the Void
medium, send their probes into the multidimensional post-Hawking reality
of it, *they could not understand it*. The Void Which Binds demands a level
of sentient empathy which the Core had never bothered evolving. The first
step toward true *satori* in the Void is learning the language of the beloved
dead—*and the Core has no beloved dead*. The Void Which Binds was like a
beautiful painting to a blind man who chooses to burn it like firewood, or
like a Beethoven symphony to a deaf man who feels the vibration and
builds a stronger floor to damp it out.

"Instead of using the Void Which Binds as the medium it is, the
TechnoCore tore bits of it loose and offered it to humankind as clever
technologies. The so-called Hawking drive did not truly evolve from the
ancient master Stephen Hawking's work as the Core said, but was a perversion of his findings. The Hawking-drive ships that wove the WorldWeb and
allowed the Hegemony to exist functioned by tearing small holes in the
nonfabric at the edge of the Void—a minor vandalism, but vandalism nonetheless. Farcasters were a different thing. Here my similes will fail us, my
friends . . . for learning to step across the medium of the Void Which
Binds is a bit like learning to walk on water, if you will pardon the scrip-
tural hubris, while the TechnoCore's farcaster burrows were more like
draining the oceans so as to build highways across the seabed. Their farcaster tunneling through the boundaries of the Void was harming several
billion years of organic growth there. It was the equivalent of paving great
swaths through a vital, green forest—although that comparison also fails,
because the forest would have to be made out of the memories and voices
of the millions we have loved and lost—and the paved highways thousands
of kilometers wide—for you to understand even a hint of the damage done.

"The so-called fatline which allowed for instantaneous communication across the Hegemony was also a perversion of the Void Which Binds.
Again, my similes are clumsy and inept, but imagine some human aborigi-
nes discovering a working electromagnetic telecommunications grid—stu-
dios, holocameras, sound equipment, generators, transmitters, relay
satellites, receivers, and projectors—and then tearing down and tearing up
everything they can reach so that they can use the junk as signal flags. It is
worse than that. It is worse than pre-Hegira days on Old Earth when
humanity's giant oil tankers and ocean going ships deafened the world's
whales by filling their seas with mechanical noise, thus drowning out their
Life Songs—destroying a million years of evolving song history before human beings even knew it was being sung. The whales all decided to die out
after that; it was not the hunting of them for food and oil that killed them,
but the destruction of their songs."

Aenea takes a breath. She flexes her fingers as if her hands are cramping. When she looks around the room, her gaze touches each of us.

"I'm sorry," she says. "I'm wandering. Suffice it to say, that with the Fall of the Farcasters, the other races using the Void decided to stop the vandalism of the fatline. These other races had long since sent observers to live among us . . . ."

There is a sudden whispering and murmuring in the room. Aenea smiles and waits for it to subside.

"I know," she says. "The idea surprised me, as well, even though I knew this before I was born. These observers have an important function . . . to decide if humanity can be trusted to join them in the Void Which Binds medium, or if we are only vandals. It was one of these observers among us who recommended that Old Earth be transported away before the Core could destroy it. And it was one of these observers who designed the tests and simulations carried out on Old Earth during the last three centuries of its exile in the Lesser Magellanic Cloud to better explain our species to them and measure the empathy of which we are capable.

"These other races also sent their observers—spies, if you will—to dwell among the elements of the Core. They knew that it had been the Core tampering which had damaged the boundaries of the Void, but they also know *that we created the Core.* Many of the . . . residents is not quite the right word—collaborators? cocreators?—on the Void Which Binds are ex-silicon constructs, nonorganic autonomous intelligences in their own right. But not of the variety which rules the TechnoCore today. No sentient race can appreciate the Void medium without having evolved empathy."

Aenea raises her knees a bit and sets her elbows on them, leaning forward now as she speaks.

"My father—the John Keats cybrid—was created for this reason," she says, and although her voice is level, I can hear the subtext of emotion there. "As I have explained before, the Core is in a constant state of civil war, with almost every entity there fighting for itself and for no one else. It is a case of hyper-hyper-hyperparasitism to the tenth degree. Their prey—other Core elements—are not so much killed as absorbed, their coded genetic materials, memories, softwares, and reproductive sequences cannibalized. The cannibalized Core element still 'lives' but as a subcomponent of the victorious element or elements, which soon enough turn on one another for parts. Alliances are temporary. There are no philosophies, creeds, or ultimate goals—only contingency arrangements to optimize survival strategies. Every action in the Core is a result of the zero-sum game that has been playing there since the Core elements evolved into sentience. Most elements of the Core are capable of dealing with humankind in only those zero-sum terms . . . optimizing their parasite strategy in relation to us. Their gain, our loss. Our gain, their loss.

"Over the centuries, however, some of these Core elements have come to understand the true potential of the Void Which Binds. They understand that their empathy-free species of intelligence can never be part of that amalgam of living and past races. They have come to understand that the Void Which Binds was not so much constructed as evolved, like a coral reef, and that they will never find shelter there unless they change some of the parameters of their own existence.

"Thus evolved some members of the Core—not altruists, but desperate survivalists who realized that the only way ultimately to win their never-ending zero-sum game was to stop the game. And to stop the game they needed to evolve into a species capable of empathy.

"The Core knows what Teilhard de Chardin and other sentimentalists refused to acknowledge: that evolution is not progress, that there is no 'goal' or direction to evolution. Evolution is change. Evolution 'succeeds' if that change best adapts some leaf or branch of its tree of life to conditions of the universe. For that evolution to 'succeed' for these elements of the Core, they would have to abandon zero-sum parasitism and discover true symbiosis. They would have to enter into honest co-evolution with our human race.

"First the renegade Core elements continued cannibalizing to evolve more empathy-prone Core elements. They rewrote their own code as far as they were able. Then they created the John Keats cybrid—a full attempt at simulating an empathic organism with the body and DNA of a human being, and the Core-stored memories and personality of a cybrid. Opposing elements destroyed the first Keats cybrid. The second one was created in the first's image. It hired my mother—a private detective—to help him unravel the mystery of the first cybrid's death."

Aenea is smiling and for a moment she seems oblivious of us or even of her own storytelling. She seems to be reliving old memories. I remember then what she once casually mentioned during our trip from Hyperion in the Consul's old ship—"Raul, I had my mother's and father's memories poured into me before I was born . . . before I'd become a real fetus even. Can you imagine anything more destructive to a child's personality than to be inundated with someone else's lives even before you've begun your own? No wonder I'm a screwed-up mess."

She does not look or act like a screwed-up mess to me at this moment. But then I love her more than life.

"He hired my mother to solve the mystery of his own persona's death," she continues softly, "but in truth he knew what had happened to his former self. His real reason for hiring my mother was to meet my mother, to be with my mother, to become my mother's lover." Aenea stops for a moment and smiles, her eyes seeing distant things. "My Uncle Martin never got that part right in his muddled-up *Cantos*. My parents were married and I don't think Uncle Martin ever told of that . . . married by the Bishop at the Shrike Temple on Lusus. It was a cult, but a legal one, and my parents' marriage would have been legal on two hundred worlds of the Hegemony." She smiles again, looking across the crowded room directly at me. "I can be a bastard, you know, but I wasn't born one.

"So they were married, I was conceived—probably before that ceremony—and then Core-backed elements murdered my father before my mother could begin the Shrike pilgrimage to Hyperion. And that should have been the end of any contact between my father and me except for two things—his Core persona was captured in a Schrön Loop implanted behind my mother's ear. For some months she was pregnant with two of us—me in her womb and my father, the second John Keats persona, in the Schrön Loop. His persona could not communicate directly to my mother while imprisoned in its endless-cycle Schrön Loop, but it communicated with me easily enough. The hard part was defining what 'me' was at that point. My father helped by entering the Void Which Binds and taking the fetal 'me' with him. I saw what was to be—who I would be—even how I would die—before my fingers were fully formed.

"And there was one other detail which Uncle Martin left out of his *Cantos*. On the day that they had gunned down my father on the steps of the Shrike Temple in the Lusian Concourse Mall, my mother was covered with his blood—the reconstructed, Core-augmented DNA of John Keats. What she did not fully understand at the time was that his blood was literally the most precious resource in the human universe at that moment. His DNA had been designed to infect others with his single gift—access to the Void. Mixed with fully human DNA in the right way, it would offer the gift of blood that would open the portal to the Void Which Binds to the entire human race.

"I am that mix. I bring the genetic ability to access the Void from the TechnoCore and the too-seldom-used human ability to perceive the universe through empathy. For better or worse, those who drink of my blood shall never see the world or the universe the same again."

So saying, Aenea rises to her knees on the tatami mat. Theo brings a white linen cloth. Rachel pours red wine from a vase into seven large goblets. Aenea takes a small packet from her sweater—I recognize it as a ship's medkit—and removes a sterile lancet and an antiseptic swab. She pauses before using the lancet and sweeps her gaze across the crowd. There is no sound—it is as if the more than hundred people there are holding their breath.

"There is no guarantee of happiness, wisdom, or long life if you drink of me this evening," she says, very softly. "There is no nirvana. There is no salvation. There is no afterlife. There is no rebirth. There is only immense knowledge—of the heart as well as the mind—and the potential for great discoveries, great adventures, and a guarantee of more of the pain and terror that make up so much of our short lives."

She looks from face to face, smiling as she meets the gaze of the eight-year-old Dalai Lama. "Some of you," she says, "have attended all of our discussion sessions over the past standard year. I have told you what I know about learning the language of the dead, learning the language of the living, learning to hear the music of the spheres, and learning how to take a first step."

She looks at me. "Some of you have heard only some of these discussions. You were not here when I discussed the real function of the Church's cruciform or the real identity of the Shrike. You have not heard the details of learning the language of the dead or the other burdens of entering the Void Which Binds. For those of you with doubts or hesitation, I urge you to wait. For the rest of you, I say again—I am not a messiah . . . but I am a teacher. If what I have taught you these months sounds like truth, and if you wish to take this chance, drink of me this night. Be warned, that the DNA which allows us to perceive the medium of the Void Which Binds cannot coexist with the cruciform. That parasite will wither and die within twenty-four hours of the time you drink of my blood. It will never grow within you again. If you seek resurrection through the cruciform cross, do not drink the blood of my body in this wine.

"And be warned that you will become, like me, the despised and sought-out enemy of the Pax. Your blood will be contagious. Those with whom you share it—those who choose to find the Void Which Binds via your shared DNA—will become despised in turn.

"And finally, be warned that, once having drunk this wine, your children will be born with the ability to enter the Void Which Binds. For better or worse, your children and their children will be born knowing the language of the dead, the language of the living, hearing the music of the spheres, and knowing that they can take a first step across the Void Which Binds."

Aenea touches her finger with the razor edge of the lancet. A tiny drop of blood is visible in the lantern light. Rachel holds a goblet up as the tiny drop of blood is squeezed into the large volume of wine. Then again with the next goblet, and so on until each of the seven cups has been . . . contaminated? Transubstantiated? My mind is reeling. My heart is pounding in something like alarm. This seems like some wild parody of the Catholic Church's Holy Communion. Has my young friend, my dear lover, my beloved . . . has she gone insane? Does she truly believe that she is a messiah? No, she said that she is not. Do *I* believe that I will be transformed forever by drinking of wine that is one part per million my beloved's blood? I do not know. I do not understand.

About half of the people there move forward to line up and sip from one of the large goblets. *Chalices? This is blasphemy. It's not right. Or is it?* One sip is all they take, then return to their places on the tatami mats. No one seems especially energized or enlightened. No horns of light shine from anyone's forehead after they partake of the wine. No one levitates or speaks in tongues. They each take a sip and sit down.

I realize that I have been holding back, trying to catch Aenea's gaze. I have so many questions . . . Belatedly, feeling like a traitor to someone I should trust without hesitation, I move toward the back of the shortening line.

Aenea sees me. She holds her hand up briefly, palm toward me. The meaning is clear—*Not now, Raul. Not yet.* I hesitate another moment, irresolute, sick at the thought of these others—these strangers—entering into an intimacy with my darling when I cannot. Then, heart pounding and face burning, I sit back on my mat.

There is no formal end to the evening. People begin to leave in twos and threes. A couple—she drank of the wine, he did not—leave together with their arms around one another as if nothing has changed. Perhaps nothing *has* changed. Perhaps the communion ritual I've just watched is all metaphor and symbolism, or autosuggestion and self-hypnosis. Perhaps those who will themselves hard enough to perceive something called the Void Which Binds will have some internal experience that convinces them that it has happened. Perhaps it's all bullshit.

I rub my forehead. I have such a headache. Good thing I didn't drink the wine, I think. Wine sometimes brings on migraines with me. I chuckle and feel ill and empty for a moment, left behind.

Rachel says, "Don't forget, the last stone will be set in place in the walkway tomorrow at noon. There'll be a party on the upper meditation platform! Bring your own refreshments."

And thus ends the evening. I go upstairs to our shared sleeping platform with a mixture of elation, anticipation, regret, embarrassment, excitement, and a throbbing headache. I confess to myself that I didn't understand half of Aenea's explanation of things, but I leave with a vague sense of letdown and inappropriateness . . . I'm sure, for instance, that Jesus Christ's Last Supper did not end with a shouted reminder of a BYOB party on the upper deck.

I chuckle and then swallow the laugh. Last Supper. That has a terrible ring to it. My heart begins pounding again and my head hurts worse. Hardly the way to enter one's lover's bedroom.

The chill air on the upper platform walkway clears my head a bit. The Oracle is just a sliver above towering cumulus to the east. The stars look cold tonight.

I am just about to enter our shared room and light the lantern when suddenly the skies explode.

21

THEY ALL CAME UP from the lower levels—all of the ones who had stayed at the Temple Hanging in Air after most of the work had been finished—Aenea and A. Bettik, Rachel and Theo, George and Jigme, Kuku and Kay, Chim Din and Gyalo Thondup, Lhomo and Labsang, Kim Byung-Soon and Viki Groselj, Kenshiro and Haruyuki, Master Abbot Kempo Ngha Wang Tashi and his master, the young Dalai Lama, Voytek Majer and Janusz Kurtyka, brooding Rimsi Kyipup and grinning Changchi Kenchung, the Dorje Phamo the Thunderbolt Sow and Carl Linga William Eiheji. Aenea came to my side and slipped her hand in mine as we watched the skies in awed silence.

I am surprised that we were not all blinded by the light show going on up there where the stars had been a moment earlier: great blossoms of white light, strobes of sulfur yellow, blazing red streaks—far brighter than a comet or meteor's tail—crisscrossed with blue, green, white, and yellow slashes—each as clear and straight as a diamond scratch on glass, then sudden bursts of orange that seemed to fold into themselves in silent implosions, followed by more white strobes and a resumption of red slashes. It was all silent, but the violence of light alone made us want to cover our ears and cringe in a sheltered place.

"What in ten hells is it?" asked Lhomo Dondrub.

"Space battle," said Aenea. Her voice sounded terribly tired.

"I do not understand," said the Dalai Lama. He did not sound afraid, merely curious. "The Pax authorities assured us that they would have only one of their starships in orbit—the *Jibril,* I believe is its name—and that it was on a diplomatic mission rather than a military one. Regent Reting Tokra also assured me of this."

The Thunderbolt Sow made a rude noise. "Your Holiness, the Regent is in the pay of the Pax bastards."

The boy looked at her.

"I believe it to be true, Your Holiness," said Eiheji, his bodyguard. "I have heard things in the palace."

The sky had faded almost to black but now it exploded again in a score of places. The rocky cliff face behind us bled reflections of red, green, and yellow.

"How can we see their laser lances if there is no dust or other colloidal particles to highlight them?" asked the Dalai Lama, his dark eyes bright. Evidently the news of his Regent's betrayal was not surprising to him . . . or at least not as interesting as the battle going on thousands of kilometers above us. I was interested to see that the supreme holy person of the Buddhist world had been tutored in basic science.

Again, it was his bodyguard who answered. "Some ships must have been hit and destroyed already, Your Holiness," said Eiheji. "The coherent beams and CPBs would become visible in the expanding fields of debris, frozen oxygen, molecular dust, and other gases."

This caused a moment of silence in our group.

"My father watched this once, on Hyperion," whispered Rachel. She rubbed her bare arms as if there had been a sudden chill.

I blinked and looked at the young woman. I had not missed Aenea's comment about her friend's father, Sol . . . I knew my *Cantos* well enough to identify Rachel as the infant on the legendary Hyperion pilgrimage, daughter of Sol Weintraub . . . but I admit that I had not completely believed it. The infant Rachel had become the almost mythical woman, Moneta, in the *Cantos*—someone who had traveled back in time in the Time Tombs with the Shrike. How could *that* Rachel be here, now?

Aenea put her arm around Rachel's shoulders. "My mother as well," she said softly. "Only then it was thought to be the Hegemony forces against the Ousters."

"Who is this, then?" demanded the Dalai Lama. "The Ousters against the Pax? And why have the Pax warships come unbidden to our system?"

Several white spheres of light pulsed, grew, dimmed, and died. We all blinked away the retinal echoes.

"I believe that the Pax warships were here since their first ship arrived, Your Holiness," said Aenea. "But I do not think that they are fighting Ousters."

"Who then?" said the boy.

Aenea turned her face back to the sky. "One of their own," she said.

Suddenly there came a series of explosions quite different than the others . . . a closer, brighter series of explosions, followed by three blazing meteor trails. One exploded quickly in the upper atmosphere, trailing a score of minor debris trails that quickly died out. The second shot to the west, blazing from yellow to red to pure white, breaking up twenty degrees above the horizon and spilling a hundred lesser trails across the cloudy western horizon. The third screeched across the sky from west of the zenith to the eastern horizon—and I say "screeched" deliberately because we could hear the noise, at first a teakettle whistle, then a howl, then a terrible tornadic roar, diminishing as quickly as it came—finally to break up into three or four large, blazing masses in the east, all but one of which died out before reaching the horizon. This last burning fragment of starship seemed to wiggle in its flight at the last moment, with yellow bursts of light preceding it, slowing it, before it was lost to sight.

We waited another half hour on the upper platform, but except for dozens of fusion-flame streaks for the first few minutes—starships accelerating away from T'ien Shan, I knew—there was nothing left to see. Eventually the stars were once again the brightest things in the sky and everyone moved off—the Dalai Lama to sleep in the monks' quarters here, others to permanent or temporary quarters on the lower levels.

Aenea bid a few of us to stay—Rachel and Theo, A. Bettik and Lhomo Dondrub, and me.

"That is the sign I've been waiting for," she said very softly when all the others had left the platform. "We must leave tomorrow."

"Leave?" I said. "To where? Why?"

Aenea touched my forearm. I interpreted this as saying, *I will explain later.* I shut up as the others spoke.

"The wings are ready, Teacher," said Lhomo.

"I have taken the liberty of checking over the skinsuits and rebreathers in M. Endymion's quarters while you were all away," said A. Bettik. "They are all serviceable."

"We'll finish up the work and organize the ceremony tomorrow," said Theo.

"I wish I were going," said Rachel.

"Going where?" I said again, despite my best efforts to shut up and listen.

"You're invited," said Aenea, still touching my arm. That did not really answer my question. "Lhomo, and A. Bettik . . . if you're both still game."

Lhomo Dondrub gave his broad grin. The android nodded. I began to think that I was the only one in the temple compound that didn't understand what was going on.

"Good night, all," said Aenea. "We'll be off at first light. You don't need to see us off."

"To hell with that," said Rachel. Theo nodded agreement. "We'll be there to say good-bye," continued Rachel.

Aenea nodded and touched their arms. Everyone clambered down ladders or slid down cables.

Aenea and I were alone on the top platform. The skies seemed dark after the battle. I realized that clouds had risen above the ridgeline and were wiping the stars away like a wet towel drawn across a black slateboard. Aenea opened the door to her sleeping room, went in, lit the lantern, and returned to stand in the entrance. "Coming, Raul?"

WE DID TALK. But not right away.

Lovemaking seems all too absurd when described—even the timing of our lovemaking seems absurd in the telling, with the sky literally falling and my lover having carried out a sort-of Last Supper convocation that night— but lovemaking is never absurd when you are making love to the person you truly love. And I was. If I had not realized that before the Last Supper night, I did then—completely, totally, and without reservation.

It was perhaps two hours later when Aenea pulled on a kimono and I donned a yukata and we moved away from the sleeping mat to the open shoji screens. Aenea brewed tea on the small burner set in the tatami, and we took our cups and sat with our backs against the opposing shoji frames, our bare toes and legs touching, my right side and her left knee extending over the kilometers-long drop. The air was cool and smelled of rain, but the storm had moved north of us. The summit of Heng Shan was shrouded with clouds, but all the lower ridges were illuminated by a constant play of lightning.

"Is Rachel really the Rachel from the *Cantos*?" I said. It was not the question I most wanted to ask, but I was afraid to ask it.

"Yes," said Aenea. "She's the daughter of Sol Weintraub—the woman who caught the Merlin Sickness on Hyperion and aged backward twenty-seven years to the infant whom Sol brought on the pilgrimage."

"And she was also known as Moneta," I said. "And Memnosyne . . ."

"*Admonisher,*" murmured Aenea. "And *Memory*. Appropriate names for her role in that time."

"That was two hundred and eighty years ago!" I said. "And scores of light-years away . . . on Hyperion. How did she get here?"

Aenea smiled. The warm tea breathed vapors that rose to her tousled hair. "I started life more than two hundred and eighty years ago," she said. "And scores of light-years away . . . on Hyperion."

"So did she get here the same way you did? Through the Time Tombs?"

"Yes and no," said Aenea. She held up one hand to stop my protest. "I know that you want straight talk, Raul . . . no parables or similes or evasions. I agree. The time for plain talk is here. But the truth is that the Sphinx Time Tombs are only part of Rachel's journey."

I waited.

"You remember the *Cantos*," she began.

"I remember that the pilgrim named Sol took his daughter . . . after the Keats persona somehow saved her from the Shrike and after she began aging normally . . . took her into the Sphinx into the future . . ." I stopped. "*This* future?"

"No," said Aenea. "The infant Rachel grew into a child again, a young woman again, in a future beyond this one. Her father raised her a second time. Their story is . . . marvelous, Raul. Literally filled with marvels."

I rubbed my forehead. The headache had gone, but now it threatened to return. "And she got here via the Time Tombs again?" I said. "Moving back in time with them?"

"Partially via the Time Tombs," said Aenea. "She is also able to move through time on her own."

I stared. This bordered on madness.

Aenea smiled as if reading my thoughts or just reading my expression. "I know it seems insane, Raul. Much of what we've yet to encounter is very strange."

"That's an understatement," I said. Another mental tumbler clicked into place. "Theo Bernard!" I said.

"Yes?"

"There was a Theo in the *Cantos,* wasn't there?" I said. "A man . . ." There were different versions of the oral tale, the poem to be sung, and many of these minor details were dropped in the short, popular versions. Grandam had made me learn most of the full poem, but the dull parts had never held my interest.

"Theo Lane," said Aenea. "At one time the Consul's aide on Hyperion, later our world's first Governor-General for the Hegemony. I met him once when I was a girl. A decent man. Quiet. He wore archaic glasses . . ."

"This Theo," I said, trying to figure it all out. *Some sort of sex change?*

Aenea shook her head. "Close, but no cigar, as Freud would have said."

"Who?"

"Theo Bernard is the great-great-great-etcetera-granddaughter of Theo Lane," said Aenea. "Her story is an adventure in itself. But she was born in this era . . . she did escape from the Pax colonies on Maui-Covenant and join the rebels . . . but she did so because of something I told the original Theo almost three hundred years ago. It had been passed down all those generations. Theo knew that I would be on Maui-Covenant when I was . . ."

"How?" I said.

"That's what I told Theo Lane," said my friend. "When I would be there. The knowledge was kept alive in his family . . . much as the Shrike Pilgrimage has been kept alive by the *Cantos.*"

"So you *can* see the future," I said flatly.

"Futures," corrected Aenea. "I've told you I can. And you heard me tonight."

"You've seen your own death?"

"Yes."

"Will you tell me what you've seen?"

"Not now, Raul. Please. When it's time."

"But if there are *futures*," I said, hearing the growl of pain in my own voice, "why do you have to see one death for yourself? If you can see it, why can't you avoid it?"

"I could avoid that particular death," she said softly, "but it would be the wrong choice."

"How can life over death *ever* be the wrong choice?" I said. I realized that I had shouted it. My hands were balled into fists.

She touched those fists with her warm hands, surrounding them with her slender fingers. "That's what all this is about," she said so softly that I had to lean forward to hear her. Lightning played on the shoulders of Heng Shan. "Death is never preferable to life, Raul, but sometimes it's necessary."

I shook my head. I realized that I must look sullen at that moment, but I didn't care. "Will you tell me when I'm going to die?" I said.

She met my gaze. Her dark eyes held depths. "I don't know," she said simply.

I blinked. I felt vaguely hurt. Didn't she care enough to look into my future?

"Of course I care," she whispered. "I've just chosen not to look at those probability waves. Seeing my death is . . . difficult. Seeing yours would be . . ." She made a strange noise and I realized that she was weeping. I moved around on the tatami mat until I could put my arms around her. She leaned in against my chest.

"I'm sorry, kiddo," I said into her hair, although I could not have said exactly what I was sorry about. It was strange to feel so happy and so miserable at the same time. The thought of losing her made me want to scream, to throw rocks at the mountainside. As if echoing my feelings, thunder rumbled from the peak to the north.

I kissed her tears away. Then we just kissed, the salt of her tears mingling with the warmth of her mouth. Then we made love again, and this time it was as slow, careful, and timeless as it had been urgent earlier.

When we were lying in the cool breeze again, our cheeks touching, her hand on my chest, she said, "You want to ask something. I can tell it. What?"

I thought of all the questions I had been filled with during her "discussion time" earlier—all of her talks I had missed that I needed to catch up on in order to understand why the communion ceremony was necessary: *What is the cruciform really about? What is the Pax up to on those worlds with missing populations? What does the Core really hope to gain in all this? What the hell is the Shrike . . . is the thing a monster or a guardian? Where did it come from? What's going to happen to us? What does she see in our future that I need to know in order for us to survive . . . in order for her to avoid the fate she has known about since before she was born? What's the giant secret behind the Void Which Binds and why is it so important to connect with it? How are we going to get off this world if the Pax really slagged the only farcaster portal under molten rock and there are Pax warships between the Consul's ship and us? Who are these "observers" she talked about who have been spying on humanity for centuries? What's all this about learning the language of the dead and so forth? Why haven't the Nemes-thing and her clone-siblings killed us yet?*

I asked, "You've been with someone else? Made love with someone before me?"

This was insanity. It was none of my business. She was almost twenty-two standard years old. I'd slept with women before—I could not remember any of their last names, but in the Home Guard, while working in the Nine Tails Casino—why should I care if—what difference did it make if—I had to know.

She hesitated only a second. "Our first time together was not my . . . first," she said.

I nodded, feeling like a swine and a voyeur for asking. There was an actual pain in my chest, much as I had imagined angina from hearing about it. I could not stop. "Did you love . . . him?" *How did I know it was a he? Theo . . . Rachel . . . she surrounds herself with women.* My own thoughts made me sick of myself.

"I love you, Raul," she whispered.

It was only the second time she had said this, the first being when we had said good-bye on Old Earth more than five and a half years earlier. My heart should have soared at the words. But it hurt too much. There was something important here that I did not understand.

"But there was a man," I said, the words like pebbles in my mouth. "You loved him . . ." *Only one? How many?* I wanted to scream at my thoughts to shut up.

Aenea put her finger on my lips. "I love you, Raul, remember that as I tell you these things. Everything is . . . complicated. By who I am. By what I must do. But I love you . . . I have loved you since the first time I saw you in the dreams of my future. I loved you when we met in the dust storm on Hyperion, with the confusion and shooting and the Shrike and the hawking mat. Do you remember how I squeezed my arms around you when we were flying on the mat, trying to escape? I loved you then . . ."

I waited in silence. Aenea's finger moved from my lips to my cheek. She sighed as if the weight of the worlds were on her shoulders. "All right," she said softly. "There was someone. I've made love before. We . . ."

"Was it serious?" I said. My voice sounded strange to me, like the ship's artificial tones.

"We were married," said Aenea.

Once, on the River Kans on Hyperion, I'd gotten into a fistfight with an older bargeman who was half again my weight with infinitely more experience in fighting. With no warning he had clipped me under the jaw with a single blow that had blacked out my vision, buckled my knees, and sent me reeling back over the barge railing into the river. The man had held no grudge and had personally dived in to fish me out. I'd regained consciousness in a minute or two, but it was hours before I could shake the ringing out of my head and truly focus my eyes.

This was worse than that. I could only lie there and look at her, at my beloved Aenea, and feel her fingers against my cheek as strange and cold and alien as a stranger's touch. She moved her hand away.

There was something worse.

"The twenty-three months, one week, and six hours that were unaccounted for," she said.

"With him?" I could not remember forming the two words but I heard them spoken in my voice.

"Yes."

"Married . . ." I said and could not go on.

Aenea actually smiled, but it was the saddest smile I think I had ever seen. "By a priest," she said. "The marriage will be legal in the eyes of the Pax and the Church."

"Will be?"

"Is."

"You are still married?" I wanted to get up then and be sick over the edge of the platform, but I could not move.

For a second Aenea seemed confused, unable to answer. "Yes . . ." she said, her eyes gleaming with tears. "I mean, no . . . I'm not married now . . . you . . . dammit, if I could only . . ."

"But the man's still alive?" I interrupted, my voice as flat and emotionless as a Holy Office Inquisition interrogator's.

"Yes." She put her hand on her own cheek. Her fingers were trembling.

"Do you love him, kiddo?"

"I love *you*, Raul."

I pulled away slightly, not consciously, not deliberately, but I could not stay in physical contact with her while we had this discussion.

"There's something else . . ." she said.

I waited.

"We had . . . I'll . . . I had a child, a baby." She looked at me as if trying to force understanding of all this through her gaze directly into my mind. It did not work.

"A child," I repeated stupidly. My dear friend . . . my child friend turned woman turned lover . . . my beloved had a child. "How old is it?" I said, hearing the banality like the thunder rumbling closer.

Again she seemed confused, as if uncertain of facts. Finally she said, "The child is . . . nowhere I can find it now."

"Oh, kiddo," I said, forgetting everything but her pain. I folded her against me as she wept. "I'm so sorry, kiddo . . . I'm so sorry," I said as I patted her head.

She pulled back, wiping away tears. "No, Raul, you don't understand. It's all right . . . it's not . . . that part's all right . . ."

I pulled away from her and stared. She was distraught, sobbing. "I understand," I lied.

"Raul . . ." Her hand felt for mine.

I patted her hand but got out of the bedclothes, pulled on my clothes, and grabbed my climbing harness and pack from their place by the door.

"Raul . . ."

"I'll be back before dawn," I said, facing in her general direction but not looking at her. "I'm just going for a walk."

"Let me go with you," she said, standing with the sheet around her. Lightning flashed behind her. Another storm was coming in.

"I'll be back before dawn," I said and went out the door before she could dress or join me.

It was raining—a cold, sleety rain. The platforms were quickly coated and made slick. I hurtled down ladders and jogged down the vibrating staircases, seeing my way by the occasional lightning flash, not slowing until I was several hundred meters down the east ledge walk headed toward the fissure where I had first landed in the ship. I did not want to go there.

Half a klick from the Temple were fixed lines rising to the top of the ridge. The sleet was pounding on the cliff face now, the red and black lines were coated with a layer of ice. I clipped carabiners onto the line and harness, pulling the powered ascenders from the pack and attaching them without double-checking the connections, then began jumaring up the icy ropes.

The wind came up, whipping my jacket and pushing me away from the rock wall. Sleet pounded at my face and hands. I ignored it and ascended, sometimes sliding back three or four meters as the jumar clamps failed on the icy line, then recovering and climbing again. Ten meters below the razor's-edge summit of the ridgeline, I emerged from the clouds like a swimmer coming up out of the water. The stars still burned coldly up there, but the billowing cloud masses were piling against the north wall of the ridge and rising like a white tide around me.

I slid the ascenders higher and jumared until I reached the relatively flat area where the fixed lines were attached. Only then did I notice that I had not tied on the safety line.

"Fuck it," I said and began walking northeast along the fifteen-centimeter-wide ridgeline. The storm was rising around me to the north. The drop to the south was kilometers of empty, black air. There were patches of ice here and it was beginning to snow.

I broke into a trot, running east, jumping icy spots and fissures, not giving a good goddamn about anything.

WHILE I WAS obsessed with my own misery, there were other things occurring in the human universe. On Hyperion, when I was a boy, news filtered slowly from the interstellar Pax to our moving caravans on the moors: an important event on Pacem or Renaissance Vector or wherever would, of necessity, be many weeks or months old from Hawking-drive time-debt, with additional weeks of transit from Port Romance or another major city to our provincial region. I was used to not paying attention to events elsewhere. The lag in news had lessened, of course, when I was guiding offworld hunters in the Fens and elsewhere, but it was still old news and of little importance to me. The Pax held no fascination for me, although offworld travel certainly had. Then there had been almost ten years of disconnection during our Old Earth hiatus and my five years of time-debt odyssey. I was not used to thinking of events elsewhere except where they affected me, such as the Pax's obsession with finding us.

But this would soon change.

That night on T'ien Shan, the Mountains of Heaven, as I ran foolishly through sleet and fog down the narrow ridgeline, these were some of the events happening elsewhere:

On the lovely world of Maui-Covenant, where the long chain of events culminating with my presence here with Aenea could be said to have begun with the courtship of Siri and Merin some four centuries ago, rebellion raged. The rebels on the motile isles had long since become followers of Aenea's philosophy, had drunk of her communion wine, had rejected the Pax and the cruciform forever, and were waging a war of sabotage and resistance while trying not to harm or kill the Pax soldiers occupying the world. For the Pax, Maui-Covenant offered special problems because it was primarily a vacation world—hundreds of thousands of wealthy born-again Christians traveled there via Hawking drive every standard year to enjoy the warm seas, the beautiful beaches of the Equatorial Archipelago isles, and the dolphin/motile isles migrations. The Pax also benefited from the hundreds of oil-drilling platforms around the mostly ocean world, situated out of sight of tourist areas but vulnerable to attack from motile isles or rebel submersibles. Now many of the Pax tourists themselves were—inexplicably—rejecting the cruciform and becoming followers of Aenea's teachings. Rejecting immortality. The planetary governor, the resident archbishop, and the Vatican officials called in for the crisis could not understand it.

On cold Sol Draconi Septem, where most of the atmosphere was frozen into a single giant glacier, there were no tourists, but the Pax attempt at colonization there over the past ten years had turned into a nightmare.

The gentle bands of Chitchatuk whom Aenea, A. Bettik, and I had befriended some nine and a half years ago had turned into implacable foes of the Pax. The skyscraper frozen into the atmospheric ice where Father Glaucus had welcomed all travelers still blazed with light despite that kind man's murder at the hand of Rhadamanth Nemes. The Chitchatuk kept the place alight like a shrine. Somehow they knew who had murdered the harmless blind man and Cuchiat's tribe—Cuchiat, Chiaku, Aichacut, Cuchtu, Chithticia, Chatchia—all of those whom Aenea, A. Bettik, and I had known by name. The other Chitchatuk blamed the Pax, who were attempting to colonize the temperate bands along the equator where the air was gaseous and the great glacier melted down to the ancient permafrost.

But the Chitchatuk, not having heard of Aenea's communion and tasted the empathy of it, descended on the Pax like a Biblical plague. Having preyed upon—and been preyed upon by—the terrible snow wraiths for millennia, the Chitchatuk now drove the tunneling white beasts south to the equatorial regions, unleashing them on the Pax colonists and missionaries. The toll was frightful. Pax military units brought in to kill the primitive Chitchatuk sent patrols out onto and into the planet glacier and never saw them again.

On the city-planet of Renaissance Vector, Aenea's word of the Void Which Binds had spread to millions of followers. Thousands of Pax faithful took communion from the changed ones every day, their cruciforms dying and falling off within twenty-four hours, sacrificing immortality for . . . what? The Pax and Vatican did not understand and at that time neither did I.

But the Pax knew that it had to contain the virus. Troopers kicked in doors and crashed through windows every day and night, usually in the poorer, old-industrial sections of the planet-wide city. These people who had rejected the cruciform did not strongly resist—they would fight fiercely, but refused to kill if there was any way to avoid it. The Pax troopers did not mind killing to carry out their orders. Thousands of Aenea's followers died the true death—former immortals who would never see resurrection again—and tens of thousands were taken into custody and sent to detention centers, where they were placed into cryogenic fugue lockers so that their blood and philosophy could not contaminate others. But for every one of Aenea's adherents killed or arrested, dozens—hundreds—stayed safe in hiding, passing along Aenea's teachings, offering communion of their own changed blood, and providing largely nonviolent resistance at every turn. The great industrial machine that was Renaissance Vector had not yet broken down, but it was lurching and grinding in a way not seen in all the centuries since the Hegemony established the world as the Web's industrial nexus.

The Vatican sent more troops and debated as to how to respond.

On Tau Ceti Center, once the political center of the WorldWeb but now just a heavily populated and popular garden planet, the rebellion took a different shape. While offworld visitors had brought Aenea's anti-cruciform contagion, the bulk of the problem there for the Vatican centered on the Archbishop Achilla Silvaski, a scheming woman who had taken over the role of governor and autocrat on TC² more than two centuries earlier. It was Archbishop Silvaski who had attempted to overthrow the reelection of the permanent pope through intrigue among the cardinals and now, having failed at that, she simply staged her own planet-wide version of the pre-Hegira Reformation, announcing that the Catholic Church on Tau Ceti

Center would henceforth recognize her as pontiff and be forever separated from the "corrupt" interstellar Church of the Pax. Because she had carefully formed an alliance with the local bishops in charge of resurrection ceremonies and machineries, she could control the Sacrament of Resurrection—and thus the local Church. More importantly, the Archbishop had wooed the local Pax military authorities with land, wealth, and power until an unprecedented event occurred—a Pax Fleet, Pax military coup that overthrew most senior officers in Tau Ceti System and replaced them with New Church advocates. No archangel starships were seized this way, but eighteen cruisers and forty-one torchships committed themselves to defending the New Church on TC^2 and its new pontiff.

Tens of thousands of faithful Church members on the planet protested. They were arrested, threatened with excommunication—i.e. immediate revocation of their cruciforms—and released on probation under the watchful eye of the Archbishop's—new pope's—New Church Security Force. Several priestly orders, most notably the Jesuits on Tau Ceti Center, refused to comply. Most were quietly arrested, excommunicated, and executed. Some hundreds escaped, however, and used their network to offer resistance to the new order—at first nonviolent, then increasingly severe. Many of the Jesuits had served as priest-officers in the Pax military before returning to civilian clerical life, and they used their military skills to create havoc in and around the planet.

Pope Urban XVI and his Pax Fleet advisors looked at their options. Already the crushing blow in the great Crusade against the Ousters had been delayed and derailed by Captain de Soya's continued harassing attacks, by the need to send Fleet units to a score of worlds to quell the Aenea contagion rebellions, by the logistical requirements for the ambush in T'ien Shan System, and now by this and other unrelated rebellions. Over Admiral Marusyn's advice to ignore the Archbishop's heresy until after other political/military goals were reached, Pope Urban XVI and his Secretary of State Lourdusamy decided to divert twenty archangels, thirty-two old-style cruisers, eight transport ships, and a hundred torchships to Tau Ceti System—although it would be many weeks of time-debt before the old Hawking-drive ships could arrive. Once formed up in that system, the task force's orders were to overcome all resistance by rebellious spacecraft, establish orbit around TC^2, demand the Archbishop's immediate surrender and the surrender of all those who supported her, and—failing compliance with that order—to slag as much of the planet as it took to destroy the New Church's infrastructure. After that, tens of thousands of Marines would drop to the planet to occupy the remaining urban centers and to reestablish the rule of the Pax and the Holy Mother Church.

On Mars, in Old Earth System, the rebellion had worsened, despite years of Pax bombardment from space and constant military incursions from orbit. Two standard months earlier, Governor Clare Palo and Archbishop Robeson had both died the true death in a nuclear suicide attack on their palace-in-exile on Phobos. The Pax response had been terrifying—

asteroids diverted from the nearby belt and dropped on Mars, carpet plasma bombing, and nightly lance attacks that sliced through the new planetary dust storm kicked up by the asteroid bombardment like so many deadly searchlights crisscrossing the frozen desert. Deathbeams would have been more efficient, but the Pax Fleet planners wanted to make an example of Mars, and wanted it to be a visible example.

The results were not exactly what the Pax had hoped for. The Martian terraforming environment, already precarious after years of poor maintenance, collapsed. Breathable atmosphere on the world was now restricted to Hellas Basin and a few other low pockets. The oceans were gone, boiled away as the pressure dropped or frozen back in the poles and permafrost subcrust. The last large plants and trees died off until only the original brandy cactus and bradberry orchards were left clinging to life in the near vacuum. The dust storms would last for years, making Pax Marine patrols on the Red Planet all but impossible.

But the Martians, especially the militant Palestinian Martians, were adapted to such a life and ready for this contingency. They hunkered down, killed the Pax troopers when they landed, and waited. Templar missionaries among the other Martian colonies urged the final nanotech adaptation to the original planetary conditions. Thousands and thousands took the gamble, allowing the molecular machines to alter their bodies and DNA to the planet.

More disturbingly to the Vatican, space battles broke out as ships once belonging to the presumably defunct Martian War Machine came out of hiding in the distant Kuiper Belt and began a series of hit-and-run attacks on the Pax Fleet convoys in Old Earth System. The kill ratio in these attacks was five to one in favor of Pax Fleet, but the losses were unacceptable and the cost of maintaining the Mars operation was frightful.

Admiral Marusyn and the Joint Chiefs advised His Holiness to cut his losses and leave Old Earth System to fester for the time being. The Admiral assured the Pope that nothing would be allowed out of the system. He pointed out that there was nothing of real value in Old Earth System any longer, now that Mars was untenable. The Pope listened but refused to authorize the pullout. At each conference, Cardinal Lourdusamy stressed the symbolic importance of keeping Old Earth's system within the Pax. His Holiness decided to wait to make his decision. The hemorrhage of ships, men, money, and materiel went on.

On Mare Infinitus, the rebellion was old—based around the submarine smugglers, poachers, and those hundreds of thousands of stubborn indigenies who had always refused the cross—but stirred up anew now that the Aenea contagion had arrived. The great fishing zones were now all but off-limits to unescorted Pax fishing fleets. The automated fishing ships and isolated floating platforms were attacked and sunk. More and more of the deadly Lantern Mouth monsters were seen in shallower waters and Archbishop Jane Kelley was furious at the Pax authorities for their failure to stop the problem. When Bishop Melandriano counseled moderation, Kelley had him excommunicated. In turn, Melandriano declared the Southern Seas seceded from the Pax and Church's authority and thousands of the faithful followed the charismatic leader. The Vatican sent more Pax Fleet ships, but there was little they could do to settle the four-way surface and subsurface struggles between the rebels, the Archbishop's forces, the Bishop's forces, and the Lantern Mouths.

And in the midst of all this confusion and carnage, Aenea's message traveled with the speed of speech and secret communion.

Rebellion—both violent and spiritual—flared elsewhere: the worlds where Aenea had traveled—Ixion, Patawpha, Amritsar, and Groombridge Dyson D; on Tsintao-Hsishuang Panna where word of the roundup of non-Christians elsewhere created first panic and then grim resistance to all things Pax, on Deneb Drei where the Jamnu Republic declared the wearing of a cruciform cause for beheading; on Fuji where Aenea's message had been brought by renegede members of the Pax Mercantilus and where it spread like a planetary firestorm; on the desert world of Vitus-Gray-Balianus B where Aenea's teachings came via refugees from Sibiatu's Bitterness and combined with the realization that the Pax way of life would destroy their culture forever—the Amoiete Spectrum Helix people led the fight. The city of Keroa Tambat was liberated in the first month of fighting, and Pax Base Bombasino soon became a fortress under siege. Base Commander Solznykov screamed for help from Pax Fleet, but the Vatican and Pax Fleet commanders—preoccupied elsewhere—ordered him to be patient and threatened excommunication if Solznykov did not end the rebellion on his own.

Solznykov did so, but not in the way Pax Fleet or His Holiness would have countenanced: he arranged for a peace treaty with the Amoiete Spectrum Helix armies in which his Pax forces would enter the countryside only with the permission of the indigenies. In return, Pax Base Bombasino was allowed to continue its existence.

Solznykov, Colonel Vinara, and the other loyal Christians settled in to wait for Vatican and Pax Fleet retribution, but the Aenea-changed civilians were among the Spectrum Helix people who came to market at Bombasino, who met and ate and drank with the troopers, who moved among the dispirited Pax men and women and told their story, and who offered their communion. Many accepted.

THIS, OF COURSE, was the tiniest slice of events on the hundreds of worlds of the Pax that last, sad night I would ever spend on T'ien Shan. I did not guess of any of these events, of course, but if I had—if I had already mastered the skill and discipline of learning these things via the Void Which Binds—I still would not have cared.

Aenea had loved another man. They had been married. She must still be married . . . she had not mentioned divorce or death. She had had a child.

I do not know why my carelessness did not send me falling to my death those wild hours on the icy ridge east of Jo-kung and Hsuan-k'ung Ssu, but it did not. Eventually I came to my senses and returned via the ridgeline and the fixed rappelling ropes so that I could be back with Aenea by first light.

I loved her. She was my dear friend. I would give my life to protect her.

An opportunity to prove that would be offered within the day, its inevitability created by the events that unfolded shortly after my return to the Temple Hanging in Air and our departure to the east.

IT WAS NOT that long after first light, in the old gompa beneath the Phallus Shiva now turned into Christian enclave, where John Domenico Cardinal Mustafa, Admiral Marget Wu, Father Farrell, Archbishop Breque, Father LeBlanc, Rhadamanth Nemes, and her two remaining siblings met in conference. In truth, it was the humans who met in conference, while Nemes and her clone sister and brother sat silently by the window looking out over the billowing cloudscapes around Otter Lake below the Shivling peak.

"And you are certain that the rogue ship *Raphael* is finished?" the Grand Inquisitor was saying.

"Absolutely," said Admiral Wu. "Although it destroyed seven of our archangel ships of the line before we slagged it." She shook her head. "De Soya was a brilliant tactician. It was the true work of the Evil One when he turned apostate."

Father Farrell leaned over the polished bonsai-wood table. "And there is no chance that de Soya or any of the others survived?"

Admiral Wu shrugged. "It was a near-orbit battle," she said. "We let *Raphael* get within cislunar distance before springing our trap. Thousands of pieces of debris—mostly from our unfortunate ships—entered the atmosphere. None of our people appear to have survived—at least no beacons have been detected. If any of de Soya's people escaped, the chances are that their pods came down in the poisonous oceans."

"Still . . ." began Archbishop Breque. He was a quiet man, cerebral and cautious.

Wu looked exhausted and irritated. "Your Eminence," she said briskly, addressing Breque but looking at Mustafa, "we can decide the issue one way or the other if you allow us to send dropships, skimmers, and EMVs into the atmosphere."

Breque blinked. Cardinal Mustafa shook his head. "No," he said, "our orders are not to show a military presence until the Vatican commands the final step in our seizure of the girl."

Wu smiled with apparent bitterness. "Last night's battle just above the atmosphere must have made that order somewhat obsolete," she said softly. "Our military presence must have been rather impressive."

"It was," said Father LeBlanc. "I have never seen anything like it."

Admiral Wu spoke to Mustafa. "Your Excellency, the people on this world have no energy weapons, no Hawking-drive detectors, no orbital defenses, no gravitonic detectors . . . hell, they don't have radar or a communications system as far as we can tell. We can send dropships or fighter aircraft into the atmosphere to search for survivors without them ever knowing. It has to be a lot less intrusive than last night's firefight and . . ."

"No," said Cardinal Mustafa and there was no doubting the finality of his decision. The Grand Inquisitor pushed back his robe to glance at his chronometer. "The Vatican courier drone should arrive any moment with final orders for the arrest of the contagion vector named Aenea. Nothing must complicate that."

Father Farrell rubbed his lean cheeks. "Regent Tokra called me this morning on the communicator channel we allocated him. It seems that their precious and precocious little Dalai Lama has gone missing . . ."

Breque and LeBlanc looked up in surprise.

"It doesn't matter," said Cardinal Mustafa, obviously aware of the news. "Nothing matters right now except receiving final go-ahead on this mission and arresting Aenea." He looked at Admiral Wu. "And you must tell your Swiss Guard and Marine officers that no harm can come to the young woman."

Wu nodded wearily. She had been briefed and rebriefed for months. "When do you think that the orders will come?" she asked the Cardinal.

Rhadamanth Nemes and her two siblings stood and walked toward the door. "The time for waiting is over," said Nemes with a thin-lipped smile. "We will bring Aenea's head back to you."

Cardinal Mustafa and the others were on their feet in an instant. "Sit down!" bellowed the Grand Inquisitor. "You have not been ordered to move."

Nemes smiled and turned toward the door.

All of the clerics in the room were shouting. Archbishop Jean Daniel Breque crossed himself. Admiral Wu went for the flechette pistol in her holster.

Things then happened too quickly to perceive. The air seemed to blur. One instant, Nemes, Scylla, and Briareus were at the doorway eight meters away, the next instant they were gone and three shimmering chrome shapes stood among the black- and red-robed figures at the table.

Scylla intercepted Admiral Marget Wu before the woman could raise her flechette pistol. A chrome arm blurred. Wu's head tumbled across the polished tabletop. The headless body stood a few seconds, some random nerve impulse ordered the fingers of the right hand to close, and the flechette pistol fired, blowing apart the legs of the heavy table and splintering the stone floor in ten thousand places.

Father LeBlanc leaped between Briareus and Archbishop Breque. The blurred, silver shape disemboweled LeBlanc. Breque dropped his glasses and ran into the adjoining room. Suddenly Briareus was gone—leaving nothing but a soft implosion of air where the blurred shape had stood a second before. There was a short scream from the other room, cut off almost before it began.

Cardinal Mustafa backed away from Rhadamanth Nemes. She took one step forward for every step he took backward. The blurred field around her had dropped away, but she looked no more human or less menacing.

"Damn you for the foul thing you are," the Cardinal said softly. "Come ahead, I'm not afraid to die."

Nemes raised one eyebrow. "Of course not, Your Excellency. But would it change your mind if I tell you that we're throwing these bodies . . . and that head"—she gestured to where Marget Wu's eyes had just stopped blinking and now stared blindly—"far out into the acid ocean, so that no resurrection will be possible?"

Cardinal Mustafa reached the wall and stopped. Nemes was only two paces in front of him. "Why are you doing this?" he said, his voice firm.

Nemes shrugged. "Our priorities diverge for the time being," she said. "Are you ready, Grand Inquisitor?"

Cardinal Mustafa crossed himself and said a hurried Act of Contrition.

Nemes smiled again, her right arm and right leg became shimmering silver things, and she stepped forward.

Mustafa watched in amazement. She did not kill him. With motions too quick to detect, she broke his left arm, shattered his right arm, kicked his legs out from under him—splintering both of them—and blinded him with two fingers that stopped just short of jabbing into his brain.

The roar of pain was without precedent for the Grand Inquisitor. Through it, he could hear her voice, still flat and lifeless. "I know your doc-in-the-box in the dropship or on the *Jibril* will fix you up," she said. "We've buzzed them. They'll be here in a few minutes. When you see the Pope and his parasites, tell them that those to whom I must report did not want the girl alive. Our apologies, but her death is necessary. And tell them to be careful in the future not to act without the consent of *all* elements of the Core. Good-bye, Your Excellency. I hope that the doc on the *Jibril* can grow you new eyes. What we are about to do will be worth seeing."

Mustafa heard footsteps, the door sliding, and then silence except for the sound of someone screaming in terrible pain. It took him several minutes to realize that it was he who was screaming.

WHEN I RETURNED to the Temple Hanging in Air, first light was seeping through the fog but the morning remained dark, drizzly, and cold. I had finally sobered up enough from my distraught and distracted state to take greater care while rappelling down the fixed lines, and it was good that I had—several times the brakes on the rappel gear slipped on the ice-shrouded rope and I would have fallen to my death if the safety lines had not arrested me.

Aenea was awake, dressed, and ready to leave when I arrived. She had

on her thermal anorak, climbing harness, and climbing boots. A. Bettik and
Lhomo Dondrub were dressed similarly, and both men carried long, heavy-
looking, nylon-wrapped packages over their shoulders. They were going
with us. Others were there to say good-bye—Theo, Rachel, the Dorje
Phamo, the Dalai Lama, George Tsarong, Jigme Norbu—and they seemed
sad and anxious. Aenea looked tired; I was sure that she had not slept
either. We made a tired-looking pair of adventurers. Lhomo walked over
and handed me one of the long, nylon-wrapped bundles. It was heavy, but I
shouldered it without question or complaint. I grabbed the rest of my own
gear, answered Lhomo's questions about the condition of the ropes to the
ridgeline—everyone evidently thought that I had unselfishly reconnoitered
our route—and stepped back to look at my friend and beloved. When she
gave me a searching look, I answered with a nod. *It's all right. I'm all right.
I'm ready to go. We'll talk about it later.*

Theo was crying. I was aware that this was an important parting—
that we might not see one another again despite Aenea's assurances to the
other two women that everyone would be reunited before nightfall—but I
was too emotionally numbed and worn out to react to it. I stepped away
from the group for a moment to take deep breaths and focus my attention.
It was probable that I would need all of my wits and alertness in the next
few hours just to survive. *The problem with being passionately in love,* I
thought, *is that it deprives you of too much sleep.*

We left by the east platform, moved in a fast trot down the icy ledge
toward the fissure, passed the ropes I'd just descended, and reached the
fissure without incident. The bonsai trees and fell fields looked ancient and
unreal in the shifting ice fog, the dark limbs and branches dripping on our
heads when they suddenly loomed out of the mist. The streams and water-
falls sounded louder than I remembered as the torrent slid over the last
overhang into the void to our left.

There were old, less reliable fixed ropes on the easternmost and
highest folds of the fissure, and Lhomo led the way up these, followed by
Aenea, then A. Bettik, and finally me. I noticed that our android friend
was climbing as quickly and competently as he always did, despite the
missing left hand. Once on the upper ridgeline, we were beyond my farthest point of my nighttime travels—the fissure acted as a barrier to ridgeline travel the way I had gone. Now the difficulty began in earnest as we
followed the narrowest of paths—worn ledges, rock outcroppings, the occasional icefield, scree slopes—on the south side of the cliff face. The
ridgeline above us was all serac of wet, heavy snow and icy overhang,
impossible to travel on. We moved silently, not even whispering, aware
that the slightest noise could trigger an avalanche that would sweep us off
these ten-centimeter ledges in a second. Finally, when the going got even
tougher, we roped up—running the line through carabiners and attaching
a doubled line to our web-sling harnesses—so that now if one fell he or
she would be caught, or we would all go over. With Lhomo leading as

strongly as ever, stepping confidently over foggy voids and icy crevasses that I would hesitate to attempt, I think that we all felt better about being connected.

I still did not know our destination. I did know that the great ridge that ran east from K'un Lun past Jo-kung would run out in a few more kilometers, dropping suddenly and dramatically into the poisonous clouds several klicks below. During certain weeks in the spring, the tides and vagaries of the ocean and clouds dropped the poisionous vapors low enough that the ridge emerged again, allowing supply caravans, pilgrims, monks, traders, and the simply curious to make their way east from the Middle Kingdom to T'ai Shan, the Great Peak of the Middle Kingdom, and the most inaccessible habitable point on the planet. The monks who lived on T'ai Shan, it was said, never returned to the Middle Kingdom or the rest of the Mountains of Heaven—for untold generations they had dedicated their lives to the mysterious tombs, gompas, ceremonies, and temples on that most holy of peaks. Now, as the weather worsened for us, I realized that if we started descending, we would not know when we left the roiling monsoon clouds and entered the roiling vaporous clouds until the poison air killed us.

We did not descend. After several hours of all but silent travel, we reached the precipice at the eastern boundary of the Middle Kingdom. The mountain of T'ai Shan was not visible, of course—even with the clouds having cleared a bit, little was visible except for the wet cliff face ahead of us and the twisting fog and cloud patterns all around.

There was a wide ledge here at the eastern edge of the world, and we sat on it gratefully as we dug cold handmeals out of our packs and drank from our water bottles. The tiny, succulent plants that carpeted this steep fell field were becoming tumescent as they gorged themselves on the first moisture of the monsoon months.

After we ate and drank, Lhomo and A. Bettik began opening our three heavy bundles. Aenea zipped open her own pack, which looked heavier than the duffels we men had carried. It did not surprise me what was wrapped in these three parcels—nylon, alloy struts and frames, rigging, and in Aenea's packet, more of the same as well as the two skinsuits and rebreathers that I'd brought with me from the ship and all but forgotten.

I sighed and looked to the east. "So we're going to try to make T'ai Shan," I said.

"Yes," said Aenea. She began stripping out of her clothes.

A. Bettik and Lhomo looked away, but I felt my heart pound with anger at the thought of other men seeing my lover naked. I controlled myself, laid out the other skinsuit, and began peeling out of my own clothes, folding them into my heavy pack as I doffed each layer. The air was cold and the fog clammy on my skin.

Lhomo and A. Bettik were assembling the parawings as Aenea and I dressed—the skinsuits were just that, almost literally a second skin, but the harness and rigging for the rebreathers allowed us some modesty. The cowl went over my head tighter than a scuba headpiece, folding my ears flat against my head. Only the filters there allowed sound to be transmitted: they would pick up the comthread transmissions once we were effectively out of real air.

Lhomo and A. Bettik had assembled four parawings from the parts we had transported. As if answering my unasked question, Lhomo said, "I can only show you the thermals and make sure you reach the jet stream. I can't survive at that altitude. And I do not want to go to T'ai Shan when there is little chance of returning."

Aenea touched the powerful man's arm. "We are grateful beyond words that you will guide us to the jet stream."

The bold flyer actually blushed.

"What about A. Bettik?" I asked and then, realizing that I was talking about our friend as if he weren't there, I turned to the android and said, "What about you? There's no skinsuit or rebreather for you."

A. Bettik smiled. I had always thought that his rare smiles were the wisest things I had ever seen on a human countenance—even if the blue-skinned man was not technically human.

"You forget, M. Endymion," he said, "I was designed to suffer a bit more abuse than the average human body."

"But the distance . . ." I began. T'ai Shan was more than a hundred kilometers east and even if we reached the jet stream, that would be almost an hour of rarified air . . . far too thin to breathe.

A. Bettik fastened the last rigging to his parawing—a pretty thing with a great blue delta wingspan almost ten meters across—and said, "If we are lucky enough to make the distance, I will survive it."

I nodded and made to get into the rigging of my own kite then, not asking any more questions, not looking at Aenea, not asking her why the four of us were risking our lives this way, when suddenly my friend was at my elbow.

"Thank you, Raul," she said, loudly enough for all to hear. "You do these things for me out of love and friendship. I thank you from the bottom of my heart."

I made some gesture, suddenly unable to speak, embarrassed that she was thanking me when the other two were ready to leap into the void for her as well. But she was not finished speaking.

"I love you, Raul," said Aenea, leaning on her tiptoes to kiss me on the lips. She rocked back and looked at me, her dark eyes fathomless. "I love you, Raul Endymion. I always have. I always will."

I stood, bewildered and overwhelmed, as we all locked in to our parawing rigs and stood at the ultimate edge of nothing. Lhomo was the last to clip on. He moved from A. Bettik to Aenea to me, checking our riggings, checking every fastened nut, bolt, tension clip, and instaweld of our kites. Satisfied, he nodded respectfully toward A. Bettik, clipped into his own red-winged rig with a speed born of infinite practice and discipline, and moved to the edge of the cliff. Even the succulents did not grow in this last meter stretch, as if terrified of the drop. I knew that I was. The last rocky ledge was steeply pitched and slick from the rain. The fog had closed in again.

"It will be hard to see each other in this soup," said Lhomo. "Keep circling to the left. Stay within five meters of the one in front of you. Same order as our march—Aenea after me in your yellow wing, then the blue man in blue, then you, Raul, in the green. Our greatest risk is losing one another in the clouds."

Aenea nodded tersely. "I'll stay close to your wing."

Lhomo looked at me. "You and Aenea can communicate via your skinsuit comthreads, but that will not help you find one another. A. Bettik and I will communicate via hand signals. Be careful. Do not lose sight of the blue man's kite. If you do, keep circling up counterclockwise until you clear the cloud tops and then try to regroup with us. Keep the circles tight while inside the clouds. If you loosen them—which is the tendency with parawings—you will strike the cliff."

My mouth was dry as I nodded.

"All right," said Lhomo. "I will see you all above the clouds. Then I will find the thermals for you, read the ridge lift, and get you to the jet stream. I will signal like this"—he made a fist and pumped his arm twice—"when I am leaving you. Keep climbing and circling. Get as deeply into the stream as you can. Rise into the upper atmospheric winds until you think that they will tear your wing apart from above you. Perhaps they will. But you will have no chance to reach T'ai Shan unless you get into the center of the stream. It is a hundred and eleven klicks to the first shoulder of the Great Peak where you can breathe true air."

We all nodded.

"May the Buddha smile on our folly today," said Lhomo. He seemed very happy.

"Amen," said Aenea.

Lhomo turned without another word and leaped out over the cliff's edge. Aenea followed a second later. A. Bettik leaned far forward in his harness, kicked off the ledge, and was swallowed up by clouds within seconds. I scurried to catch up. Suddenly there was no stone under my feet and I leaned forward until I was prone in the harness. Already I had lost sight of A. Bettik's blue wing. The swirling clouds confused and disoriented me. I pulled on the control bar, banking the hang glider as I had been taught, peering intently through the fog for a glimpse of any of the other kites. Nothing. Belatedly I realized that I had held the turn for too long. Or had I released it too soon? I leveled off the wing, feeling thermals pushing at the fabric above me but not being able to tell if I was actually gaining altitude because I was blind. The fog was like some terrible snowblindness.

Without thinking, I shouted, hoping one of the others would shout back and orient me. A man's shout hurtled back to me from just a few meters dead ahead.

It was my own voice, echoing off the vertical rock of the cliff face I was about to strike.

NEMES, SCYLLA, AND Briareus move south on foot from the Pax Enclave at the Phallus of Shiva. The sun is high and there are thick clouds to the east. To travel from the Pax Enclave to the Winter Palace at Potala, the old High Way southwest along the Koko Nor Ridge had been repaired and widened, and a special cable platform had been built where the ten-klick wire ran from Koko Nor southwest to the palace. A palanquin specially rigged for the Pax diplomats now hangs from pulleys at the new platform. Nemes pushes to the front of the line and steps into it, ignoring the stares from the little people in thick *chubas* who mill on the stairway and platform. When her clone-siblings are in the cage, she releases the two brakes and sends the palanquin hurtling across the gap. Dark clouds rise above the palace mountain.

A squad of twenty Palace Guard carrying halberds and crude energy lances greets them at the Great Terrace Steps on the west side of Yellow Hat Ridge where the palace drops away down the east face for several vertical kilometers. The captain of the Guard is deferential. "You must wait here until we bring an honor guard to escort you into the palace, Most Honored Guests," he says, bowing.

"We prefer to go in alone," says Nemes.

The twenty Guardsmen crouch with lances at port arms. They make a solid wall of iron, zygoat fur, silk, and elaborate helmets. The Guard captain bows lower. "I apologize for my unworthiness, Most Honored Guests, but it is not possible to enter the Winter Palace without an invitation and an honor guard. Both will be here in a minute. If you will be so kind as to wait in the shade under the pagoda roof here, Honored Guests, a personage of the proper rank to greet you will arrive in only a moment."

Nemes nods. "Kill them," she says to Scylla and Briareus and walks forward into the palace as her siblings phase-shift.

They shift down during the long walk through the many-leveled palace, shifting into fast time only to kill guards and servants. When they exit by the main steps and approach the Pargo Kaling, the great Western Gate on this side of the Kyi Chu Bridge, they find Regent Reting Tokra blocking the way with five hundred of his finest Palace Guard troops. A few of these elite fighters carry swords and pikes, but most hold crossbows, slug rifles, crude energy weapons, and railguns.

"Commander Nemes," says Tokra, lowering his head slightly but not bowing so much as to lose eye contact with the woman in front of him. "We have heard what you did at Shivling. You can go no farther." Tokra nods at someone high up in the gleaming eyes on the Pargo Kaling tower and the black chrome bridge of Kyi Chu slides silently back into the mountain. Only the great suspension cables remain far above, ringed about with razor wire and frictionless gel.

Nemes smiles. "What are you doing, Tokra?"

"His Holiness has gone to Hsuan-k'ung Ssu," says the thin-faced Regent. "I know why you travel that way. You cannot be allowed to harm His Holiness the Dalai Lama."

Rhadamanth Nemes shows more of her small teeth. "What are you talking about, Tokra? You sold out your dear little boy-god to the Pax secret service for thirty pieces of silver. Are we bartering here for more of your stupid six-sided coins?"

The Regent shakes his head. "The agreement with the Pax was that His Holiness would never be hurt. But you . . ."

"We want the girl's head," says Nemes. "Not your boy lama's. Get your men out of our way or lose them."

Regent Tokra turns and barks an order at his row upon row of soldiers. The men's faces are grim as they raise their weapons to their shoulders. The mass of them blocks the way to the bridge, even though the roadway of the bridge is no longer there. Dark clouds boil in the chasm.

"Kill them all," says Nemes, phase-shifting.

LHOMO HAD TRAINED us all in the hang-glider controls, but I had never had the opportunity to fly one before. Now, as the cliff rose out of the fog in front of me, I had to do the correct thing immediately or die.

The kite was controlled by manipulating the control bar that hung in front of me as I dangled in my harness, and I leaned as far left and put as much weight on it as the rigging allowed. The parawing banked, but not steeply enough, I realized at once. The kite was going to intercept the rock wall a meter or two away from the outer apex of its arc. There was another set of controls—handle grips that spilled air from the dorsal surface at the leading edge of each side of the dorsal wing—but these were dangerous and tricky and for emergency use only.

I could see the lichen on the approaching rock wall. This was an emergency.

I pulled hard on the left panic handle, the nylon on the left side of the parawing opened like a slit purse, the right wing—still catching the strong ridge lift here—banked up steeply, the parawing turned almost upside down with its useless left wing spilling air like so much empty aluminum frame, my legs were flung out sideways as the kite threatened to stall and plummet into the rocks, my boots actually brushed stone and lichen, and then the wing was falling almost straight down, I released the left handle, the active-memory fabric on the left leading surface healed itself in an instant, and I was flying again—although in a near vertical dive.

The strong thermals rising along the cliff face struck the kite like a rising elevator and I was slammed upward, the control bar swinging back against my upper chest hard enough to knock the wind out of me, and the parawing swooped, climbed, and tried to do a lazy loop with a radius of sixty or seventy meters. I found myself hanging almost upside down again, but this time with the kite and controls beneath me and the rock wall dead ahead again.

This was no good. I would conclude the loop on the cliff wall. I yanked the right panic handle, spilled lift, tumbled sideways in a sickening drop, sealed the wing, and tugged handles and control bar while shifting my weight wildly to establish balance and control. The clouds had parted enough for me to see the cliff twenty or thirty meters to my right as I fought the thermals and the kite itself for a clean line.

Then I was leveled and flying the contraption, spiraling around to my left again, but carefully this time—ever so carefully—thankful for the break in the clouds that allowed me to judge my distance from the cliff and leaning hard left on the control bar. Suddenly a whisper in my ear said, "Wow! That was fun to watch. Do it again!"

I jumped at the voice in my ear and then looked up and behind me. The bright yellow triangle of Aenea's parawing circled above me, the clouds close above it like a gray ceiling.

"No thanks," I said, allowing the comthreads on the throat of my skinsuit to pick up the subvocals. "I guess I'm through showing off." I glanced up at her again. "Why are you here? Where's A. Bettik?"

"We rendezvoused above the clouds, didn't see you, and I came down to find you," Aenea said simply, her comthreaded voice soft in my ear.

I felt a surge of nausea—more from the thought of her risking everything to do that than from the violent aerobatics of a moment earlier. "I'm all right," I said gruffly. "Just had to get the feel of the ridge lift."

"Yeah," said Aenea. "It's tricky. Why don't you follow me up?"

I did so, not allowing my pride to get in the way of survival. It was difficult to keep her yellow wing in sight with the shifting fog, but easier than flying blind near this cliff. She seemed to sense exactly where the rock wall was, cutting our circle within five meters of it—catching the strong center of the thermals there—but never coming too close or swinging too wide.

Within minutes we came out of the clouds. I admit that the experience took my breath away—first a slow brightening, then a rush of sunlight, then rising above the cloud level like a swimmer emerging from a white sea, then squinting into the bright light within the blinding freedom of blue sky and a seemingly infinite view on all sides.

Only the highest peaks and ridgelines were visible above the ocean of clouds: T'ai Shan gleaming cold and icy white so far to our east, Heng Shan about equidistant to the north, our ridgeline from Jo-kung rising like a razor's edge just above the tides of cloud running back to the west, K'un Lun Ridge a distant wall running northwest to southeast, and far, far away near the edge of the world, the brilliant summits of Chomo Lori, Mt.

Parnassus, Kangchengjunga, Mt. Koya, Mt. Kalais, and others I could not identify from this angle. There was a glimmer of sunlight on something tall beyond distant Phari Ridge, and I thought this might be the Potala or the lesser Shivling. I quit gawking and turned my attention back to our attempt to gain altitude.

A. Bettik circled close by and gave me a thumbs-up. I returned the signal and looked up to see Lhomo gesturing fifty meters above us: *Close up. Keep your circles tight. Follow me.*

We did that, Aenea easily climbing to her wingman position behind Lhomo, A. Bettik's blue kite circling across the climb circle from her, and me bringing up the rear fifteen meters below and fifty meters across the circle from the android.

Lhomo seemed to know exactly where the thermals were—sometimes we circled farther back west, caught the lift, and opened our circles to move east again. Sometimes we seemed to circle without gaining altitude, but then I would look north to Heng Shan and sense that we had covered another several hundred meters upward. Slowly we climbed and slowly we circled east, although T'ai Shan must still have been eighty or ninety klicks away.

It grew colder and harder to breathe. I sealed the last bit of osmosis mask and inhaled pure O^2 as we climbed. The skinsuit tightened around me, acting as a pressure suit and thermsuit all in one. I could see Lhomo shivering in his zygoat *chuba* and heavy mittens. There was ice on A. Bettik's bare forearm. And still we circled and rose. The sky darkened and the view grew more unbelievable—distant Nanda Devi in the southwest, Helgafell in the even more distant southeast, and Harney Peak far beyond the Shivling all coming into sight above the curve of the planet.

Finally Lhomo had had enough. A moment earlier I had unsealed the clear osmosis mask on my hood to see how thick the air was, tried to inhale what felt like hard vacuum, and quickly resealed the membrane. I could not imagine how Lhomo managed to breathe, think, and function at this altitude. Now he signaled us to keep circling higher on the thermal he had been working, gave us the ancient "good luck" sign of the circled thumb and forefinger, and then spilled the thin air out of his delta kite to drop away like a hurtling Thomas hawk. Within seconds, the red delta was several thousand meters below us and swooping toward the ridgeline to the west.

We continued circling and climbing, occasionally losing the lift for a moment, but then finding it again. We were being blown eastward by the lower edges of the jet stream, but we followed Lhomo's final advice and resisted the temptation to turn toward our destination; we did not have enough altitude or tailwind yet to make the eighty-kilometer voyage.

Encountering the jet stream was like suddenly entering a whitewater rapids in a kayak. Aenea's kite found the edge of it first, and I watched the yellow fabric vibrate as if in a powerful gale, then the aluminum superstructure flex wildly. Then A. Bettik and I were into it and it was everything we could do to hold ourselves horizontal in the swinging harness behind the control bar and continue circling for altitude.

"It's hard," came Aenea's voice in my ear. "It wants to tear loose and head east."

"We can't," I gasped, pulling the parawing into the headwind again and being thrown higher in one great vertical lift ride.

"I know," came Aenea's strained voice. I was a hundred meters away and below her now, but I could see her small form wrestling with the control bar, her legs straight, her small feet pointed backward like a cliff diver's.

I peered around. The brilliant sun was haloed by ice crystals. The ridgelines were almost invisible so far below, the summits of the highest peaks now klicks beneath us. "How is A. Bettik doing?" asked Aenea.

I twisted and strained to see. The android was circling above me. His eyes appeared to be closed, but I could see him making adjustments to the control bar. His blue flesh gleamed with frost. "All right, I think," I said. "Aenea?"

"Yes?"

"Is there any chance of the Pax at Shivling or in orbit picking up our comthread broadcasts?" The com unit/diskey journal was in my pocket, but we had decided never to use it until it was time to call the ship. It would be ironic if we were captured or killed because of using these skinsuit communicators.

"No chance," gasped Aenea. Even with the osmosis masks and the rebreather matrix woven into the skinsuits, the air was thin and cold. "The comthreads are very short range. Half a klick at most."

"Then stay close," I said and concentrated on gaining a few hundred more meters before the almost silent hurricane that was buffeting me sent the kite screaming off to the east.

Another few minutes and we could no longer resist the powerful current in this river of air. The thermal did not lessen, it just seemed to die away completely, and then we were at the mercy of the jet stream.

"Let's go!" shouted Aenea, forgetting that her slightest whisper was audible in my hearpatch.

I could see A. Bettik open his eyes and give me a thumbs-up. At the same instant, my own parawing peeled off the thermal and was swept away to the east. Even with the diminished sound, we seemed to be roaring through the air at a speed so incredible that it was audible. Aenea's yellow delta streaked east like a crossbow dart. A. Bettik's blue followed. I wrestled with the controls, realized that I did not have the strength to change course one degree, and simply held on while we rifled east and down in the pounding, flowing river of air. T'ai Shan gleamed ahead of us, but we were losing altitude quickly now and the mountain was still very far away. Kilometers beneath us, beneath the monsoon sea of white cloudtops, the greenish phosgene clouds of the acid world ocean churned away unseen but waiting.

THE PAX AUTHORITIES in T'ien Shan System were confused.

When Captain Wolmak in the *Jibril* received the strange pulsed alarm signal from the Pax Enclave at Shivling, he tried hailing Cardinal Mustafa and the others but received no answer. Within minutes he had dispatched a combat dropship with two dozen Pax Marines, including three medics.

The tightline report uplink was confusing. The conference room at their enclave gompa was a gory mess. Human blood and viscera were splashed everywhere, but the only body remaining was that of the Grand Inquisitor, who had been crippled and blinded. They DNA-typed the largest arterial spray and found it to be that of Father Farrell. Other pools of blood reportedly belonged to Archbishop Breque and his aide, LeBlanc. But no bodies. No cruciforms. The medics reported that Cardinal Mustafa was comatose, in deep shock, and near death; they stabilized him as best they could using only their fieldkits and asked for orders. Should they let the Grand Inquisitor die and be resurrected, or get him to the dropship doc-in-the-box and try to save him, knowing that it would be several days before he could regain consciousness and describe the attack? Or the medic could get him to life support, use drugs to bring the Cardinal out of the coma, and interrogate him within minutes—all the while with the patient under exquisite pain and on the verge of death.

Wolmak ordered them to wait and tightbeamed Admiral Lempriere, the task force commander. Out in the T'ien Shan System, many AUs distant, the forty-some ships that had come through the battle with *Raphael* were rescuing survivors from the terminally damaged archangels and awaiting the arrival of the papal drone and the TechnoCore robot ship that would be putting the planet's population in suspended animation. Neither had arrived. Lempriere was closer, four light-minutes away, and the tightbeam would take that long to reach him and bring him up to speed, but Wolmak felt he had no other choice. He waited while his message burned out-system.

Aboard the flagship *Raguel*, Lempriere found himself in a ticklish situation, with only minutes to decide about Mustafa. If he allowed the Grand Inquisitor to die, it was likely that a two-day resurrection would be successful. The Cardinal would suffer little pain. But the cause of the attack—Shrike, indigenies, the Aenea monster's disciples, Ousters—might remain a mystery until then. Lempriere took ten seconds to decide, but it was a four-minute tightbeam delay out and back.

"Have the medics stabilize him," he tightbeamed Wolmak on the *Jibril* in orbit around the mountain planet. "Get him to dropship life support. Bring him out of it. Interrogate him. When we know enough, have the autosurgeon give a prognosis. If it's faster to resurrect him, let him die."

"Aye, aye, sir," said Wolmak four minutes later, and passed word along to the Marines.

Meanwhile, the Marines were widening their search, using EMV reaction paks to search the vertical cliffsides around the Phallus of Shiva. They deep-radared Rhan Tso, the so-called Otter Lake, finding neither otters nor the bodies of the missing priests. There had been an honor guard of twelve Marines in the enclave with the Grand Inquisitor's party—plus the pilot of the dropship—but these men and women were also missing. Blood and viscera were found and DNA-typed—most of the missing thus accounted for—but their bodies were not found.

"Shall we spread the search to the Winter Palace?" questioned the Marine lieutenant in charge of the party. All of the Marines had specific orders not to disturb the locals—especially the Dalai Lama and his people—before the TechnoCore ship arrived to put the population asleep.

"Just a minute," said Wolmak. He saw that Admiral Lempriere's monitor telltale was on. The com diskey on his command web was also blinking. *Jibril*'s intelligence officer down in the sensor bubble. "Yes?"

"Captain, we've been visually monitoring the palace area. Something terrible has happened there."

"What?" snapped Wolmak. It was not like any member of his crew to be so vague.

"We missed it, sir," said the Intel officer. She was a young woman, but smart, Lempriere knew. "We were using the optics to check the area around the Enclave. But look at this . . ."

Wolmak turned his head slightly to watch the holopit fill with an image, knowing that it was being tightbeamed out to the Admiral. The east side of the Winter Palace, Potala, as if seen from a few hundred meters above the Kyi Chu Bridge.

The roadway of the bridge was gone, retracted. But on the steps and terraces between the palace and the bridge, and on some of the narrow ledges in the chasm between the palace and the Drepung Monastery on the east side, were scores of bodies—hundreds of bodies—bloodied and dismembered.

"Dear Lord," said Captain Wolmak and crossed himself.

"We've identified the head of Regent Tokra Reting there among the body parts," came the Intel officer's calm voice.

"The *head*?" repeated Wolmak, realizing that his useless remark was being sent to the Admiral along with all the rest of this transmission. In four minutes, Admiral Lempriere would know that Wolmak made stupid comments. No matter. "Anyone else important there?" he queried Intel.

"Negative, sir," came the young officer's voice. "But they're broadcasting on various radio frequencies now."

Wolmak raised an eyebrow. So far, the Winter Palace had maintained radio and tightbeam silence. "What are they saying?"

"It's in Mandarin and post-Hegira Tibetan, sir," said the officer. But then, quickly, "They're in a panic, Captain. The Dalai Lama is missing. So is the head of the boy lama's security team. General Surkhang Sewon Chempo, leader of the Palace Guard, is dead, sir . . . they've confirmed that his headless body was found there."

Wolmak glanced at the clock. The tightbeam broadcast was halfway to the Admiral's ship. "Who did this, Intel? The Shrike?"

"Don't know, sir. As I said, the lenses and cameras were elsewhere. We'll check the discs."

"Do that," said Wolmak. He could not wait any longer. He tightbeamed the Marine lieutenant. "Get to the palace, Lieutenant. See what the hell is going on. I'm sending down five more dropships, combat EMVs, and a thopter gunship. Search for any sign of Archbishop Breque, Father Farrell, or Father LeBlanc. And the pilot and honor guard, of course."

"Aye, aye, sir."

The tightbeam link went green. The Admiral was receiving the latest transmission. Too late to wait for his command. Wolmak tightbeamed the two closest Pax ships—torchships just beyond the outer moon—and ordered them on battle alert and to drop into matching orbit with the *Jibril.* He might need the firepower. Wolmak had seen the Shrike's work before, and the thought of that creature suddenly appearing on his ship made his skin go cold. He tightbeamed Captain Samuels on the torchship H.H.S. *St. Bonaventure.* "Carol," he said to the startled captain's image, "go tactical space, please." .

Wolmak jacked in and was standing in place above the gleaming cloud planet of T'ien Shan. Samuels suddenly appeared next to him in the starry darkness.

"Carol," said Wolmak, "something's going on down there. I think the Shrike may be loose again. If you suddenly lose transmission data from the *Jibril,* or we start screaming gibberish . . ."

"I'll launch three boats of Marines," said Samuels.

"Negative," said Wolmak. "Slag the *Jibril.* Immediately."

Captain Samuels blinked. So did the floating telltale that showed that Admiral Lempriere's flagship was tightbeaming. Wolmak jacked out of tactical.

The message was short. "I've spun the *Raguel* up for a jump in-system to just beyond the critical gravity well around T'ien Shan," said Admiral Lempriere, his thin face grave.

Wolmak opened his mouth to protest to his superior, realized that a tightbeamed protest would arrive almost three minutes after the Hawking-drive jump was executed, and shut his mouth. A jump in-system like this was sickeningly dangerous—one chance in four, at least, of a disaster that would claim all hands—but he understood the Admiral's need to get to where the information was fresh and his commands could be executed immediately.

Dear Jesus, thought Wolmak, *the Grand Inquisitor crippled, the Archbishop and the others missing, the sodding Dalai Lama's palace look-*

ing like an anthill that's been kicked over. Goddamn that Shrike-thing. Where's the papal courier probe with its command? Where's that Core ship we were promised? How can things get worse than this?

"Captain?" It was the chief Marine medic on the expeditionary force, beaming from the dropship infirmary.

"Report."

"Cardinal Mustafa is conscious, sir . . . still blind, of course . . . in terrible pain, but . . ."

"Put him on," snapped Wolmak.

A terrible visage filled the holosphere. Captain Wolmak sensed others on the bridge shrinking back.

The Grand Inquisitor's face was still bloodied. His teeth were bright red as he screamed. His eye sockets were ragged and void, except for tendrils of torn tissue and rivulets of blood.

At first, Captain Wolmak could not discern the word from the shriek. But then he realized what the Cardinal was screaming.

"Nemes! Nemes! Nemes!"

THE CONSTRUCTS CALLED Nemes, Scylla, and Briareus continue eastward.

The three remain phase-shifted, oblivious to the staggering amounts of energy this consumes. The energy is sent from elsewhere. It is not their worry. All of their existence has led to this hour.

After the timeless interlude of slaughter under the Pargo Kaling Western Gate, Nemes leads the way up the tower and across the great metal cables holding the suspension bridge in place. The three jog through Drepung Marketplace, three motile figures moving through thickened, amber air, past human forms frozen in place. At Phari Marketplace, the thousands of shopping, browsing, laughing, arguing, jostling human statues make Nemes smile her thin-lipped smile. She could decapitate all of them and they would have had no warning of their destruction. But she has an objective.

At the Phari Ridge cableway juncture, the three shift down—friction on the cable would be a problem otherwise.

Scylla, the northern High Way, Nemes sends on the common band. *Briareus, the middle bridge. I will take the cableway.*

Her siblings nod, shimmer, and are gone. The cablemaster steps forward to protest Nemes's shoving in line ahead of scores of waiting cable passengers. It is a busy time of day.

Rhadamanth Nemes picks the cablemaster up and flings him off the platform. A dozen angry men and women shove toward her, shouting, bent on revenge.

Nemes leaps from the platform and grabs the cable. She has no pulley, no brakes, no climbing harness. She phase-shifts only the palms of her inhuman hands and hurtles down the cable toward K'un Lun Ridge. The angry mob behind her clip onto the cable and give chase—a dozen, two dozen, more. The cablemaster had been liked by many.

It takes Nemes half the usual transit time to cover the great abyss between Phari and K'un Lun ridges. She brakes sloppily on the approach and slams into the rock, phase-shifting at the last instant. Pulling herself out of the crumbling indentation on the cliff behind the landing ledge, she walks back to the cable.

Pulleys whine as the first of her pursuers careen down the last few hundred meters of wire. More spread out to the horizon, black beads on a thin string. Nemes smiles, phase-shifts both her hands, reaches high, and severs the cable.

She is surprised how few of the dozens of doomed men and women scream as they slide off the twisting, falling cable to their deaths.

Nemes jogs to the fixed ropes, climbs them freehand, and cuts all of them loose—ascent lines, rappel lines, safety lines, everything. Five armed members of the K'un Lun Constabulary from Hsi wang-mu confront her on the ridgeline just south of the slideway. She phase-shifts only her left forearm and swats them off into space.

Looking northwest, Nemes adjusts her infrared and telescopic vision and zooms in on the great swinging bonsai-bamboo bridge connecting the High Way promontories between Phari Ridge and K'un Lun Ridge. The bridge falls as she watches, the slats and vines and support cables writhing as they fall back to the western ridgeline, the lower reaches of the bridge dropping into phosgene clouds.

That's that, sends Briareus.

How many on it when it fell? queries Nemes.

Many. Briareus disconnects.

A second later, Scylla logs on. *Northern bridge down. I'm destroying the High Way as I go.*

Good, sends Nemes. *I'll see you in Jo-kung.*

The three shift down as they pass through the city fissure at Jo-kung. It is raining lightly, the clouds as thick as summer fog. Nemes's thin hair is plastered to her forehead and she notices that Scylla and Briareus have the same look. The crowd parts for them. The ledge road to the Temple Hanging in Air is empty.

Nemes is leading as they approach the final, short swinging bridge before the ledge below the stairway to the Temple. This had been the first artifact repaired by Aenea—a simple, twenty-meter swinging span above a narrow fissure between dolomite spires a thousand meters above the lower crags and cloudtops—and now the monsoon clouds billow beneath and around the dripping structure.

Invisible in the thick clouds, something stands on the cliff ledge at the other side of the bridge. Nemes shifts to thermal imaging and smiles when she sees that the tall shape radiates no heat whatsoever. She pings it with her forehead-generated radar and studies the image: three meters tall, thorns, bladed fingers on four oversized hands, a perfectly radar-reflective carapace, sharp blades on chest and forehead, no respiration, razor wire rising from the shoulders and spikes from the forehead.

Perfect, sends Nemes.

Perfect, agrees Scylla and Briareus.

The figure at the other end of the dripping bridge makes no response.

WE MADE IT to the mountain with only a few meters to spare. Once we dropped out of the lower reaches of the jet stream, our descent was steady and irreversible. There were few thermals out above the cloud ocean and many downdrafts, and while we made the first half of the hundred-klick gap in a few minutes of thrilling acceleration, the second half was all heart-stopping descent—now certain that we would make it with room to spare, now more certain that we would drop into the clouds and never even see our deaths rising to surround us until the kite wings struck acid sea.

We did descend into the clouds, but these were the monsoon clouds, the water vapor clouds, the breathable clouds. The three of us flew as close as we could, blue delta, yellow delta, green delta, the metal and fabric of our parawings almost touching, more fearful of losing one another and dying alone than of striking one another and falling together.

Aenea and I had the comthreads, but we talked to each other just once during that suspenseful descent to the east. The fog had thickened, I caught the merest glimpses of her yellow wing to my left, and I was thinking, *She had a child . . . she married someone else . . . she* loved *someone else,* when I heard her voice on the hearpatch of my suit, "Raul?"

"Yes, kiddo."

"I love you, Raul."

I hesitated a few heartbeats, but the emotional vacuum that had pulled me a moment earlier was swept away in the surge of affection for my young friend and lover. "I love you, Aenea." We swept lower through the murk. I thought that I could taste an acrid scent on the wind . . . the fringes of the phosgene clouds?

"Kiddo?"

"Yes, Raul." Her voice was a whisper in my ears. We had both removed our osmosis masks, I knew . . . although they would have protected us from the phosgene. We did not know if A. Bettik could breathe the poison. If he could not, the unspoken plan between Aenea and me was to close our masks and hope that we could reach the edges of the mountain before we struck the acid sea, dragging the android up the slope and out of the poison air if we could. We both knew that it was a flimsy plan—the radar aboard the ship during my initial descent had shown me that most of the peaks and ridges dropped abruptly beneath the phosgene cloud layer and it would be only a matter of minutes between entering the poisonous clouds before we struck the sea anyway—but it was better to have a plan than to surrender to fate. In the meantime, we both had our masks up, breathing fresh air while we could.

"Kiddo," I said, "if you know that this isn't going to work . . . if you've seen what you think is . . ."

"My death?" she completed the sentence for me. I could not have said it aloud.

I nodded stupidly. She could not see me through the clouds between us.

"They're only possibilities, Raul," she said softly. "Although the one I know of with the greatest probability is not this. Don't worry, I wouldn't have asked you both to go with me if I thought this was . . . it." I heard the humor in her voice through the tension.

"I know," I said, glad that A. Bettik could not pick up this conversation. "I wasn't thinking of that." I had been thinking that perhaps she had known that the android and I would make it to the mountain, but she would not. I did not believe that now. As long as my fate was entwined with hers, I could accept about anything. "I was just wondering why we were running again, kiddo," I said. "I'm sick of running away from the Pax."

"So am I," said Aenea. "And trust me, Raul, that's not all we're doing here. Oh, shit!"

Hardly the quotable pronouncement from a messiah, but in a second I saw the reason for her shout. A rocky hillside had appeared twenty meters ahead of us, large boulders visible between scree slopes, sheer cliffs lower down.

A. Bettik led the way in, pulling up on his control bar at the last minute and dropping his legs from the stirrups of the rigging, using the kite like a parachute above him. He bounced twice on his boots and set the kite down quickly, snapping off his harness. Lhomo had shown us many times that it was important on dangerous and windy landing sites to separate yourself from the parawing quickly so that it did not drag you over some edge. And there was definitely an edge to be dragged over here.

Aenea landed next, me a few seconds later. I had the sloppiest of the three landings, bouncing high, dropping almost straight down, twisting my ankle on the small stones, and going to my knees while the parawing struck hard on a boulder above me, bending metal and rending fabric. The kite tried to tip over backward then, pulling me over the cliff's edge just as Lhomo had warned, but A. Bettik grabbed the left struts, Aenea seized the broken right spar a second later, and they stabilized it long enough for me to struggle out of my harness and hobble a few steps away from the wreckage, dragging my backpack with me.

Aenea knelt on the cold, wet rocks at my feet, loosening my boot and studying my ankle. "I don't think it's sprained badly," she said. "It may swell a bit, but you should be able to walk on it all right."

"Good," I said stupidly, aware only of her bare hands on my bare ankle. Then I jumped a bit as she sprayed something cold from her medkit on the puffy flesh.

They both helped me to my feet, we gathered our gear, and the three of us started arm-in-arm up the slick slope toward where the clouds glowed more brightly.

WE CAME UP into the sunlight high on the sacred slopes of T'ai Shan. I had pulled off the skinsuit cowl and mask, but Aenea suggested that I keep the suit on. I pulled my therm jacket on over it to feel less naked, and I noticed that my friend did the same. A. Bettik was rubbing his arms and I saw that the high altitude cold had left his flesh chilled almost white.

"Are you all right?" I asked him.

"Fine, M. Endymion," said the android. "Although another few minutes at that altitude . . ."

I looked down at the clouds where we had folded the damaged kites and left them. "I guess we're not getting off this hill with the parawings."

"Correct," said Aenea. "Look."

We had come out of the boulder fields and scree slopes to grassy highlands between great cliffs, the succulent meadows crisscrossed with zygoat trails and stepping-stone paths. Glacial melt streams trickled over rocks but there were bridges made of stone slabs. A few distant herders had watched us impassively as we climbed higher. Now we had come around a switchback below the great icefields and looked up at what could only be temples of white stone set on gray ramparts. The gleaming buildings—bright beneath the blue-white expanse of ice and snow slopes that stretched up and out of sight to the blue zenith—looked like altars. What Aenea had pointed out was a great white stone set next to the trail, with this poem carved in its smooth face:

> *With what can I compare the Great Peak?*
> *Over the surrounding provinces, its blue-green hue never*
>   *dwindles from sight.*
> *Infused by the Shaper of Forms with the soaring power of*
>   *divinity,*
> *Shaded and sunlit, its slopes divide night from day.*
> *Breast heaving as I climb toward the clouds,*
> *Eyes straining to follow birds flying home,*
> *Someday I shall reach its peerless summit,*
> *And behold all mountains in a single glance.*
>   —Tu Fu, T'ang Dynasty, China, Old Earth

And so we entered Tai'an, the City of Peace. There on the slopes were the scores of temples, hundreds of shops, inns, and homes, countless small shrines, and a busy street filled with stalls, each covered by a bright canvas awning. The people here were lovely—that is a poor word, but the only proper one, I think—all with dark hair, bright eyes, gleaming teeth, healthy skin, and a pride and vigor to their carriage and step. Their clothes were silk and dyed cotton, bright but elegantly simple, and there were many, many monks in orange and red robes. The crowds would have been forgiven if they had stared—no one visits T'ai Shan during the monsoon months—but all the glances I saw were welcoming and easy. Indeed, many of the people in the street milled around, greeting Aenea by name and touching her hand or sleeve. I remembered then that she had visited the Great Peak before.

Aenea pointed out the great slab of white rock that covered a hillside above the City of Peace. On the polished face of that slab had been carved what she explained was the *Diamond Sutra* in huge Chinese characters: one of the principle works of Buddhist philosophy, she explained, it reminded the monk and passerby of the ultimate nature of reality as symbolized in the empty expanse of blue sky overhead. Aenea also pointed out the First Heavenly Gate at the edge of the city—a gigantic stone archway under a red pagoda roof with the first of the twenty-seven thousand steps starting up toward the Jade Summit.

Incredibly, we had been expected. In the great gompa at the center of the City of Peace, more than twelve hundred red-robed monks sat cross-legged in patient files, waiting for Aenea. The resident lama greeted Aenea with a low bow—she helped him to his feet and hugged the old man—and then A. Bettik and I were sitting at one side of the low, cushioned dais while Aenea briefly addressed the waiting multitude.

"I said last spring that I would return at this time," she said softly, her voice perfectly clear in the great marble space, "and it pleases my heart to see you all again. For those of you who took communion with me during my last visit, I know that you have discovered the truth of learning the language of the dead, of learning the language of the living, and—for some of you—of hearing the music of the spheres, and—soon, I promise you—of taking that first step.

"This day is a sad day in many ways, but our future is bright with optimism and change. I am honored that you have allowed me to be your teacher. I am honored that we have shared in our exploration of a universe that is rich beyond imagining." She paused and looked at A. Bettik and me. "These are my companions . . . my friend A. Bettik and my beloved, Raul Endymion. They have shared all hardships of my longest life's voyage with me, and they will share in today's pilgrimage. When we leave you, we will pass this day through the three Heavenly Gates, enter the Mouth of the Dragon, and—Buddha and the fates of chaos willing—shall visit the Princess of Azure Clouds and see the Temple of the Jade Emperor this day."

Aenea paused again and looked at the shaven heads and bright, dark eyes. These were not religious fanatics, I saw, not mindless servants or self-punishing ascetics, but were, instead, row upon row of intelligent, questioning, alert young men and women. I say "young," but among the fresh and youthful faces were many with gray beards and subtle wrinkles.

"My dear friend the Lama tells me that there are more now who wish to share in communion with the Void Which Binds this day," said Aenea.

About one hundred of the monks in the front rows went to their knees.

Aenea nodded. "So it shall be," she said softly. The Lama brought flagons of wine and many simple bronze cups. Before filling the cups or lancing her finger for the drops of blood, Aenea said, "But before you partake of this communion, I must remind you that this is a physical change, not a spiritual one. Your individual quest for God or Enlightenment must remain just that . . . your individual quest. This moment of change will not bring *satori* or salvation. It will bring only . . . change."

My young friend held up one finger, the finger she was about to prick to draw blood. "In the cells of my blood are unique DNA and RNA arrangements along with certain viral agents which will invade your body, starting through the digestive lining of your stomachs and ending in every cell of your body. These invasive viruses are somatic . . . that is, they shall be passed along to your children.

"I have taught your teachers and they have taught you that these physical changes will allow you—after some training—to touch the Void Which Binds more directly, thus learning the language of the dead and of the living. Eventually, with much more experience and training, it may be possible for you to hear the music of the spheres and take a true step elsewhere." She raised the finger higher. "This is not metaphysics, my dear friends. This is a mutant viral agent. Be warned that you will never be able to wear the cruciform of the Pax, nor will your children nor their children's children. This basic change in the soul of your genes and chromosomes will ban you from that form of physical longevity forever.

"This communion will not offer you immortality, my dear friends. It insures that death will be our common end. I say again—I do not offer you eternal life or instant *satori*. If these are the things you seek most dearly, you must find them in your own religious searchings. I offer you only a deepening of the human experience of life and a connection to others— human or not—who have shared that commitment to living. There is no shame if you change your mind now. But there is duty, discomfort, and great danger to those who partake of this communion and, in so doing, become teachers themselves of the Void Which Binds, as well as fellow carriers of this new virus of human choice."

Aenea waited, but none of the hundred monks moved or left. All remained kneeling, heads slightly bowed as if in contemplation.

"So be it," said Aenea. "I wish you all well." And she pricked her finger, squeezing a droplet of blood into each prepared cup of wine held out by the elderly Lama.

It took only a few minutes for the hundred monks to pass the cups down their rows, each drinking but a drop. I rose from my cushion then, determined to go to the end of the row nearest me and partake of this communion, but Aenea beckoned me to her.

"Not yet, my dear," she whispered in my ear, touching my shoulder.

I was tempted to argue—why was I being excluded from this?—but instead returned to my place next to A. Bettik. I leaned over and whispered to the android, "You haven't done this so-called communion, have you?"

The blue man smiled. "No, M. Endymion. And I never shall."

I was about to ask why, but at that moment the communion ended, the twelve hundred monks rose to their feet, Aenea walked among them—chatting and touching hands—and I saw from her glance toward me over shaven heads that it was time for us to leave.

NEMES, SCYLLA, AND Briareus regard the Shrike across the expanse of the suspension bridge, not phase-shifting for a moment, appreciating the real-time view of their enemy.

It's absurd, sends Briareus. *A child's bogeyman. All spikes and thorns and teeth. How silly.*

Tell that to Gyges, responds Nemes. *Ready?*

Ready, sends Scylla.

Ready, sends Briareus.

The three phase-shift in unison. Nemes sees the air around them go thick and heavy, light becoming a sepia syrup, and she knows that even if the Shrike now does the obvious—cutting the suspension-bridge supports—that it will make no difference: in fast time, it will take ages for the bridge to begin to fall . . . time enough for the trio to cross it a thousand times.

In single file, Nemes leading, they cross it now.

The Shrike does not change position. Its head does not move to follow them. Its red eyes gleam dully, like crimson glass reflecting the last bit of sunset.

Something's not right here, sends Briareus.

Quiet, commands Nemes. *Stay off the common band unless I open contact.* She is less than ten meters from the Shrike now and still the thing has not reacted. Nemes continues forward through thick air until she steps onto solid stone. Her clone sister follows, taking up position on Nemes's left. Briareus steps off the bridge and stands on Nemes's right. They are three meters in front of the Hyperion legend. It remains quiescent.

"Move out of the way or be destroyed." Nemes shifts down long enough to speak to the chrome statue. "Your day is long past. The girl is ours today." The Shrike does not respond.

Destroy it, Nemes commands her siblings and phase shifts.

The Shrike disappears, shifting through time.

Nemes blinks as the temporal shock waves ripple over and through her and then surveys the frozen surroundings with the full spectrum of her vision. There are a few human beings still here at the Temple Hanging in Air, but no Shrike.

Shift down, she commands and her siblings obey immediately. The world brightens, the air moves, and sound returns.

"Find her," says Nemes.

In a full jog, Scylla moves to the Noble Eightfold Path axis of Wisdom and lopes up the staircase to the platform of Right Understanding. Briareus moves quickly to the axis of Morality and leaps to the pagoda of Right Speech. Nemes takes the third stairway, the highest, toward the high pavilions of Right Mindfulness and Right Meditation. Her radar shows people in the highest structure. She arrives in a few seconds, scanning the buildings and cliff wall for concealed rooms or hiding places. Nothing. There is a young woman in the pavilion for Right Meditation and for an instant Nemes thinks that the search is over, but although she is about the same age as Aenea, it is not her. There are a few others in the elegant pagoda—a very old woman—Nemes recognizes her as the Thunderbolt Sow from the Dalai Lama's reception—the Dalai Lama's Chief Crier and Head of Security, Carl Linga William Eiheji, and the boy himself—the Dalai Lama.

"Where is she?" says Nemes. "Where is the one who calls herself Aenea?"

Before any of the others can speak, the warrior Eiheji reaches into his cloak and hurls a dagger with lightning speed.

Nemes dodges it easily. Even without phase-shifting, her reactions are faster than most humans. But when Eiheji pulls a flechette pistol, Nemes shifts up, walks to the frozen man, encloses him in her shift field, and flings him out the open floor-to-ceiling window into the abyss. Of course, as soon as Eiheji leaves her field envelope, he seems to freeze in midair like some ungainly bird thrown from the nest, unable to fly but unwilling to fall.

Nemes turns back to the boy and shifts down. Behind her, Eiheji screams and plummets out of sight.

The Dalai Lama's jaw drops and his lips form an O. To him and the two women present, Eiheji had simply disappeared from next to them and reappeared in midair out the open shoji doors of the pavilion, as if he had chosen to teleport to his death.

"You can't . . ." begins the old Thunderbolt Sow.

"You are forbidden . . ." begins the Dalai Lama.

"You won't . . ." begins the woman whom Nemes guesses is either Rachel or Theo, Aenea's compatriots.

Nemes says nothing. She shifts up, walks to the boy, folds her phase field around him, lifts him, and carries him to the open door.

Nemes! It is Briareus calling from the pavilion of Right Effort.

What?

Instead of verbalizing on the common band, Briareus uses the extra energy to send the full visual image. Looking frozen in the sepia air kilometers above them, fusion flame as solid as a blue pillar, a spaceship is descending.

Shift down, commands Nemes.

THE MONKS AND the old Lama packed us a lunch in a brown bag. They also gave A. Bettik one of the old-fashioned pressure suits of the kind I had seen only in the ancient spaceflight museum at Port Romance and tried to give two more to Aenea and me, but we showed them the skinsuits under our thermal jackets. The twelve hundred monks all turned out to wave us off through the First Heavenly Gate, and there must have been two or three thousand others pressing and craning to see us leave.

The great stairway was empty except for the three of us, climbing easily now, A. Bettik with his clear helmet folded back like a cowl, Aenea and me with our osmosis masks turned up. Each of the steps was seven meters wide, but shallow, and the first section was easy enough, with a wide terrace step every hundred steps. The steps were heated from within, so even as we moved into the region of perpetual ice and snow midway up T'ai Shan, the stairway was clear.

Within an hour we had reached the Second Heavenly Gate—a huge red pagoda with a fifteen-meter archway—and then we were climbing more steeply up the near-vertical fault line known as the Mouth of the Dragon. Here the winds picked up, the temperature dropped precipitously, and the air became dangerously thin. We had redonned our harnesses at the Second Heavenly Gate, and now we clipped on to one of the buckycarbon lines that ran along each side of the staircase, adjusting the pulley grip to act like a brake if we fell or were blown off the increasingly treacherous staircase. Within minutes, A. Bettik inflated his clear helmet and gave us a thumbs-up, while Aenea and I sealed our osmosis masks.

We kept climbing toward the South Gate of Heaven still a kilometer above us, while the world fell away all around. It was the second time in a few hours that such a sight had presented itself to us, but this time we took it all in every three hundred steps as we took a break, standing and wheezing and staring out at the early afternoon light illuminating the great peaks. Tai'an, the City of Peace, was invisible now, some fifteen thousand steps and several klicks below the icefields and rock walls through which we had climbed. I realized that the skinsuit comthreads gave us privacy once again, and said, "How you doing, kiddo?"

"Tired," said Aenea, but she leavened the comment with a smile from behind her clear mask.

"Can you tell me where we're headed?" I said.

"The Temple of the Jade Emperor," said my friend. "It's on the summit."

"I guessed that," I said, setting a foot down on the wide step, then raising the next foot to the next step. The stairway passed up and through a rock-and-ice overhang at this point. I knew that if I turned around to look down, that vertigo might overcome me. This was infinitely worse than the paragliding. "Can you tell me *why* we're climbing to the Temple of the Jade Emperor when everything is going to hell behind us?"

"How do you mean going to hell?" she said.

"I mean Nemes and her ilk are probably after us. The Pax definitely is going to make its move. Things are falling apart. And we're on pilgrimage."

Aenea nodded. The wind was roaring now, as thin as it was, as we actually climbed into the jet stream. Each of us was moving forward and up with our heads bowed and our bodies arched, as if carrying a heavy load. I wondered what A. Bettik was thinking about.

"Why don't we just call the ship and get the hell out of here," I said. "If we're going to bail out, let's get it over with."

I could see Aenea's dark eyes behind the mask that reflected the deepening blue sky. "When we call the ship, there'll be two dozen Pax warships descending on us like harpy crows," said Aenea. "We can't do it until we're ready."

I gestured up the steep staircase. "And climbing this will make us ready?"

"I hope so," she said softly. I could hear the rasp of her breathing through my hearpatches.

"What's up here, kiddo?"

We had reached the next three hundredth step. All three of us stopped and panted, too tired to appreciate the view. We had climbed into the edge of space. The sky was almost black. Several of the brighter stars were visible and I could see one of the smaller moons hurtling toward the zenith. *Or was it a Pax ship?*

"I don't *know* what we'll find, Raul," said Aenea, her voice tired. "I glimpse things . . . dream things again and again . . . but then I dream the same thing in a different way. I hate to talk about it until I see which reality presents itself."

I nodded understanding, but I was lying. We began climbing again. "Aenea?" I said.

"Yes, Raul."

"Why don't you let me take . . . you know . . . communion?"

She made a face behind the osmosis mask. "I hate calling it that."

"I know, but that's what everyone calls it. But tell me this, at least . . . why don't you let me drink the wine?"

"It's not time for you to, Raul."

"Why not?" I could feel the anger and frustration just below the surface again, mixing with the roiling current of love that I felt for this woman.

"You know the four steps I talk about . . ." she began.

"Learning the language of the dead, learning the language of the living . . . yeah, yeah, I know the four steps," I said almost dismissively, setting my very real foot on a very physical marble step and taking another tired pace up the endless stairway.

I could see Aenea smile at my tone. "Those things tend to . . . preoccupy the person first encountering them," she said softly. "I need your full attention right now. I need your *help*."

That made sense to me. I reached over and touched her back through the thermal jacket and skinsuit material. A. Bettik looked across at us and nodded, as if approving of our contact. I reminded myself that he could not have heard our skinsuit transmissions.

"Aenea," I said softly, "are you the new messiah?"

I could hear her sigh. "No, Raul. I never said I was a messiah. I never wanted to be a messiah. I'm just a tired young woman right now . . . I've got a pounding headache . . . and cramps . . . it's the first day of my period . . ."

She must have seen me blink in surprise or shock. *Well, hell,* I thought, *it's not every day that you get to confront the messiah only to hear that she's suffering from what the ancients used to call PMS.*

Aenea chuckled. "I'm not the messiah, Raul. I was just chosen to be the One Who Teaches. And I'm trying to do it while . . . while I can."

Something about her last sentence made my stomach knot in anxiety. "Okay," I said. We reached the three hundredth step and paused together, wheezing more heavily now. I looked up. Still no South Gate of Heaven visible. Even though it was midday, the sky was space black. A thousand stars burned. They barely twinkled. I realized that the hiss and roar of the jet stream had gone away. T'ai Shan was the highest peak on T'ien Shan, extending into the highest fringes of the atmosphere. If it had not been for our skinsuits, our eyes, eardrums, and lungs would have exploded like overinflated balloons. Our blood would be boiling. Our . . .

I tried to shift my thoughts onto something else.

"All right," I said, "but if you *were* the messiah, what would your message to humanity be?"

Aenea chuckled again, but I noticed that it was a reflective chuckle, not a derisive one. "If *you* were a messiah," she said between breaths, "what would *your* message be?"

I laughed out loud. A. Bettik could not have heard the sound through the near vacuum separating us, but he must have seen me throw my head back, for he looked over quizzically. I waved at him and said to Aenea, "I have no fucking clue."

"Exactly," said Aenea. "When I was a kid . . . I mean a *little* kid, before I met you . . . and I knew that I'd have to go through some of this stuff . . . I was always wondering what message I was going to give humankind. Beyond the things I knew I'd have to teach, I mean. Something profound. Sort of a Sermon on the Mount."

I looked around. There was no ice or snow at this terrible altitude.

The clear, white steps rose through shelves of steep, black rock. "Well," I said, "here's the mount."

"Yeah," said Aenea, and I could hear the fatigue once again.

"So what message did you come up with?" I said, more to keep her talking and distracted than to hear the answer. It had been a while since she and I had just talked.

I could see her smile. "I kept working on it," she said at last, "trying to get it as short and important as the Sermon on the Mount. Then I realized that was no good—like Uncle Martin in his manic-poet period trying to outwrite Shakespeare—so I decided that my message would just be *shorter*."

"How short?"

"I got my message down to thirty-five words. Too long. Then down to twenty-seven. Still too long. After a few years I had it down to ten. Still too long. Eventually I boiled it down to two words."

"Two words?" I said. "Which two?"

We had reached the next resting point . . . the seventieth or eightieth three hundredth step. We stopped gratefully and panted. I bent over to rest my skinsuit-gloved hands on my skinsuit-sheathed knees and concentrated on not throwing up. It was bad form to vomit in an osmosis mask. "Which two?" I said again when I got some wind back and could hear the answer over my pounding heart and rasping lungs.

"Choose again," said Aenea.

I considered that for a wheezing, panting moment. "Choose again?" I said finally.

Aenea smiled. She had caught her wind and was actually looking down at the vertical view that I was afraid even to glance toward. She seemed to be enjoying it. I had the friendly urge to toss her off the mountain right then. Youth. It's intolerable sometimes.

"Choose again," she said firmly.

"Care to elaborate on that?"

"No," said Aenea. "That's the whole idea. Keep it simple. But name a category and you get the idea."

"Religion," I said.

"Choose again," said Aenea.

I laughed.

"I'm not being totally facetious here, Raul," she said. We began climbing again. A. Bettik seemed lost in thought.

"I know, kiddo," I said, although I had not been sure. "Categories . . . ah . . . political systems."

"Choose again."

"You don't think that the Pax is the ultimate evolution of human society? It's brought interstellar peace, fairly good government, and . . . oh, yeah . . . immortality to its citizens."

"It's time to choose again," said Aenea. "And speaking of our views of evolution . . ."

"What?"

"Choose again."

"Choose what again?" I said. "The direction of evolution?"

"No," said Aenea, "I mean our ideas about whether evolution *has* a direction. Most of our theories about evolution, for that matter."

"So, do you or don't you agree with Pope Teilhard . . . the Hyperion pilgrim, Father Duré . . . when he said three centuries ago that Teilhard de Chardin had been right, that the universe was evolving toward consciousness and a conjunction with the Godhead? What he called the Omega Point?"

Aenea looked at me. "You did do a lot of reading in the Taliesin library, didn't you?"

"Yeah."

"No, I don't agree with Teilhard . . . either the original Jesuit or the short-lived Pope. My mother knew both Father Duré and the current pretender, Father Hoyt, you know."

I blinked. I guess I had known that, but being reminded of the reality of that . . . of my friend's connections across the last three centuries . . . set me back a bit.

"Anyway," continued Aenea, "evolutionary science has really taken a bite in the butt over the last millennium. First the Core actively opposed investigation into it because of their fear of rapid human-designed genetic engineering—an explosion of our species into variant forms upon which the Core could not be parasitic. Then evolution and the biosciences were ignored by the Hegemony for centuries because of the Core's influence, and now the Pax is terrified of it."

"Why?" I said.

"Why is the Pax terrified of biological and genetic research?"

"No," I said, "I think I understand that. The Core wants to keep human beings in the form and shape they're comfortable with and so does the Church. They define being human largely by counting arms, legs, and so forth. But I mean why redefine evolution? Why open up the argument about direction or nondirection and so forth? Doesn't the ancient theory hold up pretty well?"

"No," said Aenea. We climbed several minutes in silence. Then she said, "Except for mystics such as the original Teilhard, most early evolution scientists were very careful not to think of evolution in terms of 'goals' or 'purposes.' That was religion, not science. Even the idea of a direction was anathema to the pre-Hegira scientists. They could only speak in terms of 'tendencies' in evolution, sort of statistical quirks that kept recurring."

"So?"

"So that was their shortsighted bias, just as Teilhard de Chardin's was his faith. There *are* directions in evolution."

"How do you know?" I said softly, wondering if she would answer.

She answered quickly. "Some of the data I saw before I was born," she said, "through my cybrid father's connections to the Core. The autonomous intelligences there have understood human evolution for many centuries, even while humans stayed ignorant. As hyper-hyperparasites, the AIs evolve only toward greater parasitism. They can only look at living things and their evolutionary curve and watch it . . . or try to stop it."

"So what are the directions in evolution?" I asked. "Toward greater intelligence? Toward some sort of godlike hive mind?" I was curious about her perception of the Lions and Tigers and Bears.

"Hive mind," said Aenea. "Ugghh. Can you conceive of anything more boring or distasteful?"

I said nothing. I had rather imagined that this was the direction of her teachings about learning the language of the dead and all that. I made a note to listen better the next time she taught.

"Almost everything interesting in the human experience is the result of an individual experiencing, experimenting, explaining, and sharing," said my young friend. "A hive mind would be the ancient television broadcasts, or life at the height of the datasphere . . . consensual idiocy."

"Okay," I said, still confused. "What direction *does* evolution take?"

"Toward more life," said Aenea. "Life likes life. It's pretty much that simple. But more amazingly, nonlife likes life as well . . . and wants to get into it."

"I don't understand," I said.

Aenea nodded. "Back on pre-Hegira Old Earth . . . in the 1920s . . . there was a geologist from a nation-state called Russia who understood this stuff. His name was Vladimir Vernadsky and he coined the phrase 'biosphere,' which—if things happen the way I think they will—should take on new meaning for both of us soon."

"Why?" I said.

"You'll see, my friend," said Aenea, touching my gloved hand with hers. "Anyway, Vernadsky wrote in 1926—'Atoms, once drawn into the torrent of living matter, do not readily leave it.' "

I thought about this for a moment. I did not know much science—what I had picked up came from Grandam and the Taliesin library—but this made sense to me.

"It was phrased more scientifically twelve hundred years ago as Dollo's Law," said Aenea. "The essence of it is that evolution doesn't back up . . . exceptions like the Old Earth whale trying to become a fish again after living as a land mammal are just the rare exception. Life moves on . . . it constantly finds new niches to invade."

"Yeah," I said. "Such as when humanity left Old Earth in its seedships and Hawking-drive vessels."

"Not really," said Aenea. "First of all, we did that prematurely because of the influence of the Core and the fact that Old Earth was dying because of a black hole in its belly . . . also the Core's work. Secondly, because of the Hawking drive, we could jump through our arm of the galaxy to find Earth-like worlds high on the Solmev Scale . . . most of

which we terraformed anyway and seeded with Old Earth life-forms, starting with soil bacteria and earthworms and moving up to the ducks you
used to hunt in the Hyperion fens."

I nodded. But I was thinking, *How else should we have done it as a
species moving out into space? What's wrong with going to places that
looked and smelled somewhat like home . . . especially when home
wasn't going to be there to go back to?*

"There's something more interesting in Vernadsky's observations and
Dollo's Law," said Aenea.

"What's that, kiddo?" I was still thinking about ducks.

"Life doesn't retreat."

"How so?" As soon as I asked the question I understood.

"Yeah," said my friend, seeing my understanding. "As soon as life
gets a foothold somewhere, it stays. You name it . . . arctic cold, the Old
Mars frozen desert, boiling hot springs, a sheer rockface such as here on
T'ien Shan, even in autonomous intelligence programs . . . once life gets
its proverbial foot in the door, it stays forever."

"So what are the implications of that?" I said.

"Simply that left to its own devices . . . which are clever devices
. . . life will someday fill the universe," said Aenea. "It will be a green
galaxy to begin with, then off to our neighboring clusters and galaxies."

"That's a disturbing thought," I said.

She paused to look at me. "Why, Raul? I think it's beautiful."

"Green planets I've seen," I said. "A green atmosphere is imaginable,
but weird."

She smiled. "It doesn't have to be just plants. Life adapts . . . birds,
men and women in flying machines, you and me in paragliders, people
adapted to flight . . ."

"That hasn't happened yet," I said. "But what I meant was, well, to
have a green galaxy, people and animals and . . ."

"And living machines," said Aenea. "And androids . . . artificial life
of a thousand forms . . ."

"Yeah, people, animals, machines, androids, whatever . . . would
have to adapt to space . . . I don't see how . . ."

"We have," said Aenea. "And more will before too long." We reached
the next three hundredth step and paused to pant.

"What other directions are there in evolution that we've ignored?" I
said when we began to climb again.

"Increasing diversity and complexity," said Aenea. "Scientists argued
back and forth about these directions for centuries, but there's no doubt
that evolution favors—in the very long run—both these attributes. And of
the two, diversity is the more important."

"Why?" I said. She must have been growing tired of that syllable. I
sounded like a three-year-old child even to myself.

"Scientists used to think that basic evolutionary designs kept multiplying," said Aenea. "That's called disparity. But that turned out not to be the case. Variety in basic plans tends to decrease as life's antientropic potential—evolution—increases. Look at all the orphans of Old Earth, for instance—same basic DNA, of course, but also the same basic plans: evolved from forms with tubular guts, radial symmetry, eyes, feeding mouths, two sexes . . . pretty much from the same mold."

"But I thought you said diversity was important," I said.

"It is," said Aenea. "But diversity is different than basic-plan disparity. Once evolution gets a good basic design, it tends to throw away the variants and concentrate on the near-infinite diversity within that design . . . thousands of related species . . . tens of thousands."

"Trilobites," I said, getting the idea.

"Yes," said Aenea, "and when . . ."

"Beetles," I said. "All those goddamn species of beetles."

Aenea grinned at me through her mask. "Precisely. And when . . ."

"Bugs," I said. "Every world I've been on has the same goddamn swarms of bugs. Mosquitoes. Endless varieties of . . ."

"You've got it," said Aenea. "Life shifts into high gear when the basic plan for an organism is settled and new niches open up. Life settles into those new niches by tweeking the diversity within the basic shape of those organisms. New species. There are thousands of new species of plants and animals that have come into existence in just the last millennium since interstellar flight started . . . and not all bio-engineered, some just adapted at a furious rate to the new Earth-like worlds they were dumped down on."

"Triaspens," I said, remembering just Hyperion. "Everblues. Womangrove root. Tesla trees?"

"They were native," said Aenea.

"So the diversity's good," I said, trying to find the original threads of this discussion.

"Diversity's good," agreed Aenea. "As I said, it lets life shift into high gear and get on with its mindless business of greening up the universe. But there's at least one Old Earth species that hasn't diversified much at all . . . at least not on the friendly worlds it colonized."

"Us," I said. "Humans."

Aenea nodded grimly. "We've been stuck in one species since our Cro-Magnon ancestors helped to wipe out the smarter Neanderthals," she said. "Now it's our chance to diversify rapidly, and institutions like the Hegemony, the Pax, and the Core are stopping it."

"Does the need to diversify extend to human institutions?" I said. "Religions? Social systems?" I was thinking about the people who had helped me on Vitus-Gray-Balianus B, Dem Ria, Dem Loa, and their families. I was thinking about the Amoiete Spectrum Helix and its complicated and convoluted beliefs.

"Absolutely," said Aenea. "Look over there."

A. Bettik had paused at a slab of marble upon which words were carved in Chinese and early Web English:

High rises the Eastern Peak
Soaring up to the blue sky.
Among the rocks—an empty hollow,
Secret, still, mysterious!
Uncarved and unhewn,
Screened by nature with a roof of clouds.

Time and Seasons, what things are you,
Bringing to my life ceaseless change?
I will lodge forever in this hollow
Where springs and autumns unheeded pass.

      —Tao-yun, wife of General Wang Ning-chih,
      A.D. 400

We climbed on. I thought that I could see something red at the top of this next flight of stairs. The South Gate of Heaven and entry to the summit slope? It was about time.

"Wasn't that beautiful though?" I said, speaking of the poem. "Isn't continuity like that as important or more important in human institutions as diversity?"

"It's important," agreed Aenea. "But that's almost all humanity has been doing for the last millennium, Raul . . . re-creating Old Earth institutions and ideas on different worlds. Look at the Hegemony. Look at the Church and the Pax. Look at this world . . ."

"T'ien Shan?" I said. "I think it's wonderful . . ."

"So do I," said Aenea. "But it's all borrowed. The Buddhism has evolved a bit . . . at least away from idolatry and ritual back to the open-mindedness that was its earliest hallmark . . . but everything else is pretty much an attempt to recapture things lost with Old Earth."

"Such as?" I said.

"Such as the language, dress, the names of the mountains, local customs . . . hell, Raul, even this pilgrimage trail and the Temple of the Jade Emperor, if we ever get there."

"You mean there was a T'ai Shan mountain on Old Earth?" I said.

"Absolutely," said Aenea. "With its own City of Peace and Heavenly Gates and Mouth of the Dragon. Confucius climbed it more than three thousand years ago. But the Old Earth stairway had just seven thousand steps."

"I wish we'd climbed it instead," I said, wondering if I could keep climbing. The steps were short, but there had been a hell of a lot of them. "I see your point though."

Aenea nodded. "It's wonderful to preserve tradition, but a healthy organism evolves . . . culturally and physically."

"Which brings us back to evolution," I said. "What are the other directions, tendencies, goals, or whatever that you said had been ignored the last few centuries?"

"There are just a few more," said Aenea. "One is an ever increasing number of individuals. Life likes gazillions of species, but it absolutely loves hypergazillions of individuals. In a sense, the universe is tooled up for individuals. There was a book in the Taliesin library called *Evolving Hierarchical Systems* by an Old Earth guy named Stanley Salthe. Did you see it?"

"No, I must have missed it when I was reading those early twenty-first-century holoporn novels."

"Uh-huh," said Aenea. "Well, Salthe put it sort of neatly—'An indefinite number of unique individuals can exist in a finite material world if they are nested within each other and that world is expanding.'"

"Nested within each other," I repeated, thinking about it. "Yeah, I get it. Like the Old Earth bacteria in our gut, and the paramecia we've dragged into space, and the other cells in our bodies . . . more worlds, more people . . . yeah."

"The trick is more people," said Aenea. "We have hundreds of billions, but between the Fall and the Pax, the actual human population in the galaxy—not counting Ousters—has leveled off in the last few hundred years."

"Well, birth control is important," I said, repeating what everyone on Hyperion had been taught. "I mean, especially with the cruciform capable of keeping people alive for centuries and centuries . . ."

"Exactly," said Aenea. "With artificial immortality comes more stagnation . . . physical and cultural. It's a given."

I frowned. "But that's not a reason to deny people the chance for extended life, is it?"

Aenea's voice seemed remote, as if she were contemplating something much larger. "No," she said at last, "not in itself."

"What are the evolutionary directions?" I asked, seeing the red pagoda come closer above us and praying that the conversation would keep my mind off collapsing, rolling back down the twenty-some thousand steps we had climbed.

"Just three more worth mentioning," said Aenea. "Increasing specialization, increasing codependency, and increasing evolvability. All of these are really important, but the last is most so."

"How do you mean, kiddo?"

"I mean that evolution itself evolves. It has to. Evolvability is in itself an inherited survival trait. Systems—living and otherwise—have to learn how to evolve and, to some extent, control the direction and rate of their own evolution. We . . . I mean the human species . . . were on the verge of doing that a thousand years ago, and the Core took it away from us. At least from most of us."

"What do you mean, 'most of us'?"

"I promise that you'll see in a few days, Raul."

We reached the South Gate of Heaven and passed through its arched entry, a red arch under a golden pagoda roof. Beyond it was the Heavenly Way, a gentle slope that ran to the summit that was just visible. The Heavenly Way was nothing more than path on bare, black rock. We could have been walking on an airless moon like Old Earth's—the conditions here were about as amenable to life. I started to say something to Aenea about this being a niche that life hadn't stuck its foot into, when she led the way off the path to a small stone temple set in among the sharp crags and fissures a few hundred meters below the summit. There was an air lock that looked so ancient it appeared to have come out on one of the earliest seedships. Amazingly, it worked when she activated the press pad and the three of us stood in it until it cycled and the inner door opened. We stepped inside.

It was a small room and almost bare except for an ornate bronze pot holding fresh flowers, some sprigs of green on a low dais, and a beautiful statue—once gold—of a life-size woman in robes that appeared to be made of gold. The woman was fat-cheeked and of pleasant demeanor—a sort of female Buddha—and she looked to be wearing a gilded crown of leaves and had an oddly Christian halo of hammered gold behind her head.

A. Bettik pulled off his helmet and said, "The air is good. Air pressure more than adequate."

Aenea and I folded back our skinsuit cowls. It was a pleasure to breathe regularly.

There were incense tapers and a box of matches at the statue's foot. Aenea went to one knee and used a match to light one of the tapers. The smell of incense was very strong.

"This is the Princess of the Azure Clouds," she said, smiling up at the smiling gold face. "The goddess of the dawn. By lighting this, I've just made an offering for the birth of grandchildren."

I started to smile and then froze. *She has a child. My beloved has already had a child.* My throat tightened and I looked away, but Aenea walked over and took my arm.

"Shall we eat lunch?" she said.

I had forgotten about our brown bag lunch. It would have been difficult to eat it through our helmets and osmosis masks.

We sat in the dim light, in the windowless room, amid the floating smoke and scent of incense, and ate the sandwiches packed by the monks.

"Where now?" I said as Aenea began recycling the inner lock.

"I have heard that there is a precipice on the eastern edge of the summit called Suicide Cliff," said A. Bettik. "It used to be a place for serious sacrifice. Jumping from it is said to provide instant communion with the Jade Emperor and to insure that your offering request is honored. If you really want to guarantee grandchildren, you might jump from there."

I stared at the android. I was never sure if he had a sense of humor or simply a skewed personality.

Aenea laughed. "Let's walk to the Temple of the Jade Emperor first," she said. "See if anyone's home."

Outside, I was struck first by the isolation of the skinsuit and the airless clarity of everything. The osmosis mask had gone almost opaque because of the unfiltered ferocity of the midday sun at this altitude. Shadows were harsh.

We were about fifty meters from the summit and the temple when a form stepped out of the blackness of shadow behind a boulder and blocked our way. I thought *Shrike* and foolishly clenched my hands into fists before I saw what it was.

A very tall man stood before us, dressed in lance-slashed, vacuum combat armor. Standard Pax Fleet Marine and Swiss Guard issue. I could see his face through the impact-proof visor—his skin was black, his features strong, and his short-cropped hair was white. There were fresh and livid scars on his dark face. His eyes were not friendly. He was carrying a Marine-class, multipurpose assault rifle, and now he raised it and leveled it at us. His transmission was on the skinsuit band.

"Stop!"

We stopped.

The giant did not seem to know what to do next. *The Pax finally have us,* was my first thought.

Aenea took a step forward. "Sergeant Gregorius?" came her voice on the skinsuit band.

The man cocked his head but did not lower the weapon. I had no doubt that the rifle would work perfectly in hard vacuum—either flechette cloud, energy lance, charged particle beam, solid slug, or hyper-k. The muzzle was aimed at my beloved's face.

"How do you know my . . ." began the giant and then seemed to rock backward. "You're her. The one. The girl we sought for so long, across so many systems. Aenea."

"Yes," said Aenea. "Are there others who survived?"

"Three," said the man she had called Gregorius. He gestured to his right and I could just make out a black scar on black rock, with blackened remnants of something that might have been a starship escape bulb.

"Is Father Captain de Soya among them?" said Aenea.

I remembered the name. I remembered de Soya's voice on the dropship radio when he had found us and saved us from Nemes and then let us go on God's Grove almost ten of his and Aenea's years ago.

"Aye," said Sergeant Gregorius, "the captain's alive, but just barely. He was burned bad on the poor old *Raphael*. He'd be atoms with her, if he hadn't passed out an' given me the opportunity to drag him to a lifeboat. The other two are hurt, but the father-captain's dyin'." He lowered the rifle and leaned on it wearily. "Dyin' the true death . . . we have no resurrection crèche and the darlin' father-captain made me promise to slag him to atoms when he went, rather than let him be resurrected a mindless idiot."

Aenea nodded. "Can you take me to him? I need to talk to him."

Gregorius shouldered the heavy weapon and looked suspiciously at A. Bettik and me. "And these two . . ."

"This is my dear friend," said Aenea, touching A. Bettik's arm. She took my hand. "And this is my beloved."

The giant only nodded at this, turned, and led the way up the final stretch of slope to the summit to the Temple of the Jade Emperor.

Part Three

22

ON HYPERION, SEVERAL hundred light-years toward galactic center from the events and the people on T'ien Shan, a forgotten old man rose out of the dreamless sleep of long-term cryogenic fugue and slowly became aware of his surroundings. His surroundings were a no-touch suspension bed, a gaggle of life-support modules encircling him and nuzzling him like so many feeding raptors, and uncountable tubes, wires, and umbilicals finishing their work of feeding him, detoxifying his blood, stimulating his kidneys, carrying antibiotics to fight infection, monitoring his life signs, and generally invading his body and dignity in order to revive him and keep him alive.

"Ah, fuck," rasped the old man. "Waking up is a fucking, goddamn, dung-eating, corpse-buggering, shit storm of a nightmare for the terminally old. I'd pay a million marks if I could just get out of bed and go piss."

"And good morning to you, M. Silenus," said the female android monitoring the old poet's life signs on the floating biomonitor. "You seem to be in good spirits today."

"Bugger all blue-skinned wenches," mumbled Martin Silenus. "Where are my teeth?"

"You haven't grown them back yet, M. Silenus," said the android. She was named A. Raddik and was a little over three centuries old . . . less than one-third the age of the ancient human mummy floating in the suspension bed.

"No need to," mumbled the old man. "Won't fucking be awake long enough. How long was I under?"

"Two years, three months, eight days," said A. Raddik.

Martin Silenus peered up at the open sky above his tower. The canvas roof on this highest level of his stone turret had been rolled back. Deep lapis blue. The low light of early morning or late evening. The shimmer and

flit of radiant gossamers not yet illuminating their fragile half-meter butterfly wings.

"What season?" managed Silenus.

"Late spring," said the female android. Other blue-skinned servants
of the old poet moved in and out of the circular room, bent on obscure
errands. Only A. Raddik monitored the last stages of the poet's revival
from fugue.

"How long since they left?" He did not have to specify who the
"they" were. A. Raddik knew that the old poet meant not only Raul Endymion, the last visitor to their abandoned university city, but the girl
Aenea—whom Silenus had known three centuries earlier—and whom he
still hoped to see again someday.

"Nine years, eight months, one week, one day," said A. Raddik. "All
Earth standard, of course."

"Hggrhh," grunted the old poet. He continued peering at the sky. The
sunlight was filtered through canvas rolled to the east, pouring light onto
the south wall of the stone turret while not striking him directly, but the
brightness still brought tears to his ancient eyes. "I've become a thing of
darkness," he mumbled. "Like Dracula. Rising from my fucking grave every few years to check on the world of the living."

"Yes, M. Silenus," agreed A. Raddik, changing several settings on the
control panel.

"Shut up, wench," said the poet.

"Yes, M. Silenus."

The old man moaned. "How long until I can get into my hoverchair,
Raddik?"

The hairless android pursed her lips. "Two more days, M. Silenus.
Perhaps two and a half."

"Aw, hell and damn," muttered Martin Silenus. "Recovery gets
slower each time. One of these times, I won't wake at all . . . the fugue
machinery won't bring me back."

"Yes, M. Silenus," agreed the android. "Each cold sleep is harder on
your system. The resuscitation and life-support equipment is quite old. It is
true that you will not survive many more awakenings."

"Oh, shut up," growled Martin Silenus. "You are a morbid, gloomy
old bitch."

"Yes, M. Silenus."

"How long have you been with me, Raddik?"

"Two hundred forty-one years, eleven months, nineteen days," said
the android. "Standard."

"And you still haven't learned to make a decent cup of coffee."

"No, M. Silenus."

"But you *have* put a pot on, correct?"

"Yes, M. Silenus. As per your standing instructions."

"Fucking aye," said the poet.

"But you will not be able to ingest liquids orally for at least another twelve hours, M. Silenus," said A. Raddik.

"Arrrggghhh!" said the poet.

"Yes, M. Silenus."

After several minutes in which it looked like the old man had drifted back to sleep, Martin Silenus said, "Any word from the boy or child?"

"No, sir," said A. Raddik. "But then, of course, we only have access to the in-system Pax com network these days. And most of their new encrypting is quite good."

"Any gossip about them?"

"None that we are sure of, M. Silenus," said the android. "Things are very troubled for the Pax . . . revolution in many systems, problems with their Outback Crusade against the Ousters, a constant movement of warships and troopships within the Pax boundaries . . . and there is talk of the viral contagion, highly coded and circumspect."

"The contagion," repeated Martin Silenus and smiled a toothless smile. "The child, I would guess."

"Quite possibly, M. Silenus," said A. Raddik, "although it is quite possible that there is a real viral plague on those worlds where . . ."

"No," said the poet, shaking his head almost violently. "It's Aenea. And her teachings. Spreading like the Beijing Flu. You don't remember the Beijing Flu, do you, Raddik?"

"No, sir," said the female, finishing her check of the readouts and setting the module to auto. "That was before my time. It was before anyone's time. Anyone but you, sir."

Normally there would have been some obscene outburst from the poet, but now he merely nodded. "I know. I'm a freak of nature. Pay your two bits and come into the sideshow . . . see the oldest man in the galaxy . . . see the mummy that walks and talks . . . sort of . . . see the disgusting thing that refuses to die. Bizarre, aren't I, A. Raddik?"

"Yes, M. Silenus."

The poet grunted. "Well, don't get your hopes up, blue thing. I'm not going to croak until I hear from Raul and Aenea. I have to finish the *Cantos* and I don't know the ending until they create it for me. How do I know what I think until I see what they do?"

"Precisely, M. Silenus."

"Don't humor me, blue woman."

"Yes, M. Silenus."

"The boy . . . Raul . . . asked me what his orders were almost ten years ago. I told him . . . save the child, Aenea . . . topple the Pax . . . destroy the Church's power . . . and bring the Earth back from wherever the fuck it went. He said he'd do it. Of course, he was stinking drunk with me at the time."

"Yes, M. Silenus."

"Well?" said the poet.

"Well what, sir?" said A. Raddik.

"Well, any sign of him having *done* any of the things he's promised, Raddik?"

"We know from the Pax transmissions nine years and eight months ago that he and the Consul's ship escaped Hyperion," said the android. "We can hope that the child Aenea is still safe and well."

"Yes, yes," muttered Silenus, waving his hand feebly, "but is the Pax toppled?"

"Not that we can notice, M. Silenus," said Raddik. "There were the mild troubles I mentioned earlier, and offworld, born-again tourism here on Hyperion is down a bit, but . . ."

"And the sodding Church is still in the zombie business?" demanded the poet, his thin voice stronger now.

"The Church remains ascendant," said A. Raddik. "More of the moor people and the mountain people accept the cruciform every year."

"Bugger all," said the poet. "And I don't suppose that Earth has returned to its proper place."

"We have not heard of that improbability occurring," said A. Raddik. "Of course, as I mentioned, our electronic eavesdropping is restricted to in-system transmissions these days, and since the Consul's ship left with M. Endymion and M. Aenea almost ten years ago, our decryption capabilities have not been . . ."

"All right, all right," said the old man, sounding terribly tired again. "Get me into my hoverchair."

"Not for another two days, at least, I am afraid," repeated the android, her voice gentle.

"Piss up a rope," said the ancient figure floating amid tubes and sensor wires. "Can you wheel me over to a window, Raddik? Please? I want to look at the spring chalma trees and the ruins of this old city."

"Yes, M. Silenus," said the android, sincerely pleased to be doing something for the old man besides keeping his body working.

Martin Silenus watched out the window for one full hour, fighting the tides of reawakening pain and the terrible sleepy urge to return to fugue state. It was morning light. His audio implants relayed the birdsong to him. The old poet thought of his adopted young niece, the child who had decided to call herself Aenea . . . he thought of his dear friend, Brawne Lamia, Aenea's mother . . . how they had been enemies for so long, had hated each other during parts of that last great Shrike Pilgrimage so long ago . . . about the stories they had told one another and the things they had seen . . . the Shrike in the Valley of the Time Tombs, its red eyes blazing . . . the scholar . . . what was his name? . . . Sol . . . Sol and his little swaddled brat aging backward to nothing . . . and the soldier . . . Kassad . . . that was it . . . Colonel Kassad. The old poet had never given a shit about the military . . . idiots, all of them . . . but Kassad had told an interesting tale, lived an interesting life . . . the other priest, Lenar Hoyt, had been a prig and an asshole, but the first one . . . the one with the sad eyes and the leather journal . . . Paul Duré . . . there had been a man worth writing about . . .

Martin Silenus drifted back to sleep with the light of morning flooding in on him, illuminating his countless wrinkles and translucent, parchment flesh, his blue veins visible and pulsing weakly in the rich light. He did not dream . . . but part of his poet's mind was already outlining the next sections of his never-finished *Cantos*.

SERGEANT GREGORIUS HAD not been exaggerating. Father Captain de Soya had been terribly battered and burned in the last battle of his ship, the *Raphael,* and was near death.

The sergeant had led A. Bettik, Aenea, and me into the temple. The structure was as strange as this encounter—outside there was a large, blank stone tablet, a smooth-faced monolith—Aenea mentioned briefly that it had been brought from Old Earth, had stood outside the original Temple of the Jade Emperor, and had never been inscribed during its thousands of years on the pilgrims' trail—while inside the sealed and pressurized courtyard of the echoing temple itself, a stone railing ran around a boulder that was actually the summit of T'ai Shan, the sacred Great Peak of the Middle Kingdom. There were small sleeping and eating rooms for pilgrims in the back of the huge temple, and it was in one of these that we found Father Captain de Soya and the other two survivors. Besides Gregorius and the dying de Soya, there were two other men—Carel Shan, a Weapons Systems Officer, now terribly burned and unconscious, and Hoagan Liebler, introduced by Sergeant Gregorius as the "former" Executive Officer of the *Raphael.* Liebler was the least injured of the four—his left forearm had been broken and was in a sling, but he had no burns or other impact bruises—but there was something quiet and withdrawn about the thin man, as if he were in shock or mulling something over.

Aenea's attention went immediately to Captain Federico de Soya.

The priest-captain was on one of the uncomfortable pilgrim cots, either stripped to the waist by Gregorius or he had lost all of his upper uniform in the blast and reentry. His trousers were shredded. His feet were bare. The only place on his body where he had not been terribly burned was the parasite cruciform on his chest—it was a healthy, sickening pink. De Soya's hair had been burned away and his face was splashed with liquid metal burns and radiation slashes, but I could see that he had been a striking man, mostly because of his liquid, troubled brown eyes, not dulled even by the pain that must be overwhelming him at this moment. Someone had applied burn cream, temporary dermheal, and liquid disinfectant all over the visible portions of the dying priest-captain's body—and started a standard lifeboat medkit IV drip—but this would have little effect on the outcome. I had seen combat burns like this before, not all from starship encounters. Three friends of mine during the Iceshelf fighting had died within hours when we had not been able to medevac them out. Their screams had been horrible to the point of unendurable.

Father Captain de Soya was not screaming. I could see that he was straining not to cry out from the pain, but he remained silent, his eyes focused only on the terrible concentration to silence until Aenea knelt by his side.

At first he did not recognize her. "Bettz?" he mumbled. "VIRO Argyle? No . . . you died at your station. The others too . . . Pol Denish . . . Elijah trying to free the aft boat . . . the young troopers when the starboard hull failed . . . but you look . . . familiar."

Aenea started to take his hand, saw that three of de Soya's fingers were missing, and set her own hand on the stained blanket next to his. "Father Captain," she said very softly.

"Aenea," said de Soya, his dark eyes really looking at her for the first time. "You're the child . . . so many months, chasing you . . . looked at you when you stepped out of the Sphinx. Incredible child. So glad you survived." His gaze moved to me. "You are Raul Endymion. I saw your Home Guard dossier. Almost caught up to you on Mare Infinitus." A wave of pain rolled over him and the priest-captain closed his eyes and bit into his burned and bloodied lower lip. After a moment, he opened his eyes and said to me, "I have something of yours. Personal gear on the *Raphael*. The Holy Office let me have it after they ended their investigation. Sergeant Gregorius will give it to you after I am dead."

I nodded, having no idea what he was talking about.

"Father Captain de Soya," whispered Aenea, "Federico . . . can you hear and understand me?"

"Yes," murmured the priest-captain. "Painkillers . . . said no to Sergeant Gregorius . . . didn't want to slip away forever in my sleep. Not go gently." The pain returned. I saw that much of de Soya's neck and chest had cracked and opened, like burned scales. Pus and fluid flowed down to the blankets beneath him. The man closed his eyes until the tide of agony receded; it took longer this time. I thought of how I had folded up under just the pain of a kidney stone and tried to imagine this man's torment. I could not.

"Father Captain," said Aenea, "there is a way for you to live . . ."

De Soya shook his head vigorously, despite the pain that must have caused. I noticed that his left ear was little more than carbon. Part of it flaked off on the pillow as I watched. "No!" he cried. "I told Gregorius . . . no partial resurrection . . . idiot, sexless idiot . . ." A cough that might have been a laugh from behind scorched teeth. "Had enough of that as a priest. Anyway . . . tired . . . tired of . . ." His blackened stubs of fingers on his right hand batted at the pink double cross on his flaked and oozing chest. "Let the thing die with me."

Aenea nodded. "I didn't mean be reborn, Father Captain. I meant *live*. Be healed."

De Soya was trying to blink, but his eyelids were burned ragged. "Not a prisoner of the Pax . . ." he managed, finding the air to speak only each time he exhaled with a wracking gasp. "Will . . . execute . . . me. I deserve . . . it. Killed many innocent . . . men . . . women . . . in defense of . . . friends."

Aenea leaned closer so that he could focus on her eyes. "Father Captain, the Pax is still after us as well. But we have a ship. It has an autosurgeon."

Sergeant Gregorius stepped forward from where he had been leaning wearily against the wall. The man named Carel Shan remained unconscious. Hoag Liebler, apparently lost in some private misery, did not respond.

Aenea had to repeat it before de Soya understood.

"Ship?" said the priest-captain. "The ancient Hegemony ship you escaped in? Not armed, was it?"

"No," said Aenea. "It never has been."

De Soya shook his head again. "There must have been . . . fifty archangel-class . . . ships . . . jumped us. Got . . . a few . . . rest . . . still there. No chance . . . get . . . to . . . any translation point . . . before . . ." He closed his torn eyelids again while the pain washed over him. This time, it seemed, it almost carried him away. He returned as if from a far place.

"It's all right," whispered Aenea. "I'll worry about that. You'll be in the doc-in-the-box. But there's something you would have to do."

Father Captain de Soya seemed too tired to speak, but he shifted his head to listen.

"You have to renounce the cruciform," said Aenea. "You have to surrender this type of immortality."

The priest-captain's blackened lips pulled back from his teeth. "Gladly . . ." he rasped. "But sorry . . . can't . . . once accepted . . . cruciform . . . can't be . . . surrendered."

"Yes," whispered Aenea, "it can. If you choose that, I can make it go away. Our autosurgeon is old. It would not be able to heal you with the cruciform parasite throughout your body. We have no resurrection crèche aboard the ship . . ."

De Soya reached for her then, his flaking and three-fingerless hand still gripping tightly the sleeve of her therm jacket. "Doesn't matter . . . doesn't matter if I die . . . get it off. Get if *off*. Will die a real . . . Catholic . . . again . . . if you . . . can help me . . . get it . . . OFF!" He almost shouted the final word.

Aenea turned to the sergeant. "Do you have a cup or glass?"

"There's the mug in the medkit," rumbled the giant, fumbling for it. "But we have no water . . ."

"I brought some," said my friend and removed the insulated bottle from her belt.

I expected wine, but it was only the water we had bottled up before leaving the Temple Hanging in Air those endless hours ago. Aenea did not bother with alcohol swabs or sterile lancets; she beckoned me closer, removed the hunting knife from my belt, and drew the blade across three of her fingertips in a swift move that made me flinch. Her blood flowed red. Aenea dipped her fingers in the clear plastic drinking mug for just a second, but long enough to send currents of thick crimson spiraling and twisting in the water.

"Drink this," she said to Father Captain de Soya, helping to lift the dying man's head.

The priest-captain drank, coughed, drank again. His eyes closed when she eased him back onto the stained pillow.

"The cruciform will be gone within twenty-four hours," whispered my friend.

Father Captain de Soya made that rough chuckling sound again. "I'll be dead within an hour."

"You'll be in the autosurgeon within fifteen minutes," said Aenea, touching his better hand. "Sleep now . . . but don't die on me, Federico de Soya . . . don't die on me. We have much to talk about. And you have one great service to perform for me . . . for us."

Sergeant Gregorius was standing closer. "M. Aenea . . ." he said, halted, shuffled his feet, and tried again. "M. Aenea, may I partake of that . . . water?"

Aenea looked at him. "Yes, Sergeant . . . but once you drink, you can never again carry a cruciform. Never. There will be no resurrection. And there are other . . . side effects."

Gregorius waved away any further discussion. "I have followed my captain for ten years. I will follow him now." The giant drank deeply of the pinkish water.

De Soya's eyes had been closed, and I had assumed that he was asleep or unconscious from the pain, but now he opened them and said to Gregorius, "Sergeant, would you please bring M. Endymion the parcel we dragged from the lifeboat?"

"Aye, Capt'n," said the giant and rummaged through the litter of debris in one corner of the room. He handed me a sealed tube, a little over a meter high.

I looked at the priest-captain. De Soya seemed to be floating between delirium and shock. "I'll open it when he's better," I said to the sergeant.

Gregorius nodded, carried the glass over to Carel Shan, and poured some water into the unconscious Weapons Officer's gaping mouth. "Carel may die before your ship arrives," said the sergeant. He looked up. "Or does the ship have two doc-in-the-boxes?"

"No," said Aenea, "but the one we have has three compartments. You can heal your wounds as well."

Gregorius shrugged. He went to the man named Liebler and offered the glass. The thin man with the broken arm only looked at it.

"Perhaps later," said Aenea.

Gregorius nodded and handed the glass back to her. "The XO was a prisoner on our ship," said the sergeant. "A spy. An enemy of the captain. Father-captain still risked his last life to get Liebler out of the brig . . . got his burns retrieving him. I don't think Hoag quite understands what's happened."

Liebler looked up then. "I understand it," he said softly. "I just don't *understand* it."

Aenea stood. "Raul, I hope you haven't lost the ship communicator."

I fumbled in my pockets only a few seconds before coming up with the com unit/diskey journal. "I'll go outside and tightbeam visually," I said. "Use the skinsuit jack. Any instructions for the ship?"

"Tell it to hurry," said Aenea.

IT WAS TRICKY getting the semiconscious de Soya and the unconscious Carel Shan to the ship. They had no spacesuits and it was still near vacuum outside. Sergeant Gregorius told us that he had used an inflatable transfer ball to drag them from the lifeboat wreckage to the Temple of the Jade Emperor, but the ball itself had been damaged. I had about fifteen minutes to think about the problem before the ship became visible, descending on its EM repellors and blue fusion-flame tail, so when it arrived I ordered it to land directly in front of the temple air lock, to morph its escalator ramp to the air-lock door, and to extend its containment field around the door and stairway. Then it was just a matter of getting the float litters from the medbay in the ship and transferring the men to them without hurting them too much. Shan remained unconscious, but some of de Soya's skin peeled away as we moved him onto the litter. The priest-captain stirred and opened his eyes but did not cry out.

After months on T'ien Shan, the interior of the Consul's ship was still familiar, but familiar like a recurring dream one has about a house one has lived in long ago. After de Soya and the Weapons Officer were tucked away in the autosurgeon, it was strange to stand on the carpeted holopit deck with its ancient Steinway piano with Aenea and A. Bettik there as always, but also with a burned giant still holding his assault weapon and the former XO brooding silently on the holopit stairs.

"Diagnostics completed on the autosurgeons," said the ship. "The presence of the cross-shaped parasite nodes makes treatment impossible at this time. Shall I terminate treatment or commence cryogenic fugue?"

"Cryogenic fugue," said Aenea. "The doc-in-the-box should be able to operate on them in twenty-four hours. Please keep them alive and in stasis until then."

"Affirmative," said the ship. And then, "M. Aenea? M. Endymion?"

"Yes," I said.

"Are you aware that I was tracked by long-range sensors from the time I left the third moon? There are at least thirty-seven Pax warships heading this way as we speak. One is already in parking orbit around this planet and another has just committed the highly unusual tactic of jumping on Hawking drive within the system's gravity well."

"Okay," said Aenea. "Don't worry about it."

"I believe they intend to intercept and destroy us," said the ship. "And they can do this before we clear atmosphere."

"We know," sighed Aenea. "I repeat, don't worry about it."

"Affirmative," said the ship in the most businesslike tone I had ever heard from it. "Destination?"

"The bonsai fissure six kilometers east of Hsuan-k'ung Ssu," said Aenea. "East of the Temple Hanging in Air. Quickly." She glanced at her wrist chronometer. "But stay low, Ship. Within the cloud layers."

"The phosgene clouds or the water particle clouds?" inquired the ship.

"The lowest possible," said my friend. "Unless the phosgene clouds create a problem for you."

"Of course not," said the ship. "Would you like me to plot a course that would take us through the acid seas? It would make no difference to the Pax deep radar, but it could be done with only a small addition of time and . . ."

"No," interrupted Aenea, "just the clouds."

We watched on the holopit sphereview as the ship flung itself off Suicide Cliff and dived ten kilometers through gray cloud and then into green clouds. We would be at the fissure within minutes.

We all sat on the carpeted holopit steps then. I realized that I still had the sealed tube that de Soya had given me. I rotated it through my hands.

"Go ahead and open it," said Sergeant Gregorius. The big man was slowly removing the outer layers of his scarred combat armor. Lance burns had melted the lower layers. I was afraid to see his chest and left arm.

I hesitated. I had said that I'd wait until the priest-captain had recovered.

"Go ahead," Gregorius said again. "The Captain's been waiting to give this back to you for nine years."

I had no idea what it could be. How could this man have known he would see me someday? I owned nothing . . . how could he have something of mine to return?

I broke the seal on the tube and looked within. Some sort of tightly rolled fabric. With a slow realization, I pulled the thing out and unrolled it on the floor.

Aenea laughed delightedly. "My God," she said. "In all my various dreams about this time, I never foresaw this. How wonderful."

It was the hawking mat . . . the flying carpet that had carried Aenea and me from the Valley of the Time Tombs almost ten years earlier. I had lost it . . . it took me a second or two to remember. I had lost it on Mare Infinitus nine years ago when the Pax lieutenant I had been fighting had pulled a knife, cut me, pushed me off the mat into the sea. What had happened next? The lieutenant's own men on the floating sea platform had mistakenly killed him with a cloud of flechette darts, the dead man had fallen into the violet sea, and the hawking mat had flown on . . . no, I remembered that someone on the platform had intercepted it.

"How did the father-captain get it?" I asked, knowing the answer as soon as I articulated the question. De Soya had been our relentless pursuer then.

Gregorius nodded. "The Father-Captain used it to find your blood and DNA samples. It's how we got your Pax service record from Hyperion. If we'd had pressure suits, I would have used the damn thing to get us off that airless mountain."

"You mean it works?" I tapped the flight threads. The hawking mat— more tattered than I remembered it—hovered ten centimeters off the floor. "I'll be damned," I said.

"We're rising to the fissure at the coordinates you gave me," came the ship's voice.

The holopit view cleared and showed the Jo-kung ridge rushing past. We slowed and hovered a hundred meters out. We had returned to the same forested valley fissure where the ship had dropped me more than three months earlier. Only now the green valley was filled with people. I saw Theo, Lhomo, many of the others from the Temple Hanging in Air. The ship floated lower, hovered, and waited for directions.

"Lower the escalator," said Aenea. "Let them all aboard."

"May I remind you," said the ship, "that I have fugue couches and life support for a maximum of six people for an extended interstellar jump? There are at least fifty people there on the . . ."

"Lower the escalator and let them all aboard," commanded Aenea. "Immediately."

The ship did as it was told without another word. Theo led the refugees up the ramp and the circular stairs to where we waited.

Most of those who had stayed behind at the Temple Hanging in Air were there: many of the temple monks, the Tromo Trochi of Dhomu, the ex-soldier Gyalo Thondup, Lhomo Dondrub—we were delighted to see that his paraglider had brought him safely back, and from his grins and hugs, the delight was reciprocated—Abbot Kempo Ngha Wang Tashi, Chim Din, Jigme Taring, Kuku and Kay, George and Jigme, the Dalai Lama's brother Labsang, the brickworkers Viki and Kim, Overseer Tsipon Shakabpa, Rimsi Kyipup—less dour than I had ever seen him—and high riggers Haruyuki and Kenshiro, as well as the bamboo experts Voytek and Janusz, even the Mayor of Jo-kung, Charles Chi-kyap Kempo. But no Dalai Lama. And the Dorje Phamo was also missing.

"Rachel went back to fetch them," said Theo, the last to come aboard. "The Dalai Lama insisted on being the last to leave and the Sow stayed behind to keep him company until it was time to go. But they should have been back by now. I was just ready to go back along the ledge to check . . ."

Aenea shook her head. "We'll all go."

There was no way to get everyone seated or situated. People milled on the stairways, stood around the library level, had wandered up to the bedroom at the apex of the ship to look outside via the viewing walls, while others were on the fugue cubby level and down in the engine room.

"Let's go, Ship," said Aenea. "The Temple Hanging in Air. Make a direct approach."

For the ship, a direct approach was a burst of thruster fire, a lob fifteen klicks into the atmosphere, and then a vertical drop with repellors and main engine burning at the last second. The entire process took about thirty seconds, but while the internal containment field kept us from being smashed to jelly, the view through the clear apex walls must have been disorienting for those watching upstairs. Aenea, A. Bettik, Theo, and I were watching the holopit and even that small view almost sent me to clutching the bulkheads or clinging to the carpet. We dropped lower and hovered fifty meters above the temple complex.

"Ah, damn," said Theo.

The view had shown us a man falling to his death in the clouds below. There was no possibility of swooping down to catch him. One second he was freefalling, the next he had been swallowed by the clouds.

"Who was it?" said Theo.

"Ship," said Aenea. "Playback and enhance."

Carl Linga William Eiheji, the Dalai Lama's bodyguard.

A few seconds later several figures emerged from the Right Meditation pavilion onto the highest platform, the one I had helped build to Aenea's plans less than a month ago.

"Shit," I said aloud. The Nemes-thing was carrying the Dalai Lama in one hand, holding him over the edge of the platform. Behind her . . . behind it . . . came her male and female clone-siblings. Then Rachel and the Dorje Phamo stepped out of the shadows onto the platform.

Aenea gripped my arm. "Raul, do you want to come outside with me?"

She had activated the balcony beyond the Steinway, but I knew that this was not all that she meant. "Of course," I said, thinking, *Is this her death? Is this what she has foreseen since before birth? Is it my death?* "Of course I'll come," I said.

A. Bettik and Theo started out onto the ship's balcony with us. "No," said Aenea. "Please." She took the android's hand for a second. "You can see everything from inside, my friend."

"I would prefer to be with you, M. Aenea," said A. Bettik.

Aenea nodded. "But this is for Raul and me alone."

A. Bettik lowered his head a second and returned to the holopit image. None of the rest of the score of people in the library level and on the spiral stairs said a word. The ship was dead silent. I walked out onto the balcony with my friend.

Nemes still held the boy out over the drop. We were twenty meters above her and her siblings now. I wondered idly how high they could jump.

"Hey!" shouted Aenea.

Nemes looked up. I was reminded that the effect of her gaze was like being stared at by empty eye sockets. Nothing human lived there.

"Put him down," said Aenea.

Nemes smiled and dropped the Dalai Lama, catching him with her left hand at the last second. "Be careful what you ask for, child," said the pale woman.

"Let him and the other two go and I'll come down," said Aenea.

Nemes shrugged. "You won't leave here anyway," she said, her voice not raised but perfectly audible across the gap.

"Let them go and I'll come down," repeated Aenea.

Nemes shrugged but threw the Dalai Lama across the platform like an unwanted wad of paper.

Rachel ran to the boy, saw that he was hurt and bleeding but alive, lifted him, and turned back angrily toward Nemes and her siblings.

"NO!" shouted Aenea. I had never heard her use that tone before. It froze both Rachel and me in our tracks.

"Rachel," said Aenea, her voice level again, "please bring His Holiness and the Dorje Phamo up to the ship now." It was polite, but an imperative that I could not have resisted. Rachel did not.

Aenea gave the command and the ship dropped lower, morphing and extending a stairway from the balcony. Aenea started down. I hurried to follow her. We stepped onto the bonsai cedar platform . . . I had helped to place all of the planks . . . and Rachel led the child and old woman past us, up the stairway. Aenea touched Rachel's head as the other woman went past. The stairway flowed uphill and shaped itself back into a balcony. Theo and A. Bettik joined Rachel and the Dorje Phamo on it. Someone had taken the bleeding child into the ship.

We stood two meters from Rhadamanth Nemes. Her siblings stepped up to the creature's side.

"This is not quite complete," said Nemes. "Where is your . . . ah, there."

The Shrike flowed from the shadows of the pavilion. I say "flowed," for although it moved, I had not seen it walk.

I was clenching and unclenching my hands. Everything was wrong for this showdown. I had peeled off my therm jacket in the ship, but still wore the stupid skinsuit and climbing harness, although most of the hardware had been left in the ship. The harness and multiple layers would still slow me down.

Slow me down from what? I thought. I had seen Nemes fight. Or rather, I had *not* seen her. When she and the Shrike had struggled on God's Grove, there had been a blur, then explosions, then nothing. She could decapitate Aenea and have my guts for garters before I got my hands clenched into fists.

Fists. The ship was unarmed, but I had left it with Sergeant Gregorius's Swiss Guard assault rifle still on the library level. The first thing they had taught us in the Home Guard was never to fight with fists when you could scrounge up a weapon.

I looked around. The platform was clean and bare, not even a railing I could wrench free to use as a club. This structure was too well built to rip anything loose.

I glanced at the cliff wall to our left. No loose rocks there. There were a few pitons and climbing bolts still imbedded in the fissures there, I knew—we had clipped on to them while building this level and pavilion and we hadn't got around to clearing all of them—but they were driven in far too tight for me to pull out and use as a weapon, although Nemes could probably do so with one finger. And what good would a piton or chock nut do against this monster?

There were no weapons to find here. I would die bare-handed. I hoped that I would get one blow in before she took me down . . . or at least one swing.

Aenea and Nemes were looking only at each other. Nemes did not spare more than a glance at the Shrike ten paces to her right. The female-thing said, "You know that I am not going to take you back to the Pax, don't you, child bitch?"

"Yes," said Aenea. She returned the creature's stare with a solid intensity.

Nemes smiled. "But you believe that your spiked creature will save you again."

"No," said Aenea.

"Good," said Nemes. "Because it will not." She nodded to her clone-siblings.

I know their names now—Scylla and Briareus. And I know what I saw next.

I should not have been able to see it, for all three of the Nemes-things phase-shifted at that instant. There should have been the briefest glimpse of a chrome blur, then chaos, then nothing . . . but Aenea reached over and touched the back of my neck, there was the usual electric tingle I received whenever her skin touched mine, and suddenly the light was different—deeper, darker—and the air was as thick as water around us. I realized that my heart did not seem to be beating and that I did not blink or take a breath. As alarming as that sounds, it seemed irrelevant then.

Aenea's voice whispered from the hearpatch on my folded-back skin-suit cowl . . . or perhaps it spoke directly through her touch on my neck. I could not tell. *We cannot phase-shift with them or use it to fight them,* she said. *It is an abuse of the energy of the Void Which Binds. But I can help us watch this.*

And what we watched was incredible enough.

At Nemes's command, Scylla and Briareus threw themselves at the Shrike, while the Hyperion demon raised four arms and threw itself in the direction of Nemes—only to be intercepted by the siblings. Even with our altered vision—the ship hanging frozen in midair, our friends on the balcony frozen into unblinking statues, a bird above the cliff face locked in to the thick air like an insect in amber—the sudden movement of Shrike and the two cloned creatures was almost too fast to follow.

There was a terrible impact just a meter short of Nemes, who had turned into a silver-surfaced effigy of herself, and who did not flinch. Briareus threw a blow that I am convinced would have split our ship in two. It reverberated off the Shrike's thorned neck with a sound like an underwater earthquake played back in slow motion, and then Scylla kicked the Shrike's legs out from under it. The Shrike went down, but not before two of its arms seized Scylla and two other razor-fingered claws sank deep into Briareus.

The Nemes siblings seemed to welcome the embrace, throwing themselves onto the tumbling Shrike with clacking teeth and flying nails. I could see that the hurtling edges of their rigid hands and forearms were razor-sharp, guillotine surfaces sharper than the Shrike's blades and thorns.

The three beat and chewed on each other in a wild frenzy, rolling across the platform, throwing bonsai cedar chips three meters into the air, and slamming against the rock wall. In a second, all three were on their feet, the Shrike's great jaws clamping on Briareus's neck even as Scylla slashed at one of the creature's four arms, bent it backward, and seemed to break it at a joint. Still holding Briareus in its jaws, the huge teeth chewing and scraping at the silver form's head, the Shrike whirled to confront Scylla, but by then both clone-siblings had their hands on the blades and thorns on the Shrike's skull, bending it backward until I waited to hear the neck snap and see its head roll away.

Instead, Nemes somehow communicated, *Now! Do it!* and without an instant's hesitation, the two siblings threw themselves away from the cliff face, toward the railing at the abyss-end side of the platform. I saw what they were going to do—throw the Shrike into space, just as they had done to the Dalai Lama's bodyguard.

Perhaps the Shrike saw this as well, for the tall creature slammed the two chrome bodies against it, its chest spikes and wrist thorns sinking deep into the forcefields around the struggling, clawing siblings. The trio whirled and tumbled and bounced up like some demented, three-part wind-up toy locked into hyperfast berserk mode, until finally the Shrike with its kicking, clawing, visibly impaled forms slammed into the sturdy cedar railing, tore through it as though it were wet cardboard, and went hurtling out over and into the drop, still fighting.

Aenea and I watched as the tall silver form with flashing spikes and the shorter silver forms with flailing limbs fell, fell, grew smaller and smaller, fell into clouds, and were swallowed. I knew that those watching from the ship would have seen nothing except a sudden disappearance of three of the figures on our platform, and then a broken railing and an emptier platform with just Nemes, Aenea, and me remaining. The silver thing that was Rhadamanth Nemes turned its featureless chrome face toward us.

The light changed. The breeze blew again. The air thinned. I felt my heart suddenly beating again . . . pounding loudly . . . and I blinked rapidly.

Nemes was in her human form again. "So," she said to Aenea, "shall we finish this little farce?"

"Yes," said Aenea.

Nemes smiled and went to phase-shift.

Nothing happened. The creature frowned and seemed to concentrate. Still nothing occurred.

"I can't stop you from phase-shifting," said Aenea. "But others can . . . and have."

Nemes looked irritated for a second but then laughed. "Those who created me will attend to that in a second, but I do not wish to wait that long, and I do not need to shift up to kill you, bitch child."

"That's true," said Aenea. She had stood her ground through all of this violence and confusion, her legs apart, feet firmly planted, arms easy at her sides.

Nemes showed her small teeth, but I saw that these teeth were elongating, growing sharper, as if being extruded farther from her gums and jawbone. There were at least three rows of them.

Nemes held up her hands and her fingernails—already pale and long—extended another ten centimeters, flowing into gleaming spikes.

Nemes reached down with those sharpened nails and peeled back the skin and flesh of her right forearm, revealing some sort of metallic endoskeleton that was the color of steel but which looked infinitely sharper.

"Now," said Nemes. She stepped toward Aenea.

I stepped between them.

"No," I said, and raised my fists like a boxer ready to start.

Nemes showed all of her rows of teeth.

23

IME AND MOTION seem to slow again, as if I can once again see in the phase-shift mode, but this time it is merely the effect of adrenaline and total concentration. My mind shifts into over-drive. My senses become preternaturally alert. I see, feel, and calculate every microsecond with uncanny clarity.

Nemes takes a step . . . more toward Aenea to my left than toward me.

This is a chess match more than a fight. I win if I kill the unfeeling bitch or fling her off the platform long enough for us to escape. She does not have to kill me to win . . . only neutralize me long enough to kill *Aenea.* Aenea is her target. Aenea has *always* been her target. This monster was created to kill Aenea.

Chess match. Nemes has just sacrificed two of her strongest pieces—her monster siblings—to neutralize our knight, the Shrike. Now all three pieces are off the board. Only Nemes—the dark queen—Aenea, human-kind's queen, and Aenea's lowly pawn . . . me.

This pawn may have to sacrifice himself, but not without taking out the dark queen. Of that he is determined.

Nemes is smiling. Her teeth are sharp and redundant. Her arms are still at her sides, long nails gleaming, her right forearm exposed like some obscene surgical exhibit . . . the interior not human . . . no, not human at all. The cutting edge of her forearm endoskeleton catches the afternoon sunlight.

"Aenea," I say softly, "step back, please." This highest of platforms connects to the stone walkway and staircase we had cut to climb to the overhang walkway. I want my friend off the platform.

"Raul, I . . ."

"Do it now," I say, not raising my voice but putting into it every bit

of command I have learned and earned in my thirty-two standard years of life.

Aenea takes four steps back onto the stone ledge. The ship continues to hover fifty meters out and above us. There are many faces peering from the balcony. I try to will Sergeant Gregorius to step out and use his assault rifle to blow this Nemes bitch-thing away, but I do not see his dark face among those staring. Perhaps he has been weakened by his wounds. Perhaps he feels that this should be a fair fight.

Fuck that, I think. I do not want a fair fight. I want to kill this Nemes creature any way I can. I would gladly accept any help from anywhere right now. *Is the Shrike really dead? Can this be? Martin Silenus's Cantos seemed to tell of the Shrike being defeated in some far-future battle with Colonel Fedmahn Kassad. But how did Silenus know this? And what does the future mean to a monster capable of traveling through time?* If the Shrike was not dead, I would appreciate its return about now.

Nemes takes another step to her right, my left. I step left to block her access to Aenea. Under phase-shift, this thing has superhuman strength and can move so fast as to be literally invisible. *She can't phase-shift now.* I hope to God. But she still may be faster and stronger than me . . . than any human. I have to assume that she is. And she has the teeth, claws, and cutting arm.

"Ready to die, Raul Endymion?" says Nemes, her lips sliding back from those rows of teeth.

Her strengths—probable speed, strength, and inhuman construction. She may be more robot or android than human. It is almost certain that she does not feel pain. She may have other built-in weapons that she has not revealed. I have no idea how to kill or disable her . . . her skeleton is metal, not bone . . . the muscles visible in her forearm look real enough, but may be made of plastic fibers or pink steel mesh. It is unlikely that normal fighting techniques will stop her.

Her weaknesses—I do not know. Perhaps overconfidence. Perhaps she has become too used to phase-shifting—to killing her enemies when they cannot fight back. But she had taken on the Shrike and fought it to a draw nine and a half years ago—beaten it, actually, since she had gotten it out of the way to get to Aenea. Only the intervention of Father Captain de Soya's ship, lancing her with every gigavolt available on the starship, had prevented her from killing all of us.

Nemes raises her arms now and crouches, clawed fingers extended. How far can the thing jump? Can it jump over me to get to Aenea?

My strengths—two years boxing for the regiment during my Home Guard tour—I hated it, lost about a third of my matches. The others in my regiment kept betting on me, though. Pain never stopped me. I certainly felt it, but it never stopped me. Blows to the face made me see red—early on, I would forget all of my training when someone hit me in the face, and when the red mist of fury cleared, if I was still standing, I tended to have won the match. But I know that blind fury will not help me now. If I lose focus for an instant, this thing will kill me.

I was fast when I boxed . . . but that was more than a decade ago. I was strong . . . but I have not formally trained or worked out in all the intervening years. I could take hard blows in the ring, which is different than giving in to pain . . . I'd never been knocked out in the ring, even when a better fighter had sent me down a dozen times before the fight was called.

Besides boxing, I'd been a bouncer at one of the bigger Nine Tails casinos on Felix. But that was mostly psychology, knowing how to avoid fighting while moving the obnoxious drunk out the door. I had made sure that the few actual fights were over in a few seconds.

I had been trained for hand-to-hand fighting in the Home Guard, taught to kill at close range, but that sort of business was about as rare as a bayonet charge.

While working as a bargeman, I had gotten into my most serious fights—once with a man ready and willing to carve me up with a long knife. I had survived that. But that other bargeman had knocked me out. As a hunting guide, I'd survived an offworlder coming at me with a flechette gun. But I had accidentally killed him, and he had testified against me after he was resurrected. Come to think of it, that's how all this started.

Of all my weaknesses, this was the most serious—I do not really want to hurt anyone. In all of my fights—with the possible exception of the bargemaster with the knife and the Christian hunter with his flechette gun—I had held something back, not wanting to hit them as hard as I could, not wanting to hurt them too badly.

I have to change that way of thinking immediately. This is no person . . . this is a killing machine, and if I do not disable or destroy it quickly, it will kill me even more quickly.

Nemes jumps at me, claws raking, her right arm pulling back and then slashing like a scythe.

I jump back, dodge the scythe, almost dodge all the claws, see the shirt on my left upper arm shred, see blood mist the air, and then I step in quickly and hit her—fast—hard—three times to the face.

Nemes jumps back as quickly as she came in. There is blood on the long nails of her left hand. My blood. Her nose has been smashed flat so that it lies sideways on her thin face. I have broken something—bone, cartilage, metal fiber—where her left brow was. There is no blood on her face. She does not seem to notice any of the damage. She is still grinning.

I glance at my left arm. It burns ferociously. Poison? Perhaps—it makes sense—but if she uses poison, I should be dead in seconds. No reason she would use long-acting agents.

Still here. Just burns because of the slashes. Four, I think . . . deep, but not muscle deep. They don't matter. Concentrate on her eyes. Guess what she'll do next.

Never use your bare hands. Home Guard teaching. Always find a weapon for close-in fighting. If one's personal weapon is destroyed or missing, find something else, improvise—a rock, a heavy branch, a torn piece of metal—even stones wrapped in one's fist or keys between the fingers are preferable to one's bare hands. Knuckles break more quickly than jawbones, the drill instructor always reminded us. If you absolutely *have* to use only hands, use the flat of your hand to chop. Use rigid fingers to impale. Use clawed fingers to go for the eyes and Adam's apple.

No loose rocks here, no branches, no keys . . . no weapons at all. This thing has no Adam's apple. I suspect that her eyes are as cool and hard as marbles.

Nemes moves to the left again, glancing toward Aenea. "I'm coming, sweetheart," hisses the thing to my friend.

I catch a glimpse of Aenea out of the corner of my eye. She is standing on the ledge just beyond the platform. She is not moving. Her face is impassive. This is unlike my beloved . . . normally she would be throwing stones, leaping on an enemy's back . . . anything but allowing me to fight this thing alone.

This is your moment, Raul, my darling. Her voice is as clear as a whisper in my mind.

It *is* a whisper. Coming from the auditory pickups in my folded-back skinsuit cowl. I am still wearing the damned thing, as well as my useless climbing harness. I start to subvocalize in response, but remember that I'd jacked into the ship's communicator in my upper pocket when I called the ship from the summit of T'ien Shan and I will be broadcasting to the ship as well as Aenea if I use it now.

I move to my left, blocking the creature's way again. Less room to maneuver now.

Nemes moves faster this time, feinting left and slashing in from my right, swinging her right arm backhand toward my ribs.

I leap back but the blade slices meat just below my lowest right rib. I duck, but her claws flash—her left claws go for my eyes—I duck again, but her fingers slice a section of my scalp away. For an instant the air is filled with atomized blood again.

I take one step and swing my own right arm backhand, chopping down as if I were swinging a sledgehammer, my fist connecting with the side of her neck just below her right jawline. Synthetic flesh pulps and tears. The metal and tubes beneath do not bend.

Nemes slashes backhand again with her scythe arm and claws with her left hand. I leap away. She misses completely.

I step in quickly and kick the back of her knees, hoping to sweep her legs out from under her. It is eight meters to the broken railing at the far edge. If I could get her rolling . . . even if we both go over . . .

It is like kicking a steel stanchion. My leg goes numb at the force of my kick, but she does not budge. Fluids and flesh collapse over her endoskeleton, but she does not lose her footing. She must weigh twice what I do.

She kicks back and breaks a left rib or two of mine. I hear them crack. The wind goes out of me suddenly, explosively.

I reel backward, half expecting a ring rope to be there, but there is only the cliff face, a wall of hard, slick, vertical rock. A piton bolt slams into my back, stunning me for an instant.

I know now what I will do.

The next breath is like breathing through fire, so I quickly take several more painful breaths, confirming that I can breathe, trying to get my wind back. I feel lucky—I don't think the broken ribs have penetrated my left lung.

Nemes opens her arms to prevent my escape and moves in closer.

I step into her foul embrace, getting inside the killing sweep of the bladed forearm, and bring my fists together as hard as I can on either side of her head. Her ears pulp—this time there is a yellow fluid filling the air— but I feel the permasteel solidity of the skull under the bruised flesh. My hands rebound. I stagger backward, hands and arms and fists temporarily useless.

Nemes leaps.

I lean back on the rock, raise both legs, catch her on the chest as she descends, and kick out with all of the strength in my body.

She slashes as she flies backward, slicing through part of my harness, most of my jacket and skinsuit, and the muscle above my chest. It is on the right side of my chest. She has not cut through the comlink. Good.

She backflips and lands on her feet, still five meters from the edge. There is no way that I am going to get her to and over the platform edge. She will not play the game under my rules.

I rush her, fists raised.

Nemes brings her left hand up, cupped and clawed, in a quick, disembowling scoop. I have slid to a stop millimeters short of that death blow and now, as she pulls her right arm back in preparation to scythe me in two, I pivot on one foot and kick her in her flat chest with all the strength of my body.

Nemes grunts and bites at my leg, her jaws snapping forward like a large dog's. Her teeth chew off the heel and sole of my boot, but miss flesh.

Catching my balance, I lunge forward again, gripping her right wrist with my left hand to keep the scythe arm from scraping my back clear of flesh down to my spine, and stepping in close to get a handful of her hair. She is snapping at my face, her rows of teeth directly in front of my eyes, the air between us filled with her yellow saliva or blood substitute. I am bending her head back as we pivot, two violent dancers straining against one another, but her lank, short hair is slippery with my blood and her lubricant and my fingers are slipping.

Lunging against her again to keep her off balance, I shift my fingers to her eye sockets and pull back with all of the strength in my arms and upper body.

Her head tilts back, thirty degrees—fifty—sixty—I should be hearing the snap of her spinal cord—eighty degrees—ninety. Her neck is bent backward at right angles to her torso, her marble eyes cold against my straining fingers, her wide lips stretching wider as the teeth snap at my forearm.

I release her.

She comes forward as if propelled by a giant spring. Her claws sink into my back, scrape bone at the right shoulder and left shoulder blade.

I crouch and swing short, hard blows, pounding her ribs and belly. Two—four—six fast shots, pivoting inside, the top of my head against her torn and oily chest, blood from my lacerated scalp flowing over both of us. Something in her chest or diaphragm snaps with a metallic twang and Nemes vomits yellow fluid over my neck and shoulders.

I stagger back and she grins at me, sharpened teeth gleaming through the bubbling yellow bile that drips from her chin onto the already slippery boards of the platform.

She screams—steam hissing from a dying boiler—and rushes again, scythe arm slicing through the air in an invisible arc.

I leap back. Three meters to the rock wall or ledge where Aenea stands.

Nemes swings backarm, her forearm a propeller, a whizzing pendulum of steel. She can herd me anywhere she wants me now.

She wants me dead or out of the way. She wants Aenea.

I jump back again, the blade cutting through the fabric just above belt line this time. I have jumped left this time, more toward the rock wall than the ledge.

Aenea is unprotected for this second. I am no longer between her and the creature.

Nemes's weakness. I am betting everything . . . Aenea . . . on this: she is a born predator. This close to a kill, she cannot resist finishing me.

Nemes swings to her right, keeping the option open of leaping toward Aenea, but also pursuing me toward the cliff face. The scythe swings backhand at my head for a clean decapitation.

I trip and roll farther to my left, away from Aenea. I am on the boards now, legs flailing.

Nemes straddles me, yellow fluid spattering my face and chest. She raises the scythe arm, screams, and brings the arm down.

"Ship! Land on this platform. Immediately. No discussion!"

I gasp this into the comthread pickup as I roll against Nemes's legs. Her bladed forearm slams into the tough bonsai cedar where my head was a second before.

I am under her. The blade of her arm is sunk deep into the dense wood. For just a few seconds, she is bent over to claw at me and does not have the leverage to free the cutting edge. A shadow falls over both of us.

The nails of her left hand slash the right side of my head—almost severing my ear, slicing along the jawbone, and just missing my jugular. My right hand is palm up under her jaw, trying to keep those teeth from open-ing and closing on my neck or face. She is stronger than I am.

My life depends upon getting out from under her.

Her forearm is still stuck in the platform floor, but this serves her purpose, anchoring her to me.

The shadow deepens. Ten seconds. No more.

Nemes claws my restraining hands away and wrenches the blade from the wood, staggering to her feet. Her eyes move left to where Aenea stands unguarded.

I roll away from Nemes . . . and away from Aenea . . . leaving my friend undefended. Claw cold rock to get to my feet. My right hand is useless—some tendon slashed in these final seconds—so I raise my left hand, pull the safety line from my harness—I can only hope it is still in-tact—and clip the carabiner onto the piton bolt with a metallic slap, like handcuffs slamming home.

Nemes pivots to her left, dismissing me now, black marble eyes on Aenea. My friend stands her ground.

The ship lands on the platform, turning off its EM repellors as or-dered, allowing its full weight to rest on the wood, crushing the pavilion of Right Meditation with a terrible splintering, the ship's archaic fins filling most of the space, just missing Nemes and me.

The creature glances once over her shoulder at the huge black ship looming above her, obviously dismisses it, and crouches to leap at Aenea.

For a second I think that the bonsai cedar will hold . . . that the platform is even stronger than Aenea's calculations and my experience sug-gest . . . but then there is one horrendous, tearing, splintering sound, and the entire top Right Meditation platform and much of the stairway down to the Right Mindfulness pavilion tear away from the mountain.

I see the people watching from the ship's balcony thrown back into the interior of the ship as it falls.

"Ship!" I gasp into the comthread pickup. "Hover!" Then I turn my attention back to Nemes.

The platform falls away beneath her. She leaps toward Aenea. My friend does not step back.

Only the platform falling out from beneath her keeps Nemes from completing her leap. She falls just short, but her claws strike the stone ledge, throw sparks, find a hold.

The platform rips and tears away, disintegrating as it tumbles into the abyss, some parts striking the main platform below, tearing it away in places, piling debris at other places.

Nemes is dangling from the rock, scrambling with her claws and feet, just a meter below where Aenea stands.

I have eight meters of safety line. Using my workable left arm, my blood making the rope dangerously slippery, I let out several meters and kick away from the cliff where I dangle.

Nemes pulls herself up to where she can get her clawed fingers over the top of the ledge. She finds a ridge or fissure and pulls herself up and out, an expert climber overcoming an overhang. Her body is arched like a bow as her feet scramble on the stone, pulling her higher so that she can throw herself up and over the ledge at Aenea, who has not moved.

I swing back away from Nemes, bouncing across the rock—feeling the slick stone against my lacerated bare sole where Nemes has torn away my boot—seeing that the rope I am depending upon has been frayed in the struggle, not knowing if it will hold for another few seconds.

I put more stress on it, swinging high away from Nemes in a pendulum arc.

Nemes pulls herself up onto Aenea's ledge, to her knees, getting to her feet a meter from my darling.

I swing high, rocks scraping my right shoulder, thinking for one sickening second that I do not have enough speed and line, but then feeling that I do—just enough—just barely enough—

Nemes swivels just as I swing up behind her, my legs opening in embrace, then closing around her, ankles crossing.

She screams and raises her scythe arm. My groin and belly are unprotected.

Ignoring that—ignoring the unraveling line and the pain everywhere—I cling tight as gravity and momentum swing us back—she is heavier than I—for another terrible second I hang connected and she does not budge—but she has not found her balance yet—she teeters on the edge—I arc backward, trying to move my center of gravity toward my bleeding shoulders—and Nemes comes off the ledge.

I open my legs immediately, releasing her.

She swings her scythe arm, missing my belly by millimeters as I swing back and out, but the motion sends her hurtling forward, farther away from the ledge and rock wall, out over the hole where the platform had been.

I scrape out and back along the cliff wall, trying to arrest my momentum. The safety line breaks.

I spread-eagle across the rockface, begin sliding down. My right hand is useless. My left fingers find a narrow hold . . . lose it . . . I am sliding faster . . . my left foot finds a ledge a centimeter wide. That and friction hold me against the rock long enough for me to look over my left shoulder.

Nemes is twisting as she falls, trying to change her trajectory enough to sink claws or scythe into the remaining edges of the lowest platform.

She misses by four or five centimeters. A hundred meters farther down, she strikes a rock outcropping and is propelled farther out above the clouds. Steps, posts, beams, and platform pillars are falling into cloud a kilometer below her.

Nemes screams—a shattered calliope scream of pure rage and frustration—and the echo bounces from rock to rock around me.

I can no longer hold on. I've lost too much blood and had too many muscles torn away. I feel the rock sliding away under my chest, cheek, palm, and straining left foot.

I look to my left to say good-bye to Aenea, if only with a gaze.

Her arm catches me as I begin to slide away. She has free-climbed out above me along the sheer face as I watched Nemes fall.

My heart pounds with the terror that my weight will pull both of us off. I feel myself slipping . . . feel Aenea's strong hands slipping . . . I am covered in blood. She does not let go.

"Raul," she says and her voice is shaking, but with emotion, not fatigue or terror.

With her foot on the ledge the only thing holding us against the cliff, she releases her left hand, sweeps it up, and clamps her safety line on to my dangling carabiner still attached to the piton.

We both slide off and away, scraping skin. Aenea instantly hugs me with both arms, wraps both legs around me. It is a repeat of my tight embrace of Nemes, but fueled by love and the passion to survive this time, not hate and the urge to destroy.

We fall eight meters to the end of her safety line. I think that my extra weight will pull the piton out or snap the line.

We rebound, bounce three times, and hang above nothing. The piton holds. The safety line holds. Aenea's grip holds.

"Raul," she says again. "My God, my God." I think that she is patting my head, but realize that she is trying to pull my torn scalp back into place, trying to keep my torn ear from coming off.

"It's all right," I try to say, but find that my lips are bleeding and swollen. I can't enunciate the words I need to say to the ship.

Aenea understands. She leans forward and whispers into the com-thread pickup on my cowl. "Ship—hover and pick us up. Quickly."

The shadow descends, moving in as if to crush us. The crowd is on the balcony again, eyes wide, as the giant ship floats to within three me-ters—gray cliffs on either side of us now—and extrudes a plank from the balcony. Friendly hands pull us in to safety.

Aenea does not release her grip with arms or legs until we are carried in off the balcony, into the carpeted interior, away from the drop.

I dimly hear the ship's voice. "There are warships hurrying in-system toward us. Another is just above the atmosphere ten thousand kilometers to the west and closing . . ."

"Get us out of here," orders Aenea. "Straight up and out. I'll give you the in-system coordinates in a minute. *Go!*"

I feel dizzy and close my eyes to the sound of the fusion engines roaring. I have a faint impression of Aenea kissing me, holding me, kissing my eyelids and bloody forehead and cheek. My friend is crying.

"Rachel," comes Aenea's voice from a distance, "can you diagnose him?"

Fingers other than my beloved's touch me briefly. There are stabs of pain, but these are increasingly remote. A coldness is descending. I try to open my eyes but find both of them sealed shut by blood or swelling or both.

"What looks worse is the least threatening," I hear Rachel say in her soft but no-nonsense voice. "The scalp wound, ear, broken leg, and so forth. But I think that there are internal injuries . . . not just the ribs, but internal bleeding. And the claw wounds on his back go to the spinal cord."

Aenea is still crying, but her tone is still in command. "Some of you . . . Lhomo . . . A. Bettik . . . help me get him to the doc-in-the-box."

"I'm sorry," comes the ship's voice, just at the edge of my consciousness, "but all three receptacles in the autosurgeon are in use. Sergeant Gregorius collapsed from his internal injuries and was brought to the third niche. All three patients are currently on full life support."

"Damn," I hear Aenea say under her breath. "Raul? My dear, can you hear me?"

I start to reply, to say that I'm fine, don't worry about me, but all I hear from my own swollen lips and dislocated jaw is a garbled moan.

"Raul," continues Aenea, "we've got to get away from these Pax ships. We're going to carry you down to one of the cryogenic fugue cubbies, my dear. We're going to let you sleep awhile until there's a slot free in the doc-in-the-box. Can you hear me, Raul?"

I decide against speaking and manage to nod. I feel something loose hanging down on my forehead, like a wet, displaced cap. My scalp.

"All right," says Aenea. She leans close and whispers in my remaining ear. "I love you, my dear friend. You're going to be all right. I *know* that."

Hands lift me, carry me, eventually lay me on something hard and cool. The pain rages, but it is a distant thing and does not concern me.

Before they slide the lid closed on the cryogenic fugue cubby, I can distinctly hear the ship's voice saying calmly, "Four Pax warships hailing us. They say that if we do not cut power in ten minutes, they will destroy us. May I point out that we are at least eleven hours from any translation point? And all four Pax warships are within firing distance."

I hear Aenea's tired voice. "Continue on this heading toward the coordinates I gave you, Ship. No reply to Pax warships."

I try to smile. We have done this before—trying to outrun Pax ships against great odds. But there is one thing that I am learning that I would love to explain to Aenea, if my mouth worked and if my mind would clear a bit—it's just that however long one beats those odds, they catch up to you eventually. I consider this a minor revelation, overdue *satori*.

But now the cold is creeping over me, into me, through me—chilling my heart and mind and bones and belly. I can only hope that it is the cryogenic fugue coils cycling faster than I remember from my last trip. If it is death, then . . . well, it's death. But I want to see Aenea again.

This is my last thought.

24

ALLING! HEART POUNDING wildly, I awoke in what seemed to be a different universe.

I was floating, not falling. At first I thought that I was in an ocean, a salt ocean with positive buoyancy, floating like a fetus in a sepia-tinged salt sea, but then I realized that there was no gravity at all, no waves or currents, and that the medium was not water but thick sepia light. *The ship?* No, I was in a large, empty, darkened but light-circled space—an empty ovoid some fifteen meters or more across, with parchment walls through which I could see both the filtered light of a blazing sun and something more complicated, a vast organic structure curving away on all sides. I weakly moved my hands from their floating position to touch my face, head, body, and arms . . .

I *was* floating, tethered by only the lightest harness straps to some sort of sticktite strip on the curved inner wall. I was barefoot and wearing only a soft cotton tunic that I did not recognize—pajamas? hospital gown?

My face was tender and I could feel new ridges that might be scars. My hair was gone, the flesh above my skull was raw and definitely scarred, and my ear was there but very tender. My arms had several faint scars that I could see in the dim light. I pulled up my trouser leg and looked at what had been a badly broken lower leg. Healed and firm. I felt my ribs—tender but intact. I had made it to the doc-in-the-box after all.

I must have spoken aloud, for a dark figure floating nearby said, "Eventually you did, Raul Endymion. But some of the surgery was done the old-fashioned way . . . and by me."

I started—floating up against the sticktite strips. It had not been Aenea's voice.

The dark form floated closer and I recognized the shape, the hair, and—finally—the voice. "Rachel," I said. My tongue was dry, my lips cracked. I croaked the word rather than spoke it.

Rachel came closer and offered me a squeeze bottle. The first few drops came out as tumbling spheres—most of which splashed me on the face—but I soon got the knack of it and squeezed drops into my open mouth. The water tasted cool and wonderful.

"You've been getting liquids and sustenance via IV for two weeks," said Rachel, "but it's better if you drink directly."

"Two weeks!" I said. I looked around. "Aenea? Is she . . . are they . . ."

"Everyone's all right," said Rachel. "Aenea's busy. She's spent much of the last couple of weeks in here with you . . . watching over you . . . but when she had to go out with Minmun and the others, she had me stay with you."

"Minmun?" I said. I peered through the translucent wall. One bright star—smaller than Hyperion's sun. The incredible geometries of the structure spreading away, curving out, from this ovoid room. "Where am I?" I said. "How did we get here?"

Rachel chuckled. "I'll answer the second question first, let you see the answer to the first yourself in a few minutes. Aenea had the ship jump to this place. Father Captain de Soya, his Sergeant Gregorius, and the officer, Carel Shan, knew the coordinates for this star system. They were all unconscious, but the other survivor—their former prisoner, Hoag Liebler—knew where this place was hiding."

I looked through the wall again. The structure seemed huge—a light and shadow latticework stretching out in all directions from this pod. How could they hide anything this large? And *who* hid it?

"How did we get to a translation point in time?" I croaked, taking a few more globules of water. "I thought the Pax warships were closing in."

"They were," said Rachel. "They did. We could never have gotten to a Hawking-drive translation point before they destroyed us. Here—you don't need to be stuck to the wall any longer." She ripped off the sticktite strips and I floated free. Even in zero-g, I felt very weak.

Orienting myself so that I could still see Rachel's face in the dim sepia light, I said, "So how did we do it?"

"We didn't translate," said the young woman. "Aenea directed the ship to a point in space where we farcasted directly to this system."

"*Farcast?* There was an active space farcast portal? Like one of the kinds that the Hegemony FORCE ships used to transit? I didn't think that any of those had survived the Fall."

Rachel was shaking her head. "There was no farcaster portal. Nothing. Just an arbitrary point a few hundred thousand klicks from the second moon. It was quite a chase . . . the Pax ships kept hailing us and threatening to fire. Finally they did . . . lance beams leaping toward us from a dozen sources—we wouldn't even have been a debris field, just gas on a widening trajectory—but then we reached the point Aenea had pointed us toward and suddenly we were . . . here."

I did not say *Where is here?* again, but I floated to the curved wall and tried to peer through it. The wall felt warm, spongy, organic, and it was filtering most of the sunlight. The resulting interior light was soft and beautiful, but it made it difficult to see out—just the one blazing star was visible and the hint of that incredible geometric structure beyond our pod.

"Ready to see the 'where'?" said Rachel.

"Yeah."

"Pod," said Rachel, "transparent surface, please."

Suddenly there was nothing separating us from the outside. I almost shouted in terror. Instead, I flailed my arms and legs trying to find a solid surface to cling to until Rachel kicked closer and steadied me with a firm hand.

We were in space. The surrounding pod had simply disappeared. We were floating in space—seemed to be floating in space, except for the presence of air to breathe—and we were far out on a branch of a . . .

Tree is not the right word. I had seen trees. This was not a tree.

I had heard much about the old Templar worldtrees, had seen the stump of *the* Worldtree on God's Grove—and I'd heard about the kilometers-long shiptrees that had traveled between the star systems back in Martin Silenus's pilgrim days.

This was not a worldtree or a shiptree.

I had heard wild legends—from Aenea actually, so they were probably not legends—of a tree-ring around a star, a fantastical braided ring of living material stretching all the way around an Old Earth System-like sun. I had once tried to calculate how much living material that would require, and decided that it had to be nonsense.

This was no tree-ring.

What stretched out on every side of me, curving inward across expanses too large for my planet-formed mind to take in, was a branched and interwoven sphere of living plant material—trunks tens or hundreds of kilometers across, branches klicks wide, leaves hundreds of meters across, trailing root systems stretching like God's synapses for hundreds, no . . . thousands of kilometers into space—trellised and wrapped branches stretching out and inward in all directions, trunks the length of Old Earth's Mississippi River looking like tiny twigs in the distance, tree shapes the size of my home continent of Aquila on Hyperion blending into thousands of other clumps and masses of greenery, all bending inward and away, on all sides, in every direction . . . there were many black gaps, holes into space, some gaps larger than the trunks and greenery lacing through them . . . but nowhere were the gaps complete . . . everywhere the trunks and branches and roots intertwined, opening uncounted billions of green leaves to the star blazing away in the locus of vacuum at the center of . . .

I closed my eyes.

"This can't be real," I said.

"It is," said Rachel.

"The Ousters?" I said.

"Yes," said Aenea's friend, the child of the *Cantos*. "And the Templars. And the ergs. And . . . others. It's alive but a construct . . . a minded thing."

"Impossible," I said. "It would take millions of years to grow this . . . sphere."

"Biosphere," said Rachel, smiling.

I shook my head again. "Biosphere is an old term. It's just the closed vivisystem on and around a planet."

"This is a biosphere," Rachel said again. "Only there are no planets here. Comets, yes, but no planets." She pointed.

In the far distance, perhaps hundreds of thousands of kilometers away, where the interior of this living sphere began to fade to a green blur even in the unblinking vacuum, a long, white streak moved slowly through the black gap between trunks.

"A comet," I repeated stupidly.

"For watering," said Rachel. "They have to use millions of them. Luckily there are many billions in the Oört cloud. More billions in the Kuiper Belt."

I stared. There were other white specks out there, each with a long, glowing tail. Some moved between the trunks and branches as I watched, giving me some idea of the scale of this biosphere. *The comet trajectories were routed through the gaps in the plant material. If this is truly a sphere, the comets would have to pass back through the living globe on their way out-system. What kind of confidence does it take to do such a thing?*

"What is this thing we're in?" I said.

"An environmental pod," said Rachel. "Life bulb. This one is tailored for medical duty. It's not only been monitoring your IV drip, vital signs, and tissue regeneration, it's been growing and manufacturing many of the medicines and other chemicals."

I reached out and touched the nearly transparent material. "How thick is it?"

"About a millimeter," said Rachel. "But very strong. It can shield us from most micrometeorite impacts."

"Where do the Ousters get such a material?"

"They biofacture the genes and it grows itself," said Rachel. "Do you feel up to going out to see Aenea and meeting some people? Everyone's been waiting for your awakening."

"Yes," I said, and then, quickly, "no! Rachel?"

She floated there, waiting. I saw how lustrous her dark eyes were in the amazing light. Much like my darling's.

"Rachel . . ." I began awkwardly.

She waited, floating, reaching out to touch the transparent pod wall to orient herself heads-up in relation to me.

"Rachel, we haven't really talked much . . ."

"You didn't like me," said the young woman with a slight smile.

"That's not true . . . I mean, it was true, in a way . . . but it's because I just didn't understand things at first. It had been five years for Aenea that I'd been away . . . it was difficult . . . I guess that I was jealous."

She arched a dark eyebrow. "Jealous, how, Raul? Did you think that Aenea and I were lovers all those standard years you were gone?"

"Well, no . . . I mean, I didn't know . . ."

Rachel held up a hand, sparing me further flummoxing. "We aren't," she said. "We never were. Aenea would never have considered such a thing. *Theo* might have entertained the possibility, but she knew from the start that Aenea and I were destined to love certain men."

I stared. *Destined?*

Rachel smiled again. I could imagine that grin on the little girl Sol Weintraub had talked about in his Hyperion *Canto.* "Don't worry, Raul. I happen to know for a fact that Aenea has never loved anyone but you. Even when she was a little girl. Even before she met you. You've always been her chosen one." The young woman's smile became rueful. "We should all be so lucky."

I started to speak, hesitated.

Rachel's smile faded. "Oh. She told you about the one-year eleven-month one-week six-hour interregnum?"

"Yes," I said. "And about her having . . ." I stopped. It would be foolish to choke up in front of this strong woman. She would never look at me the same again.

"A baby?" finished Rachel quickly.

I looked at her as if trying to find some answer in her handsome features. "Did Aenea tell you about it?" I said, feeling like I was betraying my dear friend somewhat by trying to get this information from someone else. But I could not stop. "Did you know at the time what . . ."

"Where she was?" said Rachel, returning my intense gaze. "What was happening to her? That she was getting married?"

I could only nod.

"Yes," said Rachel. "We knew."

"Were you there with her?"

Rachel seemed to hesitate, as if weighing her answer. "No," she said at last. "A. Bettik, Theo, and I waited for almost two years for her to return. We carried on her . . . ministry? Mission? . . . Whatever it is, we carried it on while she was gone . . . sharing some of her lessons, finding people who wished to partake of communion, letting them know when she would return."

"So you knew when she would return?"

"Yes," said Rachel. "To the day."

"How?"

"That's when she *had* to return," said the dark-haired woman. "She had taken every possible minute that she could without jeopardizing her mission. The Pax was hunting for us the next day . . . they would have seized all of us if Aenea had not returned and farcast us away."

I nodded, but was not thinking about close calls with the Pax. "Did you meet . . . him?" I said, trying unsuccessfully to keep my tone neutral.

Rachel's expression remained serious. "Father to their child, you mean? Aenea's husband?"

I felt that Rachel was not trying to be cruel, but the words tore at me far worse than had Nemes's claws. "Yes," I said. "Him."

Rachel shook her head. "None of us had met him when she went away."

"But you do know why she chose him to be the father of her child?" I persisted, feeling like the Grand Inquisitor we had left behind on T'ien Shan.

"Yes," said Rachel, returning my gaze, giving me no more.

"Was it something to do with her . . . her mission?" I said, feeling my throat growing tighter and tighter, my voice more strained. "Is it something she had to do . . . some reason the child had to be born to them? Can you tell me anything, Rachel?"

She took my wrist then, gripping it strongly. "Raul, you know that Aenea will explain this when it's time to do so."

I pulled away, making a rude noise. "When it's time," I growled. "Jesus H. Christ, I'm sick of hearing that phrase. And I'm sick of waiting."

Rachel shrugged. "Confront her then. Threaten to beat her up if she doesn't tell you. You clobbered that Nemes-thing . . . Aenea shouldn't be a problem."

I glowered at the woman.

"Seriously, Raul, this is between you and Aenea. All I can tell you is that you are the only man she has ever talked about, and—as far as I can tell—the only man she has ever loved."

"How the hell can you . . ." I began angrily and then forced myself to shut up. I patted her arm awkwardly, the motion making me begin to pivot around the center of my own axis. It was hard to stay near someone in zero-g without touching them. "Thank you, Rachel," I said.

"Ready to go see everyone?"

I took a breath. "Almost," I said. "Can this pod surface be made reflective?"

"Pod," said Rachel, "ninety percent translucence. High interior reflectivity." To me she said, "Checking in the mirror before your big date?"

The surface had become about as reflective as a still puddle of water—not a perfect mirror, but clear enough and bright enough to show me a Raul Endymion with scars on his face and bare scalp, the skin on his skull a babyish pink, traces of bruise and swelling under and around his eyes, and thin . . . very thin. The bones and muscles of my face and upper body seemed to have been sketched in bold pencil strokes. My eyes looked different.

"Jesus H. Christ," I said again.

Rachel made a motion with her hand. "The autosurgeon wanted you for another week, but Aenea couldn't wait. The scars aren't permanent . . . at least most of them. The pod medicine in the IV is taking care of the regeneration. Your hair will start growing back in two or three standard weeks."

I touched my scalp. It was like patting the scarred and especially tender butt of an ugly newborn. "Two or three weeks," I said. "Great. Fucking great."

"Don't sweat it," said Rachel. "I think it looks rather dashing, actually. I'd keep that look if I were you, Raul. Besides, I hear that Aenea is a pushover for older men. And right now, you certainly look older."

"Thanks," I said dryly.

"You're welcome," said Rachel. "Pod. Open iris. Access to main pressurized stem connector."

She led the way out, kicking and floating ahead of me through the irising wall.

AENEA HUGGED ME so hard when I came into the room . . . pod . . . that I wondered if my broken ribs might have given way again. I hugged her back just as hard.

The trip through the pressurized stem connector had been commonplace enough, if one counted being shot down a flexible, translucent, two-meter-wide pipeline at speeds up to what I estimated as sixty klicks per hour—they used currents of oxygen flowing at high speeds in opposite directions to give a boost to one's kicking and swimming through air—all the while other people, mostly very thin, hairless, and exceptionally tall other people, whizzed by silently in the opposite direction at closing speeds in excess of 120 klicks per hour, missing us by centimeters. Then there were the hub pods, into which Rachel and I were accelerated at high speed, like corpuscles being blasted into ventricles and auricles of a huge heart, and through which we tumbled, kicked, avoided other high-speed travelers, and exited via one of a dozen other stem connector openings. I was lost within minutes, but Rachel seemed to know her way—she pointed out that there were subtle colors embedded in the plant flesh over each exit—and soon we had entered a pod not much larger than mine, but crowded with cubbies, sticktite seating areas, and people. Some of the people—like Aenea, A. Bettik, Theo, the Dorje Phamo, and Lhomo Dondrub—I knew well: other people there—Father Captain de Soya, obviously renewed and recovered from his terrible wounds and wearing a priest's black trousers, tunic, and Roman collar, Sergeant Gregorius in his Swiss Guard combat fatigues—I had met recently and knew by sight; other people, like the long, thin, otherworldly Ousters and the hooded Templars were wondrous and strange, but well within my range of understanding; while still other individuals there—quickly introduced by Aenea as the Templar True Voice of the Tree Het

Masteen and the former Hegemony FORCE Colonel Fedmahn Kassad, I knew of but did not actually believe I was meeting. More than Rachel or the fact of Aenea's mother, Brawne Lamia, these were figures not just from the old poet's *Cantos* but archetypes from deep myth, long dead at the very least, and probably never real to begin with in the fixed, everyday, eat-sleep-and-use-the-toilet firmament of things.

And finally in this zero-gravity Ouster pod there were the other people who were not people at all, at least from my frame of reference: such as the willowy green beings who were introduced by Aenea as LLeeoonn and OOeeaall, two of the few surviving Seneschai empaths from Hebron—*alien and intelligent beings.* I looked at these strange creatures—the palest cypress-green skin and eyes; bodies so thin that I could have encircled their torso with my fingers; symmetrical like us with two arms, two legs, a head, but, of course, not really like us at all; limbs articulated more like single, unbroken, fluid lines than evolved of hinged bone and gristle; splayed digits like toads' hands; and heads more like a human fetus's than a human adult's. Their eyes were little more than shadowy spots on the green flesh of their faces.

The Seneschai had been reported to have died out during the early days of the Hegira . . . they were little more than legend, even less real than the tale of the soldier Kassad or the Templar Het Masteen.

One of these green legends brushed its three-fingered hand over my palm as we were introduced.

There were other non-human, non-Ouster, non-android entities in the pod.

Floating near the translucent wall of the pod were what looked to be large, greenish-white platelets—soft, shuddering saucers of soft material—each almost two meters across. I had seen these life-forms before . . . on the cloud world where I had been eaten by the sky squid.

Not eaten, M. Endymion, came surges of language echoing in my head, *only transported.*

Telepathy? I thought, half directing the query to the platelets. I remembered the surge of language-thought on the cloud world, and how I had wondered where it had originated.

It was Aenea who answered. "It feels like telepathy," she said softly, "but there's nothing mystical about. The Akerataeli learned our language the old-fashioned way—their zeplin symbiotes heard the sound vibrations and the Akerataeli broke it down and analyzed it. They control the zeplins by a form of long-distance, very tightly focused microwave pulses . . ."

"The zeplin was the thing that swallowed me on the cloud world," I said.

"Yes," said Aenea.

"Like the zeplins on Whirl?"

"Yes, and in Jupiter's atmosphere as well."

"I thought that they were hunted to extinction during the early Hegira years."

"They were eradicated on Whirl," said Aenea. "And even before the Hegira on Jupiter. But you weren't paragliding your kayak on Jupiter or Whirl . . . but on another oxygen-rich gas giant six hundred light-years into the Outback."

I nodded. "I'm sorry I interrupted. You were saying . . . microwave impulses . . ."

Aenea made that graceful throwing-away gesture I'd known since she was a child. "Just that they control their zeplin symbiote partners' actions by precise microwave stimulation of certain nerve and brain centers. We've given the Akerataeli permission to stimulate our speech centers so that we 'hear' their messages. I take it that it's rather like playing a complicated piano for them . . ."

I nodded but did not really understand.

"The Akerataeli are also a spacefaring race," said Father Captain de Soya. "Over the eons, they have colonized more than ten thousand oxygen-rich gas giant worlds."

"Ten thousand!" I said. I think that for a moment my jaw actually hung slack. In humankind's more than twelve hundred years of traveling in space we had explored and settled on less than ten percent of that number of planets.

"The Akerataeli have been at it longer than we," said de Soya softly.

I looked at the gently vibrating platelets. They had no eyes that I could see, certainly no ears. Were they hearing us? They must . . . one of them had responded to my thoughts. Could they *read* minds as well as stimulate language-thoughts?

While I was staring at them, the conversation between the humans and Ousters in the room resumed.

"The intelligence is reliable," said the pale Ouster whom I later learned was named Navson Hamnim. "There were at least three hundred archangel-class ships gathering at System Lacaille 9352. Each ship has a representative of the Order of the Knights of Jerusalem or Malta. It is definitely a major Crusade."

"Lacaille 9352," mused de Soya. "Sibiatu's Bitterness. I know the place. How old is this intelligence?"

"Twenty hours," said Navson Hamnim. "The data was sent via the only Gideon-drive courier drone we have left . . . of the three drones captured during your raids, two have been destroyed. We are fairly sure that the scoutship which sent this drone was detected and destroyed seconds after launching the courier."

"Three hundred archangels," said de Soya. He rubbed his cheeks. "If they are aware we know about them, they could make a Gideon jump this direction within days . . . hours. Assume two days' resurrection time, we may have less than three days to prepare. Have defenses been improved since I left?"

Another Ouster whom I later knew as Systenj Coredwell opened his hands in a gesture that I would discover meant "in no way." I noticed that there was webbing between the long fingers. "Most of the fighting ships have had to jump to the Great Wall salient to hold off their Task Force HORSEHEAD. The fighting is very bitter there. Few of the ships are expected to return."

"Does your intelligence say whether the Pax knows what you have here?" asked Aenea.

Navson Hamnim opened his hands in a subtle variation of Coredwell's gesture. "We think not. But they know now that this has been a major staging area for our recent defensive battles. I would venture that they think this is just another base—perhaps with a partial orbital forest ring."

"Is there anything we can do to break up the Crusade before it jumps this way?" said Aenea, speaking to everyone in the room.

"No." The flat syllable came from the tall man who had been introduced as Colonel Fedmahn Kassad. His Web English had a strange accent. He was a tall man, extremely thin but muscular, with an equally thin beard along his jawline and around his mouth. In the old poet's *Cantos*, Kassad had been described as a reasonably young man, but this warrior was in his standard sixties, at least, with heavy lines around his thin mouth and small eyes, his dark complexion burned even darker by long exposure to desert-world sun or deep-space UV, the spiked hair on top of his head rising like short silver nails.

Everyone looked at Kassad and waited.

"With de Soya's ship destroyed," said the Colonel, "our only chance at successful hit-and-run operations is gone. The few Hawking-drive warships we have left would take a time-debt of at least two months to jump to Lacaille 9352 and back. The Crusade archangels would almost certainly be here and gone by then . . . and we would be defenseless."

Navson Hamnim kicked away from the pod wall and oriented himself right side up in relation to Kassad. "These few warships do not offer us a defense in any case," he said softly, his own Web English more musical than accented. "Should we not consider dying while on the attack?"

Aenea floated between the two men. "I think that we should consider not dying at all," she said. "Nor allowing the biosphere to be destroyed."

A positive sentiment, a voice spoke in my head. *But not all positive sentiments can be supported by updrafts of possible action.*

"True," said Aenea, looking at the platelets, "but perhaps in this case the updrafts will build."

Good thermals to you all, said the voice in my head. The platelets moved toward the pod wall, which irised open for them. Then they were gone.

Aenea took a breath. "Shall we meet on the *Yggdrasill* to share the main meal in seven hours and continue this discussion? Perhaps someone will have an idea."

There was no dissension. People, Ousters, and Seneschai exited by a score of openings that had not been there a moment before.

Aenea floated over and hugged me again. I patted her hair.

"My friend," she said softly. "Come with me."

IT WAS HER private living pod—*our* private living pod, she informed me—and it was much like the one in which I awoke, except that there were organic shelves, niches, writing surfaces, storage cubbies, and facilities for comlog interface. Some of my clothes from the ship were folded neatly in a cubby and my extra boots were in a fiberplastic drawer.

Aenea pulled food from a cold-box cubby and began making sandwiches. "You must be hungry, my dear," she said, tearing off pieces of rough bread. I saw zygoat cheese on the sticktite zero-g work surface, some wrapped pieces of roast beef that must have come from the ship, bulbs of mustard, and several tankards of T'ien Shan rice beer. Suddenly I was starved.

The sandwiches were large and thick. She set them on catchplates made of some strong fiber, lifted her own meal and a beer bulb, and kicked toward the outer wall. A portal appeared and began to iris open.

"Uh . . ." I said alertly, meaning—*Excuse me, Aenea, but that's space out there. Aren't we both going to explosively decompress and die horribly?*

She kicked out through the organic portal and I shrugged and followed.

There were catwalks, suspension bridges, sticktite stairways, balconies, and terraces out there—made of steel-hard plant fiber and winding around the pods, stalks, branches, and trunks like so much ivy. There was also air to breathe. It smelled of a forest after a rain.

"Containment field," I said, thinking that I should have expected this. After all, if the Consul's ancient starship could have a balcony . . .

I looked around. "What powers it?" I said. "Solar receptors?"

"Indirectly," said Aenea, finding us a sticktite bench and mat. There were no railings on this tiny, intricately woven balcony. The huge branch—at least thirty meters across—ended in a profusion of leaves above us and the latticework web of the trunks and branches "beneath" us convinced my inner ear that we were many kilometers up on a wall made of crisscrossed, green girders. I resisted the urge to throw myself down on the sticktite mat and cling for dear life. A radiant gossamer fluttered by, followed by some type of small bird with a v-shaped tail.

"Indirectly?" I said, my mouth full as I took a huge bite of sandwich.

"The sunlight—for the most part—is converted to containment fields by ergs," continued my friend, sipping her beer and looking out at the seemingly infinite expanse of leaves above us, below us, to all sides of us, their green faces all turned toward the brilliant star. There was not enough air to give us a blue sky, but the containment field polarized the view toward the sun just enough to keep us from being blinded when we glanced that direction.

I almost spit my food out, managed to swallow instead, and said, "Ergs? As in Aldebaren energy binders? You were serious? Ergs like the one taken on the last Hyperion pilgrimage?"

"Yes," said Aenea. Her dark eyes were focused on me now.

"I thought they were extinct."

"Nope," said Aenea.

I took a long drink from the beer bulb and shook my head. "I'm confused."

"You have a right to be, my dear friend," Aenea said softly.

"This place . . ." I made a weak gesture toward the wall of branches and leaves trailing away so much farther than a planetary horizon, the infinitely distant curve of green and black far above us. "It's impossible," I said.

"Not quite," said Aenea. "The Templars and Ousters have been working on it—and others like it—for a thousand years."

I began chewing again. The cheese and roast beef were delicious. "So this is where the thousands and millions of trees went when they abandoned God's Grove during the Fall."

"Some of them," said Aenea. "But the Templars had been working with the Ousters to develop orbital forest rings and biospheres long before that."

I peered up. The distances made me dizzy. The sense of being on this small, leafy platform so many kilometers above nothing made me reel. Far below us and to our right, something that looked like a tiny, green sprig moved slowly between the latticed branches. I saw the film of energy field around it and realized that I was looking at one of the fabled Templar treeships, almost certainly kilometers long. "Is this finished then?" I said. "A true Dyson sphere? A globe around a star?"

Aenea shook her head. "Far from it, although about twenty standard years ago, they made contact with all the primary trunk tendrils. Technically it's a sphere, but most of it is comprised of holes at this point—some many millions of klicks across."

"Fan-fucking-tastic," I said, realizing that I could have been more eloquent. I rubbed my cheeks, feeling the heavy growth of beard there. "I've been out of it for two weeks?" I said.

"Fifteen standard days," said Aenea.

"Usually the doc-in-the-box works more quickly than that," I said. I finished the sandwich, stuck the catchplate to the table surface, and concentrated on the beer.

"Usually it does," agreed Aenea. "Rachel must have told you that you spent a relatively short time in the autosurgeon. She did most of the initial surgery herself."

"Why?" I said.

"The box was full," said Aenea. "We defrosted you from fugue as soon as we got here, but the three in the doc ahead of you were in bad shape. De Soya was near death for a full week. The sergeant . . . Gregorius . . . was much more seriously injured than he had let on when we met him on the Great Peak. And the third officer—Carel Shan—died despite the box's and the Ouster medics' best efforts."

"Shit," I said, lowering the beer. "I'm sorry to hear that." One got used to autosurgeons fixing almost anything.

Aenea looked at me with such intensity that I could feel her gaze warming my skin as surely as I could feel the powerful sunlight. "How *are* you, Raul?"

"Great," I said. "I ache a bit. I can feel the healing ribs. The scars itch. And I feel like I overslept by two weeks . . . but I feel good."

She took my hand. I realized that her eyes were moist. "I would have been really pissed if you'd died on me," she said after a moment, her voice thick.

"Me too." I squeezed her hand, looked up, and suddenly leaped to my feet, sending the beer bulb spiraling off into thin air and almost launching myself. Only the sticktite velcro soles on my soft shoes kept me anchored. "Holy *shit*!" I said, pointing.

From this distance, it looked like a squid, perhaps only a meter or two long. From experience and a growing sense of perspective here, I knew better.

"One of the zeplins," said Aenea. "The Akerataeli have tens of thousands working on the Biosphere. They stay inside the CO_2 and O_2 envelopes."

"It's not going to eat me again, is it?" I said.

Aenea grinned. "I doubt it. The one that got a taste of you has probably spread the word."

I looked for my beer, saw the bulb tumbling away a hundred meters below us, considered leaping after it, thought better of it, and sat down on the sticktite bench.

Aenea gave me her bulb. "Go ahead. I can never finish those things." She watched me drink. "Any other questions while we're talking?"

I swallowed and made a dismissive gesture. "Well, there happens to be a bunch of extinct, mythical, and dead people around. Care to explain that?"

"By extinct you mean the zeplins, Seneschai, and Templars?" she said.

"Yeah. And the ergs . . . although I haven't seen one of those yet."

"The Templars and Ousters have been working to preserve such hunted sentient species the way the colonists on Maui-Covenant tried to save the Old Earth dolphins," she said. "From the early Hegira colonists, then the Hegemony, and now the Pax."

"And the mythical and dead people?" I said.

"By that you mean Colonel Kassad?"

"And Het Masteen," I said. "And, for that matter, Rachel. We seem to have the whole cast of the friggin' Hyperion *Cantos* showing up here."

"Not quite," said Aenea, her voice soft and a bit sad. "The Consul is dead. Father Duré is never allowed to live. And my mother is gone."

"Sorry, kiddo . . ."

She touched my hand again. "That's all right. I know what you mean . . . it's disconcerting."

"Did you know Colonel Kassad or Het Masteen before this?" I said.

Aenea shook her head. "My mother told me about them, of course . . . and Uncle Martin had things to add to his poem's description. But they were gone before I was born."

"Gone," I repeated. "Don't you mean *dead*?" I worked to remember the *Cantos* stanzas. According to the old poet's tale, Het Masteen, the tall Templar, the True Voice of the Tree, had disappeared on the windwagon trip across Hyperion's Sea of Grass shortly after his treeship, the *Yggdrasill*, had burned in orbit. Blood in the Templar's cabin suggested the Shrike. He had left behind the erg in a Mobius cube. Sometime later, they had found Masteen in the Valley of the Time Tombs. He had not been able to explain his absence—had said only that the blood in the windwagon had not been his—had cried out that it was his job to be the Voice of the Tree of Pain— and had died.

Colonel Kassad had disappeared at about that same time—shortly after entering the Valley of the Time Tombs—but the FORCE Colonel had, according to Martin Silenus's *Cantos*, followed his phantom lover, Moneta, into the far future where he was to die in combat with the Shrike. I closed my eyes and recited aloud:

". . . *Later, in the death carnage of the valley,*
Moneta and a few of the Chosen Warriors,
Wounded all,
Torn and tossed themselves by the Shrike horde's fury,
Found the body of Fedmahn Kassad
Still wrapped in death's embrace with the
Silent Shrike.
Lifting the warrior, carrying him, touching him
With reverence born of loss and battle,
They washed and tended his ravaged body,
And bore him to the Crystal Monolith.
Here the hero was laid on a bier of white marble,
Weapons were set at his feet.
In the valley beyond, a great bonfire filled
The air with light.
Human men and women carried torches
Through the dark,
While others descended, wingsoft, through
Morning lapis lazuli,
And some others arrived in faery craft, bubbles of light,
While still others descended on wings of energy
Or wrapped in circles of green and gold.
Later, as the stars burned in place,

*Moneta made her farewells to her future's
Friends and entered the Sphinx.
Multitudes sang.
Rat things poked among fallen pennants
In the field where heroes fell,
While the wind whispered among carapace
And blade, steel and thorn.
And thus,
In the Valley,
The great Tombs shimmered,
Faded from gold to bronze,
And started their long voyage back."*

"Impressive memory," said Aenea.

"Grandam used to cuff me if I screwed it up," I said. "Don't change the subject. The Templar and the Colonel sound dead to me."

"And so they will be," said Aenea. "And so shall we all."

I waited for her to shift out of her Delphic phase.

"The *Cantos* say that Het Masteen was carried away some-where . . . some*when* by the Shrike," she said. "He later died in the Valley of the Time Tombs after returning. The poem did not say if he was gone an hour or thirty years. Uncle Martin did not know."

I squinted at her. "What about Kassad, kiddo? The *Cantos* are fairly specific there . . . the Colonel follows Moneta into the far future, engages in a battle with the Shrike . . ."

"With legions of Shrikes, actually," corrected my friend.

"Yeah," I said. I had never really understood that. "But it seems continuous·enough . . . he follows her, he fights, he dies, his body is put in the Crystal Monolith, and it and Moneta begin the long trip back through time."

Aenea nodded and smiled. "With the Shrike," she said.

I paused. The Shrike had emerged from the Tombs . . . Moneta had traveled with it somehow . . . so although the *Cantos* clearly said that Kassad had destroyed the Shrike in that great, final battle, the monster was somehow alive and traveling with Moneta and Kassad's body back through . . .

Damn. Did the poem ever actually say that Kassad was dead?

"Uncle Martin had to fake parts of the tale, you know," said Aenea. "He had some descriptions from Rachel, but he took poetic license on the parts he did not understand."

"Uh-huh," I said. *Rachel. Moneta. The* Cantos *had clearly suggested that the girl-child Rachel, who went forward with her father, Sol, to the future, would return as the woman Moneta. Colonel Kassad's phantom lover. The woman he would follow into the future to his fate . . .* And what had Rachel said to me a few hours earlier when I was suspicious that

she and Aenea were lovers? "I happen to be involved with a certain soldier . . . male . . . whom you'll meet today. Well, actually, I *will* be involved with him someday. I mean . . . shit, it's complicated."

Indeed. My head hurt. I set down the beer bulb and held my head in
my hands.

"It's more complicated than that," said Aenea.

I peered up at her through my fingers. "Care to explain?"

"Yes, but . . ."

"I know," I said. "At some other time."

"Yes," said Aenea, her hand on mine.

"Any reason why we can't talk about it now?" I said.

Aenea nodded. "We have to go in our pod now and opaque the
walls," she said.

"We do?" I said.

"Yes."

"And then what?" I said.

"Then," said Aenea, floating free of the sticktite mat and pulling me
with her, "we make love for hours."

25

ERO-G. WEIGHTLESSNESS.

      I had never really appreciated those terms and that reality before.

Our living pod was opaqued to the point that the rich evening light glowed as if through thick parchment. Once again, I had the impression of being in a warm heart. Once again I realized how much Aenea was in *my* heart.

At first the encounter bordered on the clinical as Aenea carefully removed my clothes and inspected the healing surgical scars, gently touched my repaired ribs, and ran her palm down my back.

"I should shave," I said, "and shower."

"Nonsense," whispered my friend. "I've given you sponge and sonic baths every day . . . including this morning. You're perfectly clean, my dear. And I like the whiskers." She moved her fingers across my cheek.

We floated above the soft and rounded cubby shelves. I helped Aenea out of her shirt, trousers, and underwear. As each piece came clear, she kicked it through the air into the cubby drawer, shutting the fiber panel with her bare foot when everything was inside. We both chuckled. My own clothes were still floating in the quiet air, the sleeves of my shirt gesturing in slow motion.

"I'll get the . . ." I began.

"No you won't," said Aenea and pulled me closer.

Even kissing demands new skills in zero-g. Aenea's hair coiled around her head in a sunlit corona as I held her face in my hands and kissed her— her lips, eyes, cheeks, forehead, and lips again. We began tumbling slowly, brushing the smooth and glowing wall. It was as warm as my dear friend's flesh. One of us pushed off and we tumbled together into the middle of the oval pod space.

Our kissing became more urgent. Each time we moved to hold the other more tightly, we would begin to pivot around an invisible center of mass, arms and legs entangled as we pressed tighter and rotated more quickly. Without disentangling or interrupting our kiss, I held out one arm, waited for the flesh-warm walls to reach us, and stopped our tumble. The contact pushed us away from the curved, warmly glowing wall and sent us spinning very slowly toward the center again.

Aenea broke our kiss and moved her head back a moment, still holding my arms, regarding me from arm's length. I had seen her smile ten thousand times in the last ten years of her life—had thought that I knew all of her smiles—but this one was deeper, older, more mysterious, and more mischievous than any I had seen before.

"Don't move," she whispered, and, pushing softly against my arm for leverage, rotated in space.

"Aenea . . ." was all I could say and then I could say nothing. I closed my eyes, oblivious of everything except sensation. I could feel my darling's hands tight on the backs of my legs, pulling me closer to her.

After a moment, her knees came to rest against my shoulders, her thighs bumping softly against my chest. I reached out to the hollow of her back and pulled her closer, sliding my cheek along the strong muscle of her inner thigh. At Taliesin West, one of the cooks had owned a tabby cat. Many evenings, when I was sitting alone out on the western terrace watching the sunset and feeling the stones lose their day's heat, waiting for the hour when Aenea and I could sit in her shelter and talk about everything and nothing, I would watch the cat lap slowly from her bowl of cream. I visualized that cat now, but within minutes I could visualize nothing but the immediate and overpowering sense of my dear friend opening to me, of the subtle taste of the sea, of our movements like the tide rising, of all of my senses being centered in the slow but growing sensation at the core of me.

How long we floated this way, I have no idea. Such overwhelming excitement is like a fire that consumes time. Total intimacy is an exemption from the space/time demands of the universe. Only the growing prerogatives of our passion and the ineluctable need to be even closer than this penultimate closeness marked the minutes of our lovemaking.

Aenea opened her legs wider, moved away, released me with her mouth but not her hand. We pivoted again in the sepia light, her tight fingers and my excitement the center of our slow rotation. We kissed, lips moist, Aenea's grasp tightening around me. "Now," she whispered. I obeyed.

If there is a true secret to the universe, it is this . . . these first few seconds of warmth and entry and complete acceptance by one's beloved. We kissed again, oblivious of our slow tumbling, the rich light taking on a heart warmth around us. I opened my eyes long enough to see Aenea's hair swirling like Ophelia's cloak in the wine-dark sea of air in which we floated. It was indeed like holding my beloved in deep, salty water—buoyed up and weightless, the warmth of her around me like the rising tide, our movements as regular as the surf against warm sand.

"Oops . . ." whispered Aenea after only a moment of this perfection.

I paused in my kissing long enough to assess what was separating us. "Newton's Law," I whispered against her cheek.

"For every action . . ." whispered Aenea, chuckling softly, holding my shoulders like a swimmer pausing to rest.

". . . an equal and opposite reaction . . ." I said, smiling until she kissed me again.

"Solution," whispered Aenea. Her legs closed tight around my hips. Her breasts floated between us, the nipples teasing my chest.

Then she lay back, again the swimmer, floating this time, her arms spread but her fingers still interlaced with mine. We continued to pivot slowly around our common center of gravity, a slow tumble, my head coming over and down and around like a rider on a porpoise doing slow cartwheels in the sunlit depths, but I was no longer interested or aware of the elegant ballistics of our lovemaking, but only in the lovemaking. We moved faster in the warm sea of air.

Some minutes later, Aenea released my hands, moved upright and forward as we tumbled together, still moving, sank her short nails into my back even while she kissed me with a wild urgency, and then moved her mouth away to gasp and cry out, once, softly. At the same instant as her cry, I felt the warm universe of her close around me with that short, tight throb, that intimate, shared pulse. A second later it was my turn to gasp, to cling to her as I throbbed within her, to whisper into her salty neck and floating hair—"Aenea . . . Aenea." A prayer. My only prayer then. My only prayer now.

For a long time we floated together even after we had become two people again rather than one. Our legs were still intertwined, our fingers stroking and holding one another. I kissed her throat and felt her pulse like a memory echo against my lips. She ran her fingers through my sweaty hair.

I realized that for this moment, nothing in the past mattered. Nothing terrible in the future mattered. What mattered was her skin against me, her hand holding me, the perfume of her hair and skin and the warmth of her breath against my chest. *This* was *satori*. *This* was truth.

Aenea kicked away to the pod cubby just long enough to return with a small, warm, and wet towel. We took turns wiping some of the sweat and slickness from us. My shirt floated by, the empty sleeves attempting to swim in the gentle air currents. Aenea laughed and lingered in her washing and drying, the simple act quickly turning into something else.

"Oops," said Aenea, smiling at me. "How did that happen?"

"Newton's Law?" I said.

"That makes sense," she whispered. "Then what would be the reaction if I were to do . . . this?"

I think we were both surprised by the instant result of her experiment.

"We have hours until we have to meet the others on the treeship," she said softly. She said something to the living pod and the curved wall went absolutely transparent. It was as if we were floating among these countless branches and sail-sized leaves, the sun's warmth bathing us one moment and then being submerged in night and stars when we looked out the other side of the clear pod.

"Don't worry," said Aenea, "we can see out, but the exterior is opaque on the outside. Reflective."

"How can you be sure?" I whispered, kissing her neck again, seeking the soft pulse.

Aenea sighed. "I guess we can't without going out to look in. Sort of a David Hume problem."

I tried to remember my philosophy readings at Taliesin, recalled our discussions of Berkeley, Hume, and Kant, and chuckled. "There's another way we can check," I said, rubbing my bare feet along her calves and the backs of her legs.

"How's that?" murmured my friend, her eyes closed.

"If anyone can see in," I said, floating behind her, rubbing her back without letting her float away, "there's going to be a huge crowd of Ouster angels and Templar treeships and comet farmers hanging out there in about thirty minutes."

"Really," said Aenea, eyes still closed. "And why is that?"

I began to show her.

She opened her eyes. "Oh, my," she said softly.

I was afraid that I was shocking her.

"Raul?" she whispered.

"Hmmm?" I said, not stopping what I was doing. I closed my eyes.

"Maybe you're right about the pod being reflective on the outside," she whispered and then sighed again, more deeply this time.

"Mmmhmm?" I said.

She grabbed my ears and floated around, pulled herself closer, and whispered, "Why don't we leave the outside transparent and make the *inside* wall reflective?"

My eyes snapped open.

"Just kidding," she whispered and pushed away from the pod wall, pulling me with her into the central sphere of warm air.

The stars blazed around us.

WE WORE FORMAL black outfits to the dinner party and conference on the *Yggdrasill*. I was tense with excitement to be aboard one of the legendary treeships and it was a bit of an anticlimax when I realized that I had not noticed when we had crossed from the biosphere branches to the treeship trunk. It was only when hundreds of us were gathered on a series of plat-forms and opened pods, when the treeship had actually cast off and moved away from the encircling city-sized leaves, province-sized branches, and continent-sized trunks that I realized that we were aboard and moving.

The *Yggdrasill* must have been a bit more than a kilometer in length, from the narrowed crown of the tree to the resplendent root system of boiling fusion energy at its base. A bit of gravity returned under drive—probably only a few percentage points of microgravity—but it was still disconcerting after so much zero-g. It did help with our orientation though, the scores of us able to sit at tables and look one another in the eyes rather than float for a polite position . . . I thought of Aenea and our last hours together and blushed at this thought. There were tables and chairs on the multitiered platforms and many who were not seated there thronged on the flimsy suspension bridges that connected platforms to more far-flung branches, or on the helixes of spiral stairways winding up through branches, leaves, and binding the central trunk like vines, or hung from swingvines and leafy bowers.

Aenea and I were seated at the round central table along with the True Voice of the Tree Het Masteen, the Ouster leaders, and two score of other Templars, refugees from T'ien Shan, and others. I was on Aenea's immediate left. The Templar dignitaries were seated to her right. Even now I can remember the names of most of the others present at the central table.

Besides the captain of the treeship, Het Masteen, there were half a dozen other Templars there, including Ket Rosteen—introduced as the True Voice of the Startree, High Priest of the Muir, and Spokesman of the Templar Brotherhood. The dozen Ousters at the main table included Systenj Coredwell and Navson Hamnim, but there were others who looked little like these tall, thin Ouster archetypes: Am Chipeta and Kent Quinkent, two shorter, darker Ousters—a married couple, I thought—with lively eyes and no webs between their fingers; Sian Quintana Ka'an, a female who was either wearing a resplendent robe of bright feathers or who had been born with them, and her blue-feathered partners Paul Uray and Morgan Bottoms. Two others better fit the Ouster image—Drivenj Nicaagat and Palou Koror—for they were vacuum-adapted and wore their silvery skinsuits through the entire banquet.

There were four of the Hebronese Seneschai Aluit present—LLeeoonn and OOeeaall, whom I had met at the earlier gathering, as well as another pair of the willowy green figures introduced by Aenea as AAllooee and NNeelloo. I could only assume that the four were related or marriage-bound in some complex way.

The alien Akerataeli appeared to be missing until Aenea pointed to a place far out among the branches where the microgravity was even less, and there—between the gossamers and glowbirds—floated the platelet beings. Even the erg binders who were controlling the treeship's containment field were present by proxy in the form of three Mobius cubes with translator discs embedded in their black matrices.

Father Captain Federico de Soya sat to my left and his aide, Sergeant Gregorius, sat to the left of him. Next to the sergeant sat Colonel Fedmahn

Kassad in his formal FORCE black uniform, looking like a holo from the deep Hegemony past. Beyond Kassad sat the Thunderbolt Sow, as upright and proud as the old FORCE warrior to her right, while next to her—eyes bright and attentive—sat Getswang Ngwang Lobsang Tengin Gyapso Sisunwangyur Tshungpa Mapai Dhepal Sangpo, the boy Dalai Lama.

All of the other refugees from T'ien Shan were somewhere on the dining platform, and I saw Lhomo Dondrub, Labsang Samten, George and Jigme, Haruyuki, Kenshiro, Voytek, Viki, Kuku, Kay, and others present at the main table. Just beyond the Templars around the table from us were A. Bettik, Rachel, and Theo Bernard. Rachel never took her eyes off Colonel Kassad, except to look at Aenea when she spoke. It was as if the rest of us were not there.

Tiny Templar servants whom Aenea whisperingly described as crew clones served water and stronger drinks and for a while there was the usual murmuring and polite, predinner conversation. Then there was a silence as thick as prayer. When Ket Rosteen, the True Voice of the Startree, stood to speak, everyone else rose as well.

"My friends," said the small, hooded figure, "fellow Brothers in the Muir, honored Ouster allies, sentient sisters and brothers of the ultimate Lifetree, human refugees from the Pax, and"—the True Voice of the Startree bowed in Aenea's direction—"the most revered One Who Teaches.

"As most of us gathered here know, what the Shrike Church once called the Days of Atonement—with us now for almost three centuries— are almost done. The True Voices of the Brotherhood of the Muir have followed the path of both prophecy and conservation, awaiting events as they came to pass, planting seeds as the soil of revelation has proved fertile.

"In these coming months and years, the future of many races—not just the human race—will be determined. Although there are those among us now who have been granted the gift of being able to glimpse patterns of the future, probabilities tossed like dice on the uneven blanket of space and time, even these gifted ones know that no single future has been pre-ordained for us or our posterity. Events are fluid. The future is like smoke from a burning forest, waiting for the wind of specific events and personal courage to blow the sparks and embers of reality this way or that.

"This day, on this treeship . . . on the reborn and rechristened *Ygg-drasill* . . . we shall determine our own paths to our own futures. My own prayer to the Lifeforce glimpsed by the Muir is not just that the Star-tree Biosphere survives, not just that the Brotherhood survives, not just that our Ouster brethren survive, not just that our hunted and harried sentient cousins of the Seneschai and the Akerataeli and the erg and the zeplin survive, not just that the species known as humankind survives, but that our prophecies begin to be realized this day and that all species of beloved life—humanity no more than the soft-shelled turtle or Mare Infinitus Lantern Mouth, the jumping spider and the tesla tree, the Old Earth raccoon and the Maui-Covenant Thomas hawk—that all species beloved of life join in rebirth of respect as distinct partners in the universe's growing cycle of life."

The True Voice of the Startree turned to Aenea and bowed. "Revered One Who Teaches, we are gathered here today because of you. We know from our prophecies—from those in our Brotherhood and elsewhere who have touched the nexus known as the Void Which Binds—that you are the best, single hope of reconciliation between humanity and Core, between humankind and otherkind. We also know that time is short and that the immediate future holds the potential for both the beginnings of this reconciliation and our liberation . . . or for near total destruction. Before any decisions can be made, there are those among us who must ask their final questions. Will you join in discussion with us now? Is this the time to speak of those things which must be spoken of and understood before all the worlds and abodes of Ouster and Templar and Pax and disparate humankind join in the final battle for humanity's soul?"

"Yes," said Aenea.

The True Voice of the Startree sat down. Aenea stood, waited. I slipped my 'scriber from my vest pocket.

OUSTER SYSTENJ COREDWELL: M. Aenea, Most Respected One Who Teaches, can you tell us with any certainty whether the Biosphere, our Startree, will be spared destruction and the Pax assault?
AENEA: I cannot, Freeman Coredwell. And if I could, it would be wrong for me to speak of it. It is not my role to predict probabilities in the great epicycles of chaos which are the futures. I can say without doubt that the next few days and weeks will determine whether this amazing Biosphere shall survive or not. Our own actions will, to a great extent, determine this. But there is no single correct course of action.

And if I may ask a question . . . there are friends of mine here new to the Startree and to Ouster space. It would help in our discussion if one of our hosts were to explain the background of the Ouster race, of the Biosphere and other projects, and of the Ouster and Templar philosophy.
OUSTER SIAN QUINTANA KA'AN: I would be pleased to speak to our new guests, Friend Aenea. It is important that all present in these deliberations understand our stake in the outcome.

As all of our Ouster and Templar brethren here well know, the Ouster race was created more than eight hundred years ago in scores of star systems far-flung from one another. Human seedships with colonists trained in the genetic arts were sent out from Old Earth System in the great pre-Hegira expansions. These seedships were—for the most part—slower-than-light craft: fleets of crude Bussard ramjets, solar sailing ships, ion scoops, nuclear-pulse propulsion craft, gravity-launched Dyson spherelets, laser-driven containment sailing ships . . . only a few dozen of the later seedships were early Hawking-drive C-plus craft.

These colonists, our ancestors—most traveling in cold sleep deeper than cryogenic fugue—were among the best ARNists, nanotechs, and genetic engineers Old Earth System had to offer. Their missions were to find habitable worlds and—in the absence of terraforming technology—to bioengineer and nanotech the millions of Old Earth life-forms frozen aboard their ships into viable adaptations for those worlds.

As we know, a few of the seedships reached habitable worlds—New Earth, Tau Ceti, Barnard's World. Most, however, reached worlds in systems where no life-forms could survive. The colonists had a choice—they could continue on, hoping that their ship life-support systems would sustain them for more long decades or centuries of travel—or they could use their gene-engineering skills to adapt themselves and their ark's embryos to conditions far harsher than the original seedship planners had imagined.

And so they did. Using the most advanced methods of nanotechnology—methods quashed on Old Earth and the early Hegemony by the TechnoCore—these human beings adapted themselves to wildly inhospitable worlds and to the even less hospitable dark spaces between worlds and stars. Within centuries, the use of Hawking drive had spread to most of these far-flung Swarms of Ouster colonists, but their urge to find friendlier worlds had faded. What they now wanted was to continue to adapt—to allow all of Old Earth's orphans to adapt—to whatever conditions the place and space offered them.

And with this new mission grew their philosophy . . . our philosophy, almost religious in fervor, of spreading life throughout the galaxy . . . throughout the universe. Not just human life . . . not just Old Earth life-forms . . . but life in all of its infinite and complex variations.

A few of our visitors here tonight may not know that the end goal of both us Ousters and our Templar brethren is not just the Biosphere Startree which we can see above us even as we speak . . . but a day in which air and water and life shall fill almost all of the space between the Startree and the yellow sun we see burning above us.

The Brotherhood of the Muir and our loose confederations of Ousters want nothing less than to turn the surface, seas, and atmosphere of every world around every star green with life. *More than that,* we work to see the galaxy grow green . . . tendrils reaching to nearby galaxies . . . superstrings of life.

One by-product of this philosophy, and the reason that the Church and the Pax seek to destroy us, is that for centuries we have been tailoring human evolution to fit the demands the environment gives us. So far, there are no distinct and separate species of humankind different than *Homo sapiens*—that is, all of us here could, if both parties were willing, interbreed with any Pax human or Templar human. But the differences are growing, the genetic separation widening. Already there are forms of Ouster humanity so different that we border on new human species . . . and *those differences are passed along genetically to our offspring.*

This the Church cannot abide. And so we are engaged in this terrible war, deciding whether humankind must remain one species forever, or whether our celebration of diversity in the universe can be allowed to continue.

AENEA: Thank you, Freewoman Sian Quintana Ka'an. I am sure that this has been helpful for my friends who are new to Ouster space, as well as important for the rest of us to remember as we make these momentous decisions. Does anyone else wish to speak?

DALAI LAMA: Friend Aenea, I have a comment and a question of you. The Pax's promise of immortality seduced even me into considering—for a few moments only—converting to their Christian faith. All here love life, it is the bright thread of our commonality. Can you tell us why the cruciform is bad for us? And I must say—the fact that it is a symbiote or parasite does not make it that unthinkable to me or many others. Our bodies have many life-forms—the bacteria in our gut, for instance—which feed off us yet allow us to live. Friend Aenea, what *is* the cruciform? And why should we shun it?

AENEA: (closes her eyes for only a second, sighs, and opens them to face the boy)

Your Holiness, the cruciform was born out of the TechnoCore's desperation following Meina Gladstone's attack on them in the hours before the Fall of the Farcasters.

The TechnoCore, as I have discussed with all of you in different forums, lives and thinks only as a parasite. In that sense, humankind has long been a symbiotic partner of the Core. Our technology was created and limited by Core designs. Our societies have been created, altered, and destroyed by Core plans and Core fears. Our existence as human beings has largely been defined by the endless dance of fear and parasitism with the Core AI entities.

After the Fall, after the Core lost control of the Hegemony via its dataspheres and farcasters, after the Core lost its greatest computing engine—its direct parasitism on the billions of human brains as they transited the Void Which Binds via the so-called farcasters—the TechnoCore had to find a new way to exploit humankind. And it had to find it quickly.

Thus the cruciform. This is nanotechnology at its most refined and most injurious. Where our Ouster friends use advanced genetic engineering combined with nanotechnology to advance the cause of life in the universe, the TechnoCore uses it to advance the cause of Core hyperparasitism.

Each cruciform is made up of billions of Core-connected nanotech entities, each in contact with other cruciforms and the Core via a terrible misuse of the Void Which Binds medium. The TechnoCore has known of the Void for a millennium and used it—misused it—for almost as long. The so-called Hawking drive tore holes in the Void. Then farcasters ripped at the essential fabric of the Void. The Core-driven information metasphere and instantaneous fatline medium stole information from the Void Which

Binds in ways that blinded entire races, destroyed millennia of memories. But it is the cruciform that is the Core's most cynical and terrible misuse of the Void medium.

What makes the cruciform seem most miraculous to most of us is not its ability to restore some form of life—technology has offered variations of that for centuries—but its ability to restore the *personality* and *memories* of the deceased person. When one realizes that this demands information storage capabilities in excess of 6×10^{23} bytes *for each human resurrected*, the fact of cruciform seems truly miraculous. Those in the hierarchy of the Catholic Church who know the Core's secret role in all resurrections ascribe this staggering—impossible—computing power to the Core's megasphere storage potential.

But the Core has nowhere near that computing power. Indeed, even in the heyday of the Ultimates' attempt to create the perfect artificial computing entity, the Ultimate Intelligence, the analyzer of all variables, no AI or series of AIs in the Core had the ability to store sufficient bytes for even one human body/personality to be recorded and resurrected. In fact, even if the Core had such information storage capability, it would never have the energy necessary to re-form atoms and molecules into the precise living entity that is the body of a human being, much less reproduce the intricate wave-form dance that is a human personality.

Resurrection of a single person was and remains impossible for the Core.

That is, it was impossible unless they further ravaged the Void Which Binds—that transtemporal, interstellar medium for the memory and emotions of all sentient races.

Which the Core did without a backward glance. It is the Void Which Binds that records the individual wave-front personalities of those humans wearing cruciforms . . . the cruciform itself is little more than a Core-spawned nanotech data-transfer device.

But every time a person is resurrected, parts of thousands of personalities—human and otherwise—are erased from the more permanent record that is the Void Which Binds. Those of you who have taken communion with me, who have learned the language of the dead and of the living, who have attempted to hear the music of the spheres and have pondered the potential of taking that first step through the Void Which Binds, you understand the terrible savagery this vandalism represents. It must stop. I must stop it.

(Aenea closes her eyes for a long moment, then opens them again and continues.)

But this is not the only evil of the cruciform.

I say again, the Core AI entities are parasites. They cannot stop themselves from being parasites. Besides providing control of humanity via the Church—and, if all else fails, by administering pain to individuals via the cruciforms—there is another reason the AIs have offered humanity resurrection via these cruciform parasites.

With the Fall of the Farcasters, the use of trillions of human neurons in the Core's ultimate datasphere-connected Ultimate Intelligence effort was interrupted. Without the ruse of the farcasters by which to attach themselves like leeches on human brains, to steal the very life energy of neurons and holistic wave fronts from their human hosts, to hook billions of human minds into parallel computing devices, the Ultimate Intelligence project had to stop. With the cruciforms, this parasitism on the human brain has been resumed.

But it is now more complex than mere dataspace connections of billions of human minds in parallel for the Core's purposes. Centuries ago—as far back as the twentieth century A.D.—human researchers dealing with similar neural networks comprised of pre-AI silicon intelligences discovered that the best way to make a neural network creative was to kill it. In those dying seconds—even in the last nanoseconds of a sentient or near-sentient conscience's existence—the linear, essentially binary processes of neural net computing jumped barriers, became wildly creative in the near-death liberation from off-on, binary-based processing.

War-game computer simulations as far back as the late twentieth century showed that dying neural nets made unexpected but highly creative decisions: a primitive, presentient AI controlling a battered seagoing fleet in a simulated war game, for instance, suddenly sank its own damaged ships so that the remnants of its fleet could escape. Such was the genius of dying, nonlinear, neural-net creativity.

The Core has always lacked such creativity. Essentially, it has the linear, serial architecture of the serial CPUs from which it evolved, coupled with the obsessive, noncreative mentality of the ultimate parasite.

But with the cruciform, that great neural-networked Core computing device which is the Christian-cruciformed part of the human race has found a source for almost unlimited creativity. All they need for a creativity catalyst is the death of large parts of the neural net. And humans provide that in abundance.

The Core AIs hover like vampires, waiting to feed off the dying human brains, sucking the marrow of creativity from humankind's mental bones. And when the deaths fall below the needed level or when their Core-computing demand for creative solutions rises . . . they orchestrate a few million more deaths.

Odd accidents occur. Humans' health is not what it was a few centuries ago. Death from cancer, heart disease, and the like are on the rise. And there are more clever forms of arranged mortality. Even with the Pax imposition of peace within the human interstellar empire, the incidents of violent death are on the rise. New forms of death are introduced. The archangel starships are such a beginning. Death is a cheap commodity for the born-again Christian. But it is a rich source of orchestrated creativity for the Core.

And thus the cruciform. And thus . . . I believe . . . at least one reason to eliminate the things from the human body and the human soul.

(When Aenea quits speaking, there is a long silence. Leaves on the treeship whisper in the breeze of circulating air. None of the hundreds of humans or hominids on the many platforms, branches, bridges, or stairways seem to blink, so intense are their gazes as they stare at my friend. Finally a single, strong voice speaks . . .)

FATHER CAPTAIN DE SOYA: I still wear the collar and carry the vows of a Catholic priest. Is there no hope for my Church . . . not the Church of the Pax, held under TechnoCore control and the conceit of greedy men and women . . . but the Church of Jesus Christ and the hundreds of millions who followed His word?

AENEA: Federico . . . Father de Soya . . . it is for you to answer this question. You and the faithful like you. But I can tell you that there are billions of men and women today . . . some who wear the cruciform, more who do not . . . who yearn to return to a Church which concerns itself with spiritual matters, with the teachings of Christ and the deepest matters of the heart, rather than with this obsession with false resurrection.

TEMPLAR HET MASTEEN: Revered One Who Teaches, if I may change the subject from the cosmic and theological to the most personal and petty . . .

AENEA: Nothing of which you speak could be petty, True Voice of the Tree Het Masteen.

TEMPLAR HET MASTEEN: I was on the Hyperion pilgrimage with your mother, Revered One Who Teaches . . .

AENEA: She spoke to me of you often, True Voice of the Tree Het Masteen.

TEMPLAR HET MASTEEN: Then you know that the Lord of Pain . . . the Shrike . . . came to me as the pilgrims were crossing Hyperion's Sea of Grass on the windwagon, One Who Teaches. It came to me and carried me forward in time and across space . . . to this time, to this place.

AENEA: Yes.

TEMPLAR HET MASTEEN: And in my conversations with you and with my brethren in the Brotherhood of the Muir, I have come to understand that it is my fate to serve the Muir and the cause of Life in this age, as it was prophesied centuries ago by our own seers into the Void Which Binds. But in these days, and despite the best efforts of my Brothers and other kind friends among the Ousters, I have heard of Martin Silenus's epic poem and found an edition of the *Cantos* . . .

AENEA: That is unfortunate, True Voice of the Tree Het Masteen. My Uncle Martin wrote that to the best of his knowledge, but his knowledge was incomplete.

TEMPLAR HET MASTEEN: But in the *Cantos,* Revered One Who Teaches, it says that the pilgrims in their day . . . and my friend Colonel Kassad has confirmed that this was the case . . . that they find me on Hyperion, in the Valley of the Time Tombs, and that I die shortly after they find me . . .

AENEA: This is true in the context of the *Cantos,* but . . .

TEMPLAR HET MASTEEN: (holding up one hand to silence my friend)
It is not the inevitability of my return through time to the pilgrimage on Hyperion nor my inevitable death that worries me, Revered One Who Teaches. I understand that this is just one possible future for me . . . however probable or desirable. But what I wish to clarify is the truth of my last words according to the old poet's *Cantos.* Is it true that immediately before dying I will cry out, *I am the True Chosen. I must guide the Tree of Pain during the time of Atonement.*

AENEA: This is what is written in the *Cantos,* True Voice of the Tree Het Masteen.

TEMPLAR HET MASTEEN: (smiling under his hood)
And this time is near, Revered One Who Teaches? Will you be using this *Yggdrasill* as the Tree of Pain for our Atonement as the prophecies attest?

AENEA: I will, True Voice of the Tree Het Masteen. I will be leaving to carry out that Atonement within standard days. I formally ask that the *Yggdrasill* be the instrument of our voyage and the instrument of that Atonement. I will be inviting many among us here tonight to join me on that final voyage. And I formally ask you, True Voice of the Tree Het Masteen, if you will captain the treeship *Yggdrasill*—forever after known as the Tree of Pain—on this voyage.

TEMPLAR HET MASTEEN: I formally accept your invitation and agree to captain the treeship *Yggdrasill* on this mission of Atonement, O Revered One Who Teaches. *(There are several minutes of silence.)*

FOREMAN JIGME NORBU: Aenea, George and I have a question.

AENEA: Yes, Jigme.

FOREMAN JIGME NORBU: You have taught us about the TechnoCore's quiet genocide on such worlds as Hebron, Qom-Riyadh, and others. Well . . . not genocide, exactly, because the populations have been put in a sort of sleeping death, but a terrible kidnapping.

AENEA: Yes.

FOREMAN JIGME NORBU: Has this happened to our beloved T'ien Shan, the Mountains of Heaven, since we left, Aenea? Have our friends and families been silenced with this Core deathwand and been carried away to some Labyrinthine world?

AENEA: Yes, Jigme, I am sad to say that it has happened. The bodies are being transported offworld even as we speak.

KUKU SE: Why? For what reason are these populations being kidnapped? The Jews, the Muslims, the Hindus, the atheists, the Marxists, and now our beautiful Buddhist world. Is the Pax intent on destroying all other faiths?

AENEA: That is the Pax and Church's motivation, Kuku. For the TechnoCore it is a much more complicated matter. Without the cruciform parasite on these non-Christian populations, the Core cannot use these humans in its dying neural net. But by storing these billions of people in their false death, the Core can utilize their minds in its huge, parallel-processing neural network. It is a mutually beneficial deal—the Church, who carries out much of the removal work, is no longer threatened by nonbelievers—the Core, who brings the sleep death and carries out the storage in the Labyrinths, gains new circuits in its Ultimate Intelligence network.

FOREMAN GEORGE TSARONG: Is there no hope then? Can we do nothing to help our friends?

OUSTER NAVSON HAMNIM: Excuse me for interrupting, M. Tsarong, M. Aenea, but we should explain to our friends that when the time comes for our Ouster Swarms and Templar allies to take the offensive against the Pax, our first objective is to liberate the many Labyrinthine worlds where these populations are kept in silent storage and to attempt to revive them.

THE DORJE PHAMO: (loudly)
Revive them? How is this to happen? How can anyone revive them?

AENEA: By striking directly at the TechnoCore.

LHOMO DONDRUB: And where *is* the TechnoCore, Aenea? Tell me and I will go there now and do battle with these AI cowards.

AENEA: The true location of the TechnoCore has been the AIs' best-kept secret since the entities left Old Earth a thousand standard years ago, Lhomo. Their actual, physical location has been hidden since then . . . their secrecy is their best defense against the hosts which might turn against their parasites.

COLONEL FEDMAHN KASSAD: CEO Meina Gladstone was convinced that the Core dwelt in the interstices of the farcaster medium . . . like invisible spiders in an unseen web. It is the reason she authorized the deathbombing of the space-portal farcaster network . . . to strike at the Core. Was she wrong? Were the farcasters destroyed for nothing?

AENEA: She was wrong, Fedmahn. The physical location of the Core was not within the farcaster medium . . . which is the fabric of the Void Which Binds. But the destruction of the farcasters was not in vain . . . it deprived the Core of the parasite medium upon which they fed on human minds, while silencing part of their megasphere data network.

LHOMO DONDRUB: But, Aenea, *you* know where the Core resides?

AENEA: I believe I do.

LHOMO DONDRUB: Will you tell us so that we can attack them with our teeth and nails and bullets and plasma weapons?

AENEA: I will not say at this time, Lhomo. Not until I am certain. And the Core cannot be attacked with physical weapons, just as it cannot be entered by physical entities.

COLONEL FEDMAHN KASSAD: So once again they are impervious to our attacks? Free from confrontation?

AENEA: No, neither impervious nor free from confrontation. If the fates allow, I will personally carry the attack to the physical Core. Indeed, that attack has already begun in ways that I hope to make clear later. And I promise you that I will confront the AIs in their lair.

COLONEL FEDMAHN KASSAD: M. Aenea, Brawne's child, may I ask another question relating to my own fate and future?

AENEA: I will endeavor to answer, Colonel, while repeating my reluctance to discuss specifics of a topic as fluid as our future.

COLONEL FEDMAHN KASSAD: Reluctant or no, child, I believe I deserve an answer to this question. I, too, have read these damned *Cantos*. In them, it says that I followed the apparition Moneta into the future while fighting the Shrike . . . trying to prevent it from slaughtering the other pilgrims. This was true . . . some months ago I arrived here. Moneta disappeared, but has reappeared in the younger version of this woman who calls herself Rachel Weintraub. But the *Cantos* also state that I will soon join in terrible battle with legions of Shrikes, will die, and will be entombed in the newly built Time Tomb called the Crystal Monolith on Hyperion, where my body travels back in time with Moneta as my companion. How can this be, M. Aenea? Have I come to the wrong time? The wrong place?

AENEA: Colonel Kassad, friend and protector of my mother and the other pilgrims, be assured that all proceeds according to whatever plan there is. Uncle Martin wrote the *Cantos* given what revelation there was granted to him. Not all details of your life . . . or mine . . . were available to him. Indeed, he was told precious little of what was to transpire outside of his presence.

I can say this to you, Colonel Kassad . . . the battle with the Shrike is true, however metaphorically rendered. One possible future is for you to die in battle with the Shrike . . . with many Shrike-like warriors . . . and to be placed in the Crystal Monolith after a hero's funeral. But if this were to come to pass, it would be after many years and many other battles. There is work for you to do in the days, months, years, and decades yet to come. I ask you now to accompany me on the *Yggdrasill* when I depart in three days . . . that will be the first step toward these battles.

COLONEL FEDMAHN KASSAD: (smiling)

But you deflect the question somewhat, M. Aenea. May I ask you . . . will the Shrike be on your Tree of Pain when it leaves in three standard days' time?

AENEA: I believe it will, Colonel Kassad.

COLONEL FEDMAHN KASSAD: You have not told us here tonight, M. Aenea, *what* the Shrike is . . . where it truly comes from . . . what its role in this centuries-old and centuries-to-come game is.

AENEA: That is correct, Colonel. I have not told anyone here tonight.

COLONEL FEDMAHN KASSAD: Have you ever told anyone, child?

AENEA: No.

COLONEL FEDMAHN KASSAD: But you *know* the origin of the Shrike.

AENEA: Yes.

COLONEL FEDMAHN KASSAD: Will you tell us, Brawne Lamia's child?

AENEA: I would prefer not to, Colonel.

COLONEL FEDMAHN KASSAD: But you *will* if asked again, will you not? At least you will answer my direct questions on the matter?

AENEA: (nods silently . . . I see tears in her eyes)

COLONEL FEDMAHN KASSAD: The Shrike first appears in that same far future in which I do battle with it as per the *Cantos,* is this not correct, M. Aenea? That future in which the Core is making its last-ditch stand against its enemies?

AENEA: Yes.

COLONEL FEDMAHN KASSAD: And the Shrike is . . . will be . . . a construct, is it not? A created thing. A *Core*-created thing.

AENEA: This is accurate.

COLONEL FEDMAHN KASSAD: It will be a strange amalgam of Core technological wizardry, Void Which Binds energy, and the cybrid-recycled personality of a real human being, won't it, M. Aenea?

AENEA: Yes, Colonel. It will be all those things and more.

COLONEL FEDMAHN KASSAD: And the Shrike will be created by the Core but will become a servant and Avatar of other . . . powers . . . entities, will it not?

AENEA: Yes.

COLONEL FEDMAHN KASSAD: In truth, Aenea, would you agree that the Shrike will be a pawn of both sides . . . of *all* sides . . . in this war for the soul of humankind . . . this war that leaps back and forth across time like a four-dimensional chess game?

AENEA: Yes, Colonel . . . although not a pawn. A knight, perhaps.

COLONEL FEDMAHN KASSAD: All right, a knight. And this cybrid, Void Which Binds–connected, ARNied, DNA-engineered, nanotech-enhanced, terribly mutated knight . . . it starts with the personality of a single warrior, does it not? Perhaps an opponent in this thousand-year game?

AENEA: Do you need to know this, Colonel? There is no greater hell than seeing the precise details of one's . . .

COLONEL FEDMAHN KASSAD: (softly)

Of one's future? Of one's own death? Of one's fate? I know that, Aenea, daughter of my friend Brawne Lamia. I know that you have carried such terrible certitudes and visions with you since before you were born . . . since the days when your mother and I crossed the seas and mountains of Hyperion toward what we thought was our fate with the Shrike. I know that it has been very difficult for you, Aenea, my young friend . . . harder than any of us here could imagine. None of us could have borne up under such a burden.

But still I want to know this part of my own fate. And I believe that my years of service in the cause of this battle . . . years past and years yet to be given . . . have earned me the right to an answer.

Is the Shrike based on a single human warrior's personality?

AENEA: Yes.

COLONEL FEDMAHN KASSAD: Mine? After my death in battle, the Core elements . . . or some power . . . will incorporate my will, my soul, my persona into that . . . monster . . . and send it back in time through the Crystal Monolith?

AENEA: Yes, Colonel. Parts of your persona . . . but only *parts* of it . . . will be incorporated into the living construct called the Shrike.

COLONEL FEDMAHN KASSAD: (laughing)

But I can also live to *beat* it in battle?

AENEA: Yes.

COLONEL FEDMAHN KASSAD: (laughing harder now, the laughter sounding sincere and unforced)

By God . . . by the will of Allah . . . if the universe has any soul, it is the soul of irony. I kill mine enemy, I eat his heart, and the enemy becomes me . . . and I become him. *(There are several more minutes of silence. I see that the treeship* Yggdrasill *has turned around and that we are approaching the great curve of the Biosphere Startree again.)*

RACHEL WEINTRAUB: Friend Aenea, Beloved Teacher, in the years I have listened to you teach and learned from you, one great mystery has haunted me.

AENEA: What is that, Rachel?

RACHEL WEINTRAUB: Through the Void Which Binds, you have heard the voices of the Others . . . the sentient races beyond our space and time whose memories and personalities resonate in the Void medium. Through communion with your blood, some of us have learned to hear the whispers of the echoes of those voices . . . of the Lions and Tigers and Bears, as some call them.

AENEA: You are one of my best students, Rachel. You will someday hear these voices clearly. Just as you will learn to hear the music of the spheres and to take that first step.

RACHEL WEINTRAUB: (shaking her head)

That is not my question, friend Aenea. The mystery to me has been the presence in human space of an Observer or Observers sent by those . . . Others . . . those Lions and Tigers and Bears . . . to study humankind and report back to these distant races. Is the presence of this Observer . . . or these Observers . . . a literal fact?

AENEA: It is.

RACHEL WEINTRAUB: And they were able to take on the form of human or Ouster or Templar?

AENEA: The Observer or Observers are not shapeshifters, Rachel. They chose to come among us in some sort of mortal form, that is true . . . much as my father was mortal but cybrid born.

RACHEL WEINTRAUB: And this Observer or these Observers have been watching us for centuries?

AENEA: Yes.

RACHEL WEINTRAUB: Is that Observer . . . or one of these Observers . . . with us here today, on this treeship, or at this table?

AENEA: (hesitates)

Rachel, it is best that I say nothing more at this time. There are those who would kill such an Observer in an instant to protect the Pax or to defend what they think it means to be "human." Even saying that such an

Observer exists puts that entity at great risk. I am sorry . . . I promise you that this . . . this mystery . . . will be solved in the not-too-distant future and the Observer or Observers' identity revealed. Not by me, but by the Observer or Observers themselves.

TEMPLAR TRUE VOICE OF THE STARTREE KET ROS-TEEN: Brothers in the Muir, respected Ouster allies, honored human guests, beloved sentient friends, Revered One Who Teaches . . . we shall finish this discussion at another time and in another place. I take it as a consensus of those among us that M. Aenea's request for the treeship *Yggdrasill* to depart for Pax space in three standard days is agreed to . . . and that, with luck and courage, thus shall be fulfilled the ancient Templar prophecies of the Tree of Pain and the time of Atonement for all children of Old Earth.

Now we will finish our meal and speak of other things. This formal meeting is adjourned, and what remains of our short voyage must be friendly conversation, good food, and the sacrament of real coffee grown from beans harvested on Old Earth . . . our common home . . . the good Earth.

This meeting is adjourned. I have spoken.

LATER THAT EVENING, in the warm light of our private cubby, Aenea and I made love, spoke of personal things, and had a late, second supper of wine and zygoat cheese and fresh bread.

Aenea had gone off to the kitchen cubby for a moment and returned with two cystal bulbs of wine. Offering me one, she said, "Here, Raul, my beloved . . . take this and drink."

"Thanks," I said without thinking and started to raise the bulb to my lips. Then I froze. "Is this . . . did you . . ."

"Yes," said Aenea. "It is the communion that I have delayed so long for you. Now it is yours if you choose to drink. But you do not have to do this, my love. It will not change the way I feel about you if you choose not to."

Still looking into her eyes, I drained the wine in the bulb. It tasted only of wine.

Aenea was weeping. She turned her head away, but I had already seen the tears in her lovely, dark eyes. I swept her up in my arms and we floated together in the warm womb light.

"Kiddo?" I whispered. "What's wrong?" My heart ached as I wondered if she was thinking of the other man in her past, her marriage, the child . . . The wine had made me dizzy and a bit sick. Or perhaps it was not the wine.

She shook her head. "I love you, Raul."

"I love you, Aenea."

She kissed my neck and clung to me. "For what you have just done, for me, in my name, you will be hunted and persecuted . . ."

I forced a chuckle. "Hey, kiddo, I've been hunted and persecuted since the day we rode the hawking mat out of the Valley of the Time Tombs together. Nothing new there. I'd miss it if the Pax quit chasing us."

She did not smile. I felt her tears against my throat and chest as she clung more tightly. "You will be the first among all those who follow me, Raul. You will be the leader in the decades and decades of struggle to come. You will be respected and hated, obeyed and despised . . . they will want to make a god of you, my darling."

"Bullshit," I whispered into my friend's hair. "You know I'm no leader, kiddo. I haven't done anything except follow in all the years we've known each other. Hell . . . I spend most of my time just trying to catch up."

Aenea raised her face to mine. "You were my Chosen One before I was born, Raul Endymion. When I fall, you will continue on for us. Both of us must live through you . . ."

I put my heavy finger against her lips. I kissed the tears from her cheeks and lashes. "No talking of falling or living without the other," I commanded her. "My plan is simple . . . to stay with you forever . . . through everything . . . to share everything. What happens to you, happens to me, kiddo. I love you, Aenea." We floated in the warm air together. I was cradling her in my arms.

"Yes," whispered my friend, hugging me fiercely, "I love you, Raul. Together. Time. Yes."

We quit talking then. I tasted wine and the salt from her tears in our kisses. We made love for more hours, then drifted off to sleep together, floating entwined in the other's embrace like two sea creatures, like one wonderfully complex sea creature, drifting on a warm and friendly tide.

26

THE NEXT DAY we took the Consul's ship out toward the sun.

I had awakened expecting to be feeling some sort of enlightenment, overnight *satori* from the communion wine, a deeper understanding of the universe at the very least, omniscience and omnipotence at best. Instead, I awoke with a full bladder, a slight headache, but pleasant memories of the night before.

Aenea was awake before me and by the time I came out of the toilet cubby, she had coffee hot in the brewing bulb, fruit in its serving globe, and fresh, warm rolls ready.

"Don't expect this service every morning," she said with a smile.

"Okay, kiddo. Tomorrow I'll make breakfast."

"Omelet?" she said, handing me a coffee bulb.

I broke the seal, inhaled the aroma, and squeezed out a drop, taking care not to burn my lips or to let the globule of hot coffee get away. "Sure," I said. "Anything you like."

"Good luck in finding the eggs," she said, finishing her roll in two bites. "This Startree is neat, but short on chickens."

"Pity," I said, looking through the transparent pod wall. "And so many places to roost." I changed tones to serious. "Kiddo, about the wine . . . I mean, it's been about eight standard hours and . . ."

"You don't feel any different," said Aenea. "Hmm, I guess you're one of those rare individuals on which the magic doesn't work."

"Really?"

My voice must have sounded alarmed, or relieved, or both, because Aenea shook her head. "Uh-uh, just kidding. About twenty-four standard hours. You'll feel something. I guarantee it."

"What if we're . . . ah . . . busy when the time comes?" I said, wiggling my eyebrows for emphasis. The motion made me float free a bit from the sticktite table.

Aenea sighed. "Down, boy, before I staple those eyebrows in place."

"Mmm," I said, grinning at her over the coffee bulb. "I love it when you talk dirty."

"Hurry," said Aenea, setting her bulb in the sonic washer bin and recycling the eating mat.

I was content to munch my roll and look at the incredible view through the wall. "Hurry? Why? Are we going somewhere?"

"Meeting on the ship," said Aenea. "*Our* ship. Then we have to get back and see to the last provisioning of the *Yggdrasill* for departure tomorrow evening."

"Why on our ship?" I said. "Won't it just be crowded compared to all these other places?"

"You'll see," said Aenea. She had slipped into soft blue zero-g trousers, pulled tight at the ankle, with a tucked-in white shirt with several sticktite-sealing pockets. She wore gray slippers. I had gotten used to going barefoot around the cubby and in the various stems and pods.

"Hurry," she said again. "Ship's leaving in ten minutes and it's a long vine ride to the docking pod."

IT WAS CROWDED. And although the internal containment field held the gravity to one-sixth-g, it felt like a Jovian pull after sleeping in freefall. It seemed strange to be crowded in on one dimensional plane with everyone, letting all that airspace overhead go to waste. On the library deck of the Consul's ship with us, seated at the piano, on benches, in overstuffed chairs, and along holopit ledges, were the Ousters Navson Hamnim, Systenj Coredwell, Sian Quintana Ka'an resplendent in her feathers, the two silver, vacuum-adapted Ousters Palou Koror and Drivenj Nicaagat, as well as Paul Uray, and Am Chipeta. Het Masteen was there, as was his superior, Ket Rosteen. Colonel Kassad was present—as tall as the towering Ousters—and so were the Dorje Phamo, looking ancient and regal in an ice-gray gown that billowed beautifully in the low gravity, as well as Lhomo, Rachel, Theo, A. Bettik, and the Dalai Lama. None of the other sentient beings were there.

Several of us stepped out on the balcony to watch the inner surface of the Startree fall behind as the ship climbed toward the central star on its pillar of blue fusion flame.

"Welcome back, Colonel Kassad," the ship said as we gathered on the library level.

I raised an eyebrow at Aenea, surprised that the ship had managed to remember his passenger from the old days.

"Thank you, Ship," said the Colonel. The tall, dark man seemed distracted to the point of brooding.

Climbing away from the inner shell of the Biosphere Startree gave me a sense of vertigo quite distinct from watching the sphere of a planet grow smaller and fall behind. Here we were *inside* the orbital structure, and while the view from within the branches of the Startree had been one of open gaps between the leaves and trunks, glimpses of starfields on the side opposite the sun and everywhere great spaces, the view from a hundred thousand klicks and climbing was of a seemingly solid surface, the huge leaves reduced to a shimmering surface—looking for all the world like a great green, concave ocean—and the sense of being *in* some huge bowl and unable to escape was almost overwhelming.

The branches were glowing blue from the trapped atmosphere within the containment fields there, giving thousands of klicks of vinous wood and flickering leaves a sort of blue, electric glow, as if the entire inner surface were charged with voltage. And everywhere was life and motion: Ouster angels with hundred-klick wings not only flitted among the branches and beyond the leaves, but were hurled deeper into space—inward toward the sun, more quickly outward past the ten-thousand-klick root systems; a myriad of smaller life-forms shimmered in the blue envelope of atmosphere—radiant gossamers, faery chains, parrots, blue arboreals, Old Earth monkeys, vast schools of tropical fish swimming along in zero-g, seeking out the comet-misted regions, blue herons, flights of geese and Martian brandy fowl, Old Earth porpoises—we passed out of range before I could categorize a fraction of what I was seeing.

Farther out, the size of the largest life-forms and swarms of life-forms became apparent. From several thousand klicks "up," I could see the shimmering herds of blue platelets, the sentient Akerataeli traveling together. After our first meeting here with the creatures from my cloud planet, I had asked Aenea if there were any more on the Biosphere Startree than the two in the conference. "A few more," my friend had said. "About six hundred million more." Now I could see the Akerataeli moving effortlessly on the air currents from trunk to trunk—hundreds of kilometers apart—in swarms of thousands, perhaps tens of thousands.

And with them came their obedient servants: the sky squids and zeplins and transparent medusae and vast, tendriled gas bags similar to the one that had eaten me on the cloud world. But larger. I had estimated that original monster as perhaps ten klicks long—these zeplinlike work beasts must have been several hundred klicks long, perhaps longer when one factored in the countless tentacles, tendrils, flagella, whips, tails, probes, and proboscises the things sported. I realized as I watched that all of the Akerataeli's giant beasts of burden were busy with tasks—weaving branches and stems and pods into elaborate bio-designs, pruning dead branches and city-sized leaves from the Startree, wrestling Ouster-designed structures into place or hauling material from one part of the Biosphere to another.

"How many zeplin things are the Akerataeli controlling on the Startree?" I asked Aenea when she was free for a second.

"I don't know," she said. "Let's ask Navson."

The Ouster said, "We have no idea. They breed as needed for tasks. The Akerataeli themselves are a perfect example of a swarm organism, a hive mind . . . none of the disc-entities alone is sentient . . . in parallel, they are brilliant. The sky squids and other ex-Jovian-world creatures have been reproducing as needed here for more than seven hundred standard years. I would venture that there are several hundred million working around the Biosphere . . . perhaps a billion at this point."

I stared down at the tiny forms on the dwindling Biosphere surface. A billion creatures each the size of the Pinion Plateau on my homeworld.

Farther out and the gaps between the branches a million klicks overhead and a half million klicks underfoot became apparent enough. The section from which we had come was the oldest and densest, but far along the great inner curve of the Biosphere there were gaps and divisions—some planned, others yet to be filled in with living material. But even here space was busy and filled with motion—comets arcing between roots, branches, leaves, and trunks on precise trajectories, their gift of water being volatilized from the surface by Ouster-aimed and erg-powered heat beams from the trunks and from genetically adapted reflective leaves creating mirrors hundreds of klicks across. Once turned to water vapor, the great clouds drifted across the trailing roots and misted the billion square klicks of leaf surface.

Larger than the comets were the scores of carefully placed asteroids and shepherd moons moving a few thousand or tens of thousands of kilometers above the inner and outer surface of the living sphere—correcting for orbital drift, providing tides and tugs to help the branches grow correctly, throwing shadow on the Biosphere's inner surface where shade was needed, and serving as observation bases and work shacks for the countless Ouster and Templar gardeners who watched over the project from decade to decade and century to century.

And now, a half a light-minute out and accelerating toward the sun as if the ship were searching for a Hawking-drive translation point, there appeared to be even more traffic in the vast hollow of the green sphere: Ouster warships, all obsolete by Pax standards, with Hawking-drive blisters or giant ramscoop containment fields, old-fashioned high-g destroyers and C_3 ships from a long-gone era, elegant sunjammer cargo craft with great curved sails of gleaming monofilm—and everywhere the individual Ouster angels, wings flapping and shimmering as they tacked in toward the sun or hurtled back out toward the Biosphere.

Aenea and the others stepped back inside to continue their discussion. The topic was important—still trying to find a way to stall the Pax from attacking, some sort of feint or distraction that would keep the massing fleet from hurling itself this way—but I had more important things on my mind.

As A. Bettik turned to leave the balcony, I touched the android's right sleeve. "Can you stay and talk a minute?"

"Of course, M. Endymion." The blue-skinned man's voice was as gentle as always.

I waited until we were alone on the balcony, the drone of conversation from within affording us privacy outside, and leaned on the railing. "I'm sorry we haven't had more chance to talk since arriving here at the Startree," I said.

A. Bettik's bald scalp gleamed in the rich sunlight. His blue-eyed gaze was calm and friendly. "That's perfectly all right, M. Endymion. Events have proven quite hectic since our arrival. I do concur, however, that this artifact does cause one to find opportunities to discuss it." He waved his remaining hand at the huge curve of the Startree to where it seemed to fade away near the central sun's brilliance.

"It's not the Startree or the Ousters I want to talk about," I said softly, leaning a bit closer.

A. Bettik nodded and waited.

"You were with Aenea on all of the worlds between Old Earth and T'ien Shan," I said. "Ixion, Maui-Covenant, Renaissance Vector, and the others?"

"Yes, M. Endymion. I had the privilege to travel with her during all the time she allowed others to travel with her."

I chewed my lip, realizing that I was about to make a fool of myself but having no choice. "And what about the time when she did *not* allow you to travel with her," I said.

"While M. Rachel, M. Theo, and the others remained with me on Groombridge Dyson D?" said A. Bettik. "We carried on with M. Aenea's work, M. Endymion. I was especially busy working on the construction of . . ."

"No, no," I interrupted, "I mean what do you know about her absence?"

A. Bettik paused. "Virtually nothing, M. Endymion. She had told us that she would be away for some time. She had made provisions for our employment and continued work with her . . . students. One day she was gone and she was to stay away for approximately two standard years . . ."

"One year, eleven months, one week, six hours," I said.

"Yes, M. Endymion. That is precisely correct."

"And after she returned, she never told you where she had been?"

"No, M. Endymion. As far as I know, she never mentioned it to any of us."

I wanted to grab A. Bettik's shoulders, to make him understand, to explain why this was of life and death importance to me. Would he have understood? I didn't know. Instead, attempting to sound calm, almost disinterested—and failing miserably—I said, "Did you notice anything different about Aenea when she returned from that sabbatical, A. Bettik?"

My android friend paused, not, it seemed, out of hesitation to speak, but as if laboring to remember nuances of human emotion. "We left for T'ien Shan almost immediately after that, M. Endymion, but my best recollection is that M. Aenea was very emotional for some months—elated one minute, absolutely wracked with despair the next. By the time you arrived on T'ien Shan, these emotional swings had seemed to have abated."

"And she never mentioned what caused them?" I felt like a swine going behind my beloved's back like this, but I knew that she would not talk to me about these things.

"No, M. Endymion," said the android. "She never talked to me about the cause. I presumed it was some event or events she experienced during her absence."

I took a deep breath. "Before she left . . . on the other worlds . . . Amritsar, Patawpha . . . any of the worlds before she left Groombridge Dyson D . . . had she . . . was she . . . had there been anyone?"

"I don't understand, M. Endymion."

"Was there a man in her life, A. Bettik? Someone she showed affection for? Someone who seemed especially close to her?"

"Ah," said the android. "No, M. Endymion, there seemed to be no male who showed any special interest in M. Aenea . . . other than as a teacher and possible messiah, of course."

"Yeah," I said. "And no one came back with her after the one year, eleven months, one week, and six hours?"

"No, M. Endymion."

I gripped A. Bettik's shoulder. "Thank you, my friend. I'm sorry I'm asking these stupid questions. It's just that . . . I don't understand . . . somewhere there's a . . . shit, it doesn't matter. It's just stupid human emotion." I turned to go in to join the others.

A. Bettik stopped me with a hand on my wrist. "M. Endymion," he said softly, "if love is the human emotion to which you refer, I feel that I have watched humankind long enough during my existence to know that love is never a stupid emotion. I feel that M. Aenea is correct when she teaches that it may well be the mainspring energy of the universe."

I stood and watched, gaping, as the android left the balcony and went into the crowded library level.

THEY WERE CLOSE to making a decision.

"I think we should send the Gideon-drive courier drone with a message," Aenea was saying as I came into the lounge. "Send it direct and within the hour."

"They'll confiscate the drone," said Sian Quintana Ka'an in her musical contralto. "And it's the only ship we have left with the instantaneous drive."

"Good," said Aenea. "They're an abomination. Every time they are used, part of the Void is destroyed."

"Still," said Paul Uray, his thick Ouster dialect sounding like someone speaking through radio static, "there remains the option of using the
drone as a delivery system."

"To launch nuclear warheads, or plasma weapons, against the armada?" said Aenea. "I thought that we had dismissed that possibility."

"It's our only way of striking at them before they strike at us," said
Colonel Kassad.

"It would do no good," said the Templar True Voice of the Startree
Ket Rosteen. "The drones are not built for precise targeting. An archangel-
class warship would destroy it light-minutes away from target. I agree with
the One Who Teaches. Send the message."

"But will the message stop their attack?" said Systenj Coredwell.

Aenea made the little gesture that I knew so well. "There are no
guarantees . . . but if it puts them off balance, at least *they* will use their
instantaneous drive drones to postpone the attack. It is worth a try, I
think."

"And what will the message say?" said Rachel.

"Please hand me that vellum and stylus," said Aenea.

Theo brought the items and set them on the Steinway. Everyone—
including me—crowded close as Aenea wrote:

> To Pope Urban XVI and Cardinal Lourdusamy:
> I am coming to Pacem, to the Vatican.
> Aenea

"There," said my young friend, handing the vellum to Navson
Hamnim. "Please set this in the courier drone when we dock, set the transponder to 'carrying hardcopy message,' and launch it to Pacem System."

The Ouster took the vellum. I had not yet developed the knack of
reading the Ouster's facial expressions, but I could tell that something was
giving him pause. Perhaps it was a lesser form of the same sort of panic and
confusion that was filling my chest at the moment.

I am coming to Pacem. What the goddamn hell did that mean? How
could Aenea go to Pacem and survive? She could not. And wherever she
was going, I was certain of only one thing . . . that I would be at her side.
Which meant that she was going to kill me as well, if she was as good as
her word. Which she always had been. *I am coming to Pacem.* Was it just a
ploy to deter their fleet? An empty threat . . . a way of stalling them? I
wanted to shake my beloved until her teeth fell out or until she explained
everything to me.

"Raul," she said, gesturing me closer.

I thought that perhaps this was the explanation I wanted, that she
was reading my expression from across the room and saw the turmoil
within me, but all she said was, "Palou Koror and Drivenj Nicaagat are
going to show me what it means to fly like an angel, do you want to come
with me? Lhomo's coming."

Fly like an angel? For a moment I was sure that she was speaking gibberish.

"They have an extra skinsuit if you want to come," Aenea was saying. "But we have to go now. We're almost back to the Startree and the ship will be docking in a few minutes. Het Masteen has to get on with the loading and provisioning of the *Yggdrasill* and I have a hundred things to do before tomorrow."

"Yeah," I said, not knowing what I was agreeing to. "I'll come along." At the time I was feeling surly enough to think that this response was a wonderful metaphor for my entire ten-year odyssey: *yeah, I don't know what I'm doing or getting into, but count me in.*

One of the space-adapted Ousters, Palou Koror, handed us the skinsuits. I had used skinsuits before, of course—the last time being just a few weeks earlier when Aenea and I had climbed T'ai Shan, the Great Peak of the Middle Kingdom—although it seemed like months or years ago—but I had never seen or felt a skinsuit like these.

Skinsuits go back many centuries, the working concept being that the best way to keep from exploding in vacuum is not a bulky pressure suit as in the earliest days of spaceflight, but a covering so thin that it allows perspiration to pass even while it protects the skin from the terrible heat, cold, and vacuum of space. Skinsuits had not changed much in all those centuries, except to incorporate rebreathing filaments and osmosis panels. Of course, my last skinsuit had been a Hegemony artifact, workable enough until Rhadamanth Nemes had clawed it to shreds.

But this was no ordinary skinsuit. Silver, malleable as mercury, the thing felt like a warm but weightless blob of protoplasm when Palou Koror dropped it in my hand. It *shifted* like mercury. No, it shifted and flowed like a living, fluid thing. I almost dropped it in my shock, catching it with my other hand only to watch it flow several centimeters up my wrist and arm like some flesh-eating alien.

I must have said something out loud, because Aenea said, "It *is* alive, Raul. The skinsuit's an organism . . . gene-tailored and nanoteched . . . but only three molecules thick."

"How do I put it on?" I said, watching it flow up my arm to the sleeve of my tunic, then retreat. I had the impression that the thing was more carnivore than garment. And the problem with any skinsuit was that they had to be worn next to the *skin*: one did not wear layers *under* a skinsuit. Anywhere.

"Uh-huh," said Aenea. "It's easy . . . none of the pulling and tugging we had to do with the old skinsuits. Just strip naked, stand very still, and drop the thing on your head. It'll flow down over you. And we have to hurry."

This inspired something less than great enthusiasm in me.

Aenea and I excused ourselves and jogged up the spiral stairs to the bedroom level at the apex of the ship. Once there we hurried out of our clothes. I looked at my beloved—standing naked next to the Consul's ancient (and quite comfortable, as I remembered) bed—and was about to suggest a better use of our time before the treeship docked. But Aenea just waggled a finger at me, held the blob of silver protoplasm above her, and dropped it in her hair.

It was alarming watching the silver organism engulf her—flowing down over her brown-blond hair like liquid metal, covering her eyes and mouth and chin, flowing down her neck like reflective lava, then covering her shoulders, breasts, belly, hipbones, pubis, thighs, knees . . . finally she lifted first one foot and then the other and the engulfment was complete.

"Are you all right?" I said, my voice small, my own blob of silver still pulsing in my hand, eager to get at me.

Aenea—or the chrome statue that had been Aenea—gave me a thumbs-up and gestured to her throat. I understood: as with the Hegemony skinsuits, communication from now on would be via subvocalization pick-ups.

I lifted the pulsing mass in both hands, held my breath, closed my eyes, and dropped it on my head.

It took less than five seconds. For a terrible instant I was sure that I could not breathe, feeling the slick mass over my nose and mouth, but then I remembered to inhale and the oxygen came cool and fresh.

Can you hear me, Raul? Her voice was much more distinct than the hearpatch pickups on the old suit.

I nodded, then subvocalized, *Yeah. Weird feeling.*

Are you ready, M. Aenea, M. Endymion? It took me a second to realize that it was the other adapted Ouster, Drivenj Nicaagat on the suit-line. I had heard his voice before, but translated via speech synthesizer. On the direct line, his voice was even more clear and melodious than the bird-song of Sian Quintana Ka'an.

Ready, responded Aenea, and we went down the spiral stairs, through the throng, and out onto the balcony.

Good luck, M. Aenea, M. Endymion. It was A. Bettik speaking to us through one of the ship's comlinks. The android touched each of us on our respective silver shoulders as we stepped next to Koror and Nicaagat at the balcony railing.

Lhomo was also waiting, his silver skinsuit showing every ridge of delineated muscle on his arms, thighs, and flat belly. I felt awkward for a moment, wishing either that I was wearing something over this micron-thin layer of silver fluid or that I worked harder at keeping in shape. Aenea looked beautiful, the body that I loved sculpted in chrome. I was glad that no one but the android had followed the five of us onto the balcony.

The ship was within a couple thousand klicks of the Startree and decelerating hard. Palou Koror made a motion and jumped easily onto the thin balcony rail, balancing against the one-sixth-g. Drivenj Nicaagat fol-lowed suit, and then Lhomo, then Aenea, and finally—much less grace-fully—I joined them. The sense of height and exposure was all but overwhelming—the great green basin of the Startree beneath us, the leafy walls rising into the unblinking distance on all sides, the bulk of the ship curving away beneath us, balancing on the slim column of fusion fire like a building teetering on a fragile blue column. I realized with a sickening feeling that we were going to jump.

Do not worry, I will open the containment field at the precise instant you pass through and go to EM repulsors until you are clear of the drive exhaust. I realized that it was the ship speaking. I had no idea of what we were doing.

The suits should give you a rough idea of our adaptation, Palou Koror was saying. *Of course, for those of us who have chosen full integration, it is not the semisentient suits and their molecular microprocessors that allow us to live and travel in space, but the adapted circuits in our skin, our blood, our vision, and brains.*

How do we . . . I began, having some trouble subvocalizing, as if the dryness in my mouth would have any affect on my throat muscles.

Do not worry, said Nicaagat. *We will not deploy our wings until proper separation is achieved. They will not collide . . . the fields would not allow it. Controls are quite intuitive. Your suit's optical systems should interface with your nervous system and neurosensors, calling up data when required.*

Data? What data? I had only meant to think that, but the suitcom sent it out.

Aenea took my silver hand in hers. *This will be fun, Raul. The only free minutes we're going to have today, I think. Or for a while.*

At that moment, poised on the railing on the edge of a terrifying vertical drop through fusion flame and vacuum, I did not really focus on the meaning of her words.

Come, said Palou Koror and leaped from the railing.

Still holding hands, Aenea and I jumped together.

SHE LET GO of my hand and we spun away from one another. The containment field parted and ejected us a safe distance, the fusion drive paused as the five of us spun away from the ship, then it relit—the ship seeming to hurtle upward and away from us as its deceleration outpaced our own— and we continued dropping, that sensation was overwhelming, five silver, spread-eagled forms, separating farther and farther from each other, all plummeting toward the Startree lattice still several thousand klicks beneath. Then our wings opened.

For our purposes today, the lightwings need only be a kilometer or so across, came Palou Koror's voice in my ears. *Were we traveling farther or faster, they would extend much farther . . . perhaps several hundred kilometers.*

When I raised my arms, the panels of energy extruding from my skinsuit unfurled like butterfly wings. I *felt* the sudden push of sunlight.

What we feel is more the current of the primary magnetic field line we are following, said Palou Koror. *If I may slave your suits for a second . . . there.*

Vision shifted. I looked to my left to where Aenea fell, already several klicks away—a shining silver chrysalis set within expanding gold wings. The others glowed beyond her. I could *see* the solar wind, see the charged particles and currents of plasma flowing and spiraling outward along the infinitely complex geometry of the heliosphere—red lines of twisting magnetic field coiling as if painted on the inner surfaces of an ever-shifting chambered nautilus, all this convoluted, multilayered, multicolored writhing of plasma streams flowing back to a sun that no longer seemed a pale star but was the locus of millions of converging field lines, entire sheets of plasma being evicted at 400 kilometers a second and being drawn into these shapes by the pulsing magnetic fields in its north and south equators, ` I could see the violet streamers of the inward-rushing magnetic lines, weaving and interlacing with the crimson red of the outward-exploding sheets of field current, I could see the blue vortices of heliospheric shock wave around the outer edges of the Startree, the moons and comets cutting through plasma medium like ocean-going ships at night plowing through a glowing, phosphorescent sea, and could see our gold wings interacting with this plasma and magnetic medium, catching photons like billions of fireflies in our nets, sail surfaces surging to the plasma currents, our silver bodies accelerating out along the great shimmering folds and spiral magnetic geometries of the heliosphere matrix.

In addition to this enhanced vision, the suit opticals were overlaying trajectory information and computational data that meant nothing to me, but must have meant life or death to these space-adapted Ousters. The equations and functions flashed by, seemingly floating in the distance at critical focus, and I remember only a sampling:

$$\frac{GM_3M_c}{r^2} = \frac{M_cV^2_{cir}}{r}$$

and

$$P_r = \frac{(1+k)\, S_r}{c}$$

and

$$k = \frac{R_a}{(R_a + A)}$$

and

$$a_s \quad\rule{2cm}{0.4pt}\quad a_3 = \frac{(1+k)\,(6.3 \times 10^{17})\, R_s^2}{2Mr^2} \quad\rule{2cm}{0.4pt}\quad m\,/\,sec^2$$

and

$$V_1^2 + \triangle V^2 + 2\triangle V(V_i^2 + V_e^2)^{1/2} > V_i^2 + \triangle V^2 + 2\triangle VV_i$$

Even without understanding any of these equations, I knew that we were approaching the Startree too fast. In addition to the ship's velocity, we had picked up our own speed from the solar wind and the plasma stream. I began to see how these Ouster energy wings could move one *out* from a star—and at an impressive velocity—but how did one *stop* within what looked to be less than a thousand kilometers?

This is fantastic, came Lhomo's voice. *Amazing.*

I rotated my head far enough to see our flyer friend from T'ien Shan far to our left and many kilometers below us. He had already entered the leaf zone and was swooping and soaring just above the blue blur of the containment field that surrounded the branches and spaces between the branches like an osmotic membrane.

How the hell did he do that? I wondered.

Again, I must have subvocalized the thought, for I heard Lhomo's deep, distinctive laugh and he sent, USE *the wings, Raul. And cooperate with the tree and the ergs!*

Cooperate with the tree and the ergs? My friend must have lost his reason.

Then I saw Aenea extending her wings, manipulating them by both thought and the movement of her arms, I looked beyond her to the world of branches approaching us at horrifying velocity, and then I began to see the trick.

That's good, came Drivenj Nicaagat's voice. *Catch the repelling wind. Good.*

I watched the two adapted Ousters flutter like butterflies, saw the torrent of plasma energy rising from the Startree to surround them, and suddenly hurtled past them as if they had opened parachutes and I was still in freefall.

Panting against the skinsuit field, my heart pounding, I spread my arms and legs and willed the wings wider. The energy folds shimmered and expanded to at least two klicks. Beneath me, an expanse of leaves shifted, turned slowly and purposefully as if in a time-lapse nature holo of flowers seeking the light, folded over one another to form a smooth, parabolic dish at least five klicks across, and then went perfectly reflective.

Sunlight blazed against me. If I had been watching with unshielded eyes, I would have been instantly blinded. As it was, the suit optics polarized. I *heard* the sunlight striking my skinsuit and wings, like hard rain on a metal roof. I opened my wings wider to catch the blazing gust of light at the same instant the ergs on the Startree below folded the heliosphere matrix, bending the plasma stream back against Aenea and me, decelerating both of us rapidly but not painfully so. Wings flapping, we passed into the bowering outbranches of the Startree while the suit optics continued to flow data across my field of vision.

$$v_f = \sqrt{V_c^2} = \frac{2(J - GM_{star}M_c)}{r_i M_c}$$

Which somehow assured me that the tree was providing the proper amount of the sun's light based on its mass and luminosity, while the erg was providing just enough heliospheric plasma and magnetic feedback to bring us to near zero delta-v before we struck one of the huge main branches or interdicted the containment field.

Aenea and I followed the Ousters, using our wings in the same way they used theirs, soaring and then flapping, braking and then expanding to catch the true sun's light to accelerate again, swooping in among the outer branches, soaring over the leafy outer layer of the Startree, then diving deep among the branches again, folding our wings to pass between pods or covered bridges out beyond the core containment fields, swooping around busily working space squids whose tentacles were ten times longer than the Consul's ship now decelerating carefully through the leaf level, then opening our wings again to surge past floating schools of thousands of blue-pulsing Akerataeli platelets, which seemed to be waving at us as we passed.

There was a huge platform branch just below the containment field shimmer. I did not know if the wings would work through the field, but Palou Koror passed through with only a shimmer—like a graceful diver cutting through still water—followed by Drivenj Nicaagat, then by Lhomo, then Aenea, and finally I joined them, folding my wings to a dozen or so meters across as I crossed the energy barrier into air and sound and scent and cool breezes once again.

We landed on the platform.

"Very nice for a first flight," said Palou Koror, her voice synthesized for the atmosphere. "We wanted to share just a moment of our lives with you."

Aenea deactivated the skinsuit around her face, allowing it to flow into a collar of fluid mercury. Her eyes were bright, as alive as I had ever seen them. Her fair skin was flushed and her hair was damp with sweat. "Wonderful!" she cried and turned to squeeze my hand. "Wonderful . . . thank you so much. Thank you, thank you, thank you, Freeman Nicaagat, Freewoman Koror."

"It was our pleasure, Revered One Who Teaches," said Nicaagat with a bow.

I looked up and realized that the *Yggdrasill* was docked with the Startree just above us, the treeship's kilometer of branches and trunk mingling perfectly with the Biosphere branches. Only the fact that the Consul's ship had slowly docked and was being pulled into a storage pod by a worker squid allowed me to see the treeship. Crew clones were visible, working feverishly, carrying provisions and Mobius cubes onto Het Masteen's treeship, and I could see scores of plantstem life-support umbilicals and connector stems running from the Startree to the treeship.

Aenea had not released my hand. When I turned my gaze from the treeship hanging above us to my friend, she leaned closer and kissed me on the lips. "Can you imagine, Raul? Millions of the space-adapted Ousters *living* out there . . . seeing all that energy all the time . . . flying for weeks and months in the empty spaces . . . running the bowshock rapids of magnetospheres and vortexes around planets . . . riding the solar-wind plasma shock waves out ten AUs or more, and then flying farther . . . to the heliopause termination-shock boundary seventy-five to a hundred and fifty AUs from the star, out to where the solar wind ends and the interstellar medium begins. *Hearing* the hiss and whispers and surf-crash of the universe's ocean? Can you *imagine*?"

"No," I said. I could not. I did not know what she was talking about. Not then.

A. Bettik, Rachel, Theo, Kassad, and the others descended from a transit vine. Rachel carried clothes for Aenea. A. Bettik brought my clothes.

Ousters and others surrounded my friend again, demanding answers to urgent questions, seeking clarifications of orders, reporting on the imminent launch of the Gideon-drive drone. We were swept apart by the press of other people.

Aenea looked back and waved. I raised my hand—still silver from the skinsuit—to wave back, but she was gone.

THAT EVENING SEVERAL hundred of us took a transport pod pulled by a squid to a site many thousands of klicks to the northwest above the plane of the ecliptic along the inner shell of the Biosphere Startree, but the voyage lasted less than thirty minutes because the squid took a shortcut, cutting an arc through space from our section of the sphere to the new one.

The architecture of living pods and communal platforms, branch towers and connecting bridges on this section of the tree, while still so close to our region by any meaningful geography of this huge structure, looked different—larger, more baroque, *alien*—and the Ousters and Templars here spoke a slightly different dialect, while the space-adapted Ousters ornamented themselves with bands of shimmering color that I had not seen before. There were different birds and beasts in the atmosphere zones here—exotic fish swimming through misted air, great herds of something that looked like Old Earth killer whales with short arms and elegant hands. And this was only a few thousand klicks from the region I knew. I could not imagine the diversity of cultures and life-forms throughout this Biosphere. For the first time I realized what Aenea and the others had been telling me over and over . . . there was more internal surface on the sections of the completed Biosphere than the total of all the planetary surfaces discovered by humankind in the past thousand years of interstellar flight. When the Startree was completed, the internal Biosphere quickened, the volume of habitable space would exceed all the inhabitable worlds in the Milky Way galaxy.

We were met by officials, feted for a few moments on crowded one-sixth-g platforms among hundreds of Ouster and Templar dignitaries, then taken into a pod so large that it might have been a small moon.

A crowd of several hundred thousand Ousters and Templars waited, with a few hundred Seneschai Aluit and hovering crowds of Akerataeli near the central dais. Blinking, I realized that the ergs had set the internal containment field at a comfortable one-sixth-g, pulling everyone toward the surface of the sphere, but then I noticed *that the seats continued up and over and around* the full interior of the sphere. I revised my estimate of the crowd to well over a million.

Ouster Freeman Navson Hamnim and Templar True Voice of the Startree Ket Rosteen introduced Aenea, saying that she brought with her the message that their people had awaited for centuries.

My young friend walked to the podium, looking up and around and down, as if making eye contact with every person in the huge space. The sound system was so sophisticated that we could have heard her swallow or breathe. My beloved looked calm.

"Choose again," said Aenea. And she turned, walked away from the podium, and went down to where the chalices lay on the long table.

Hundreds of us donated our blood, mere drops, as the chalices of wine were passed out to the waiting multitudes. I knew that there was no way that a million waiting Ouster and Templar communicants could be served by a few hundred of us who had already received communion from Aenea, but the aides drew a few drops with sterile lancets, the drops were transferred to the reservoir of wine, scores of helpers passed chalice bulbs under the spigots, and within the hour, those who wished communion with Aenea's wine-blood had received it. The great sphere began emptying.

After her two words, nothing else had been said through the entire evening. For the first time on that long—endless—day, there was silence in the transport pod traveling home . . . home, back to our region of the Startree under the shadow of the *Yggdrasill* destined to depart within twenty hours.

I had felt like a fraud. I had drunk the wine almost twenty-four hours earlier, but I had felt nothing this day . . . nothing except my usual love for Aenea, which is to say, my absolutely *un*usual, unique, totally without referent or equal love for Aenea.

The multitudes who wanted to drink had drunk. The great sphere had emptied, with even those who had not come to the communion silent— whether with disappointment at my beloved's two-word speech, or pondering something beyond and beneath that, I did not know.

We took the transport pod back to our region of the Startree and we were silent except for the most necessary of communications. It was not an awkward or disappointed silence, more a silence of awe bordering on fear at the terminus of one part of one's life and the beginning . . . the hope for a beginning . . . of another.

Choose again. Aenea and I made love in the darkened living pod, despite our fatigue and the late hour. Our lovemaking was slow and tender and almost unbearably sweet.

Choose again. They were the last words in my mind as I finally drifted . . . literally . . . off to sleep. *Choose again.* I understood. I chose Aenea and life with Aenea. And I believe that she had chosen me.

And I would choose her and she would choose me again tomorrow, and the tomorrow after that, and in every hour during those tomorrows.

Choose again. Yes. Yes.

27

Y NAME IS Jacob Schulmann. I write this letter to my friends in Lodz:

> My very dear friends, I waited to write to confirm what I'd heard. Alas, to our great grief, we now know it all. I spoke to an eyewitness who escaped. He told me everything. They're exterminated in Chelmno, near Dombie, and they're all buried in Rzuszow forest. The Jews are killed in two ways: by shooting or gas. It's just happened to thousands of Lodz Jews. Do not think that this is being written by a madman. Alas, it is the tragic, horrible truth.
>
> "Horror, horror! Man, shed thy clothes, cover thy head with ashes, run in the streets and dance in thy madness." I am so weary that my pen can no longer write. Creator of the universe, help us!

I write the letter on January 19, A.D. 1942. A few weeks later, during a February thaw when there is a false scent of spring to the woods around our city of Grabow, we—the men in the camp—are loaded into vans. Some of the vans have brightly painted pictures of tropical trees and jungle animals on them. These are the children's vans from last summer when they took the children from the camp. The paint has faded over this past winter, and the Germans have not bothered to retouch the images so that the gay pictures seem to be fading like last summer's dreams.

They drive us fifteen kilometers to Chelmno, which the Germans call Kulmhof. Here they order us out of the vans and demand that we relieve ourselves in the forest. I cannot do it . . . not with the guards and the other men looking on, but I pretend that I have urinated and button my pants again.

They put us back in the big vans and drive us to an old castle. Here they order us out again and we are marched through a courtyard littered with clothes and shoes and down into a cellar. On the wall of the cellar, in Yiddish, is written "No one leaves here alive." There are hundreds of us in the cellar now, all men, all Poles, most of us from the nearby villages such as Gradow and Kolo, but many from Lodz. The air smells of dampness and rot and cold stone and mildew.

After several hours, as the light is waning, we do leave the cellar alive. More vans have arrived, larger vans, with double-leaf doors. These larger vans are green. They have no pictures painted on their sides. The guards open the van doors and I can see that most of these larger vans are almost full, each holding seventy to eighty men. I recognize none of the men in them.

The Germans push and beat us to hurry us into the large vans. I hear many of the men I know crying out so I lead them in prayer as we are packed into the foul-smelling vans—*Shema Israel,* we are praying. We are still praying as the van doors are slammed shut.

Outside, the Germans are shouting at the Polish driver and his Polish helpers. I hear one of the helpers shout "Gas!" in Polish and there comes the sound of a pipe or hose being coupled somewhere under our truck. The engine starts again with a roar.

Some of those around me continue praying with me, but most of the men begin screaming. The van starts to move, very slowly. I know that we are taking the narrow, asphalted road that the Germans built from Chelmno into the forest. All of the villagers marveled at this, because the road goes nowhere . . . it stops in the forest where the road widens so that there is room for the vans to turn around. But there is nothing there but the forest and the ovens the Germans ordered built and the pits the Germans ordered dug. The Jews in the camp who worked on that road and who dug the pits out there and who worked to build the ovens in the forest have told us this. We had not believed them when they told us, and then they were gone . . . transported.

The air thickens. The screams rise. My head hurts. It is hard to breathe. My heart is pounding wildly. I am holding the hands of a young man—a boy—on my left, and an old man to my right. Both are praying with me.

Somewhere in our van, someone is singing above the screams, singing in Yiddish, singing in a baritone that has been trained for opera:

"My God, my God,
 why hast Thou forsaken us?
 We have been thrust into the fire before,
 but we have never denied Thy Holy Law."

Aenea! My God! What?
Shhh. It's all right, my dear. I'm here.
I don't . . . what?

My name is Kaltryn Cateyen Endymion and I am the wife of Trorbe Endymion, who died five local months ago in a hunting accident. I am also the mother of the child named Raul, now three Hyperion-years old, who is playing by the campfire in the caravan circle as aunts watch him.

I climb the grassy hill above the valley where the caravan wagons have circled for the night. There are a few triaspen along the stream in the valley, but otherwise the moors are empty of any landmarks except short grass, heather, sedge, rocks, boulders, and lichen. And sheep. Hundreds of the caravan's sheep are visible and audible on the hills to the east as they mill and surge to the sheepdogs' herding.

Grandam is mending clothes on a rock outcropping with a grand view down the valley to the west. There is a haze over the western horizon that means open water, the sea, but the immediate world is bound about by the moors, the evening sky of deepening lapis, the meteor streaks silently crossing and crisscrossing that sky, and the sound of the wind in the grass.

I take a seat on a rock next to Grandam. She is my late mother's mother, and her face is our face but older, with weathered skin, short white hair, firm bones in a strong face, a blade of a nose, and brown eyes with laugh lines at the corners.

"You're back at last," says the older woman. "Was the voyage home smooth?"

"Aye," I say. "Tom took us along the coast from Port Romance and then up the Beak Highway rather than paying the ferry toll through the Fens. We stayed at the Benbroke Inn the first night, camped along the Suiss the second."

Grandam nods. Her fingers are busy with the sewing. There is a basket of clothes next to her on the rock. "And the doctors?"

"The clinic was large," I say. "The Christians have added to it since last we were in Port Romance. The sisters . . . the nurses . . . were very kind during the tests."

Grandam waits.

I look down the valley to where the sun is breaking free from the dark clouds. Light streaks the valley tops, throws subtle shadows behind the low boulders and rocky hilltops, and sets the heather aflame. "It is cancer," I say. "The new strain."

"We knew that from the Moor's Edge doctor," says Grandam. "What did they say the prognosis is?"

I pick up a shirt—it is one of Trorbe's, but belongs to his brother, Raul's Uncle Ley. I pull my own needle and thread from my apron and begin to sew on the button that Trorbe had lost just before his last hunting trip north. My cheeks are hot at the thought that I gave this shirt to Ley with the button missing. "They recommend that I accept the cross," I say.

"There is no cure?" says Grandam. "With all their machines and serums?"

"There used to be," I say. "But evidently it used the molecular technology . . ."

"Nanotech," says Grandam.

"Yes. And the Church banned it some time ago. The more advanced worlds have other treatments."

"But Hyperion does not," says Grandam and sets the clothes in her lap aside.

"Correct." As I speak, I feel very tired, still a little ill from the tests and the trip, and very calm. But also very sad. I can hear Raul and the other boys laughing on the breeze.

"And they counsel accepting their cross," says Grandam, the last word sounding short and sharp-edged.

"Yes. A very nice young priest talked to me for hours yesterday."

Grandam looks me in the eye. "And will you do it, Kaltryn?"

I return her gaze. "No."

"You are sure?"

"Absolutely."

"Trorbe would be alive again and with us now if he had accepted the cruciform last spring as the missionary pleaded."

"Not *my* Trorbe," I say and turn away. For the first time since the pain began seven weeks ago, I am crying. Not for me, I know, but at the memory of Trorbe smiling and waving that last sunrise morn when he set out with his brothers to hunt salt ibson near the coast.

Grandam is holding my hand. "You're thinking of Raul?"

I shake my head. "Not yet. In a few weeks, I'll think of nothing else."

"You do not have to worry about that, you know," Grandam says softly. "I still remember how to raise a young one. I still have tales to tell and skills to teach. And I will keep your memory alive in him."

"He will be so young when . . ." I say and stop.

Grandam is squeezing my hand. "The young remember most deeply," she says softly. "When we are old and failing, it is the memories of childhood which can be summoned most clearly."

The sunset is brilliant but distorted by my tears. I keep my face half turned away from Grandam's gaze. "I don't want him remembering me only when he is old. I want to *see* him . . . every day . . . see him play and grow up."

"Do you remember the verse of Ryokan that I taught you when you were barely older than Raul?" says Grandam.

I have to laugh. "You taught me dozens of Ryokan verses, Grandam."

"The first one," says the old woman.

It takes me only a moment to recall it. I say the verse, avoiding the singsong quality to my voice just as Grandam taught me when I was little older than Raul is now:

> "How happy I am
> As I go hand in hand
> With the children,

To gather young greens
In the fields of spring!"

Grandam has closed her eyes. I can see how thin the parchment of her eyelids is. "You used to like that verse, Kaltryn."

"I still do."

"And does it say anything about the need to gather greens next week or next year or ten years from now in order to be happy now?"

I smile. "Easy for you to say, old woman," I say, my voice soft and affectionate to temper the disrespect in the words. "You've been gathering greens for seventy-four springs and plan to do so for another seventy."

"Not so many to come, I think." She squeezes my hand a final time and releases it. "But the important thing is to walk with the children now, in this evening's spring sunlight, and to gather the greens quickly, for tonight's dinner. I am having your favorite meal."

I actually clap my hands at this. "The Northwind soup? But the leeks are not ripe."

"They are in the south swards, where I sent Lee and his boys to search. And they have a pot full. Go now, get the spring greens to add to the mix. Take your child and be back before true dark."

"I love you, Grandam."

"I know. And Raul loves you, Little One. And I shall take care that the circle remains unbroken. Run on now."

I come awake falling. I have been awake. The leaves of the Startree have shaded the pods for night and the stars to the out-system side are blazing. The voices do not diminish. The images do not fade. This is not like dreaming. This is a maelstrom of images and voices . . . thousands of voices in chorus, all clamoring to be heard. I had not remembered my mother's voice until this moment. When Rabbi Schulmann cried out in Old Earth Polish and prayed in Yiddish, I had understood not only his voice but his thoughts.

I am going mad.

"No, my dear, you are not going mad," whispers Aenea. She is floating against the warm pod wall with me, holding me. The chronometer on my comlog says that the sleep period along this region of the Biosphere Startree is almost over, that the leaves will be shifting to allow the sunlight in within the hour.

The voices whisper and murmur and argue and sob. The images flit at the back of my brain like colors after a terrible blow to the head. I realize that I am holding myself stiffly, fists clenched, teeth clenched, neck veins straining, as against a terrible wind or wave of pain.

"No, no," Aenea is saying, her soft hands stroking my cheek and temples. Sweat floats around me like a sour nimbus. "No, Raul, relax. You are so sensitive to this, my dear, just as I thought. Relax and allow the voices to subside. You can control this, my darling. You can listen when you wish, quiet them when you must."

"But they never go away?" I say.

"Not far away," whispers Aenea. Ouster angels float in the sunlight beyond the leaf barrier sunward.

"And you have listened to this since you were an infant?" I say.

"Since before I was born," says my darling.

"My God, my God," I say, holding my fists against my eyes. "My God."

My name is Amnye Machen Al Ata and I am eleven standard years old when the Pax comes to my village of Qom-Riyadh. Our village is far from the cities, far from the few highways and skyways, far, even, from the caravan routes that crisscross the rock desert and the Burning Plains.

For two days the evening skies have shown the Pax ships burning like embers as they pass from east to west in what my father says is a place above the air. Yesterday the village radio carried orders from the imam at Al-Ghazali who heard over the phone lines from Omar that everyone in the High Reaches and the Burning Plains Oasis Camps are to assemble outside their yurts and wait. Father has gone to the meeting of the men inside the mud-walled mosque in our village.

The rest of my family stands outside our yurt. The other thirty families also wait. Our village poet, Farid ud-Din Attar, walks among us, trying to settle our nerves with verse, but even the adults are fearful.

My father has returned. He tells Mother that the mullah has decided that we cannot wait for the infidels to kill us. The village radio has not been able to raise the mosque at Al-Ghazali or Omar. Father thinks that the radio is broken again, but the mullah believes that the infidels have killed everyone west of the Burning Plains.

We hear the sound of shots from the front of the other yurts. Mother and my oldest sister want to run, but Father orders them to stay. There are screams. I watch the sky, waiting for the infidel Pax ships to reappear. When I look down again, the mullah's enforcers are coming around the side of our yurt, setting new magazines in their rifles. Their faces are grim.

Father has us all hold hands. "God is great," he says and we respond, "God is great." Even I know that "Islam" means submission to the merciful will of Allah.

At the last second, I see the embers in the sky—the Pax ships floating east to west across the zenith so high above.

"God is great!" cries Father.

I hear the shots.

"Aenea, I don't know what these things mean."

"Raul, they do not mean, they are."

"They are real?"

"As real as any memories can be, my love."

"But how? I can hear the voices . . . so many voices . . . as soon as I . . . touch one with my mind . . . these are stronger than my own memories, clearer."

"They are memories, nonetheless, my love."

"Of the dead . . ."

"These are, yes."

"Learning their language . . ."

"In many ways we must learn their language, Raul. Their actual tongues . . . English, Yiddish, Polish, Parsi, Tamal, Greek, Mandarin . . . but also their hearts. The soul of their memory."

"Are these ghosts speaking, Aenea?"

"There are no ghosts, my love. Death is final. The soul is that ineffable combination of memory and personality which we carry through life . . . when life departs, the soul also dies. Except for what we leave in the memory of those who loved us."

"And these memories . . ."

"Resonate in the Void Which Binds."

"How? All those billions of lives . . ."

"And thousands of races and billions of years, my love. Some of your mother's memories are there . . . and my mother's . . . but so are the life impressions of beings terribly far removed from us in space and time."

"Can I touch those as well, Aenea?"

"Perhaps. With time and practice. It took me years to understand them. Even the sense impressions of life-forms so differently evolved are difficult to comprehend, much less their thoughts, memories, and emotions."

"But you have done it?"

"I have tried."

"Alien life-forms like the Seneschai Aluit or the Akerataeli?"

"Much more alien than that, Raul. The Seneschai lived hidden on Hebron near the human settlers for generations. And they are empaths— emotions were their primary language. The Akerataeli are quite different from us, but not so different from the Core entities whom my father visited."

"My head hurts, kiddo. Can you help me stop these voices and images?"

"I can help you quiet them, my love. They will never really stop as long as we live. This is the blessing and burden of the communion with my blood. But before I show you how to quiet them, listen a few more minutes. It is almost leafturn and sunrise."

My name was Lenar Hoyt, priest, but now I am Pope Urban XVI, and I am celebrating the Mass of Resurrection for John Domenico Cardinal Mustafa in St. Peter's Basilica with more than five hundred of the Vatican's most important faithful in attendance.

Standing at the altar, my hands outstretched, I read from the *Prayer of the Faithful*—

"Let us confidently call upon God our Almighty Father
Who raised Christ His Son from the dead
for the salvation of all."

Cardinal Lourdusamy, who serves as my deacon for this Mass, intones—

"That He may return into the perpetual company of the Faithful,
this deceased Cardinal, John Domenico Mustafa,
who once received the seed of eternal life through Baptism,
we pray to the Lord.

"That he, who exercised the episcopal office in the Church
and in the Holy Office while alive,
may once again serve God in his renewed life,
we pray to the Lord.

"That He may give to the souls of our brothers, sisters, relatives,
and benefactors
the reward of their labor,
we pray to the Lord.

"That He may welcome into the light of His countenance
all who sleep in the hope of the resurrection,
and grant them that resurrection,
that they may better serve Him,
we pray to the Lord.

"That He may assist and graciously console
our brothers and sisters who are suffering affliction
from the assaults of the godless and the
derision of the fallen away,
we pray to the Lord.

"That He may one day call into His glorious kingdom,
all who are assembled here in faith and devotion,
and award unto us that same blessing
of temporal resurrection in Christ's name,
we pray to the Lord."

Now, as the choir sings the Offertory Antiphon and the congregation kneels in echoing silence in anticipation of the Holy Eucharist, I turn back from the altar and say—

"Receive, Lord, these gifts which we offer You on behalf of Your servant, John Domenico Mustafa, Cardinal; You gave the reward of the high priesthood in this world; may he be briefly united with the company of Your Saints in the Kingdom of Heaven and return to us via Your Sacrament of Resurrection. Through Christ our Lord."

The congregation responds in unison—

"Amen."

I walk to Cardinal Mustafa's coffin and resurrection crèche near the communion altar and sprinkle holy water on it, while praying—

"Father, all-powerful and ever-living God,
we do well always and everywhere to give You thanks
through Jesus Christ our Lord.

"In Him, Who rose from the dead,
our hope of resurrection dawned.
The sadness of death gives way
to the bright promise of immortality.

"Lord, for your faithful people life is changed and renewed, not ended.
When the body of our earthly dwelling lies in death
we trust in Your mercy and Your miracle to renew it to us.

"And so, with all the choirs of angels in Heaven
we proclaim Your glory
and join in their unending hymn of praise:"

The great organ in the Basilica thunders while the choir immediately begins singing the *Sanctus:*

"Holy, holy, holy Lord God of power and might,
Heaven and earth are full of Your glory.
    Hosanna in the highest.
Blessed is He who comes in the name of the Lord.
    Hosanna in the highest."

After Communion, after the Mass ends and the congregation departs, I walk slowly to the sacristy. I am sad and my heart hurts—literally. The heart disease has advanced once again, clogging my arteries and making every step and word painful. I think—*I must not tell Lourdusamy.*

That Cardinal appears as acolytes and altar boys help divest me of my garments.

"We have received a Gideon-drone courier, Your Holiness."

"From which front?" I inquire.

"Not from the fleet, Holy Father," says the Cardinal, frowning at a hardcopy message that he holds in his fat hands.

"From where then?" I say, holding out my hand impatiently. The message is written on thin vellum.

I am coming to Pacem, to the Vatican.
Aenea.

I look up at my Secretary of State. "Can you stop the fleet, Simon Augustino?"

His jowls seem to quiver. "No, Your Holiness. They made the jump more than twenty-four hours ago. They should be almost finished with their accelerated resurrection schedule and commencing the attack within moments. We cannot outfit a drone and send it in time to recall them."

I realize that my hand is shaking. I give the message back to Cardinal Lourdusamy. "Call in Marusyn and the other fleet commanders," I say. "Tell them to bring every remaining capital fighting ship back to Pacem System. Immediately."

"But Your Holiness," says Lourdusamy, his voice urgent, "there are so many important task force missions under way at the present . . ."

"Immediately!" I snap.

Lourdusamy bows. "Immediately, Your Holiness."

As I turn away, the pain in my chest and the shortness in my breath are like warnings from God that time is short.

"Aenea! The Pope . . ."

"Easy, my love. I'm here."

"I was with the Pope . . . Lenar Hoyt . . . but he's not dead, is he?"

"You are also learning the language of the living, Raul. Incredible that your first contact with another living person's memories is with him. I think . . ."

"No time, Aenea! No time. His cardinal . . . Lourdusamy . . . brought your message. The Pope tried to recall the fleet, but Lourdusamy said that it was too late . . . that they jumped twenty-four hours ago and would be attacking any moment. That could be here, Aenea. It could be the fleet massing at Lacaille 9352 . . ."

"No!" Aenea's cry brings me out of the cacophony of images and voices, memories and sense overlays, not banishing them completely, but making them recede to something not unlike loud music in an adjoining room.

Aenea has summoned a comlog unit from the cubby shelf and is calling both our ship and Navson Hamnim at the same time.

I try to focus on my friend and the moment, pulling clothes on as I do so, but like a person emerging from a vivid dream, the murmur of voices and other memories is still with me.

Father Captain Federico de Soya kneeling in prayer in his private cubby pod on the treeship Yggdrasill, *only de Soya no longer thinks of himself as "Father-Captain," but simply as "Father." And he is unsure of even this title as he kneels and prays, prays as he has for hours this night, and longer hours in the days and nights since the cruciform was removed from his chest and body by the communion with Aenea's blood.*

Father de Soya prays for forgiveness of which—he knows beyond doubt—he is unworthy. He prays for forgiveness for his years as a Pax Fleet captain, his many battles, the lives he has taken, the beautiful works of man and God he has destroyed. Father Federico de Soya kneels in the one-sixth-g silence of his cubby and asks his Lord and Savior . . .

the God of Mercy in which he had learned to believe and which he now doubts . . . to forgive him, not for his own sake, but so that his thoughts and actions in the months and years to come, or hours if his life is to be that short, might better serve his Lord . . .

I pull away from this contact with the sudden revulsion of someone realizing that he is becoming a voyeur. I understand immediately that if Aenea has known this "language of the living" for years, for her entire life, that she has almost certainly spent more energy denying it—avoiding these unsolicited entries into other people's lives—than mastering it.

Aenea has irised an opening in the pod wall and taken the comlog out to the organic tuft of balcony there. I float through and join her, floating down to the balcony's surface under the gentle one-tenth-g pull of the containment field there. There are several faces floating above the diskey of the comlog—Het Masteen's, Ket Rosteen's, and Navson Hamnim's—but all are looking away from the visual pickups, as is Aenea.

It takes me a second to look up at what she is seeing.

Blazing streaks are cutting through the Startree past beautiful rosettes of orange and red flame. For an instant I think that it is just leafturn sunrise along the inner curve of the Biosphere, squids and angels and watering comets catching the light the way Aenea and I had hours earlier when riding the heliosphere matrix, but then I realize what I am seeing.

Pax ships cutting through the Startree in a hundred places, their fusion tails slicing away branches and trunk like cold, bright knives.

Explosions of leaves and debris hundreds of thousands of kilometers away sending earthquake tremors through the branch and pod and balcony on which we stand.

Bright confusion. Energy lances leaping through space, visible because of the billions of particles of escaping atmosphere, pulverized organic matter, burning leaves, and Ouster and Templar blood. Lances cutting and burning everything they touch.

More explosions blossom outward within a few kilometers. The containment field still holds and sound pounds us back against the pod wall that ripples like the flesh of an injured beast. Aenea's comlog goes off at the same instant the Startree curve above us bursts into flame and explodes into silent space. There are shouts and screams and roars audible, but I know that within seconds the containment field must fail and Aenea and I will be sucked out into space with the other tons of debris flying past us.

I try to pull her back into the pod, which is sealing itself in a vain attempt to survive.

"No, Raul, look!"

I look to where she points. Above us, then beneath us, around us, the Startree is burning and exploding, vines and branches snapping, Ouster angels consumed in flame, ten-klick worker squids imploding, treeships burning as they attempt to get under way.

"They're killing the ergs!" shouts Aenea above the wind roar and explosions.

I pound on the pod wall, shouting commands. The door irises open for just a second, but long enough for me to pull my beloved inside.

There is no shelter here. The plasma blasts are visible through the polarized pod walls.

Aenea has pulled her pack out of the cubby and tugged it on. I grab mine, thrust my sheath knife in my belt as if it would help fight off the marauders.

"We have to get to the *Yggdrasill*!" cries Aenea.

We kick off to the stemway wall, but the pod will not let us out. There is a roaring through the pod hull.

"Stemway's breached," gasps Aenea. She still carries the comlog—I see that it is the ancient one from the Consul's ship—and is calling up data from the Startree grid. "Bridges are out. We have to get to the treeship."

I look through the wall. Orange blossoms of flame. The *Yggdrasill* is ten klicks up and inner surface–east of us. With the swaying bridges and stemways gone, it might as well be a thousand light-years away.

"Send the ship for us," I say. "The Consul's ship."

Aenea shakes her head. "Het Masteen is getting the *Yggdrasill* under way now . . . no time to undock our ship. We have to be there in the next three or four minutes or . . . What about the Ouster skinsuits? We can fly over."

It is my turn for headshaking. "They're not here. When we got out of them at the landing platform, I had A. Bettik carry both of them to the treeship."

The pod shakes wildly and Aenea turns away to look. The pod wall is a bright red, melting.

I pull open my storage cubby, throw clothes and gear aside, and pull out the one extraneous artifact I own, tugging it out of its leather storage tube. Father Captain de Soya's gift.

I tap the activator threads. The hawking mat stiffens and hovers in zero-g. The EM field around this section of the Startree is still intact.

"Come on," I shout as the wall melts. I pull my beloved onto the hawking mat.

We are swept out through the fissure, into vacuum and madness.

28

THE ERG-FOLDED MAGNETIC fields were still standing but strangely scrambled. Instead of flying along and above the boulevard-wide swath of branch toward the *Yggdrasill,* the hawking mat wanted to align itself at right angles to the branch, so that our faces seemed to be pointing *down* as the mat rose like an elevator through shaking branches, dangling bridges, severed stemways, globes of flame, and hordes of Ousters leaping off into space to do battle and die. As long as we made progress toward the treeship, I let the hawking mat do what it wanted.

There were bubbles of containment-field atmosphere remaining, but most of the erg-fields had died along with the ergs who maintained them. Despite multiple redundancies, air was either leaking or explosively decompressing all along this region of the Startree. We had no suits. What I had remembered in the pod at the last moment was that the ancient hawking mat had its own low-level field for holding passengers or air in. It was never meant as a long-term pressurization device, but we had used it nine years ago on the unnamed jungle planet when we'd flown too high to breathe, and I hoped the systems were still working.

They still worked . . . at least after a fashion. As soon as we were out of the pod and rising like a parawing through the chaos, the hawking mat's low-level field kicked in. I could almost feel the thin air leaking out, but I told myself that it should last us the length of time it would take to reach the *Yggdrasill.*

We almost did not reach the *Yggdrasill.*

It was not the first space battle I had witnessed—Aenea and I had sat on the high platform of the Temple Hanging in Air not that many standard days, eons, ago and watched the light show in cislunar space as the Pax task force had destroyed Father de Soya's ship—but this was the first space battle I had seen where someone was trying to kill me.

Where there was air, the noise was deafening: explosions, implosions, shattering trunks and stemways, rupturing branches and dying squids, the howl of alarms and babble and squeal of comlogs and other communicators. Where there was vacuum, the silence was even more deafening: Ouster and Templar bodies being blown noiselessly into space—women and children, warriors unable to reach their weapons or battle stations, robed priests of the Muir tumbling toward the sun while wrapped in the ultimate indignity of violent death—flames with no crackling, screams with no sound, cyclones with no windrush warning.

Aenea was huddled over Siri's ancient comlog as we rose through the maelstrom. I saw Systenj Coredwell shouting from the tiny holo display above the diskey, and then Kent Quinkent and Sian Quintana Ka'an speaking earnestly. I was too busy guiding the hawking mat to listen to their desperate conversations.

I could no longer see the fusion tails of the Pax Fleet archangels, only their lances cutting through gas clouds and debris fields, slicing the Startree like scalpels through living flesh. The great trunks and winding branches actually bled, their sap and other vital fluids mixing with the kilometers of fiber-optic vine and Ouster blood as they exploded into space or boiled away in vacuum. A ten-klick worker squid was sliced through and then sliced through again as I watched, its delicate tentacles spasming in a destructive dance as it died. Ouster angels took flight by the thousands and died by the thousands. A treeship tried to get under way and was lanced through in seconds, its rich oxygen atmosphere igniting within the containment field, its crew dying in the time it took for the energy globe to fill with swirling smoke.

"Not the *Yggdrasill*," shouted Aenea.

I nodded. The dying treeship had been coming from sphere north, but the *Yggdrasill* should be close now, a klick or less above us along the vibrating, splintering branch.

Unless I had taken a wrong turn. Or unless it had already been destroyed. Or unless it had left without us.

"I talked to Het Masteen," Aenea shouted. We were in a globe of escaping air now and the din was terrible. "Only about three hundred of the thousand are aboard."

"All right," I said. I had no idea what she was talking about. What thousand? No time to ask. I caught a glimpse of the deeper green of a treeship a klick or more above us and to the left—on another branch helix altogether—and swept the hawking mat in that direction. If it was not the *Yggdrasill* we would have to seek shelter there anyway. The Startree EM fields were failing, the hawking mat losing energy and inertia.

The EM field failed. The hawking mat surged a final time and then began tumbling in the blackness between shattered branches, a kilometer or more from the nearest burning stemways. Far below and behind us I could see the cluster of environment pods from which we had come: they were all shattered, leaking air and bodies, the podstems and connecting branches writhing in blind Newtonian response.

"That's it," I said, my voice low because there was no more air or noise outside our failing bubble of energy. The hawking mat had been designed seven centuries ago to seduce a teenage niece into loving an old man, not to keep its flyers alive in outer space. "We tried, kiddo." I moved back from the flight threads and put my arm around Aenea.

"No," said Aenea, rejecting not my hug but the death sentence. She gripped my arm so fiercely that her fingers sank into the flesh of my bicep. "No, no," she said to herself and tapped the comlog diskey.

Het Masteen's cowled face appeared against the tumbling starfield. "Yes," he said. "I see you."

The huge treeship now hung a thousand meters above us, a single great ceiling of branches and leaves green behind the flickering violet containment field, the bulk of it slowly separating from the burning Startree. There was a sudden, violent tug, and for a second I was sure that one of the archangel lances had found us.

"The ergs are pulling us in," said Aenea, still grasping my arm.

"Ergs?" I said. "I thought a treeship only had one erg aboard to handle the drive and fields."

"Usually they do," said Aenea. "Sometimes two if it's an extraordinary voyage . . . into the outer envelope of a star, for instance, or through the shock wave of a binary's heliosphere."

"So there are two aboard the *Yggdrasill*?" I said, watching the tree grow and fill the sky. Plasma explosions unfolded silently behind us.

"No," said Aenea, "there are twenty-seven."

The extended field pulled us in. Up rearranged itself and became down. We were lowered onto a high deck, just beneath the bridge platform near the crown of the treeship. Even before I tapped the flight threads to collapse our own puny containment field, Aenea was scooping up her comlog and backpack and was racing toward the stairway.

I rolled the hawking mat neatly, shoved it into its leather carrier, flung the tube on my back, and rushed to catch up.

ONLY THE TEMPLAR treeship captain Het Masteen and a few of his lieutenants were on the crown bridge, but the platforms and stairways beneath the bridge level were crowded with people I knew and did not know: Rachel, Theo, A. Bettik, Father de Soya, Sergeant Gregorius, Lhomo Dondrub, and the dozens of other familiar refugees from T'ien Shan, but there were also scores of other non-Ouster, non-Templar humans, men, women, and children whom I had not seen previously. "Refugees fleeing a hundred Pax worlds, picked up by Father Captain de Soya in the *Raphael* over the past few years," said Aenea. "We'd expected hundreds more to arrive to-day before departure, but it's too late now."

I followed her up to the bridge level. Het Masteen stood at the locus of a circle of organic control diskeys—displays from the fiber-optic nerves running throughout the ship, holo displays from onboard, astern, and ahead of the treeship, a communicator nexus to put him in touch with the Templars standing duty with the ergs, in the singularity containment core, at the drive roots, and elsewhere, and the central holo-simulacrum of the treeship itself, which he could touch with his long fingers to call up interactives or change headings. The Templar looked up as Aenea walked quickly across the sacred bridge toward him. His countenance—shaped from Old Earth Asian stock—was calm beneath his cowl.

"I am pleased that you were not left behind, One Who Teaches," he said dryly. "Where do you wish us to go?"

"Out-system," said Aenea without hesitation.

Het Masteen nodded. "We will draw fire, of course. The Pax Fleet firepower is formidable."

Aenea only nodded. I saw the treeship simulacrum turning slowly and looked up to see the starfield rotating above us. We had moved in-system only a few hundred kilometers and were now turning back toward the battered inner surface of the Biosphere Startree. Where our meeting and environment pods had been there was now a ragged hole in the braided branches. All across the thousands of square klicks of this region were gaping wounds and denuded branches. The *Yggdrasill* moved slowly through billions of tumbling leaves—those still in containment-field atmosphere burning brightly and painting the containment-field perimeter gray with ash—as the treeship returned to the sphere wall and carefully passed through.

Emerging from the far side and picking up speed as the erg-controlled fusion drive flared, we could see even more of the battle now. Space here was a myriad of winking pinpoints of light, fiery sparks appearing as defensive containment fields came alight under lance attack, countless thermonuclear and plasma explosions, the drive tails of missiles, hyperkinetic weapons, small attack craft, and archangels. The curving-away outer surface of the Startree looked like a fibrous volcano world erupting with flames and geysers of debris. Watering comets and shepherd asteroids, knocked from their perfect balancing act by Pax weapon blasts, tore through the Startree like cannonballs through kindling. Het Masteen called up tactical holos and we stared at the image of the entire Biosphere, pocked now with ten thousand fires—many individual conflagrations as large as my homeworld of Hyperion—and a hundred thousand visible rents and tears in the sphere fabric that had taken almost a thousand years to weave. There were thousands of under-drive objects being plotted on the radar and deep distance sensors, but fewer each second as the powerful archangels picked off Ouster ramscouts, torchships, destroyers, and treeships with their lances at distances of several AUs. Millions of space-adapted Ousters threw themselves at the attackers, but they died like moths in a flame-thrower.

Lhomo Dondrub strode onto the bridge. He was wearing an Ouster skinsuit and carrying a long, class-four assault weapon. "Aenea, where the goddamned hell are we going?"

"Away," said my beloved. "We have to leave, Lhomo."

The flyer shook his head. "No, we don't. We have to stay and fight. We can't just abandon our friends to these Pax carrion birds."

"Lhomo," said Aenea, "we can't help the Startree. I have to leave here in order to fight the Pax."

"Run again if you have to," said Lhomo, his handsome features contorted by rage and frustration. He molded the silvery skinsuit cowl up over his head. "*I* am going to stay and fight."

"They'll kill you, my friend," said Aenea. "You can't fight archangel-class starships."

"Watch me," said Lhomo, the silvery suit covering everything but his face now. He shook my hand. "Good luck, Raul."

"And to you," I said, feeling my throat tighten and face flush as much from my own shame at fleeing as from bidding farewell to this brave man.

Aenea touched the powerful silver arm. "Lhomo, you can help the fight more if you come with us . . ."

Lhomo Dondrub shook his head and lowered the fluid cowl. The audio pickups sounded metallic as they spoke for him. "Good luck to you, Aenea. May God and the Buddha help you. May God and the Buddha help us all." He stepped to the edge of the platform and looked back at Het Masteen. The Templar nodded, touched the control simulacrum near the crown of the tree, and whispered into one of the fiberthreads.

I felt gravity lessen. The outer field shimmered and shifted. Lhomo was lifted, turned, and catapulted out into space beyond our branches and air and lights. I saw his silver wings unfold, saw the light fill his wings, and watched him form up with a score of other Ouster angels carrying their puny weapons and riding sunlight toward the nearest archangel.

Others were coming onto the bridge now—Rachel, Theo, the Dorje Phamo, Father de Soya and his sergeant, A. Bettik, the Dalai Lama—but all held back, keeping a respectful distance from the busy Templar captain.

"They've acquired us," said Het Masteen. "Firing."

The containment field exploded red. I could hear the sizzling. It was as if we had fallen into the heart of a star.

Displays flickered. "Holding," said the True Voice of the Tree Het Masteen. "Holding."

He meant the defensive fields, but the Pax ships were also holding—maintaining their energy lance fire even as we accelerated out-system. Except for the display holos, there was no sign of our movement—no stars visible—only the crackling, hissing, boiling ovoid of destructive energy bubbling and slithering a few dozen meters above and around us.

"What is our course, please?" asked Het Masteen of Aenea.

My friend touched her forehead briefly as if tired or lost. "Just out where we can see the stars."

"We will never reach a translation point while under this severity of attack," said the Templar.

"I know," said Aenea. "Just . . . out . . . where I can see the stars."

Het Masteen looked up at the inferno above us. "We may never see the stars again."

"We have to," Aenea said simply.

There was a sudden flurry of shouts. I looked up at where the commotion was centered.

There were only a few small platforms above the control bridge—tiny structures looking like crow's nests on a holodrama pirate ship or like a treehouse I had seen once in the Hyperion fens—and it was on one of these that the figure stood. Crew clones were shouting and pointing. Het Masteen peered up toward the tiny platform fifteen meters above us and turned to Aenea. "The Lord of Pain rides with us."

I could see the colors from the inferno beyond the containment field reflecting on the Shrike's forehead and chest carapace.

"I thought it died on T'ien Shan," I said.

Aenea looked more weary than I had ever seen her. "The thing moves through time more easily than we move through space, Raul. It may have died on T'ien Shan . . . it may die a thousand years hence in a battle with Colonel Kassad . . . it may not be capable of dying . . . we will never know."

As if her use of his name had summoned him, Colonel Fedmahn Kassad came up the stairs to the bridge platform. The Colonel was in archaic Hegemony-era battle dress and was carrying the assault rifle I had once seen in the Consul's ship armory. He stared at the Shrike like a man possessed.

"Can I get up there?" Kassad asked the Templar captain.

Still absorbed with issuing commands and monitoring displays, Het Masteen pointed to some ratlines and rope ladders that rose to the highest platform.

"No shooting on this treeship," Het Masteen called after the Colonel. Kassad nodded and began climbing.

The rest of us turned our attention back to the simulacra displays. There were at least three archangels directing some of their fire at us from distances of less than a million klicks. They would take turns lancing us, each then directing some of its fire at other targets. But our odd refusal to die seemed to increase their anger at us and the lances would return, creeping across the four to ten light-seconds and exploding on the containment field above us. One of the ships was about to pass around the curve of the blazing Startree, but the two others were still decelerating in-system toward us with clear fields of fire.

"Missiles launched against us," said one of the captain's Templar lieutenants in a voice no more excited than I would use to announce the arrival of dinner. "Two . . . four . . . nine. Sublight. Presumably plasma warheads."

"Can we survive that?" asked Theo. Rachel had walked over to watch the Colonel climb toward the Shrike.

Het Masteen was too occupied to answer, so Aenea said, "We don't know. It depends on the binders . . . the ergs."

"Sixty seconds to missile impact," said the same Templar lieutenant in the same flat tones.

Het Masteen touched a comwand. His voice sounded normal, but I realized that it was being amplified all over the klick-long treeship. "Everyone will please shield their eyes and avoid looking toward the field. The binders will polarize the flash as much as possible, but please do not look up. May the peace of the Muir be with us."

I looked at Aenea. "Kiddo, does this treeship carry weapons?"

"No," she said. Her eyes looked as weary as her voice had sounded.

"So we're not going to fight . . . just run?"

"Yes, Raul."

I ground my molars. "Then I agree with Lhomo," I said. "We've run too much. It's time to help our friends here. Time to . . ."

At least three of the missiles exploded. Later, I recall the light so blinding that I could see Aenea's skull and vertebrae through her skin and flesh, but that must be impossible. There was a sense of falling . . . of the bottom falling out of everything . . . and then the one-sixth-g field was restored. A subsonic rumble made my teeth and bones hurt.

I blinked away retinal afterimages. Aenea's face was still before me—her cheeks flushed and sweaty, her hair pulled back by a hastily tied band, her eyes tired but infinitely alive, her forearms bare and sunburned—and in a thick moment of sentimentality I thought that it would not have been unthinkable to die like that, with Aenea's face seared into my soul and memory.

Two more plasma warheads made the treeship shudder. Then four more. "Holding," said Het Masteen's lieutenant. "All fields holding."

"Lhomo and Raul are right, Aenea," said the Dorje Phamo, stepping forward with regal elegance in her simple cotton robe. "You have run away from the Pax for years. It is time to fight them . . . time for all of us to fight them."

I was staring at the old woman with something close to rude intensity. I had realized that there was an aura about her . . . no, wrong word, too mystical . . . but a feeling of strong color emanating from her, a deep carmine as strong as the Thunderbolt Sow's personality. I also realized that I had been noticing that with everyone on the platform that evening—the bright blue of Lhomo's courage, the golden confidence of Het Masteen's command, the shimmering violet of Colonel Kassad's shock at seeing the Shrike—and I wondered if this was some artifact of learning the language of the living. Or perhaps it was a result of the overload of light from the plasma explosions. Whatever it was, I knew that the colors were not real—I was not hallucinating and my vision was not clouded—but I also thought that I knew that my mind was making these connections, these shorthand glimpses into the true spirit of the person, on some level below and above sight.

And I knew that the colors surrounding Aenea covered the spectrum and beyond—a glow so pervasive that it filled the treeship as surely as the plasma explosions filled the world outside it.

Father de Soya spoke. "No, ma'am," he said to the Dorje Phamo, his voice soft and respectful. "Lhomo and Raul are not correct. In spite of all of our anger and our wish to strike back, Aenea is correct. Lhomo may learn—if he lives—what we all will learn if we live. That is, after communion with Aenea, we share the pain of those we attack. Truly share it. Literally share it. Physically share it. Share it as part of having learned the language of the living."

The Dorje Phamo looked down at the shorter priest. "I know this is true, Christian. But this does not mean that we cannot strike back when others hurt *us*." She swept one arm upward to include the slowly clearing containment field and the starfield of fusion trails and burning embers beyond it. "These Pax . . . monsters . . . are destroying one of the greatest achievements of the human race. We must *stop* them!"

"Not now," said Father de Soya. "Not by fighting them here. Trust Aenea."

The giant named Sergeant Gregorius stepped into the circle. "Every fiber of my being, every moment of my training, every scar from my years of fighting . . . everything urges me to fight *now*," he growled. "But I trusted my captain. Now I trust him as my priest. And if he says we must trust the young woman . . . then we must trust her."

Het Masteen held up a hand. The group fell into silence. "This argument is a waste of time. As the One Who Teaches told you, the *Yggdrasill* has no weapons and the ergs are our only defense. But they cannot phase-shift the fusion drive while providing this level of shield. Effectively, we have no propulsion . . . we are drifting on our former course only a few light-minutes beyond our original position. And five of the archangels have changed course to intercept us." The Templar turned to face us. "Please, everyone except the Revered One Who Teaches and her tall friend Raul, please leave the bridge platform and wait below."

The others left without another word. I saw the direction of Rachel's gaze before she turned away and I looked up. Colonel Kassad was at the top crow's nest, standing next to the Shrike, the tall man still dwarfed by the three-meter sculpture of chrome and blades and thorns. Neither the Colonel nor the killing machine moved as they regarded one another from less than a meter's distance.

I looked back at the simulacra display. The Pax ship embers were closing fast. Above us the containment field cleared.

"Take my hand, Raul," said Aenea.

I took her hand, remembering all of the other times I had touched it in the last ten standard years.

"The stars," she whispered. "Look up at the stars. And listen to them."

THE TREESHIP *YGGDRASILL* hung in low orbit around an orange-red world with white polar caps, ancient volcanoes larger than my world's Pinion Plateau, and a river valley running for more than five thousand kilometers like an appendectomy scar around the world's belly.

"This is Mars," said Aenea. "Colonel Kassad will leave us here."

The Colonel had come down from his close regard of the Shrike after the quantum-shift jump. There was no word or phrase for what we did: one moment the treeship was in the Biosphere System, coasting at low velocity, drives dead, under attack by a swarm of archangels, and the next instant we were in low and stable orbit around this dead world in Old Earth System.

"How did you do that?" I had asked Aenea a second after she had done it. I'd had no doubt whatsoever that she had . . . shifted . . . us there.

"I learned to hear the music of the spheres," she said. "And then to take a step."

I kept staring at her. I was still holding her hand. I had no plans to release it until she spoke to me in plain language.

"One can *understand* a place, Raul," she said, knowing that so many others were undoubtedly listening at that moment, "and when you do, it is like hearing the music of it. Each world a different chord. Each star system a different sonata. Each specific place a clear and distinct note."

I did not release her hand. "And the farcasting without a farcaster?" I said.

Aenea nodded. "Freecasting. A quantum leap in the real sense of the term," she said. "Moving in the macro universe the way an electron moves in the infinitely micro. Taking a step with the help of the Void Which Binds."

I was shaking my head. "Energy. Where does the energy come from, kiddo? Nothing comes from nothing."

"But everything comes from everything."

"What does that *mean*, Aenea?"

She pulled her fingers from mine but touched my cheek. "Remember our discussion long, long ago about the Newtonian physics of love?"

"Love is an emotion, kiddo. Not a form of energy."

"It's both, Raul. It truly is. And it is the only key to unlocking the universe's greatest supply of energy."

"Are you talking about religion?" I said, half furious at either her opacity or my denseness or both.

"No," she said, "I'm talking about quasars deliberately ignited, about pulsars tamed, about the exploding cores of galaxies tapped for energy like steam turbines. I'm talking about an engineering project two and a half billion years old and barely begun."

I could only stare.

She shook her head. "Later, my love. For now understand that farcasting without a farcaster really works. There were *never* any real farcasters . . . never any magical doors opening onto different worlds . . . only the TechnoCore's perversion of this form of the Void's second most wonderful gift."

I should have said, *What is the Void's first most wonderful gift?* but I assumed then that it was the learning-the-language-of-the-dead recording of sentient races' memories . . . my mother's voice, to be more precise. But what I did say then was, "So this is how you moved Rachel and Theo and you from world to world without time-debt."

"Yes."

"And took the Consul's ship from T'ien Shan System to Biosphere with no Hawking drive."

"Yes."

I was about to say, *And traveled to whatever world where you met your lover, were married, and had a child,* but the words would not form.

"This is Mars," she said next, filling the silence. "Colonel Kassad will leave us here."

The tall warrior stepped to Aenea's side. Rachel came closer, stood on her tiptoes, and kissed him.

"Someday you will be called Moneta," Kassad said softly. "And we will be lovers."

"Yes," said Rachel and stepped back.

Aenea took the tall man's hand. He was still in quaint battle garb, the assault rifle held comfortably in the crook of his arm. Smiling slightly, the Colonel looked up at the highest platform where the Shrike still stood, the blood light of Mars on his carapace.

"Raul," said Aenea, "will you come as well?"

I took her other hand.

THE WIND WAS blowing sand into my eyes and I could not breathe. Aenea handed me an osmosis mask and I slipped mine on as she set hers in place.

The sand was red, the rocks were red, and the sky was a stormy pink. We were standing in a dry river valley bounded by rocky cliffs. The riverbed was strewn with boulders—some as big as the Consul's ship. Colonel Kassad pulled on the helmet cowl of his combat suit and static rasped in our comthread pickups. "Where I started," he said. "In the Tharsis Relocation Slums a few hundred klicks that direction." He gestured toward where the sun hung low and small above the cliffs. The suited figure, ominous in its size and bulk, the heavy assault weapon looking anything but obsolete here on the plain of Mars, turned toward Aenea. "What would you have me do, woman?"

Aenea spoke in the crisp, quick, sure syllables of command. "The Pax has retreated from Mars and Old Earth System temporarily because of the Palestinian uprising here and the resurgence of the Martian War Machine in space. There is nothing strategic enough to hold them here now while their resources are stretched so thin."

Kassad nodded.

"But they'll be back," said Aenea. "Back in force. Not just to pacify Mars, but to occupy the entire system." She paused to look around. I followed her gaze and saw the dark human figures moving down the boulder field toward us. They carried weapons.

"You must keep them out of the system, Colonel," said my friend. "Do whatever you must . . . sacrifice whomever you must . . . but keep them out of Old Earth System for the next five standard years."

I had never heard Aenea sound so adamant or ruthless.

"Five *standard* years," said Colonel Kassad. I could see his thin smile behind the cowl visor. "No problem. If it was five *Martian* years, I might have to strain a bit."

Aenea smiled. The figures were moving closer through the blowing sand. "You'll have to take the leadership of the Martian resistance movement," she said, her voice deadly serious. "Take it any way you can."

"I will," said Kassad and the firmness in his voice matched Aenea's.

"Consolidate the various tribes and warrior factions," said Aenea.

"I will."

"Form a more permanent alliance with the War Machine spacers."

Kassad nodded. The figures were less than a hundred meters away now. I could see weapons raised.

"*Protect Old Earth,*" said Aenea. "Keep the Pax away at all costs."

I was shocked. Colonel Kassad must have been surprised as well. "You mean Old Earth *System,*" he said.

Aenea shook her head. "Old Earth, Fedmahn. Keep the Pax away. You have approximately a year to consolidate control of the entire system. Good luck."

The two shook hands.

"Your mother was a fine, brave woman," said the Colonel. "I valued her friendship."

"And she valued yours."

The dark figures were moving closer, keeping to the cover of boulders and dunes. Colonel Kassad walked toward them, his right hand high, the assault weapon still easy in his arm.

Aenea came closer and took my hand again. "It's cold, isn't it, Raul?"

It was. There was a flash of light like a painless blow to the back of one's head and we were on the bridge platform of the *Yggdrasill*. Our friends backed away at the sight of our appearance; the fear of magic dies hard in a species. Mars turned red and cold beyond our branches and containment field.

"What course, Revered One Who Teaches?" said Het Masteen.

"Just turn outward to where we can clearly see the stars," said Aenea.

29

T HE *Yggdrasill* CONTINUED on. The Tree of Pain its captain, the Templar True Voice of the Tree Het Masteen, called it. I could not argue. Each jump took more energy from my Aenea, my love, my poor, tired Aenea, and each separation filled the depleting pool of energy with a growing reservoir of sadness. And through it all the Shrike stood useless and alone on its high platform, like a hideous bowsprit on a doomed ship or a macabre dark angel on the top of a mirthless Christmas tree.

After leaving Colonel Kassad on Mars, the treeship jumped to orbit around Maui-Covenant. The world was in rebellion but deep within Pax space and I expected hordes of Pax warships to rise up in challenge, but there was no attack during the few hours we were there.

"One of the benefits of the armada attack on the Biosphere Startree," Aenea said with sad irony. "They've stripped the inner systems of fighting ships."

It was Theo whose hand Aenea took for the step down to Maui-Covenant. Again, I accompanied my friend and her friend.

I blinked away the white light and we were on a motile isle, its treesails filling with warm tropical wind, the sky and sea a breathtaking blue. Other isles kept pace while dolphin outriders left white wakes on either side of the convoy.

There were people on the high platform and although they were mystified by our appearance, they were not alarmed. Theo hugged the tall blond man and his dark-haired wife who came forward to greet us.

"Aenea, Raul," she said, "I am pleased to introduce Merin and Deneb Aspic-Coreau."

"Merin?" I said, feeling the strength in the man's handshake.

He smiled. "Ten generations removed from *the* Merin Aspic," he said.

"But a direct descendant. As Deneb is of our famed lady, Siri." He put his hand on Aenea's shoulder. "You have come back just as promised. And brought our fiercest fighter back with you."

"I have," said Aenea. "And you must keep her safe. For the next days and months, you must keep clear of contact with the Pax."

Deneb Aspic-Coreau laughed. I noticed without a trace of desire that she might be the healthiest, most beautiful woman I had ever seen. "We're running for our lives as it is, One Who Teaches. Thrice we've tried to destroy the oil platform complex at Three Currents, and thrice they have cut us down like Thomas hawks. Now we are just hoping to reach the Equatorial Archipelago and hide among the isle migration, eventually to regroup at the submersible base at Lat Zero."

"Protect her at all costs," repeated Aenea. She turned to Theo. "I will miss you, my friend."

Theo Bernard visibly attempted to keep from weeping, failed, and hugged Aenea fiercely. "All the time . . . was *good*," Theo said and stood back. "I pray for your success. And I pray that you fail . . . for your own good."

Aenea shook her head. "Pray for all of our success." She held her hand up in farewell and walked back to the lower platform with me.

I could smell the intoxicating salt-and-fish scent of the sea. The sun was so fierce it made me squint, but the air temperature was perfect. The water on the dolphins' skin was as clear to me as the sweat on my own forearms. I could imagine staying in this place forever.

"We have to go," said Aenea. She took my hand.

A torchship did appear on radar just as we climbed out of Maui-Covenant's gravity well, but we ignored it as Aenea stood alone on the bridge platform, staring at the stars.

I went over to stand next to her.

"Can you hear them?" she whispered.

"The stars?" I said.

"The worlds," she said. "The people on them. Their secrets and silences. So many heartbeats."

I shook my head. "When I am not concentrating on something else," I said, "I am still haunted by voices and images from elsewhere. Other times. My father hunting in the moors with his brothers. Father Glaucus being thrown to his death by Rhadamanth Nemes."

She looked at me. "You saw that?"

"Yes. It was horrible. He could not see who it was who had attacked him. The fall . . . the darkness . . . the cold . . . the moments of pain before he died. He had refused to accept the cruciform. It was why the Church sent him to Sol Draconi Septem . . . exile in the ice."

"Yes," said Aenea. "I've touched those last memories of his many times in the past ten years. But there are other memories of Father Glaucus, Raul. Warm and beautiful memories . . . filled with light. I hope you find them."

"I just want the voices to stop," I said truthfully. "This . . ." I gestured around at the treeship, the people we knew, Het Masteen at his bridge controls. "This is all too important."

Aenea smiled. "It's all too important. That's the damned problem, isn't it?" She turned her face back to the stars. "No, Raul, what you have to hear before you take a step is not the resonance of the language of the dead . . . or even of the living. It is . . . the essence of things." I hesitated, not wanting to make a fool of myself, but went on:

". . . So
A million times ocean must ebb and flow,
And he oppressed. Yet he shall not die,
These things accomplished. If he utterly . . ."

Aenea broke in:

". . . Scans all depths of magic, and expounds
The meanings of all motions, shapes, and sounds;
If he explores all forms and substances
Straight homeward to their symbol-essences;
He shall not die . . ."

She smiled again. "I wonder how Uncle Martin is. Is he cold-sleeping the years away? Railing at his poor android servants? Still working on his unfinished Cantos? In all my dreams, I never manage to see Uncle Martin."

"He's dying," I said.

Aenea blinked in shock.

"I dreamed of him . . . saw him . . . this morning," I said. "He's defrosted himself for the last time, he's told his faithful servants. The machines are keeping him alive. The Poulsen treatments have finally worn off. He's . . ." I stopped.

"Tell me," said Aenea.

"He's staying alive until he can see you again," I said. "But he's very frail."

Aenea looked away. "It's strange," she said. "My mother fought with Uncle Martin during the entire pilgrimage. At times they could have killed one another. Before she died, he was her closest friend. Now . . ." She stopped, her voice thick.

"You'll just have to stay alive, kiddo," I said, my own voice strange. "Stay alive, stay healthy, and go back to see the old man. You owe him that."

"Take my hand, Raul."

The ship farcast through light.

AROUND TAU CETI Center we were immediately attacked, not only by Pax ships but by rebel torchships fighting for the planetary secession started by the ambitious female Archbishop Achilla Silvaski. The containment field flared like a nova.

"Surely you can't 'cast through this," I said to Aenea when she offered the Tromo Trochi of Dhomu and me her hands.

"One does not 'cast *through* anything," said my friend, and took our hands, and we were on the surface of the former capital of the late and unlamented Hegemony.

The Tromo Trochi had never been to TC^2, indeed, had never been off the world of T'ien Shan, but his merchant interests were aroused by the tales of this onetime capitalist capital of the human universe.

"It is a pity that I have nothing to trade," said the clever trader. "In six months on so fecund a world, I would have built a commercial empire."

Aenea reached into the shoulder pack she had carried and lifted out a heavy bar of gold. "This should get you started," she said. "But remember your true duties here."

Holding the bar, the little man bowed. "I will never forget, One Who Teaches. I have not suffered to learn the language of the dead to no avail."

"Just stay safe for the next few months," said Aenea. "And then, I am confident, you will be able to afford transport to any world you choose."

"I would come to wherever you are, M. Aenea," said the trader with the only visible show of emotion I had ever seen from him. "And I would pay all of my wealth—past, future, and fantasized—to do so."

I had to blink at this. It occurred to me for the first time that many of Aenea's disciples might be—probably were—a little bit in love with her, as well as very much in awe of her. To hear it from this coin-obsessed merchant, though, was a shock.

Aenea touched his arm. "Be safe and stay well."

The *Yggdrasill* was still under attack when we returned. It was under attack when Aenea 'cast us away from the Tau Ceti System.

The inner city-world of Lusus was much as I remembered it from my brief sojourn there: a series of Hive towers above the vertical canyons of gray metal. George Tsarong and Jigme Norbu bade us farewell there. The stocky, heavily muscled George—weeping as he hugged Aenea—might have passed for an average Lusian in dim light, but the skeletal Jigme would stand out in the Hive-bound crowds. But Lusus was used to off-worlders and our two foremen would do well as long as they had money. But Lusus was one of the few Pax worlds to have returned to universal credit cards and Aenea did not have one of these in her backpack.

A few minutes after we stepped from the empty Dreg's Hive corridors, however, seven figures in crimson cloaks approached. I stepped between Aenea and these ominous figures, but rather than attack, the seven men went to their knees on the greasy floor, bowed their heads, and chanted:

"BLESSED BE SHE
BLESSED BE THE SOURCE OF OUR SALVATION
BLESSED BE THE INSTRUMENT OF OUR ATONEMENT
BLESSED BE THE FRUIT OF OUR RECONCILIATION
BLESSED BE SHE."

"The Shrike Cult," I said stupidly. "I thought they were gone—wiped out during the Fall."

"We prefer to be referred to as the Church of the Final Atonement," said the first man, rising from his knees but still bowing in Aenea's direction. "And no . . . we were not 'wiped out' as you put it . . . merely driven underground. Welcome, Daughter of Light. Welcome, Bride of the Avatar."

Aenea shook her head with visible impatience. "I am bride of no one, Bishop Duruyen. These are the two men I have brought to entrust to your protection for the next ten months."

The Bishop in red bowed his bald head. "Just as your prophecies said, Daughter of Light."

"Not prophecies," said Aenea. "Promises." She turned and hugged George and Jigme a final time.

"Will we see you again, Architect?" said Jigme.

"I cannot promise that," said Aenea. "But I do promise that if it is in my power, we will be in contact again."

I followed her back to the empty hall in the dripping corridors of Dreg's Hive, where our departure would not seem so miraculous as to add to the Shrike Cult's already fertile canon.

ON TSINTAO-HSISHUANG PANNA, we said good-bye to the Dalai Lama and his brother, Labsang Samten. Labsang wept. The boy Lama did not.

"The local people's Mandarin dialect is atrocious," said the Dalai Lama.

"But they will understand you, Your Holiness," said Aenea. "And they will listen."

"But you are my teacher," said the boy, his voice near anger. "How can I teach them without your help?"

"I will help," said Aenea. "I will try to help. And then it is your job. And theirs."

"But we may share communion with them?" asked Labsang.

"If they ask for it," said Aenea. To the boy she said, "Would you give me your blessing, Your Holiness?"

The child smiled. "It is I who should be asking for a blessing, Teacher."

"Please," said Aenea, and again I could hear the weariness in her voice.

The Dalai Lama bowed and, with his eyes closed, said:

"This is from the 'Prayer of Kuntu Sangpo,' as revealed to me through the vision of my *terton* in a previous life—

"HO! The phenomenal world and all existence, samsara *and*
     nirvana,
All has one foundation, but there are two paths and two results—
Displays of both ignorance and Knowledge.
Through Kuntu Sangpo's aspiration,
In the Palace of the Primal Space of Emptiness
Let all beings attain perfect consummation and Buddhahood.

"The universal foundation is unconditioned,
Spontaneously arising, a vast immanent expanse, beyond
     expression,
Where neither samsara *nor* nirvana *exist.*
Knowledge of this reality is Buddhahood,
While ignorant beings wander in samsara.
Let all sentient beings of the three realms
Attain Knowledge of the nature of the ineffable foundation."

Aenea bowed toward the boy. "The Palace of the Primal Space of Emptiness," she murmured. "How much more elegant than my clumsy description of the 'Void Which Binds.' Thank you, Your Holiness."

The child bowed. "Thank *you*, Revered Teacher. May your death be more quick and less painful than we both expect."

Aenea and I returned to the treeship. "What did he *mean*?" I demanded, both of my hands on her shoulders. " 'Death more quick and less painful'? What the hell does that mean? Are you planning to be crucified? Does this goddamned messiah impersonation have to go to the same bizarre end? *Tell me, Aenea!*" I realized that I was shaking her . . . shaking my dear friend, my beloved girl. I dropped my hands.

Aenea put her arms around me. "Just stay with me, Raul. Stay with me as long as you can."

"I will," I said, patting her back. "I swear to you I will."

ON FUJI WE said good-bye to Kenshiro Endo and Haruyuki Otaki. On Deneb Drei it was a child whom I had never met—a ten-year-old girl named Katherine—who stayed behind, alone and seemingly unafraid. On Sol Draconi Septem, that world of frozen air and deadly wraiths where Father Glaucus and our Chitchatuk friends had been foully murdered, the sad and brooding scaffold rigger, Rimsi Kyipup, volunteered almost happily to be left behind. On Nevermore it was another man I had not had the privilege of meeting—a soft-spoken, elderly gentleman who seemed like Martin Silenus's kindlier younger brother. On God's Grove, where A. Bettik had lost part of his arm ten standard years earlier, the two Templar lieutenants of Het Masteen 'cast down with Aenea and me and did not return. On Hebron, empty now of its Jewish settlers but filled now with good Christian colonists sent there by the Pax, the Seneschai Aluit empaths, Lleeoonn and Ooeeaall 'cast down to say good-bye to us on an empty desert evening where the rocks still held the daytime's glow.

On Parvati, the usually happy sisters Kuku Se and Kay Se wept and hugged the both of us good-bye. On Asquith, a family of two parents and their five golden-haired children stayed behind. Above the white cloud-swirl and blue ocean world of Mare Infinitus—a world whose mere name haunted me with memories of pain and friendship—Aenea asked Sergeant Gregorius if he would 'cast down with her to meet the rebels and support her cause.

"And leave the captain?" asked the giant, obviously shocked by the suggestion.

De Soya stepped forward. "There is no more captain, Sergeant. My dear friend. Only this priest without a Church. And I suspect that we would do more good now apart than together. Am I right, M. Aenea?"

My friend nodded. "I had hoped that Lhomo would be my representative on Mare Infinitus," she said. "The smugglers and rebels and Lantern Mouth hunters on this world would respect a man of strength. But it will be difficult and dangerous . . . the rebellion still rages here and the Pax takes no prisoners."

" 'Tis not th' danger I object to!" cried Gregorius. "I'm willin' to die the true death a hundred times over for a good cause."

"I know that, Sergeant," said Aenea.

The giant looked at his former captain and then back to Aenea. "Lass, I know ye do not like to tell the future, even though we know you spy it now and then. But tell me this . . . is there a chance of reunion with my captain?"

"Yes," said Aenea. "And with some you thought dead . . . such as Corporal Kee."

"Then I'll go. I'll do your will. I may not be of the Corps Helvetica anymore, but the obedience they taught me runs deep."

"It's not obedience we ask now," said Father de Soya. "It is something harder and deeper."

Sergeant Gregorius thought a moment. "Aye," he said at last and turned his back on everyone a moment. "Let's go, lass," he said, holding out his hand for Aenea's touch.

We left him on an abandoned platform somewhere in the South Littoral, but Aenea told him that submersibles would put in there within a day.

ABOVE MADREDEDIOS, FATHER de Soya stepped forward, but Aenea held up her hand to stop him.

"Surely this is my world," said the priest. "I was born here. My diocese was here. I imagine that I will die here."

"Perhaps," said Aenea, "but I need you for a more difficult place and a more dangerous job, Federico."

"Where is that?" said the sad-eyed priest.

"Pacem," said Aenea. "Our last stop."

I stepped closer. "Wait, kiddo," I said. "I'm going with you to Pacem if you insist on going there. You said that I could stay with you." My voice sounded querulous and desperate even to me.

"Yes," said Aenea, touching my wrist with her cool fingers. "But I would like Father de Soya to come with us when it is time."

The Jesuit looked confused and a bit disappointed, but he bowed his head. Evidently obedience ran even deeper in the Society of Jesus than it did in the Corps Helvetica.

In the end, the T'ien Shan bamboo worker Voytek Majer and his new fiancée, the brickmaker Viki Groselj, volunteered to stay on MadredeDios.

On Freeholm, we said good-bye to Janusz Kurtyka. On Kastrop-Rauxel, recently reterraformed and settled by the Pax, it was the soldier Jigme Paring who volunteered to find the rebel population. Above Parsimony, while Pax warships turned the containment field into a torrent of noise and light, a woman named Helen Dean O'Brian stepped forward and took Aenea's hand. On Esperance, Aenea and I bid farewell to the former mayor of Jo-kung, Charles Chi-kyap Kempo. On Grass, standing shoulder high in the yellow world prairie, we waved good-bye to Isher Perpet, one of the bolder rebels once rescued from a Pax prison galley and gathered in by Father de Soya. On Qom-Riyadh, where the mosques were quickly being bulldozed or converted to cathedrals by the new Pax settlers, we 'cast down in the dead of night and whispered our farewells to a former refugee from that world named Merwin Muhammed Ali and to our former interpreter on T'ien Shan, the clever Perri Samdup.

Above Renaissance Minor, with a horde of in-system warships accelerating toward us with murderous intent, it was the silent ex-prisoner, Hoagan Liebler who stepped forward. "I was a spy," said the pale man. He was speaking to Aenea but looking directly at Father de Soya. "I sold my allegiance for money, so that I could return to this world to renew my family's lost lands and wealth. I betrayed my captain and my soul."

"My son," said Father de Soya, "you have long since been forgiven those sins, if sins they were . . . by both your captain and, more importantly, by God. No harm was done."

Liebler nodded slowly. "The voices I have been listening to since I drank the wine with M. Aenea . . ." He trailed off. "I know many people on this world," he said, his voice stronger. "I wish to return home to start this new life."

"Yes," said Aenea and offered her hand.

ON VITUS-GRAY-BALIANUS B, Aenea, the Dorje Phamo, and I 'cast down to a desert wasteland, far from the river with its farm fields and brightly painted cottages lining the way where the kind people of the Amoiete Spectrum Helix had nursed me to health and helped me escape the Pax. Here there was only a tumble of boulders and dried fissures, mazes of tunnel entrances in the rock, and dust storms blowing in from the bloody sunset on the black-cloud horizon. It reminded me of Mars with warmer, thicker air and more of a stench of death and cordite to it.

The shrouded figures surrounded us almost immediately, flechette guns and hellwhips at the ready. I tried again to step between Aenea and the danger, but the figures in the blowing red wind surrounded us and raised their weapons.

"Wait!" cried a voice familiar to me, and one of the shrouded soldiers slid down a red dune to stand in front of us. "Wait!" she called again to those eager to shoot, and this time she unwrapped the bands of her cowl.

"Dem Loa!" I cried and stepped forward to hug the short woman in her bulky battle garb. I saw tears leaving muddy streaks on her cheeks.

"You have brought back your special one," said the woman who had saved me. "Just as you promised."

I introduced her to Aenea and then to the Dorje Phamo, feeling silly and happy at the same moment. Dem Loa and Aenea regarded one another for a moment, and then hugged.

I looked around at the other figures who still hung back in the red twilight. "Where is Dem Ria?" I asked. "Alem Mikail Dem Alem? And your children—Bin and Ces Ambre?"

"Dead," said Dem Loa. "All dead, except Ces Ambre, who is missing after the last attack from the Bombasino Pax."

I stood speechless, stunned.

"Bin Ria Dem Loa Alem died of his illness," continued Dem Loa, "but the rest died in our war with the Pax."

"War with the Pax," I repeated. "I hope to God that I did not start it . . ."

Dem Loa raised her hand. "No, Raul Endymion. You did not start it. Those of us in the Amoiete Spectrum Helix who prized our own ways refused the cross . . . that is what started it. The rebellion had already begun when you were with us. After you left, we thought we had it won. The cowardly troops at Pax Base Bombasino sued for peace, ignored the orders from their commanders in space, and made treaties with us. More Pax ships arrived. They bombed their own base . . . then came after our villages. It has been war since then. When they land and try to occupy the land, we kill many of them. They send more."

"Dem Loa," I said, "I am so, so sorry."

She set her hand on my chest and nodded. I saw the smile that I remembered from our hours together. She looked at Aenea again. "You are the one he spoke of in his delirium and his pain. You are the one whom he loved. Do you love him as well, child?"

"I do," said Aenea.

"Good," said Dem Loa. "It would be sad if a man who thought he was dying expressed such love for someone who did not feel the same about him." Dem Loa looked at the Thunderbolt Sow, silent and regal. "You are a priestess?"

"Not a priestess," said the Thunderbolt Sow, "but the abbess of the Samden Gompa monastery."

Dem Loa showed her teeth. "You rule over monks? Over men?"

"I . . . instruct them," said the Dorje Phamo. The wind ruffled her steel-gray hair.

"Just as good as ruling them." Dem Loa laughed. "Welcome then, Dorje Phamo." To Aenea she said, "And are you staying with us, child? Or just touching us and passing on as our prophecies predict?"

"I must go on," said Aenea. "But I would like to leave the Dorje Phamo here as your ally and our . . . liaison."

Dem Loa nodded. "It is dangerous here now," she said to the Thunderbolt Sow.

The Dorje Phamo smiled at the shorter woman. The strength of the two was almost a palpable energy in the air around us.

"Good," said Dem Loa. She hugged me. "Be kind to your love, Raul Endymion. Be good to her in the hours granted to you by the cycles of life and chaos."

"I will," I said.

To Aenea, Dem Loa said, "Thank you for coming, child. It was our wish. It was our hope." The two women hugged again. I felt suddenly shy, as if I had brought Aenea home to meet my own mother or Grandam.

The Dorje Phamo touched both of us in benediction. *"Kale pe a,"* she said to Aenea.

We moved away in the twilight dust storm and 'cast through the burst of white light. On the quiet of the *Yggdrasill's* bridge, I said to Aenea, "What was that she said?"

"Kale pe a," repeated my friend. "It is an ancient Tibetan farewell when a caravan sets out to climb the high peaks. It means—go slowly if you wish to return."

AND SO IT went for a hundred other worlds, each one visited only for moments, but each farewell moving and stirring in its own way. It is hard for me to say how many days and nights were spent on this final voyage with Aenea, because there was only the 'casting down and 'casting up, the treeship entering the light one place and emerging elsewhere, and when everyone was too tired to go on, the *Yggdrasill* was allowed to drift in empty space for a few hours while the ergs rested and the rest of us tried to sleep.

I remember at least three of these sleep periods, so perhaps we traveled for only three days and nights. Or perhaps we traveled for a week or more and slept only three times. But I remember that Aenea and I slept little and loved one another tenderly, as if each time we held each other it might be our last.

It was during one of these brief interludes alone that I whispered to her, "Why are you doing this, kiddo? Not just so we can all become like the Ousters and catch sunlight in our wings. I mean . . . it was beautiful . . . but I *like* planets. I like dirt under my boots. I like just being . . . human. Being a man."

Aenea had chuckled and touched my cheek. I remember that the light was dim but that I could see the perspiration still beaded between her breasts. "I like your being a man too, Raul my love."

"I mean . . ." I began awkwardly.

"I know what you mean," whispered Aenea. "I like planets too. And I like being human . . . just being a woman. It's not for some utopian evolution of humankind into Ouster angels or Seneschai empaths that I'm doing . . . what I have to do."

"What then?" I whispered into her hair.

"Just for the chance to choose," she said softly. "Just for the opportunity to continue being human, whatever that means to each person who chooses."

"To choose again?" I said.

"Yes," said Aenea. "Even if that means choosing what one has had before. Even if it means choosing the Pax, the cruciform, and alliance with the Core."

I did not understand, but at that moment I was more interested in holding her than in fully understanding.

After moments of silence, Aenea said, "Raul . . . I also love the dirt under my boots, the sound of the wind in the grass. Would you do something for me?"

"Anything," I said fiercely.

"If I die before you," she whispered, "would you return my ashes to Old Earth and sprinkle them where we were happiest together?"

If she had stabbed me in the heart, it would not have hurt as much. "You said that I could stay with you," I said at last, my voice thick and angry and lost. "That I could go anywhere you go."

"And I meant it, my love," whispered Aenea. "But if I go ahead of you into death, will you do that for me? Wait a few years, and then set my ashes free where we had been happiest on Old Earth?"

I felt like squeezing her until she cried out then. Until she renounced her request. Instead, I whispered, "How the goddamned hell am I supposed to get back to Old Earth? It's in the Lesser Magellanic Cloud, isn't it? Some hundred-sixty thousand light-years away, isn't it?"

"Yes," said Aenea.

"Well, are you going to open the farcaster doors again so I can get back there?"

"No," said Aenea. "Those doors are closed forever."

"Then how the hell do you expect me to . . ." I closed my eyes. "Don't ask me to do this, Aenea."

"I've already asked you, my love."

"Ask me to die with you instead."

"No," she said. "I'm asking you to live for me. To do this for me."

"Shit," I said.

"Does that mean yes, Raul?"

"It means *shit*," I said. "I hate martyrs. I hate predestination. I hate love stories with sad endings."

"So do I," whispered Aenea. "Will you do this for me?"

I made a noise. "Where were we happiest on Old Earth?" I said at last. "You must mean Taliesin West, because we didn't see much else of the planet together."

"You'll know," whispered Aenea. "Let's go to sleep."

"I don't want to go to sleep," I said roughly.

She put her arms around me. It had been delightful sleeping together in zero gravity on the Startree. It was even more delightful sleeping together in our small bed in our private cubby in the slight gravity field of the *Yggdrasill*. I could not conceive of a time when I would have to sleep without her next to me.

"Sprinkle your ashes, eh?" I whispered eventually.

"Yes," she murmured, more asleep than awake.

"Kiddo, my dear, my love," I said, "you're a morbid little bitch."

"Yes," murmured my Aenea. "But I'm your morbid little bitch."

By and by, we did get to sleep.

ON OUR LAST day, Aenea 'cast us to a star system with an M3 class red dwarf at its core and a sweet Earth-like world swinging in close orbit.

"No," said Rachel as our small group stood on Het Masteen's bridge. The three hundred had left us one by one, Aenea's many disciples left sprinkled among the Pax worlds like so many bottles cast into a great ocean but without their messages. Now Father de Soya remained, Rachel, Aenea, the captain Het Masteen, A. Bettik, a few crew clones, the ergs below, and me. And the Shrike, silent and motionless on its high platform.

"No," Rachel said again. "I've changed my mind. I want to go on with you."

Aenea stood with her arms folded. She had been especially quiet all this long morning of 'casting and bidding farewells to disciples. "As you will," she said softly. "You know I would not demand that you do anything, Rache."

"Damn you," Rachel said softly.

"Yes," said Aenea.

Rachel clenched her fists. "Is this ever going to fucking end?"

"What do you mean?" said Aenea.

"You know what I mean. My father . . . my mother . . . *your* mother . . . their lives filled with this. My life . . . lived twice now . . . always fighting this unseen enemy. Running and running and waiting and waiting. Backward and forward through time like some accursed, out-of-control dreidel . . . oh, damn."

Aenea waited.

"One request," said Rachel. She looked at me. "No offense, Raul. I've come to like you a lot. But could Aenea bring me down to Barnard's World alone."

I looked at Aenea. "It's all right with me," I said.

Rachel sighed. "Back to this backward world again . . . cornfields and sunsets and tiny little towns with big white houses and big wide porches. It bored me when I was eight."

"You loved it when you were eight," said Aenea.

"Yeah," said Rachel. "I did." She shook the priest's hand, then Het Masteen's, then mine.

On a whim, remembering the most obscure verses of the old poet's *Cantos,* remembering laughing about them at the edge of the campfire's light with Grandam having me repeat them line for line, wondering if people ever really said such things, I said to Rachel, "See you later, alligator."

The young woman looked at me strangely, her green eyes catching the light from the world hanging above us. "After a while, crocodile."

She took Aenea's hand and they were gone. No flash of light when one was not traveling with Aenea. Just a sudden . . . absence.

Aenea returned within five minutes. Het Masteen stepped back from the control circle and folded his hands in the sleeves of his robe. "One Who Teaches?"

"Pacem System, please, True Voice of the Tree Het Masteen."

The Templar did not move. "You know, dear friend and teacher, that by now the Pax will have recalled half of their fighting ships to the Vatican's home system."

Aenea looked up and around at the gently rustling leaves of the beautiful tree on which we rode. A kilometer behind us, the glow of the fusion drive was pushing us slowly out of Barnard's World's gravity well. No Pax ships had challenged us here. "Will the ergs be able to hold the fields until we get close to Pacem?" she asked.

The captain's small hands came out of the sleeves of his robe and gestured palms up. "It is doubtful. They are exhausted. The toll these attacks have taken on them . . ."

"I know," Aenea said. "And I am very sorry. You need only be in-system for a minute or two. Perhaps if you accelerate now and are ready for full-drive maneuvers when we appear in Pacem System, the treeship can 'cast out before the fields are overwhelmed."

"We will try," said Het Masteen. "But be prepared to 'cast away immediately. The life of the treeship may be measured in seconds after we arrive."

"First, we have to send the Consul's ship away," said Aenea. "We will have to do it now, here. Just a few moments, Het Masteen."

The Templar nodded and went back to his displays and touch panels.

"Oh, no," I said when she turned to me. "I'm not going to Hyperion in the ship."

Aenea looked surprised. "You thought that I was sending you away after I said that you could accompany me?"

I folded my arms. "We've visited most of the Pax and Outback worlds . . . except Hyperion. Whatever you're planning, I can't believe that you'll leave our homeworld out of it."

"I'm not going to," said Aenea. "But I'm also not 'casting us there."

I did not understand.

"A. Bettik," said Aenea, "the ship should be about ready to depart. Do you have the letter I wrote to Uncle Martin?"

"I do, M. Aenea," said the android. The blue-skinned man did not look happy, but neither did he look distressed.

"Please give him my love," said Aenea.

"Wait, wait," I said. "A. Bettik is your . . . your envoy . . . to Hyperion?"

Aenea rubbed her cheek. I sensed that she was more exhausted than I could imagine, but saving her strength for something important yet to come. "My envoy?" she said. "You mean like Rachel and Theo and the Dorje Phamo and George and Jigme?"

"Yeah," I said. "And the three hundred others."

"No," said Aenea, "A. Bettik will not be my envoy to Hyperion. Not in that sense. And the Consul's ship has a deep time-debt to pay via Hawking drive. It . . . and A. Bettik . . . will not arrive for months of our time."

"Then who is the envoy . . . the liaison on Hyperion?" I asked, certain that this world would not be exempted.

"Can't you guess?" My friend smiled. "Dear Uncle Martin. The poet and critic once again becomes a player in this endless chess game with the Core."

"But the others," I said, "all took communion with you and . . ." I stopped.

"Yes," said Aenea. "When I was still a child. Uncle Martin understood. He drank the wine. It was not hard for him to adapt . . . he has been hearing the language of the dead and of the living for centuries in his own poet's way. It is how he came to write the *Cantos* in the first place. Why he thought the Shrike was his muse."

"So why is A. Bettik taking the ship back there?" I said. "Just to bring your message?"

"More than that," said Aenea. "If things work out, we will see." She hugged the android and he awkwardly patted her back with his one hand.

A moment later, welling up with more emotion than I had imagined possible, I shook that blue hand. "I will miss you," I said stupidly.

The android looked at me for a long moment, nodded, and turned toward the waiting ship.

"A. Bettik!" I called just as he was about to enter the ship.

He turned back and waited while I ran to my small pile of belongings on the lower platform, then jogged back up the steps. "Will you take this?" I said, handing him the leather tube.

"The hawking mat," said A. Bettik. "Yes, of course, M. Endymion. I will be happy to keep this for you until I see you again."

"And if we don't see each other again," I said and paused. I was about to say, *Please give it to Martin Silenus,* but I knew from my own waking visions that the old poet was near death. "If we don't happen to see each other again, A. Bettik," I said, "please keep the mat as a memento of our trip together. And of our friendship."

A. Bettik looked at me for another quiet moment, nodded again, and went into the Consul's ship. I half expected the ship to say its good-byes, filled with malapropisms and misinformation, but it simply conferred with the treeship's ergs, rose silently on repellors until it cleared the containment field, and then moved away on low thrusters until it was a safe distance from us. Its fusion tail was so bright that it made my eyes water as I watched it accelerate out and away from Barnard's World and the *Yggdrasill.* I wished then with all of my heart and will that Aenea and I were going back to Hyperion with A. Bettik, ready to sleep for days on the large bed at the apex of the ship, then listen to music on the Steinway and swim in a zero-g pool above the balcony—

"We have to go," Aenea said to Het Masteen. "Could you please prepare the ergs for what we are about to encounter."

"As you wish, Revered One Who Teaches," said the True Voice of the Tree.

"And Het Masteen . . ." said Aenea.

The Templar turned and awaited further orders.

"Thank you, Het Masteen," she said. "On behalf of all of those who traveled with you on this voyage and all those who will tell of your voyage for generations to come, thank you, Het Masteen."

The Templar bowed and went back to his panels. "Full fusion drive to point nine-two. Prepare for evasive maneuvers. Prepare for Pacem System," he said to his beloved ergs wrapped around the invisible singularity three quarters of a kilometer below us. "Prepare for Pacem System."

Father de Soya had been standing quietly nearby, but now he took Aenea's right hand in his left hand. With his right hand, he gave a quiet benediction in the direction of the Templar and the crew clones—*"In nomine Patris et Filii et Spiritu Sanctus."*

"Amen," I said, taking Aenea's left hand.

"Amen," said Aenea.

30

HEY HIT US less than two seconds after we 'cast into the system, the torchships and archangels converging fire on us much as the rainbow sharks had once converged on me in the seas of Mare Infinitus.

"Go!" cried the True Voice of the Tree Het Masteen above the torrent of field noise around us. "The ergs are dying! The containment field will drop in seconds. Go! May the Muir guide your thoughts. Go!"

Aenea had had only two seconds to glimpse the yellow star at the center of Pacem System and the smaller star that was Pacem proper, but it was enough. The three of us held hands as we 'cast through light and noise as if rising through the cauldron of lance fire boiling the ship's fields, spirits rising from Hell's burning lakes.

The light faded and then resumed as diffuse sunlight. It was cloudy above the Vatican, chilly, almost wintry, and a light, cool rain fell on cobblestone streets. Aenea had dressed this day in a soft tan shirt, a brown leather vest, and more formal black trousers than I was used to seeing her wear. Her hair was brushed back and held in place by two tortoiseshell barrettes. Her skin looked fresh and clean and young and her eyes—so tired in recent days—were bright and calm. She still held my hand as the three of us turned to look at the streets and people around us.

We were at the edge of an alley looking onto a wide boulevard. Small groups of people—men and women in formal black, groups of priests, flocks of nuns, a row of children in tow behind two nuns, everywhere black and red umbrellas—moved to and fro on the pedestrian walkways while low, black groundcars glided silently down the streets. I caught a glimpse of bishops and archbishops in the backseats of the groundcars, their visages distorted by beads and rivulets of rain on the cars' bubble tops. No one seemed to be taking any notice of us or our arrival.

Aenea was looking up toward the low clouds. "The *Yggdrasill* just 'cast out of system. Did either of you feel it?"

I closed my eyes to concentrate on the dream flow of voices and images that were ever under the surface there now. There was . . . an absence. A vision of flame as the outer branches began to burn. "The fields collapsed just as they 'cast away," I said. "How did they 'cast without you, Aenea?" I saw the answer as soon as I had verbalized the question. "The Shrike," I said.

"Yes." Aenea was still holding my hand. The rain was cold on us and I could hear it gurgling down gutters and drainpipes behind us. She spoke very quietly. "The Shrike will carry the *Yggdrasill* and the True Voice of the Tree away through space and time. To his . . . destiny."

I remembered bits of the *Cantos*. The treeship burning as the pilgrims watched from the Sea of Grass shortly before Het Masteen had mysteriously disappeared with the Shrike during the windwagon crossing. Then the Templar reappearing in the presence of the Shrike some days later near the Valley of the Time Tombs, dying from his wounds shortly after that, his tale the only one of the seven pilgrims' not to be told on the voyage. The Hyperion pilgrims: Colonel Kassad; the Hegemony Consul, Sol—Rachel's father; Brawne Lamia—Aenea's mother; the Templar Het Masteen; Martin Silenus; Father Hoyt—the current Pope; all at a loss to explain events at the time. For me as a child, just old words from a myth. Verses about strangers. How they must have thought their efforts and adventures over, only to have to pick up their burdens again. How often, I realized now as an adult in my standard thirties, how often that is the case in all of our lives.

"See that church across the street?" said Father de Soya.

I had to shake my head to focus on the *now* and to ignore the thoughts and voices whispering to me. "Yeah," I said, wiping the rain from my brow. "Is that St. Peter's Basilica?"

"No," said the priest. "That is St. Anne's Parish Church and the entrance to the Vatican next to it is the Porta Sant'Anna. The main entrance to St. Peter's Square is down the boulevard there and around those colonnades."

"Are we going to St. Peter's Square?" I asked Aenea. "Into the Vatican?"

"Let's see if we can," she said.

We started down the pedestrian walkway, just a man and a younger woman walking with a priest on a cool, rainy day. Across the street from us was a sign indicating that the imposing, windowless structure there was the barracks for the Swiss Guard. Troopers from that barracks in formal, Renaissance-era black cloaks, white ruffled collars, and yellow-and-black leggings stood holding pikes at the Porta Sant'Anna and at the intersections while Pax security police in no-nonsense black impact armor manned roadblocks and floated overhead in black skimmers.

St. Peter's Square was closed off to foot traffic except for several security gates where guards were carefully checking passes and chipcard IDs.

"We won't get through there," said Father de Soya. It was dark enough that the lights had come on atop Bernini's colonnade to illuminate statuary and the stone papal coats of arms there. The priest pointed to two windows glowing above the colonnade and to the right of St. Peter's facade topped by statues of Christ, John the Baptist, and the Apostles. "Those are the Pope's private offices."

"Just a rifle shot away," I said, although I had no thoughts of attacking the Pope.

Father de Soya shook his head. "Class-ten containment field." He glanced around. Much of the pedestrian traffic had passed through the security gates into St. Peter's Square and we were becoming more obvious on the street. "We're going to get our ID checked if we don't do something," he said.

"Is this level of security common?" asked Aenea.

"No," said Father de Soya. "It may be because of your message that you were coming but it is more probable that it is the usual security when His Holiness is saying a papal Mass. Those bells we heard were a call to an afternoon Mass at which he is presiding."

"How do you know that?" I said, amazed that he could read so much from the sound of a few bells.

Father de Soya looked surprised. "I know that because it is Holy Thursday," he said, looking shocked either because we did not know such an elementary fact or because he had managed to forget it until this moment. "This is Holy Week," he went on, talking softly as if to himself. "All this week His Holiness must carry out both his papal and diocesan duties. Today . . . this afternoon . . . certainly at this Mass, he performs the ceremony of washing the feet of twelve priests who symbolize the twelve disciples whose feet Jesus washed at the Last Supper. The ceremony was always held at the Pope's diocese church, the Basilica of St. John Lateran, which used to be beyond the Vatican walls, but ever since the Vatican was moved to Pacem it's been held in St. Peter's Basilica. The Basilica of St. John Lateran was left behind during the Hegira because it had been destroyed during the Seven Nation Wars in the twenty-first century and . . ." De Soya stopped what I had thought was nervous chatter. His face had gone blank in that way common to mild epileptics or deeply thoughtful people.

Aenea and I waited. I admit that I was glancing with some anxiety toward the patrol of black-armored Pax security men moving toward us down the long boulevard.

"I know how we can get into the Vatican," said Father de Soya and turned back toward an alley opposite the Vatican Boulevard.

"Good," said Aenea, following quickly.

The Jesuit stopped suddenly. "I think that I can get us in," he said. "But I have no idea how to get us out."

"Just get us in, please," said Aenea.

THE STEEL DOOR was at the rear of a ruined, windowless stone chapel three blocks from the Vatican. It was locked with a small padlock and a large chain. The sign on the sealed door said TOURS ON ALTERNATE SATURDAYS ONLY: Closed During Holy Week: CONTACT VATICAN TOUR OFFICE 3888 SQUARE OF THE FIRST CHRISTIAN MARTYRS.

"Can you break this chain?" Father de Soya asked me.

I felt the massive chain and the solid padlock. My only tool or weapon was the small hunting knife still in my belt sheath. "No," I said. "But maybe I can pick the lock. See if you can find some wire in that garbage module there . . . baling wire would do."

We stood there in the drizzle for at least ten minutes, with the light fading around us and the sound of traffic on nearby boulevards seeming to grow louder, waiting every minute for the Swiss Guard or security people to swoop down on us. Everything I had learned about picking locks had come from an old riverboat gambler on the Kans who had turned to gambling after the Port Romance authorities had removed two of his fingers for thieving. As I worked, I thought of the ten years of odyssey for Aenea and me, of Father de Soya's long voyage to this place, of the hundreds of light-years traveled and tens of thousands of hours of tension and pain and sacrifice and terror.

And the goddamn ten-florin lock would not budge.

Finally the point of my knife broke. I cursed, threw the knife away, and slammed the stinking lousy cretinous piece-of-shit lock and chain against the grimy stone wall. The padlock clicked open.

It was dark inside. If there was a light switch, none of us could find it. If there was an idiot AI somewhere controlling the lights, it did not respond to our commands. None of us had brought a light. After carrying a flash-light laser for years, I had left mine behind in my backpack this day. When the time had come to leave the *Yggdrasill*, I had stepped forward and taken Aenea's hand without a thought to weapons or other necessary items.

"Is this the Basilica of St. John Lateran?" whispered Aenea. It was impossible to speak in anything above a whisper in the oppressive darkness.

"No, no," whispered Father de Soya. "Just a tiny memorial chapel built near the original basilica in the twenty-first . . ." He stopped and I could imagine his thoughtful expression returning. "It *is* a working chapel, I believe," he said. "Wait here."

Aenea and I stood with shoulders touching as we heard Father de Soya moving around the perimeter of the tiny building. Once something heavy fell with the sound of iron on stone and we all stood holding our breath. A minute later we heard the sound of his hands sliding along the inside walls again and the rustle of his cassock. There was a muffled "Ahhh . . ." and a second later light flared.

The Jesuit was standing less than ten meters from us, holding a lighted match. A box of matches was in his left hand. "A chapel," he explained. "They still had the stand for votive candles." I could see that the candles themselves had been melted to uselessness and never replaced, but the tapers and this one box of matches had remained for God knows how long in this dark, abandoned place. We joined him in the small circle of light, waited while he lighted a second match, and followed him to a heavy wooden door set behind rotting curtains.

"Father Baggio, my resurrection chaplain, told me about this tour when I was under house arrest near here some years ago," whispered Father de Soya. This door was not locked, but opened with a squeal of ancient, unoiled hinges. "I believe he thought it would appeal to my sense of the macabre," went on Father de Soya, leading us down a narrow, spiraling stone stairway not much wider than my shoulders. Aenea followed the priest. I kept close to Aenea.

The stairway continued down, then down some more, and then more. I estimated that we were at least twenty meters beneath street level when the stairway ended and we passed through a series of narrow corridors into a wider, echoing hallway. The priest had gone through a half-dozen matches by this point, dropping each only after it had burned his fingers. I did not ask him how many matches were left in the small matchbox.

"When the Church decided to move St. Peter's and the Vatican during the Hegira," said de Soya, his voice loud enough now to empty in the black space, "they brought it en masse to Pacem using heavy field lifters and tractor-field towers. Since mass was not a problem, they brought half of Rome with them, including the huge Castel Sant'Angelo and everything under the old city down to a depth of sixty meters. This was the twentieth-century subway system."

Father de Soya began walking down what I realized was an abandoned railway platform. At places the ceiling tiles had fallen in and everywhere except on a narrow pathway there were centuries of dust, fallen rocks, broken plastic, unreadable signs lying in the grime, and shattered benches. We went down several corroded steel stairways—escalators halted more than a millennium ago, I realized—through a narrow corridor that continued downward along an echoing ramp, and then onto another platform. At the end of this platform, I could see a fiberplastic ladder leading down to where the tracks had been . . . where the tracks still were under the layers of dust, rubble, and rust.

We had just climbed down the ladder and stepped into the subway tunnel when the next match went out. But not before Aenea and I had seen what lay ahead.

Bones. Human bones. Bones and skulls stacked neatly almost two meters high on either side of a narrow passage between the rusted tracks. Great heaps of bones, the socket ends out, skulls neatly placed at meter-intervals or arranged in geometric designs within the knobby walls of human bones.

Father de Soya lit the next match and began striding between the walls of skeletal human remains. The breeze of his motion flickered the tiny flame that he held aloft. "After the Seven Nations War in the early twenty-first century," he said, his voice at a normal conversational volume now, "the cemeteries of Rome were overflowing. There had been mass graves dug all around the suburbs of the city and in the large parks. It became quite a health problem what with the global warming and constant flooding. All of the bio and chem warheads, you know. The subways had ceased to run anyway, so the powers-that-be authorized a removal of the remains and their reinterment in the old metro systems."

This time when the match burned out, we were in a section where the bones were stacked five layers high, each layer marked by a row of skulls, their white brows reflecting the light but the sightless sockets indifferent to our passing. The neat walls of bones went back for at least six meters on either side and rose to the vaulted ceiling ten meters above us. In a few places, there had been a small avalanche of bones and skulls and we had to pick our way over them carefully. Still there was the crunching underfoot. We did not move during the interludes of darkness between matches, but waited quietly. There was no other noise . . . not the scurry of rats nor the drip of water. Only our breathing and soft words disturbed the silence here.

"Oddly enough," said Father de Soya after we had gone another two hundred meters, "they did not get the idea from Rome's ancient catacombs, which lie all about us here, but from the so-called catacombs of Paris . . . old quarry tunnels deep under that city. The Parisians had to move bones from their overflowing cemeteries to those tunnels between the late eighteenth to mid-nineteenth centuries. They found that they could easily accommodate six million dead in just a few kilometers of corridors. Ahh . . . here we are . . ."

To our left, through an even narrower corridor of bones, was a path with a few boot marks in the dust, leading to another steel door, this one unlocked. It took all three of us to leverage the door open. The priest led the way down another set of rusting spiral stairs to a depth I estimated at being at least thirty-five meters beneath the street above. The match went out just as we stepped into another tunnel—much older than the subway vault, its edges and ceiling unfinished and tumbledown. I had caught a glimpse of side passages running off, of bones spilled haphazardly everywhere in these passages, of skulls upside down, of bits of rotted garments.

"According to Father Baggio," whispered the priest, "this is where the real catacombs begin. The Christian catacombs which go back to the first century A.D." A new match flared. I heard a rattle in the matchbox that sounded like very few matches indeed. "This way, I would guess," said Father de Soya and led us to his right.

"We're under the Vatican now?" whispered Aenea a few minutes later. I could feel her impatience. The match flared and died.

"Soon, soon," said de Soya in the darkness. He lit another one. I heard no rattle in the box.

After another 150 meters or so, the corridor simply ended. There were no tumbled bones here, no skulls, only rough stone walls and a hint of masonry where the tunnel ended. The match went out. Aenea touched my hand as we waited in the darkness.

"I am sorry," said the priest. "There are no more matches."

I fought back the rise of panic in my chest. I was sure that I heard noises now . . . distant rat feet scurrying at the least, boots on stairs at the worst. "Do we backtrack?" I said, my whisper sounding far too loud in the absolute darkness.

"I was sure that Father Baggio said that these catacombs to the north had once connected to the older ones under the Vatican," whispered Father de Soya. "Under St. Peter's Basilica, to be precise."

"Well, it doesn't seem to . . ." I began and stopped. In the few seconds of light before the match had gone out, I had glimpsed the relative newness of the brick wall between stones . . . a few centuries old as opposed to the millennia since the stone had been cut away. I crawled forward, feeling ahead of me until my fingers found stone, brick, loose mortar.

"This was hastily done," I said, speaking with only the authority I had gained as an assistant landscape worker on the Beak estates years and years before. "The mortar's cracked and some of the bricks have crumbled," I said, my fingers moving quickly. "Give me something to dig with. Damn, I wish I hadn't thrown away my knife . . ."

Aenea handed me a sharp-edged stick or branch in the dark and I was digging away for several minutes before I realized that I was working with a thigh bone broken at one end. The two of them joined me, digging with bones, scrabbling at the cold brick with our fingernails until the nails broke and our fingers bled. After some time at this, we paused to pant and catch our breath. Our eyes had not adapted to the darkness. There was no light here.

"The Mass will be over," whispered Aenea. The tone in her voice made it sound like a tragic event.

"It is a High Mass," whispered the priest. "A long ceremony."

"Wait!" I said. My fingers had remembered a slight movement in the bricks—not in one or a few of them, but in the entire casement.

"Get back," I said aloud. "Crawl to the side of the tunnel." I backed up myself, but straight back, raised my left shoulder, lowered my head, and charged forward in a crouch, half expecting to bash my head on the stone and knock myself out.

I hit the bricks with a mighty grunt and a shower of dust and small debris. The bricks had not fallen away. But I had felt them sag away from me.

Aenea and de Soya joined me and in another minute we had pushed loose the center bricks, tumbled the entire mass away from us.

There was the faintest glimmer of light on the other side of the passage, but enough to show us a ramp of debris leading to an even deeper tunnel. We crawled down on our hands and knees, found room to stand, and moved through the earth-smelling corridor. Two more turns and we came into a catacomb as roughly hewn as the one above but illuminated by a narrow strip of glowtape running along the right wall at belt height. Another fifty meters of twisting and turning, always following the main passage illuminated by glowtape, and we came into a wider tunnel with modern glowglobes set every five meters. These globes were not lit, but the ancient glowtape continued on.

"We're under St. Peter's," whispered Father de Soya. "This area was first rediscovered in 1939, after they buried Pope Pius XI in a nearby grotto. The excavations were carried on for another twenty years or so before being abandoned. They have not been reopened to archaeologists."

We came into an even wider corridor—wide enough for the three of us to walk side by side for the first time. Here the ancient rock and plastered walls with the occasional marble inset were covered with frescoes, early Christian mosaics, and broken statues set above grottoes in which bones and skulls were clearly visible. Someone had once placed plastic across many of these grottoes and the material had yellowed and opaqued to make the mortal remains within almost unviewable, but by bending and peering we could see empty eye sockets and pelvic ovals peering back at us.

The frescoes showed Christian images—doves carrying olive branches, women drawing water, the ubiquitous fish—but were next to older grottoes, cremation urns, and graves offering pre-Christian images of Isis and Apollo, Bacchus welcoming the dead to the afterlife with great, overflowing flagons of wine, a scene of oxen and rams cavorting, another with satyrs dancing—I immediately noticed the likeness to Martin Silenus and turned just in time to catch Aenea's knowing glance—and still more with beings Father de Soya described as maenads, some rural scenes, partridges all in a row, a preening peacock with feathers of lapis chips that still caught the light in bright blue.

Peering through the ancient, mottled plastic and plastiglass at these things made me think that we were passing through some terrestrial aquarium of death. Finally we came to a red wall at right angles to a lower wall of faded, mottled blue with the remnants of graffiti in Latin still visible. Here the sheet of plastic was newer, fresher, and the small container of bones within quite visible. The skull had been set atop the neat pile of bones and seemed to be regarding us with some interest.

Father de Soya went to his knees in the dust, crossed himself, and bent his head in prayer. Aenea and I stood back and watched with the quiet embarrassment common to the unbeliever in the presence of any true faith.

When the priest arose, his eyes were moist. "According to Church history and Father Baggio, the workers uncovered these poor bones in

1949 A.D. Later analysis showed that they belong to a robust man who died sometime in his sixties. We are directly under the high altar of St. Peter's Basilica, which was built here because of the legend that St. Peter had been interred secretly at just this spot. In 1968 A.D., Pope Paul VI announced that the Vatican was convinced that these were indeed the bones of the fisherman, the same Peter who walked with Jesus and was the Rock upon which Christ built his Church."

We looked at the silent heap of bones and then back at the priest.

"Federico, you know that I am not trying to bring down the Church," Aenea said. "Only this current aberration of it."

"Yes," said Father de Soya, wiping his eyes roughly, leaving muddy streaks there. "I know that, Aenea." He looked around, went to a door, opened it. A metal staircase led upward.

"There will be guards," I whispered.

"I think not," said Aenea. "The Vatican has spent eight hundred years fearing attack from space . . . from above. I do not believe they give much thought to their catacombs." She stepped in front of the priest and started quickly but quietly up the metal steps. I hurried to follow her. I saw Father de Soya glance back toward the dim grotto, cross himself a final time, and follow us up toward St. Peter's Basilica.

THE LIGHT IN the main basilica, although softened by evening, stained glass, and candlelight, was all but blinding after the catacombs.

We had climbed up through the subterranean shrine, up past a memorial basilica marked in stone as the Trophy of Gaius, through side corridors and service entrances, through the anteroom to the sacristy, past standing priests and craning altar boys, and out into the echoing expanse at the rear of the nave of St. Peter's Basilica. Here were scores of dignitaries not important enough to have been awarded a place in the pews but still honored by being allowed to stand in the rear of the Basilica to witness this important celebration. It took only a glance to see that there were Swiss Guard and security people at all the entrances to the Basilica and in all the outer rooms with exits. Here at the back of the congregation, we were inconspicuous for the moment, just another priest and two somewhat underdressed parishioners allowed to crane their necks to see the Holy Father on Holy Thursday.

Mass was still being celebrated. The air smelled of incense and candlewax. Hundreds of brightly robed bishops and VIPs lined the gleaming rows of pews. At the marble altar rail before the baroque splendor canopy of the Throne of St. Peter, the Holy Father himself knelt to finish his menial work of washing the feet of twelve seated priests—eight men and four women. An unseen but large choir was singing—

"O Holy Ghost, through Thee alone
    Know we the Father and the Son;

Be this our firm unchanging creed.
That Thou dost from them both proceed.
That Thou dost from them both proceed.

"Praise be the Lord, Father and Son
And Holy Spirit with them one;
And may the Son on us bestow.
All gifts that from the Spirit flow.
All gifts that from the Spirit flow."

I hesitated then, wondering what we were doing here, why this end-less battle of Aenea's had brought us to the center of these people's faith. I believed everything she had taught us, valued everything she had shared with us, but three thousand years of tradition and faith had formed the words of this beautiful song and had built the walls of this mighty cathe-dral. I could not help but remember the simple wooden platforms, the firm but inelegant bridges and stairways of Aenea's rebuilt Temple Hanging in Air. What was it . . . what were we . . . compared to this splendor and humility? Aenea was an architect, largely self-trained except for her adoles-cent years with the cybrid Mr. Wright, building stone walls out of desert rock and mixing concrete by hand. *Michelangelo* had helped to design this Basilica.

The Mass was almost over. Some of the standing crowd in the rear of the longitudinal nave were beginning to leave, walking lightly so as not to interrupt the end of the service with their footfalls, whispering only when they reached the stairs to the piazza outside. I saw that Aenea was whisper-ing in Father de Soya's ear and I leaned against them to hear, afraid that I might miss some vital instruction.

"Will you do me one final great service, Father?" she asked.

"Anything," whispered the sad-eyed priest.

"Please leave the Basilica now," Aenea whispered in his ear. "Please go now, quietly, with these others. Leave now and lose yourself in Rome until the day comes to cease being lost."

Father de Soya pulled his head back in shock, looking at Aenea from half a meter away with an expression of someone who has been aban-doned. He leaned close to her ear. "Ask anything else of me, Teacher."

"This is all I ask, Father. And I ask it with love and respect."

The choir began singing another hymn. Above the heads in front of me, I could see the Holy Father completing the washing of the priests' feet and moving back to the altar under the gilded canopy. Everyone in the pews stood in anticipation of the closing litanies and final benediction.

Father de Soya gave his own benediction of my friend, turned, and left the Basilica with a group of monks whose beads rattled as they walked.

I stared at Aenea with enough intensity to set wood aflame, trying to send her the mental message *DO NOT ASK ME TO LEAVE!*

She beckoned me close and whispered in my ear, "Do one final thing for me, Raul, my love."

I almost shouted "No, goddammit!" at the top of my lungs in the echoing nave of St. Peter's Basilica during the holiest moments of Holy Thursday's High Mass. Instead I waited.

Aenea fumbled in the pockets of her vest and came out with a small vial. The liquid in it was clear but somehow looked heavier than water. "Would you drink this?" she whispered and handed me the vial.

I thought of Romeo and Juliet, Caesar and Cleopatra, Abelard and Heloise, George Wu and Howard Sung. All star-crossed lovers. Suicide and poison. I drank down the potion in one gulp, setting the empty vial in my own shirt pocket, waiting for Aenea to take out and drink a similar potion. She did not.

"What was it?" I whispered, not fearing any answer.

Aenea was watching the final moments of the Mass. She leaned very close to whisper. "Antidote to the Pax's birth control medication that you took when you joined the Home Guard."

What the hell!!??!! I came close to shouting over the Holy Father's closing words. *You're worried about family planning NOW?? Are you out of your goddamn MIND???*

She leaned back, her breath warm on my neck as she whispered again. "Thank God, I've been carrying that for two days and almost forgot it. Don't worry, it'll take about three weeks to take effect. Then you'll never be shooting blanks again."

I blinked at her. Was this blasphemy in St. Peter's Basilica or just extraordinarily bad taste? Then my mind shifted into high gear—*This is wonderful news . . . whatever happens next, Aenea sees a future for us . . . for herself . . . wants to have a child with me. But what about her first child? And why do I assume she's doing this so that she and I can . . . why would she . . . perhaps it's her idea of a farewell present . . . why would she . . . why . . .*

"Kiss me, Raul," she whispered, loud enough to make the elderly nun standing in front of us turn around with a severe expression.

I did not question her. I kissed her. Her lips were soft and slightly moist, just as they were the first time we had kissed standing on the bank of the Mississippi River at a place called Hannibal. The kiss seemed to last a long time. She touched the back of my neck with her cool fingers before our lips parted.

The Pope was moving to the front of the apse, facing each of the two arms of the transept, then the short nave, and finally the longitudinal nave as he gave his final benediction.

Aenea walked out into the main aisle, pushing people gently aside until she was in the open space and striding toward the distant altar. "Lenar Hoyt!" she shouted, and her voice echoed the hundred meters to the dome above. It was more than 150 meters from where we had been

standing to where the Pope now paused in his benediction, and I knew
Aenea had no chance of making that distance before being intercepted, but
I hurried to catch up to her.

"Lenar Hoyt!" she shouted again and hundreds of heads turned in
her direction. I saw movement in the arched shadows along the sides of the
nave as Swiss Guard leaped into action. "Lenar Hoyt, I am Aenea, daughter of Brawne Lamia who traveled to Hyperion with you to face the Shrike.
I am the daughter of the John Keats cybrid whom your Core masters have
twice killed in the flesh!"

The Pope stood as if transfixed, one bony finger raised in benediction
a moment before now pointing, shaking as if palsied. His other hand
clutched his vestments above his chest. His miter trembled as his head
bobbed back and forth. "You!" he cried, his voice high, thin, and weak.
"The Abomination!"

"*You* are the abomination," shouted Aenea, she was running now,
shrugging off dark-robed figures that rose from the pews to grab at her. I
pulled two men from her back and she ran on. I leaped over a lunging
figure and ran at her side, watching the Swiss Guard shoving through the
crowd, energy pikes aimed but hesitant to fire with so many Vatican and
Mercantilus dignitaries in the line of fire. I knew that they would not hesitate if she got within ten meters of the Pope. "You are the abomination,"
she shouted again, running hard now, dodging grasping hands and lunging
arms. "You are the Judas of the Catholic Church, Lenar Hoyt, selling its
sacred history to the . . ."

A heavy man in a Pax Fleet admiral's uniform pulled a ceremonial
sword from his scabbard and swung it at my beloved's head. She ducked. I
blocked the Admiral's arm, broke it, kicked the sword aside, and threw him
halfway down the length of the pew into his subordinates.

Colonel Kassad had said that after learning the language of the living,
that he had *felt* the pain he administered to others. I experienced that now,
feeling the torn nerves and muscle and shattered bone of my forearm and
the collision of my body as the Admiral struck his men. But when I looked
down, my forearm was firm and the only penalty was pain. I did not care
about the pain.

A cordon of priests, monks, and bishops put themselves between
Aenea and the Pope. I saw the Pontiff clutch his chest more tightly and fall,
but several of the deacons standing near him caught him, carried him back
under the canopy of Bernini's throne. Swiss Guardsmen hurtled into the
space at the end of the aisle, blocking Aenea's way with their pikes and
bodies. More filled the space behind us, roughly shoving away the onlookers with brutal swings of their pikes. Pax security in black armor and
compact repulsor flying belts came hurtling in ten meters above the heads
of the congregation. Laser dots danced on Aenea's face and chest.

I threw myself between her and the imminent energy bolts and
flechette clouds. The laser beam blinded my right eye as the target dot

swept across it. I threw my arms wide and bellowed something . . . a challenge perhaps . . . defiance certainly.

"No! Keep them alive!" It was a huge cardinal shouting in a bass rumble like the voice of God.

A Swiss Guardsman rushed at Aenea with his pike raised to stun her with a blow to the head. She threw herself down, slid across the tile, clipped him at his knees, and sent him sprawling toward me. I kicked him in the head and turned to wrestle the pike out of another Guardsman's hands, knocking him backward into the crowd and swinging the long weapon at the five Guardsmen rushing us from the rear. They gave way.

A flying security trooper fired two darts into my left shoulder. I presumed they were tranquilizers, but I ripped them away, threw them at the flying form, and felt nothing. Two guards—a large man and a larger woman—grabbed my arms. I swung them through the air until their skulls collided and dropped them onto tile. "Aenea!"

She was on her feet again, pulling free of one Guardsman only to have two forms in black armor block her way. The congregation was screaming. The great cathedral organ suddenly screamed like a woman in labor. A security man shot her at five-meter range. Aenea spun around. A woman in black armor clubbed my darling down, straddling her and pulling her arms behind her.

I used my forearm to swat the Pax security bitch five meters backward through the air. A Guardsman clubbed me in the stomach with his pike. A flying security shape zapped me with a neural stunner. Stunners are supposed to work instantly, guaranteed to work instantly, but I had time to close my hands on the nearest Guardsman's throat before they stunned me again, and then a third time. My body spasmed and fell and I pissed my pants as all voluntary functions ceased, my last conscious sensation being the cold flow of urine down my pant leg onto the perfect tiles of St. Peter's Basilica.

I was not really aware of the dozen heavy forms landing on my back, pinning my arms, pulling me away. I did not really hear or feel the crack of my forehead striking tile or the rip it opened from my brow to hairline.

In the last three or four seconds of semiconsciousness, I saw black feet, combat boots, a fallen Swiss Guardsman's cap, more feet. I knew that Aenea had fallen to my left but I could not turn my head to see her one last time.

They dragged me away, leaving a trail of blood, urine, and saliva as they did so. I was far beyond caring.

And so ends my tale.

I was conscious but restrained with neural locks during my "trial," a ten-minute appearance before the black-robed judges of the Holy Office. I was condemned to death. No human being would sully his or her soul by executing me; I was to be transferred to a Schrödinger cat box in orbit around the quarantined labyrinth world of Armaghast. The immutable laws of physics and quantum chance would execute the sentence.

As soon as the trial ended they shipped me via a Hawking-drive, high-g, robot torchship to Armaghast System—a two-month time-debt. Wherever Aenea was, whatever had happened to her, I was already two months too late to help her when I awoke just as they finished sealing the fused-energy shell of my prison.

And for uncounted days . . . perhaps months, I went insane. And then for more uncounted days, certainly more months, I have been using the 'scriber they included in my tiny egg of a cell to tell this tale. They must have known that the 'scriber would be an additional punishment as I waited to die, writing my story on my few pages of recycled microvellum like the snake devouring its own tail, knowing that no one will ever access the story in the memory chip.

I said at the beginning of all this that you, my impossible reader, were reading it for the wrong reason. I said at the beginning that if you were reading this to discover her fate, or my own, that you were reading the wrong document. I was not with her when her fate was played out, and my own is closer now to its final act than when I first wrote these words.

I was not with her.

I was not with her.

Oh, Jesus God, God of Moses, Allah, dear Buddha, Zeus, Muir, Elvis, Christ . . . if any of you exist or ever existed or retain a shred of power in your dead gray hands . . . please let me die now. Now. Let the particle be detected and the gas released. Now.

I was not with her.

31

I LIED TO you.

I said at the beginning of this narrative that I was not with her when Aenea's fate was played out—implying that I did not know what that fate might be—and I repeated it some sleep periods ago when I 'scribed what I was sure must be the last installment of that same narrative.

But I lied by omission, as some priest of the Church might say.

I lied because I did not want to discuss it, to describe it, to relive it, to believe it. But I know now that I must do all of these things. I have relived it every hour of my incarceration here in this Schrödinger cat box prison. I have believed it since the moment I shared the experience with my dear friend, my dear Aenea.

I knew before they shipped me out of Pacem System what the fate of my dear girl had been. Having believed it and relived it, I owe it to the truth of this narrative and to the memory of our love to discuss it and describe it.

All this came to me while I was drugged and docile, tethered in a high-g tank aboard the robot shuttle an hour after my ten-minute trial in front of the Inquisition on a Pax base asteroid ten light-minutes from Pacem. I knew soon as I heard and felt and saw these things that they were real, that they were happening at the moment I shared them, and that only my closeness to Aenea and my slow progress in learning the language of the living had allowed such a powerful sharing. When the sharing was over, I began screaming in my high-g tank, ripping at life-support umbilicals and banging the bulkhead with my head and fists, until the water-filled tank was swirling with my blood. I tried tearing at the osmosis mask that covered my face like some parasite sucking away my breath; it would not tear. For a full three hours I screamed and protested, battering myself into a state of semiconsciousness at best, reliving the shared moments with Aenea a thousand times and screaming in agony a thousand times, and then the robot ship injected sleep drugs through the leechlike umbilicals, the high-g tank drained, and I drifted away into cryogenic fugue as the torchship reached the translation point for the jump to nearby Armaghast System.

I awoke in the Schrödinger cat box. The robot ship had loaded me into the fused-energy satellite and launched it without human intervention. For a few moments I was disoriented, believing that the shared moments with Aenea had all been nightmare. Then the reality of those moments flooded back and I began screaming again. I believe that I was not sane again for some months.

Here is what drove me to madness.

AENEA HAD ALSO been taken bleeding and unconscious from St. Peter's Basilica, but unlike me she awoke the next day neither drugged nor shunted. She came to consciousness—and I shared this awakening more clearly than I have recalled any memory of mine, as sharp and real as a second set of sense impressions—in a huge stone room, round, some thirty meters across, with a ceiling fifty meters above the stone floor. Set in the ceiling was a glowing frosted glass that gave the sense of a skylight, although Aenea guessed that this was an illusion and that the room was deep within a larger structure.

The medics had cleaned me up for my ten-minute trial while I was unconscious, but no one had touched Aenea's wounds: the left side of her face was tender, swollen with bruises, her clothes had been torn away from her body and she was naked, her lips were swollen, her left eye was almost shut—she could see out of it only with effort and the vision from her right eye was blurred from concussion—and there were cuts and bruises on her chest, thighs, forearm, and belly. Some of these cuts had caked over, but a few were deep enough to require stitches that no one had provided. They still bled.

She was strapped in what appeared to be a rusted iron skeleton of crossed metal that hung by chains from the high ceiling and that allowed her to lean back and rest her weight against it but still kept her almost standing, her arms held low along the rusted girders, a near-vertical asterisk of cold metal hanging in air with her wrists and ankles cruelly clamped and bolted to the frame. Her toes hung about ten centimeters above a grated floor. She could move her head. The round room was empty except for this and two other objects. A broad wastebasket sat to the right of the chair. There was a plastic liner in the wastebasket. Also next to the right arm of the asterisk was a rusted metal tray with various instruments on it: ancient dental picks and pliers, circular blades, scalpels, bone saws, a long forceps of some kind, pieces of wire with barbs at three-centimeter intervals, long-bladed shears, shorter, serrated shears, bottles of dark fluid, tubes of paste, needles, heavy thread, and a hammer. Even more disturbing was the round grate some two and a half meters across beneath her, through which she could see dozens of tiny, blue flames burning like pilot lights. There was the faint smell of natural gas.

Aenea tried the restraints—they gave not at all—felt her bruised wrists and ankles throb at the attempts, and put her head back against the iron girder to wait. Her hair was matted there and she could feel a huge lump high on her scalp and another near the base of her skull. She felt nauseous and concentrated on not throwing up on herself.

After a few minutes, a hidden door in the stone wall opened and Rhadamanth Nemes came in and walked to a place just beyond the grate to the right side of Aenea. A second Rhadamanth Nemes came in and took her place on Aenea's left side. Two more Nemeses came in and took up positions farther back. They did not speak. Aenea did not speak to them.

A few minutes later, John Domenico Cardinal Mustafa shimmered into existence—his life-size holographic image taking on solidity directly in front of Aenea. The illusion of his physical presence was perfect except for the fact that the Cardinal was sitting on a chair not represented in the hologram, giving the illusion that he was floating in midair. Mustafa looked younger and healthier than he had on T'ien Shan. A few seconds later he was joined by the holo of a more massive cardinal in a red robe, and then by the holo of a thin, tubercular-looking priest. A moment after that, a tall, handsome man dressed all in gray came through the physical door in the wall of the physical dungeon and stood with the holos. Mustafa and the other Cardinal continued sitting on unseen chairs while the monsignor's holo and the physically present man in gray stood behind the chairs like servants.

"M. Aenea," said the Grand Inquisitor, "allow me to introduce the Vatican Secretary of State His Eminence Cardinal Lourdusamy, his aide Monsignor Lucas Oddi, and our esteemed Councillor Albedo."

"Where am I?" asked Aenea. She had to attempt the sentence a second time because of her swollen lips and bruised jaw.

The Grand Inquisitor smiled. "We will answer all of your questions for the moment, my dear. And then you will answer all of ours. I guarantee this. To answer your first question, you are in the deepest . . . ah . . . interview room . . . in the Castel Sant'Angelo, on the right bank of the new Tiber, near the Ponte Sant'Angelo, quite near the Vatican, still on the world of Pacem."

"Where is Raul?"

"Raul?" said the Grand Inquisitor. "Oh, you mean your rather useless bodyguard. At the moment, I believe he has completed his own meeting with the Holy Office and is aboard a ship preparing to leave our fair system. Is he important to you, my dear? We could make arrangements to return him to Castel Sant'Angelo."

"He's not important," murmured Aenea, and after my first second of hurt and anguish at the words, I could *feel* her thoughts beneath them . . . concern for me, terror for me, hope that they would not threaten me as a means to coerce her.

"As you wish," said Cardinal Mustafa. "It is you we want to interview today. How do you feel?"

Aenea stared at them through her good eye.

"Well," said the Grand Inquisitor, "one should not hope to attack the Holy Father in St. Peter's Basilica and come away with impunity."

Aenea mumbled something.

"What was that, my dear? We could not make it out." Mustafa was smiling slightly—a toad's self-satisfied leer.

"I . . . did . . . not . . . attack . . . the . . . Pope."

Mustafa opened his hands. "If you insist, M. Aenea . . . but your intentions did not seem friendly. What is it that you had in mind as you ran down the central aisle toward the Holy Father?"

"Warn him," said Aenea. Part of her mind was assessing her injuries even as she listened to the Grand Inquisitor's prattle: serious bruises but nothing broken, the sword cut on her thigh needed stitching, as did the cut on her upper chest. But something was wrong in her system—internal bleeding? She did not think so. Something alien had been administered to her via injection.

"Warn him of what?" said Cardinal Mustafa with butter smoothness.

Aenea moved her head to look with her good eye at Cardinal Lourdusamy and then at Councillor Albedo. She said nothing.

"Warn him of what?" asked Cardinal Mustafa again. When Aenea did not respond, the Grand Inquisitor nodded to the nearest Nemes clone. The pale woman walked slowly to the side of Aenea's chair, took up the smaller of the two shears, seemed to think twice about it, set the instrument back on the tray, came closer, went to one knee on the grate next to Aenea's right arm, bent back my darling's little finger, and bit it off. Nemes smiled, stood, and spit the bloody finger into the wastebasket.

Aenea screamed with the shock and pain and half swooned against the headrest.

The Nemes-thing took tourniquet paste from the tube and smeared it on the stump of Aenea's little finger.

The holo of Cardinal Mustafa looked sad. "We do not desire to administer pain, my dear, but we also shall not hesitate to do so. You shall answer our questions quickly and honestly, or more parts of you will end up in the basket. Your tongue will be the last to go."

Aenea fought back the nausea. The pain from her mutilated hand was incredible—ten light-minutes away, I screamed with the secondhand shock of it.

"I was going to warn the Pope . . . about . . . your *coup*," gasped Aenea, still looking at Lourdusamy and Albedo. "Heart attack."

Cardinal Mustafa blinked in surprise. "You *are* a witch," he said softly.

"And you're a traitorous asshole," Aenea said strongly and clearly. "All of you are. You sold out your Church. Now you're selling out your puppet Lenar Hoyt."

"Oh?" said Cardinal Lourdusamy. He looked mildly amused. "How are we doing that, child?"

Aenea jerked her head at Councillor Albedo. "The Core controls everyone's life and death via the cruciforms. People die when it's convenient for the Core to have them dead . . . neural networks in the process of dying are more creative than living ones. You're going to kill the Pope again, but this time his resurrection won't be successful, will it?"

"Very perceptive, my dear," rumbled Cardinal Lourdusamy. He shrugged. "Perhaps it *is* time for a new pontiff." He moved his hand in the air and a fifth hologram appeared behind them in the room: Pope Urban XVI comatose in a hospital bed, nursing nuns, human doctors, and medical machines hovering around him. Lourdusamy waved his pudgy hand again and the image disappeared.

"Your turn to be pope?" said Aenea and closed her eyes. Red spots were dancing in her vision. When she opened her eyes again, Lourdusamy was making a modest shrug.

"Enough of this," said Councillor Albedo. He walked directly through the holos of the seated cardinals and stood at the edge of the grate, directly in front of Aenea. "How have you been manipulating the farcaster medium? How do you farcast without the portals?"

Aenea looked at the Core representative. "It scares you, doesn't it, Councillor? In the same way that the cardinals are too frightened to be here with me in person."

The gray man showed his perfect teeth. "Not at all, Aenea. But you have the ability to farcast yourself—and those near you—without portals. His Eminence Cardinal Lourdusamy and Cardinal Mustafa, as well as Monsignor Oddi, have no wish to suddenly vanish from Pacem with you. As for me . . . I would be delighted if you farcast us somewhere else." He waited. Aenea said nothing. She did not move. Councillor Albedo smiled again. "We know that you're the only one who has learned how to do this type of farcasting," he said softly. "None of your so-called disciples are close to learning the technique. But what *is* the technique? The only way we've managed to use the Void for farcasting is by wedging open permanent rifts in the medium . . . and that takes far too much energy."

"And they don't allow you to do that anymore," muttered Aenea, blinking away the red dots so she could meet the gray man's gaze. The pain from her hand rose and fell in and around her like long swells on an uneasy sea.

Councillor Albedo's eyebrow moved up a fraction. "*They* won't allow us to? Who is *they*, child? Describe your masters to us."

"No masters," murmured Aenea. She had to concentrate in order to banish the dizziness. "Lions and Tigers and Bears," she whispered.

"No more double talk," rumbled Lourdusamy. The fat man nodded to the second Nemes clone, who walked to the tray, removed the rusty pair of pliers, walked around to Aenea's left hand, held it steady at the wrist, and pulled out all of my darling's fingernails.

Aenea screamed, passed out briefly, awoke, tried to turn her head away in time but failed, vomited on herself, and moaned softly.

"There is no dignity in pain, my child," said Cardinal Mustafa. "Tell us what the Councillor wishes to know and we will end this sad charade. You will be taken from here, your wounds will be attended to, your finger regrown, you will be cleaned and dressed and reunited with your body-guard or disciple or whatever. This ugly episode will be over."

At that moment, reeling in agony, Aenea's body still was aware of the alien substance that had been injected into her while she was unconscious hours earlier. Her cells recognized it. Poison. A sure, slow, terminal poison with no antidote—it would activate in twenty-four hours no matter what anyone did. She knew then what they wanted her to do and why.

Aenea had always been in contact with the Core, even before she was born, via the Schrön Loop in her mother's skull linked to her father's cybrid persona. It allowed her to touch primitive dataspheres directly, and she did this now—sensing the solid array of exotic Core machinery that lined this subterranean cell: instruments within instruments, sensors be-yond human understanding or description, devices working in four dimen-sions and more, waiting, sniffing, waiting.

The cardinals and Councillor Albedo and the Core wanted her to escape. Everything was predicated upon her 'casting out of this intolerable situation: thus the holodrama coarseness of the torture, the melodramatic absurdity of the dungeon cell in Castel Sant'Angelo and the heavy-handed Inquisition. They would hurt her until she could not stand it any longer, and when she 'cast away, the Core instruments would measure everything to the billionth of a nanosecond, analyze her use of the Void, and come up with a way to replicate it. The Core would finally have their farcasters back—not in their crude wormhole or Gideon-drive manner, but instant and elegant and eternally theirs.

Aenea ignored the Grand Inquisitor, licked her dry, cracked lips, and said distinctly to Councillor Albedo, "I know where you live."

The handsome gray man's mouth twitched. "What do you mean?"

"I know where the Core—the physical elements of the Core—are," said Aenea.

Albedo smiled but Aenea saw the quick glance toward the two cardi-nals and tall priest. "Nonsense," he said. "No human being has ever known the location of the Core."

"In the beginning," said Aenea, her voice slurred only slightly by pain and shock, "the Core was a transient entity floating in the crude datasphere on Old Earth known as the Internet. Then, even before the Hegira, you moved your bubble memories and servers and core storage nexus to a cluster of asteroids in long orbit around the sun, far from the Old Earth you planned to destroy . . ."

"Silence her," snapped Albedo, turning back toward Lourdusamy, Mustafa, and Oddi. "She is trying to distract us from our questioning. This is not important."

The expressions of the Mustafa, Lourdusamy, and Oddi holos suggested otherwise.

"During the days of the Hegemony," continued Aenea, her good eyelid fluttering with the effort to focus her attention and steady her voice through the long, slow swells of pain, "the Core decided that it was prudent to diversify the physical Core components—bubble-memory matrices deep underground on the nine Labyrinthine worlds, fatline servers in the orbital industrial complexes around Tau Ceti Center, Core entity personae traveling along farcaster combands, and the megasphere connecting it all laced through the farcaster rifts in the Void Which Binds."

Albedo folded his arms. "You're raving."

"But after the Fall," continued Aenea, holding her good eyelid open and defying the gray man with her stare, "the Core got worried. Meina Gladstone's attack on the farcaster medium gave you pause, even if the damage to your megasphere was repairable. You decided to diversify further. Multiply your personae, miniaturize essential Core memories, and make your parasitism on the human neural networks more direct . . ."

Albedo turned his back on her and gestured toward the nearest Nemes-thing. "She's raving. Sew her lips shut."

"No!" commanded Cardinal Lourdusamy. The fat man's eyes were bright and attentive. "Don't touch her until I command it."

The Nemes on Aenea's right had already picked up a needle and roll of heavy thread. Now the pale-faced female paused and looked to Albedo for instructions.

"Wait," said the Councillor.

"You wanted your neural parasitism to be more direct," said Aenea. "So your billions of Core entities each formed its surrounding matrix in cruciform shape and attached themselves directly to your human hosts. Every one of your Core individuals now has a human host of its own to live in and destroy at will. You remain connected via the old dataspheres and new Gideon-drive megasphere nodes, but you enjoy dwelling so close to your food source . . ."

Albedo threw his head back and laughed, showing perfect teeth. He opened his arms and turned back to the three human holos. "This is marvelous entertainment," he said, still chuckling. "You've arranged all this for her interrogation"—he flicked manicured nails in the general direction of the dungeon chamber, the skylight, the iron crossbeams upon which Aenea was clamped—"and the *girl* ends up playing with *your* minds. Pure nonsense. But wonderfully entertaining."

Cardinal Mustafa, Cardinal Lourdusamy, and Monsignor Oddi were looking at Councillor Albedo most attentively, but their holographic fingers were touching their holographic chests.

The red-robed holo of Lourdusamy rose from its invisible chair and walked over to the edge of the grate. The holographic illusion was so perfect that Aenea could hear the slight rustling of the pectoral cross as it swung from its cord of red silk; the cord was intertwined with gold thread and ended in a large red and gold tuft. Aenea concentrated on watching the swinging cross and its clean silk cord rather than paying attention to the agony in her mutilated hands. She could feel the poison quietly spreading its way through her limbs and torso like the tumors and nematodes of a growing cruciform. She smiled. Whatever else they did to her, the cells of her body and blood would never accept the cruciform.

"This is interesting but irrelevant, my child," murmured Cardinal Lourdusamy. "And this"—he flicked his short, fat fingers in the direction of her wounds and nakedness as if repulsed by it—"is most unpleasant." The holo leaned closer and his intelligent little pig eyes bored into her. "And most unnecessary. Tell the Councillor what he wishes to know."

Aenea raised her head to look into the big man's eyes. "How to 'cast without a farcaster?"

Cardinal Lourdusamy licked his thin lips. "Yes, yes."

Aenea smiled. "It is simple, Your Eminence. All you have to do is come to a few classes, learn about learning . . . the language of the dead, of the living, how to hear the music of the spheres . . . and then take communion with my blood or the blood of one of my followers who has drunk the wine."

Lourdusamy backed away as if slapped. He raised the pectoral cross and held it in front of him like a shield. "Blasphemy!" he bellowed. *"Jesus Christus est primogenitus mortuorum; ipsi gloria et imperium in saecula saeculorum!"*

"Jesus Christ *was* the first born of the dead," Aenea said softly, the reflected light from the cross glaring in her good eye. "And you *should* offer him glory. And dominion, if you choose. But it was never his intention that human beings should be revived from death like laboratory mice at the whim of thinking machines . . ."

"Nemes," snapped Councillor Albedo and this time there was no countermand. The Nemes female near the wall walked over to the grate, extended five-centimeter nails, and raked them down Aenea's cheeks from just under each eye, slicing through muscle and exposing my dear friend's cheekbones to the harsh light. Aenea let out a long, terrible sigh and slumped back against the girder. Nemes moved her face closer and showed her small, sharp teeth in a wide grin. Her breath was carrion.

"Chew off her nose and eyelids," said Albedo. "Slowly."

"No!" shouted Mustafa, leaping to his feet, hurrying forward and reaching out to stop Nemes. His holographic hands passed through Nemes's all too solid flesh.

"A moment," said Councillor Albedo, holding up one finger. Nemes paused with her mouth open above Aenea's eyes.

"This is monstrous," said the Grand Inquisitor. "As was your treatment of me."

Albedo shrugged. "It was decided that you needed a lesson, Your Eminence."

Mustafa was quivering with outrage. "Do you truly believe you are our masters?"

Councillor Albedo sighed. "We have always been your masters. You are rotting flesh wrapped around chimpanzee brains . . . gibbering primates decaying toward death from the moment of your birth. Your only role in the universe was as midwives to a higher form of self-awareness. A truly immortal life-form."

"The Core . . ." said Cardinal Mustafa with great disdain.

"Move aside," ordered Councillor Albedo. "Or . . ."

"Or what?" The Grand Inquisitor laughed. "Or you will torture me as you are torturing this deluded woman? Or will you have your monster beat me unto death again?" Mustafa swung his holographic arm back and forth through Nemes's tensed torso, then through Albedo's hard form. The Grand Inquisitor laughed and turned toward Aenea. "You are dead anyway, child. Tell this soulless creature what it needs to know and we will put you out of your misery in seconds with no . . ."

"Silence!" shouted Albedo and held up one hand like a curled claw.

The holo of Cardinal Mustafa screamed, clutched its chest, rolled across the grate through Aenea's bleeding feet and the iron girder, rolled through one of the Nemeses' legs, screamed again, and winked out of existence.

Cardinal Lourdusamy and Monsignor Oddi looked at Albedo. Their faces were expressionless. "Councillor," said the Secretary of State in a soft, respectful tone, "could I interrogate her for a moment? If we are not successful, you can do what you wish with her."

Albedo stared coolly at the Cardinal, but after a second he clapped Nemes on her shoulder and the killing thing stepped back three paces and closed her wide mouth.

Lourdusamy reached toward Aenea's mutilated right hand as if to hold it. His holographic fingers seemed to sink into my darling's torn flesh. *"Quod petis?"* whispered the Cardinal, and ten light-minutes away, screaming and writhing in my high-g tank, I understood him through Aenea: *What do you seek?*

"Virtutes," whispered Aenea. *"Concede mihi virtutes, quibus indigeo, valeum impere."*

And drowning in fury and sorrow and the sloshing fluids of my high-g tank, accelerating farther from Aenea every second, I understood— *Strength. That I be given the strength I need to carry out this, my resolve.*

"Desiderium tuum grave est," whispered Cardinal Lourdusamy. *Your desire is a serious one. "Quod ultra quaeris?" What else do you seek?*

Aenea blinked blood out of her good eye so that she could see the Cardinal's face. *"Quaero togam pacem,"* she said softly, her voice firm. *I seek peace.*

Councillor Albedo laughed again. "Your Eminence," he said, his voice sarcastic, "do you think that I do not understand Latin?"

Lourdusamy looked in the direction of the gray man. "On the contrary, Councillor, I was sure that you did. She is near breaking, you know. I see it in her face. But it is the flames she fears most . . . not the animal to which you are feeding her."

Albedo looked skeptical.

"Give me five minutes with the flames, Councillor," said the Cardinal. "If that fails, turn your beast loose again."

"Three minutes," said Albedo, stepping back next to the Nemes that had raked furrows into Aenea's face.

Lourdusamy stepped back several paces. "Child," he said, speaking Web English again, "this will hurt very much, I am afraid." He moved his holographic hands and a jet of blue flame beneath the grate spurted into a column of flame that singed the bare soles of Aenea's clamped feet. Skin burned, blackened, and curled. The stench of burning flesh filled the cell.

Aenea screamed and attempted to pull free of the clamps. They did not budge. The hanging bar of iron on which she was pinned began to glow at the bottom, sending pain up her bare calves and thighs. She felt her skin blister there as well. She screamed again.

Cardinal Lourdusamy waved his hand again and the flame dropped back beneath the grate, becoming a pilot light watching like the blue eye of a hungry carnivore.

"That is just a taste of the pain you will feel," murmured the Cardinal. "And, unfortunately, when one is seriously burned, the pain continues even after the flesh and nerves are irreparably burned away. They say that it is the most painful way to die."

Aenea gritted her teeth to keep from screaming again. Blood dripped from her torn cheeks to her pale breasts . . . those breasts I had held and kissed and fallen asleep against. Imprisoned in my high-g crèche, millions of kilometers away and preparing to spin up to C-plus and fugue oblivion, I screamed and raged into silence.

Albedo stepped onto the grate and said to my dear friend, " 'Cast away from all this. 'Cast to the ship that is taking Raul to certain death and free him. 'Cast to the Consul's ship. The autosurgeon there will heal you. You will live for years with the man you love. It is either that or a slow and terrible death here for you, and a slow and terrible death for Raul elsewhere. You will never see him again. Never hear his voice. 'Cast away, Aenea. Save yourself while there is still time. Save the one you love. In a minute, this man will burn the flesh from your legs and arms until your bones blacken. But we will not let you die. I will turn Nemes loose to feed on you. 'Cast away, Aenea. 'Cast away now."

"Aenea," said Cardinal Lourdusamy, *"es igitur paratus?"* Are you ready, therefore?

"In nomine Humanitus, ego paratus sum," said Aenea, looking into the Cardinal's eyes with her one good eye. *In the name of Humanitus, I am ready.*

Cardinal Lourdusamy waved his hand. All of the gas jets flamed high at once. Flame engulfed my darling and the Albedo cybrid.

Aenea stretched in agony as the heat engulfed her.

"No!" screamed Albedo from the midst of flames and walked from the burning grate, his synthetic flesh burning away from his false bones. His expensive gray clothes rose toward the distant ceiling in burning wads of cloth and his handsome features were melting onto his chest. "No, damn you!" he screamed again and reached for Lourdusamy's throat with blazing fingers.

Albedo's hands went through the hologram. The Cardinal was staring at Aenea's face through the flames. He raised his right hand. *"Miser-ecordiam Dei . . . in nomine Patris, et Filia, et Spiritu Sanctus."*

These were the last words that Aenea ever heard as the flames closed on her ears and throat and face. Her hair exploded in flame. Her vision burned a bright orange and faded as her eyes were fused with flames.

But I felt her pain in the few seconds of life left to her. And I heard her thoughts like a shout—no, like a whisper in my mind.

Raul, I love you.

Then the heat expanded, the pain expanded, her sense of life and love and mission expanded and lifted through the flames like smoke rising toward the unseen ceiling skylight, and my darling Aenea died.

I felt the second of her death like an implosion of all sight and sound and symbol essence. Everything in the universe worth loving and living for disappeared at that second.

I did not scream again. I quit pounding the walls of my high-g tank. I floated in weightlessness, feeling the tank drain, feeling the drugs and umbilicals for cryogenic fugue fall into me and onto me like worms at my flesh. I did not fight. I did not care.

Aenea was dead.

The torchship translated to quantum state. When I awoke, I was in this Schrödinger cat box death cell.

It did not matter. Aenea was dead.

32

THERE WAS NEITHER clock nor calendar in my cell. I do not know how many standard days, weeks, or months I was beyond the reach of sanity. I may have gone many days without sleeping or slept for weeks on end. It is difficult or impossible to tell.

But eventually, when the cyanide and the laws of quantum chance continued to spare me from day to day, hour to hour, minute to minute, I began this narrative. I do not know why my imprisoners provided me with a slate text 'scriber and stylus and the ability to print a few pages of re-cycled microvellum. Perhaps they saw the possibility of the condemned man writing his confession or using the 'scriber stylus as an impotent way to rage at his judges and jailers. Or perhaps they saw the condemned man's writing of his sins and injuries, joys and losses of joy as an additional source of punishment. And perhaps in a way it was.

But it was also my salvation. At first it saved me from the insanity and self-destruction of uncontrollable grief and remorse. Then it saved my memories of Aenea—pulling them from the quagmire of horror at her terri-ble death to the firmer ground of our days together, her joy of living, her mission, our travels, and her complex but terribly straightforward message to me and all humankind. Eventually it simply saved my life.

Soon after beginning the narrative, I discovered that I could share the thoughts and actions of any of the participants in our long odyssey and failed struggle. I knew that this was a function of what Aenea had taught me through discussion and communion—with learning the language of the dead and the language of the living. I still encountered the dead in my sleeping and waking dreams: my mother often spoke to me and I tasted the agony and wisdom of uncounted others who had lived and died long ago, but it was not these lost souls who obsessed me now—it was those with some parallel view of my own experiences in all my years of knowing Aenea.

Never during my time waiting for death in the Schrödinger cat box did I believe that I could hear the current thoughts of the living beyond my prison—I assumed that the fused-energy shell of the orbital egg somehow prevented that—but I soon learned how to shut out the clamor of all those countless older voices resonating in the Void Which Binds and concentrate on the memories of those—those dead as well as presumably still living—who had been part of Aenea's story. Thus I entered into at least some of the thoughts and motives of human beings so different from my own way of thinking as to be literally alien creatures: Cardinals Simon Augustino Lourdusamy and John Domenico Mustafa, Lenar Hoyt in his incarnations as Pope Julius and Pope Urban XVI, Mercantilus traders such as Kenzo Isozaki and Anna Pelli Cognani, priests and warriors such as Father de Soya, Sergeant Gregorius, Captain Marget Wu, and Executive Officer Hoagan Liebler. Some of the characters in my tale are present in the Void Which Bind largely as scars, holes, vacancies—the Nemes creatures are such vacuums, as are Councillor Albedo and the other Core entities—but I was able to track some of the movements and actions of these beings simply by the movement of that vacancy through the matrix of sentient emotion that was the Void, much as one would see the outline of an invisible man in a hard rain. Thus, in combination with listening to the soft murmurings of the human dead, I could reconstruct Rhadamanth Nemes's slaughter of the innocents on Sol Draconi Septem and hear the sibilant hissings and see the deadly actions of Scylla, Gyges, Briareus, and Nemes on Vitus-Gray-Balianus B. But as distasteful and disorienting as these descents into moral vacuum and mental nightmare were to me, they were balanced by a taste again of the warmth of such friends as Dem Loa, Dem Ria, Father Glaucus, Het Masteen, A. Bettik, and all the rest. Many of these participants in the tale I sought out only through my own memory—wonderful people such as Lhomo Dondrub, last seen flying off on his wings of pure light in his gallant and hopeless battle against the Pax warships, and Rachel, living the second of several lives she was destined to fill with adventure, and the regal Dorje Phamo and the wise young Dalai Lama. In this way, I was using the Void Which Binds to hear my own voice, to clarify memory beyond the ability and clarity of memory, and in that sense I often saw myself as a minor character in my own tale, a not-too-intelligent follower, usually reacting rather than leading, often failing to ask questions when he should or accepting answers all too inadequate. But I also saw the lumbering Raul Endymion of the tale as a man discovering love with a person he had waited for all of his life, and in that sense his willingness to follow without question was often balanced by his willingness to give his life in an instant for his dear friend.

Although I know without doubt that Aenea is dead, I never sought her voice among the chorus of those speaking the language of the dead.

Rather, I felt her presence throughout the Void Which Binds, felt her touch in the minds and hearts of all the good people who wandered through our odyssey or had their lives changed forever in our long struggle with the Pax. As I learned to dim the insensate clamor and pick out specific voices among the chorus of the dead, I realized that I often visualized these human resonances in the Void as stars—some dim but visible when one knew where to look, others blazing like supernovas, still others existing in binary combinations with other former living souls, or set forever in a constellation of love and relationship with specific individuals, others—like Mustafa and Lourdusamy and Hoyt—all but burned out and imploded by the terrible gravity of their ambition or greed or lust for power, their human radiance all but lost as they collapsed into black holes of the spirit.

But Aenea was not one of these stars. She was like the sunlight that had surrounded us during a walk on a warming spring day in the meadows above Taliesin West—constant, diffuse, flowing from a single source but warming everything and everyone around us, a source of life and energy. And as when winter comes or night falls, the absence of that sunlight brings the cold and darkness and we wait for spring and morning.

But I knew that there would be no morning for Aenea now, no resurrection for her and our love affair. The great power of her message is that the Pax version of resurrection was a lie—as sterile as the required birth-control injections administered by the Pax. In a finite universe of would-be immortals, there is almost no room for children. The Pax universe was ordered and static, unchanging and sterile. Children bring chaos and clutter and an infinite potential for the future that was anathema to the Pax.

As I thought of this and pondered Aenea's last gift to me—the antidote to the Pax birth-control implant within me—I wondered if it had been a primarily metaphorical gesture. I hoped that Aenea had not been suggesting that I use it literally; that I find another love, a wife, have children with someone else. In one of our many conversations, she and I had discussed that once—I remember it was while sitting in the vestibule of her shelter near Taliesin as the evening wind blew the scent of yucca and primrose to us—that strange elasticity of the human heart in finding new relationships, new people to share one's life with, new potentials. But I hope that Aenea's gift of fertility in that last few minutes we were together in St. Peter's Basilica *was* a metaphor for the wider gift she had already given humanity, the option for chaos and clutter and wonderful, unseen options. If it was a literal gift, a suggestion that I find a new love, have children with someone else, then Aenea had not known me at all. In my writing of this narrative, I had seen all too well through the eyes of too many others that Raul Endymion was a likable enough fellow, trustworthy, awkwardly valiant on occasion, but not known for his insight or intelligence. But I was smart enough and insightful enough—at least into my own soul—to know for certain that this one love had been enough for my lifetime, and while I grew to realize—as the days and weeks and then, almost certainly, months passed in my death cell with no arrival of death—that if I somehow miraculously returned to the universe of the living I would seek out joy and laughter and friendship again, but not a pale shadow of the love I had felt. Not children. No.

For a few wonderful days while writing the text, I convinced myself that Aenea had returned from the dead . . . that some sort of miracle had been possible. I had just reached the part of my narrative where we had reached Old Earth—passing through the farcaster on God's Grove after the terrible encounter with the first Nemes-thing—and had finished that section with a description of our arrival at Taliesin West.

The night after finishing that first chunk of our story, I dreamed that Aenea had come to me there—in the Schrödinger death cell—had called my name in the dark, touched my cheek, and whispered to me, "We're leaving here, Raul, my darling. Not soon, but as soon as you finish your tale. As soon as you remember it all and understand it all." When I awoke, I had found that the stylus 'scriber had been activated and on its pages, in Aenea's distinctive handwriting, was a long note from her including some excerpts from her father's poetry.

For days—weeks—I was convinced that this had been a real visitation, a miracle of the sort the later apostles had insisted was visited on the original disciples after Jesus's execution—and I worked on the narrative at a fever pitch, desperate to see it all, record it all, and understand it all. But the process took me more months, and in that time I came to realize that the visit from Aenea must have been something else altogether—my first experience of hearing a whisper of her among the voices of the dead in the Void, almost certainly, and possibly, somehow, an actual message from her stored in the memory of the 'scriber and set to be triggered when I wrote those pages. It was not beyond possibility. One thing that had been certain was my darling friend's ability to catch glimpses of the future—*futures*, she always said, emphasizing the plural. It might have been possible for her to store that beautiful note in a 'scriber and somehow see to it that the instrument was included in my Schrödinger cat box cell.

Or . . . and this is the explanation I have come to accept . . . I wrote that note myself while totally immersed, although "possessed" might be a better word, in Aenea's persona as I pursued its essence through the Void and my own memories. This theory is the least pleasing to me, but it conforms with Aenea's only expressed view of the afterlife, based as it was more or less on the Judaic tradition of believing that people live on after death only in the hearts and memories of those they loved and those they served and those they saved.

At any rate, I wrote for more months, began to see the true immensity—and futility—of Aenea's brave quest and hopeless sacrifice, and then I finished the frenzied scribbling, found the courage to describe Aenea's terrible death and my own helplessness as she died, wept as I printed out the last few pages of microvellum, read them, recycled them, ordered the 'scriber to keep the complete narrative in its memory, and shut the stylus off for what I thought was the final time.

Aenea did not appear. She did not lead me out of captivity. She was dead. I *felt* her absence from the universe as clearly as I had felt any resonance from the Void Which Binds since my communion.

So I lay in my Schrödinger cat box, tried to sleep, forgot to eat, and waited for death.

SOME OF MY explorations among the voices of the dead had led to revelations that had no direct relevance to my narrative. Some were personal and private—waking dreams of my long-dead father hunting with his brothers, for instance, and an insight into the generosity of that quiet man I had never known, or chronicles of human cruelty that, like the memories of Jacob Schulmann from the forgotten twentieth century, acted only as subtext for my deeper understanding of today's barbarisms.

But other voices . . .

So I had finished the narrative of my life with Aenea and was waiting to die, spending longer and longer sleep periods, hoping that the decisive quantum event would occur while I was asleep, aware of the text in the memory of my 'scriber and wondering vaguely if anyone would ever figure out a way through the fixed-to-explode-if-tampered-with shell of my Schrödinger box and find my narrative someday, perhaps centuries hence, when I fell asleep again and had this dream. I knew at once that this was not a regular dream—that wave-front dance of possibilities—but was a call from one of the voices of the dead.

In my dream, the Hegemony Consul was playing the Steinway on the balcony of his ebony spaceship—that spaceship that I knew so well—while great, green, saurian things surged and bellowed in the nearby swamps. He was playing Schubert. I did not recognize the world beyond the balcony, but it was a place of huge, primitive plants, towering storm clouds, and frightening animal roars.

The Consul was a smaller man than I had always imagined. When he was finished with the piece, he sat quietly for a moment in the twilight until the ship spoke in a voice I did not recognize—a smarter, more human voice.

"Very nice," said the ship. "Very nice indeed."

"Thank you, John," said the Consul, rising from the bench and bringing the balcony into the ship with him. It was beginning to rain.

"Do you still insist on going hunting in the morning?" asked the disembodied voice that was not the ship's as I knew it.

"Yes," said the Consul. "It is something I do here upon occasion."

"Do you like the taste of dinosaur meat?" asked the ship's AI.

"Not at all," said the Consul. "Almost inedible. It is the hunt I enjoy."

"You mean the risk," said the ship.

"That too." The Consul chuckled. "Although I do take care."

"But what if you don't come back from your hunt tomorrow?" asked the ship. His voice was of a young man with an Old Earth British accent.

The Consul shrugged. "We've spent—what?—more than six years exploring the old Hegemony worlds. We know the pattern . . . chaos, civil war, starvation, fragmentation. We've seen the fruit of the Fall of the Farcaster system."

"Do you think that Gladstone was wrong in ordering the attack?" asked the ship softly.

The Consul had poured himself a brandy at the sideboard and now carried it to the chess table set near the bookcase. He took a seat and looked at the game pieces already engaged in battle on the board in front of him. "Not at all," he said. "She did the right thing. But the result is sad. It will be decades, perhaps centuries before the Web begins to weave itself together in a new form." He had been warming the brandy and sloshing it gently as he spoke, now he inhaled it and sipped. Looking up, the Consul said, "Would you like to join me for the completion of our game, John?"

The holo of a young man appeared in the seat opposite. He was a striking young man with clear hazel-colored eyes, low brow, hollow cheeks, a compact nose and stubborn jaw, and a wide mouth that suggested both a calm masculinity and a hint of pugnaciousness. The young man was dressed in a loose blouse and high-cut breeches. His hair was auburn-colored, thick, and very curly. The Consul knew that his guest had once been described as having ". . . a brisk, winning face," and he put that down to the easy mobility of expression that came with the young man's great intelligence and vitality.

"Your move," said John.

The Consul studied his options for several moments and then moved a bishop.

John responded at once, pointing to a pawn that the Consul obediently moved one rank forward for him. The young man looked up with sincere curiosity in his eyes. "What if you don't come back from the hunt tomorrow?" he said softly.

Startled out of his reverie, the Consul smiled. "Then the ship is yours, which it obviously is anyway." He moved his bishop back. "What will you do, John, if this should be the end of our travels together?"

John gestured to have his rook moved forward at the same lightning speed with which he replied. "Take it back to Hyperion," he said. "Program it to return to Brawne if all is well. Or possibly to Martin Silenus, if the old man is still alive and working on his *Cantos*."

"Program it?" said the Consul, frowning at the board. "You mean you'd leave the ship's AI?" He moved his bishop diagonally another square.

"Yes," said John, pointing to have his pawn advanced again. "I will do that in the next few days, at any rate."

His frown deepening, the Consul looked at the board, then at the hologram across from him, and then at the board again. "Where will you go?" he said and moved his queen to protect his king.

"Back into the Core," said John, moving the rook two spaces.

"To confront your maker again?" asked the Consul, attacking again with his bishop.

John shook his head. His bearing was very upright and he had the habit of clearing his forehead of curls with an elegant, backward toss of his head. "No," he said softly, "to start raising hell with the Core entities. To accelerate their endless civil wars and internecine rivalries. To be what my template had been to the poetic community—an irritant." He pointed to where he wanted his remaining knight moved.

The Consul considered that move, found it not a threat, and frowned at his own bishop. "For what reason?" he said at last.

John smiled again and pointed to the square where his rook should next appear. "My daughter will need the help in a few years," he said. He chuckled. "Well, in two hundred and seventy-some years, actually. Checkmate."

"What?" said the Consul, startled, and studied the board. "It can't be . . ."

John waited.

"Damn," said the Hegemony Consul at last, tipping over his king. "Goddamn and spit and hell."

"Yes," said John, extending his hand. "Thank you again for a pleasant game. And I do hope that tomorrow's hunt turns out more agreeably for you."

"Damn," said the Consul and, without thinking, attempted to shake the hologram's thin-fingered hand. For the hundredth time, his solid fingers went through the other's insubstantial palm. "Damn," he said again.

THAT NIGHT IN the Schrödinger cell, I awoke with two words echoing in my mind. "The child!"

The knowledge that Aenea had been married before our relationship had become a full-fledged love affair, the knowledge that she had given birth to a child, had burned in my soul and gut like a painful ember, but except for my almost obsessive curiosity about *who* and *why*—curiosity unsatisfied by my questioning of A. Bettik, Rachel, and the others who had seen her leave during her odyssey with them but who had no idea themselves where she had gone or with whom—I had not considered the reality of that child alive somewhere in the same universe I inhabited. *Her child.* The thought made me want to weep for several reasons.

"The child is nowhere I can find it now," Aenea had said.

Where might that child be now? How old? I sat on my bunk in the Schrödinger cat box and pondered this. Aenea had just turned twenty-three standard years old when she died . . . correction: when she had been brutally murdered by the Core and its Pax puppets. She had disappeared from sight for the one year, eleven months, one week, and six hours when she had just turned twenty years old. That would make the infant about three standard years old . . . plus the time I had spent here in the Schrödinger execution egg . . . eight months? Ten? I simply did not know, but if the child were still alive, he or she . . . my God, I had never asked Aenea whether her baby had been a boy or girl and she had not mentioned it the one time she had discussed the matter with me. I had been so involved with my own hurt and childish sense of injustice that I had not thought to ask her. What an idiot I had been. The child—Aenea's son or Aenea's daughter—would now be about four standard years old. Walking . . . certainly. Talking . . . yes. My God, I realized, her child would be a rational human being at this point, talking, asking questions . . . a *lot* of questions if my few experiences with young children were any indication . . . learning to hike and fish and to love nature . . .

I had never asked Aenea her child's name. My eyes burned and my throat closed with the painful recognition of this fact. Again, she had shown no inclination to talk about that period in her life and I had not asked, telling myself in the weeks we had had together afterward that I did not want to upset her with questions or probings that would make her feel guilty and make me feel murderous. But Aenea had shown no guilt when she had briefly told me about her marriage and child. To be honest, that is part of the reason I'd felt so furious and helpless at the knowledge. But somehow, incredibly, it had not stopped us from being lovers . . . how had it been phrased on the note I had found on my stylus screen months ago, the note I was sure was from Aenea? "Lovers of whom the poets would sing." That was it. The knowledge of her brief marriage and the child had not stopped us from feeling toward one another like lovers who had never experienced such emotion with another person.

And perhaps she had not, I realized. I had always assumed that her marriage was one of sudden passion, almost impulse, but now I looked at it in another way. Who *was* the father? Aenea's note had said that she loved me backward and forward in time, which is precisely the way I had discovered I felt about her—it was as if I had *always* loved her, had waited my entire life to discover the reality of that love. What if Aenea's marriage had not been one of love or passion or impulse but . . . convenience? No, not the right word. *Necessity?*

It had been prophesied by the Templars, the Ousters, the Shrike Cult Church of the Final Atonement and others that Aenea's mother, Brawne Lamia, would bear a child—the One Who Teaches—Aenea, as it turned out. According to the old poet's *Cantos,* on the day that the second John Keats cybrid had died a physical death and Brawne Lamia had fought her way to the Shrike Temple for refuge, the Shrike cultists had chanted— "Blessed be the Mother of Our Salvation—Blessed be the Instrument of Our Atonement"—the salvation being Aenea herself.

What if Aenea had been destined to have a child to continue this line of prophets . . . of messiahs? I had not heard any of these prophecies of another in Aenea's line, but there was one thing I had discovered beyond argument during my months writing of Aenea's life—Raul Endymion was slow and thick-witted, usually the last to understand anything. Perhaps there had been as many prophecies of another One Who Teaches as there had been preceding Aenea herself. Or perhaps this child would have completely different powers and insights that the universe and humanity had been awaiting.

Obviously I would not be the father of such a second messiah. The union of the second John Keats cybrid and Brawne Lamia had been, by Aenea's own accounts, the great reconciliation between the best elements of the TechnoCore and humanity itself. It had taken the abilities and perceptions of both AIs and human beings to create the hybrid ability to see directly into the Void Which Binds . . . for humanity finally to learn the language of the dead and of the living. Empathy was another name for that ability, and Aenea had been the Child of Empathy, if any title suited her.

Who could the father of her child be?

The answer struck me like a thunderbolt. For a second there in the Schrödinger cat box, I was so shaken by the logic of it that I was sure that the particle detector clicking away periodically in the frozen-energy wall of my prison had detected the emitted particle at exactly the right time and the cyanide had been released. What irony to figure things out and to die in the same moment.

But it was not poison in the air, only the growing strength of my certainty on this matter and the even stronger impulse to some action.

There was one other player in the cosmic chess game Aenea and the others had been playing for three hundred standard years now: that near-mythical Observer from the alien sentient races whom Aenea had mentioned briefly in several different contexts. The Lions and Tigers and Bears, the beings so powerful that they could kidnap Old Earth to the Lesser Magellanic Cloud rather than watch it be destroyed, had—according to Aenea—sent among us one or more Observers over the past few centuries, entities who had, according to my interpretation of what Aenea had said, taken on human form and walked among us for all this time. This would have been relatively easy during the Pax era with the virtual immortality of the cruciform so widespread. And there were certainly others who, like the ancient poet Martin Silenus, had stayed alive through a combination of WorldWeb-era medicine, Poulsen treatments, and sheer determination.

Martin Silenus was old, that was certain, perhaps the oldest human being in the galaxy—but he had not been the Observer, that was equally certain. The author of the *Cantos* was too opinionated, too active, too visible to the public at large, too obscene, and generally just too damned cantankerous to be a cool observer representing alien races so powerful that they could destroy us in an eye blink. Or so I hoped.

But somewhere—probably somewhere I had never visited and could not imagine—that Observer had been waiting and watching in human form. It made sense that Aenea might have been compelled—by both prophecy and the necessity of unhindered human evolution she had taught about and believed in—to 'cast away from her odyssey to that distant world where the Observer waited, meet him, mate with him, and bring that child into the universe. Thus would be reconciled the Core, humanity, and the distant Others.

The idea was unsettling, definitely disturbing to me, but also exciting in a way that nothing had been since Aenea's death.

I knew Aenea. Her child would be a human child—filled with life and laughter and a love of everything from nature to old holodramas. I had never understood how Aenea could have left her child behind, but now I realized that she would have had no choice. She *knew* the terrible fate that awaited her in the basement cell of Castel Sant'Angelo. She *knew* that she would die by fire and torture while surrounded by inhuman enemies and the Nemes monsters. She had known this since before she was born.

The fact of this made my knees weak. How could my dear friend have laughed with me so often, gone optimistically into new days so happily, celebrated life so thoroughly, when she knew that every day passing was another day closer to such a terrible death? I shook my head at the strength of will this implied. I did not have it—this I knew. Aenea had.

But she could not have kept the child with her, knowing when and how this terrible ending would take place. Presumably then, the father was raising the child. The Other in human form. The Observer.

I found this even more upsetting than my earlier revelations. I was struck then with the additional certainty that Aenea would have wanted me to have some role in her child's life if she had thought it possible. Her own glimpses into possible futures presumably ended with her own death. Perhaps she did not know that I would not be executed at the same time. But then, she *had* asked me to scatter her ashes on Old Earth . . . which assumed my survival. Perhaps she had thought it too much of a request to make—for me to find her child and to help in any way I could as the boy or girl came of age, to help protect it in a universe of sharp edges.

I realized that I was weeping—not softly, but with great, ragged sobs. It was the first time I had wept like this since Aenea's death, and—oddly enough—it was not primarily out of grief for Aenea's absence, but at the thought of this second chance to hold a child's hand as I had once held Aenea's when she was still twelve standard, of protecting this child of my beloved's as I had tried to protect my beloved.

And failed. The indictment was my own.

Yes, I had failed to protect Aenea in the end, but she *knew* that I would fail, that she would fail in her quest to bring down the Pax. She had loved me and loved life while knowing that we would fail.

There was no reason I had to fail with this other child. Perhaps the

Observer would welcome my help, my sharing of the human experience with this almost certainly more-than-human little boy or girl. I felt it safe to say that no one had known Aenea better than I had. This would be important for the child's—for the new *messiah*'s—upbringing. I would bring this narrative now sitting useless in my 'scriber and share bits and pieces of it with the boy or girl as he or she grew older, giving it all to him or her someday.

I picked up the slate and 'scriber and paced back and forth in my Schrödinger cell. There was this small matter of my unavoidable execution. No one was coming to rescue me. The explosive shell of the egg had decided that, and if there were a way around that problem, someone would have been here by now. It was the most staggering improbability and good luck that I had survived this long when every few hours there was another crap shoot with death as the detector sniffed for the particle emission. I had beaten the laws of quantum chance for this long, but the luck could not hold.

I stopped in my pacing.

There had been four steps in Aenea's teaching of our race's new relationship with the Void Which Binds. Even before coming to my cell I had experienced, if not mastered, learning the language of the dead and of the living. I had shown in my writing of the narrative that I could gain access to the Void for at least old memories of those still living, even if the shell somehow interfered with my ability to sense what was happening now with friends such as Father de Soya or Rachel or Lhomo or Martin Silenus.

Or was there interference? Perhaps I had subconsciously refused to *try* to contact the world of the living—at least for anything beyond memories of Aenea—since I knew that I now inhabited the world of the dead.

No longer. I wanted out of here.

There were two other steps that Aenea had mentioned in her teaching but never fully explained—hearing the music of the spheres and taking the first step.

I now understood both these concepts. Without seeing Aenea 'cast, and without that great rush of gestalt understanding that had come with the terrible sharing of her death, I would not have understood. But I did now.

I had thought of hearing the music of the spheres as a sort of para-normal-radio-telescope trick—actually hearing the pop and crack and whistle of the stars as radio telescopes had for eleven centuries or more. But that had not been what Aenea had meant at all, I realized. It was not the *stars* she was listening to and for, but the resonance of those people—human and otherwise—who dwelt among and around those stars. She had been using the Void as a sort of directional beacon before farcasting herself.

Much of her personal 'casting had not made sense to me. The core-controlled farcaster doors had been rough holes torn through the Void—and thus through space/time—held open by the portals that were like crude clamps holding open the raw edges of a wound in the old days of scalpel surgery. Aenea's farcasting, I now understood, was an infinitely more graceful device.

I had wondered in the busy time when Aenea and I were freecasting down to planet surfaces and from star system to star system in the *Yggdrasill* how she had avoided having us blink into existence inside a hill or fifty meters above the surface, or the treeship inside a star. It seemed to me that blind freecasting, like unplanned Hawking-drive jumps, would be haphazard and disastrous. But we had always emerged exactly where we had to be when Aenea 'cast us. Now I saw why.

Aenea heard the music of the spheres. She resonated with the Void Which Binds, which resonates in turn to sentient life and thought, and then she used the almost illimitable energy of the Void to . . . to take the first step. To travel via the Void to where those voices waited. Aenea had once said that the Void tapped into the energy of quasars, of the exploding centers of galaxies, of black holes and black matter. Enough, perhaps, to move a few organic life-forms through space/time and deposit them in the proper place.

Love was the prime mover in the universe, Aenea had once said to me. She had joked about being the Newton who someday explained the basic physics of that largely untapped energy source. She had not lived to do so.

But I saw now what she had meant and how it worked. Much of the music of the spheres was created by the elegant harmonies and chord changes of love. Freecasting to where one's loved one waits. Learning a place after having traveled there with the one or ones you love. Loving to see new places.

Suddenly I understood why our first months together had been what had seemed at the time like useless farcaster wanderings from world to world: Mare Infinitus, Qom-Riyadh, Hebron, Sol Draconi Septem, the unnamed world where we had left the ship, all of the others, even Old Earth. There had been no working farcaster portals. Aenea had swept A. Bettik and me with her to these places—touching them, sniffing their air, feeling their sunlight on her skin, seeing them all with friends—with someone she loved—learning the music of the spheres so that it could be played later.

And my own solo odyssey, I thought: the kayak farcasting from Old Earth to Lusus and the cloud planet and all the other places. Aenea had been the energy behind that 'casting. Sending me to places so that I could taste them and find them again someday on my own.

I had thought—even as I wrote the narrative in the 'scriber that I held under my arm there in the Schrödinger death cell—that I had been little more than a fellow traveler in a series of picaresque adventures. But it had all held a purpose. I had been a lover traveling with my love—or *to* my love—through a musical score of worlds. A score that I had to learn by heart so that I could play it again someday.

I CLOSED MY eyes in the Schrödinger cat box and concentrated, then went beyond concentration to the empty mind state I had learned in meditation on T'ien Shan. *Every world had its purpose. Every minute had its purpose.*

In that unhurried emptiness, I opened myself to the Void Which Binds and the universe to which it resonated. I could not do this, I realized, without communion with Aenea's blood, without the nanotech tailored organisms that now dwelt in my cells and would dwell in my children's cells. *No,* I thought at once, *not my children. But in the cells of those in the human race who escape the cruciform. In their children's cells.* I could not do this without having learned from Aenea. I could not have heard the voices I heard then—greater choruses than I had ever heard before—without having honed my own grammar and syntax of the language of the dead and living during the months I worked on the narrative while waiting to die.

I could not do this, I realized, if I were immortal. This degree of love of life and of one another is granted, I saw for once and for ever, not to immortals, but to those who live briefly and always under the shadow of death and loss.

As I stood there, listening to the swelling chords of the music of the spheres, able now to pick out separate star-voices in the chorus—Martin Silenus's, still alive but failing on my homeworld of Hyperion, Theo's on beautiful Maui-Covenant, Rachel's on Barnard's World, Colonel Kassad's on red Mars, Father de Soya's on Pacem—and even the lovely chords of the dead, Dem Ria's on Vitus-Gray-Balianus B, dear Father Glaucus's on cold Sol Draconi Septem, my mother's voice, again on distant Hyperion—I also heard John Keats's words, in his voice, and in Martin Silenus's, and in Aenea's:

> "But this is human life: the war, the deeds,
> The disappointment, the anxiety,
> Imagination's struggles, far and nigh,
> All human; bearing in themselves this good,
> That they are still the air, the subtle food,
> To make us feel existence, and to show
> How quiet death is. Where soil is men grow,
> Whether to weeds or flowers; but for me,
> There is no depth to strike in . . ."

But the opposite was true of me at that moment—there was more than enough depth to strike in. The universe deepened at that moment, the music of the spheres grew from a mere chorus to a symphony as triumphant as Beethoven's Ninth, and I knew that I would always be able to hear it when I wished or needed to, always be able to use it to take the step I needed to see the one I loved, or, failing that, step to the place where I had been with the one I loved, or, failing that, find a place to love for its own beauty and richness.

The energy of quasars and exploding stellar nuclei filled me then. I was borne up on waves of energy more lovely and more lyrical even than the Ouster angels' wings seen sliding along corridors of sunlight. The shell of deadly energy that was my prison and execution cell seemed laughable now, Schrödinger's original joke, a child's jump rope laid around me on the ground as restraining walls.

I stepped out of the Schrödinger cat box and out of Armaghast System.

For a moment, feeling the confines of the Schrödinger prison fall away and behind me forever, existing nowhere and everywhere in space but remaining physically intact in my body and stylus and 'scriber, I felt a surge of sheer exhilaration as powerful as the dizzying effect of solo-farcasting itself. *Free! I was free!* The wave of joy was so intense that it made me want to weep, to shout into the surrounding light of no-space, to join my voice with the chorus of voices of the living and dead, to sing along with the crystal-clear symphonies of the spheres rising and plunging like a solid, acoustic surf all around me. *Free at last!*

And then I remembered that the one reason to be free, the one person who would make such freedom worthwhile, was gone. Aenea was dead. The sheer joy of escape faded suddenly and absolutely, replaced by a simple but profound satisfaction at my release from so many months of imprisonment. The universe might have had the color drained out of it for me, but at least now I was free to go anywhere I wanted within that monotone realm.

But where was I going? Floating on light, freecasting into the universe with my stylus and 'scriber tucked under my arm, I still had not decided.

Hyperion? I had promised to return to Martin Silenus. I could hear his voice resonating strong in the Void, past and present, but it would not be part of the current chorus for long. His life remaining could now be counted in days or less. But not to Hyperion. Not yet.

The Biosphere Startree? I was shocked to hear that it still existed in some form, although Lhomo's voice was absent from the choral symphony there. The place had been important to Aenea and me, and I had to return someday. But not now.

Old Earth? Amazingly, I heard the music of that sphere quite clearly, in Aenea's former voice and in mine, in the song of the friends at Taliesin with whom we had tallied there. Distance meant nothing in the Void Which Binds. Time there seasons but does not destroy. But not to Old Earth. Not now.

I heard scores of possibilities, more scores of voices I wanted to hear in person, people to hug and weep with, but the music I reacted to most strongly now was from the world where Aenea had been tortured and killed. Pacem. Home of the Church and nest of our enemies—not, I saw now, the same thing. Pacem. There was, I knew, nothing of Aenea for me on Pacem but ashes of the past.

But she had asked me to take her ashes and spread them on Old Earth. Spread them where we had laughed and loved most well.

Pacem. In the vortex of Void energy, already stepping beyond the Schrödinger cell but existing nowhere else except as pure quantum probability, I made my decision and freecast for Pacem.

33

HE VATICAN IS broken as surely as if the fist of God had smashed down from the sky in an anger beyond human understanding. The endless bureaucratic city around it is crushed. The spaceport is destroyed. The grand boulevards are slagged and melted and rimmed with ruin. The Egyptian obelisk that had stood at the center of St. Peter's Square has been snapped off at the base and the scores of colonnades around the oval space are tumbled like petrified logs. The dome of St. Peter's Basilica is shattered and has fallen through the central loggia and grand facade to lie in pieces on the broken steps. The Vatican wall is tumbled down in a hundred places, completely missing for long stretches. The buildings once protected within its medieval confines—the Apostolic Palace, the Secret Archives, the barracks of the Swiss Guard, St. Mother Teresa's Hospice, the papal apartments, the Sistine Chapel—are all exposed and smashed, scorched and tumbled and scattered.

Castel Sant'Angelo on this side of the river has been slagged. The towering cylinder—twenty meters of towering stone rising from its huge square base—has been melted to a mound of cooled lava.

I see all this while walking along the boulevard of broken slabs on the east side of the river. Ahead of me, the bridge, the Ponte Sant'Angelo, has been cracked into three sections and dropped into the river. Into the riverbed, I should say, for it looks as if the New Tiber has been boiled away, leaving glass where the sandy river bottom and riverbanks had been. Someone has rigged a rope suspension bridge across the debris-filled gap between the banks.

This is Pacem; I do not doubt it. The thin, cool atmosphere feels and tastes the same as when Father de Soya, Aenea, and I came through here on the day before my dear girl died, although it was raining and gray then and now the sky is rich with a sunset that manages to make even the broken, fallen-away dome of St. Peter's look beautiful.

It is almost overwhelming to be walking free under an open sky after my uncounted months of tight incarceration. I clutch my 'scriber to me like a shield, like some talisman, like a Bible, and walk the once-proud boulevard with shaky legs. For months my mind has been sharing memories of many places and many people, but my own eyes and lungs and legs and skin have forgotten the feeling of real freedom. Even in my sadness, there is an exultation.

Freecasting had been superficially the same as when Aenea had freecast us both, but on a deeper level it was profoundly different. The flash of white light had been the same, the ease of sudden transition, the slight shock of different air pressure or gravity or light. But this time I had *heard* the light rather than seen it. I had been carried up by the music of the stars and their myriad worlds and chosen the one to which I wanted to step. There had been no effort on my part, no great expenditure of energy, other than the need to focus and to choose carefully. And the music had not faded completely away—I guessed that it never would—but even now played in the background like musicians practicing just beyond the hill for a summer evening's concert.

I can see signs of survivors in the city-wide wreckage. In the gold distance, two oxcarts move along the horizon with human silhouettes walking behind. On this side of the river, I can see huts, simple brick homes among the tumbles of old stone, a church, another small church. From somewhere far behind me comes the smell of meat cooking on an open fire and the unmistakable sound of children laughing.

I am just turning toward that smell and sound when a man steps out from behind a mass of debris that may have once been a guard post at the entrance to Castel Sant'Angelo. He is a small man, quick of hand, his face half-hidden behind a beard and his hair combed back to a queue, but his eyes are alert. He carries a solid slug rifle of the sort once used for ceremony by the Swiss Guard.

We stare at each other for a moment—the unarmed, weakened man carrying nothing but a 'scriber and the sun-bronzed hunter with his ready weapon—and then each recognizes the other. I have never met this man, nor he me, but I have seen him through others' memories via the Void Which Binds, although he was uniformed, armored, and clean-shaven the first time I saw him—naked and in the act of being tortured the last time. I do not know how he recognizes me, but I see that recognition in his eyes an instant before he sets the weapon aside and steps forward to seize my hand and forearm in both his hands.

"Raul Endymion!" he cries. "The day has come! Praise be. Welcome." The bearded apparition actually hugs me before stepping back to look at me again and grin.

"You're Corporal Kee," I say stupidly. I remember the eyes most of all, seen from Father de Soya's point of view as he and Kee and Sergeant

Gregorius and Lancer Rettiq chased Aenea and me across this arm of the galaxy for years.

"Formerly Corporal Kee," says the grinning man. "Now just Bassin Kee, citizen of New Rome, member of the diocese of St. Anne's, hunter for tomorrow's meal." He shakes his head as he stares at me. "Raul Endymion. My God. Some thought you would never escape that cursed Schrödinger cat–thing."

"You know about the Schrödinger egg?"

"Of course," says Kee. "It was part of the Shared Moment. Aenea knew where they were taking you. So we all knew. And we've sensed your presence there through the Void, of course."

I felt suddenly dizzy and a bit sick to my stomach. The light, the air, the great distance to the horizon . . . That horizon became unstable, as if I were looking at it from aboard a small ship in a rough sea, so I closed my eyes. When I opened them, Kee was holding my arm and helping me sit on a large, white stone that looked as if it been blasted from the cathedral far across the glass river.

"My God, Raul," he says, "have you just freecast from there? You've been nowhere else?"

"Yes," I say. "No." I take two slow breaths and say, "What is the Shared Moment?" I had heard the formal capital letters in his voice.

The small man studies me with his bright, intelligent gaze. His voice is soft. "Aenea's Shared Moment," he says. "It is what we all call it, although of course it was more than a single moment. All the moments of her torture and death."

"You felt that too?" I say. I suddenly feel a fist closing around my heart, although whether the emotion is joy or terrible sadness remains to be discovered.

"Everyone felt it," says Kee. "Everyone shared it. Everyone, that is, except her torturers."

"Everyone else on Pacem?" I ask.

"On Pacem," says Kee. "On Lusus and Renaissance Vector. On Mars and Qom-Riyadh and Renaissance Minor and Tau Ceti Center. On Fuji and Ixion and Deneb Drei and Sibitu's Bitterness. On Barnard's World and God's Grove and Mare Infinitus. On Tsingtao Hsishuang Panna and Patawpha and Groombridge Dyson D." Kee pauses and smiles at the sound of his own litany. "On almost every world, Raul. And in places in between. We know that the Startree felt the Shared Moment . . . all the startree biospheres did."

I blink. "There are other startrees?"

Kee nods.

"How did all these worlds . . . share that moment?" I ask, seeing the answer even as I pose the question.

"Yes," murmurs the former Corporal Kee. "All of the places Aenea visited, often with you. All of the worlds where she left disciples who had partaken of communion and renounced the cruciform. Her Shared Moment . . . the hour of her death . . . was like a signal broadcast and rebroadcast through all of these worlds."

I rub my face. It feels numb. "So only those who had already taken communion or studied with Aenea shared in that moment?" I say.

Kee is shaking his head. "No . . . they were the transponders, the relay stations. They pulled the Shared Moment from the Void Which Binds and rebroadcast it to everyone."

"Everyone?" I repeat stupidly. "Even those tens and hundreds of billions in the Pax who wear the cross?"

"Who *wore* the cross," amends Bassin Kee. "Many of those faithful have since decided not to carry a Core parasite in their bodies."

I begin to understand then. Aenea's last shared moments had been more than words and torture and pain and horror—I had sensed her thoughts, shared her understanding of the Core's motives, of the true parasitism of the cruciform, of the cynical use of human death to tweak their neural networks, of Lourdusamy's lust for power and Mustafa's confusion and Albedo's absolute inhumanity . . . If *everyone* had shared the same Shared Moment that I had screamed and fought my way through in the high-g tank on the outward-bound robot prison torchship, then it had been a bright and terrible moment for the human race. And every living human being must have heard her final *I love you, Raul* as the flames swept high.

The sun is setting. Rays of gold light shine through the ruins on the west side of the river and throw a maze of shadows across the east bank. The molten mass of Castel Sant'Angelo runs down toward us like a mountain of melted glass. *She asked me to spread her ashes on Old Earth. And I can't even do that for her. I fail her even in death.*

I look up at Bassin Kee. "On Pacem?" I say. "She had no disciples on Pacem when . . . Oh." She had sent Father de Soya away immediately before our doomed charge up the aisle in St. Peter's Basilica, asking him to leave with the monks and blend into the city he knew so well, to avoid the Pax whatever else happened. When he had argued, Aenea's words had been—*"This is all I ask, Father. And I ask it with love and respect."* And Father de Soya had gone out into the rain. And he had been the broadcast relay, carrying my darling girl's last agony and insight to several billion people on Pacem.

"Oh," I say, still looking at Kee. "But the last time I saw you . . . through the Void . . . you were being kept captive in cryogenic fugue there in that . . . ." I sweep my hand in disgust toward the melted heap of Castel Sant'Angelo.

Kee nods again. "I *was* in cryogenic fugue, Raul. I *was* stored like a sleeping slab of meat in a cold locker in a basement dungeon not far from where they murdered Aenea. But I felt the Shared Moment. Every human alive did—whether sleeping or drunk or dying or lost in madness."

I can only stare at the man, my heart breaking again in understanding. Eventually I say, "How did you get out? Away from there?" We are both looking at the ruins of the Holy Office headquarters now.

Kee sighs. "There was a revolution very soon after the Shared Moment. Many people—the majority here on Pacem—no longer wanted anything to do with the cruciforms and the betrayed Church which had implanted them. Some still were cynical enough to make that trade with the devil in exchange for physical resurrection, but millions . . . hundreds of millions . . . sought out communion and freedom from the Core cross just in the first week. The Pax loyalists attempted to stop them. There was fighting . . . revolution . . . civil war."

"Again," I say. "Just like the Fall of the Farcasters three centuries ago."

"No," says Kee. "Nothing that bad. Remember, once one has learned the language of the dead and the living, it's *painful* to hurt someone else. The Pax loyalists did not have that restraint, but then, they were in the minority everywhere."

I gesture toward the world of ruins. "You call this restraint? You call this not so bad?"

"The revolution against the Vatican and the Pax and the Holy Office did not do this," says Kee grimly. "That was relatively bloodless. The loyalists fled in archangel starships. Their New Vatican is on a world called Madhya . . . a real shithole of a planet, guarded now by half the old fleet and several million loyalists."

"Who then?" I say, still looking at the devastation everywhere around us.

"The Core did this," says Kee. "The Nemes-things destroyed the city and then seized four archangel ships. Slagged us from space after the loyalists left. The Core was pissed off. Probably still is. We don't care."

I carefully set the 'scriber down on the white stone and look around. More men and women are coming out of the ruins, staying a respectful distance from us but watching with great interest. They are dressed in work clothes and hunting garb, but not in bearskins or rags. These are obviously people living in a rough place during a hard time, but not savages. A young blond boy waves at me shyly. I wave back.

"I never really answered your question," says Kee. "The guards released me . . . released all of the prisoners . . . during the confusion in the week after the Shared Moment. A lot of prisoners around this arm of the galaxy found doors opening that week. After communion . . . well, it's hard to imprison or torture someone else when you end up sharing half their pain through the Void Which Binds. And the Ousters have been busy since the Shared Moment reviving the billions of Jews and Muslims and others kidnapped by the Core . . . and ferrying them home from the Labyrinthine planets to their homeworlds."

I think about this for a minute. Then I say, "Did Father de Soya survive?"

Kee grins even more broadly. "I guess you can say he survived. He's our priest in the parish of St. Anne's. Come on, I'll take you to him. He knows you're here by now. It's only a five-minute walk."

DE SOYA HUGS me so fiercely that my ribs ache for an hour. The priest is wearing a plain black cassock and Roman collar. St. Anne's is not the large parish church we had glimpsed in the Vatican, but a small brick and adobe chapel set in a cleared area on the east bank. It seems that the parish consists of about a hundred families who make their livelihood hunting and farming in what had been a large park on this side of the spaceport. I am introduced to most of these hundred families as we eat outside in the lighted space near the foyer of the church and it seems that they all know of me—they act as if they know me personally, and all seem sincerely grateful that I am alive and returned to the world of the living.

As night deepens, Kee, de Soya, and I adjourn to the priest's private quarters: a spartan room adjoining the back of the church. Father de Soya brings out a bottle of wine and pours a full glass for each of us.

"One of the few benefits of the fall of civilization as we know it," he says, "is that there are private cellars with fine vintages everywhere one digs. It is not theft. It is archaeology."

Kee lifts his glass as if in toast and then hesitates. "To Aenea?" he suggests.

"To Aenea," say Father de Soya and I. We drain our glasses and the priest pours more.

"How long was I gone?" I ask. The wine makes my face flush, as it always does. Aenea used to kid me about it.

"It has been thirteen standard months since the Shared Moment," says de Soya.

I shake my head. I must have spent the time writing the narrative and waiting to die in work sessions of thirty hours or more, interspersed with a few hours of sleep, then another thirty or forty hours straight. I had been doing what sleep scientists call free-running: losing all connection to circadian rhythm.

"Do you have any contact with the other worlds?" I ask. I look at Kee and answer my own question. "You must. Bassin was telling me about the reaction to the Shared Moment on other worlds and the return of the kidnapped billions."

"A few ships set in here," says de Soya, "but with the archangel ships gone, travel takes time. The Templars and Ousters use their treeships to ferry the refugees home, but the rest of us hate to use the Hawking drive now that we realize how harmful it is to the Void medium. And as hard as everyone works to learn it, very few have learned how to hear the music of the spheres well enough to take that first step."

"It is not so hard," I say and chuckle to myself as I sip the smooth wine. "It's goddamn hard," I add. "Sorry, Father."

De Soya nods his indulgence. "It *is* goddamn hard. I feel that I've come close a hundred times, but always lose the focus at the last moment."

I look at the little priest. "You've stayed Catholic," I say at last.

Father de Soya sips the wine out of an old glass. "I haven't just stayed Catholic, Raul. I've rediscovered what it means to be Catholic. To be a Christian. To be a believer."

"Even after Aenea's Shared Moment?" I say. I am aware of Corporal Kee watching us from the end of the table. Shadows from the oil lights dance on the warm earth walls.

De Soya nods. "I already understood the corruption of the Church in its pact with the Core," he says very softly. "Aenea's shared insights only underlined what it meant for me to be human . . . and a child of Christ."

I am thinking about this a minute later when Father de Soya adds, "There is talk of making me a bishop, but I am quelling that. It is why I have stayed in this region of Pacem even though most of the viable communities are away from the old urban areas. One look at the ruins of our beautiful tradition across the river reminds me of the folly of staking too much on hierarchy."

"So there's no pope?" I say. "No holy father?"

De Soya shrugs and pours us all more wine. After thirteen standard months of recycled food and no alcohol, the wine is going straight to my head. "Monsignor Lucas Oddi escaped both the revolution and the Core attack and has established the papacy in exile on Madhya," the priest says with a sharp tone in his voice. "I don't believe that anyone in the former Pax except his immediate defenders and followers in that system honor him as a real pope." He sips his wine. "It is not the first time that the Mother Church has had an antipope."

"What about Pope Urban XVI?" I say. "Did he die of his heart attack?"

"Yes," says Kee, leaning forward and setting his strong forearms on the table.

"And was resurrected?" I say.

"Not exactly," says Kee.

I look at the former corporal, waiting for an explanation, but none is forthcoming.

"I've sent word across the river," says Father de Soya. "Bassin's comment should be explained any minute."

Indeed, a minute later the curtains at the entrance to de Soya's comfortable little alcove are pulled back and a tall man in a black cassock enters. It is not Lenar Hoyt. It is a man I have never met but whom I feel that I know well—his elegant hands, long face, large, sad eyes, broad forehead, and thinning silver hair. I stand to shake his hand, to bow, to kiss his ring . . . something.

"Raul, my boy, my boy," says Father Paul Duré. "What a pleasure to meet you. How thrilled we all are that you have returned."

The older priest shakes my hand with a firm grip, hugs me for good measure, and then goes to de Soya's cupboard as if he is familiar with it, finds a jar, pumps water into the sink, washes the jar, pours wine for himself, and sits in the chair opposite Kee at the end of the table.

"We're catching Raul up on what has happened in the past year and a month of his absence," says Father de Soya.

"It feels like a century," I say. My eyes are focused on something far beyond the table and this room.

"It *was* a century for me," says the older Jesuit. His accent is quaint and somehow charming—a French-speaking Outback world, perhaps? "Almost three centuries, actually."

"I saw what they did to you when you were resurrected," I say with the brazenness of the wine in me. "Lourdusamy and Albedo murdered you so that Hoyt would be reborn again from your shared cruciforms."

Father Duré has not actually tasted his wine, but he stares down into the glass as if waiting for it to transubstantiate. "Time and time again," he says in a tone that seems more wistful than anything else. "It is a strange life, being born just to be murdered."

"Aenea would agree," I say, knowing that these men are friends and good men but not feeling especially friendly to the Church in general.

"Yes," says Paul Duré and holds up his glass in a silent toast. He drinks.

Bassin Kee fills the vacuum of silence. "Most of the faithful left on Pacem would have Father Duré as our true pope."

I look at the elderly Jesuit. I have been through enough that it does not make me all tingly to be in the presence of a legend, someone who was central to the *Cantos*. As is always the case when you are with the actual human being behind the celebrity or legend, there is something human about the man or woman that makes things less than myth. In this case, it is the soft tufts of gray hair growing in the priest's large ears.

"Teilhard the Second?" I say, remembering that the man had reportedly been a fine pope as Teilhard I 279 years ago—for a short period before he was murdered for the first time.

Duré accepts more wine from Father de Soya and shakes his head. I can see that the sadness behind those large eyes is the same as de Soya's— earned and heartfelt, not assumed for character effect. "No more papacy for me," he says. "I will spend the rest of my years attempting to learn from Aenea's teachings—listening very hard for the voices of the dead and the living—while reacquainting myself with Our Lord's lessons on humility. For years I played the archaeologist and intellectual. It is time to rediscover myself as a simple parish priest."

"Amen," says de Soya and hunts in his cupboard for another bottle. The former Pax starship captain sounds a bit drunk.

"You don't wear the cruciform any longer?" I say, addressing myself to all three men while looking at Duré.

All three of them look shocked. Duré says, "Only the fools and ultimately cynical still wear the parasite, Raul. Very few on Pacem. Very few on any of the worlds where Aenea's Shared Moment was heard." He touches his thin chest as if remembering. "It was not a choice for me, actually. I was reborn in one of the Vatican resurrection crèches at the height of the fighting. I waited for Lourdusamy and Albedo to visit me as always . . . to murder me as always. Instead, this man . . ." He extends his long fingers toward Kee, who bows slightly and pours himself a bit more wine. "This man," continues the former Pope Teilhard, "came crashing in with his rebels, all combat armor and ancient rifles. He brought me a chalice of wine. I knew what it was. I had shared in the Shared Moment."

I stare at the old priest. *Even dormant in the bubble-memory matrix of the extra cruciform, even while being resurrected?* I thought.

As if reading my gaze, Father Duré nods. "Even there," he says. Looking directly at me, he says, "What will you do now, Raul Endymion?"

I hesitate only a second. "I came to Pacem to find Aenea's ashes . . . she asked me . . . she once asked . . ."

"We know, my son," says Father de Soya quietly.

"Anyway," I go on when I can, "there's no chance of that in what's left of Castel Sant'Angelo, so I'll continue with my other priority."

"Which is?" says Father Duré with infinite gentleness. Suddenly, in this dim room with the rough table and the old wine and the male smell of clean sweat all around, I can see in the old Jesuit the powerful reality behind Uncle Martin's mythic *Cantos*. I realize without doubt that *this* was indeed the man of faith who had crucified himself not once but repeated times on the lightning-filled tesla tree rather than submit to the false cross of the cruciform. This was a true defender of the faith. This was a man whom Aenea would have loved to have met and talked with and debated with. At that moment I feel her loss with such renewed pain that I have to look down into my wine to hide my eyes from Duré and the others.

"Aenea once told me that she had given birth to a child," I manage to say and then stop. I cannot remember if this fact had been in the gestalt of memories and thoughts that was transmitted in Aenea's Shared Moment. If so, they know all about this. I glance at them, but both priests and the corporal are waiting politely. They had not known this.

"I'm going to find that child," I say. "Find it and help raise it, if I am allowed."

The priests look at one another in something like wonderment. Kee is looking at me. "We did not know this," says Federico de Soya. "I am amazed. I would have wagered everything I know about human nature to say that you were the only man in her life . . . the only love. I have never seen two young people so happy."

"There was someone else," I say, raising my glass almost violently to swig down the last of the wine only to find the glass empty. I set it carefully on the table. "There was someone else," I say again, less miserably and emphatically this time. "But that's not important. The baby . . . the child . . . *is* important. I want to find it if I can."

"Do you have any idea where the child is?" says Kee.

I sigh and shake my head. "None. But I'll 'cast to every world in the old Pax and Outback, to every world in the galaxy if I have to. Beyond the galaxy . . ." I stop. I am drunk and this is too important to talk about when drunk. "Anyway, that's where I'll be going in a few minutes."

Father de Soya shakes his head. "You're exhausted, Raul. Spend the night here. Bassin has an extra cot in his house next door. We will all sleep tonight and see you off in the morning."

"Have to go now," I say and start to rise, to show them my ability to think straight and act decisively. The room tilts as if the ground has subsided suddenly on the south side of Father de Soya's little house. I grab the table for support, almost miss it, and hang on.

"Perhaps the morning would be best," says Father Duré, standing and putting a strong hand on my shoulder.

"Yes," I say, standing again and finding the ground tremors subsiding slightly. "T'morrow's better." I shake all of their hands again. Twice. I am desperately close to crying again, not from grief this time, although the grief is there, always in the background like the symphony of the spheres, but out of sheer relief at their company. I have been alone for so long now.

"Come, friend," says former Corporal Bassin Kee of the Pax Marines and the Corps Helvetica, putting his hand on my other shoulder and walking with the former Pope Teilhard and me to his little room, where I collapse onto one of the two cots there. I am drifting away when I feel someone pulling off my boots. I think it is the former Pope.

I HAD FORGOTTEN that Pacem has only a nineteen-standard-hour day. The nights are too short. In the morning I am still suffused with the exhilaration of my freedom, but my head hurts, my back hurts, my stomach aches, my teeth hurt, my hair hurts, and I am sure that a pack of small, fuzzy creatures has taken up residence in the back of my mouth.

The village beyond the chapel is bustling with early morning activity. All of it too loud. Cook fires simmer. Women and children go about chores while the men emerge from the simple homes with the same stubbled, red-eyed, roadkill expression that I know I am giving to the world.

The priests are in good form, however. I watch a dozen or so parishioners leave the chapel and realize that both de Soya and Duré have celebrated an early Mass while I was snoring. Bassin Kee comes by, greets me in much too loud a voice, and shows me a small structure that is the men's washhouse. Plumbing consists of cold water pumped to an overhead reservoir that one can spill onto oneself in one quick, bone-marrow-freezing second of shower. The morning is Pacem-cool, much like mornings at the eight-thousand-meter altitude on T'ien Shan, and the shower wakes me up very quickly. Kee has brought clean new clothes for me—softened corduroy work trousers, a finely spun blue wool shirt, thick belt, and sturdy shoes that are infinitely more comfortable than the boots I have stubbornly worn for more than a standard year in the Schrödinger cat box. Shaven, clean, wearing different clothes, holding a steaming mug of coffee that Kee's young bride has handed me, the 'scriber hanging from a strap over my shoulder, I feel like a new man. My first thought at this swell of well-being is, *Aenea would love this fresh morning* and the clouds obscure the sunlight for me again.

Fathers Duré and de Soya join me on a large rock overlooking the absent river. The rubble of the Vatican looks like a ruin from ancient days. I see the windshields of moving groundcars glinting in the sharp morning light and catch a glimpse of the occasional EMV flying high above the wrecked city and realize again that this is not another Fall—even Pacem has not been dropped back into barbarism. Kee had explained that the morning coffee had been shipped in by transport from the largely untouched agricultural cities in the west. The Vatican and the ruins of the administrative cities here are more of a localized disaster area: rather like survivors choosing to rebuild in the wake of a regional earthquake or hurricane.

Kee joins us again with several warm breakfast rolls and the four of us eat in agreeable silence, occasionally brushing crumbs away and sipping our coffee as the sun rises higher behind us, catching the many columns of smoke from campfires and cookstoves.

"I'm trying to understand this new way of looking at things," I say at last. "You're isolated here on Pacem compared to the days of the Pax empire, but you're still aware of what's going on elsewhere . . . on other worlds."

Father de Soya nods. "Just as you can touch the Void to listen to the language of the living, so can we reach out to those we know and care for. For instance, this morning I touched the thoughts of Sergeant Gregorius on Mare Infinitus."

I had also heard Gregorius's distinctive thoughts while listening to the music of the spheres before freecasting, but I say, "Is he well?"

"He is well," says de Soya. "The poachers and smugglers and deep-sea rebels on that world quickly isolated the few Pax loyalists, although the fighting between various Pax outposts did much damage to many of the civilian platforms. Gregorius has become sort of a local mayor or governor for the mid-lattoral region. Quite in opposition to his wishes, I might add. The sergeant was never interested in command . . . he would have been an officer many years ago if he had been."

"Speaking of command," I say, "who's in charge of . . . all this?" I gesture at the ruins, the distant highway with its moving vehicles, the EMV transport coming in toward the east bank.

"Actually the entire Pacem System is under the temporary governorship of a former Pax Mercantilus CEO named Kenzo Isozaki," says Father de Soya. "His headquarters is in the ruins of the old Torus Mercantilus, but he visits the planet frequently."

I show my surprise at this. "Isozaki?" I say. "The last I saw of him in preparing my narrative, he was involved in the attack on the Startree Biosphere."

"He was," agrees de Soya. "But that attack was still under way when the Shared Moment occurred. There was much confusion. Elements of the Pax Fleet rallied to Lourdusamy and his ilk, while other elements—some led by Kenzo Isozaki who held the title of Commander of the Order of the Knights of Jerusalem—fought to stop the carnage. The loyalists kept most of the archangel starships, since they could not be used without resurrection. Isozaki brought more than a hundred of the older Hawking-drive starships back to Pacem System and drove off the last of the Core attackers."

"Is he a dictator?" I ask, not caring too much if he is. It is not my problem.

"Not at all," says Kee. "Isozaki is running things temporarily with the help of elected governing councils from each of the Pacem cantons. He's excellent at arranging logistics . . . which we need. In the meantime, the local areas are running things fairly well. It's the first time there has ever been a real democracy in this system. It's sloppy, but it works. I think that Isozaki is helping to shape a sort of capitalist-with-a-conscience trading system for the days when we begin moving freely through old Pax space."

"By freecasting?" I say.

All three of the men nod.

I shake my head again. It is hard to imagine the near future: billions . . . hundreds of billions . . . of people free to move from world to world without spacecraft or farcaster. Hundreds of billions able to contact each other by touching the Void with their hearts and minds. It will be like the height of the Hegemony WorldWeb days without the Core façade of farcaster portals and fatline transmitters. No, I realize at once, it will not be like the Hegemony days at all. It will be something completely different. Something unprecedented in human experience. Aenea has changed everything forever.

"Are you leaving today, Raul?" asks Father Duré in his soft French accent.

"As soon as I finish this fine coffee." The sun is growing warm on my bare arms and neck.

"Where will you go?" asks Father de Soya.

I start to answer and then stop. I realize that I have no idea. Where do I look for Aenea's child? What if the Observer has taken the boy or girl to some distant system that I cannot reach by 'casting? What if they have returned to Old Earth . . . can I actually freecast one hundred and sixty thousand light-years? Aenea did. But she may have had the help of the Lions and Tigers and Bears. Will I someday be able to hear *those* voices in the complex chorus of the Void? It all seems too large and vague and irrelevant to me.

"I don't know where I'm going," I hear myself saying in the voice of a lost boy. "I was going to Old Earth because of Aenea's wish that I . . .

her ashes . . . but . . ." Embarrassed at showing emotion again, I wave at the mountain of melted stone that had been Castel Sant'Angelo. "Maybe I'll go back to Hyperion," I say. "See Martin Silenus." *Before he dies,* I add silently.

All of us stand on the boulder, pouring out the last drops of cold coffee from the mugs and brushing away the last crumbs from the delicious rolls. I am suddenly struck by an obvious thought. "Do any of you want to come with me?" I say. "Or go anywhere else, for that matter. I *think* that I will remember how to freecast . . . and Aenea took us with her just by holding the person's hand. No, she freecast the entire *Yggdrasill* with her just by willing it."

"If you are going to Hyperion," says Father de Soya, "I may wish to accompany you. But first I have something to show you. Excuse us, Father Duré. Bassin."

I follow the short priest back to the village and into his little church. In the tiny sacristy, barely large enough for a wooden wardrobe cupboard for vestments and the small secondary altar in which to store the sacramental hosts and wine, de Soya pushes back a curtain on a small alcove and removes a short metal cylinder, smaller than a coffee thermos. He holds it out to me and I am reaching for it, my fingers just centimeters away, when suddenly I freeze in midmotion, unable to touch it.

"Yes," says the priest. "Aenea's ashes. What we could recover. Not much, I am afraid."

My fingers trembling, still unable to touch the dull metal cylinder, I stammer, "How? When?"

"Before the final Core attack," de Soya says softly. "Some of us who liberated the prisoners thought it prudent to remove our young friend's cremated remains. There are actually those who wanted to find them and hold them as holy relics . . . the start of another cult. I felt strongly that Aenea would not have wished that. Was I correct, Raul?"

"Yes," I say, my hand shaking visibly now. I am still unable to touch the cylinder and almost unable to speak. "Yes, absolutely, completely," I say vehemently. "She would have hated that. She would have cursed at the thought. I can't tell you how many times she and I discussed the tragedy of Buddha's followers treating him like a god and his remains as relics. The Buddha also asked that his body be cremated and his ashes scattered so that . . ." I have to stop there.

"Yes," says de Soya. He pulls a black canvas shoulder bag from his cupboard and sets the cylinder in it. He shoulders the bag. "If you would like, I could bring this with us if we are to travel together."

"Thank you," is all I can say. I cannot reconcile the life and energy and skin and flashing eyes and clean, female scent of Aenea, her touch and laugh and voice and hair and ultimate physical presence with that small metal cylinder. I lower my hand before the priest can see how badly it is shaking.

"Are you ready to go?" I say at last.

De Soya nods. "Please allow me to tell a few of my village friends that I will be absent for a few days. Would it be possible for you to drop me off here later on your way . . . wherever you go?"

I blink at that. Of course it will be possible. I had thought of my leave-taking today as final, an interstellar voyage. But Pacem . . . as everywhere else in the known universe . . . will never be farther than a step away for me as long as I live. *If I remember how to hear the music of the spheres and freecast again. If I can take someone with me. If it was not a onetime gift which I have lost without knowing it.* Now my entire frame is shaking. I tell myself it is just too much coffee and say raggedly, "Yeah, no problem. I'll go chat with Father Duré and Bassin until you're ready."

The old Jesuit and the young soldier are at the edge of a small cornfield, arguing about whether it is the optimum time to pick the ears. I can hear Paul Duré admitting that much of his opinion to pick immediately is swayed by his love of corn on the cob. They smile at me as I approach. "Father de Soya is accompanying you?" says Duré.

I nod.

"Please give my warmest regards to Martin Silenus," says the Jesuit. "He and I shared some interesting experiences in a roundabout way, long ago and worlds away. I have heard of his so-called *Cantos,* but I confess that I am loath to read them." Duré grins. "I understand that the Hegemony libel laws have lapsed."

"I think he's fought to stay alive this long to finish those *Cantos,*" I say softly. "Now he never will."

Father Duré sighs. "No lifetime is long enough for those who wish to create, Raul. Or for those who simply wish to understand themselves and their lives. It is, perhaps, the curse of being human, but also a blessing."

"How so?" I ask, but before Duré can answer, Father de Soya and several of the villagers come up and there is a buzz of discussion and farewells and invitations for me to return. I look at the black shoulder bag and see that the priest has filled it with other things as well as the canister holding Aenea's ashes.

"A fresh cassock," says de Soya, seeing the direction of my glance. "Some clean underwear. Socks. A few peaches. My Bible and missal and the essentials for saying Mass. I am not sure when I will be back." He gestures toward the others crowding in. "I forget exactly how this is done. Do we need more room?"

"I don't think so," I say. "You and I should be in physical contact, maybe. At least for this first try." I turn and shake hands with Kee and Duré. "Thank you," I say.

Kee grins and steps back as if I'm going to rise on a rocket exhaust and he does not want to get burned. Father Duré clasps my shoulder a final time. "I think that we will see each other again, Raul Endymion," he says. "Although perhaps not for two years or so."

I do not understand. I've just promised to return Father de Soya within a few days. But I nod as if I do comprehend, shake the priest's hand a second time, and move away from his touch.

"Shall we hold hands?" says de Soya.

I put my hand on the smaller priest's shoulder much as Duré had gripped mine a second earlier and check to make sure that my 'scriber is secure on its strap. "This should do it," I say.

"Homophobia?" says de Soya with a mischievous boy's grin.

"A reluctance to look silly more often than I have to," I say and close my eyes, quite certain that the music of the spheres will not be there this time, that I will have forgotten completely how to take that step through the Void. *Well,* I think, *at least the coffee and conversation are good here if I have to stay forever.*

The white light surrounds and subsumes us.

34

HAD ASSUMED that the priest and I would step out of the light into the abandoned city of Endymion, probably right next to the old poet's tower, but when we blinked away the glare of the Void, it was quite dark and we were on a rolling plain with wind whistling through grass that came to my knees and to Father de Soya's cassocked thighs.

"Did we do it?" asked the Jesuit in excited tones. "Are we on Hyperion? It doesn't look familiar, but then I saw only portions of the northern continent more than eleven standard years ago. Is this right? The gravity feels as I remember it. The air is . . . sweeter."

I let my eyes adapt to the night for a moment. Then I said, "This is right." I pointed skyward. "Those constellations? That's the Swan. Over there are the Twin Archers. That one is actually called the Water Bearer, but Grandam always used to kid that it was named Raul's Caravan after a little cart I used to pull around." I took a breath and looked at the rolling plain again. "This was one of our favorite camping spots," I said. "Our nomad caravan's. When I was a child." I went to one knee to study the ground in the starlight. "Still rubber tire marks. A few weeks old. The caravans still come this way, I guess."

De Soya's cassock made rustling sounds in the grass as he strode back and forth, as restless as a penned night hunter. "Are we close?" he asked. "Can we walk to Martin Silenus's place from here?"

"About four hundred klicks," I said. "We're on the eastern expanse of the moors, south of the Beak. Uncle Martin is in the foothills of the Pinion Plateau." I winced inwardly when I realized that I had used Aenea's pet name for the old poet.

"Whatever," said the priest impatiently. "In which direction shall we set out?"

The Jesuit was actually ready to start walking, but I put my hand back on his shoulder to stop him. "I don't think we'll have to hike," I said softly. Something was occluding the stars to the southeast and I picked up the high hum of turbofans above the wind whistle. A minute later we could see the blinking red and green navigation lights as the skimmer turned north across the grassland and obscured the Swan.

"Is this good?" asked de Soya, his shoulder tensing slightly under my palm.

I shrugged. "When I lived here it wouldn't be," I said. "Most of the skimmers belonged to the Pax. To Pax Security, to be exact."

We waited only another moment. The skimmer landed, the fans hummed down and died, and the left bubble at the front hinged open. The interior lights came on. I saw the blue skin, the blue eyes, the missing left hand, the blue right hand raised in greeting.

"It's good," I said.

"HOW IS HE?" I asked A. Bettik as we flew southeast at three thousand meters. From the paling above the Pinions on the horizon, I guessed that it was about an hour before dawn.

"He's dying," said the android. For a moment then we flew in silence.

A. Bettik had seemed delighted to see me again, although he stood awkwardly when I hugged him. Androids were never comfortable with such shows of emotion between servants and the humans they had been biofactured to serve. I asked as many questions as I could in the short flight time we had.

He had immediately expressed his regrets about Aenea's death, which gave me the opportunity to ask the question uppermost in my mind. "Did you feel the Shared Moment?"

"Not exactly, M. Endymion," said the android, which did not serve to enlighten me at all. But then A. Bettik was catching us up with the last standard year and month on Hyperion since that Moment.

Martin Silenus had been, just as Aenea had known he would be, the beacon relay for the Shared Moment. Everyone on my homeworld had felt it. The majority of the born-again and Pax military had deserted outright, seeking out communion to rid themselves of the cruciform parasites and shunning the Pax loyalists. Uncle Martin had supplied the wine and blood, both out of his personal stock. He had been hoarding the wine for decades and drawing off blood since his communion with the 10-year-old Aenea 250 years earlier.

The few remaining Pax loyalists had fled in the three remaining starships and their last occupied city—Port Romance—had been liberated four months after the Moment. From his continued seclusion in the old university city of Endymion, Uncle Martin had begun broadcasting old holos of Aenea—Aenea as a youngster I had never met—explaining how to use their new access to the Void Which Binds and pleading for nonviolence. The millions of indigenies and ex-Pax faithful, who were just discovering the voices of their dead and the language of the living, did not disobey her wishes.

A. Bettik also informed me that there was a single, gigantic Templar treeship in orbit now—the *Sequoia Sempervirens*—and that it was captained by the True Voice of the Startree Ket Rosteen and was carrying several of our old friends, including Rachel, Theo, the Dorje Phamo, the Dalai Lama, and the Ousters Navson Hamnim and Sian Quintana Ka'an. George Tsarong and Jigme Norbu were also aboard. Rosteen had been radioing the old poet for permission to land for two days, said A. Bettik, but Silenus had refused—saying that he did not want to see them or any-one else until I arrived.

"Me?" I said. "Martin Silenus knew I was coming?"

"Of course," said the android and left it at that.

"How did Rachel and the Dorje Phamo and the others get to the treeship?" I said. "Did the *Sequoia Sempervirens* stop by Barnard's World and Vitus-Gray-Balianus B and the other systems to pick them up?"

"It is my understanding, M. Endymion, that the Ousters traveled with the treeship from what remains of the Biosphere Startree which we were fortunate enough to visit. The others, as I am given to understand from M. Rosteen's increasingly frustrated transmissions to M. Silenus, freecast to the treeship much as you have 'cast here to us."

I sat straight up in my seat. This was shocking news. For some rea-son, I had assumed that I was the only person clever enough, blessed enough, or whatever enough to have learned the freecasting trick. Now I learn that Rachel and Theo and the old abbot had done so, the young Dalai Lama, and . . . well, a Dalai Lama, maybe, and Rachel and Theo had been Aenea's earliest disciples . . . but George and Jigme? I admit to feeling a bit deflated, yet also excited by the news. Thousands of others—perhaps those, at first, whom Aenea had known and touched and taught directly—must be on the verge of their first steps. And then . . . the mind again reeled at the thought of all those billions traveling freely wherever they wished.

We landed at the abandoned mountain city just as the sky was paling in earnest to the east of the peaks. I jumped out of the skimmer, holding the 'scriber against my side as I ran up the tower steps and leaving the android and the priest behind in my eagerness to see Martin Silenus. The old man had to be happy to see me and grateful that I had done so much to help meet all his impossible requests—Aenea rescued from the original Pax ambush in the Valley of the Time Tombs, now the Pax destroyed, the corrupt Church toppled, the Shrike evidently stopped from hurting Aenea or attacking humanity—just as the old poet had requested that last drunken evening we had spent together here more than a standard decade earlier. He would *have* to be happy and grateful.

"IT TOOK YOU goddamn fucking long enough to get your lazy ass here," said the mummy in the web of life-support tubes and filaments. "I thought I'd have to go out and drag you back from wherever you were lazing around like some fucking twentieth-century welfare queen."

The emaciated thing in the hoverbed at the locus of all the machines, monitors, respirators, and android nurses did not look much like the Poulsen-rejuvenated old man I had said good-bye to less than a decade of mine and only two waking years of his ago. This was a corpse that had neglected to be buried. Even his voice was an electronic restructuring of his subvocalized gasps and rattles.

"Are you finished fucking gawking, or do you want to buy another ticket for the freak show?" asked the voice synthesizer above the mummy's head.

"Sorry," I mumbled, feeling like a rude child caught staring.

"Sorry doesn't feed the bulldog," said the old poet. "Are you going to report to me or just stand there like the indigenie hick you are?"

"Report?" I said, opening my hands and setting the 'scriber on a table tray. "I think you know the essential things."

"*Essential* things?" roared the synthesizer, interpreting the torrent of chokes and rattles. "What the fuck do you know about essential things, boy?" The last of the android nurses had scurried out of sight.

I felt a flush of anger. Perhaps age had rotted the old bastard's mind as well as his manners, if he ever had any manners. After a minute of silence broken only by the rasp of the mechanical bellows below the bed, bellows that moved air in and out of the dying man's useless lungs, I said, "Report. All right. Most of the things you asked are done, M. Silenus. Aenea ended the rule of the Pax and the Church. The Shrike seems to have disappeared. The human universe has changed forever."

"The human universe has changed forever," mimicked the old poet in his synthesizer's attempt at a sarcastic falsetto. "Did I fucking ask you . . . or the girl for that matter . . . to change the fucking universe for fucking ever?"

I thought back to our conversations here a standard decade earlier. "No," I said at last.

"There you go," snarled the old man. "Your brain cells are beginning to stir again. Jesus H. Christ, kid, I think that Schrödinger litter box made you stupider than you were."

I stood and waited. Perhaps if I waited long enough he would just die quietly.

"What *did* I ask you to do before you left, boy wonder?" he demanded in the tone of a furious schoolmaster.

I tried to remember details other than his demand that Aenea and I destroy the Pax's iron rule and topple a Church that controlled hundreds of worlds. The Shrike . . . well, that wasn't what he meant. By touching the Void Which Binds rather than my own fallible memory, I finally retrieved his last words before I had flown off on the hawking mat to meet the girl.

"Get going," the old poet had said. "Give my love to Aenea. Tell her that Uncle Martin is waiting to see Old Earth before he dies. Tell her that the old fart is eager to hear her expound the meanings of all motions, shapes, and sounds." *The essence of things.*

"Oh," I said aloud. "I'm sorry that Aenea is not here to talk to you."

"So am I, boy," whispered the old man in his own voice. "So am I. And don't bring up that thermos of ashes the priest is carrying. That isn't what I meant when I said I wanted to see my niece again before I died."

I could only nod, feeling the pain in my throat and chest.

"What about the rest?" he demanded. "You goin' to carry out my final request, or just let me die while you stand there with your big disciple's thumb up your stupid ass?"

"Final request?" I repeated. My IQ seemed to drop fifty points when I was in the presence of Martin Silenus.

The voice synthesizer sighed. "Give me your stylus 'scriber there if you want me to spell it out in big block letters for you, boy. I want to see Old Earth before I croak. I want to go back there. I want to go home."

IN THE END, it was decided that we should not move him from his tower. The android medics conferred with the Ouster medics who finally were permitted to land who conferred with the autosurgeon aboard the Consul's ship . . . which was parked just beyond the tower, exactly where A. Bettik had landed it some two months earlier after paying his time-debt for translation from Pacem System—which conferred electronically with the medical monitors surrounding the poet, as it had been constantly, and the verdict remained the same. It would probably kill him to take him aboard either the Consul's ship or the treeship by removing him from his tower and submitting him to even the most subtle changes of gravity or pressure.

So we brought the tower and a large chunk of Endymion with us.

Ket Rosteen and the Ousters handled the details, bringing down half a dozen ergs from their lair on the giant treeship. I estimated later that about ten hectares actually rose into the air during that lovely Hyperion sunrise, including the tower, the Consul's parked spaceship, the pulsing Mobius cubes that had transported the ergs, the parked skimmer, the kitchen and laundry annexes next to the tower, part of the old chemistry building on the Endymion campus, several stone dwellings, precisely half of the bridge over the Pinion River, and a few million metric tons of rock and subsoil. The liftoff was undetectable—the containment fields and lift fields were handled so perfectly by the ergs and their Ouster and Templar handlers that there was no hint of movement whatsoever, except for the morning sky becoming an unblinking starfield in the circular opening of Uncle Martin's tower above our heads, and the holos in the sickroom that showed our progress. Standing in that room, the stars burning and rotating overhead, A. Bettik, Father de Soya, a few other android nurses, and I watched those direct-feed holos as I held the old man's hand.

Endymion, our world's oldest city and the source of my indigenie family's name, slid silently up through sunrise and atmosphere to be embraced by the ten kilometers of perfect treeship waiting for us in high orbit. The *Sequoia Sempervirens* had parted its branches to make a perfect berth for us, so we could walk from Hyperion soil to the great bridges and branches and walkways of the ship with no sense of transition. Then the treeship turned out toward the stars.

"You will have to do the next part, Raul," said the Dorje Phamo. "M. Silenus will not survive a Hawking-drive shift or the fugue or the time-debt necessary."

"This is a damned big treeship," I said. "Lots of people and machines aboard. You'll help, I hope?"

"Of course," said the tall woman with the wild, gray hair.

"Yes," said the Dalai Lama and George and Jigme.

"We'll help," said Rachel as she stood next to Theo. Both women looked older.

"We will also try," said Father de Soya, speaking for Ket Rosteen and the others gathered near.

High on the bridge of the ship, while A. Bettik tended to his former master some hundred meters below, the Dorje Phamo, Rachel, Theo, the Dalai Lama, George, Jigme, Father de Soya, the Templar captain, and the others held hands. I completed the rough circle. We closed our eyes and listened to the stars.

I HAD EXPECTED the sky-river of stars that was the Lesser Magellanic Cloud to hang above the treeship as we emerged from light, but it was obvious that we were still in the Milky Way, still in our arm of the Milky Way, not that many light-years from Hyperion System, if the familiar constellations were to be believed. We had gone *somewhere*. But the world that burned above the branches was not the sea blue and cloud white of Old Earth, or even an Earth-like planet, but was a red and oceanless desert world with scattered pocks of volcanic or impact-crater acne and a gleaming white polar cap.

"Mars," said A. Bettik. "We have returned to Old Earth System near the star named Sol."

All of us heard the Void-voice resonance of Fedmahn Kassad on that world. We freecast down, found him, explained the voyage—he did not need the explanation because he had heard us coming through his own listening—and brought him back to the *Sequoia Sempervirens* with us.

Martin Silenus sent up word that he wanted to speak to his old pilgrimage partner, and I walked the stairways and bridges to the tower with the soldier.

"Old Earth System is secure, just as the One Who Teaches commanded me," said Kassad as we stepped onto the Hyperion soil where the fragment of city nestled in the treeship's branches. "No Pax ships have tested our defenses for ten months. No one in-system, not even our own warships, will be allowed to approach closer than twenty million kilometers to Old Earth."

"To Old Earth?" I repeated. I stopped in my tracks. Kassad stopped and turned his thin, dark visage toward me.

"You don't know?" he said. The soldier pointed skyward, straight up toward where the treeship was accelerating under smooth, erg-managed full thrust.

It looked like a double star, as all planets with one large moon look. But I could see the pale glow of Luna, smaller, colder. And the warm blue and white pulse of life that was Old Earth.

A. Bettik joined us at the entrance to the tower. "When was it . . . when did they . . . how . . . when did it return?" I said, still looking up at Old Earth as it grew into a true sphere.

"At the time of the Shared Moment," said Kassad. He brushed red dust from his black uniform, preparing himself to see the old poet.

"Does everyone know?" I said. Poor dumb Raul Endymion. Always the last one to get the word.

"Now they do," said Colonel Fedmahn Kassad.

The three of us went up to see the dying man.

MARTIN SILENUS WAS in good humor upon meeting his old friend after almost 280 years of separation.

"So your black killer's soul is going to become the seed crystal when they build the Shrike a millennium hence, heh?" cackled the old man through his laboring speech synthesizer. "Well, thanks a shitload, Kassad."

The soldier frowned down at the grinning mummy. "Why aren't you dead, Martin?" the Colonel said at last.

"I am, I am," said Silenus, coughing. "I quit breathing ages and eons ago. They just haven't been smart enough to push me over and bury me yet." The synthesizer did not try to articulate the chokes and rattles that followed.

"Did you ever finish your worthless prose poem?" asked the soldier as the old man continued to cough, sending the web of tubes and wires shaking.

"No," I said, speaking for the coughing form in the bed. "He couldn't."

"Yes," said Martin Silenus clearly through his throat mike. "I did."

I just stood there.

"Actually," cackled the poet, "*he* finished it for me." The bony arm with its wrapping of parchment flesh rose slightly from the bed. A thumb distorted by arthritis jerked in my direction.

Colonel Kassad gave me a glance. I shook my head.

"Don't be so fucking dense, boy," said Martin Silenus with what translated as an affectionate tone over the speaker. "See your 'scriber any-where?"

I whirled and looked at the bedside tray where I had left it earlier. It was gone.

"All printed out. About a billion backup memories cut. Sent it out on the datasphere before we 'cast here," rasped Silenus.

"There is no datasphere," I said.

Martin Silenus laughed himself into a coughing fit. Eventually the synthesizer translated some of those coughs as, "You aren't just dumb, boy. You're helpless. What do you think the Void is? It's the goddamn universe's goddamn datasphere, boy. I been listenin' to it for centuries before the kid gave me communion to do it with nanotech bugs in me. That's what writers and artists and creators *do,* boy. Listen to the Void and try to hear dead folks' thoughts. Feel their pain. The pain of living folks too. Finding a muse is just an artist or holy man's way of getting a foot in the Void Which Binds' front door. Aenea knew that. You should have too."

"You had no right to transmit my narrative," I said. "It's mine. I wrote it. It's not part of your *Cantos.*" If I had known for sure which tube passing to him was his oxygen hose, I would have stepped on it till the rattling stopped.

"Bullshit, boy," said Martin Silenus. "Why do you think I sent you on this eleven-year vacation?"

"To rescue Aenea," I said.

The poet cackled and coughed. "She didn't need rescuing, Raul. Hell, the way I saw it while it was happening, she pulled *your* worthless ass out of the fire more often than not. Even when the Shrike was doing the sav-ing, it was only because that girl-child had tamed it for a bit." The mummy's white eyes with their video-pickup glasses turned toward Colo-nel Kassad. "Tamed *you,* I mean, you once and future killing machine."

I stepped away from the bed and touched one of the biomonitors to steady myself. Overhead, in the wide circle that was the open top of the tower, Old Earth grew large and round. Martin Silenus's voice called me back, almost taunting me. "But you haven't finished it yet, boy. The *Can-tos* aren't done."

I stared at him across the few cold meters of distance. "What do you mean, old man?"

"You've got to take me down there so we can finish it, Raul. To-gether."

WE COULD NOT freecast down to Old Earth because there was no one there for me to use as a beacon for the 'casting, so we decided to use the ergs to land the entire slab of Endymion city. This might be fatal to the old poet, but the old poet had shouted at us to for God's sake shut the fuck up and get on with it, so we were. The *Sequoia Sempervirens* had been in low orbit around Old Earth—or just plain "Earth" as Martin Silenus demanded we call it—for several hours. The treeship's optics, radar, and other sensors had shown a world empty of human life but healthy with animals, birds, fish, plants, and an atmosphere free of pollution. I had planned to land at Taliesin West, but telescopes showed the buildings gone. Only high desert remained, probably just as it was in the final days before Earth was supposed to have fallen into the Big Mistake of '08 black hole. The Rome to which the second John Keats cybrid had returned was gone. All of the cities and structures which I thought of as the Lions' and Tigers' and Bears' experimental reconstructions apparently were gone. The Earth had been scrubbed clean of cities and highways and signs of humankind. It throbbed with life and health as if awaiting our return.

I was near the base of the Consul's ship on Hyperion soil in the city-within-the-treeship, surrounded by Aenea's old friends and speaking aloud about the trip down, wondering who wanted to go and who should accompany us, thinking all the time only of the small metal canister in Father de Soya's shoulder bag, when A. Bettik stepped forward and cleared his throat.

"Excuse me, M. Endymion, I do not mean to interrupt." My old android friend seemed apologetic to the point of blushing under his blue skin, as he always did when he had to contradict one of us. "But M. Aenea left specific instructions with me should you return to Old Earth, as you obviously have."

We all waited. I had not heard her give the android instructions on the *Yggdrasill*. But then, things had been very loud and confused there toward the end.

A. Bettik cleared his throat. "M. Aenea specified that Ket Rosteen should pilot the landing, if there were a landing, with four other individuals to disembark once landed, and asked me to apologize to all of you who wish to go down to Old Earth immediately," he said. "Apologize especially, she said, to dear friends such as M. Rachel, M. Theo, and others who would be especially eager to see the planet. M. Aenea asked me to assure you that you would be welcome there two weeks from the landing day—on the last day before the treeship would leave orbit. And, she asked me to say, that in two standard years . . . that is, two Earth years, of course . . . anyone who could 'cast here on their own would be welcome to visit Old Earth."

"Two years?" I said. "Why a two-year quarantine?"

A. Bettik shook his bald head. "M. Aenea did not specify, M. Endymion. I am sorry."

I held up my hands, palms up. "Well, who does get to go down now?" I asked. If my name was not on the list, I was going to go down anyway, Aenea's last wishes or not. I'd use my fists to get aboard, if need be. Or hijack the Consul's ship and land it. Or freecast alone.

"You, sir," said A. Bettik. "She quite specifically mentioned you, M. Endymion. And M. Silenus, of course. Father de Soya. And . . ." The android hesitated as if embarrassed again.

"Go on," I said more sharply than I had intended.

"Me," said A. Bettik.

"You," I repeated. In a second it made sense to me. The android had made our long trip out with us . . . had, in fact, spent more time with Aenea than I had over the years because of the time-debt involved in my solo odyssey. More than that, A. Bettik had risked his life for her, for us, and lost his arm in Nemes's ambush on God's Grove so many years ago. He had listened to Aenea's teachings even before Rachel and Theo . . . or I . . . had signed on as disciples. Of course she would want her friend A. Bettik there when her few ashes were scattered in the breezes of Old Earth. I felt ashamed for acting surprised. "I am sorry," I said aloud. "Of course you should come."

A. Bettik nodded very slightly.

"Two weeks," I said to the others, most of whose disappointment was visible on their faces. "In two weeks we'll all be down there to look around, see what surprises the Lions and Tigers and Bears have left for us."

There were good-byes as old friends, Templars, Ousters, and others left the soil of the city Endymion to watch from the treeship's stairways and platforms. Rachel was the last to leave. To my surprise, she hugged me fiercely. "I hope to hell that you're worth it," she said in my ear. I had no idea what the feisty brunette was talking about. She—and most women— had always been a mystery to me.

"All right," I said after we had trooped up the stairs to Martin Silenus's bedside. I could see Old Earth . . . Earth . . . above us. The view grew hazy and then disappeared as the containment fields merged, thickened, and then separated, the drive fields flowed, and the city pulled away from the treeship. The Templar crew members and Ousters had rigged makeshift controls to the tower sickroom, which, with all of Martin Silenus's medical machines hovering around, had become a very crowded space. I also thought that this was as good a place as any to sit out the ergs' attempt to land a mass of rock and grass, a city with a tower and a parked spaceship, and a half stump of bridge leading nowhere, on a world that was three-fifths water and that had no spaceports or traffic control. At least, I thought, if we were going to crash and die, I might get a hint of the impending catastrophe from watching Ket Rosteen's impassive visage under his overhanging Templar hood in the seconds before impact.

We did not feel entry into Earth's atmosphere. Only the gradual change of the circle of sky above us from starfields to blueness let us know that we had entered successfully. We did not feel the landing. One moment we were standing in silence, waiting, and then Ket Rosteen looked up from his displays and monitors, whispered something through the comlines to his beloved ergs, and said to us, "We're down."

"I forgot to tell you where we should land," I said, thinking of the desert that had been Taliesin. It must be the place where Aenea had been happiest; where she would want those ashes—which I knew but still could not believe were hers—scattered in the warm Arizona winds.

Ket Rosteen glanced toward the floating deathbed.

"I told him where to fucking land," rasped the old poet's voice synthesizer. "Where I was born. Where I plan to die. Now, will you all please pull your collective thumbs out and roll me out of here so that I can see the sky?"

A. Bettik unplugged all of Silenus's monitors, everything except the most essential life-support equipment, and tied everything together within the same EM repulsor field. While we were on the treeship, the androids and the Ouster crew clones and the Templars had built a long, gradual ramp from the top tower room down to the ground, then paved an exit walk to the edge of the city slab and beyond. All of this had landed intact I noticed as we accompanied the floating sickbed out into the sunlight and down. As we passed the Consul's ebony spacecraft, a speaker on the hull of the ship said, "Good-bye, Martin Silenus. It was an honor knowing you."

The ancient figure in the bed managed to lift one skeletal arm in a rather jaunty wave. "See you in hell, Ship."

We left the city slab, stepped off the paved ramp, and looked out at grasslands and distant bluffs not so different from my childhood moors except for the line of forest to our right. The gravity and air pressure was as I remembered it from our four-year sojourn on Earth, although the air was much more humid here than in the desert.

"Where are we?" I asked of no one in particular. Ket Rosteen had stayed in the tower and only the android, the dying poet, Father de Soya, and I were outside now in what seemed to be morning sunlight in an early spring day in the northern hemisphere.

"Where my mother's estate used to be," whispered Martin Silenus's synthesizer. "In the heart of the heart of the North American Preserve."

A. Bettik looked up from checking the med-unit's readouts. "I believe that this was called Illinois in the pre–Big Mistake days," he said. "The center of that state, I believe. The prairies have returned, I see. Those trees are elms and chestnut . . . extinct by the twenty-first century here, if I am not mistaken. That river beyond the bluffs flows south-southwest into the Mississippi River. I believe you have . . . ah . . . traversed a portion of that river, M. Endymion."

"Yes," I said, remembering the flimsy little kayak and the farewell at Hannibal and Aenea's first kiss.

We waited. The sun rose higher. Wind stirred the grasses. Somewhere beyond the line of trees, a bird protested something as only birds can. I looked at Martin Silenus.

"Boy," said the old poet's synthesizer, "if you expect me to die on cue just to save you from a sunburn, fucking forget it. I'm hanging on by my fingernails, but those nails are old and tough and long."

I smiled and touched his bony shoulder.

"Boy?" whispered the poet.

"Yes, sir," I said.

"You told me years ago that your old grannie—Grandam you called her—had made you memorize the *Cantos* till they were dribbling out your ears. Was that true?"

"Yes, sir."

"Can you recollect the lines I wrote about this place . . . as it was back in my day?"

"I can try," I said. I closed my eyes. I was tempted to touch the Void, to seek the sound of those lessons in Grandam's voice in place of this struggle to recall them from memory, but instead I did it the hard way, using the mnemonic devices she had taught me to recall distinct passages of verse. Standing there, eyes still closed, I spoke the passages I could recall:

> *"Fragile twilights fading from fuchsia to purple*
> *above the crepe-paper silhouettes of trees*
> *beyond the southwest sweep of lawn.*
> *Skies as delicate as translucent china,*
> *unscarred by cloud or contrail.*
> *The presymphony hush of first light followed*
> *by the cymbal crash of sunrise.*
> *Oranges and russets igniting to gold,*
> *the long, cool descent to green:*
> *leaf shadow, shade, tendrils of cypress*
> *and weeping willow, the hushed*
> *green velvet of the glade.*

> *"Mother's estate—our estate—a thousand acres*
> *centered in a million more. Lawns the size*
> *of small prairies with grass so perfect it*
> *beckoned a body to lie on it,*
> *to nap on its soft perfection.*
> *Noble shade trees making sundials of*
> *the Earth,*
> *their shadows circling in stately procession;*
> *now mingling, now contracting to midday,*
> *finally stretching eastward with the dying of the day.*
> *Royal oak.*
> *Giant elms.*

Cottonwood and cypress and redwood and bonsai.
Banyan trees lowering new trunks
like smooth-sided columns in a temple
roofed by sky.
Willows lining carefully laid canals and haphazard
streams,
their hanging branches singing ancient dirges to
the wind."

I stopped. The next part was hazy. I'd never enjoyed those fake-lyrical bits of the *Cantos,* preferring the battle scenes instead.

I had been touching the old poet's shoulder as I recited and I had felt it relax as I spoke. I opened my eyes, expecting to see a dead man in the bed.

Martin Silenus gave me a satyr's grin. "Not bad, not bad," he rasped. "Not bad for an old hack." His video glasses turned toward the android and the priest. "See why I chose this boy to finish my *Cantos* for me? He can't write worth shit, but he's got a memory like an elephant's."

I was about to ask, *What is an elephant,* when I glanced over at A. Bettik for no special reason. For one instant, after all my years of knowing the gentle android, I actually *saw* him. My mouth dropped slack.

"What?" asked Father de Soya, his voice alarmed. Perhaps he thought I was having a heart attack.

"You," I said to A. Bettik. "You're the Observer."

"Yes," said the android.

"You're one of them . . . from them . . . from the Lions and Tigers and Bears."

The priest looked from me to A. Bettik to the still-grinning man in the bed and then back at the android.

"I have never appreciated that choice of phrase of M. Aenea's," A. Bettik said very quietly. "I have never seen a lion or tiger or bear in the flesh, but I understand that they share a certain fierceness which is alien to . . . ah . . . the alien race to which I belong."

"You took the form of an android centuries ago," I said, still staring in a deepening understanding that was as sharp and painful as a blow to the head. "You were there for all the central events . . . the rise of the Hegemony, the discovery of the Time Tombs on Hyperion, the Fall of the Farcasters . . . good Christ, you were there for most of the last Shrike Pilgrimage."

A. Bettik bowed his bald head slightly. "If one is to observe, M. Endymion, one must be in the proper place to observe."

I leaned over Martin Silenus's bed, ready to shake him alive for an answer if he had already died. "Did you know this, old man?"

"Not before he left with you, Raul," said the poet. "Not until I read your narrative through the Void and realized . . ."

I took two steps back in the soft, high grass. "I was such an idiot," I said. "I saw nothing. I understood nothing. I was a fool."

"No," said Father de Soya. "You were in love."

I advanced on A. Bettik as if I was ready to throttle him if he did not answer immediately and honestly. Perhaps I would have. "You're the father," I said. "You lied about not knowing where Aenea disappeared to for almost two years. You're the father of the child . . . of the next messiah."

"No," said the android calmly. The Observer. The Observer with one arm, the friend who almost died with us a score of times. "No," he said again. "I am not Aenea's husband. I am not the father."

"Please," I said, my hands shaking, "do not lie to me." Knowing that he would not lie. Had never lied.

A. Bettik looked me in the eye. "I am not the father," he said. "There is no father now. There was never another messiah. There is no child."

Dead. They're both dead . . . her child, her husband—whoever, whatever he was—Aenea herself. My dear girl. My darling girl. Nothing left. Ashes. Somehow, even as I had dedicated myself to finding the child, to pleading with the Observer father to allow me to be this child's friend and bodyguard and disciple as I had been Aenea's, to using that newfound hope as a means of escaping the Schrödinger box, I had known deep in my heart that there was no child of my darling's alive in the universe . . . I would have heard that soul's music echoing across the Void like a Bach fugue . . . no child. Everything was ashes.

I turned to Father de Soya now, ready to touch the cylinder holding Aenea's remains, ready to accept the fact of her being gone forever with the first touch of cold steel against my fingertips. I would go off alone to find a place to spread her ashes. Walk from Illinois to Arizona if I had to. Or perhaps just to where Hannibal had been . . . where we first kissed. Perhaps that is where she was happiest while we were here.

"Where is the canister?" I said, my voice thick.

"I did not bring it," said the priest.

"Where is it?" I said. I was not angry, just very, very tired. "I'll walk back to the tower to get it."

Father Federico de Soya took a breath and shook his head. "I left it in the treeship, Raul. I did not forget it. I left it there on purpose."

I stared at him, more puzzled than angry. Then I realized that he—and A. Bettik, and even the old poet in the bed—had turned their heads toward the bluffs above the river.

It was as if a cloud had passed over but then an especially bright ray of light had illuminated the grass for a moment. The two figures were motionless for long seconds, but then the shorter of the two forms began walking briskly toward us, breaking into a run.

The taller figure was more recognizable at this distance, of course— sunlight on its chrome carapace, the red eyes visibly glinting even at this distance, the gleam of thorns and spikes and razor fingers—but I had no time to waste looking at the motionless Shrike. It had done its job. It had farcast itself and the person with it forward through time as easily as I had learned to 'cast through space.

Aenea ran the last thirty meters. She looked younger—less worn by worry and events—her hair was almost blond in the sun and had been hastily tied back. She *was* younger, I realized, frozen in my place as she ran up to our small party on the hill. She was twenty, four years older than when I had left her in Hannibal but almost three years younger than when I saw her last.

Aenea kissed A. Bettik, hugged Father de Soya, leaned into the bed to kiss the old poet with great gentleness, and then turned to me.

I was still frozen in place.

Aenea walked closer and stood on tiptoe as she always had when she wanted to kiss me on the cheek.

She kissed me gently on the lips. "I'm sorry, Raul," she whispered. "I'm sorry this had to be so hard on you. On everyone."

So hard on me. She stood there with the full foresight of the torture to come in Castel Sant'Angelo, with the Nemes-things circling her naked body like carrion birds, with the images of the rising flames . . .

She touched my cheek again. "Raul, my dear. I'm here. This is me. For the next one year, eleven months, one week, and six hours, I'll be with you. And I will never mention the amount of time again. We have infinite time. We'll *always* be together. And our child will be there with you as well."

Our child. Not a messiah born of necessity. Not a marriage with an Observer. Our child. Our human, fallible, falling-down-and-crying child.

"Raul?" said Aenea, touching my cheek with her work-callused fingers.

"Hello, kiddo," I said. And I took her in my arms.

35

ARTIN SILENUS DIED late on the next day, several hours after Aenea and I were wed. Father de Soya performed the wedding service, of course, just as he later performed the funeral service just before sunset. The priest said that he was glad that he had brought along his vestments and missal.

We buried the old poet on one of the grassy bluffs above the river, where the view of the prairie and distant forests seemed most lovely. As far as we could tell, his mother's house would have been set somewhere nearby. A. Bettik, Aenea, and I had dug the grave deep since there were wild animals about—we had heard wolves howl the night before—and then carried heavy stones to the site to cover the earth. On the simple headstone, Aenea marked the dates of the old poet's birth and death—four months short of a full thousand years—carved his name in deep script, and in the space below, added only—OUR POET.

The Shrike had been standing on that grassy bluff where it had arrived with Aenea, and it had not moved during our wedding service that day, nor during the beautiful evening when the old poet died, nor during the sunset funeral service when we buried Martin Silenus not twenty meters from where the thing stood like a silver-spiked and thorn-shrouded sentinel, but as we moved away from the grave, the Shrike walked slowly forward until it stood over the grave, its head bowed, its four arms hanging limply, the last of the sky's dying glow reflected in its smooth carapace and red-jeweled eyes. It did not move again.

Father de Soya and Ket Rosteen urged us to spend another night in one of the tower rooms, but Aenea and I had other plans. We had liberated some camping gear from the Consul's ship, an inflatable raft, a hunting rifle, plenty of freeze-dried food if we were unsuccessful hunting, and managed to get it all in two very heavy backpacks. Now we stood at the edge of the city slab and looked out at the twilight world of grass and woods and deepening sky. The old poet's cairn was clearly visible against the fading sunset.

"It will be dark soon," fussed Father de Soya.

"We have a lantern." Aenea grinned.

"There are wild animals out there," said the priest. "That howl we heard last night . . . God knows what predators are just waking up."

"This is Earth," I said. "Anything short of a grizzly bear I can handle with the rifle."

"What if there *are* grizzly bears?" persisted the Jesuit. "Besides, you'll get lost out there. There are no roads or cities. No bridges. How will you cross the rivers . . ."

"Federico," said Aenea, setting her hand firmly but gently on the priest's forearm. "It's our wedding night."

"Oh," said the priest. He hugged her quickly, shook my hand, and stepped back.

"May I make a suggestion, M. Aenea, M. Endymion?" said A. Bettik diffidently.

I looked up from sliding the sheath knife onto my belt. "Are you going to tell us what you folks on the other side of the Void Which Binds have planned for Earth in the years to come?" I said. "Or for finally saying hello to the human race in person?"

The android looked embarrassed. "Ah . . . no," he said. "The suggestion was actually more in the line of a modest wedding present." He handed both of us the leather case.

I recognized it at once. So did Aenea. We got down on our hands and knees to take the hawking mat out and unroll it on the grass.

It activated at first tap, hovering a meter above the ground. We piled and lashed our packs on the back, set the rifle in place, and still had room for the both of us—if I sat cross-legged and Aenea sat in the cusp of my arms and legs, her back against my chest.

"This should get us across the rivers and above the beasties," said Aenea. "And we're not going far tonight to find a campsite. Just across the river there, just out of earshot."

"Out of earshot?" said the Jesuit. "But why stay so close if we can't hear you if you call? What if you cried out for help and . . . oh." He reddened.

Aenea hugged him. She shook Ket Rosteen's hand and said, "In two weeks, I would be obliged if you would let Rachel and the others 'cast down or take the Consul's ship down if they want to look around. We'll meet them at Uncle Martin's grave at high noon. They're welcome to stay until sunset. In two *years,* anyone who can 'cast here on his or her own is welcome to explore to their heart's content," she said. "But they can only stay one month, no longer. And no permanent structures allowed. No buildings. No cities. No roads. No fences. Two years . . ." She grinned at me. "Some years down the road, the Lions and Tigers and Bears and I have made some interesting plans for this world. But for these two years, it's ours . . . Raul's and mine. So please, True Voice of the Tree, please post a big KEEP OUT sign on your way up to your treeship, would you?"

"We will do so," said the Templar. He went back into the tower to ready his ergs for takeoff.

We settled onto the mat. My arms were around Aenea. I had no intention of letting her go for a very long time. One Earth year, eleven months, one week, and six hours can be an eternity if you allow it to be so. A day can be so. An hour.

Father de Soya gave us his benediction and said, "Is there anything I can do for you in the coming months? Any supplies you want sent down to Old Earth?"

I shook my head. "No thanks, Father. With our camping gear, ship's medkit, inflatable raft, and this rifle, we should be all set. I wasn't a hunting guide on Hyperion for nothing."

"There is one thing," Aenea said and I caught the slight twitch of muscle at the corner of her mouth that had always warned me that mischief was imminent.

"Anything," said Father de Soya.

"If you can come back in about a year," said Aenea, "I may have use for a good midwife. That should give you time to read up on the subject."

Father de Soya blanched, started to speak, thought better of it, and nodded grimly.

Aenea laughed and touched his hand. "Just kidding," she said. "The Dorje Phamo and Dem Loa have already agreed to freecast here if needed." She looked back at me. "And they will be needed."

Father de Soya let out a breath, set his strong hand on Aenea's head in a final benediction, and walked slowly up onto the city slab and then up the ramp to the tower. We watched him blend with the shadows.

"What's going to happen to his Church?" I said softly to Aenea.

She shook her head. "Whatever happens, it has a chance at a fresh start . . . to rediscover its soul." She smiled over her shoulder at me. "And so do we."

I felt my heart pounding with nervousness, but I spoke anyway. "Kiddo?"

Aenea turned her cheek against my chest and looked up at me.

"Boy or girl?" I said. "I never asked."

"What?" said Aenea, confused.

"The reason you'll need the Thunderbolt Sow and Dem Loa in a year or so?" I said, my voice thick. "Will it be a boy or girl?"

"Ahhh," said Aenea, understanding me now. She turned her face away again, settled back against me, and set the curve of her skull under my jawline. I could *feel* the words through bone conduction as she spoke next. "I don't know, Raul. I really don't. This is one part of my life I've always avoided peeking at. Everything that happens next will be new. Oh . . . I know from glimpses of things beyond this that we will have a healthy child and that leaving the baby . . . and you . . . will be the hardest thing I ever do . . . much harder than when I have to let myself be caught in St. Peter's Basilica and go to the Pax inquisitors. But I also know from those glimpses of myself after this period—when I am with you again on T'ien Shan, in my future and your past, and suffering because I am unable to tell you any of this—that I also will be consoled by the fact that in this future our baby is well and that you will be raising him or her. And I know that you will never let the child forget who I was or how much I loved the two of you."

She took a deep breath. "But as for knowing whether it will be a boy or girl, or what we name the baby . . . I have no clue, my darling. I have chosen not to look into this time, our time, but just to live it with you day to day. I am as blind to this future as you are."

I lifted my arms across her chest and pulled her back tightly against me.

There came an embarrassed cough and we looked up to realize that A. Bettik was still standing next to the hawking mat.

"Old friend," said Aenea, gripping his hand while I still held her tight. "What words are there?"

The android shook his head, but then said, "Have you ever read your father's sonnet 'To Homer,' M. Aenea?"

My dear girl thought, frowned, and said, "I think I have, but I don't remember it."

"Perhaps part of it is relevant to M. Endymion's query about the future of Father de Soya's Church," said the blue man. "And to other things as well. May I?"

"Please," said Aenea. I could feel through the strong muscles in her back against me, and through the squeezing of her hand on my right thigh, that she was as eager as I to get away and find a camping spot. I hoped that A. Bettik's recital would be short. The android quoted:

> *"Aye, on the shores of darkness there is light,*
> *And precipices show untrodden green;*
> *There is a budding morrow in midnight;*
> *There is triple sight in blindness keen . . ."*

"Thank you," said Aenea. "Thank you, dear friend." She freed herself enough to kiss the android a final time.

"Hey," I said, attempting the whine of an excluded child.

She kissed me a longer time. A much longer time. A very deep time.

We waved a final good-bye, I tapped the flight threads, and the centuries-old mat rose fifty meters, flew over the errant city slab and stone tower a final time, circled the Consul's ebony spaceship, and carried us away westward. Already trusting the North Star as our guide, softly discussing a likely looking campsite on high ground some kilometers west, we passed over the old poet's grave where the Shrike still stood silent guard, flew out over the river where the ripples and whirlpools caught the last glows of sunset, and gained altitude as we gazed down on the lush meadows and enticing forests of our new playground, our ancient world . . . our new world . . . our first and future and finest world.